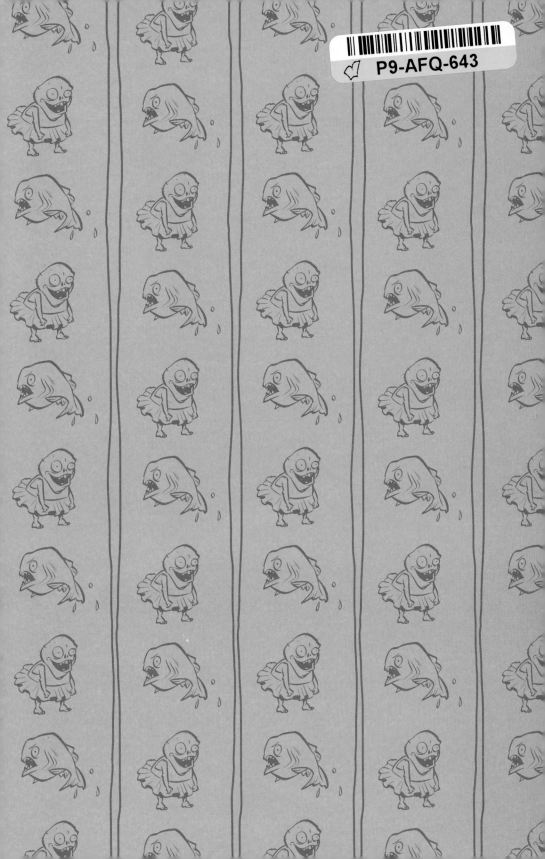

PLANTS VS. ZOMBIES™

ZOMNIBUS · VOLUME 1

Written by **PAUL TOBIN**

Art by **RON CHAN**

Colors by **MATT J. RAINWATER**

Letters by **STEVE DUTRO**

Cover by **RON CHAN**

WITH BONUS STORIES illustrated by Dustin Nguyen, Jennifer L. Meyer, and Peter Bagge!

DARK HORSE BOOKS

PLANTS VS. ZOMBIES

ZOMNIBUS · VOLUME 1

President and Publisher **MIKE RICHARDSON**
Senior Editor **PHILIP R. SIMON**
Associate Editor **JUDY KHUU**
Assistant Editor **ROSE WEITZ**
Designer **BRENNAN THOME**
Digital Art Technician **ALLYSON HALLER**

Special thanks to Nina Dobner, Joshua Franks, Kristen Star, and everyone at PopCap Games and EA Games.

First Edition: November 2021
Ebook ISBN 978-1-50672-821-6
Hardcover ISBN 978-1-50672-820-9

1 2 3 4 5 6 7 8 9 10
Printed in China

DarkHorse.com
PopCap.com

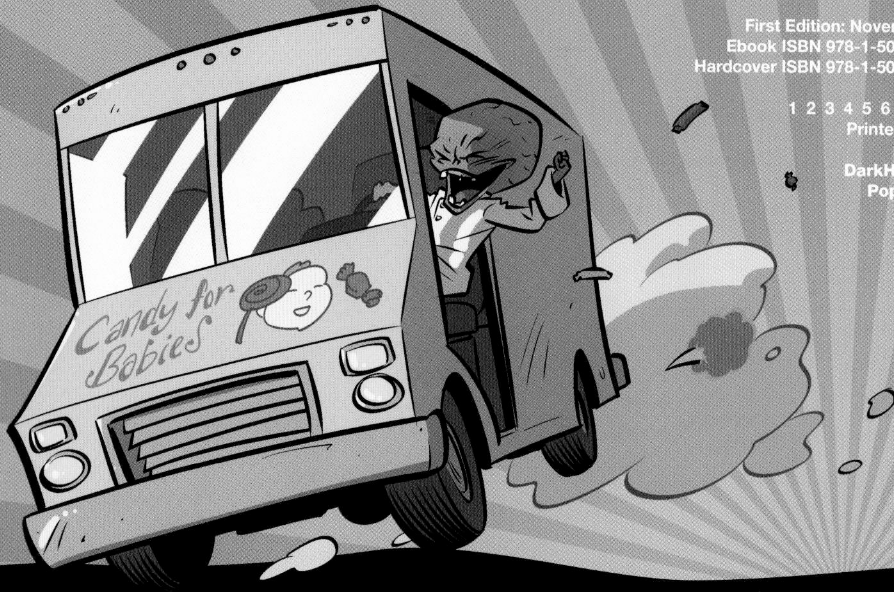
Candy for Babies

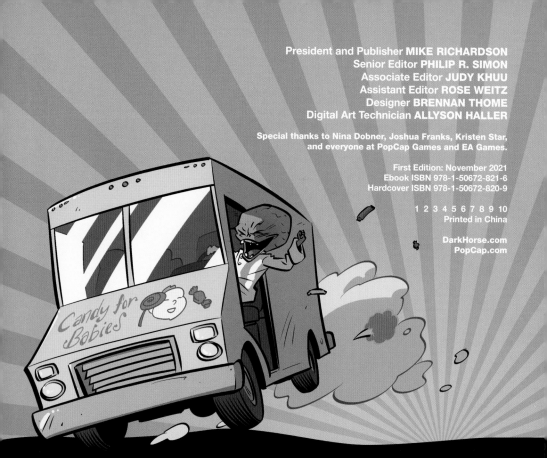

No plants were harmed in the making of these comics. Countless zombies, however, from various time periods and definitely all who tend to bully others, were indeed assailed.

This volume collects the Dark Horse digital comic book series *Plants vs. Zombies: Lawnmageddon* #1-6 and *Plants vs. Zombies: Timepocalypse* #1-6, the print comics *Plants vs. Zombies: Bully For You* #1-3, and the short story "The Curse of the Flower-Bot" from Dark Horse's Free Comic Book Day 2015 comic.

Library of Congress Cataloging-in-Publication Data

Names: Tobin, Paul, 1965- writer. | Chan, Ron, artist | Rainwater, Matthew J., colourist | Dutro, Steve, letterer.
Title: Plants vs. zombies. Zomnibus / writer, Paul Tobin ; artist, Ron Chan ; colors, Matthew J. Rainwater ; letters, Steve Dutro.
Other titles: Plants versus zombies. Zomnibus
Description: First edition. | Milwaukie, OR : Dark Horse Books, 2021- | Series: Plants vs. zombies | v.1: "This volume collects Plants vs. Zombies Volume 1: Lawnmageddon, Volume 2: Timepocalypse, and Volume 3: Bully For You, published November 2013-November 2015."
Identifiers: LCCN 2021014168 (print) | LCCN 2021014169 (ebook) | ISBN 9781506728209 (v. 1 ; hardcover) | ISBN 9781506728216 (v. 1 ; ebook)
Subjects: LCSH: Graphic novels. | CYAC: Graphic novels. | Zombies--Fiction. | Plants--Fiction. | Humorous stories.
Classification: LCC PZ7.7.T62 Prg 2021 (print) | LCC PZ7.7.T62 (ebook) | DDC 741.5/973--dc23
LC record available at https://lccn.loc.gov/2021014168
LC ebook record available at https://lccn.loc.gov/2021014169

TABLE OF CONTENTS

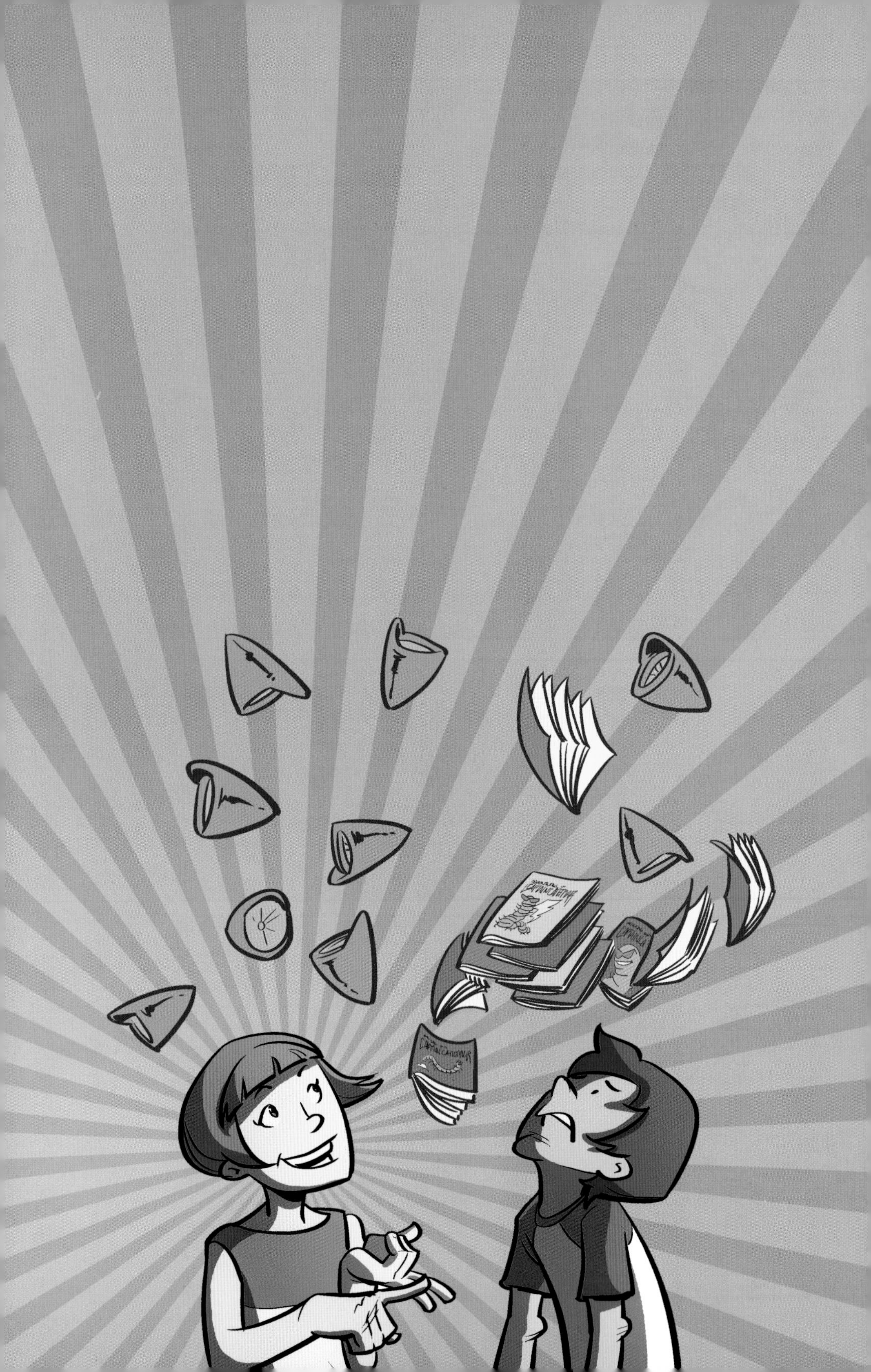

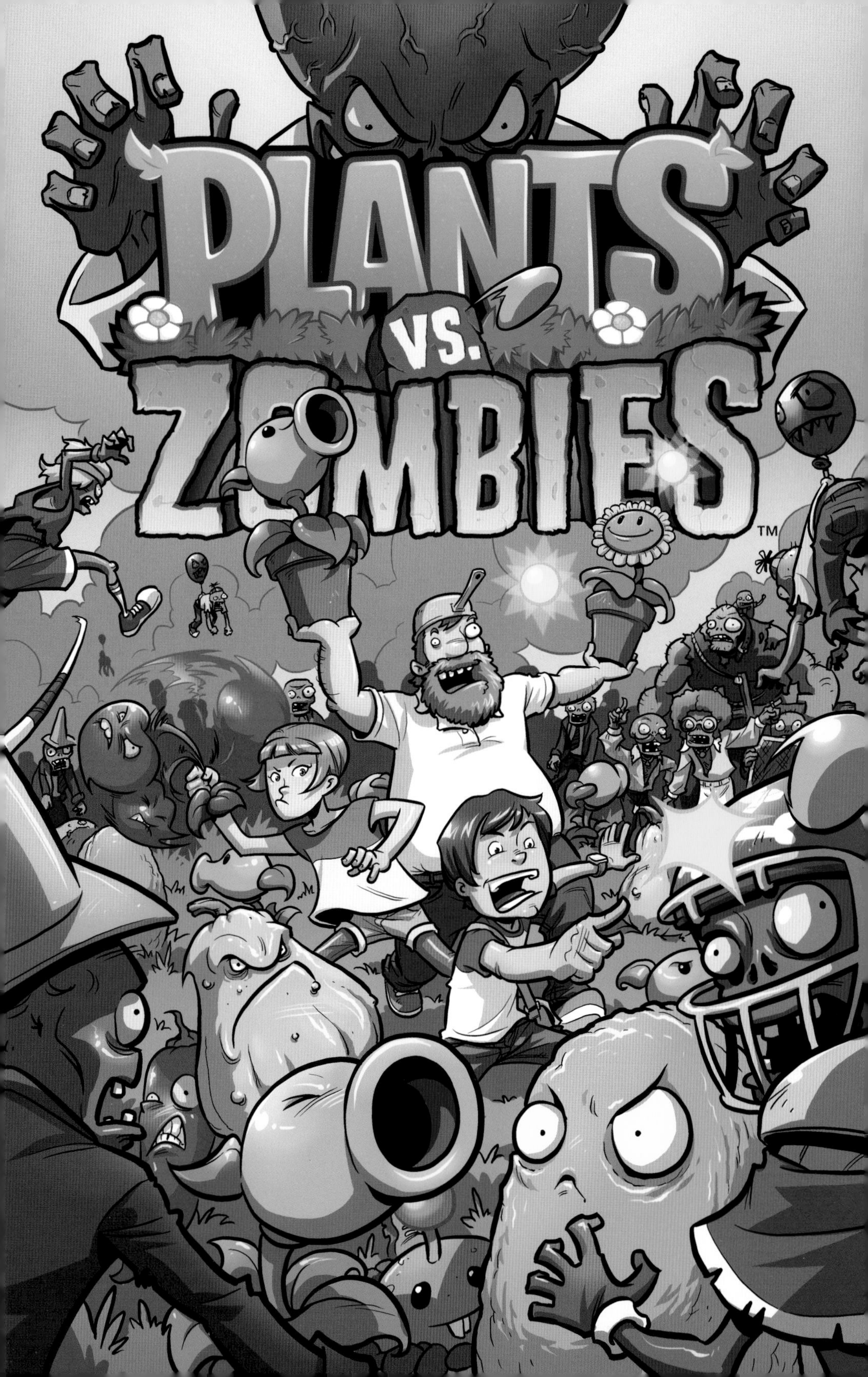
PLANTS VS. ZOMBIES™

PLANTS vs. ZOMBIES

LAWNMAGEDDON

Written by PAUL TOBIN
Art by RON CHAN
Colors by MATT J. RAINWATER
Letters by STEVE DUTRO

Plants vs. Zombies: Lawnmageddon #1 cover art
(previous page) by Ron Chan

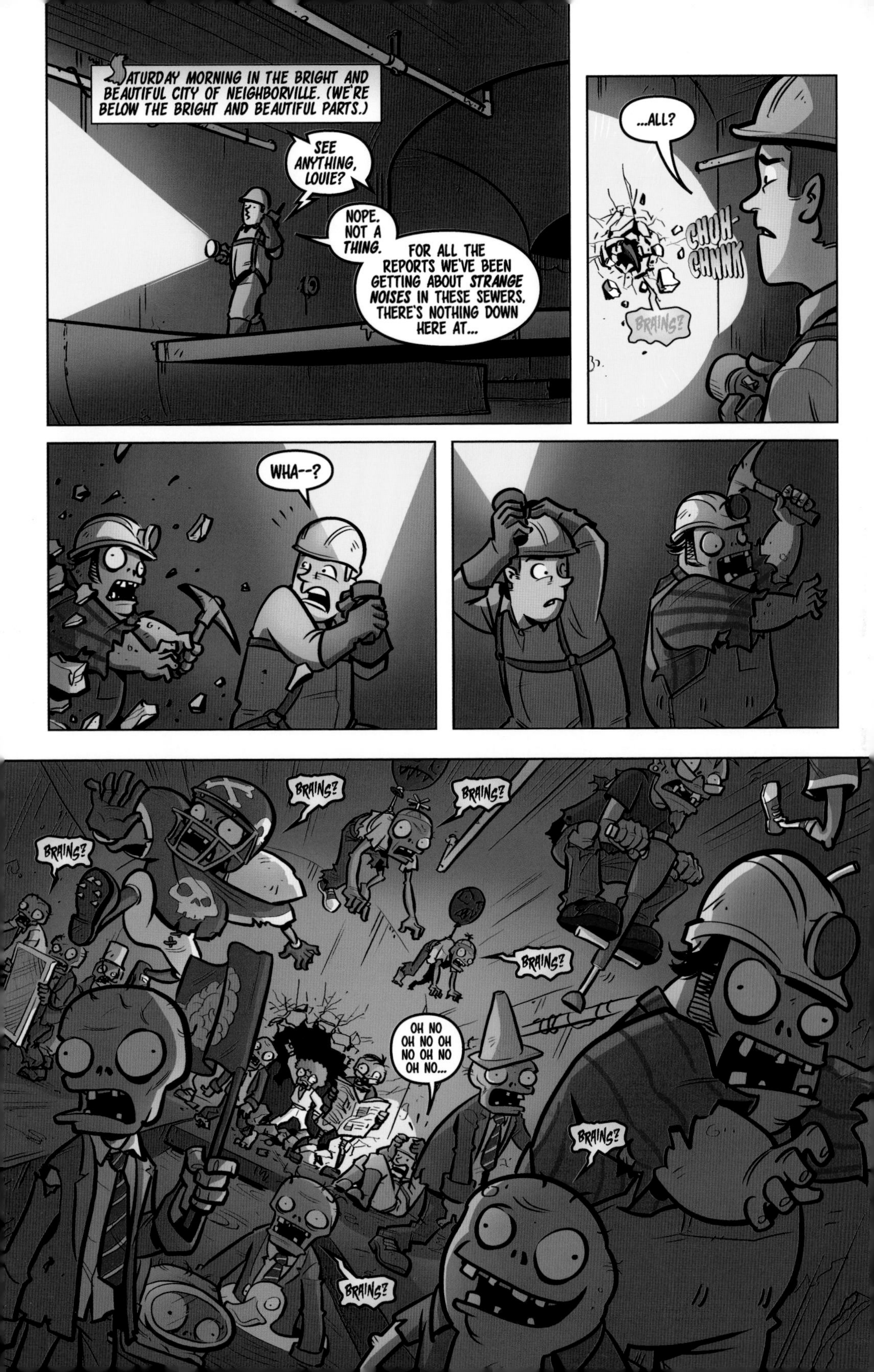
SATURDAY MORNING IN THE BRIGHT AND BEAUTIFUL CITY OF NEIGHBORVILLE. (WE'RE BELOW THE BRIGHT AND BEAUTIFUL PARTS.)
SEE ANYTHING, LOUIE?
NOPE. NOT A THING.
FOR ALL THE REPORTS WE'VE BEEN GETTING ABOUT STRANGE NOISES IN THESE SEWERS, THERE'S NOTHING DOWN HERE AT...
...ALL?
CHUH-CHNNK
BRAINS?
WHA--?
BRAINS?
BRAINS?
BRAINS?
BRAINS?
OH NO OH NO OH NO OH NO OH NO...
BRAINS?
BRAINS?

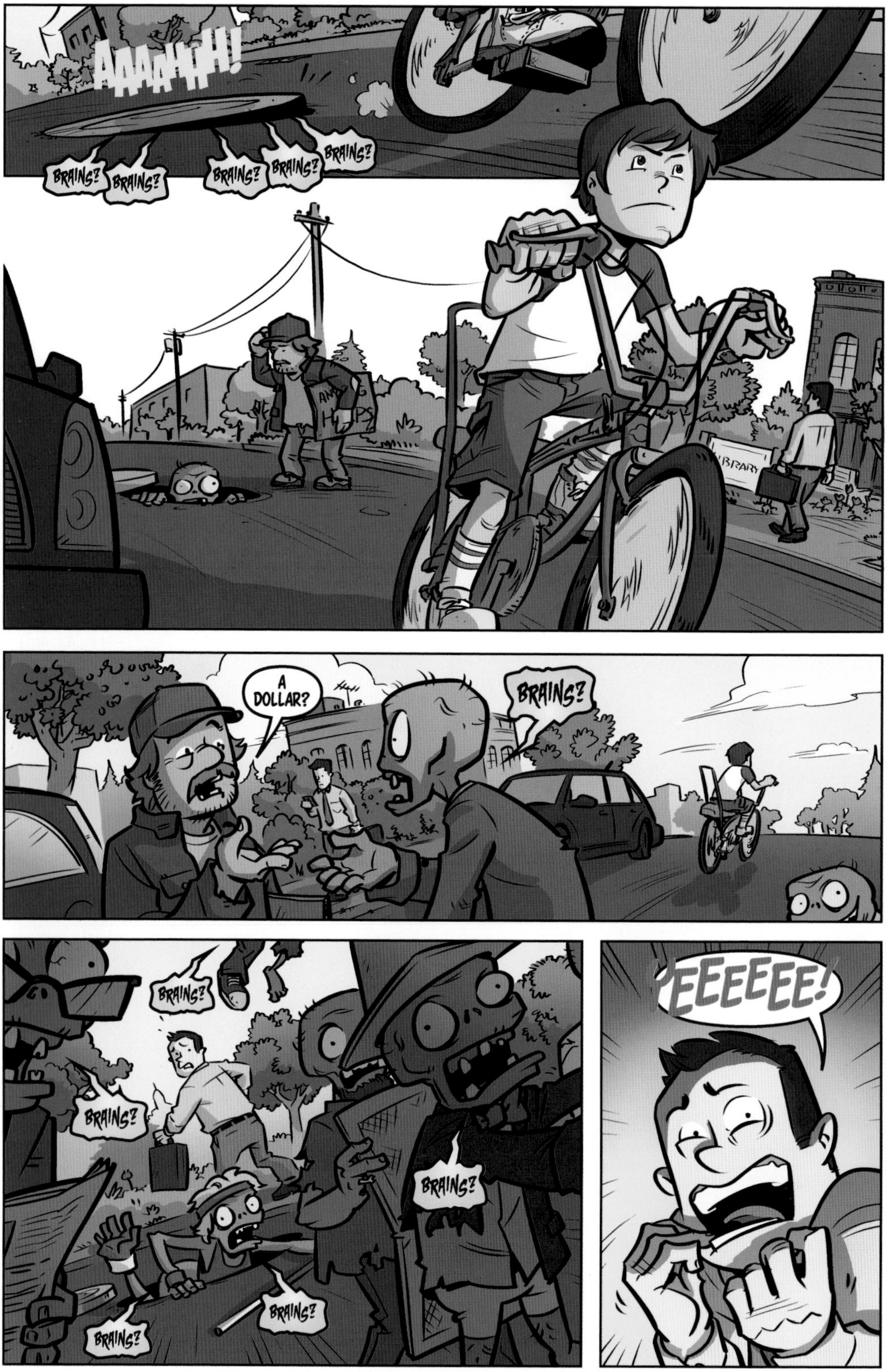
AAAHHH!
BRAINS?
BRAINS?
BRAINS?
BRAINS?
BRAINS?
LIBRARY
A DOLLAR?
BRAINS?
BRAINS?
BRAINS?
BRAINS?
BRAINS?
BRAINS?
EEEEEE!

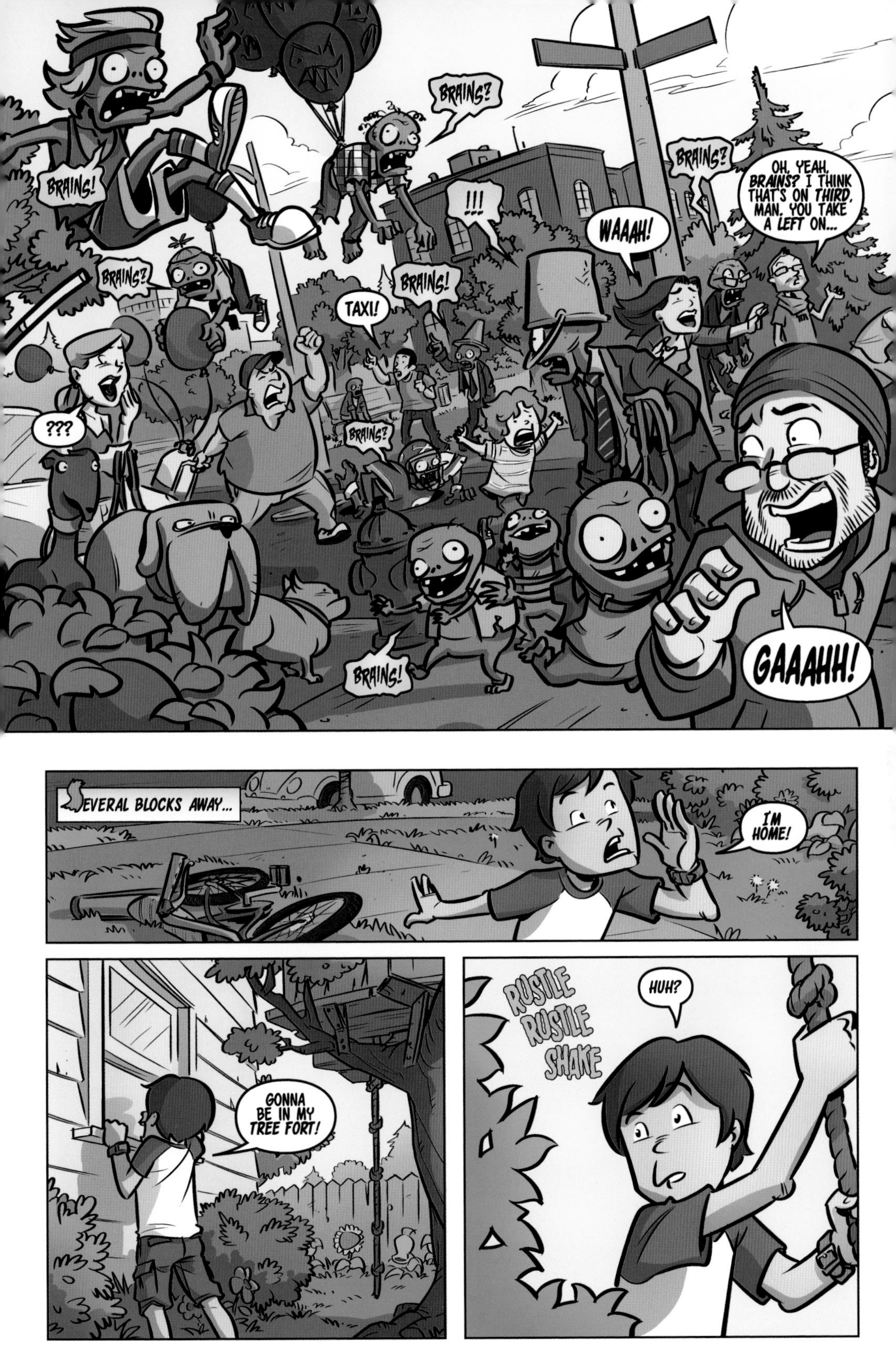
BRAINS!
BRAINS?
BRAINS?
TAXI!
BRAINS!
!!!
BRAINS?
WAAAH!
OH, YEAH, BRAINS? I THINK THAT'S ON THIRD, MAN. YOU TAKE A LEFT ON...
???
BRAINS?
BRAINS!
GAAAHH!
SEVERAL BLOCKS AWAY...
I'M HOME!
GONNA BE IN MY TREE FORT!
RUSTLE RUSTLE SHAKE
HUH?

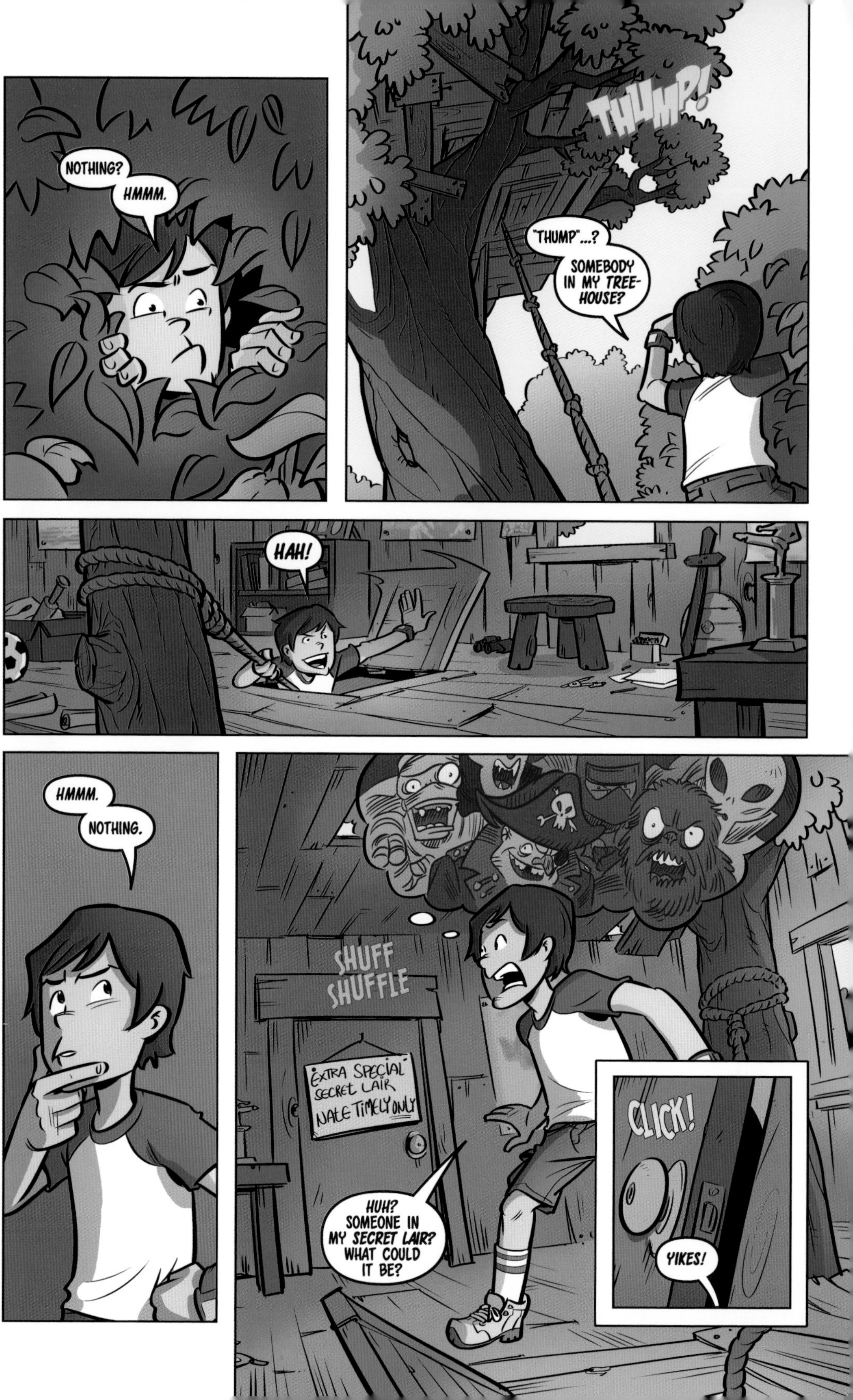

NOTHING?
HMMM.
THUMP!
"THUMP"...?
SOMEBODY IN MY TREE-HOUSE?
HAH!
HMMM.
NOTHING.
SHUFF SHUFFLE
EXTRA SPECIAL SECRET LAIR NATE TIMELY ONLY
HUH? SOMEONE IN MY SECRET LAIR? WHAT COULD IT BE?
CLICK!
YIKES!

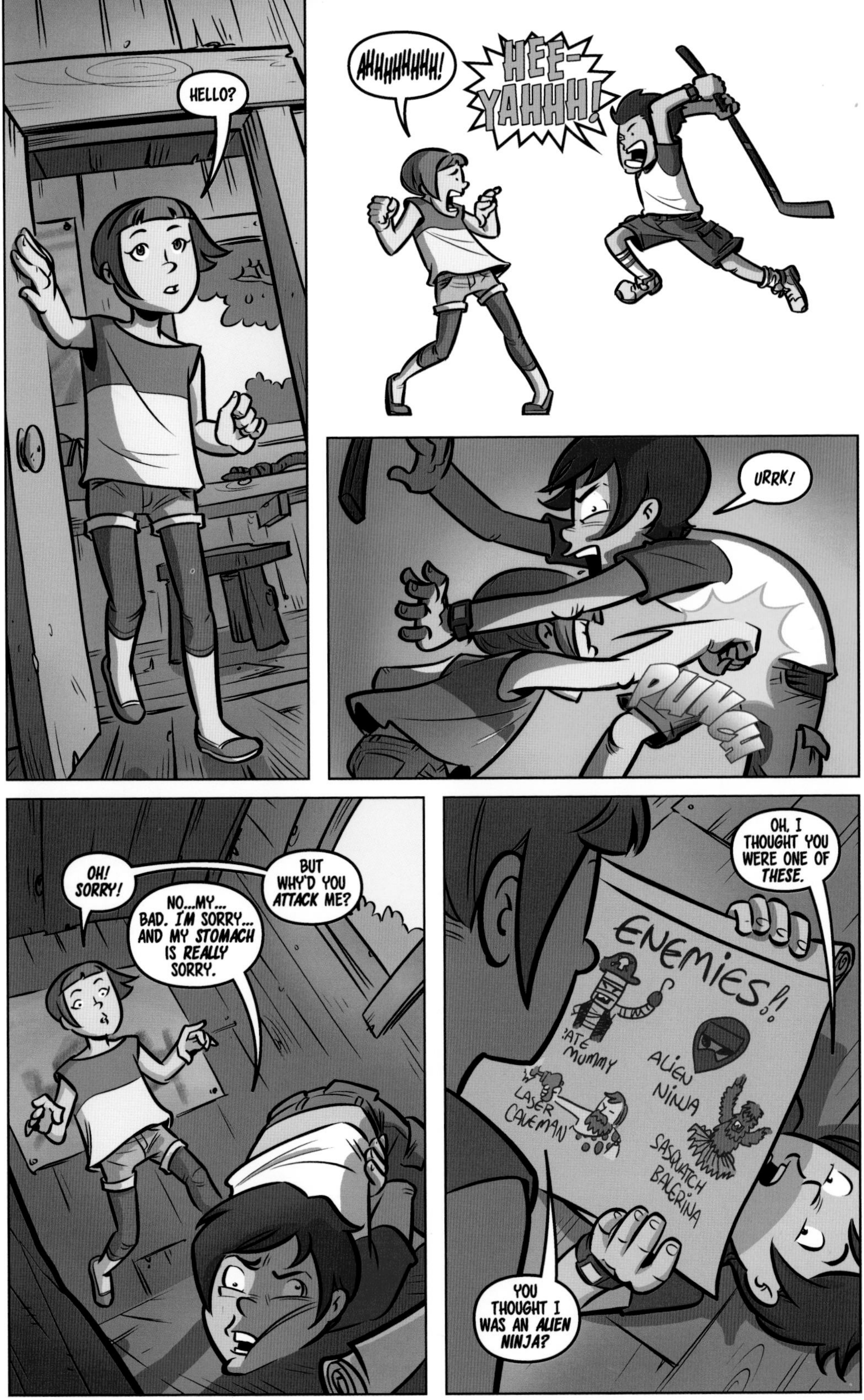
HELLO?
AHHHHHHHH!
HEE-YAHHH!
URRK!
PUNCH!
OH! SORRY!
BUT WHY'D YOU ATTACK ME?
NO...MY... BAD. I'M SORRY... AND MY STOMACH IS REALLY SORRY.
OH, I THOUGHT YOU WERE ONE OF THESE.
ENEMIES!!
PIRATE MUMMY
ALIEN NINJA
LASER CAVEMAN
SASQUATCH BALERINA
YOU THOUGHT I WAS AN ALIEN NINJA?

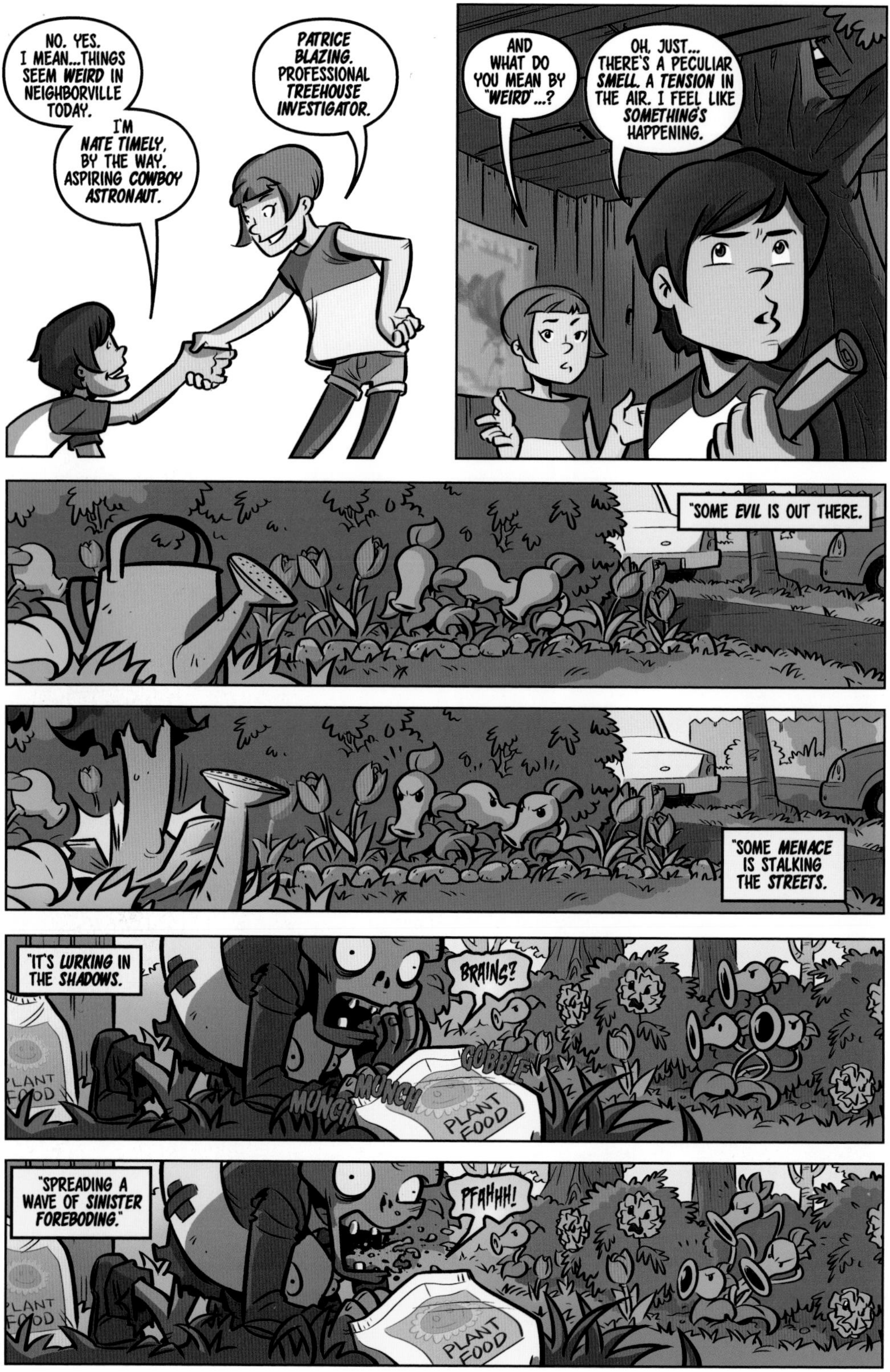
NO. YES. I MEAN...THINGS SEEM WEIRD IN NEIGHBORVILLE TODAY.
I'M NATE TIMELY, BY THE WAY. ASPIRING COWBOY ASTRONAUT.
PATRICE BLAZING. PROFESSIONAL TREEHOUSE INVESTIGATOR.
AND WHAT DO YOU MEAN BY "WEIRD"...?
OH, JUST... THERE'S A PECULIAR SMELL. A TENSION IN THE AIR. I FEEL LIKE SOMETHING'S HAPPENING.
"SOME EVIL IS OUT THERE.
"SOME MENACE IS STALKING THE STREETS.
"IT'S LURKING IN THE SHADOWS.
BRAINS?
PLANT FOOD
GOBBLE
MUNCH
MUNCH
PLANT FOOD
"SPREADING A WAVE OF SINISTER FOREBODING."
PFAHHH!
PLANT FOOD
PLANT FOOD

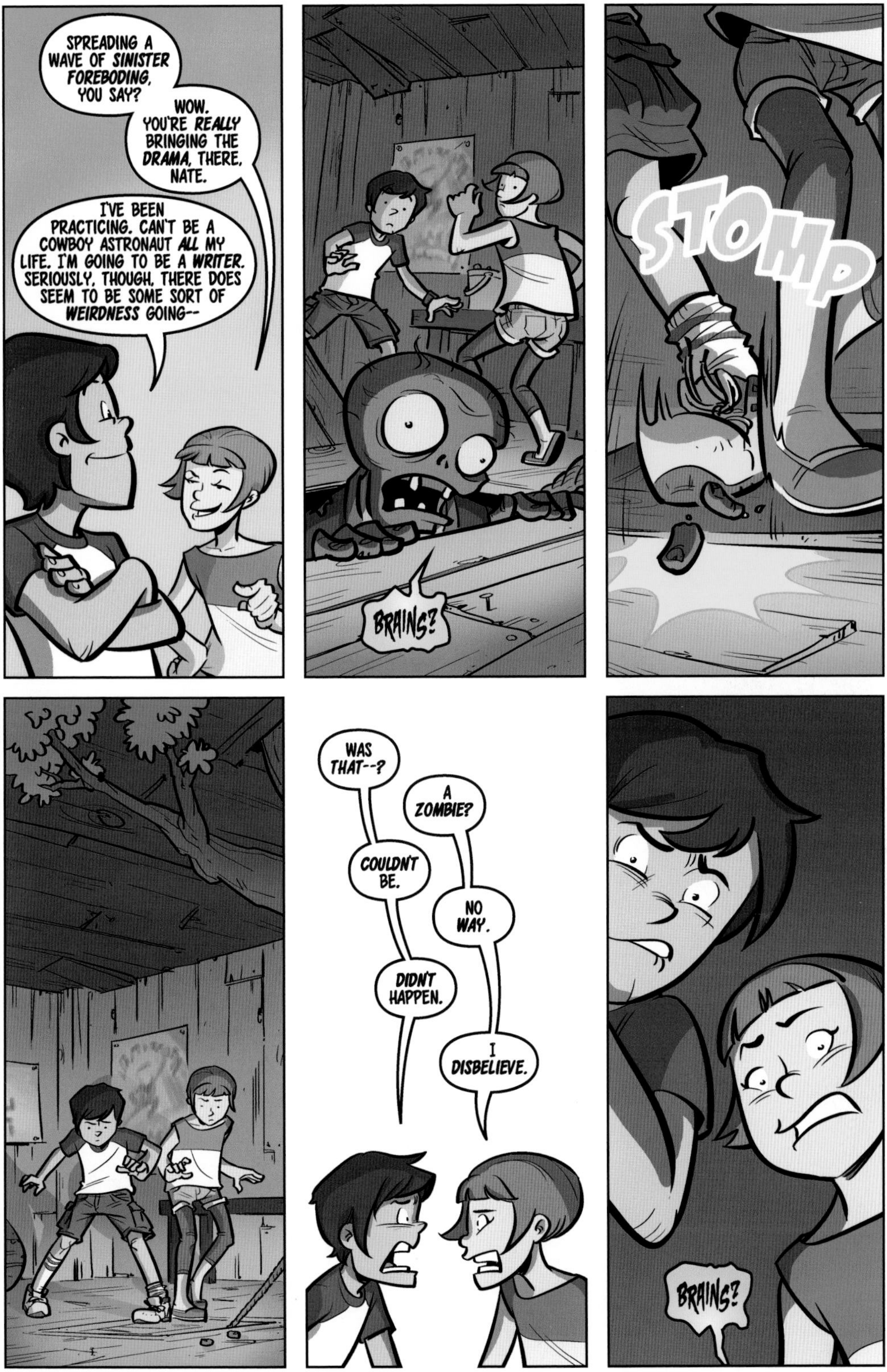
SPREADING A WAVE OF SINISTER FOREBODING, YOU SAY?
WOW. YOU'RE REALLY BRINGING THE DRAMA, THERE, NATE.
I'VE BEEN PRACTICING. CAN'T BE A COWBOY ASTRONAUT ALL MY LIFE. I'M GOING TO BE A WRITER. SERIOUSLY, THOUGH, THERE DOES SEEM TO BE SOME SORT OF WEIRDNESS GOING--
BRAINS?
STOMP
WAS THAT--?
A ZOMBIE?
COULDN'T BE.
NO WAY.
DIDN'T HAPPEN.
I DISBELIEVE.
BRAINS?

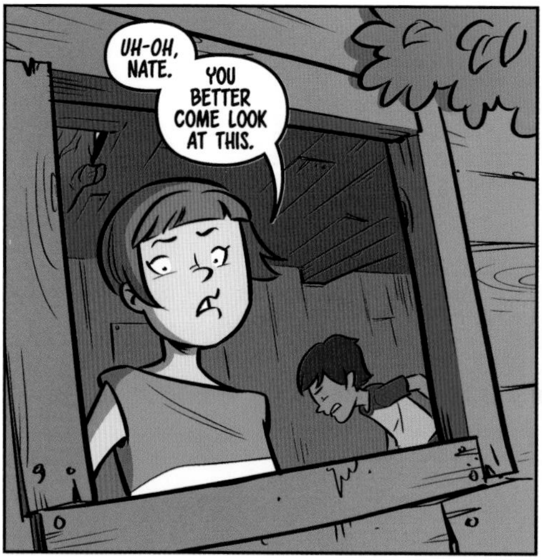
UH-OH, NATE.
YOU BETTER COME LOOK AT THIS.

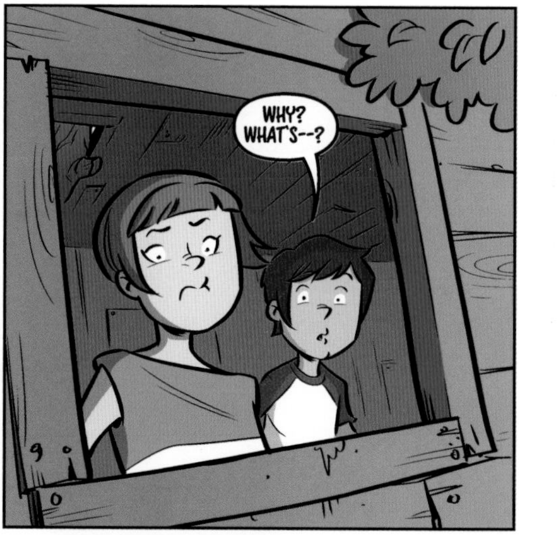
WHY? WHAT'S--?

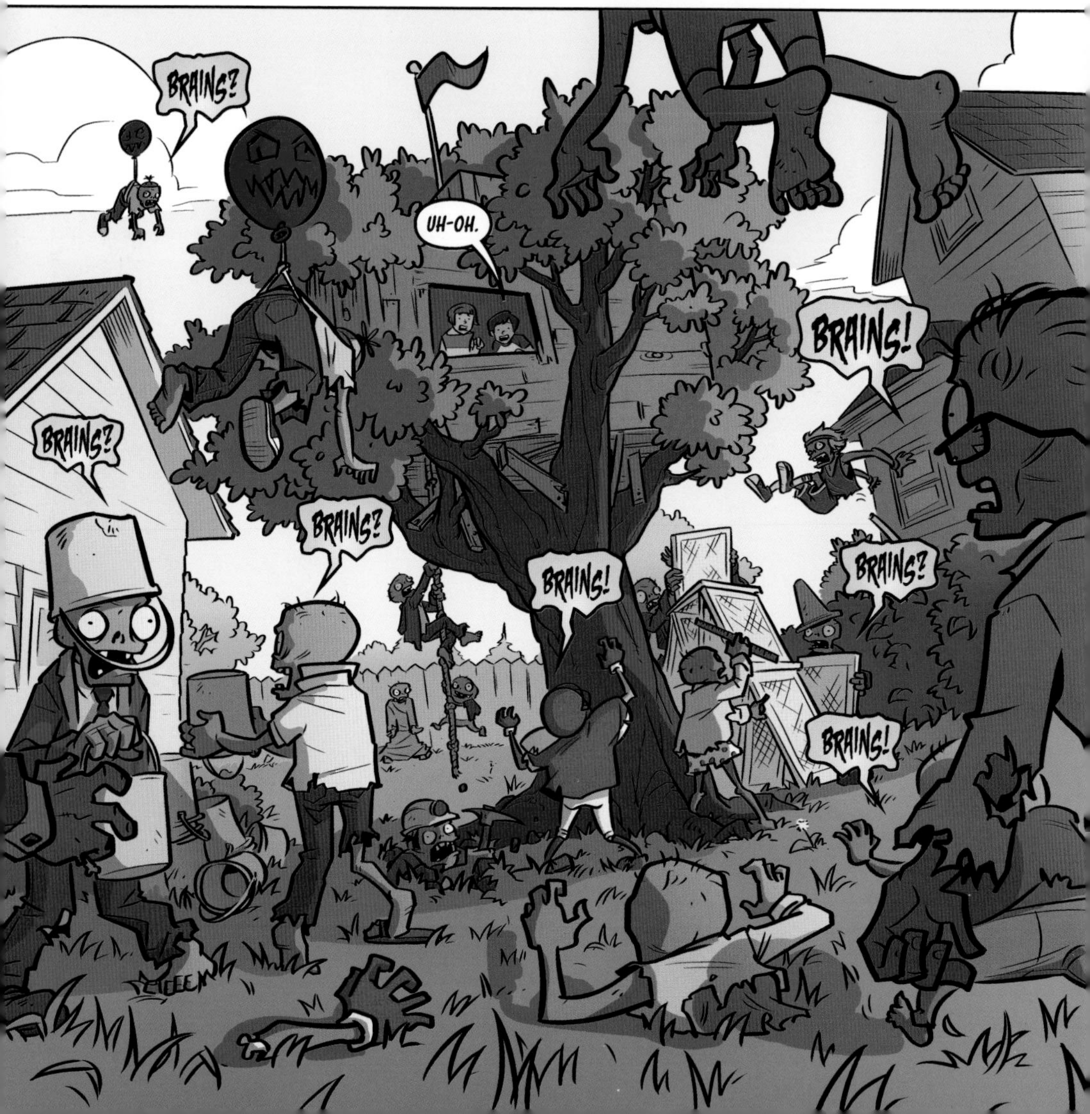
BRAINS?
UH-OH.
BRAINS!
BRAINS?
BRAINS?
BRAINS!
BRAINS?
BRAINS!

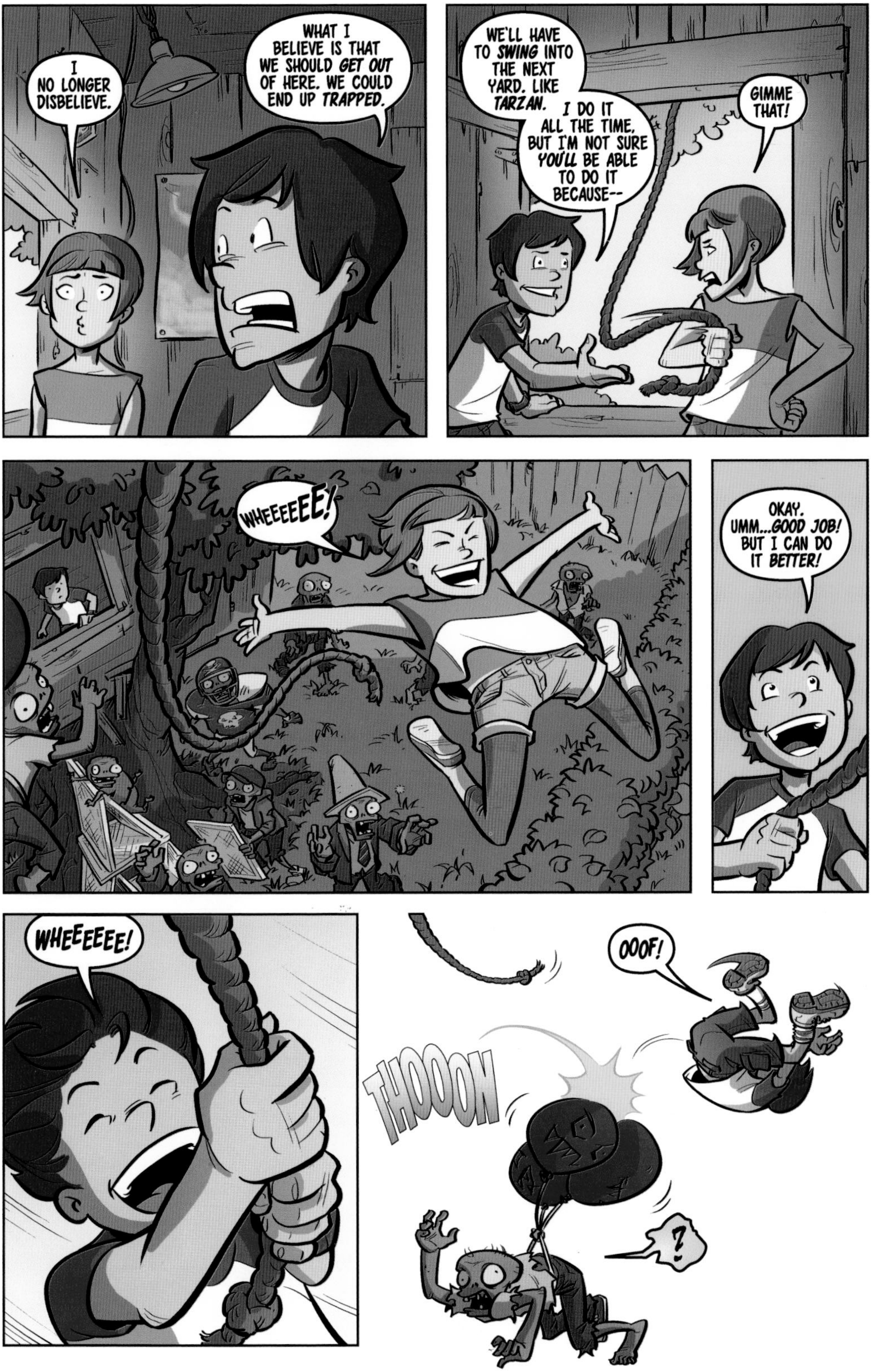
I NO LONGER DISBELIEVE.
WHAT I BELIEVE IS THAT WE SHOULD GET OUT OF HERE. WE COULD END UP TRAPPED.
WE'LL HAVE TO SWING INTO THE NEXT YARD. LIKE TARZAN.
I DO IT ALL THE TIME, BUT I'M NOT SURE YOU'LL BE ABLE TO DO IT BECAUSE--
GIMME THAT!
WHEEEEEE!
OKAY. UMM...GOOD JOB! BUT I CAN DO IT BETTER!
WHEEEEEE!
OOOF!
THOOON
?

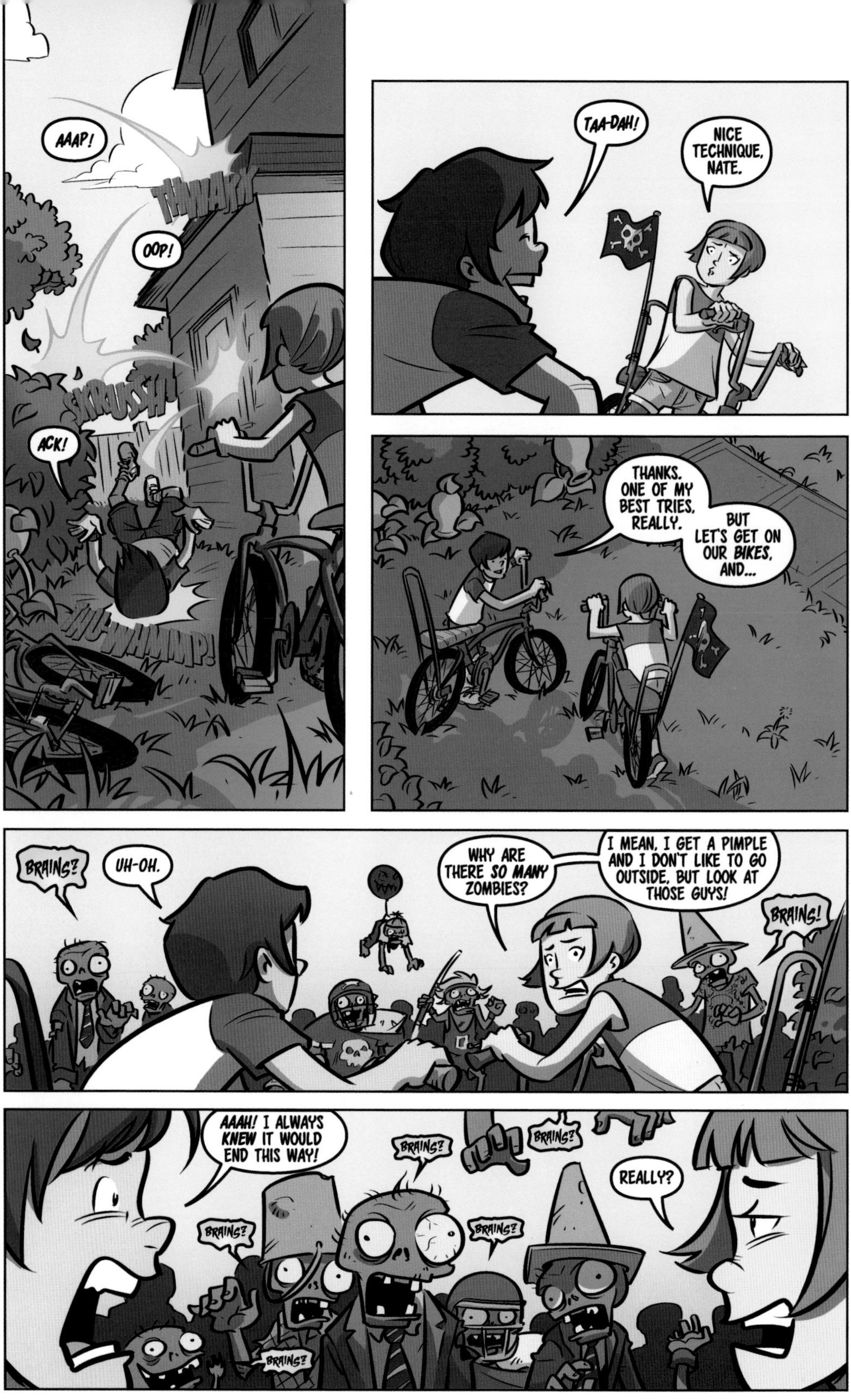
AAAP!
THWAKK
OOP!
SKRUSH!
ACK!
WHU-WHAMMP!
TAA-DAH!
NICE TECHNIQUE, NATE.
THANKS. ONE OF MY BEST TRIES, REALLY.
BUT LET'S GET ON OUR BIKES, AND...
BRAINS?
UH-OH.
WHY ARE THERE SO MANY ZOMBIES?
I MEAN, I GET A PIMPLE AND I DON'T LIKE TO GO OUTSIDE, BUT LOOK AT THOSE GUYS!
BRAINS!
AAAH! I ALWAYS KNEW IT WOULD END THIS WAY!
BRAINS?
BRAINS?
REALLY?
BRAINS?
BRAINS?
BRAINS?

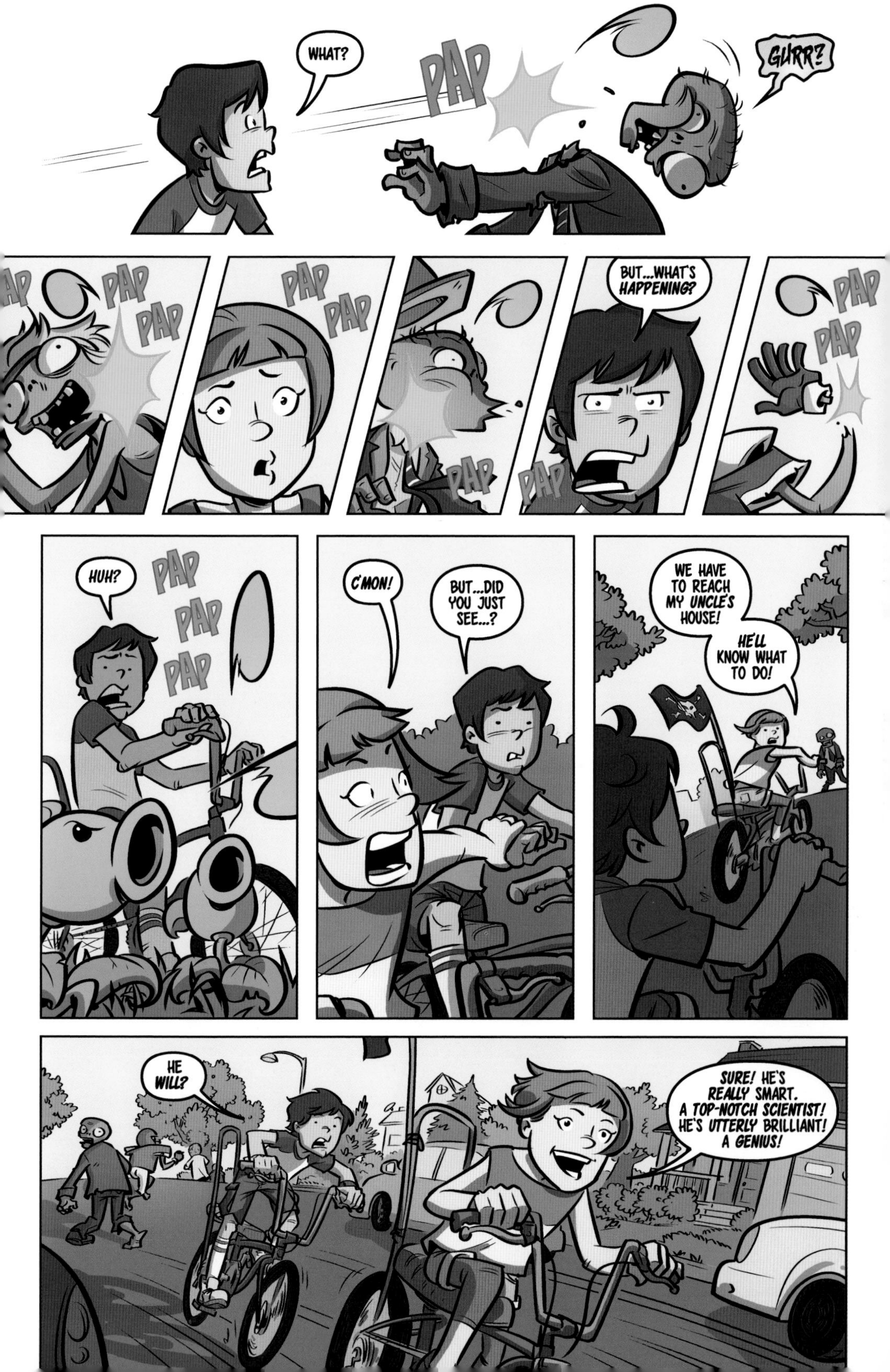
WHAT?
PAP
GURR?
PAP
PAP
PAP
PAP
PAP
PAP
BUT...WHAT'S HAPPENING?
PAP
PAP
PAP
HUH?
PAP
PAP
PAP
C'MON!
BUT...DID YOU JUST SEE...?
WE HAVE TO REACH MY UNCLE'S HOUSE!
HE'LL KNOW WHAT TO DO!
HE WILL?
SURE! HE'S REALLY SMART. A TOP-NOTCH SCIENTIST! HE'S UTTERLY BRILLIANT! A GENIUS!

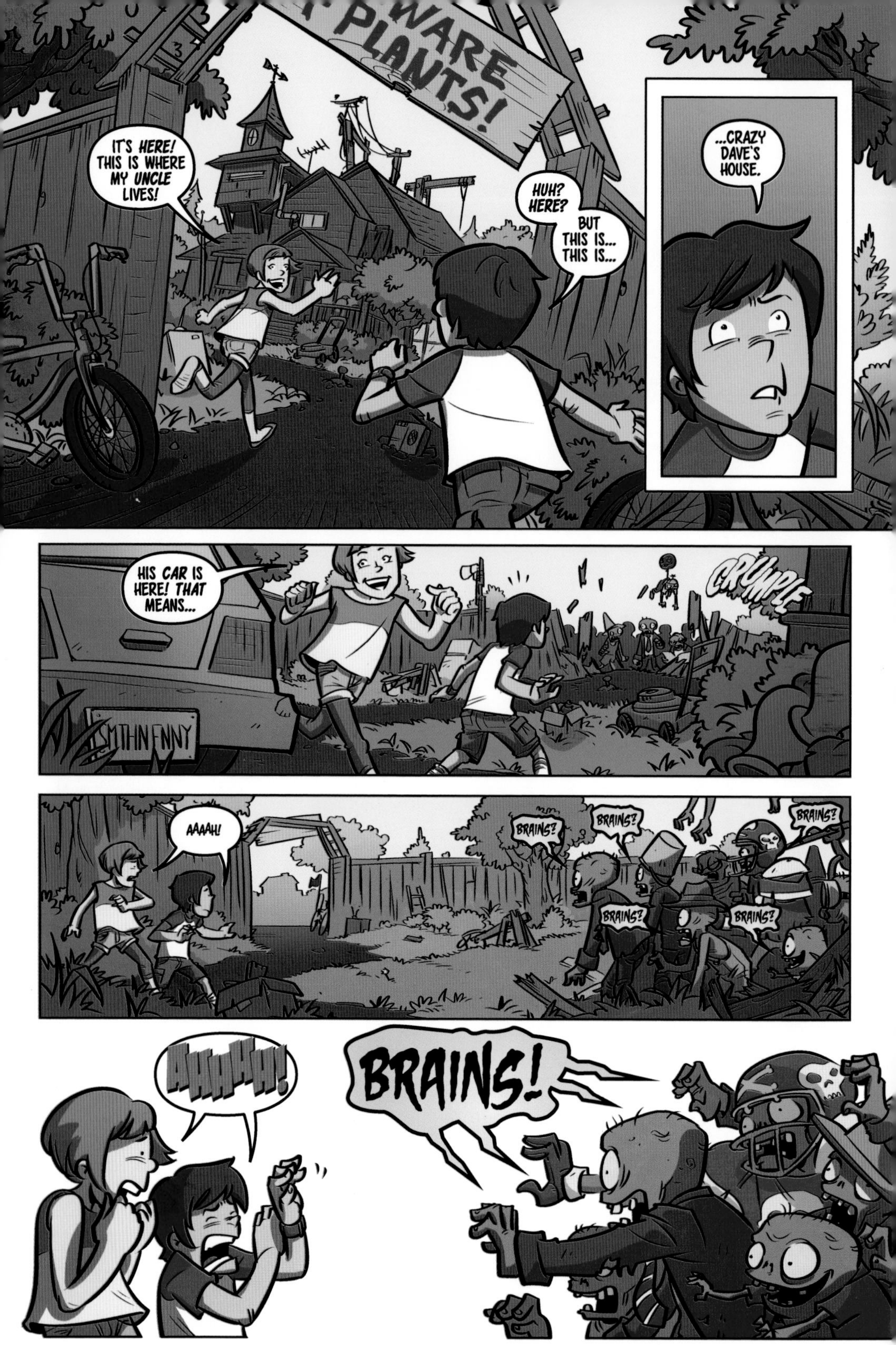
WARE PLANTS!
IT'S HERE! THIS IS WHERE MY UNCLE LIVES!
HUH? HERE?
BUT THIS IS... THIS IS...
...CRAZY DAVE'S HOUSE.
HIS CAR IS HERE! THAT MEANS...
SMTHNFNNY
CRUMPLE
AAAAH!
BRAINS?
BRAINS?
BRAINS?
BRAINS?
BRAINS?
AHHHHH!
BRAINS!

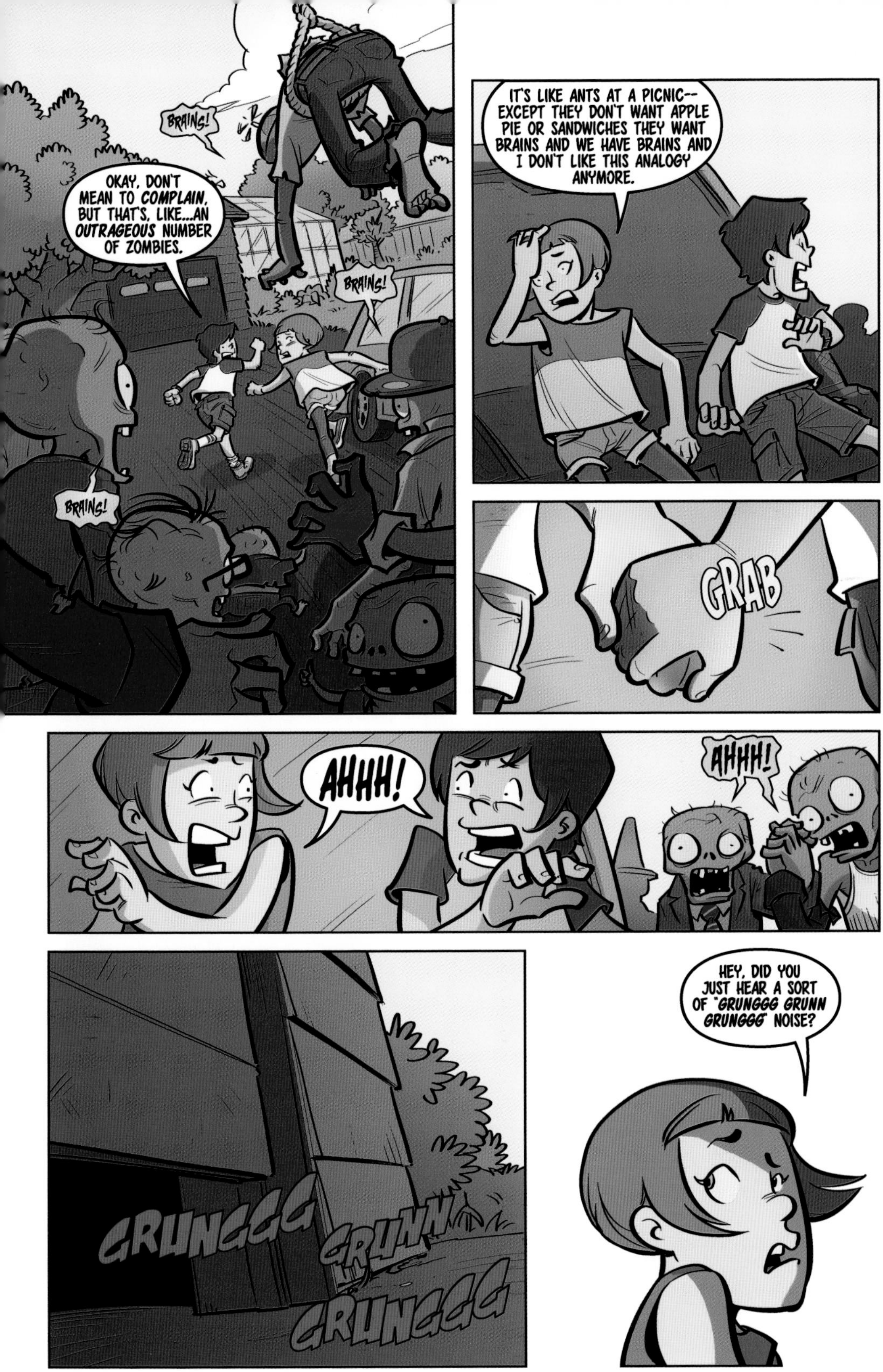
BRAINS!
OKAY, DON'T MEAN TO *COMPLAIN,* BUT THAT'S, LIKE...AN *OUTRAGEOUS* NUMBER OF ZOMBIES.
BRAINS!
BRAINS!
IT'S LIKE ANTS AT A PICNIC-- EXCEPT THEY DON'T WANT APPLE PIE OR SANDWICHES THEY WANT BRAINS AND WE HAVE BRAINS AND I DON'T LIKE THIS ANALOGY ANYMORE.
GRAB
AHHH!
AHHH!
GRUNGGG GRUNN GRUNGGG
HEY, DID YOU JUST HEAR A SORT OF "*GRUNGGG GRUNN GRUNGGG*" NOISE?

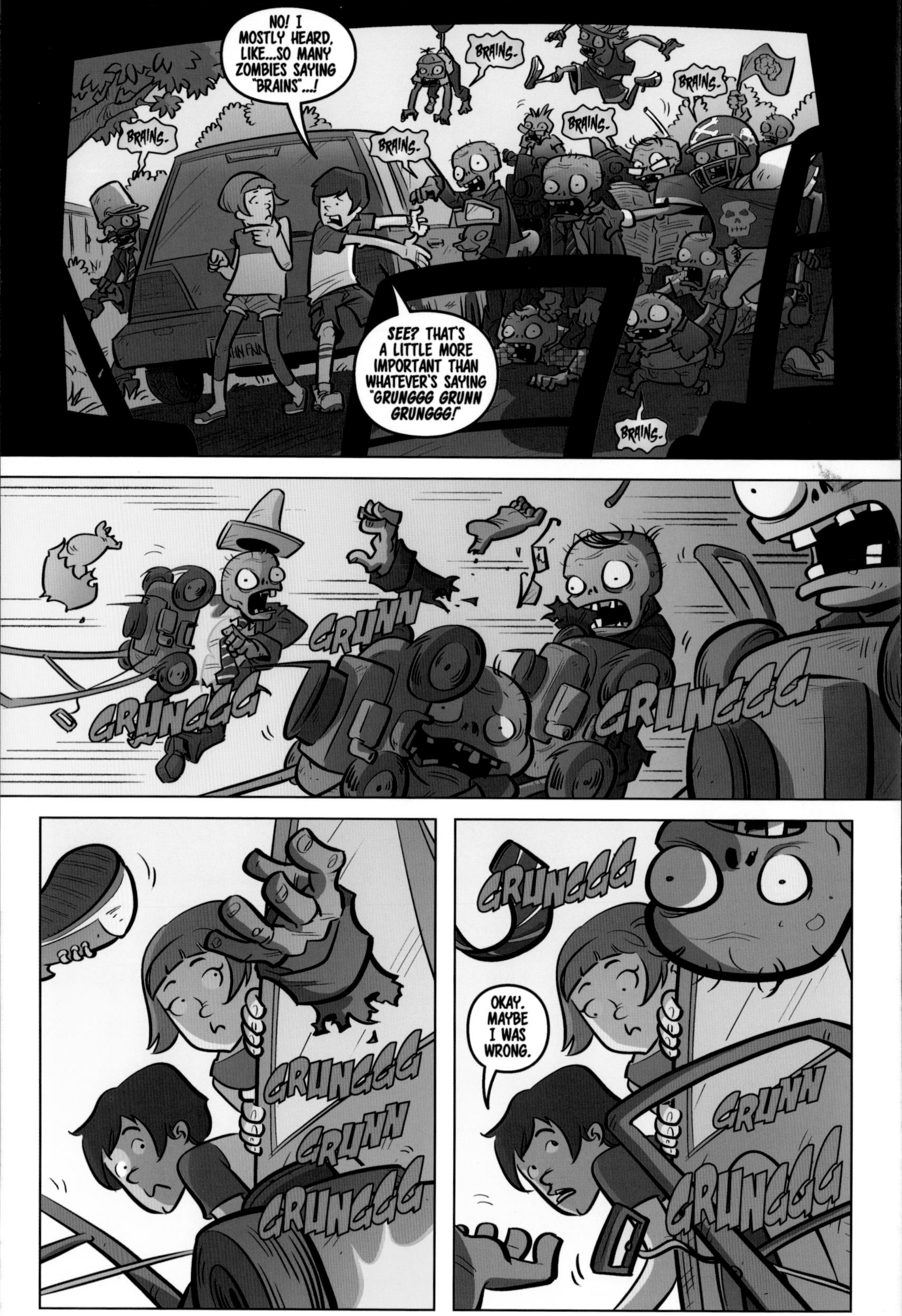
NO! I MOSTLY HEARD, LIKE...SO MANY ZOMBIES SAYING "BRAINS"...!
BRAINS.
BRAINS.
BRAINS.
BRAINS.
BRAINS.
BRAINS.
SEE? THAT'S A LITTLE MORE IMPORTANT THAN WHATEVER'S SAYING "GRUNGGG GRUNN GRUNGGG!"
BRAINS.
GRUNN
GRUNGGG
GRUNGGG
GRUNGGG
GRUNN
GRUNGGG
GRUNGGG
OKAY. MAYBE I WAS WRONG.
GRUNN
GRUNGGG

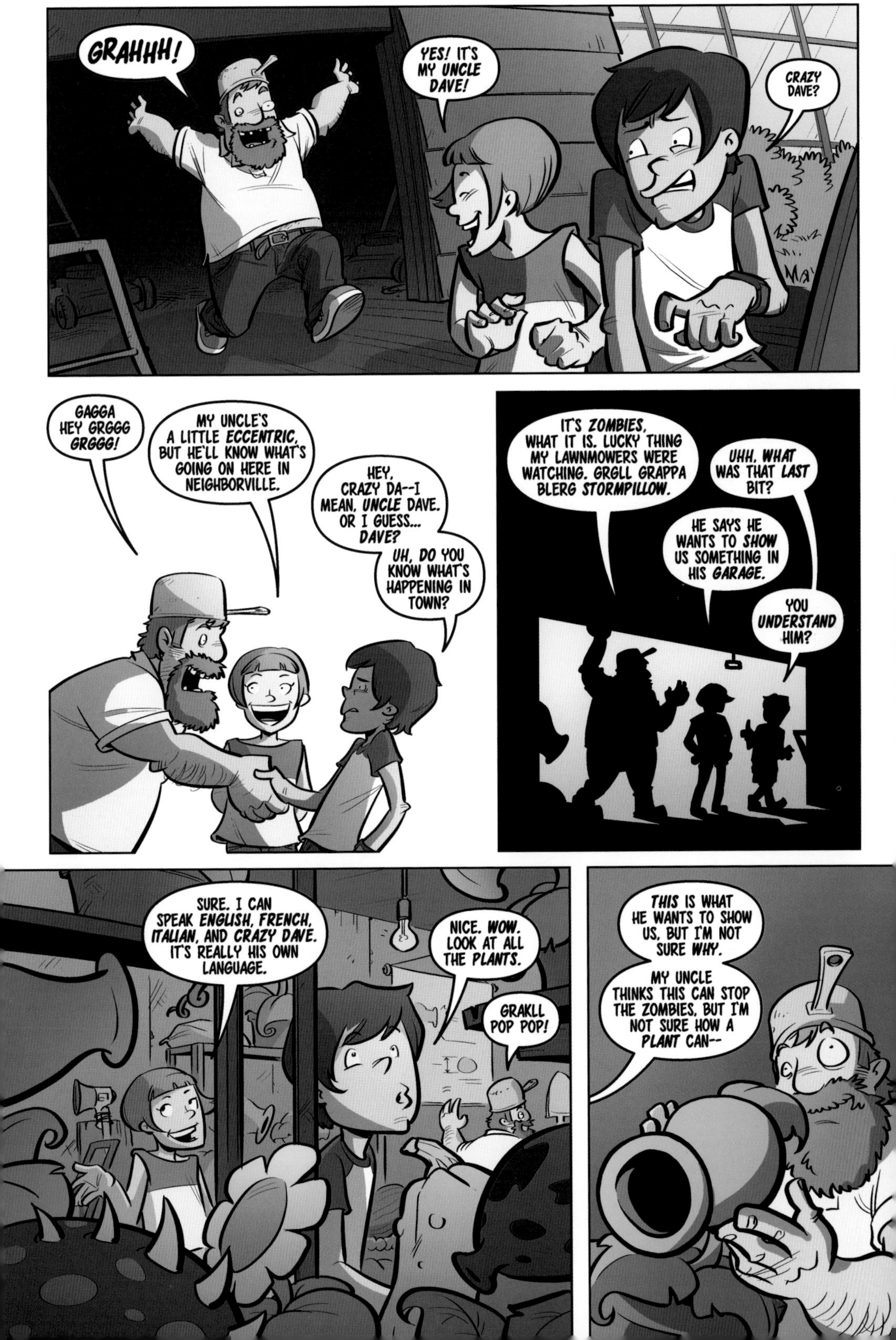
GRAHHH!
YES! IT'S MY UNCLE DAVE!
CRAZY DAVE?
GAGGA HEY GRGGG GRGGG!
MY UNCLE'S A LITTLE ECCENTRIC, BUT HE'LL KNOW WHAT'S GOING ON HERE IN NEIGHBORVILLE.
HEY, CRAZY DA--I MEAN, UNCLE DAVE. OR I GUESS... DAVE?
UH, DO YOU KNOW WHAT'S HAPPENING IN TOWN?
IT'S ZOMBIES, WHAT IT IS. LUCKY THING MY LAWNMOWERS WERE WATCHING. GRGLL GRAPPA BLERG STORMPILLOW.
UHH, WHAT WAS THAT LAST BIT?
HE SAYS HE WANTS TO SHOW US SOMETHING IN HIS GARAGE.
YOU UNDERSTAND HIM?
SURE. I CAN SPEAK ENGLISH, FRENCH, ITALIAN, AND CRAZY DAVE. IT'S REALLY HIS OWN LANGUAGE.
NICE. WOW. LOOK AT ALL THE PLANTS.
GRAKLL POP POP!
THIS IS WHAT HE WANTS TO SHOW US, BUT I'M NOT SURE WHY.
MY UNCLE THINKS THIS CAN STOP THE ZOMBIES, BUT I'M NOT SURE HOW A PLANT CAN--

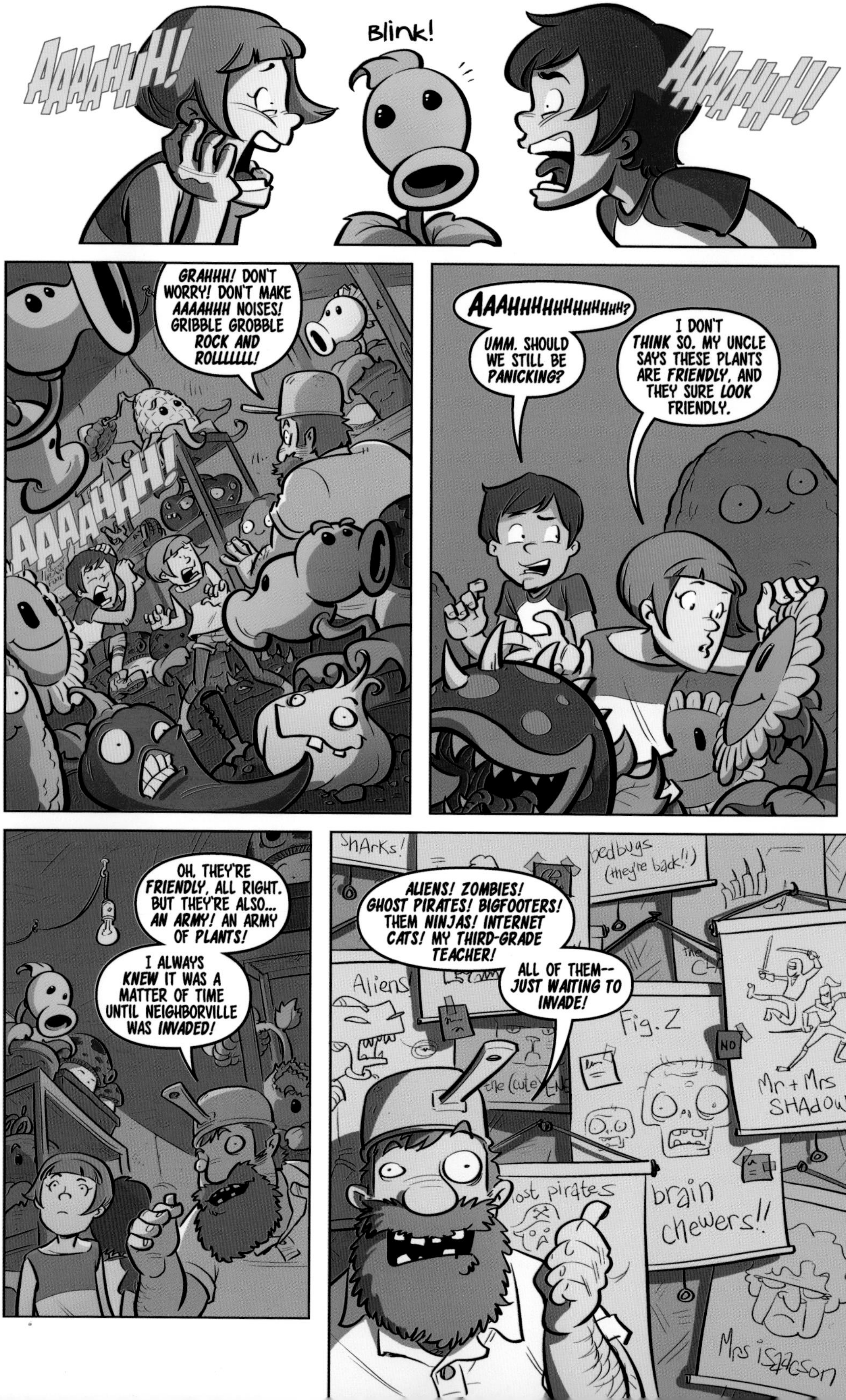
AAAAHHH!
Blink!
AAAAHHH!!
GRAHHH! DON'T WORRY! DON'T MAKE AAAAHHH NOISES! GRIBBLE GROBBLE ROCK AND ROLLLLLLL!
AAAAHHH!
AAAHHHHHHHHHHHHH?
UMM. SHOULD WE STILL BE PANICKING?
I DON'T THINK SO. MY UNCLE SAYS THESE PLANTS ARE FRIENDLY, AND THEY SURE LOOK FRIENDLY.
OH, THEY'RE FRIENDLY, ALL RIGHT. BUT THEY'RE ALSO... AN ARMY! AN ARMY OF PLANTS!
I ALWAYS KNEW IT WAS A MATTER OF TIME UNTIL NEIGHBORVILLE WAS INVADED!
ALIENS! ZOMBIES! GHOST PIRATES! BIGFOOTERS! THEM NINJAS! INTERNET CATS! MY THIRD-GRADE TEACHER!
ALL OF THEM-- JUST WAITING TO INVADE!
ShArKs!
bedbugs (they're back!!)
Aliens!
Fig. Z
NO
Mr + Mrs SHADOW...
brain chewers!!
Mrs isaacson

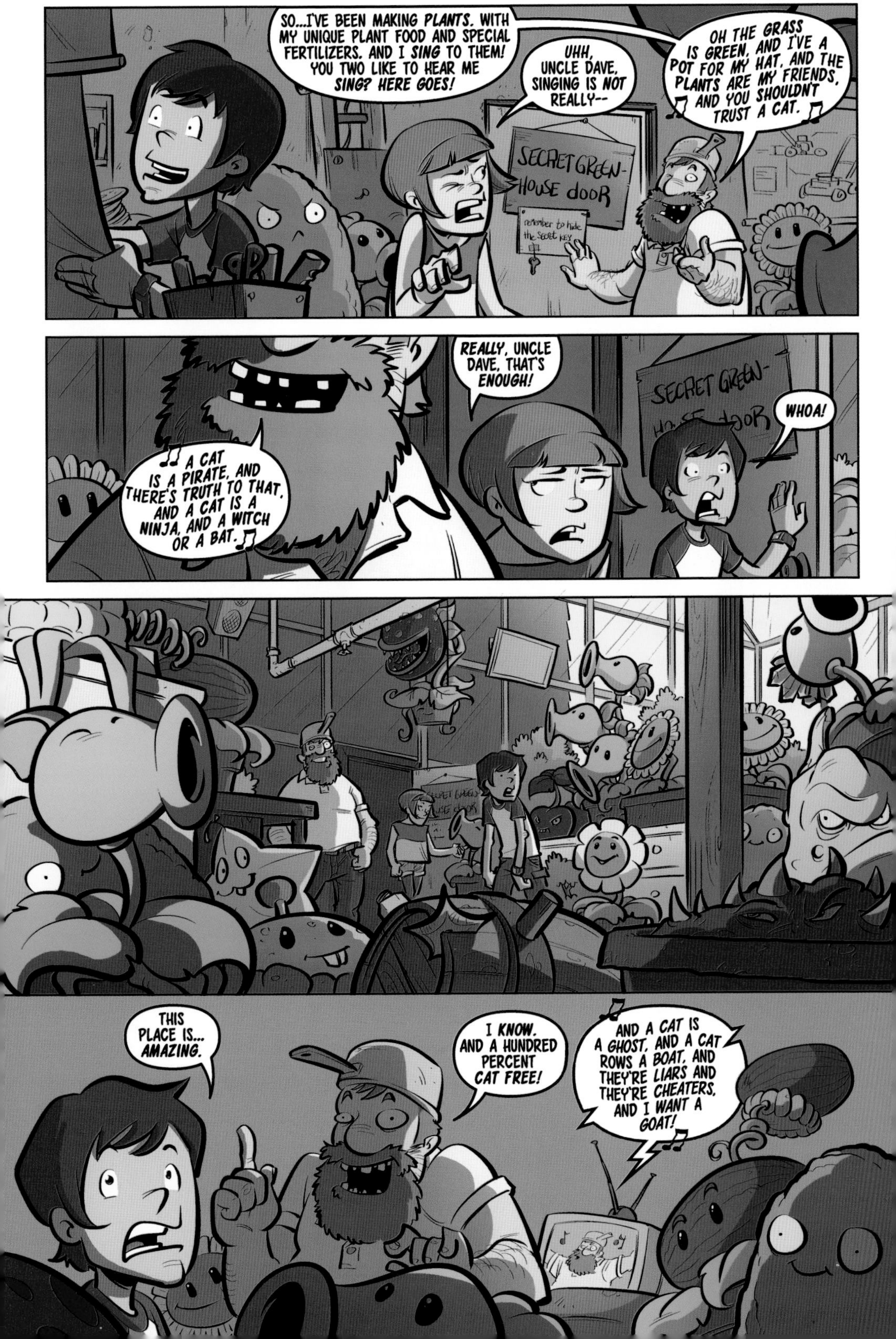
SO...I'VE BEEN MAKING PLANTS. WITH MY UNIQUE PLANT FOOD AND SPECIAL FERTILIZERS. AND I SING TO THEM! YOU TWO LIKE TO HEAR ME SING? HERE GOES!
UHH, UNCLE DAVE, SINGING IS NOT REALLY--
OH THE GRASS IS GREEN, AND I'VE A POT FOR MY HAT, AND THE PLANTS ARE MY FRIENDS, AND YOU SHOULDN'T TRUST A CAT.
SECRET GREEN-HOUSE door
remember to hide the Secret key
A CAT IS A PIRATE, AND THERE'S TRUTH TO THAT, AND A CAT IS A NINJA, AND A WITCH OR A BAT.
REALLY, UNCLE DAVE, THAT'S ENOUGH!
WHOA!
THIS PLACE IS... AMAZING.
I KNOW. AND A HUNDRED PERCENT CAT FREE!
AND A CAT IS A GHOST, AND A CAT ROWS A BOAT, AND THEY'RE LIARS AND THEY'RE CHEATERS, AND I WANT A GOAT!

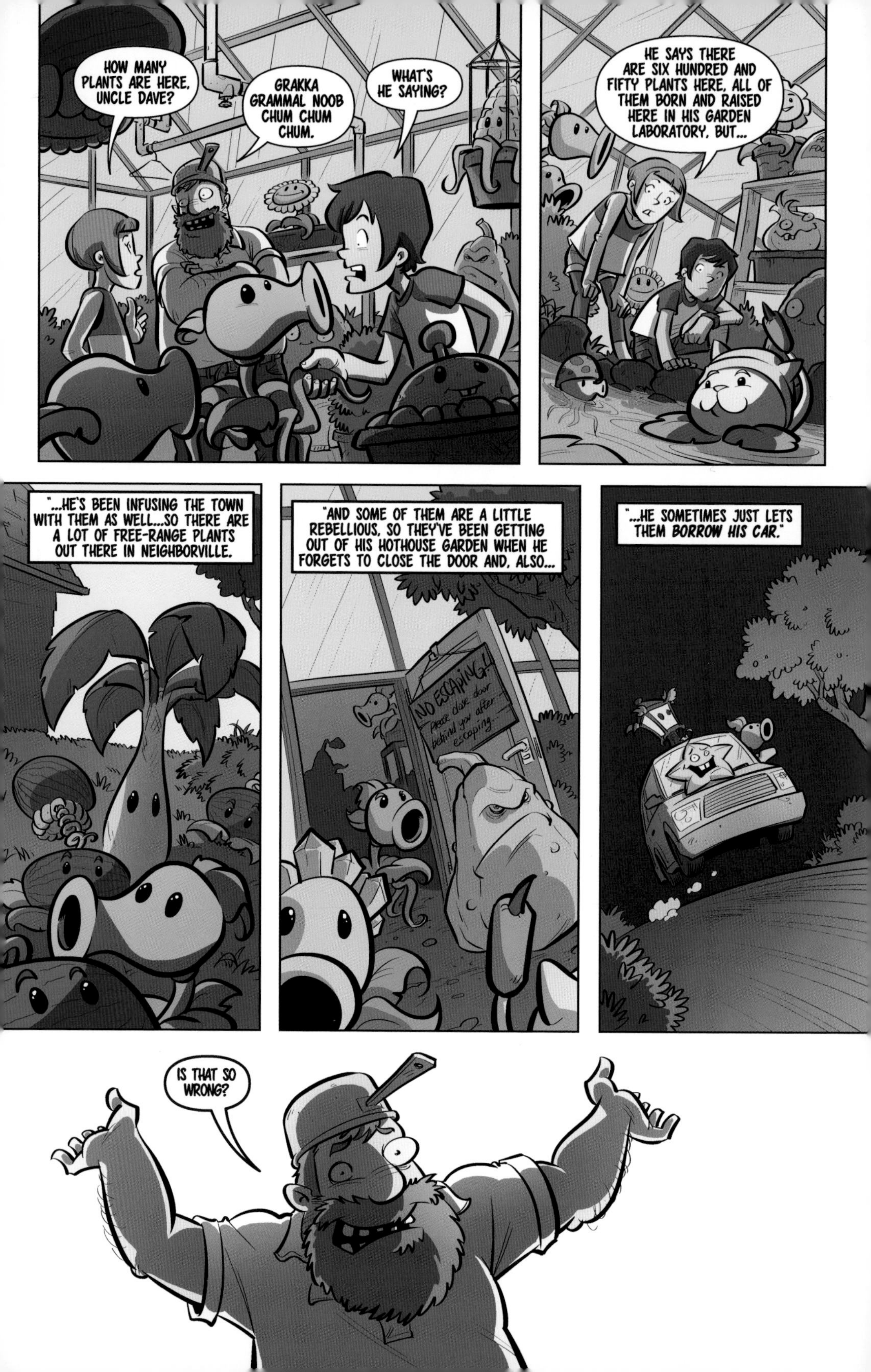
HOW MANY PLANTS ARE HERE, UNCLE DAVE?
GRAKKA GRAMMAL NOOB CHUM CHUM CHUM.
WHAT'S HE SAYING?
HE SAYS THERE ARE SIX HUNDRED AND FIFTY PLANTS HERE, ALL OF THEM BORN AND RAISED HERE IN HIS GARDEN LABORATORY, BUT...
"...HE'S BEEN INFUSING THE TOWN WITH THEM AS WELL...SO THERE ARE A LOT OF FREE-RANGE PLANTS OUT THERE IN NEIGHBORVILLE.
"AND SOME OF THEM ARE A LITTLE REBELLIOUS, SO THEY'VE BEEN GETTING OUT OF HIS HOTHOUSE GARDEN WHEN HE FORGETS TO CLOSE THE DOOR AND, ALSO...
NO ESCAPING!
Please close door behind you after escaping...
"...HE SOMETIMES JUST LETS THEM BORROW HIS CAR."
IS THAT SO WRONG?

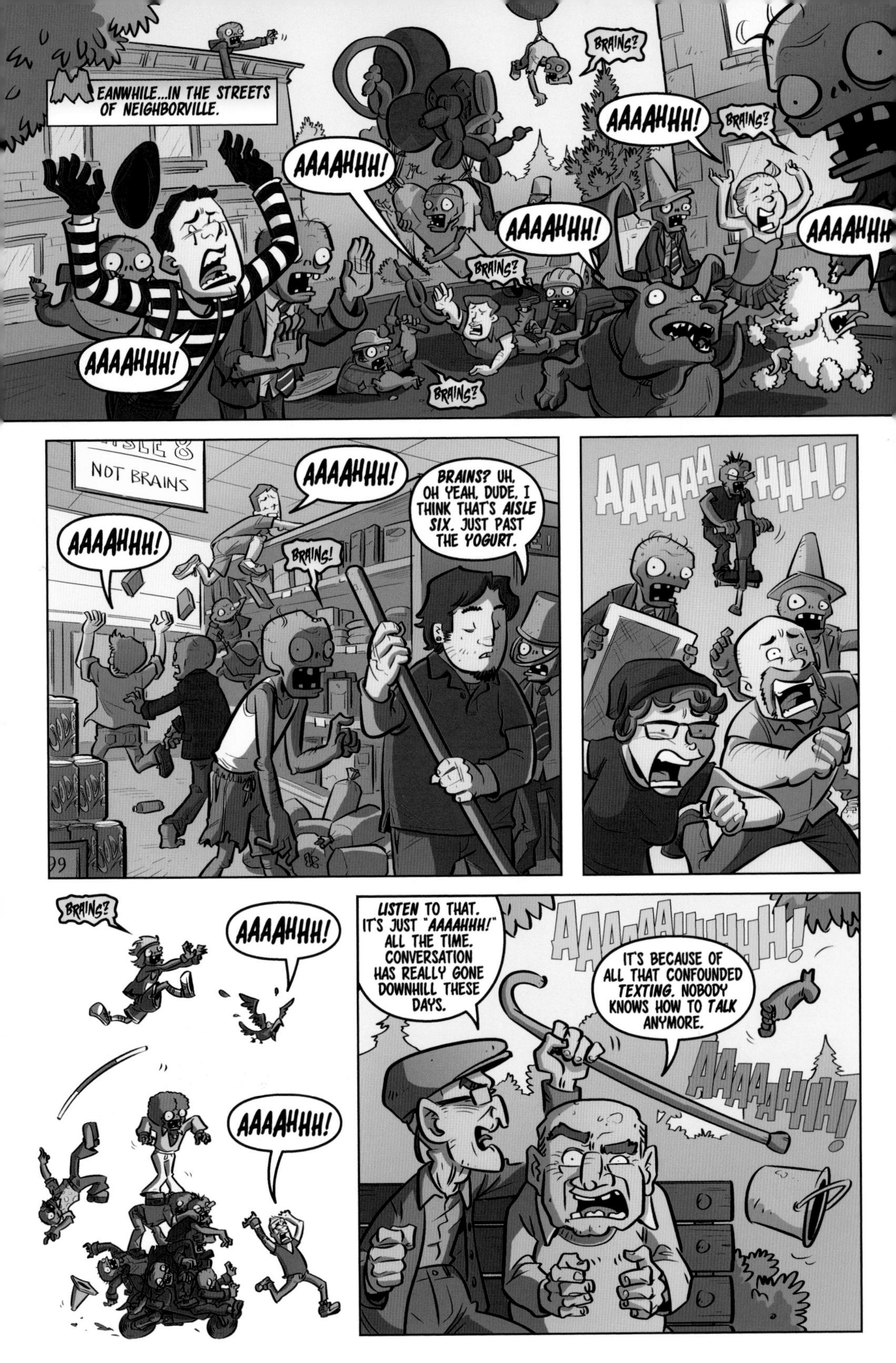
MEANWHILE...IN THE STREETS OF NEIGHBORVILLE.
BRAINS?
AAAAHHH!
AAAAHHH!
BRAINS?
AAAAHHH!
AAAAHHH
BRAINS?
AAAAHHH!
BRAINS?
NOT BRAINS
AAAAHHH!
AAAAHHH!
BRAINS? UH, OH YEAH, DUDE, I THINK THAT'S AISLE SIX. JUST PAST THE YOGURT.
BRAINS!
AAAAAAHHH!
BRAINS?
AAAAHHH!
AAAAHHH!
LISTEN TO THAT. IT'S JUST "AAAAHHH!" ALL THE TIME. CONVERSATION HAS REALLY GONE DOWNHILL THESE DAYS.
IT'S BECAUSE OF ALL THAT CONFOUNDED TEXTING. NOBODY KNOWS HOW TO TALK ANYMORE.
AAAAAHHHH!

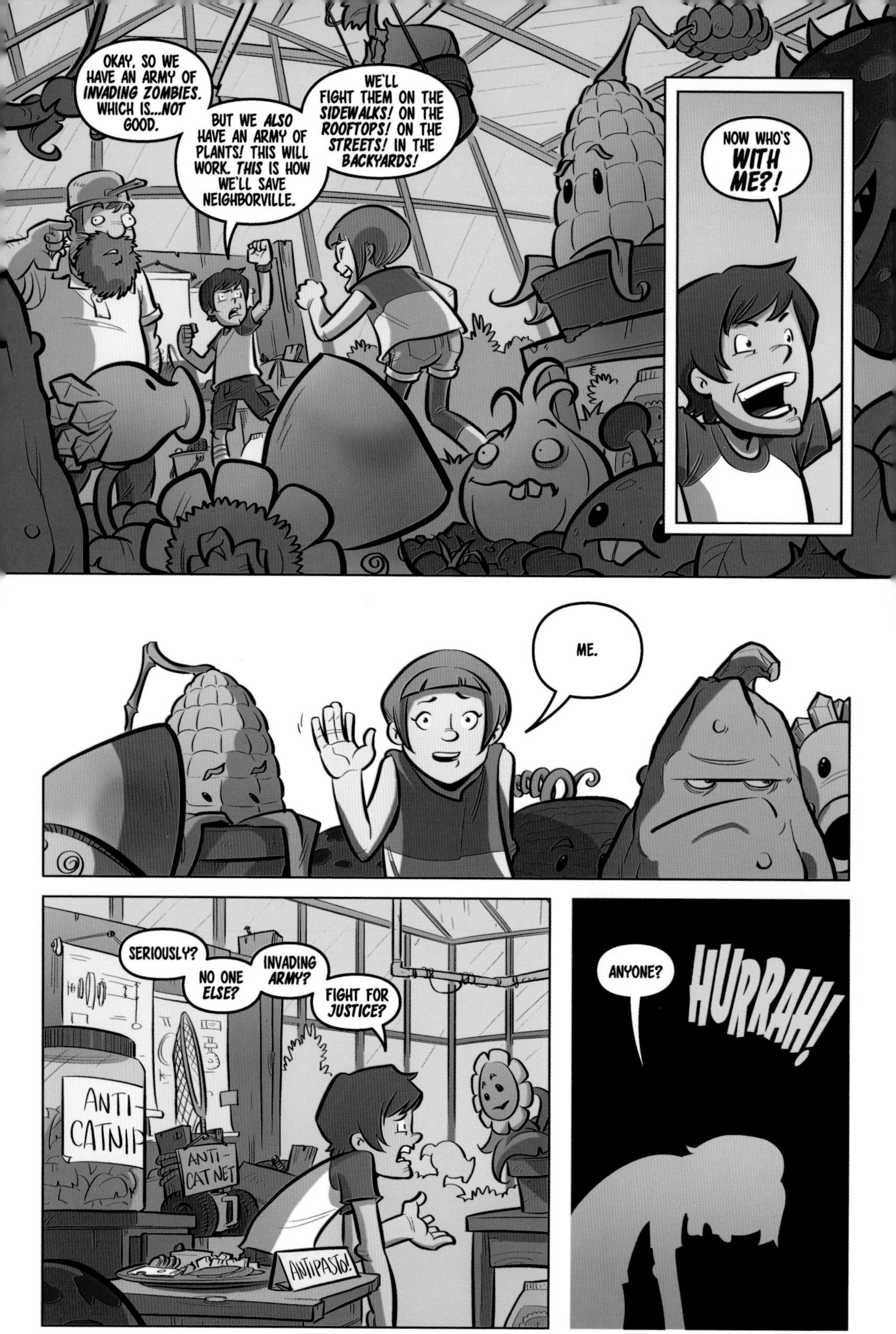
OKAY, SO WE HAVE AN ARMY OF INVADING ZOMBIES. WHICH IS...NOT GOOD.
BUT WE ALSO HAVE AN ARMY OF PLANTS! THIS WILL WORK. THIS IS HOW WE'LL SAVE NEIGHBORVILLE.
WE'LL FIGHT THEM ON THE SIDEWALKS! ON THE ROOFTOPS! ON THE STREETS! IN THE BACKYARDS!
NOW WHO'S WITH ME?!
ME.
SERIOUSLY?
NO ONE ELSE?
INVADING ARMY?
FIGHT FOR JUSTICE?
ANTI-CATNIP
ANTI-CAT NET
ANTIPASTO!
ANYONE?
HURRAH!

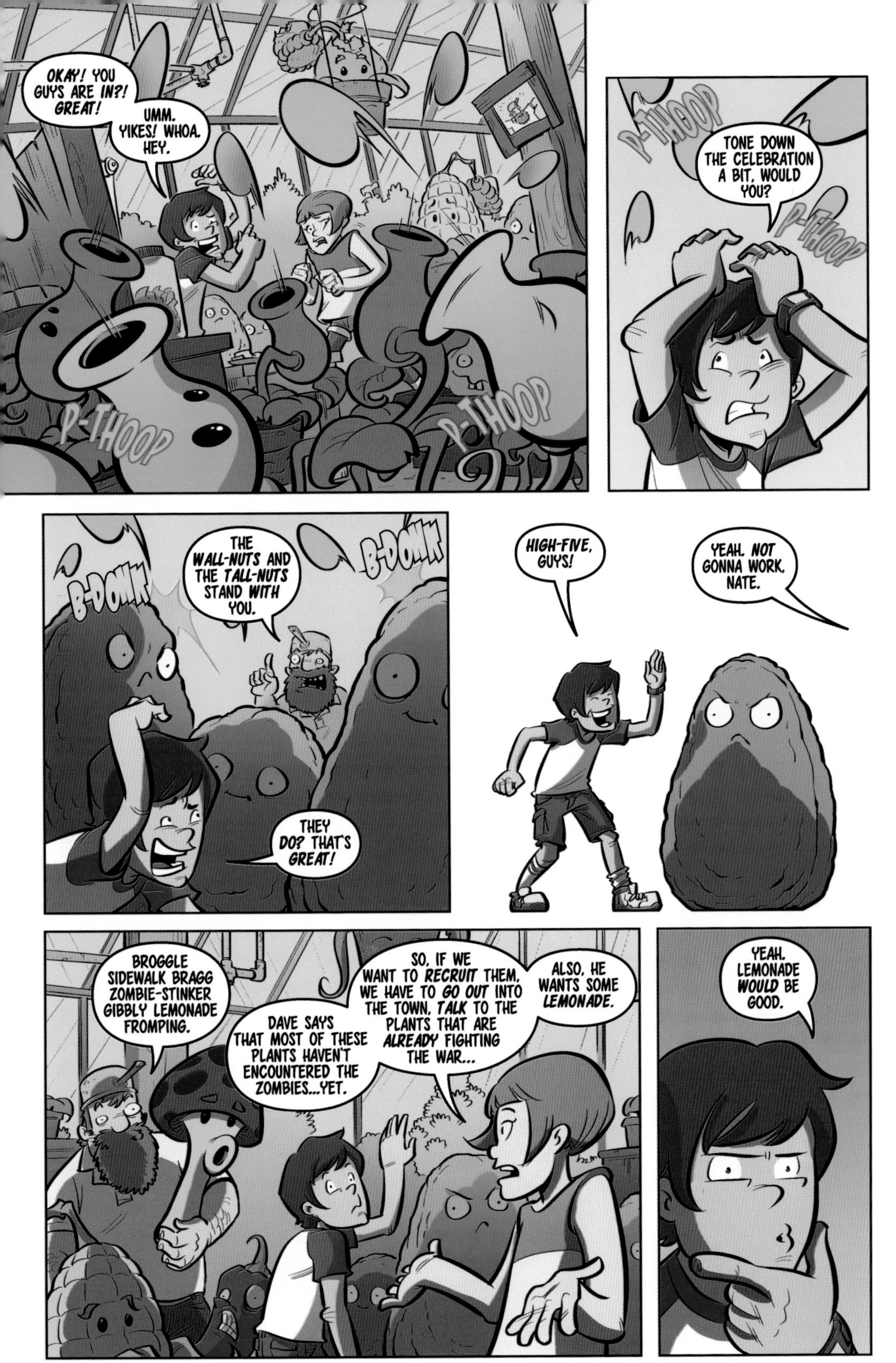
OKAY! YOU GUYS ARE IN?! GREAT!
UMM. YIKES! WHOA. HEY.
P-THOOP
P-THOOP
P-THOOP
TONE DOWN THE CELEBRATION A BIT, WOULD YOU?
P-THOOP
B-DONK
THE WALL-NUTS AND THE TALL-NUTS STAND WITH YOU.
B-DONK
THEY DO? THAT'S GREAT!
HIGH-FIVE, GUYS!
YEAH. NOT GONNA WORK, NATE.
BROGGLE SIDEWALK BRAGG ZOMBIE-STINKER GIBBLY LEMONADE FROMPING.
DAVE SAYS THAT MOST OF THESE PLANTS HAVEN'T ENCOUNTERED THE ZOMBIES...YET.
SO, IF WE WANT TO RECRUIT THEM, WE HAVE TO GO OUT INTO THE TOWN, TALK TO THE PLANTS THAT ARE ALREADY FIGHTING THE WAR...
ALSO, HE WANTS SOME LEMONADE.
YEAH. LEMONADE WOULD BE GOOD.

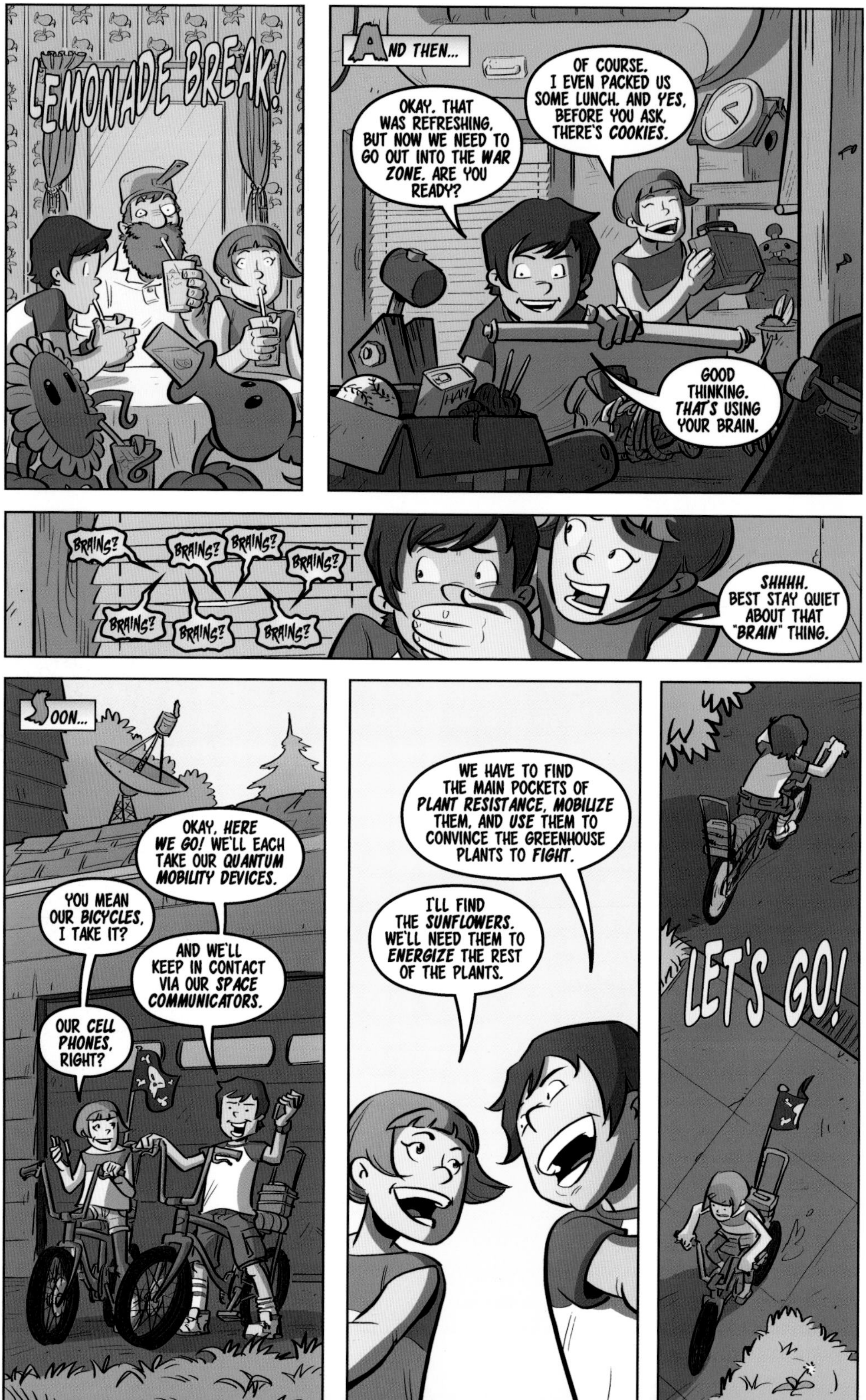
LEMONADE BREAK!
AND THEN...
OKAY. THAT WAS REFRESHING, BUT NOW WE NEED TO GO OUT INTO THE WAR ZONE. ARE YOU READY?
OF COURSE. I EVEN PACKED US SOME LUNCH. AND YES, BEFORE YOU ASK, THERE'S COOKIES.
HAM
GOOD THINKING. THAT'S USING YOUR BRAIN.
BRAINS?
BRAINS?
BRAINS?
BRAINS?
BRAINS?
BRAINS?
BRAINS?
SHHHH. BEST STAY QUIET ABOUT THAT "BRAIN" THING.
SOON...
OKAY, HERE WE GO! WE'LL EACH TAKE OUR QUANTUM MOBILITY DEVICES.
YOU MEAN OUR BICYCLES, I TAKE IT?
AND WE'LL KEEP IN CONTACT VIA OUR SPACE COMMUNICATORS.
OUR CELL PHONES, RIGHT?
WE HAVE TO FIND THE MAIN POCKETS OF PLANT RESISTANCE, MOBILIZE THEM, AND USE THEM TO CONVINCE THE GREENHOUSE PLANTS TO FIGHT.
I'LL FIND THE SUNFLOWERS. WE'LL NEED THEM TO ENERGIZE THE REST OF THE PLANTS.
LET'S GO!

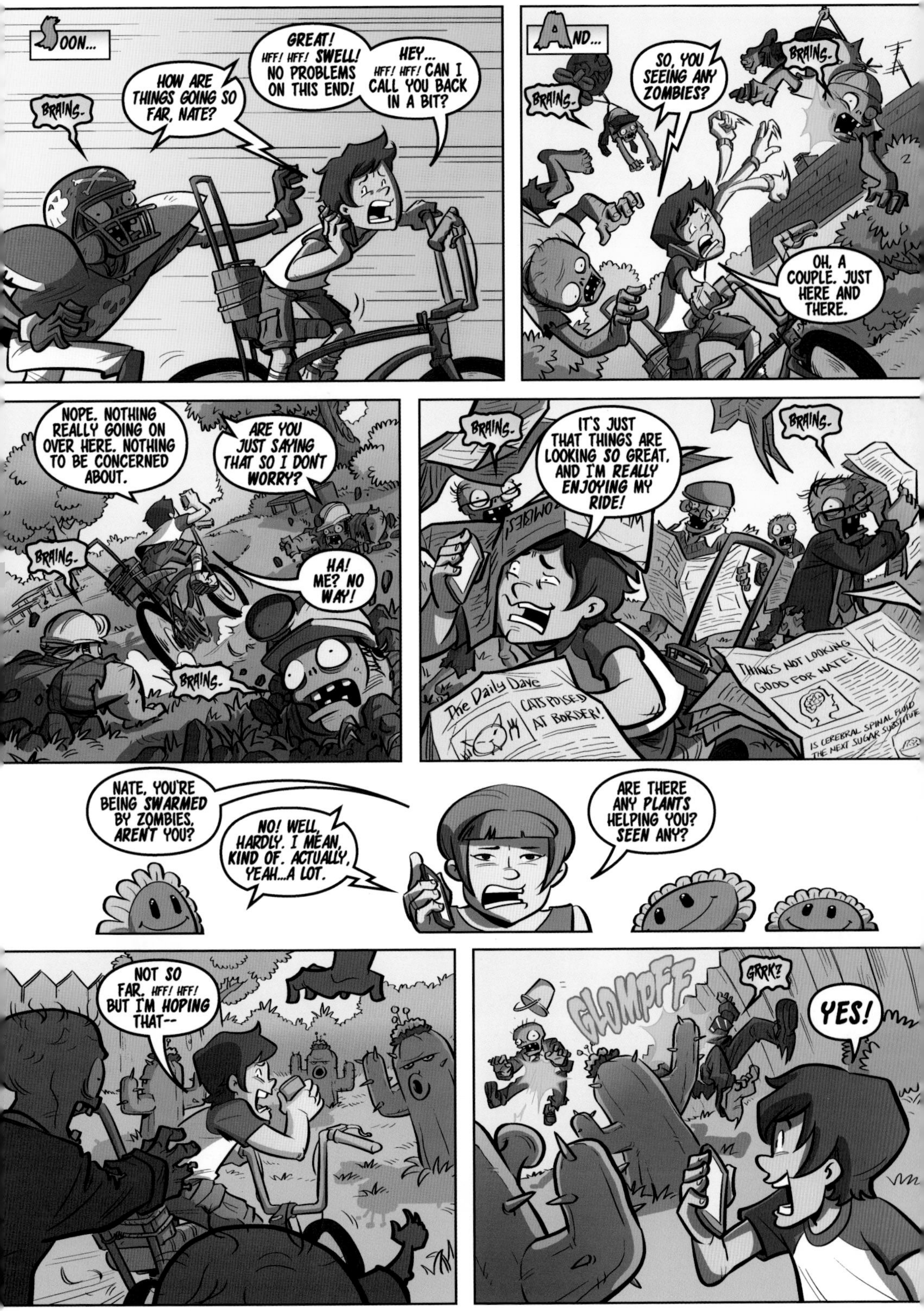
SOON...
BRAINS.
HOW ARE THINGS GOING SO FAR, NATE?
GREAT! HFF! HFF! SWELL! NO PROBLEMS ON THIS END!
HEY... HFF! HFF! CAN I CALL YOU BACK IN A BIT?
AND...
BRAINS.
SO, YOU SEEING ANY ZOMBIES?
BRAINS.
OH, A COUPLE. JUST HERE AND THERE.
NOPE. NOTHING REALLY GOING ON OVER HERE. NOTHING TO BE CONCERNED ABOUT.
ARE YOU JUST SAYING THAT SO I DON'T WORRY?
BRAINS.
HA! ME? NO WAY!
BRAINS.
BRAINS.
IT'S JUST THAT THINGS ARE LOOKING SO GREAT, AND I'M REALLY ENJOYING MY RIDE!
BRAINS.
The Daily Dave
CATS POISED AT BORDER!
THINGS NOT LOOKING GOOD FOR NATE!
IS CEREBRAL SPINAL FLUID THE NEXT SUGAR SUBSTITUTE
NATE, YOU'RE BEING SWARMED BY ZOMBIES, AREN'T YOU?
NO! WELL, HARDLY. I MEAN, KIND OF. ACTUALLY, YEAH...A LOT.
ARE THERE ANY PLANTS HELPING YOU? SEEN ANY?
NOT SO FAR. HFF! HFF! BUT I'M HOPING THAT--
GLOMPFF
GRRK?
YES!

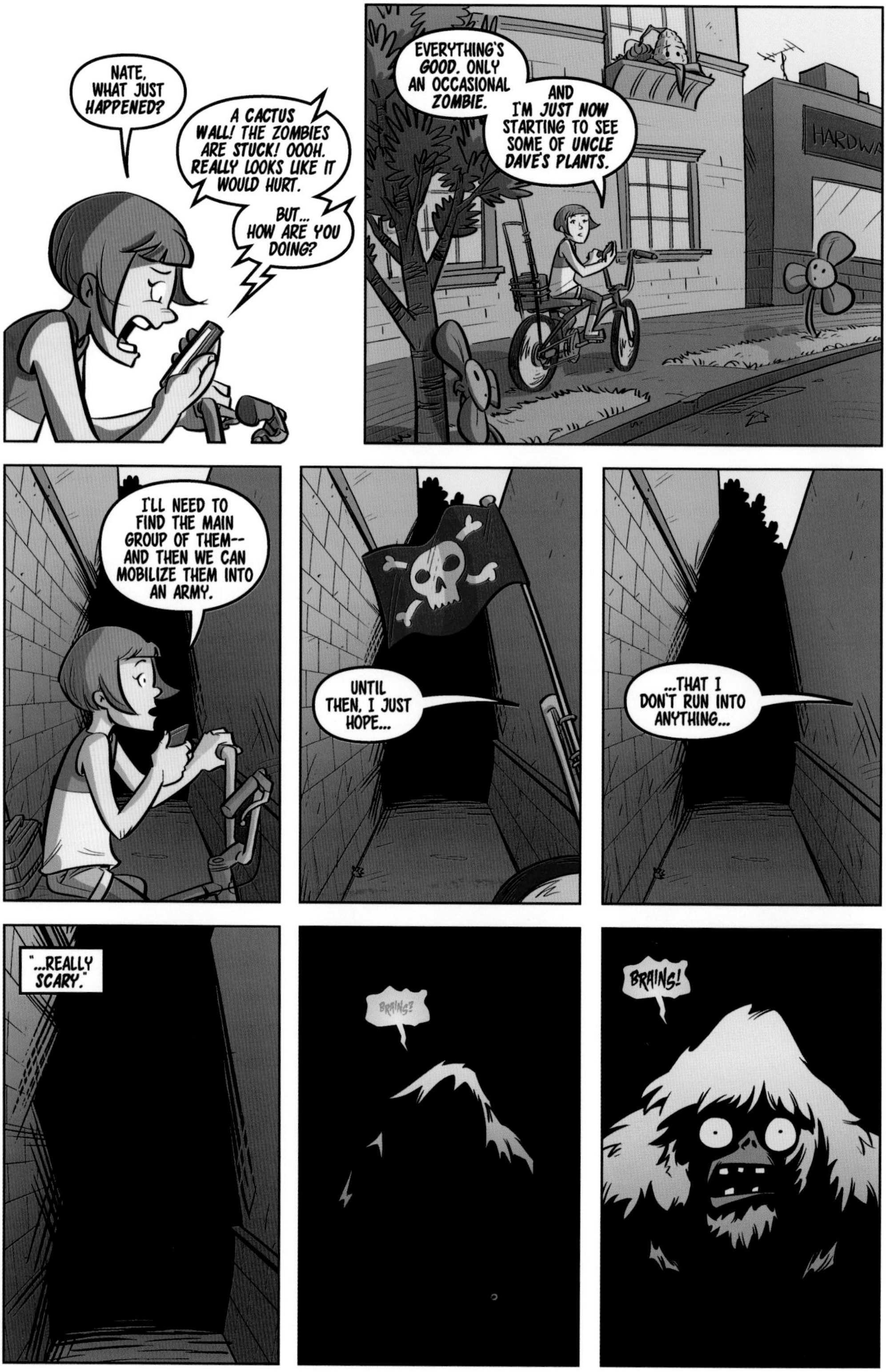
NATE, WHAT JUST HAPPENED?
A CACTUS WALL! THE ZOMBIES ARE STUCK! OOOH. REALLY LOOKS LIKE IT WOULD HURT.
BUT... HOW ARE YOU DOING?
EVERYTHING'S GOOD. ONLY AN OCCASIONAL ZOMBIE.
AND I'M JUST NOW STARTING TO SEE SOME OF UNCLE DAVE'S PLANTS.
HARDWA
I'LL NEED TO FIND THE MAIN GROUP OF THEM--AND THEN WE CAN MOBILIZE THEM INTO AN ARMY.
UNTIL THEN, I JUST HOPE...
...THAT I DON'T RUN INTO ANYTHING...
"...REALLY SCARY."
BRAINS?
BRAINS!

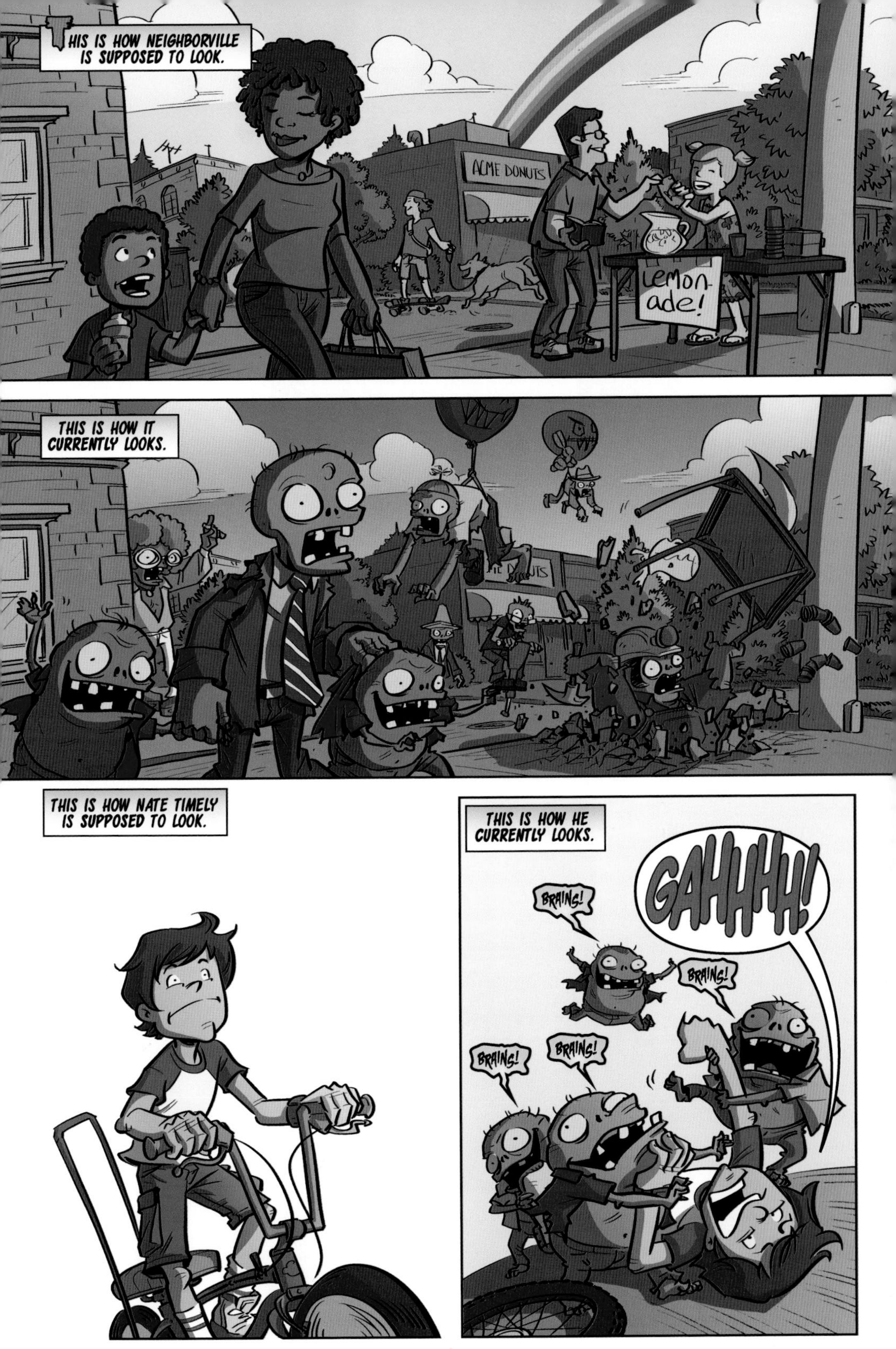
THIS IS HOW NEIGHBORVILLE IS SUPPOSED TO LOOK.
ACME DONUTS
LEMON-ADE!
THIS IS HOW IT CURRENTLY LOOKS.
THIS IS HOW NATE TIMELY IS SUPPOSED TO LOOK.
THIS IS HOW HE CURRENTLY LOOKS.
BRAINS!
GAHHHH!
BRAINS!
BRAINS!
BRAINS!

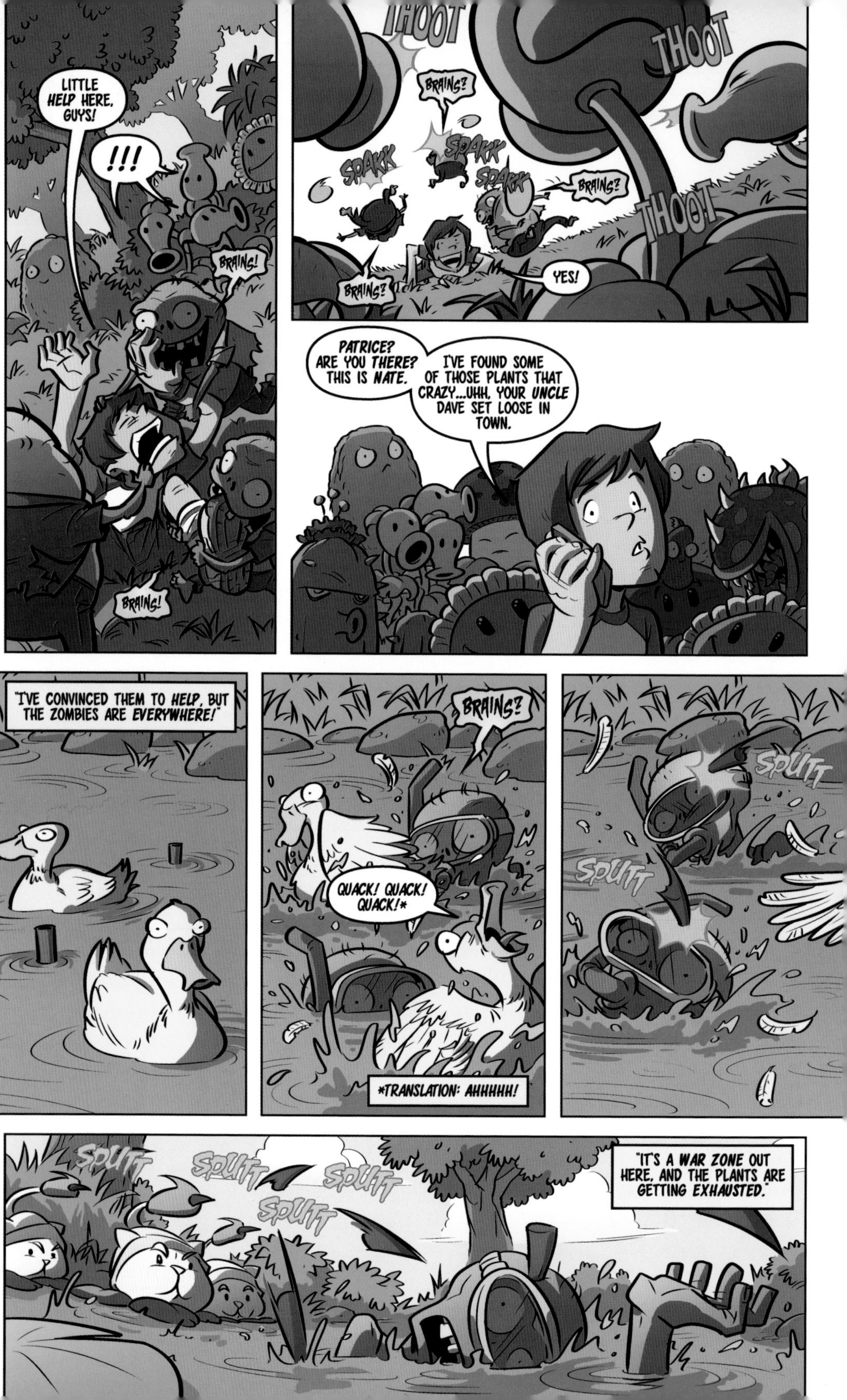
LITTLE HELP HERE, GUYS!
!!!
BRAINS!
BRAINS!
THOOT
BRAINS?
SPAKK
SPAKK
SPAKK
THOOT
BRAINS?
THOOT
BRAINS?
YES!
PATRICE? ARE YOU THERE? THIS IS NATE.
I'VE FOUND SOME OF THOSE PLANTS THAT CRAZY...UHH, YOUR UNCLE DAVE SET LOOSE IN TOWN.
"I'VE CONVINCED THEM TO HELP, BUT THE ZOMBIES ARE EVERYWHERE!"
BRAINS?
QUACK! QUACK! QUACK!*
*TRANSLATION: AHHHHH!
SPUTT
SPUTT
SPUTT
SPUTT
SPUTT
SPUTT
"IT'S A WAR ZONE OUT HERE, AND THE PLANTS ARE GETTING EXHAUSTED."

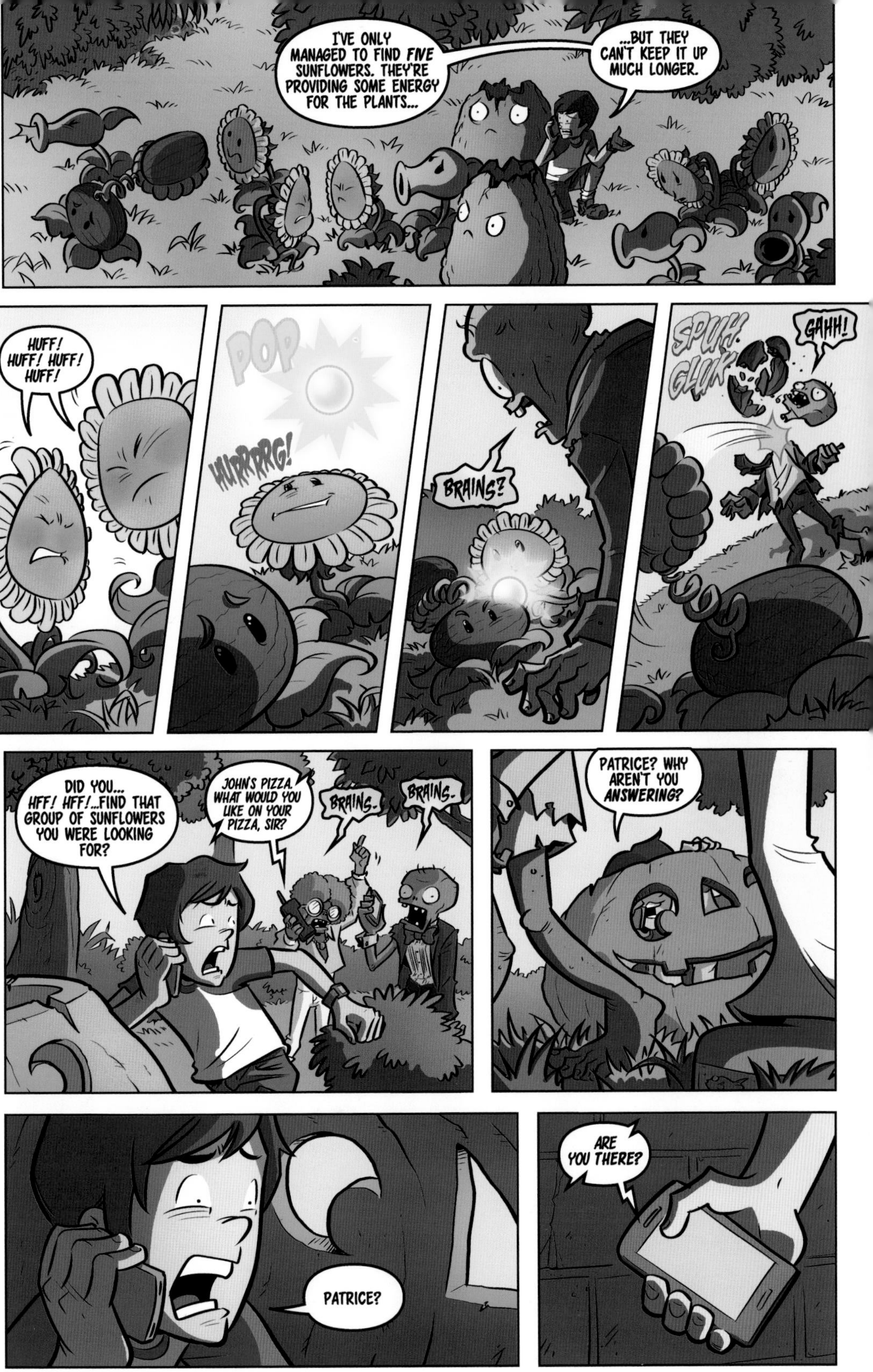
I'VE ONLY MANAGED TO FIND *FIVE* SUNFLOWERS. THEY'RE PROVIDING SOME ENERGY FOR THE PLANTS...
...BUT THEY CAN'T KEEP IT UP MUCH LONGER.
HUFF! HUFF! HUFF! HUFF!
POP
HURRRRG!
BRAINS?
SPUH. GLUK
GAHH!
DID YOU... HFF! HFF!...FIND THAT GROUP OF SUNFLOWERS YOU WERE LOOKING FOR?
JOHN'S PIZZA. WHAT WOULD YOU LIKE ON YOUR PIZZA, SIR?
BRAINS.
BRAINS.
PATRICE? WHY AREN'T YOU *ANSWERING?*
PATRICE?
ARE YOU *THERE?*

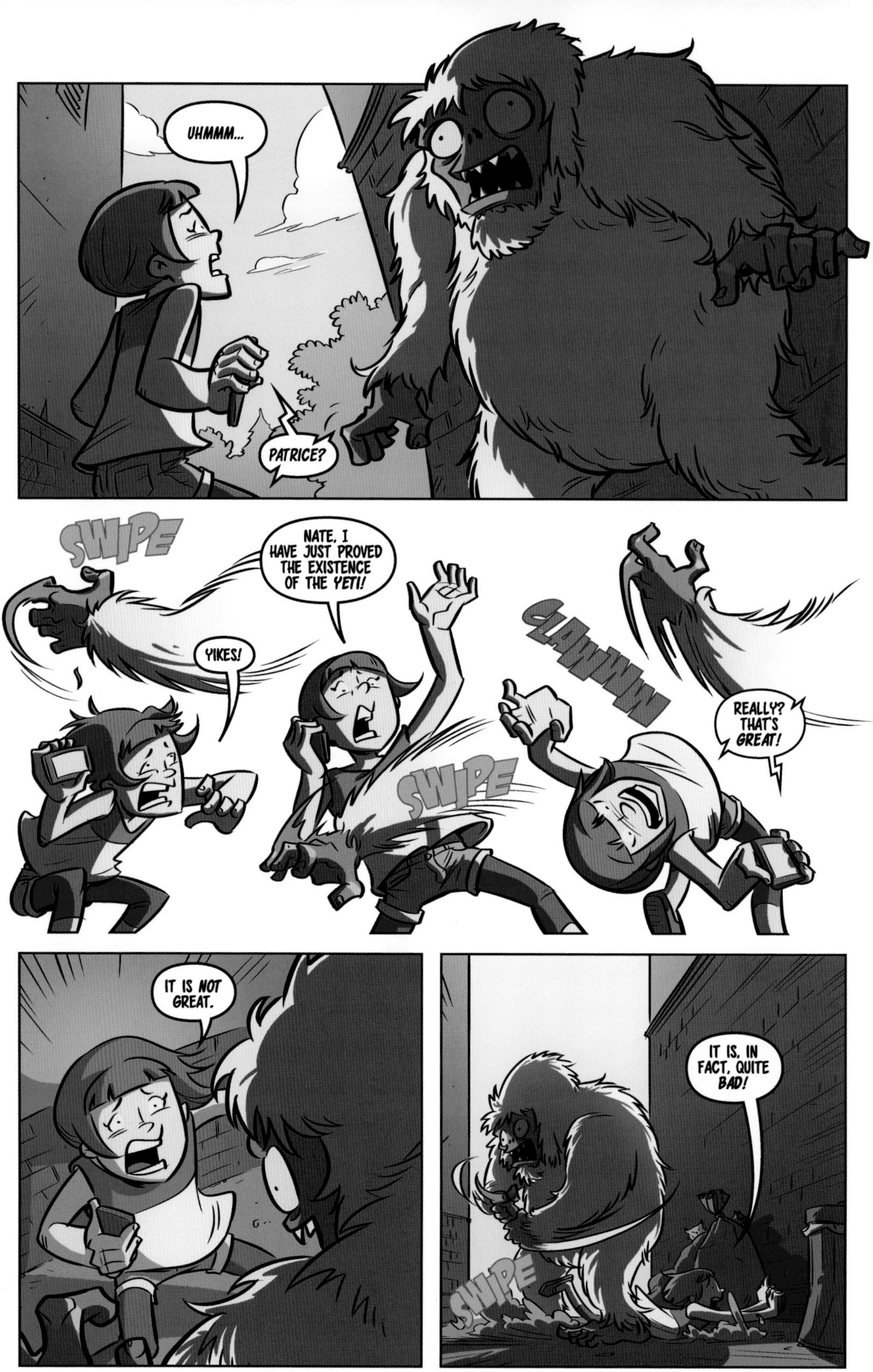
UHMMM...
PATRICE?
SWIPE
NATE, I HAVE JUST PROVED THE EXISTENCE OF THE YETI!
YIKES!
CLAWWWW
SWIPE
REALLY? THAT'S GREAT!
IT IS NOT GREAT.
IT IS, IN FACT, QUITE BAD!
SWIPE

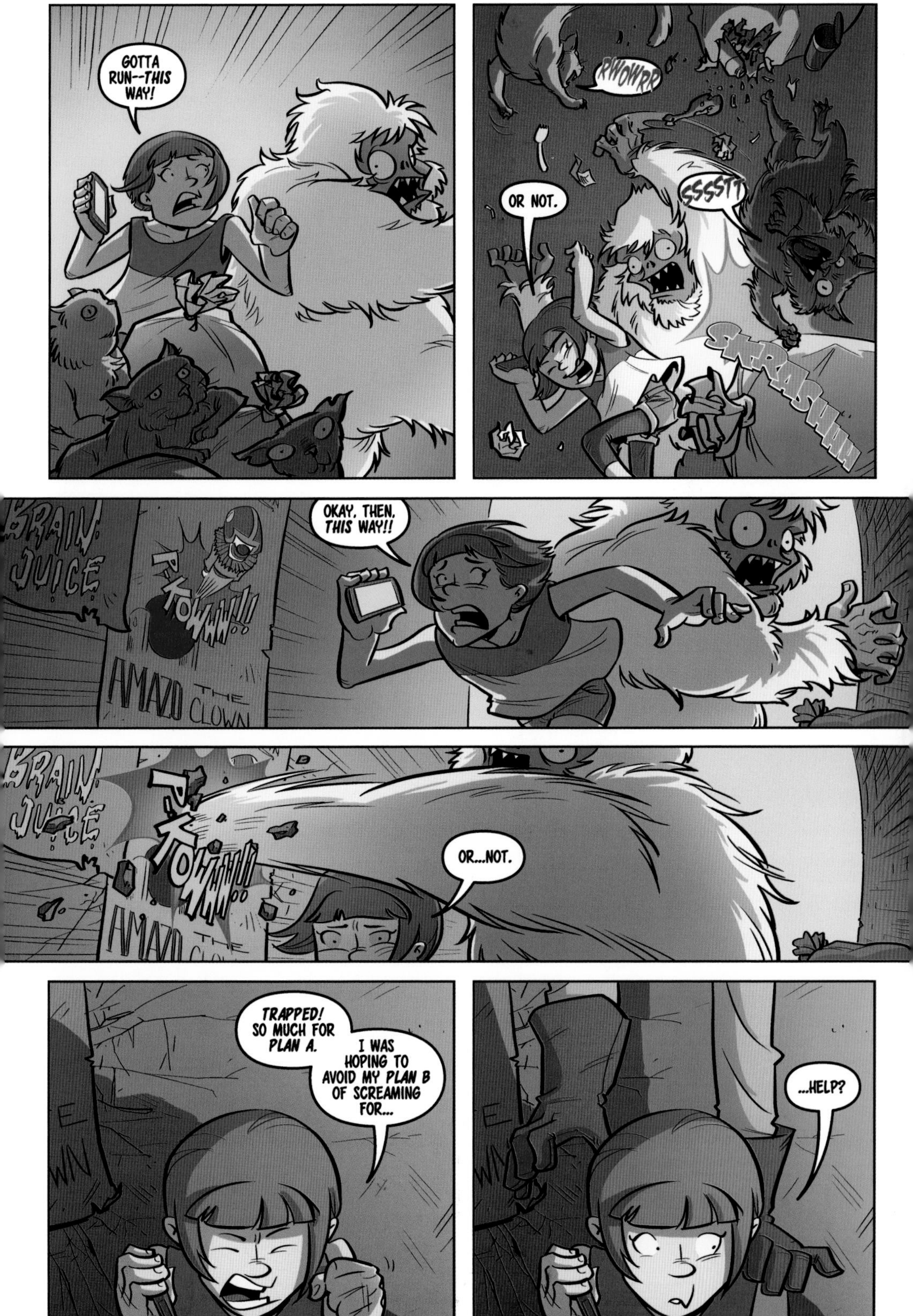
GOTTA RUN--THIS WAY!
RWOWRR
OR NOT.
SSSSTT
SKRASHHH
BRAIN JUICE
P-KOWWW!!
AMAZO THE CLOWN
OKAY, THEN, THIS WAY!!
BRAIN JUICE
P-KOWWW!!
AMAZO THE CLOWN
OR...NOT.
TRAPPED! SO MUCH FOR PLAN A.
I WAS HOPING TO AVOID MY PLAN B OF SCREAMING FOR...
...HELP?

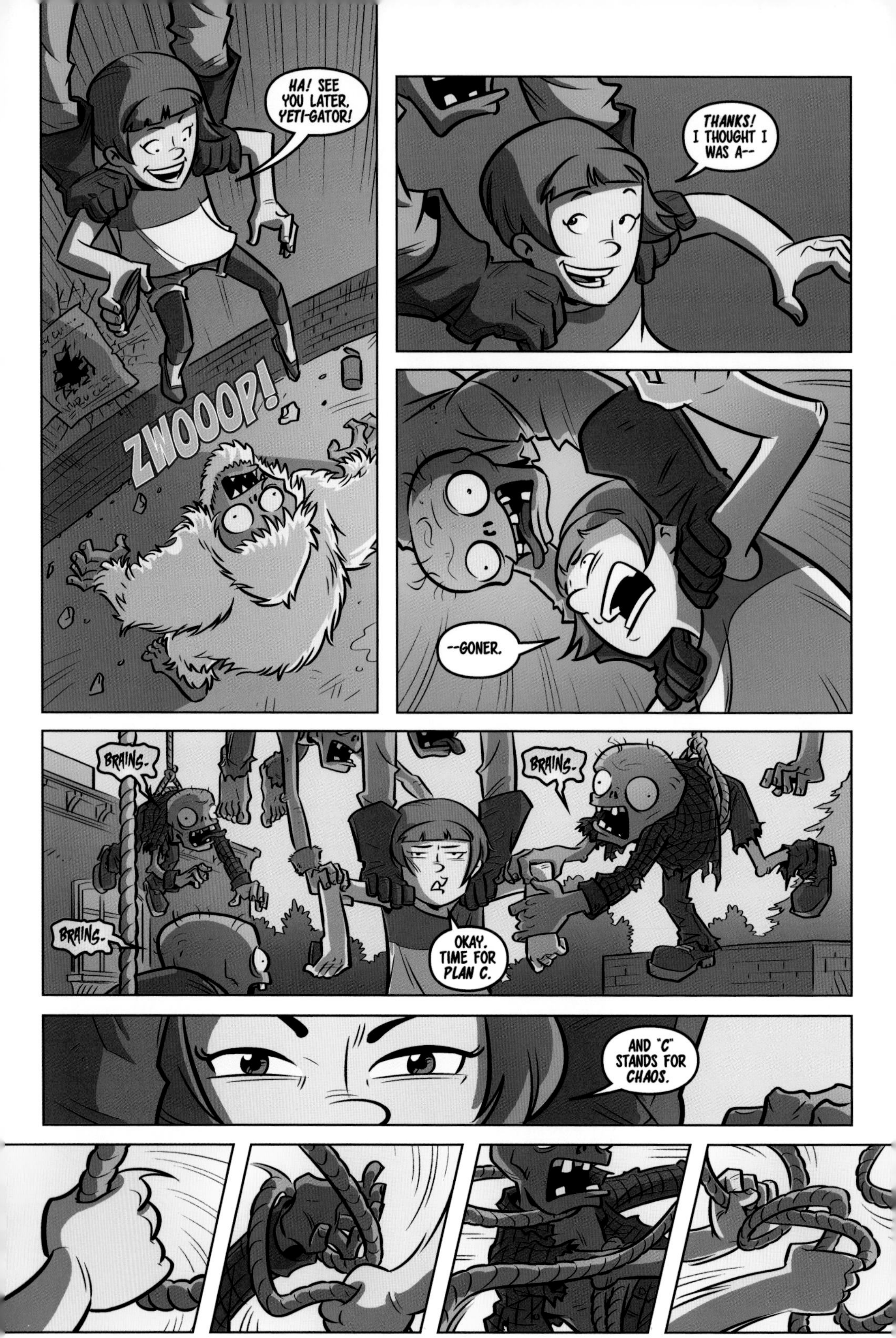
HA! SEE YOU LATER, YETI-GATOR!
ZWOOOP!
THANKS! I THOUGHT I WAS A--
--GONER.
BRAINS.
BRAINS.
BRAINS.
OKAY. TIME FOR PLAN C.
AND "C" STANDS FOR CHAOS.

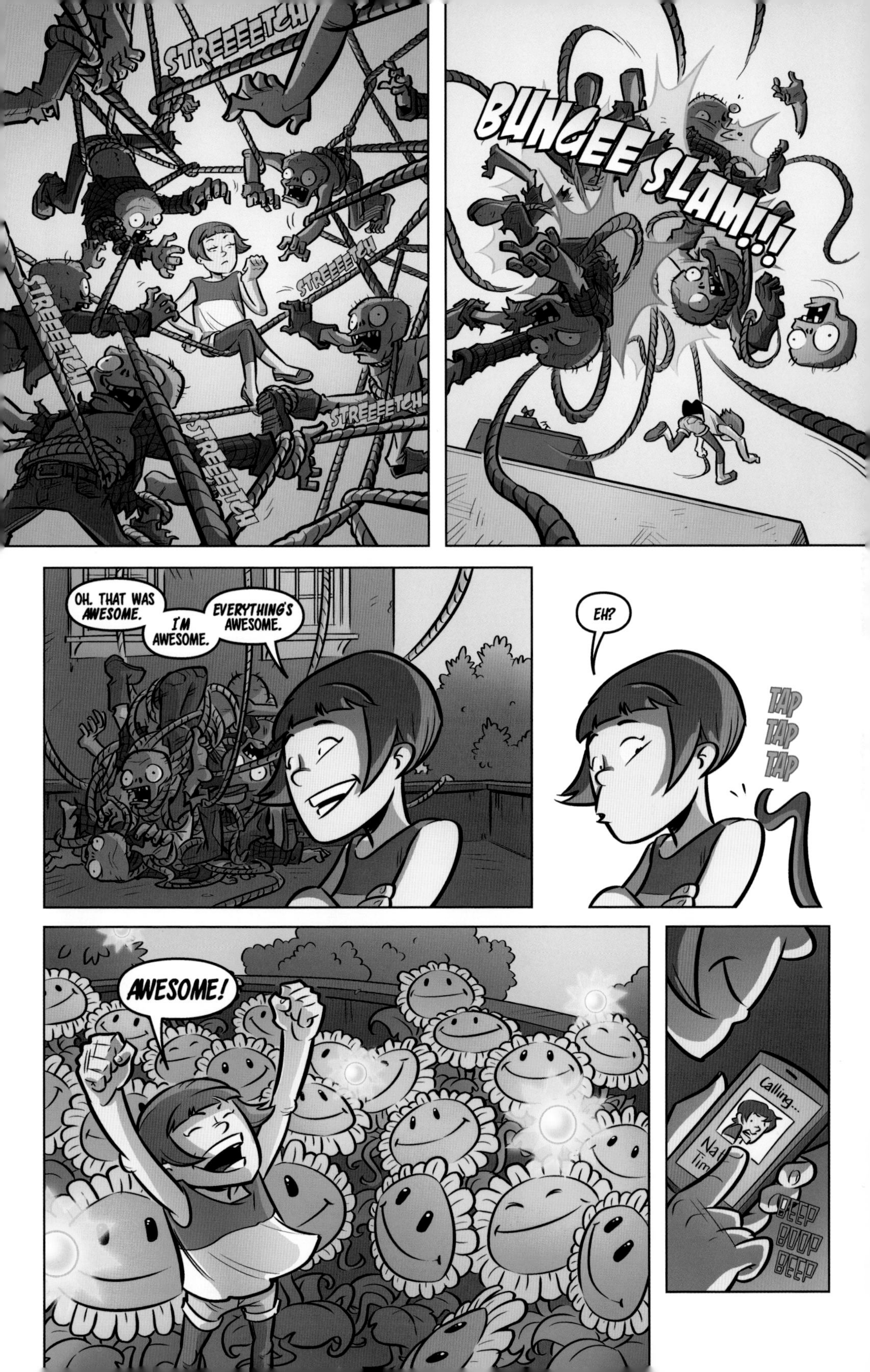
STREEEEETCH
STREEEEETCH
STREEEEETCH
STREEEETCH
STREEEETCH
BUNGEE SLAM!!!
OH. THAT WAS AWESOME.
I'M AWESOME.
EVERYTHING'S AWESOME.
EH?
TAP TAP TAP
AWESOME!
Calling...
BEEP BOOP BEEP

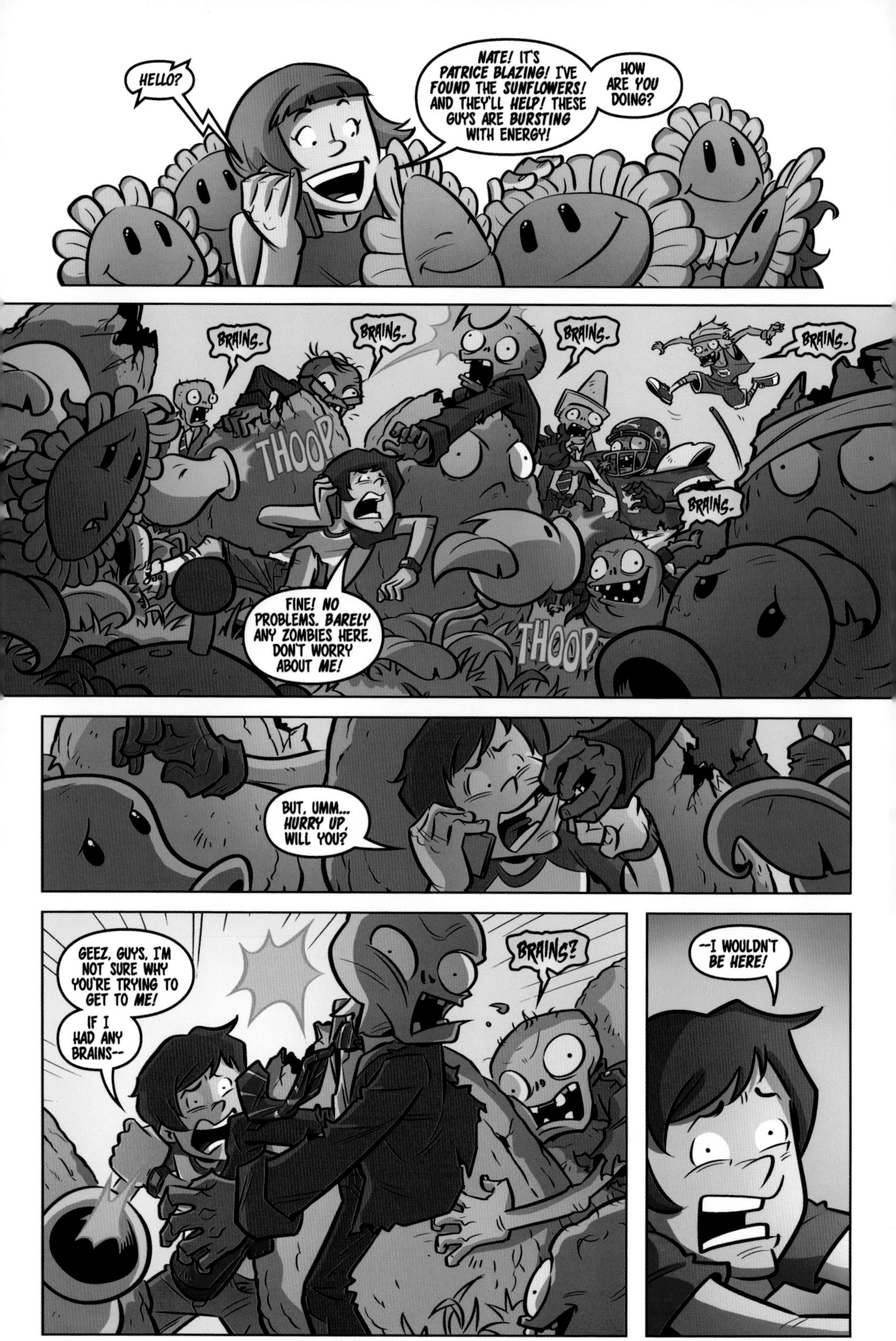
HELLO?
NATE! IT'S PATRICE BLAZING! I'VE FOUND THE SUNFLOWERS! AND THEY'LL HELP! THESE GUYS ARE BURSTING WITH ENERGY!
HOW ARE YOU DOING?
BRAINS.
BRAINS.
BRAINS.
BRAINS.
THOOP
BRAINS.
FINE! NO PROBLEMS. BARELY ANY ZOMBIES HERE. DON'T WORRY ABOUT ME!
THOOP
BUT, UMM... HURRY UP, WILL YOU?
GEEZ, GUYS, I'M NOT SURE WHY YOU'RE TRYING TO GET TO ME!
IF I HAD ANY BRAINS--
BRAINS?
--I WOULDN'T BE HERE!

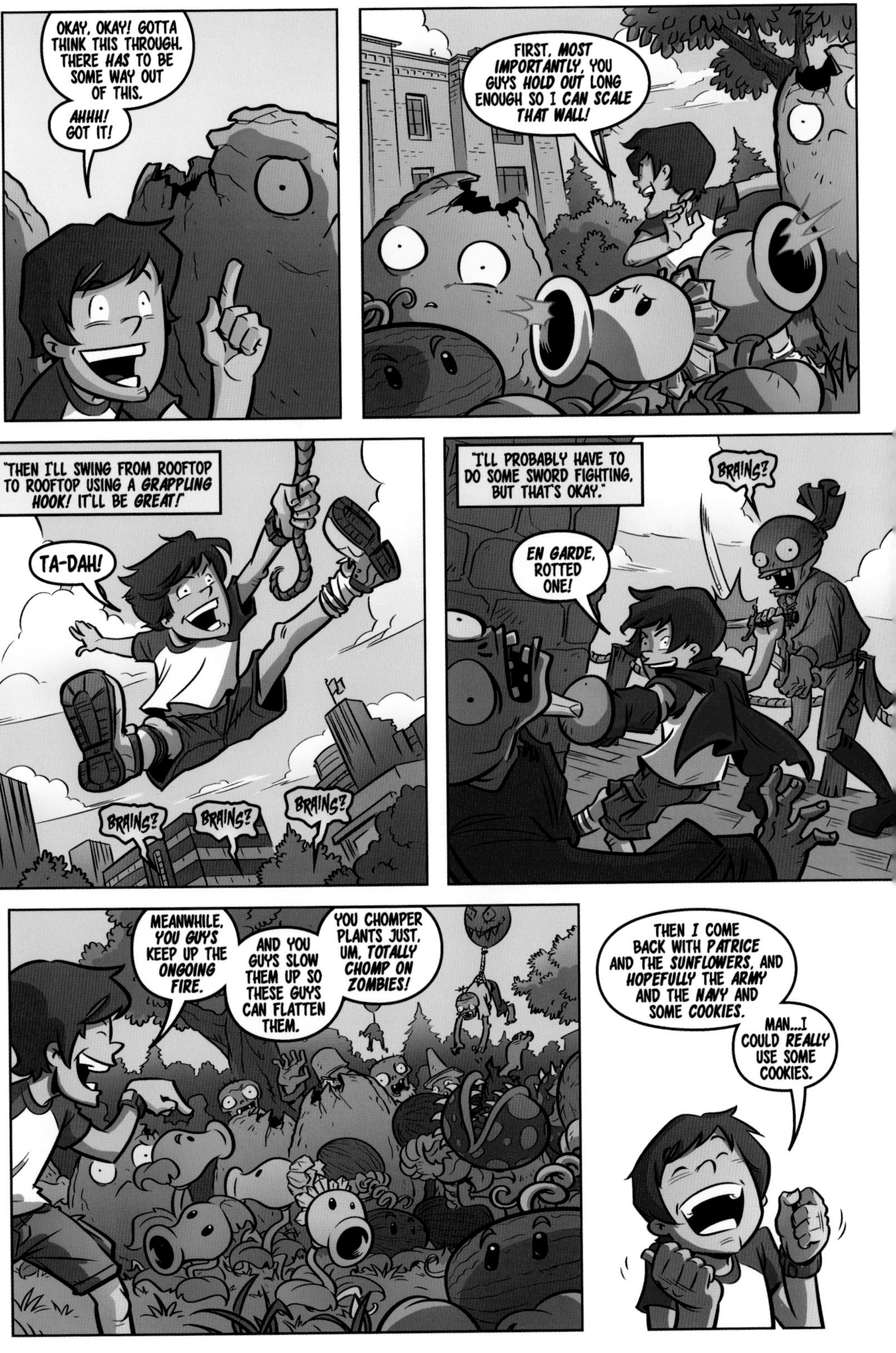
OKAY, OKAY! GOTTA THINK THIS THROUGH. THERE HAS TO BE SOME WAY OUT OF THIS.
AHHH! GOT IT!
FIRST, MOST IMPORTANTLY, YOU GUYS HOLD OUT LONG ENOUGH SO I CAN SCALE THAT WALL!
"THEN I'LL SWING FROM ROOFTOP TO ROOFTOP USING A GRAPPLING HOOK! IT'LL BE GREAT!"
TA-DAH!
BRAINS?
BRAINS?
BRAINS?
"I'LL PROBABLY HAVE TO DO SOME SWORD FIGHTING, BUT THAT'S OKAY."
BRAINS?
EN GARDE, ROTTED ONE!
MEANWHILE, YOU GUYS KEEP UP THE ONGOING FIRE.
AND YOU GUYS SLOW THEM UP SO THESE GUYS CAN FLATTEN THEM.
YOU CHOMPER PLANTS JUST, UM, TOTALLY CHOMP ON ZOMBIES!
THEN I COME BACK WITH PATRICE AND THE SUNFLOWERS, AND HOPEFULLY THE ARMY AND THE NAVY AND SOME COOKIES.
MAN...I COULD REALLY USE SOME COOKIES.

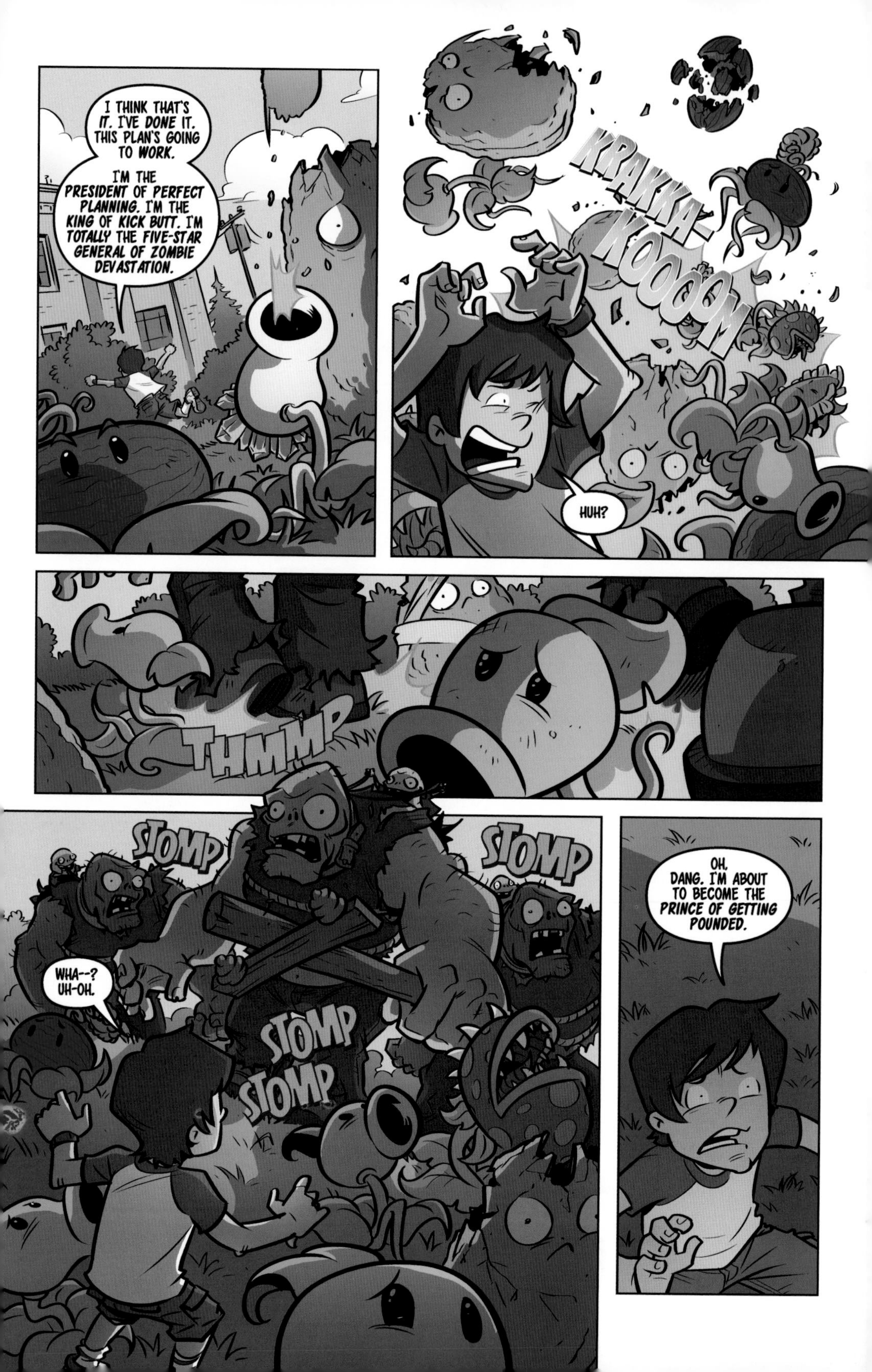
I THINK THAT'S IT. I'VE DONE IT. THIS PLAN'S GOING TO WORK.
I'M THE PRESIDENT OF PERFECT PLANNING. I'M THE KING OF KICK BUTT. I'M TOTALLY THE FIVE-STAR GENERAL OF ZOMBIE DEVASTATION.
KRAKKA-KOOOOM
HUH?
THMMP
STOMP
STOMP
WHA--? UH-OH.
STOMP
STOMP
OH, DANG. I'M ABOUT TO BECOME THE PRINCE OF GETTING POUNDED.

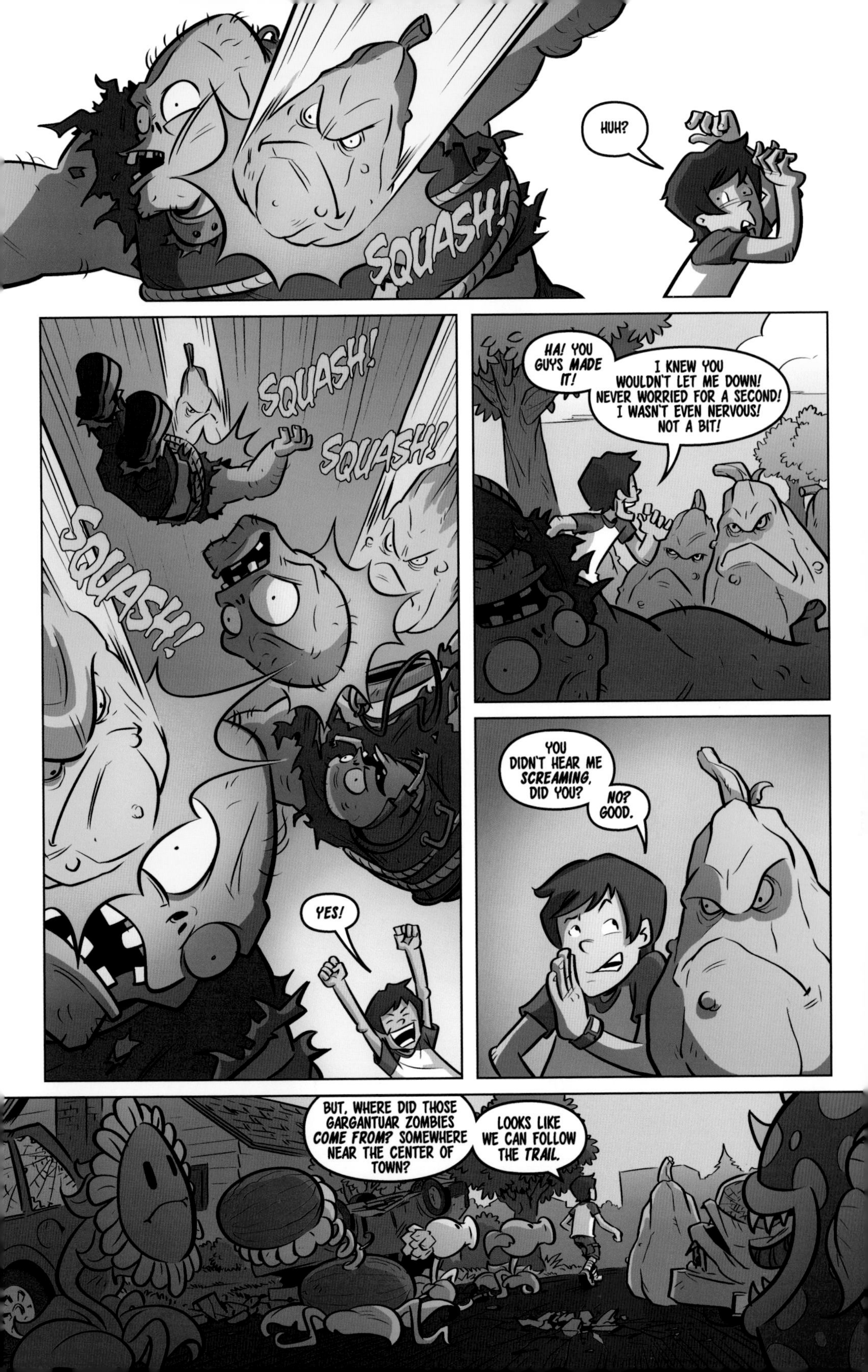
SQUASH!
HUH?
SQUASH!
SQUASH!
SQUASH!
YES!
HA! YOU GUYS *MADE* IT!
I KNEW YOU WOULDN'T LET ME DOWN! NEVER WORRIED FOR A SECOND! I WASN'T EVEN NERVOUS! NOT A BIT!
YOU DIDN'T HEAR ME *SCREAMING*, DID YOU?
NO? GOOD.
BUT, WHERE DID THOSE GARGANTUAR ZOMBIES *COME FROM?* SOMEWHERE NEAR THE CENTER OF TOWN?
LOOKS LIKE WE CAN FOLLOW THE *TRAIL*.

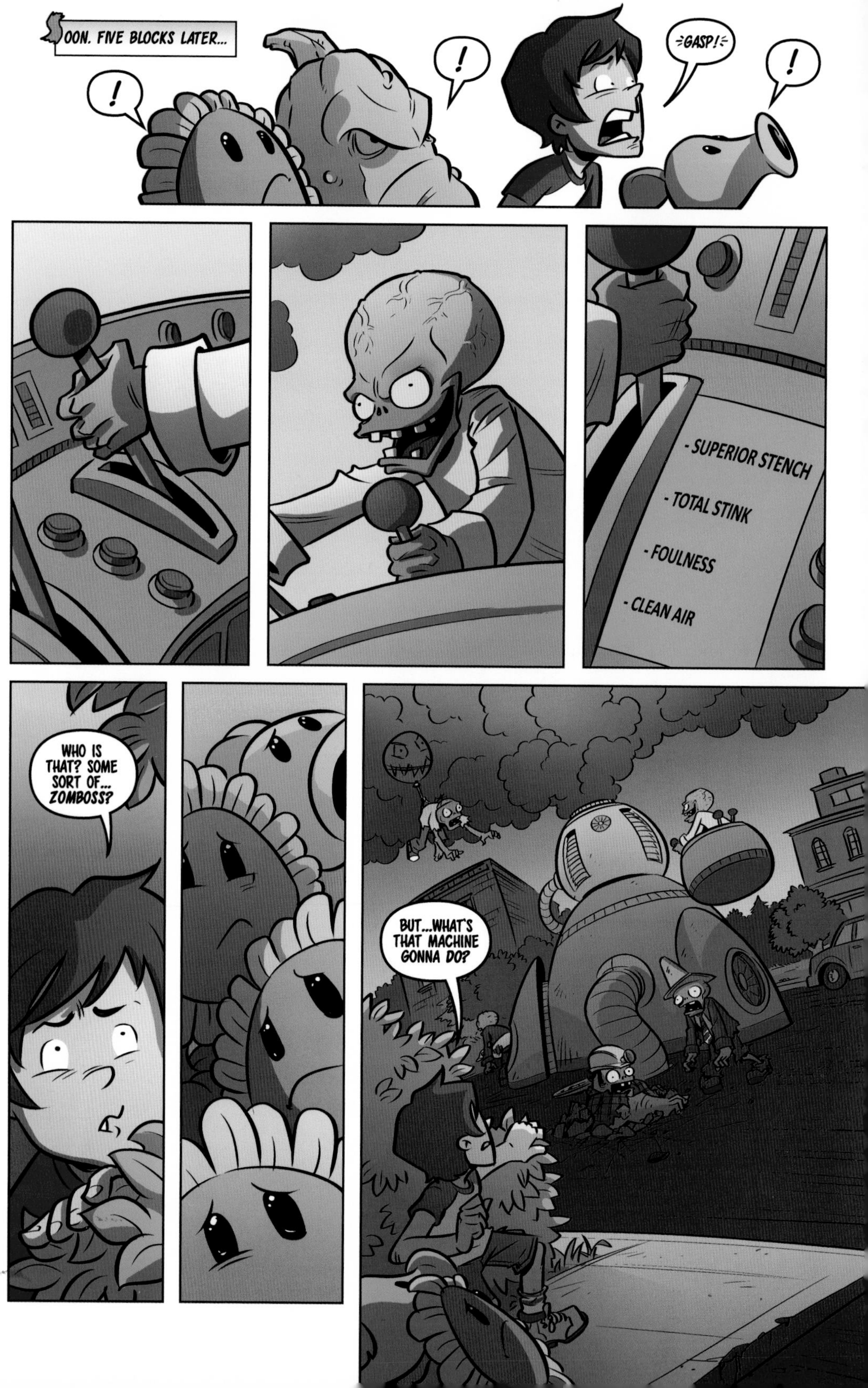
SOON. FIVE BLOCKS LATER...
!
!
=GASP!=
!
- SUPERIOR STENCH
- TOTAL STINK
- FOULNESS
- CLEAN AIR
WHO IS THAT? SOME SORT OF... ZOMBOSS?
BUT...WHAT'S THAT MACHINE GONNA DO?

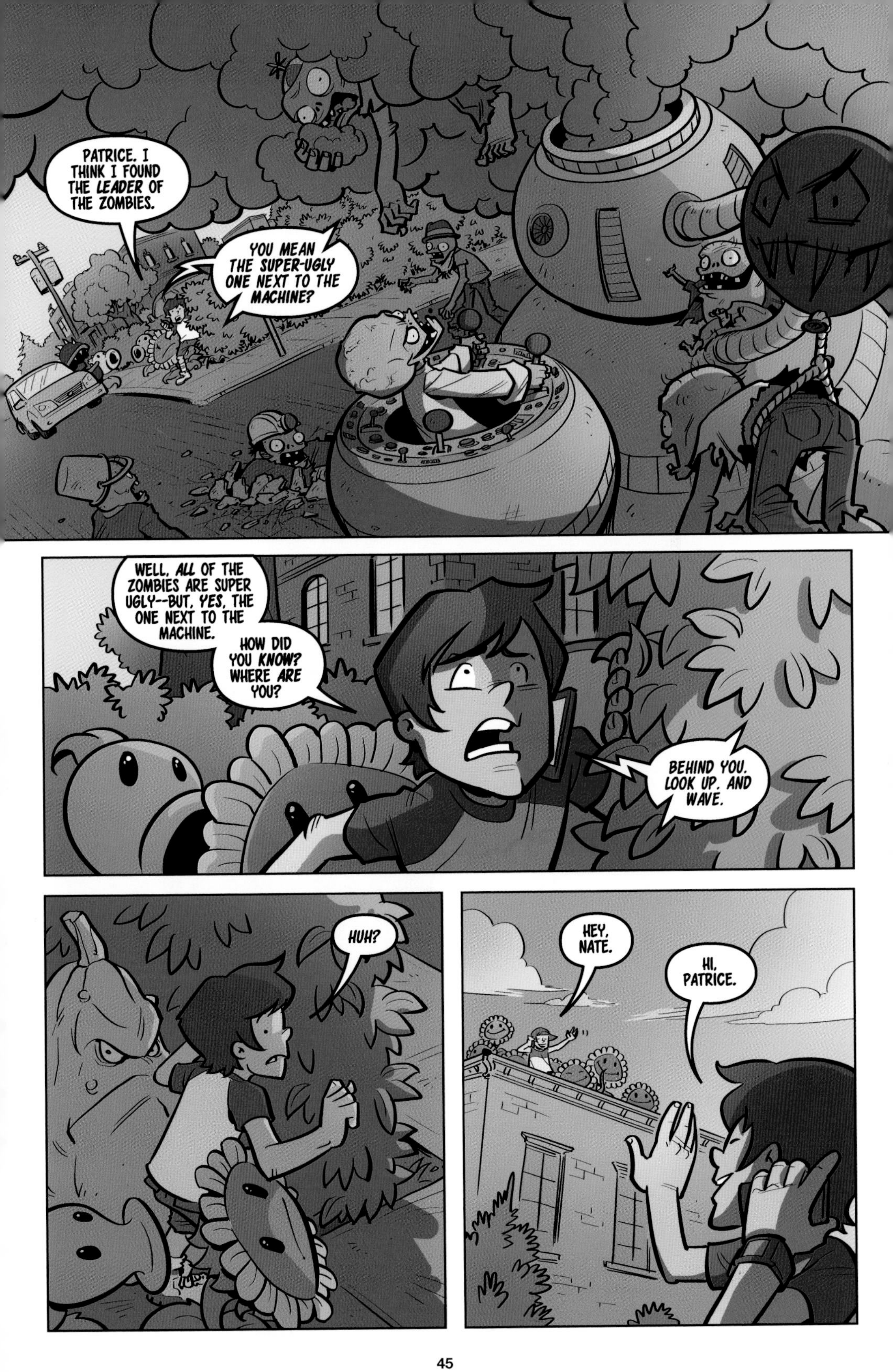

PATRICE. I THINK I FOUND THE LEADER OF THE ZOMBIES.
YOU MEAN THE SUPER-UGLY ONE NEXT TO THE MACHINE?
WELL, ALL OF THE ZOMBIES ARE SUPER UGLY--BUT, YES, THE ONE NEXT TO THE MACHINE.
HOW DID YOU KNOW? WHERE ARE YOU?
BEHIND YOU. LOOK UP. AND WAVE.
HUH?
HEY, NATE.
HI, PATRICE.

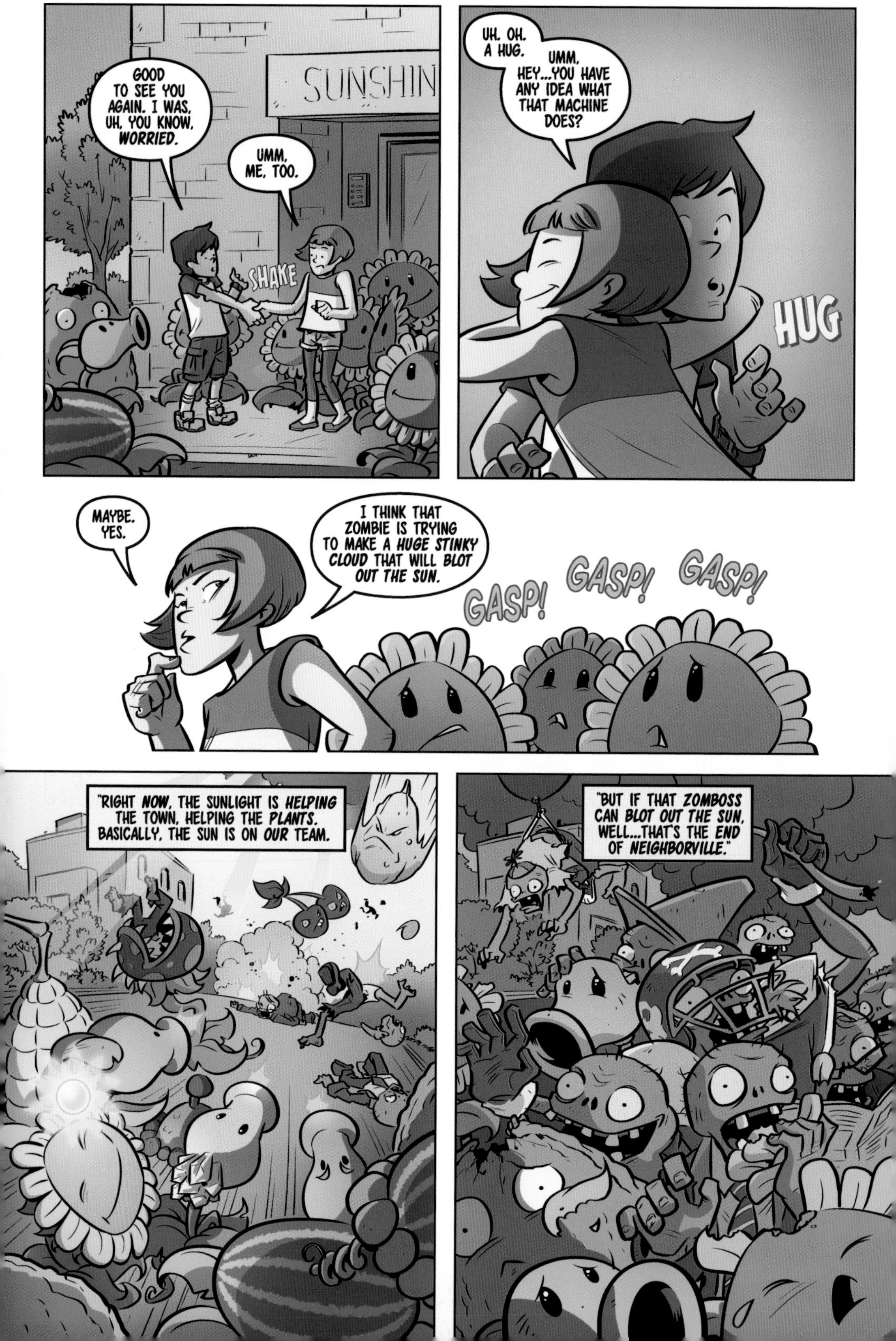

SUNSHIN
GOOD TO SEE YOU AGAIN. I WAS, UH, YOU KNOW, WORRIED.
UMM, ME, TOO.
SHAKE
UH. OH. A HUG.
UMM, HEY...YOU HAVE ANY IDEA WHAT THAT MACHINE DOES?
HUG
MAYBE. YES.
I THINK THAT ZOMBIE IS TRYING TO MAKE A HUGE STINKY CLOUD THAT WILL BLOT OUT THE SUN.
GASP!
GASP!
GASP!
"RIGHT NOW, THE SUNLIGHT IS HELPING THE TOWN, HELPING THE PLANTS. BASICALLY, THE SUN IS ON OUR TEAM.
"BUT IF THAT ZOMBOSS CAN BLOT OUT THE SUN, WELL...THAT'S THE END OF NEIGHBORVILLE."

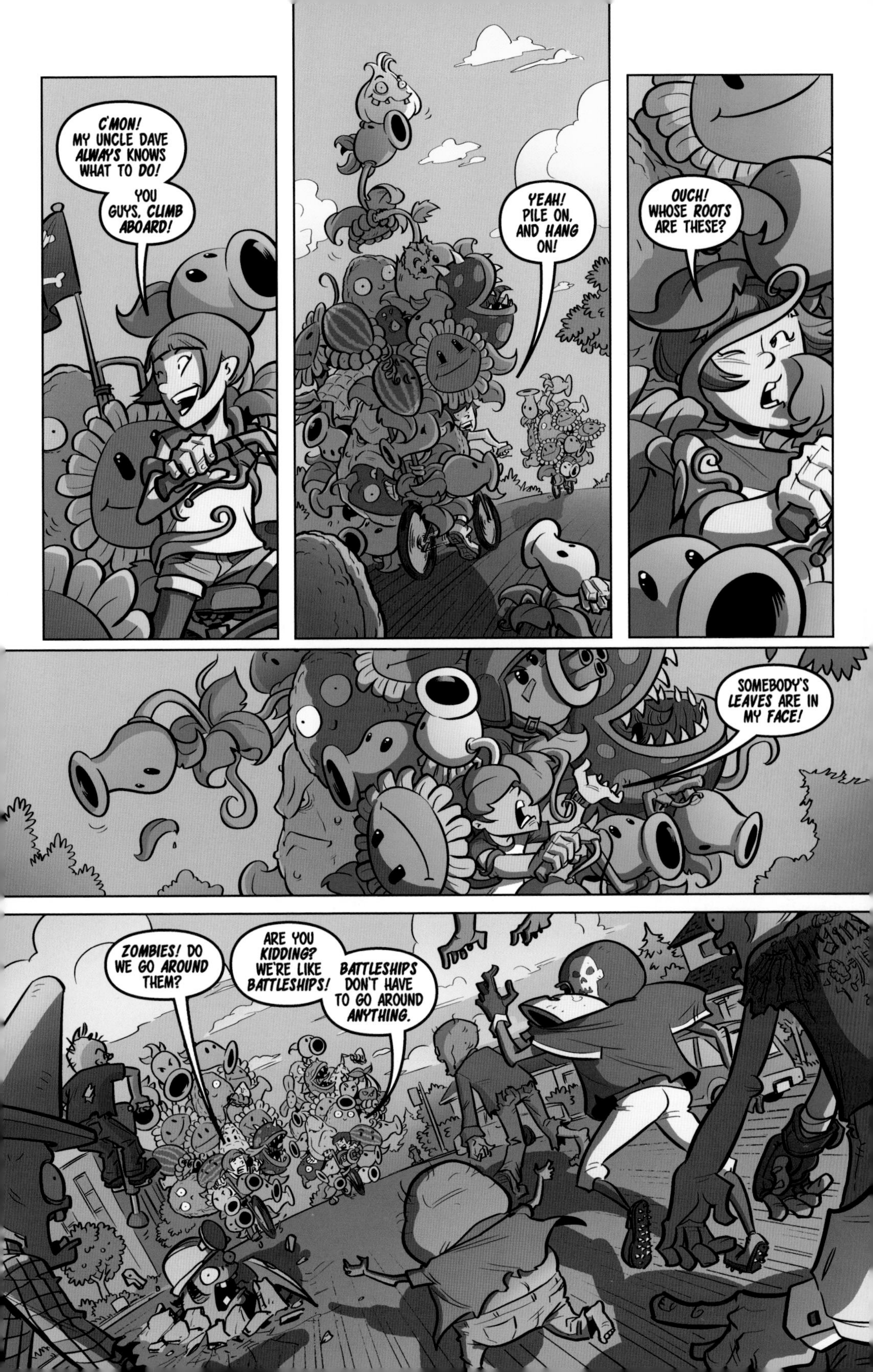

C'MON! MY UNCLE DAVE ALWAYS KNOWS WHAT TO DO!
YOU GUYS, CLIMB ABOARD!
YEAH! PILE ON, AND HANG ON!
OUCH! WHOSE ROOTS ARE THESE?
SOMEBODY'S LEAVES ARE IN MY FACE!
ZOMBIES! DO WE GO AROUND THEM?
ARE YOU KIDDING? WE'RE LIKE BATTLESHIPS!
BATTLESHIPS DON'T HAVE TO GO AROUND ANYTHING.

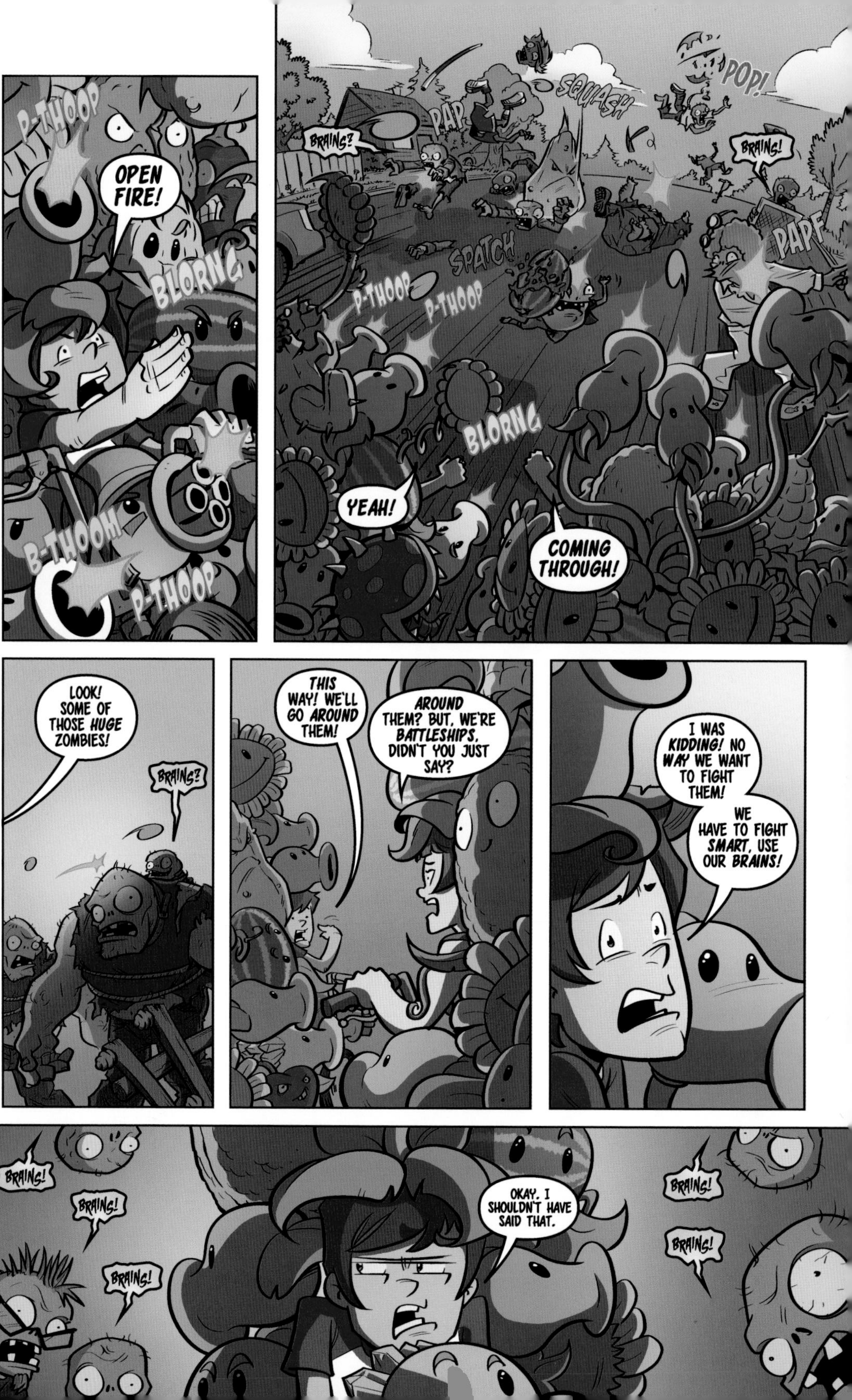
P-THOOP
OPEN FIRE!
BLORNG
B-THOOM
P-THOOP
BRAINS?
PAP
SQUASH
POP!
BRAINS!
PAPF
SPATCH
P-THOOP
P-THOOP
BLORNG
YEAH!
COMING THROUGH!
LOOK! SOME OF THOSE HUGE ZOMBIES!
BRAINS?
THIS WAY! WE'LL GO AROUND THEM!
AROUND THEM? BUT, WE'RE BATTLESHIPS, DIDN'T YOU JUST SAY?
I WAS KIDDING! NO WAY WE WANT TO FIGHT THEM!
WE HAVE TO FIGHT SMART, USE OUR BRAINS!
BRAINS!
BRAINS!
BRAINS!
OKAY, I SHOULDN'T HAVE SAID THAT.
BRAINS!
BRAINS!

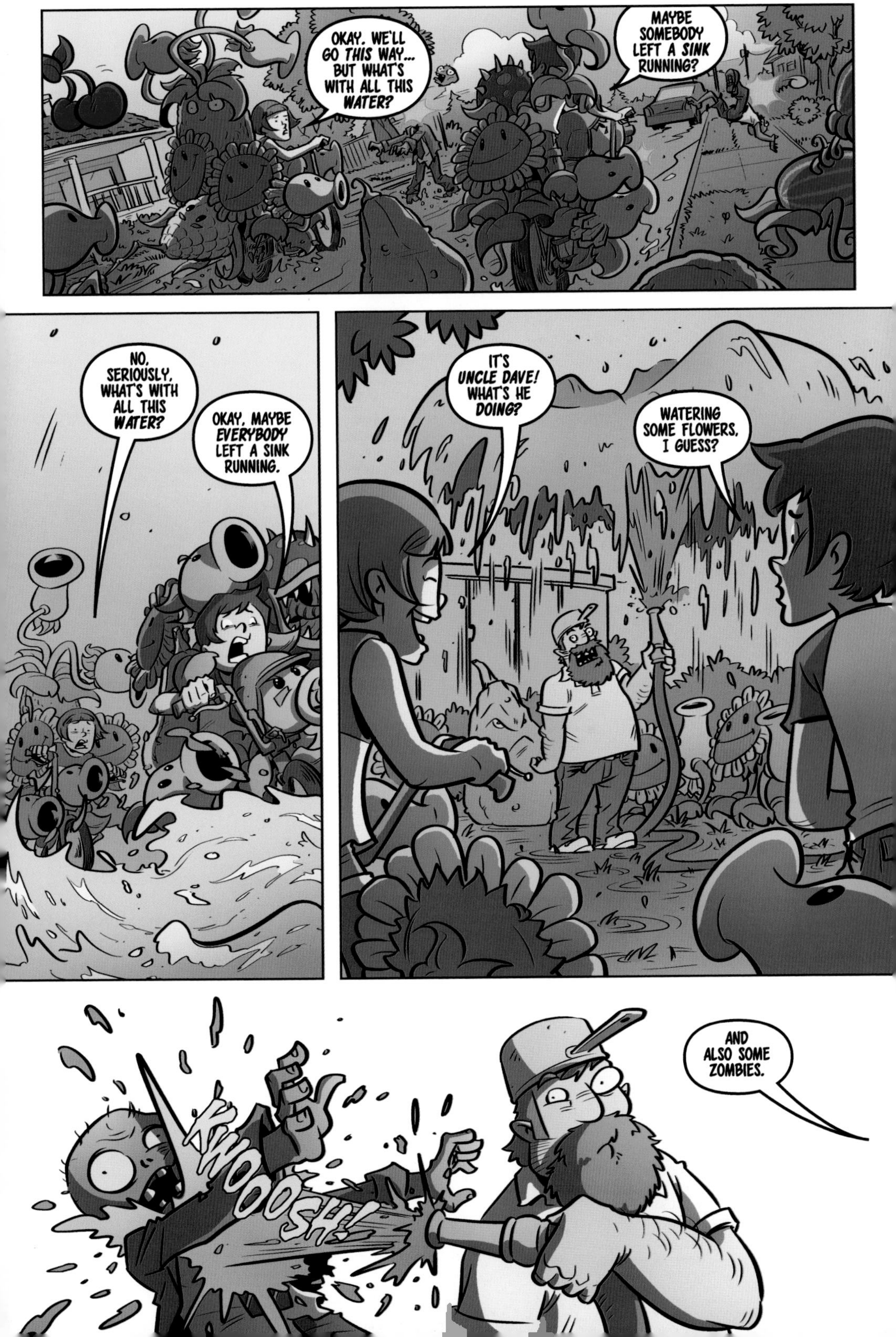
OKAY. WE'LL GO THIS WAY... BUT WHAT'S WITH ALL THIS WATER?
MAYBE SOMEBODY LEFT A SINK RUNNING?
NO, SERIOUSLY, WHAT'S WITH ALL THIS WATER?
OKAY, MAYBE EVERYBODY LEFT A SINK RUNNING.
IT'S UNCLE DAVE! WHAT'S HE DOING?
WATERING SOME FLOWERS, I GUESS?
AND ALSO SOME ZOMBIES.
KWOOOSH!

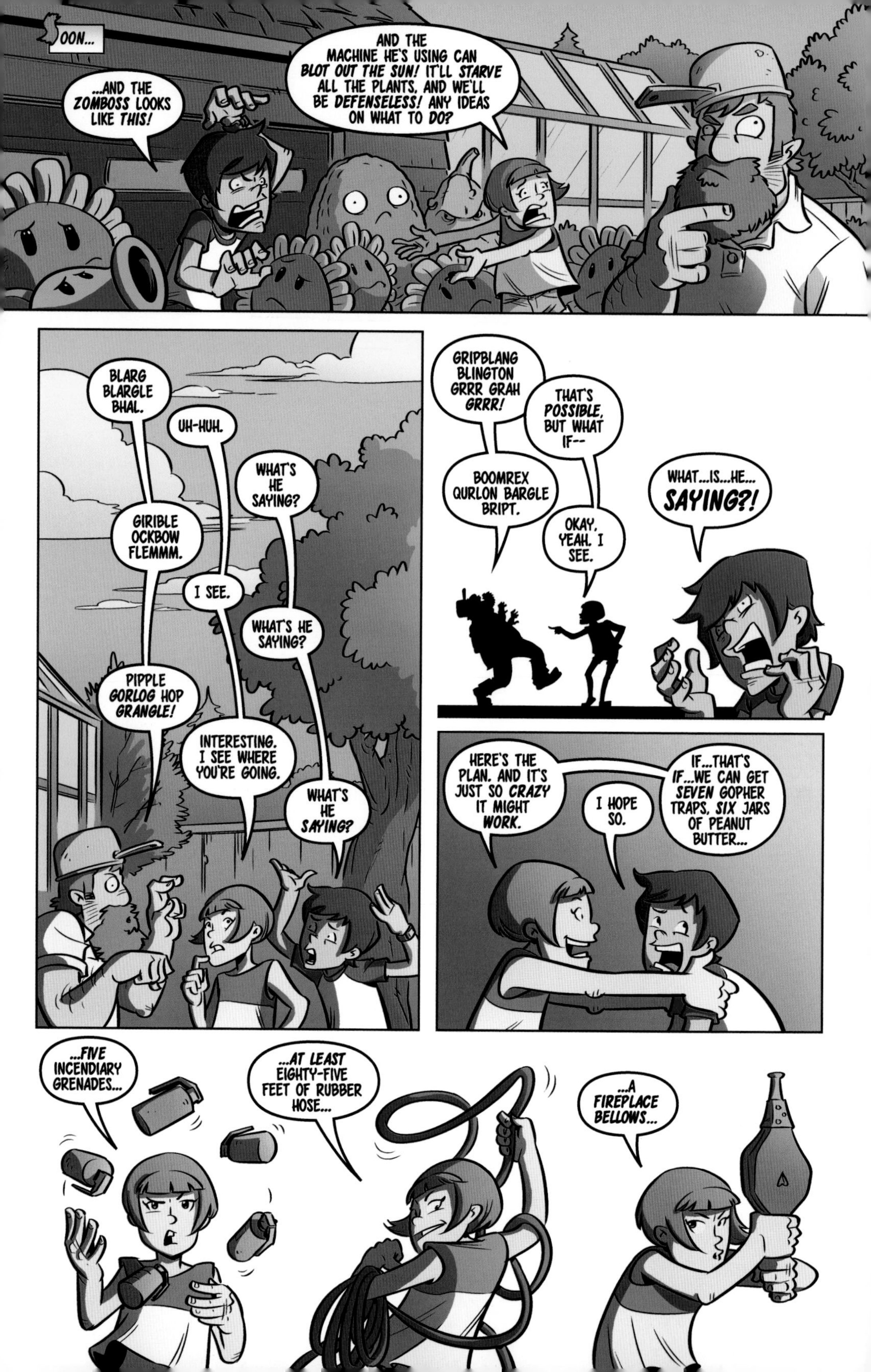
SOON...
...AND THE ZOMBOSS LOOKS LIKE THIS!
AND THE MACHINE HE'S USING CAN BLOT OUT THE SUN! IT'LL STARVE ALL THE PLANTS, AND WE'LL BE DEFENSELESS! ANY IDEAS ON WHAT TO DO?
BLARG BLARGLE BHAL.
UH-HUH.
WHAT'S HE SAYING?
GIRIBLE OCKBOW FLEMMM.
I SEE.
WHAT'S HE SAYING?
PIPPLE GORLOG HOP GRANGLE!
INTERESTING. I SEE WHERE YOU'RE GOING.
WHAT'S HE SAYING?
GRIPBLANG BLINGTON GRRR GRAH GRRR!
THAT'S POSSIBLE, BUT WHAT IF--
BOOMREX QURLON BARGLE BRIPT.
OKAY, YEAH. I SEE.
WHAT...IS...HE... SAYING?!
HERE'S THE PLAN. AND IT'S JUST SO CRAZY IT MIGHT WORK.
I HOPE SO.
IF...THAT'S IF...WE CAN GET SEVEN GOPHER TRAPS, SIX JARS OF PEANUT BUTTER...
...FIVE INCENDIARY GRENADES...
...AT LEAST EIGHTY-FIVE FEET OF RUBBER HOSE...
...A FIREPLACE BELLOWS...

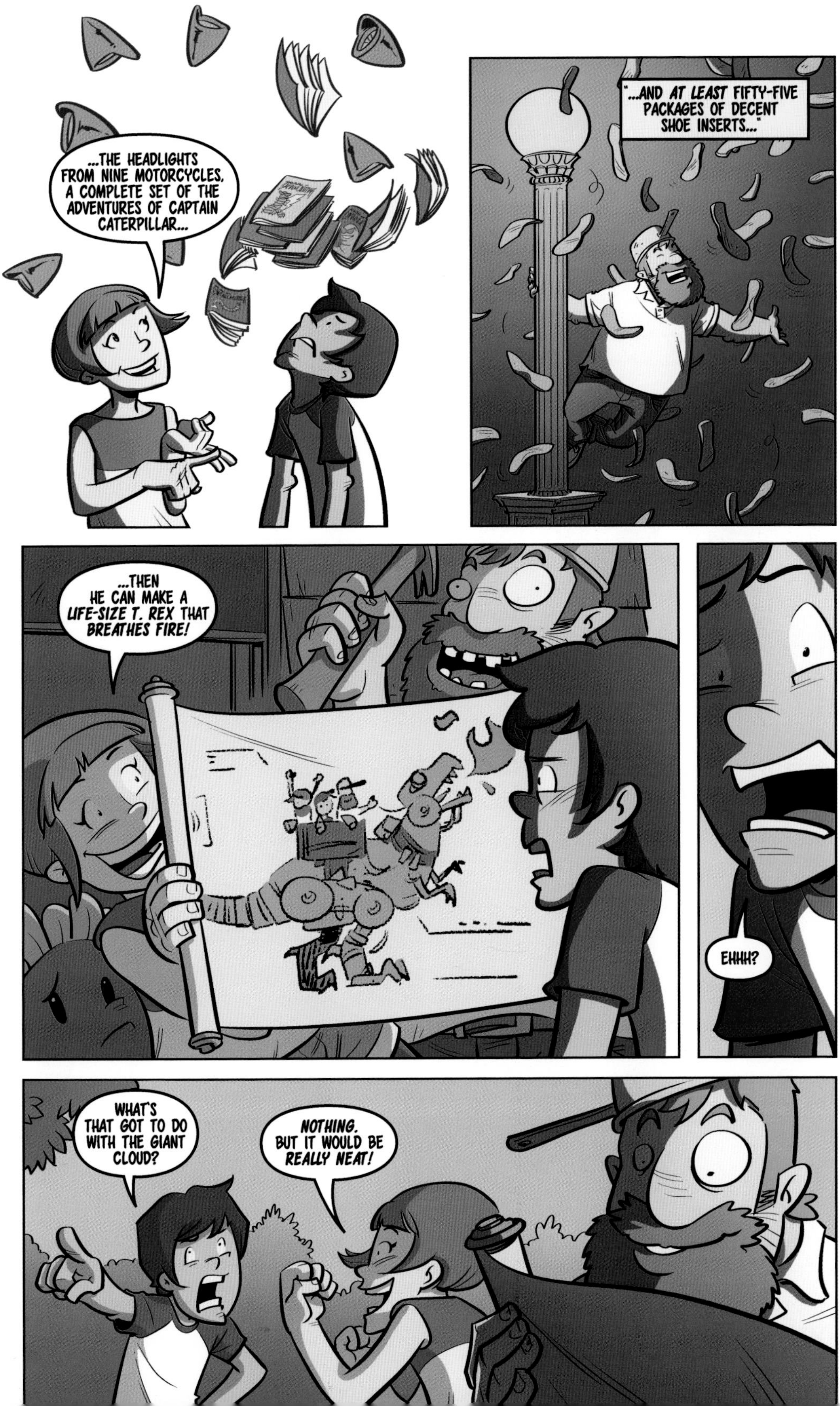
...THE HEADLIGHTS FROM NINE MOTORCYCLES, A COMPLETE SET OF THE ADVENTURES OF CAPTAIN CATERPILLAR...
"...AND AT LEAST FIFTY-FIVE PACKAGES OF DECENT SHOE INSERTS..."
...THEN HE CAN MAKE A LIFE-SIZE T. REX THAT BREATHES FIRE!
EHHH?
WHAT'S THAT GOT TO DO WITH THE GIANT CLOUD?
NOTHING. BUT IT WOULD BE REALLY NEAT!

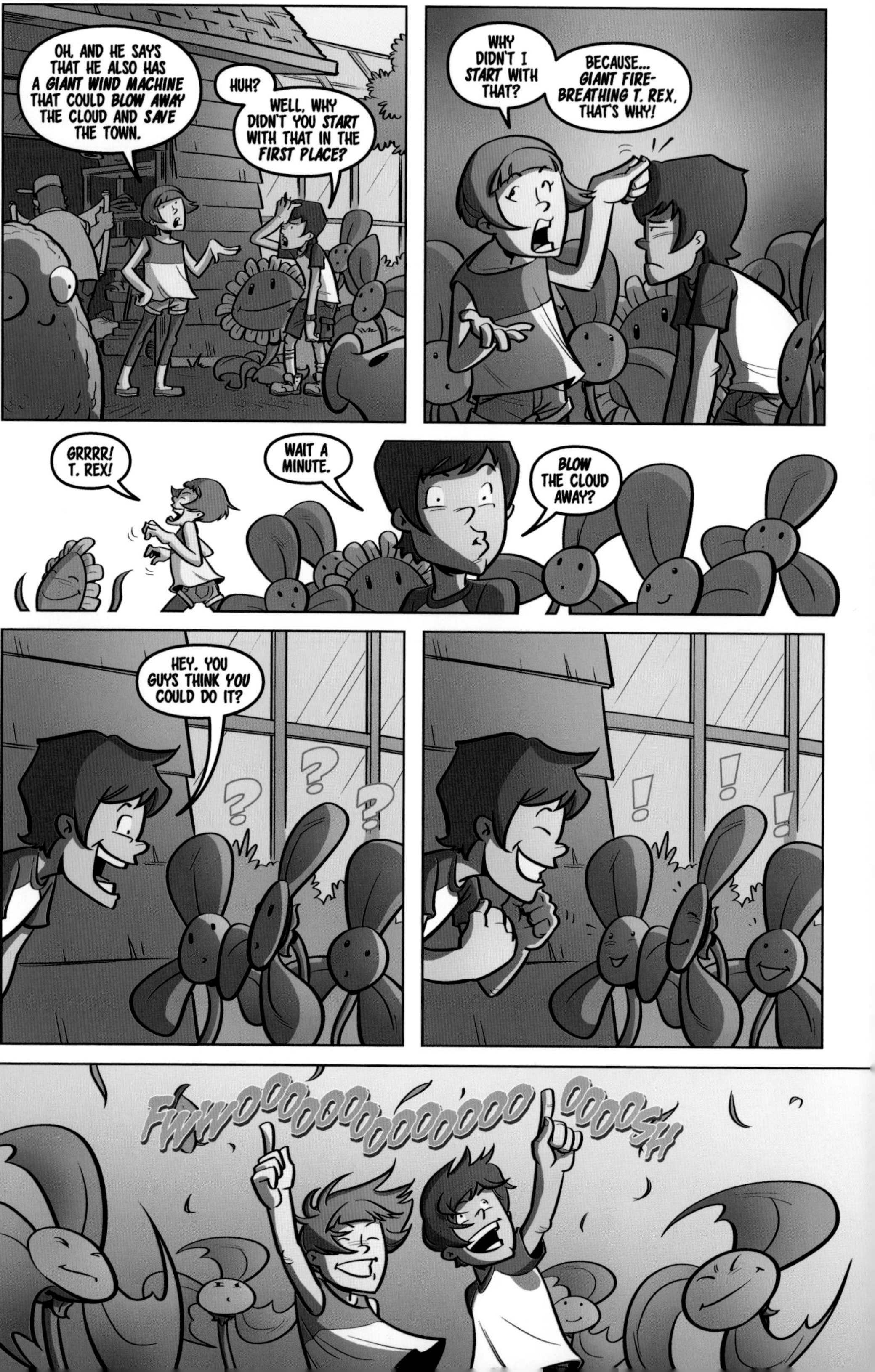
OH, AND HE SAYS THAT HE ALSO HAS A GIANT WIND MACHINE THAT COULD BLOW AWAY THE CLOUD AND SAVE THE TOWN.
HUH?
WELL, WHY DIDN'T YOU START WITH THAT IN THE FIRST PLACE?
WHY DIDN'T I START WITH THAT?
BECAUSE... GIANT FIRE-BREATHING T. REX, THAT'S WHY!
GRRRR! T. REX!
WAIT A MINUTE.
BLOW THE CLOUD AWAY?
HEY. YOU GUYS THINK YOU COULD DO IT?
FWWOOOOOOOOOOOOOOOOOOSH

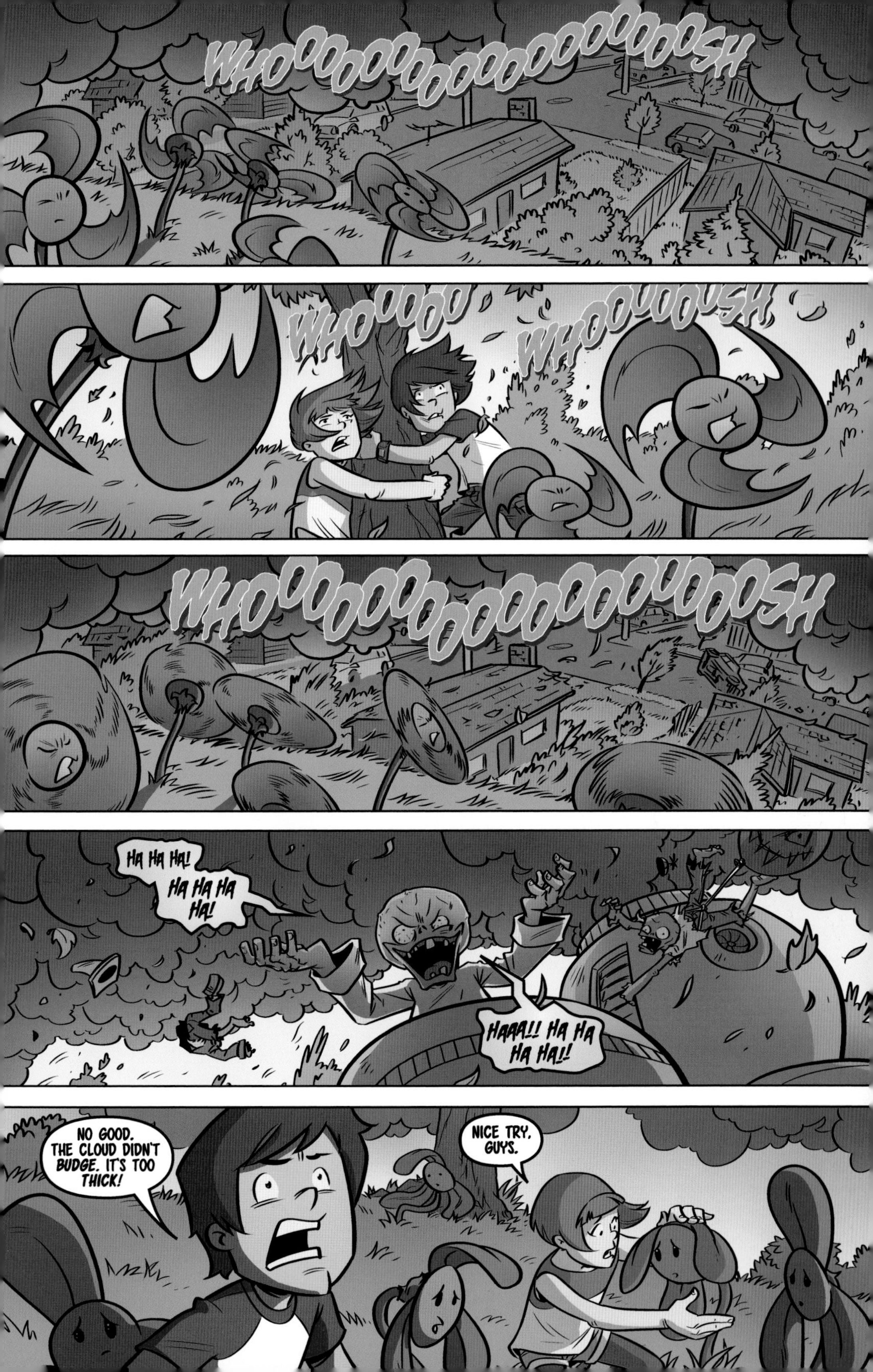
WHOOOOOOOOOOOOOOOOOOSH
WHOOOOOO
WHOOOOOOOSH
WHOOOOOOOOOOOOOOOOOOOOSH
HA HA HA!
HA HA HA HA!
HAAA!! HA HA HA HA!!
NO GOOD. THE CLOUD DIDN'T BUDGE. IT'S TOO THICK!
NICE TRY, GUYS.

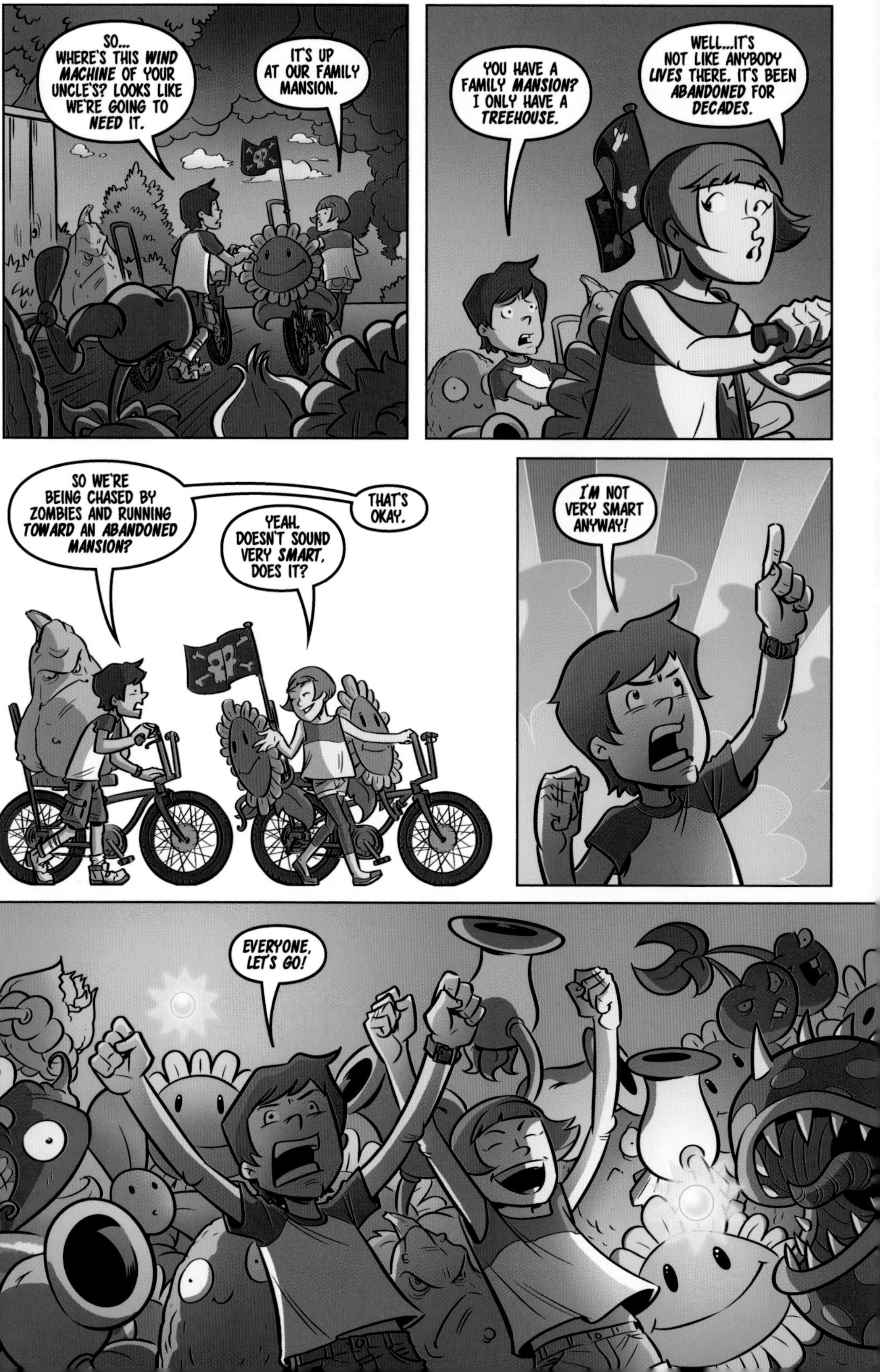
SO... WHERE'S THIS WIND MACHINE OF YOUR UNCLE'S? LOOKS LIKE WE'RE GOING TO NEED IT.
IT'S UP AT OUR FAMILY MANSION.
YOU HAVE A FAMILY MANSION? I ONLY HAVE A TREEHOUSE.
WELL...IT'S NOT LIKE ANYBODY LIVES THERE. IT'S BEEN ABANDONED FOR DECADES.
SO WE'RE BEING CHASED BY ZOMBIES AND RUNNING TOWARD AN ABANDONED MANSION?
YEAH. DOESN'T SOUND VERY SMART, DOES IT?
THAT'S OKAY.
I'M NOT VERY SMART ANYWAY!
EVERYONE, LET'S GO!

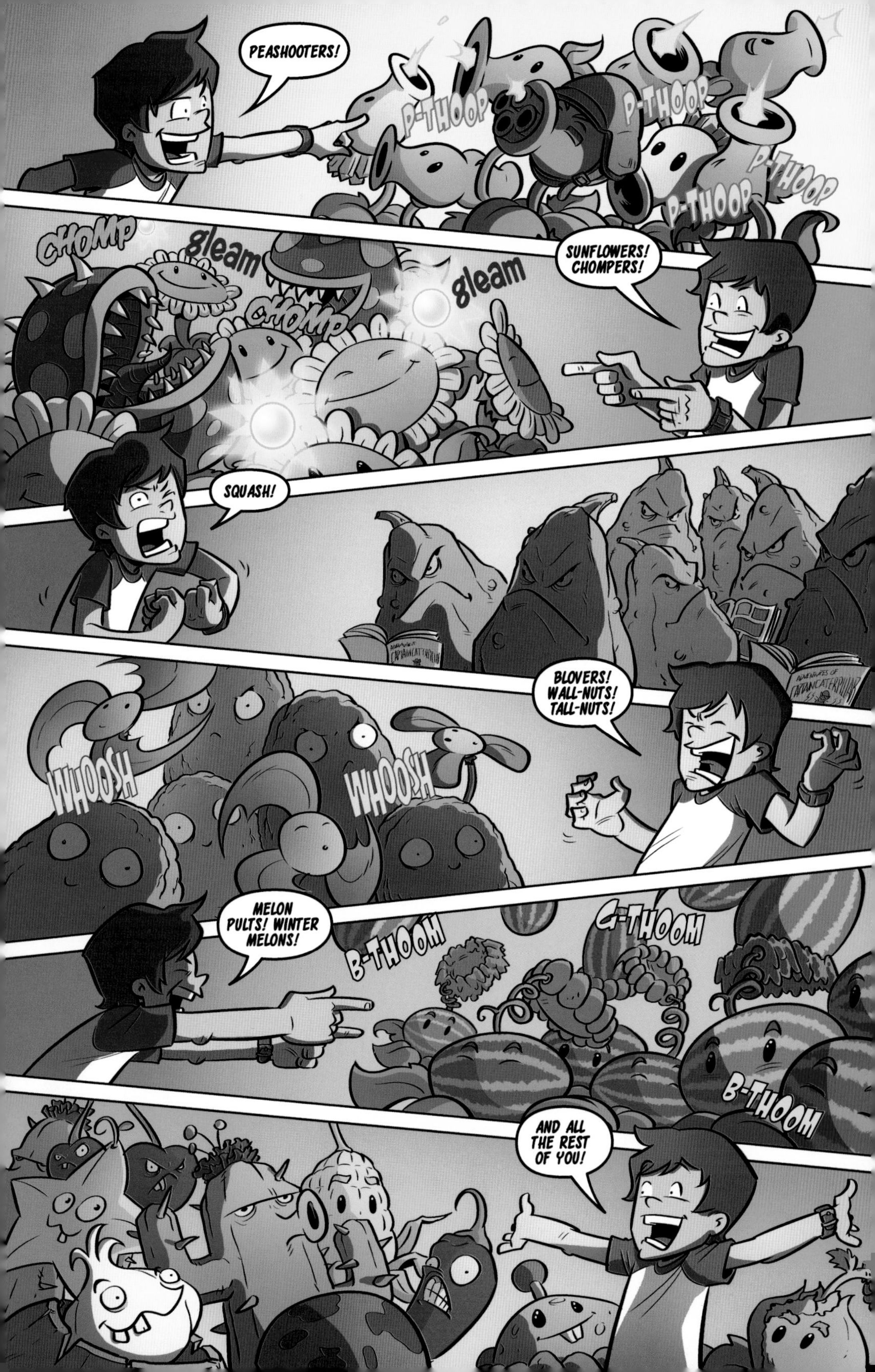
PEASHOOTERS!
P-THOOP
P-THOOP
P-THOOP
P-THOOP
CHOMP
gleam
CHOMP
gleam
SUNFLOWERS! CHOMPERS!
SQUASH!
BLOVERS! WALL-NUTS! TALL-NUTS!
WHOOSH
WHOOSH
MELON PULTS! WINTER MELONS!
B-THOOM
G-THOOM
B-THOOM
AND ALL THE REST OF YOU!

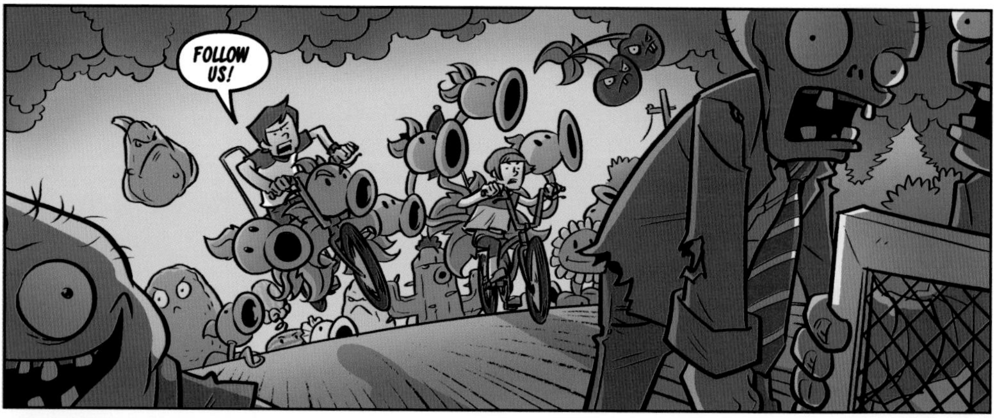
FOLLOW US!

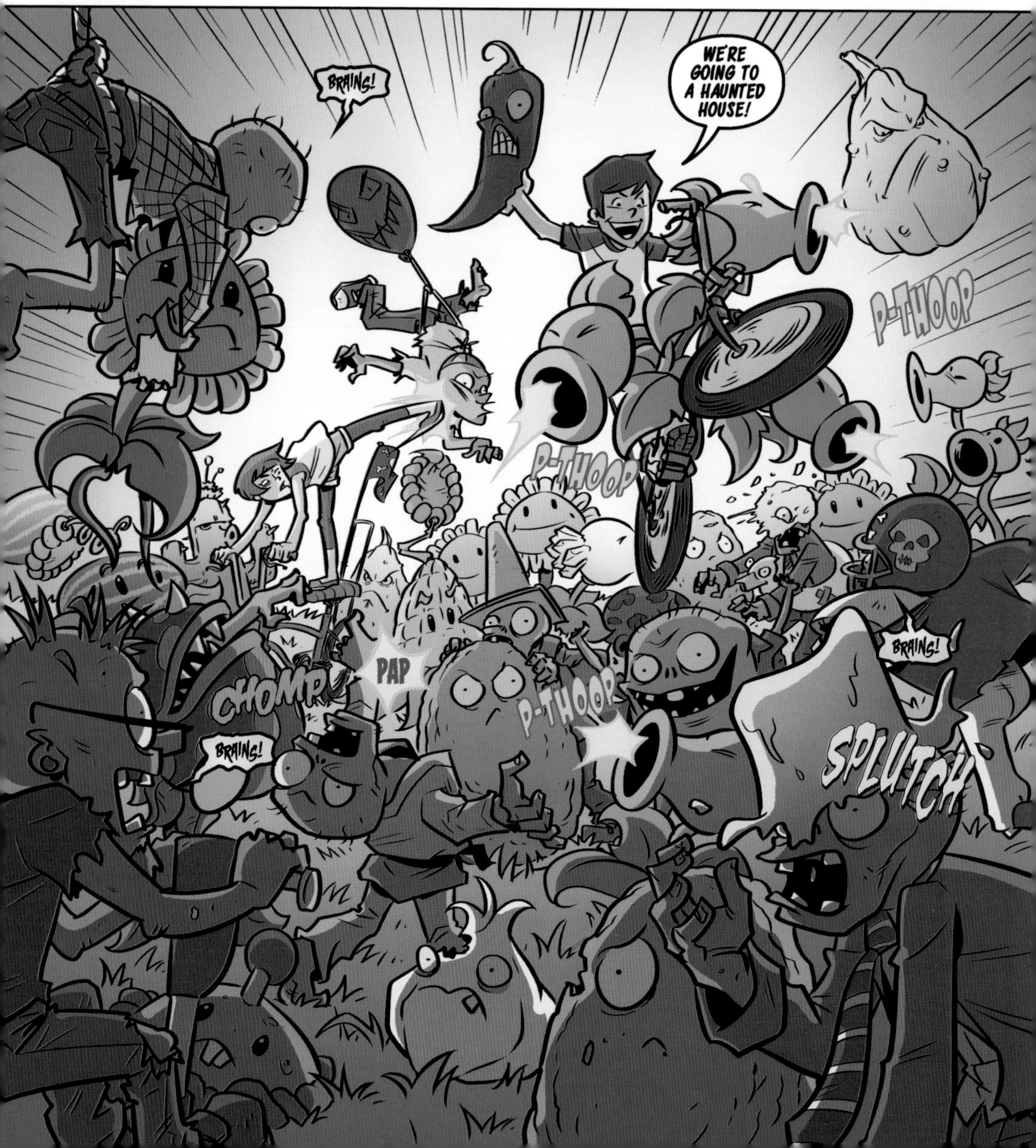
BRAINS!
WE'RE GOING TO A HAUNTED HOUSE!
P-THOOP
P-THOOP
CHOMP
PAP
P-THOOP
BRAINS!
BRAINS!
SPLUTCH

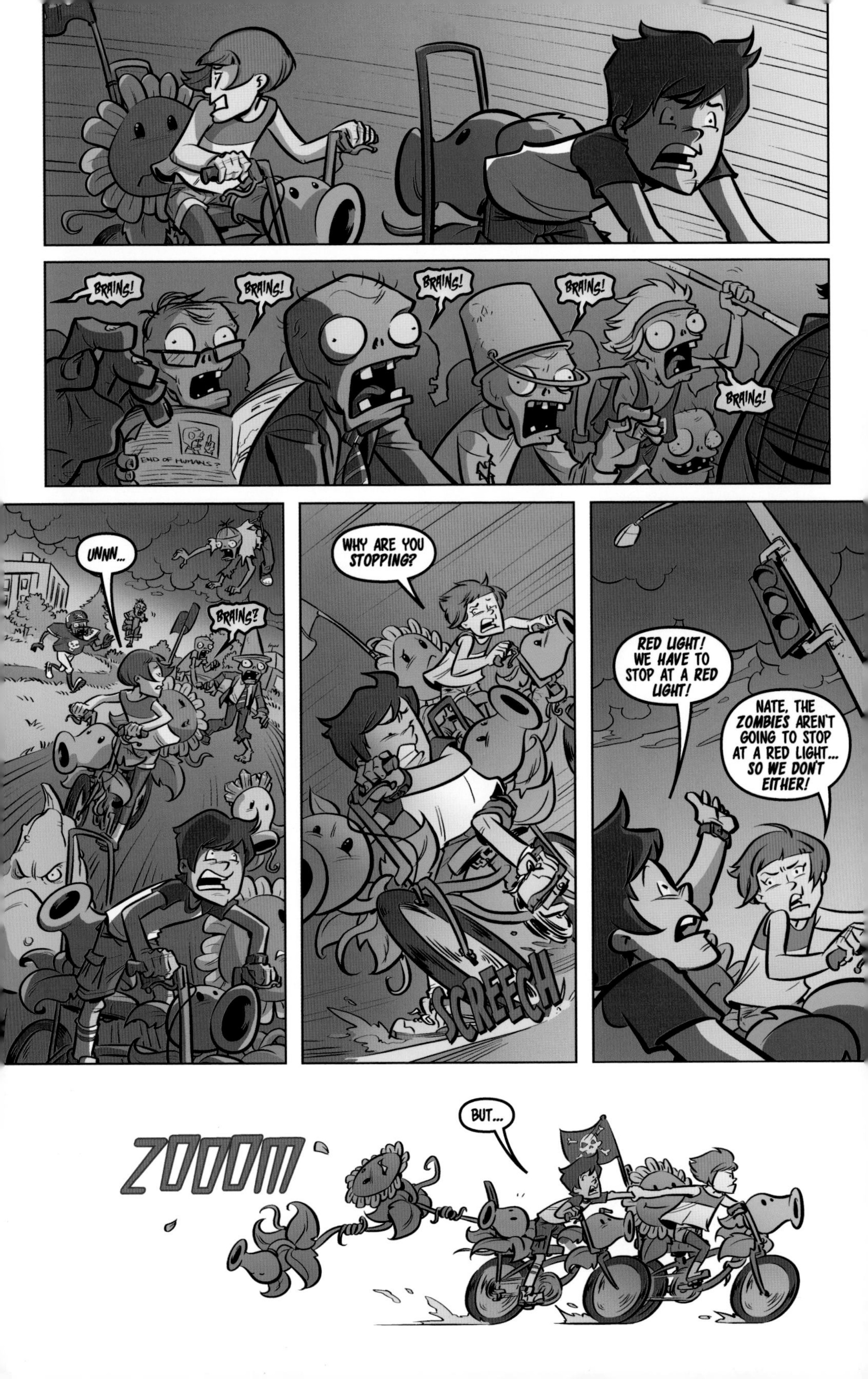
BRAINS!
BRAINS!
BRAINS!
BRAINS!
BRAINS!
END OF HUMANS?
UNNN...
BRAINS?
WHY ARE YOU STOPPING?
SCREECH
RED LIGHT! WE HAVE TO STOP AT A RED LIGHT!
NATE, THE ZOMBIES AREN'T GOING TO STOP AT A RED LIGHT... SO WE DON'T EITHER!
ZOOOM
BUT...

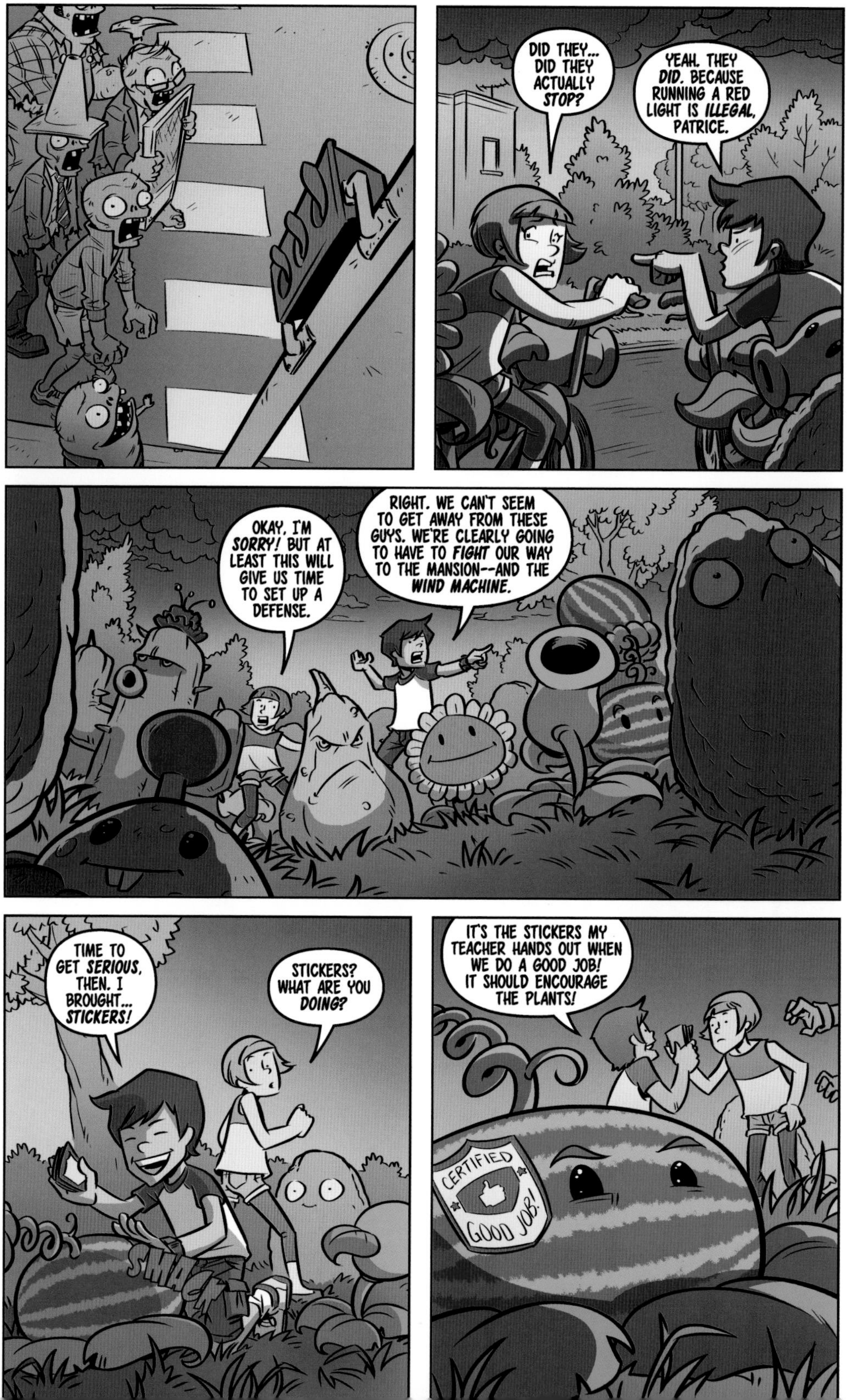
DID THEY... DID THEY ACTUALLY STOP?
YEAH. THEY DID. BECAUSE RUNNING A RED LIGHT IS ILLEGAL, PATRICE.
OKAY, I'M SORRY! BUT AT LEAST THIS WILL GIVE US TIME TO SET UP A DEFENSE.
RIGHT. WE CAN'T SEEM TO GET AWAY FROM THESE GUYS. WE'RE CLEARLY GOING TO HAVE TO FIGHT OUR WAY TO THE MANSION--AND THE WIND MACHINE.
TIME TO GET SERIOUS, THEN. I BROUGHT... STICKERS!
STICKERS? WHAT ARE YOU DOING?
IT'S THE STICKERS MY TEACHER HANDS OUT WHEN WE DO A GOOD JOB! IT SHOULD ENCOURAGE THE PLANTS!
CERTIFIED
GOOD JOB!

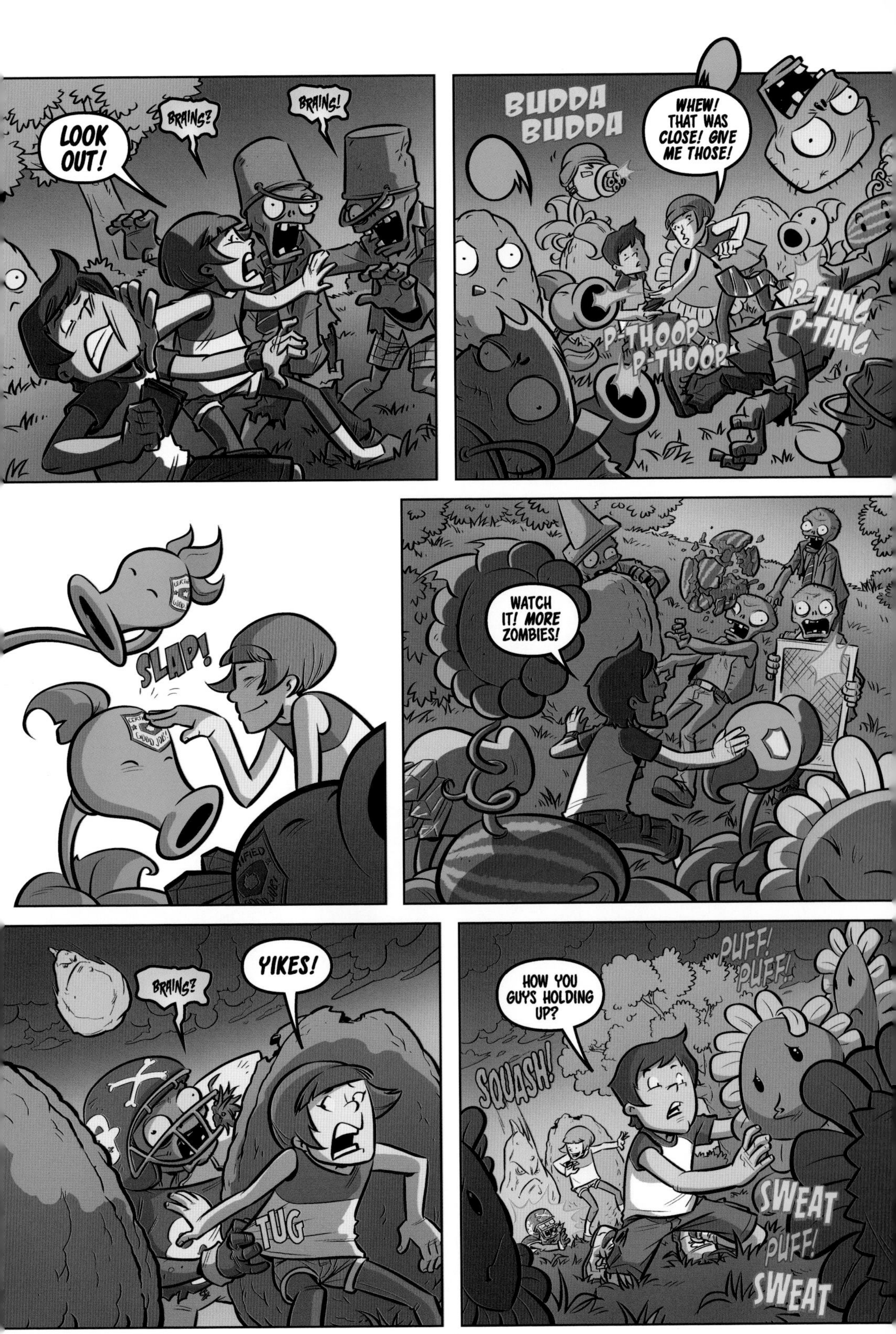
LOOK OUT!
BRAINS?
BRAINS!
BUDDA
BUDDA
WHEW! THAT WAS CLOSE! GIVE ME THOSE!
P-THOOP
P-THOOP
P-TANG
P-TANG
SLAP!
WATCH IT! MORE ZOMBIES!
BRAINS?
YIKES!
TUG
PUFF!
PUFF!
HOW YOU GUYS HOLDING UP?
SQUASH!
SWEAT
PUFF!
SWEAT

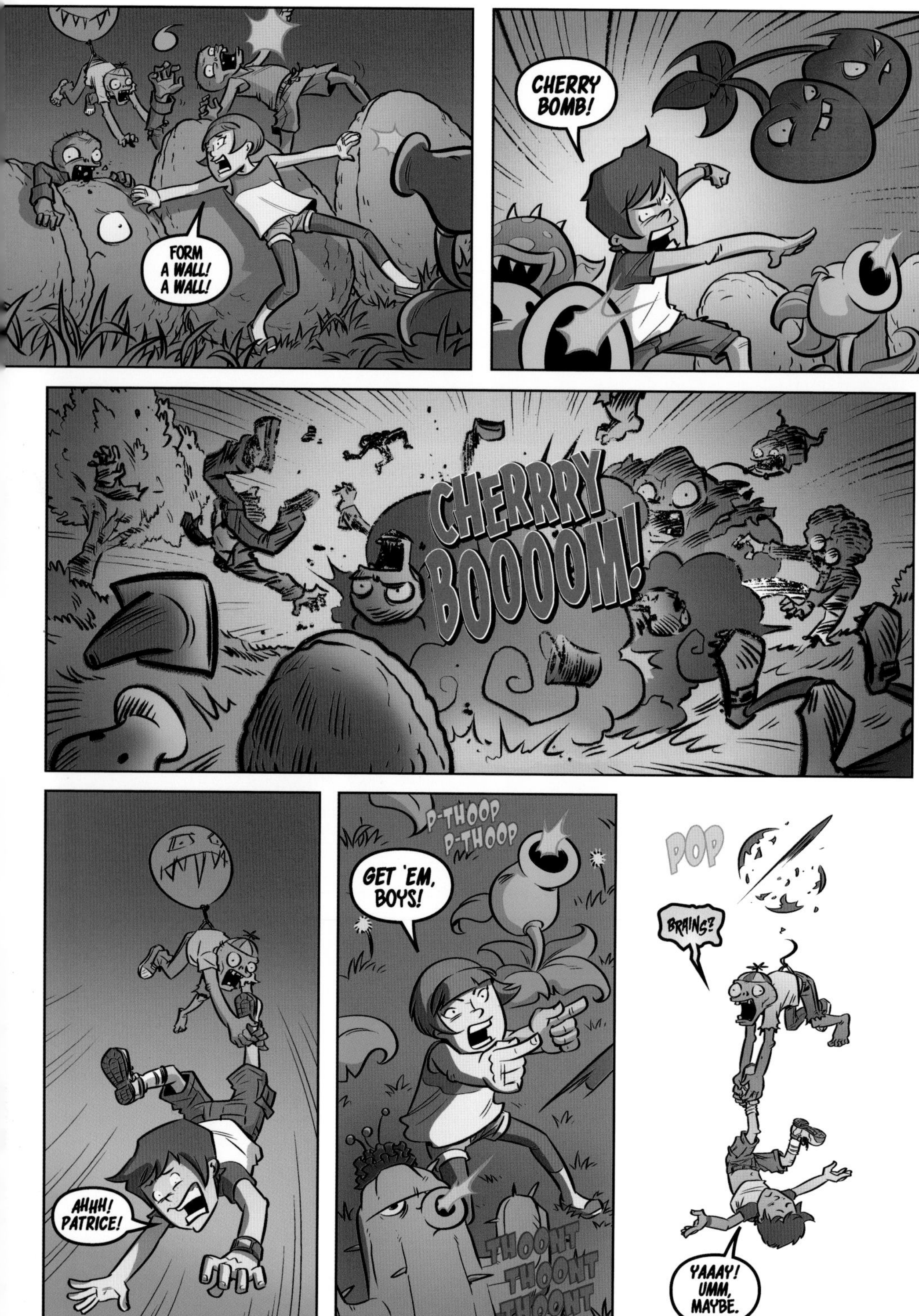
FORM A WALL! A WALL!
CHERRY BOMB!
CHERRRY BOOOOM!
AHHH! PATRICE!
P-THOOP P-THOOP
GET 'EM, BOYS!
THOONT THOONT THOONT
POP
BRAINS?
YAAAY! UMM, MAYBE.

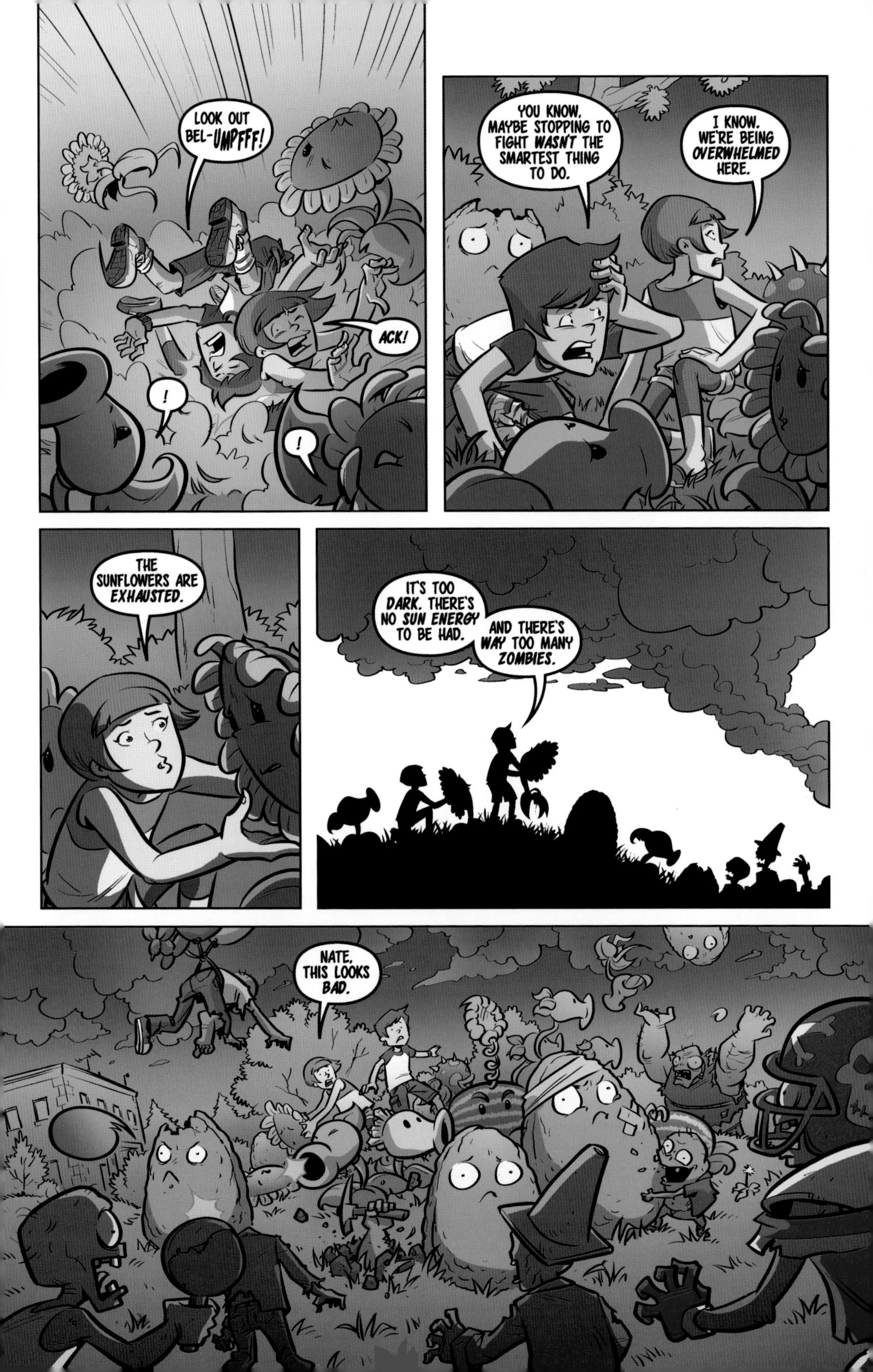
LOOK OUT BEL-UMPFFF!
ACK!
!
!
YOU KNOW, MAYBE STOPPING TO FIGHT WASN'T THE SMARTEST THING TO DO.
I KNOW. WE'RE BEING OVERWHELMED HERE.
THE SUNFLOWERS ARE EXHAUSTED.
IT'S TOO DARK. THERE'S NO SUN ENERGY TO BE HAD.
AND THERE'S WAY TOO MANY ZOMBIES.
NATE, THIS LOOKS BAD.

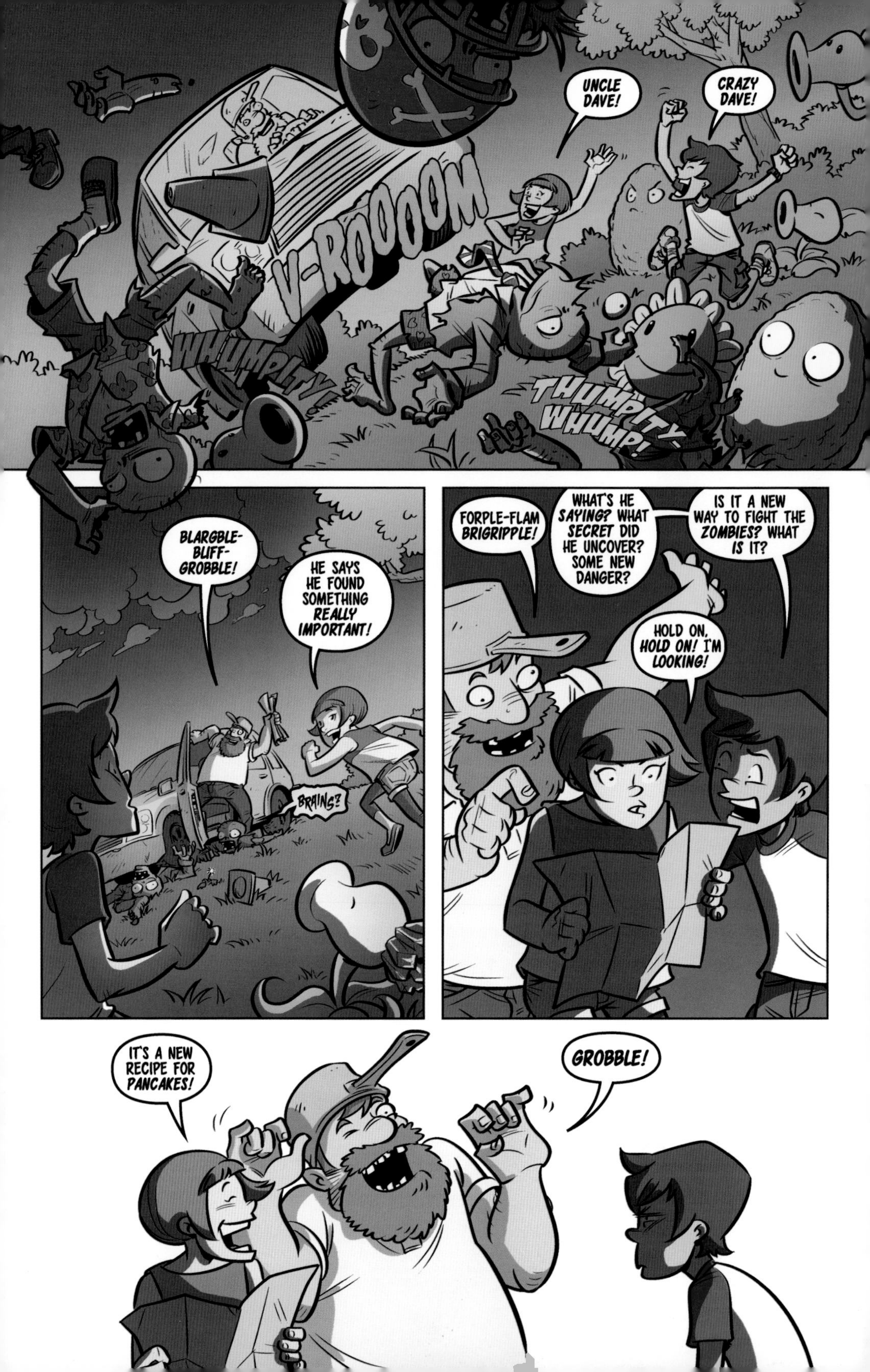
UNCLE DAVE!
CRAZY DAVE!
V-ROOOOM
WHUMPITY
THUMPITY-WHUMP!
BLARGBLE-BUFF-GROBBLE!
HE SAYS HE FOUND SOMETHING REALLY IMPORTANT!
BRAINS?
FORPLE-FLAM BRIGRIPPLE!
WHAT'S HE SAYING? WHAT SECRET DID HE UNCOVER? SOME NEW DANGER?
IS IT A NEW WAY TO FIGHT THE ZOMBIES? WHAT IS IT?
HOLD ON, HOLD ON! I'M LOOKING!
IT'S A NEW RECIPE FOR PANCAKES!
GROBBLE!

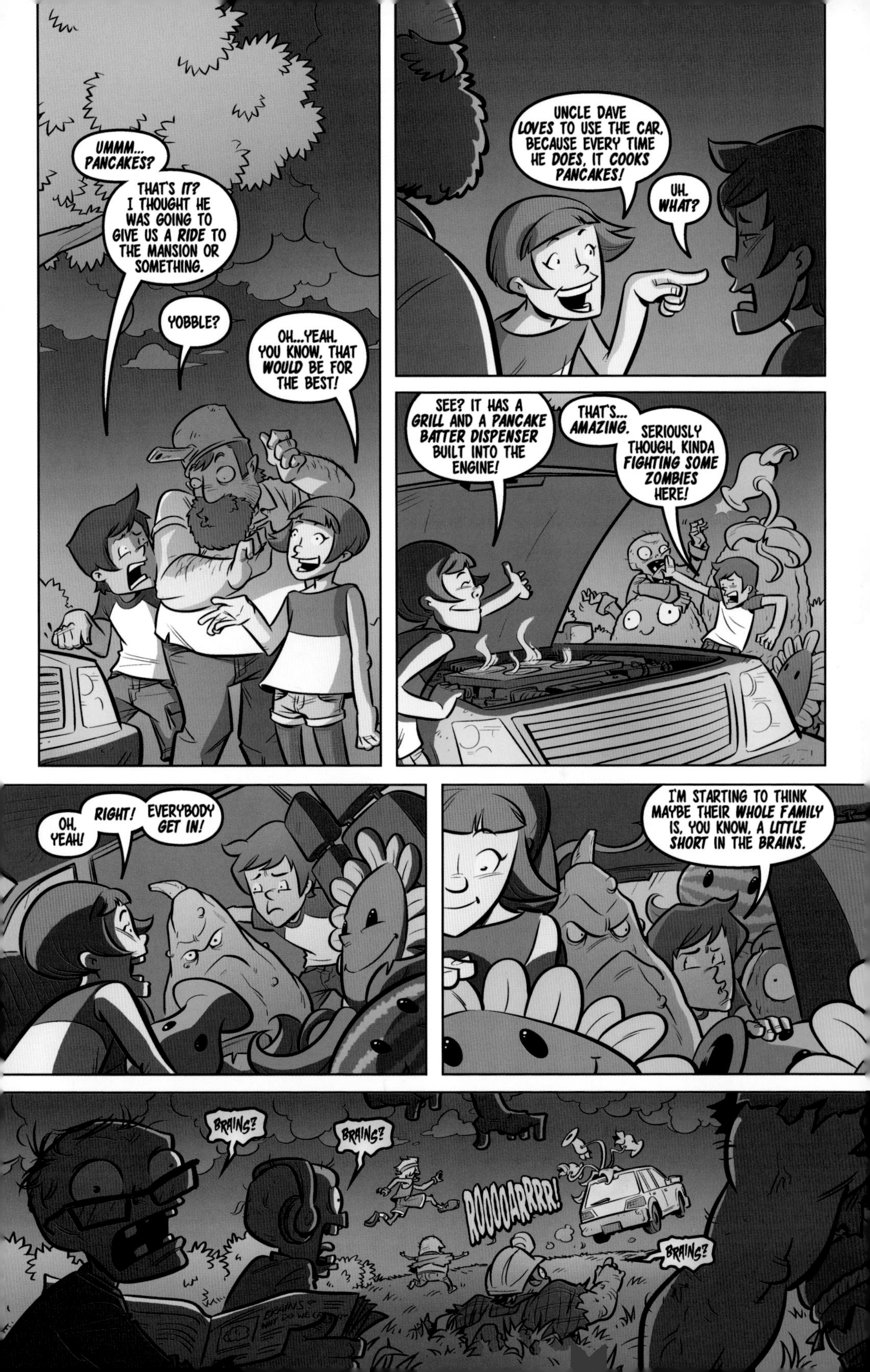
UMMM... PANCAKES?
THAT'S IT? I THOUGHT HE WAS GOING TO GIVE US A RIDE TO THE MANSION OR SOMETHING.
YOBBLE?
OH...YEAH. YOU KNOW, THAT WOULD BE FOR THE BEST!
UNCLE DAVE LOVES TO USE THE CAR, BECAUSE EVERY TIME HE DOES, IT COOKS PANCAKES!
UH. WHAT?
SEE? IT HAS A GRILL AND A PANCAKE BATTER DISPENSER BUILT INTO THE ENGINE!
THAT'S... AMAZING.
SERIOUSLY THOUGH, KINDA FIGHTING SOME ZOMBIES HERE!
OH, YEAH!
RIGHT!
EVERYBODY GET IN!
I'M STARTING TO THINK MAYBE THEIR WHOLE FAMILY IS, YOU KNOW, A LITTLE SHORT IN THE BRAINS.
BRAINS?
BRAINS?
ROOOOARRRR!
BRAINS?

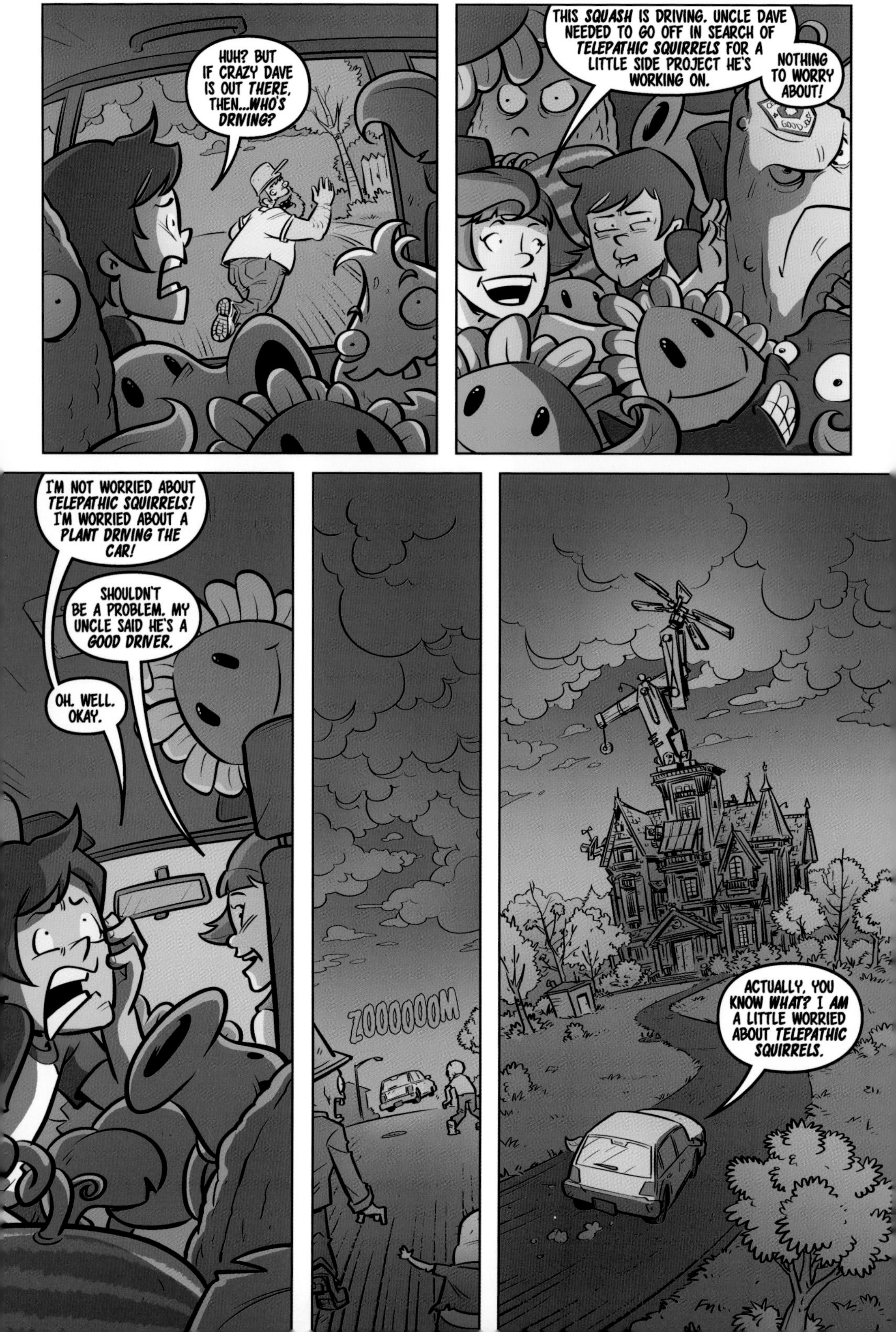

HUH? BUT IF CRAZY DAVE IS OUT THERE, THEN...WHO'S DRIVING?
THIS SQUASH IS DRIVING. UNCLE DAVE NEEDED TO GO OFF IN SEARCH OF TELEPATHIC SQUIRRELS FOR A LITTLE SIDE PROJECT HE'S WORKING ON.
NOTHING TO WORRY ABOUT!
I'M NOT WORRIED ABOUT TELEPATHIC SQUIRRELS! I'M WORRIED ABOUT A PLANT DRIVING THE CAR!
SHOULDN'T BE A PROBLEM. MY UNCLE SAID HE'S A GOOD DRIVER.
OH. WELL. OKAY.
ZOOOOOOM
ACTUALLY, YOU KNOW WHAT? I AM A LITTLE WORRIED ABOUT TELEPATHIC SQUIRRELS.

LOOKS CAN BE DECEIVING. I KNOW IT *LOOKS* LIKE A HAUNTED MANSION, BUT IT'S A GREAT HOUSE!

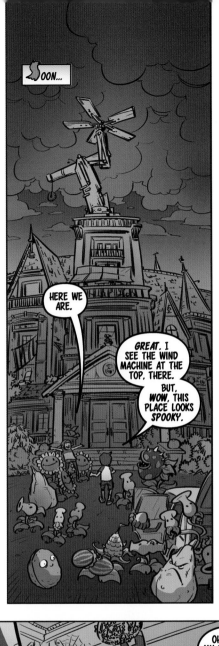

SOON...

HERE WE ARE.

GREAT. I SEE THE WIND MACHINE AT THE TOP, THERE.

BUT, WOW, THIS PLACE LOOKS SPOOKY.

THERE'S NO GHOSTS OR DEMONS OR ZOMBIES OR WEREWOLVES OR ANYTHING LIKE THAT.

WAIT...DID I SAY NO ZOMBIES?

YOU DID.

OH, WELL... MY BAD. THERE ARE A LOT OF ZOMBIES.

BRAINS?

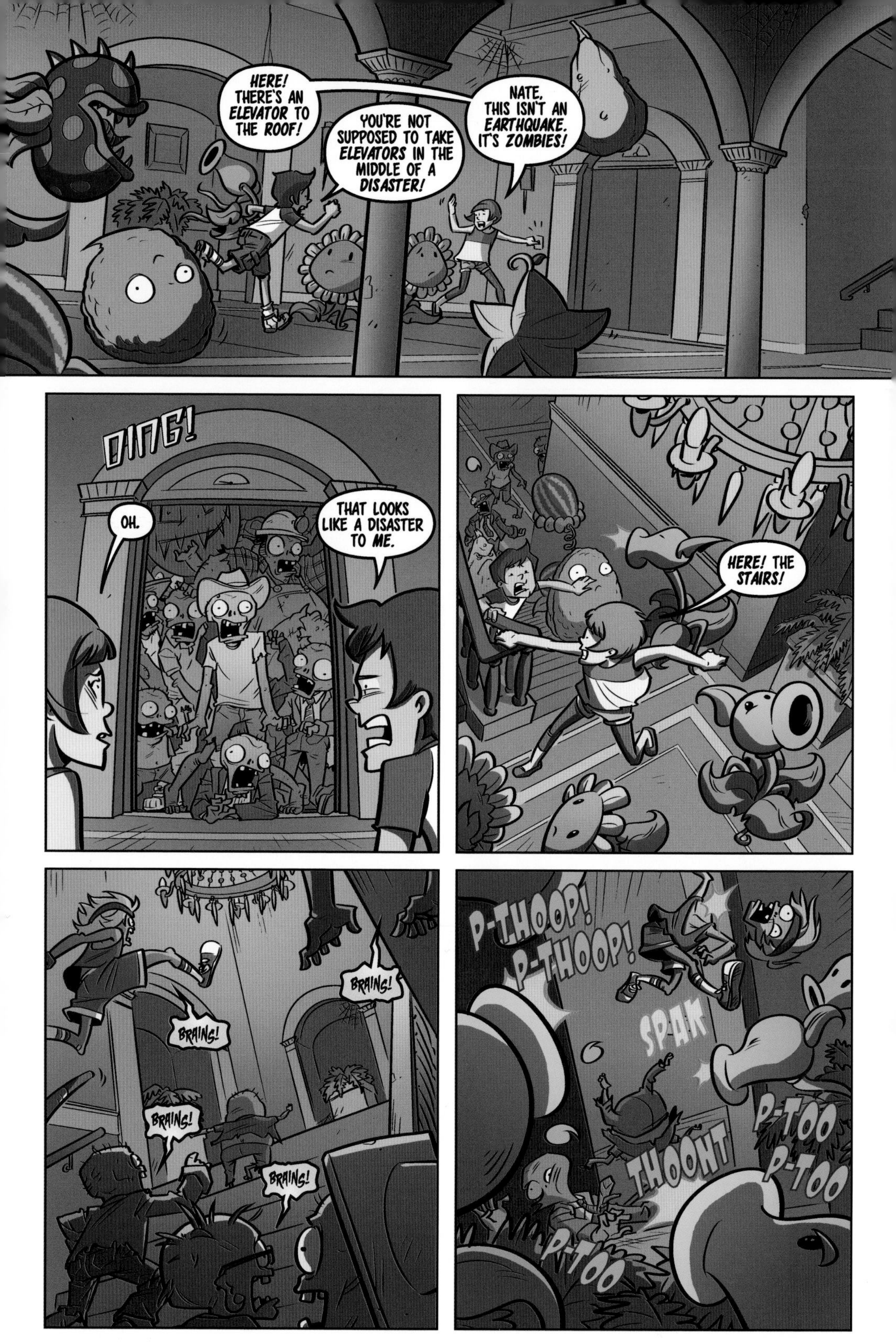
HERE! THERE'S AN ELEVATOR TO THE ROOF!
YOU'RE NOT SUPPOSED TO TAKE ELEVATORS IN THE MIDDLE OF A DISASTER!
NATE, THIS ISN'T AN EARTHQUAKE. IT'S ZOMBIES!
DING!
OH.
THAT LOOKS LIKE A DISASTER TO ME.
HERE! THE STAIRS!
BRAINS!
BRAINS!
BRAINS!
BRAINS!
P-THOOP!
P-THOOP!
SPAK
P-TOO
P-TOO
THOONT
P-TOO

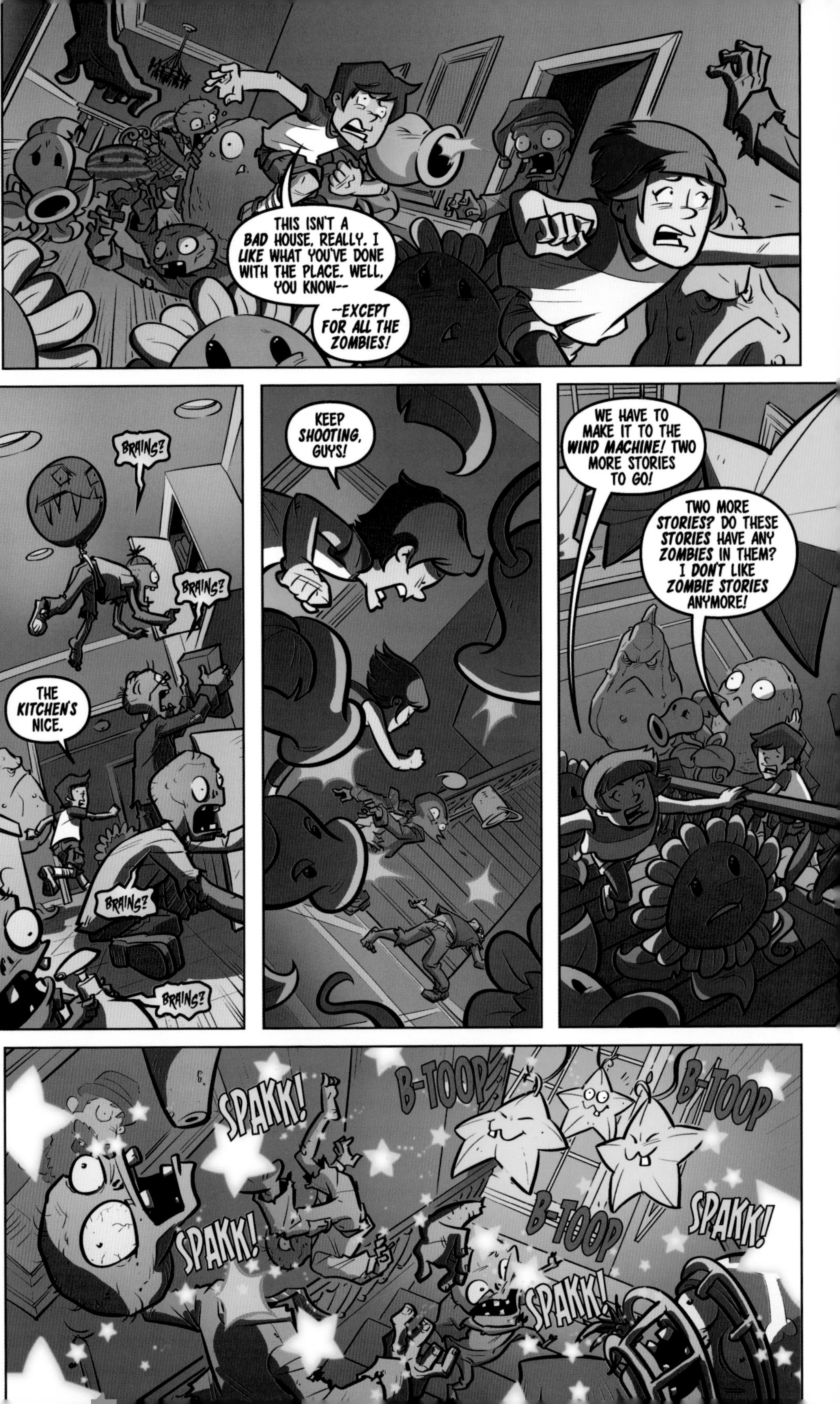
THIS ISN'T A BAD HOUSE, REALLY. I LIKE WHAT YOU'VE DONE WITH THE PLACE. WELL, YOU KNOW--
--EXCEPT FOR ALL THE ZOMBIES!
BRAINS?
BRAINS?
THE KITCHEN'S NICE.
BRAINS?
BRAINS?
KEEP SHOOTING, GUYS!
WE HAVE TO MAKE IT TO THE WIND MACHINE! TWO MORE STORIES TO GO!
TWO MORE STORIES? DO THESE STORIES HAVE ANY ZOMBIES IN THEM? I DON'T LIKE ZOMBIE STORIES ANYMORE!
SPAKK!
B-TOOP
B-TOOP
SPAKK!
B-TOOP
SPAKK!
SPAKK!

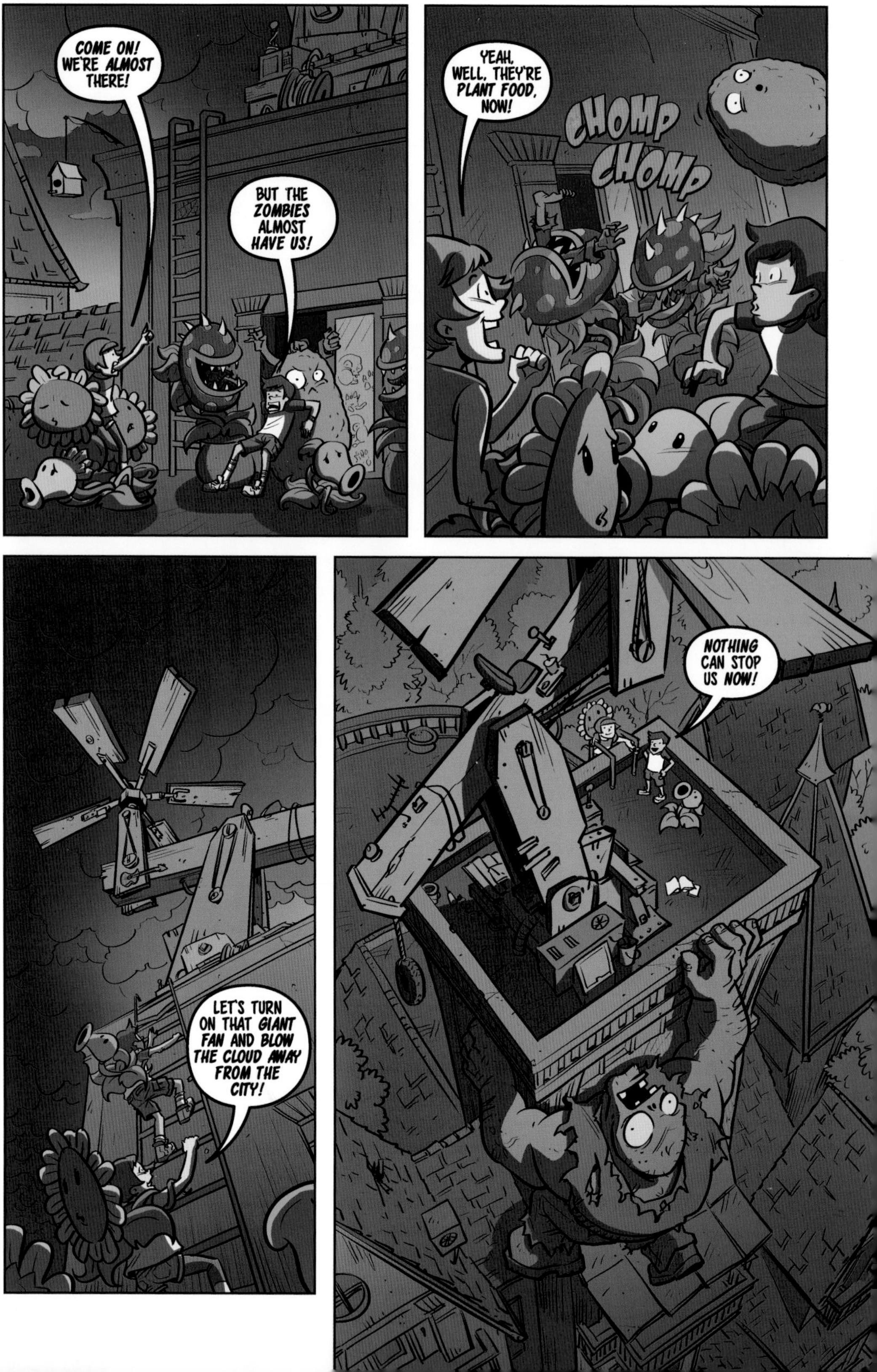
COME ON! WE'RE ALMOST THERE!
BUT THE ZOMBIES ALMOST HAVE US!
YEAH, WELL, THEY'RE PLANT FOOD, NOW!
CHOMP
CHOMP
LET'S TURN ON THAT GIANT FAN AND BLOW THE CLOUD AWAY FROM THE CITY!
NOTHING CAN STOP US NOW!

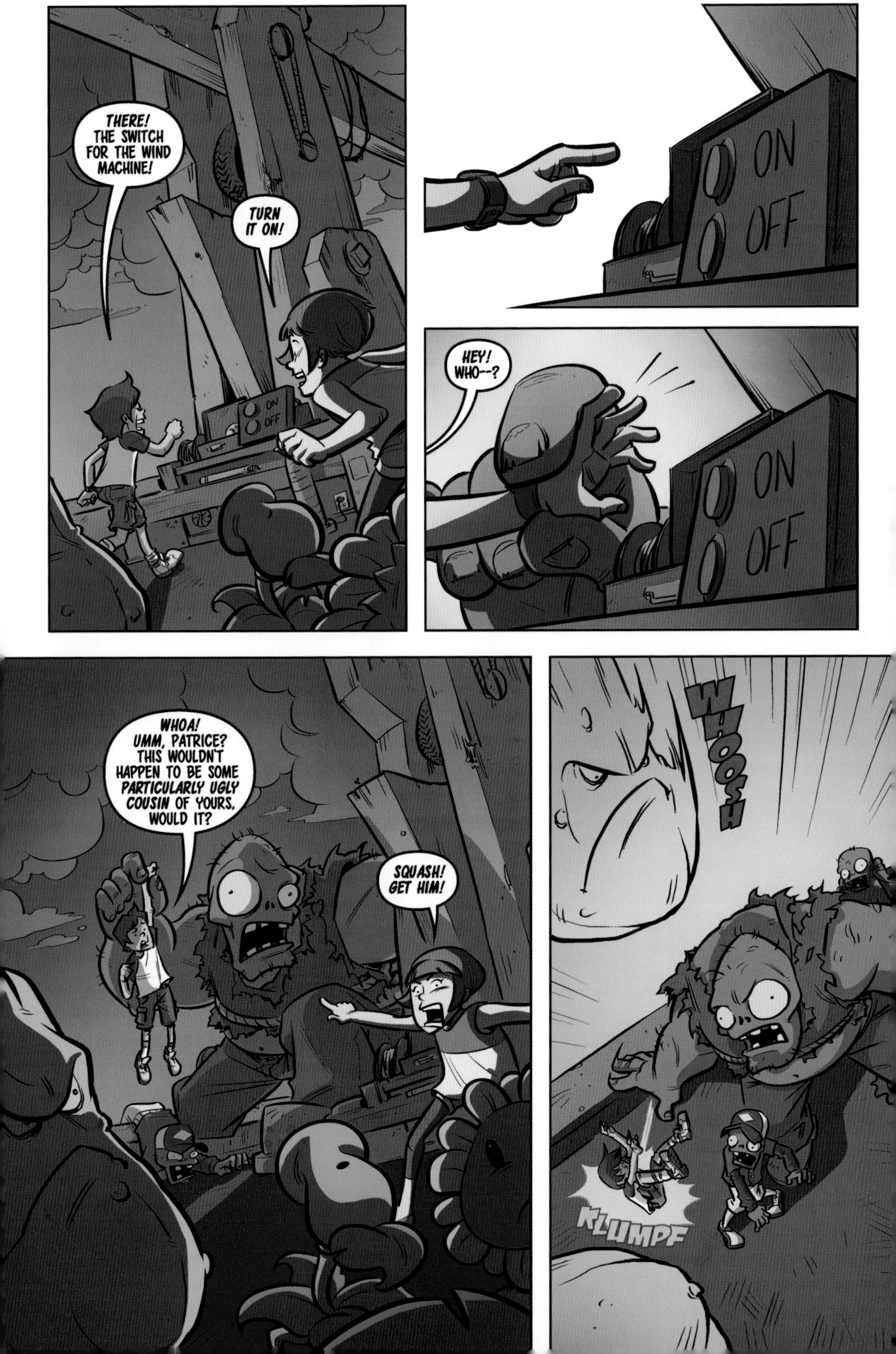
THERE! THE SWITCH FOR THE WIND MACHINE!
TURN IT ON!
ON
OFF
ON
OFF
HEY! WHO--?
ON
OFF
WHOA! UMM, PATRICE? THIS WOULDN'T HAPPEN TO BE SOME PARTICULARLY UGLY COUSIN OF YOURS, WOULD IT?
SQUASH! GET HIM!
WHOOOSH
KLUMPF

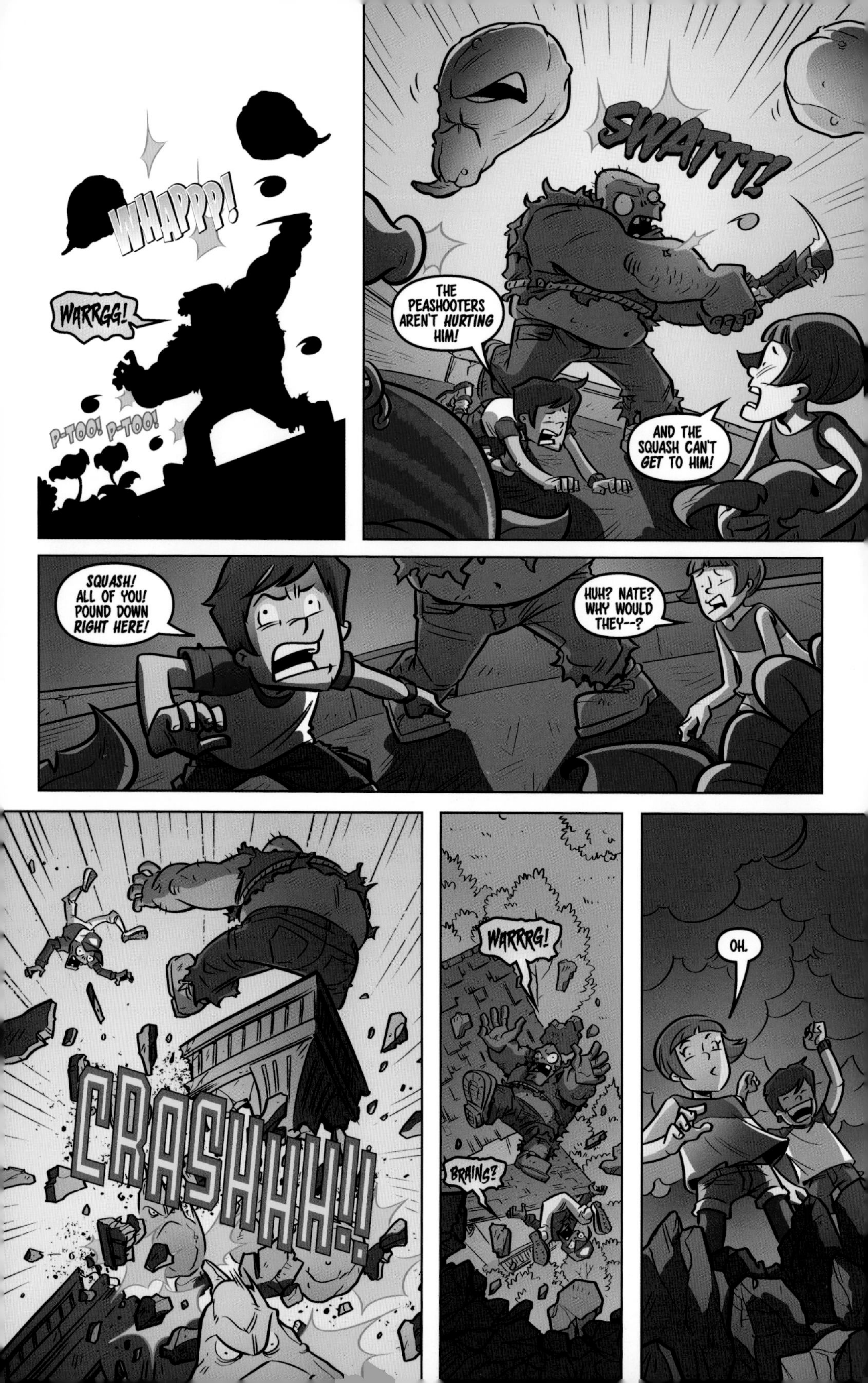
WHAPPP!
WARRGG!
P-TOO! P-TOO!
SWATTT!
THE PEASHOOTERS AREN'T HURTING HIM!
AND THE SQUASH CAN'T GET TO HIM!
SQUASH! ALL OF YOU! POUND DOWN RIGHT HERE!
HUH? NATE? WHY WOULD THEY--?
CRASHHH!!
WARRRG!
BRAINS?
OH.

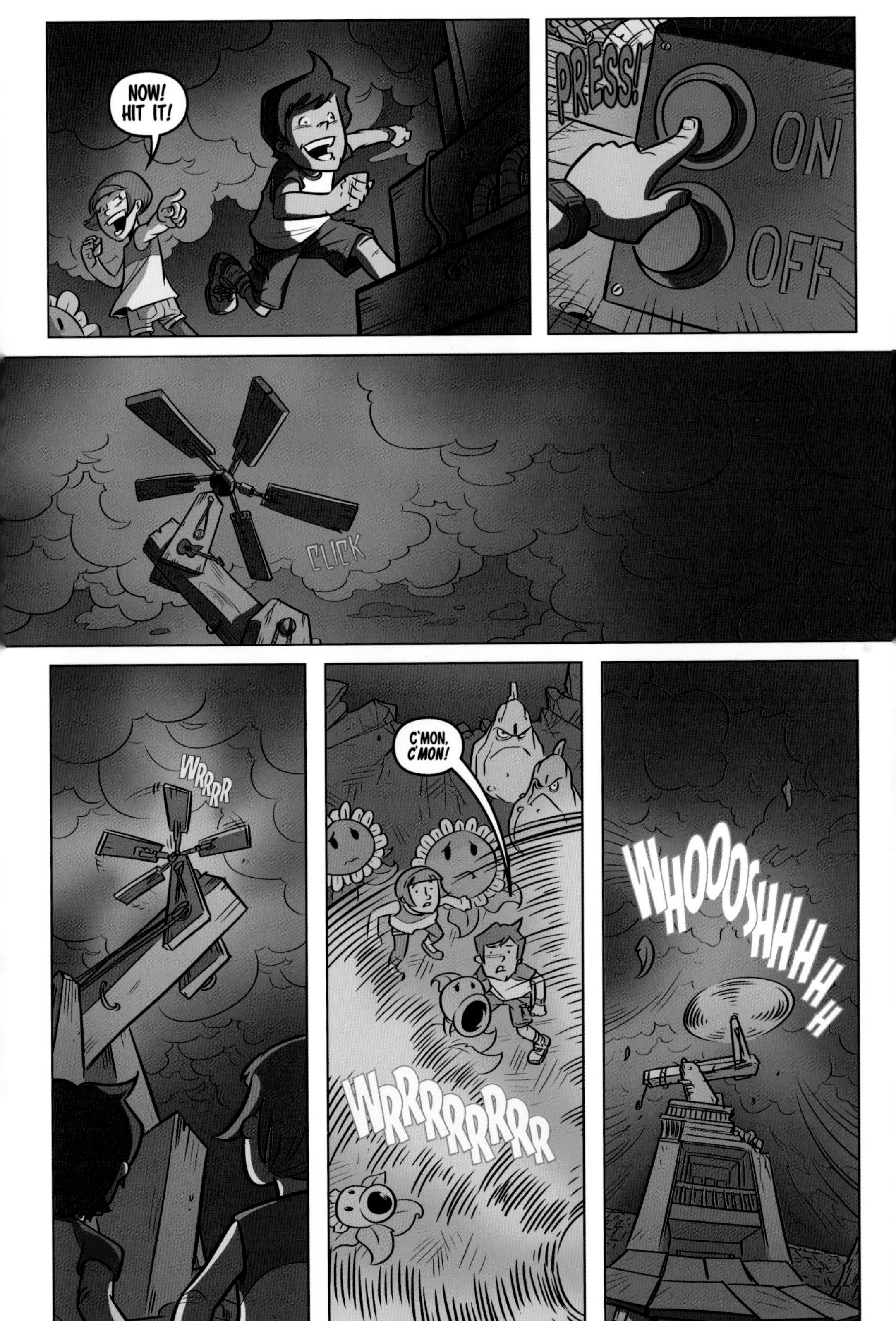
NOW! HIT IT!
PRESS!
ON
OFF
CLICK
WRRRR
C'MON, C'MON!
WRRRRRRRRR
WHOOOSHHHHHH

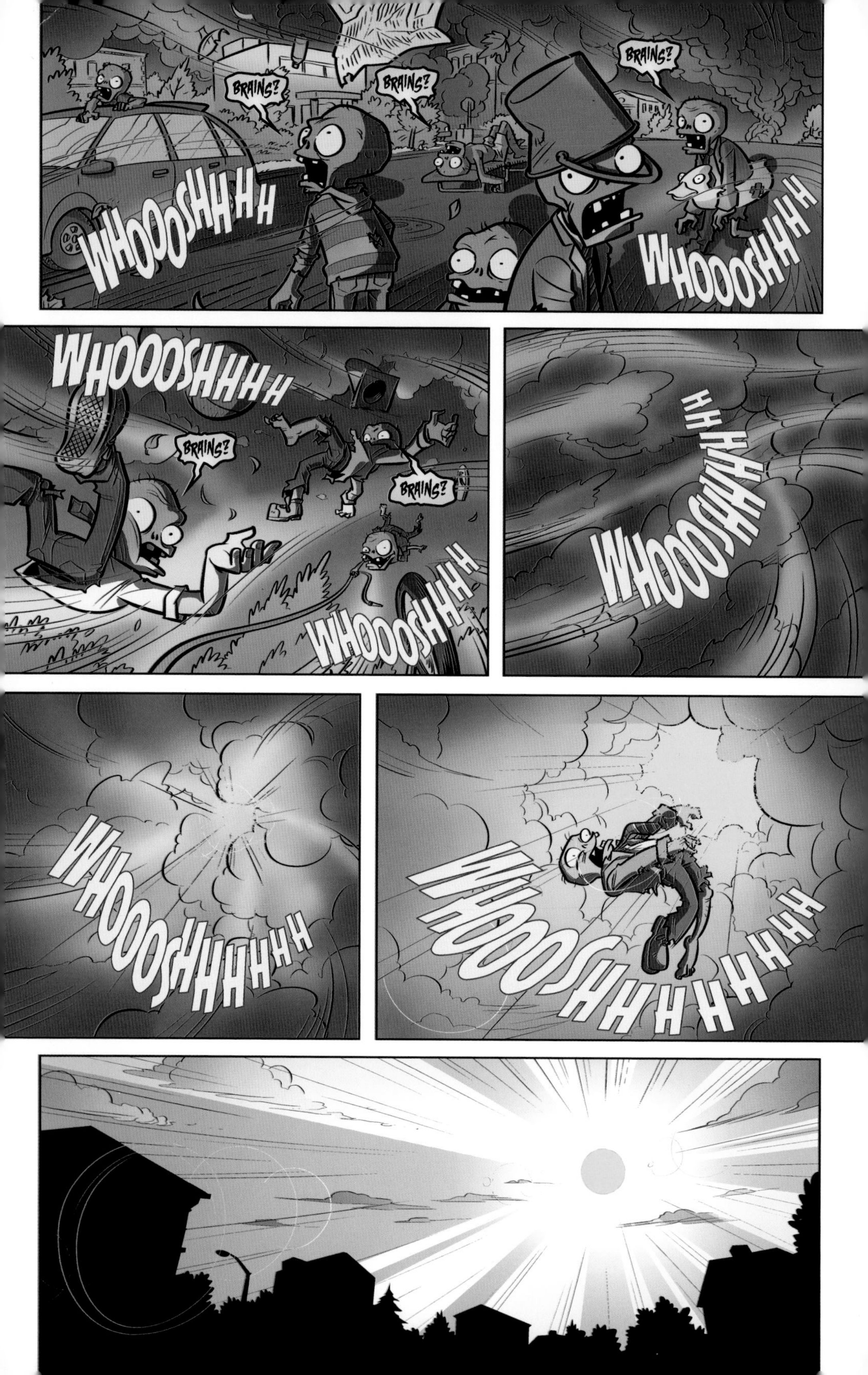
BRAINS?
BRAINS?
BRAINS?
WHOOOSHHHH
WHOOOSHHH
WHOOOSHHHHH
BRAINS?
BRAINS?
WHOOOSHHH
WHOOOSHHHHHH
WHOOOSHHHHHH
WHOOOSHHHHHHHHH

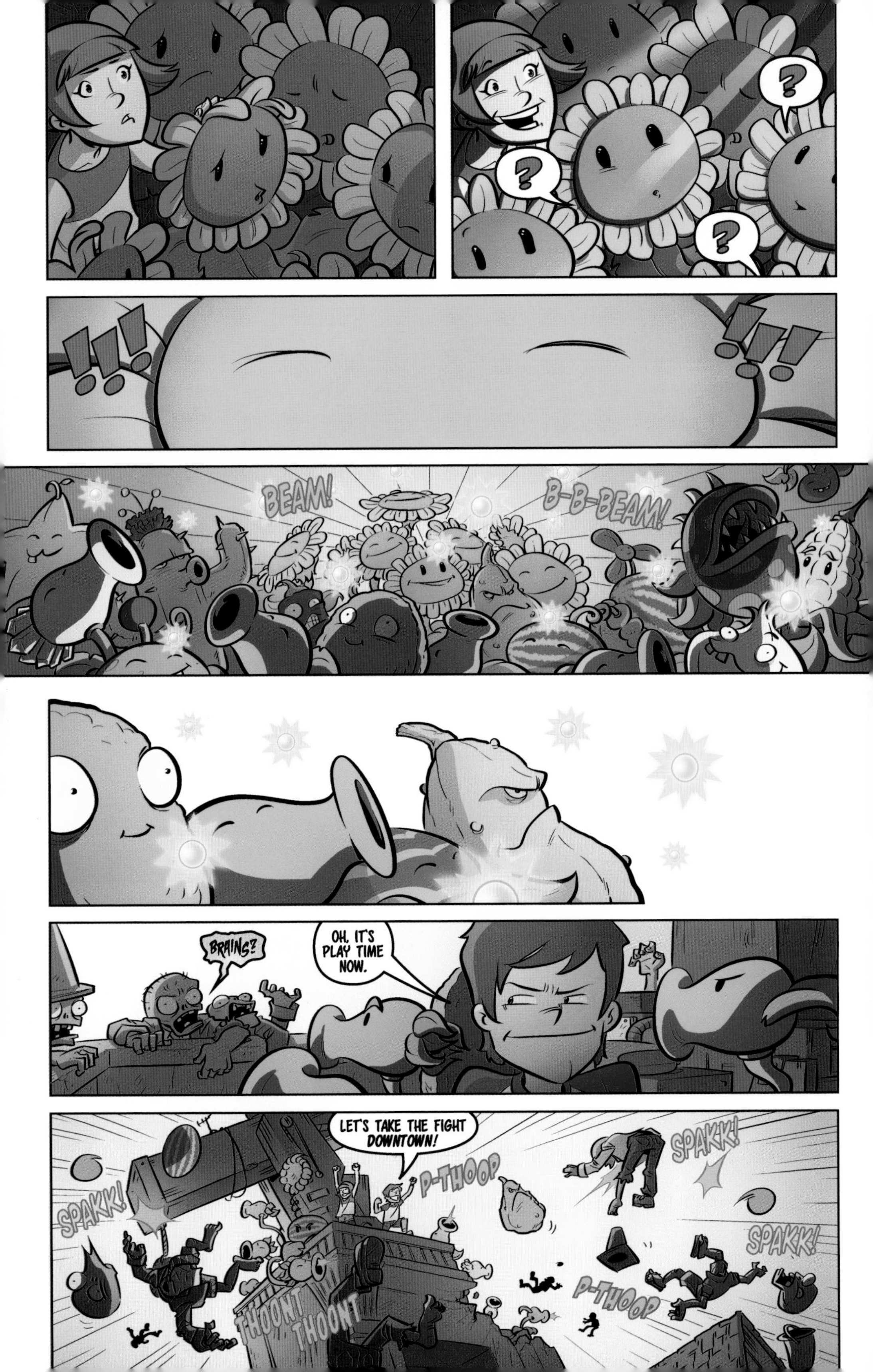
?
?
?
!!!
!!!
BEAM!
B-B-BEAM!
BRAINS?
OH, IT'S PLAY TIME NOW.
LET'S TAKE THE FIGHT DOWNTOWN!
SPAKK!
P-THOOP
SPAKK!
SPAKK!
P-THOOP
THOONT
THOONT

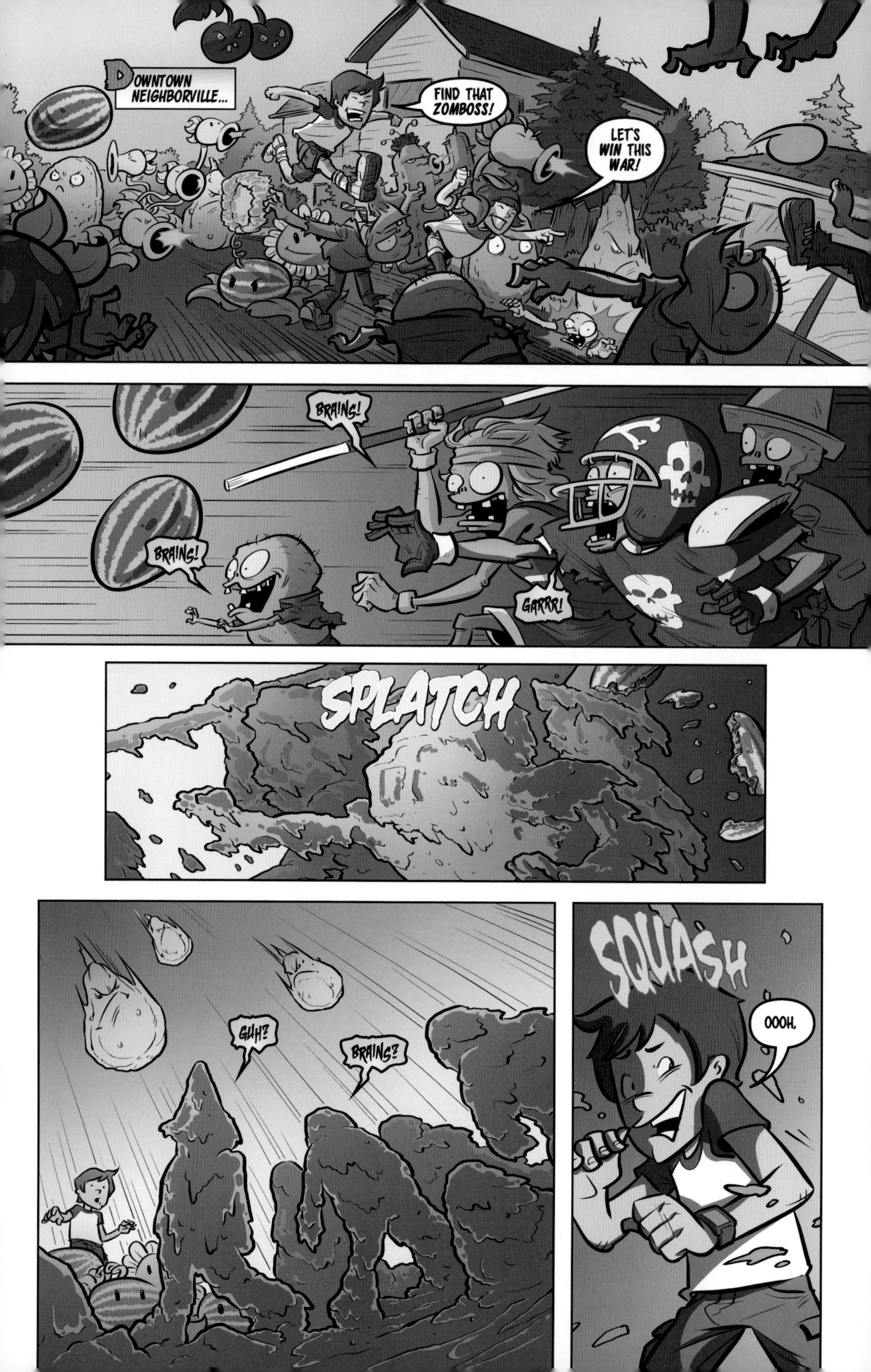
DOWNTOWN NEIGHBORVILLE...
FIND THAT ZOMBOSS!
LET'S WIN THIS WAR!
BRAINS!
BRAINS!
GARRR!
SPLATCH
GUH?
BRAINS?
SQUASH
OOOH.

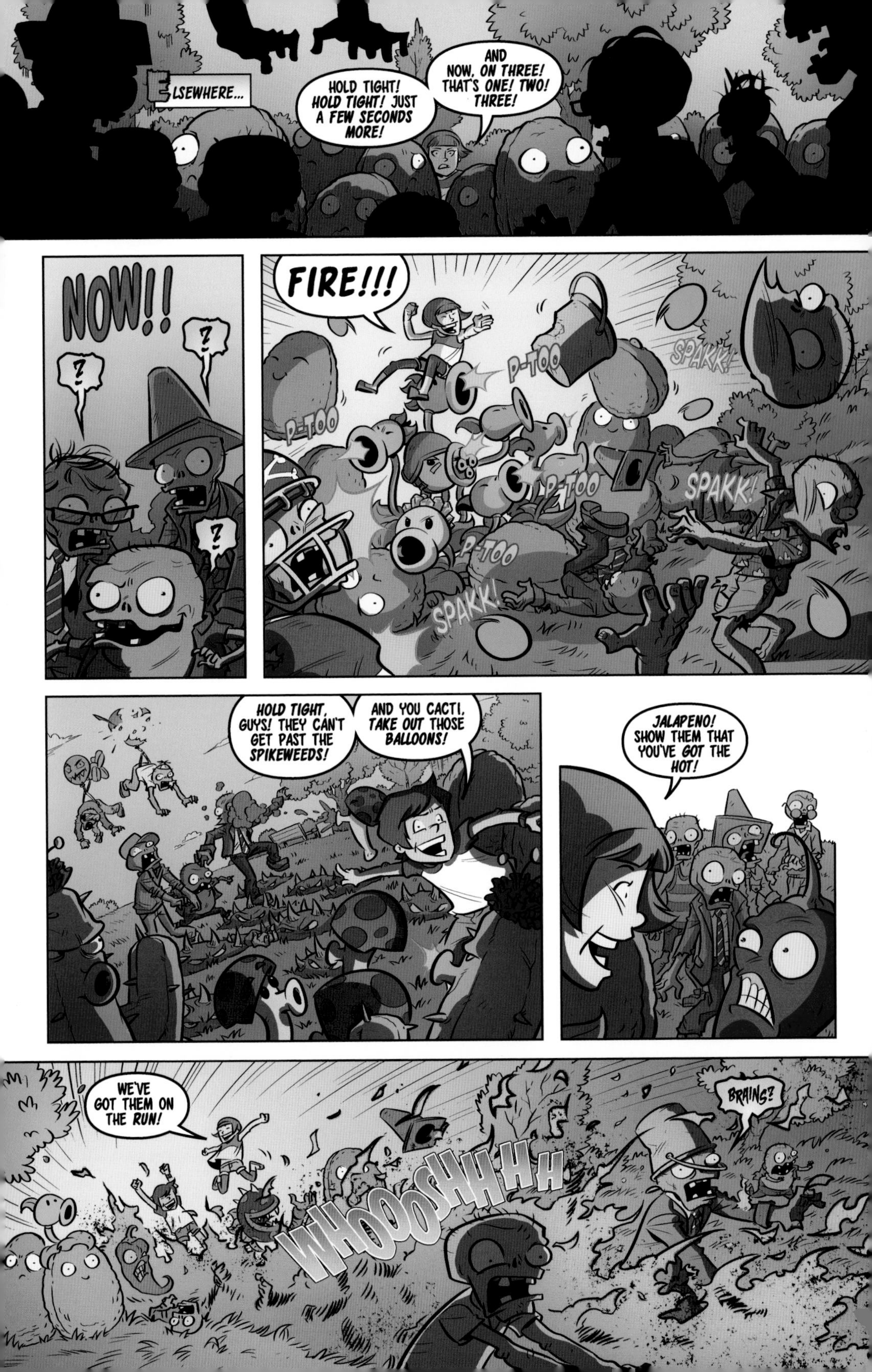
ELSEWHERE...
HOLD TIGHT! HOLD TIGHT! JUST A FEW SECONDS MORE!
AND NOW, ON THREE! THAT'S ONE! TWO! THREE!
NOW!!
?
?
?
FIRE!!!
P-TOO
P-TOO
P-TOO
P-TOO
SPAKK!
SPAKK!
SPAKK!
HOLD TIGHT, GUYS! THEY CAN'T GET PAST THE SPIKEWEEDS!
AND YOU CACTI, TAKE OUT THOSE BALLOONS!
JALAPENO! SHOW THEM THAT YOU'VE GOT THE HOT!
WE'VE GOT THEM ON THE RUN!
BRAINS?
WHOOOOSHHHHH

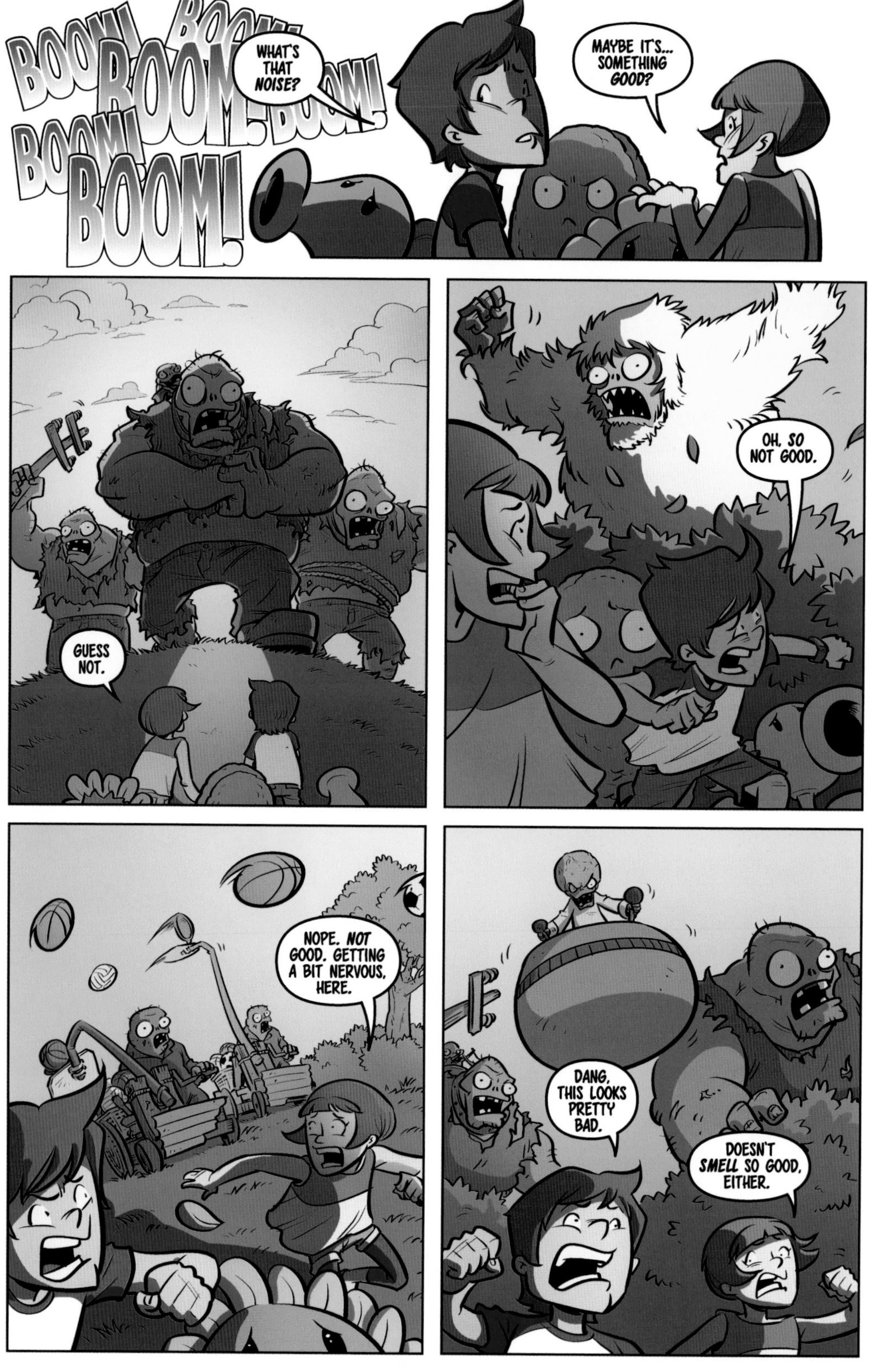
BOOM! BOOM! BOOM! BOOM! BOOM! BOOM!
WHAT'S THAT NOISE?
MAYBE IT'S... SOMETHING GOOD?
GUESS NOT.
OH, SO NOT GOOD.
NOPE. NOT GOOD. GETTING A BIT NERVOUS, HERE.
DANG, THIS LOOKS PRETTY BAD.
DOESN'T SMELL SO GOOD, EITHER.

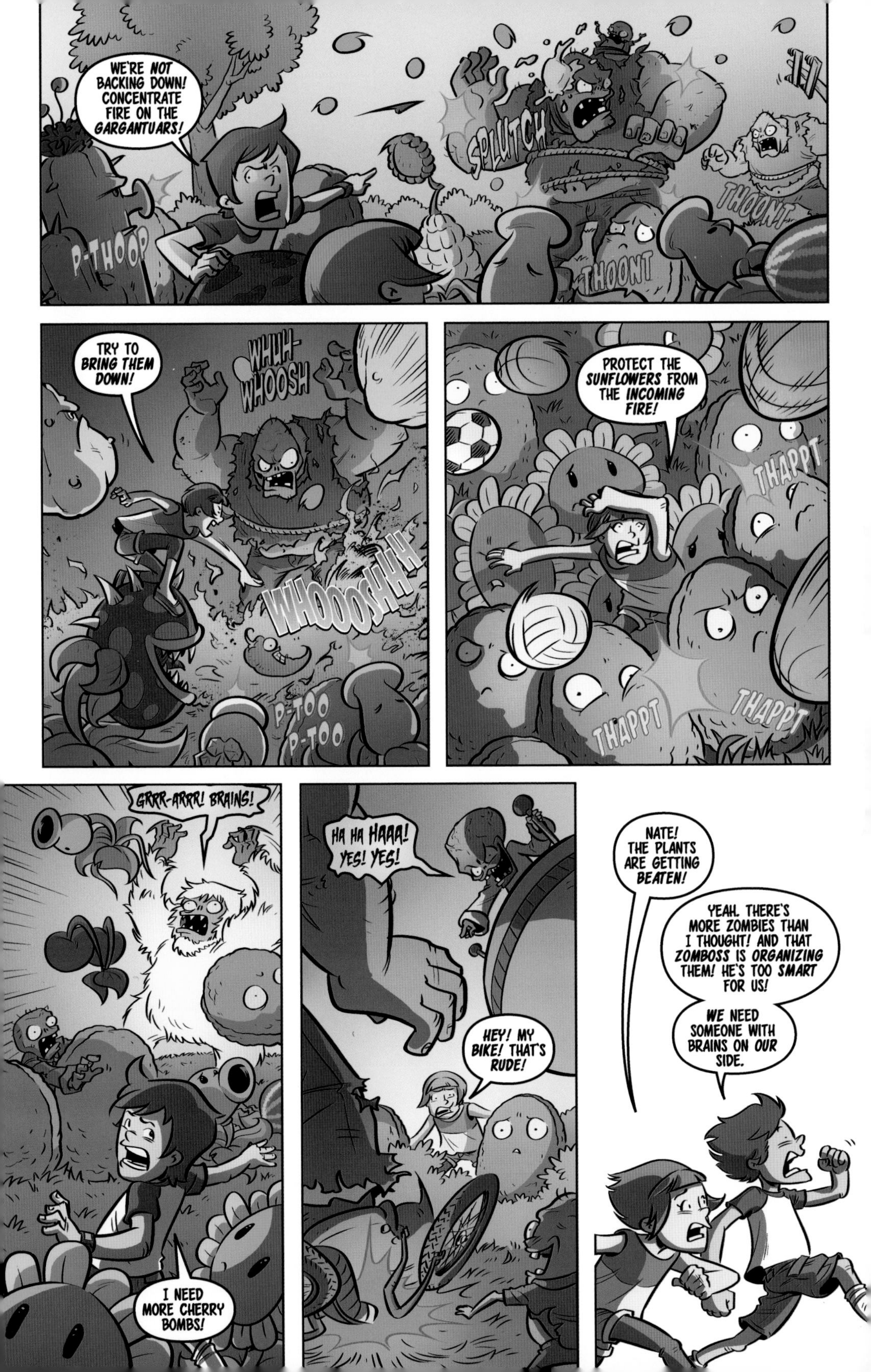
WE'RE NOT BACKING DOWN! CONCENTRATE FIRE ON THE GARGANTUARS!
SPLUTCH
P-THOOP
THOONT
THOONT
TRY TO BRING THEM DOWN!
WHUH-WHOOSH
WHOOOSHHH
P-TOO P-TOO
PROTECT THE SUNFLOWERS FROM THE INCOMING FIRE!
THAPPT
THAPPT
THAPPT
GRRR-ARRR! BRAINS!
I NEED MORE CHERRY BOMBS!
HA HA HAAA! YES! YES!
HEY! MY BIKE! THAT'S RUDE!
NATE! THE PLANTS ARE GETTING BEATEN!
YEAH. THERE'S MORE ZOMBIES THAN I THOUGHT! AND THAT ZOMBOSS IS ORGANIZING THEM! HE'S TOO SMART FOR US!
WE NEED SOMEONE WITH BRAINS ON OUR SIDE.

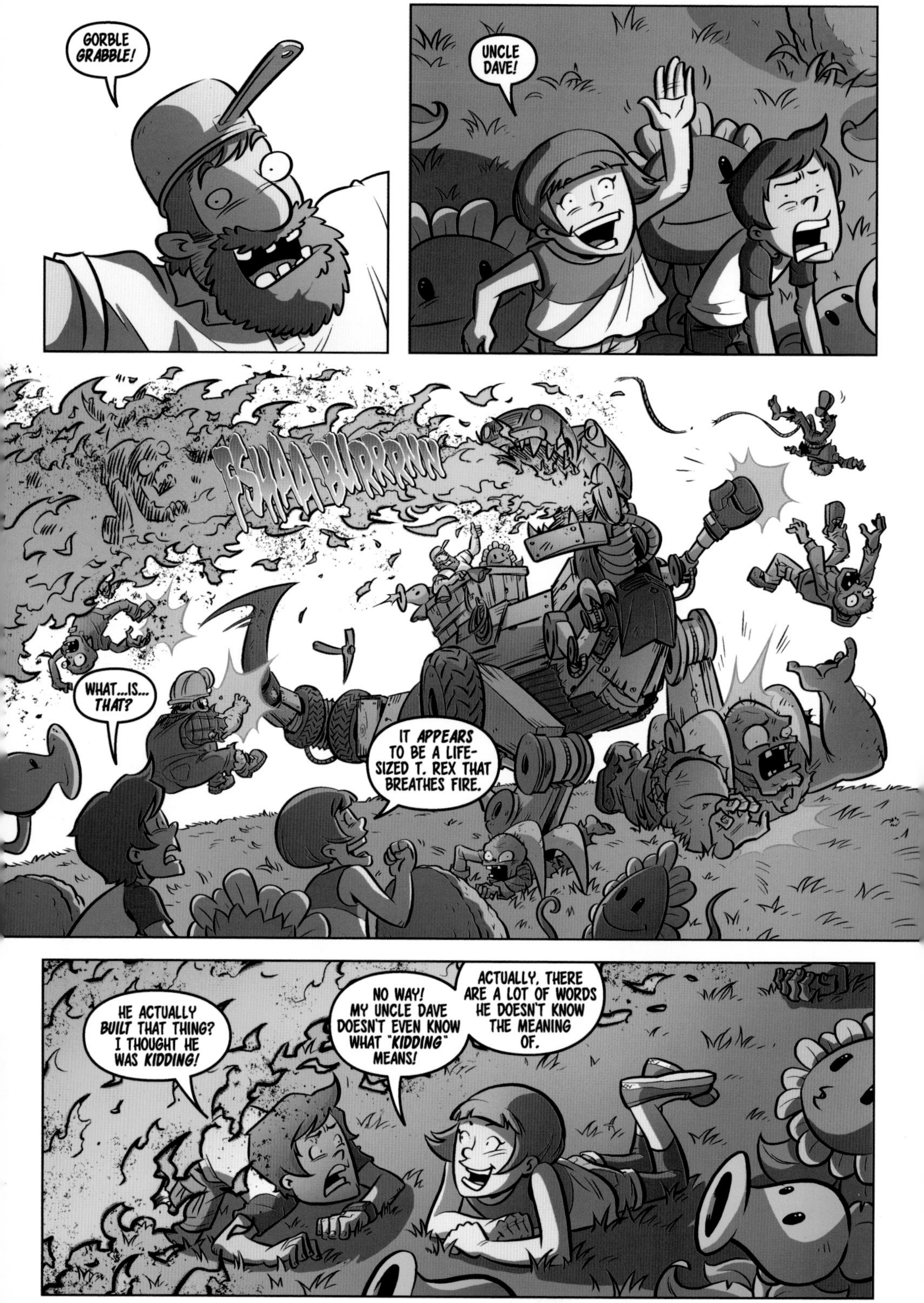
GORBLE GRABBLE!
UNCLE DAVE!
TSHAAABURRRNN
WHAT...IS... THAT?
IT APPEARS TO BE A LIFE-SIZED T. REX THAT BREATHES FIRE.
HE ACTUALLY BUILT THAT THING? I THOUGHT HE WAS KIDDING!
NO WAY! MY UNCLE DAVE DOESN'T EVEN KNOW WHAT "KIDDING" MEANS!
ACTUALLY, THERE ARE A LOT OF WORDS HE DOESN'T KNOW THE MEANING OF.

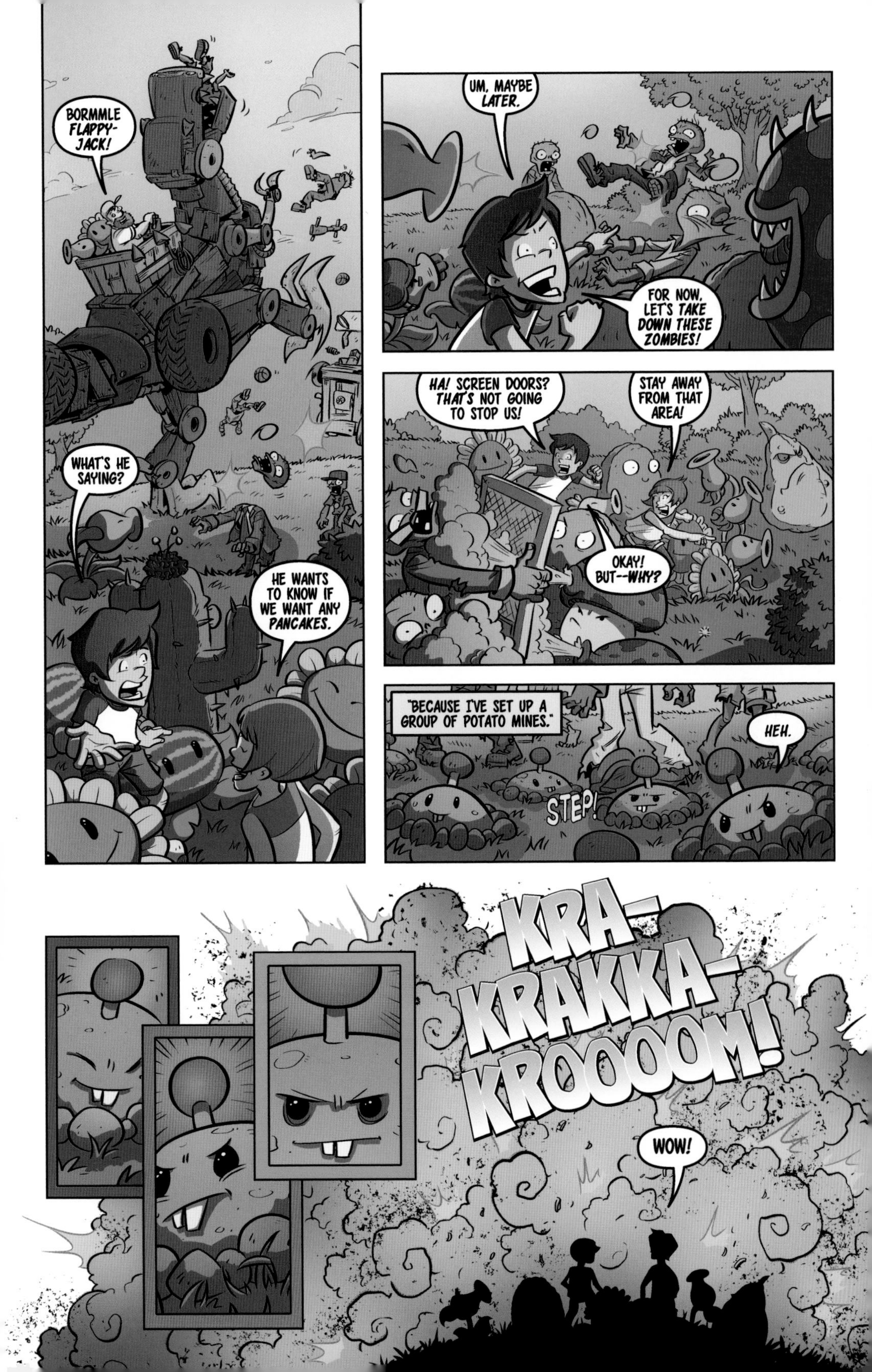
BORMMLE FLAPPY-JACK!
WHAT'S HE SAYING?
HE WANTS TO KNOW IF WE WANT ANY PANCAKES.
UM, MAYBE LATER.
FOR NOW, LET'S TAKE DOWN THESE ZOMBIES!
HA! SCREEN DOORS? THAT'S NOT GOING TO STOP US!
STAY AWAY FROM THAT AREA!
OKAY! BUT--WHY?
"BECAUSE I'VE SET UP A GROUP OF POTATO MINES."
HEH.
STEP!
KRA-KRAKKA-KROOOOM!
WOW!

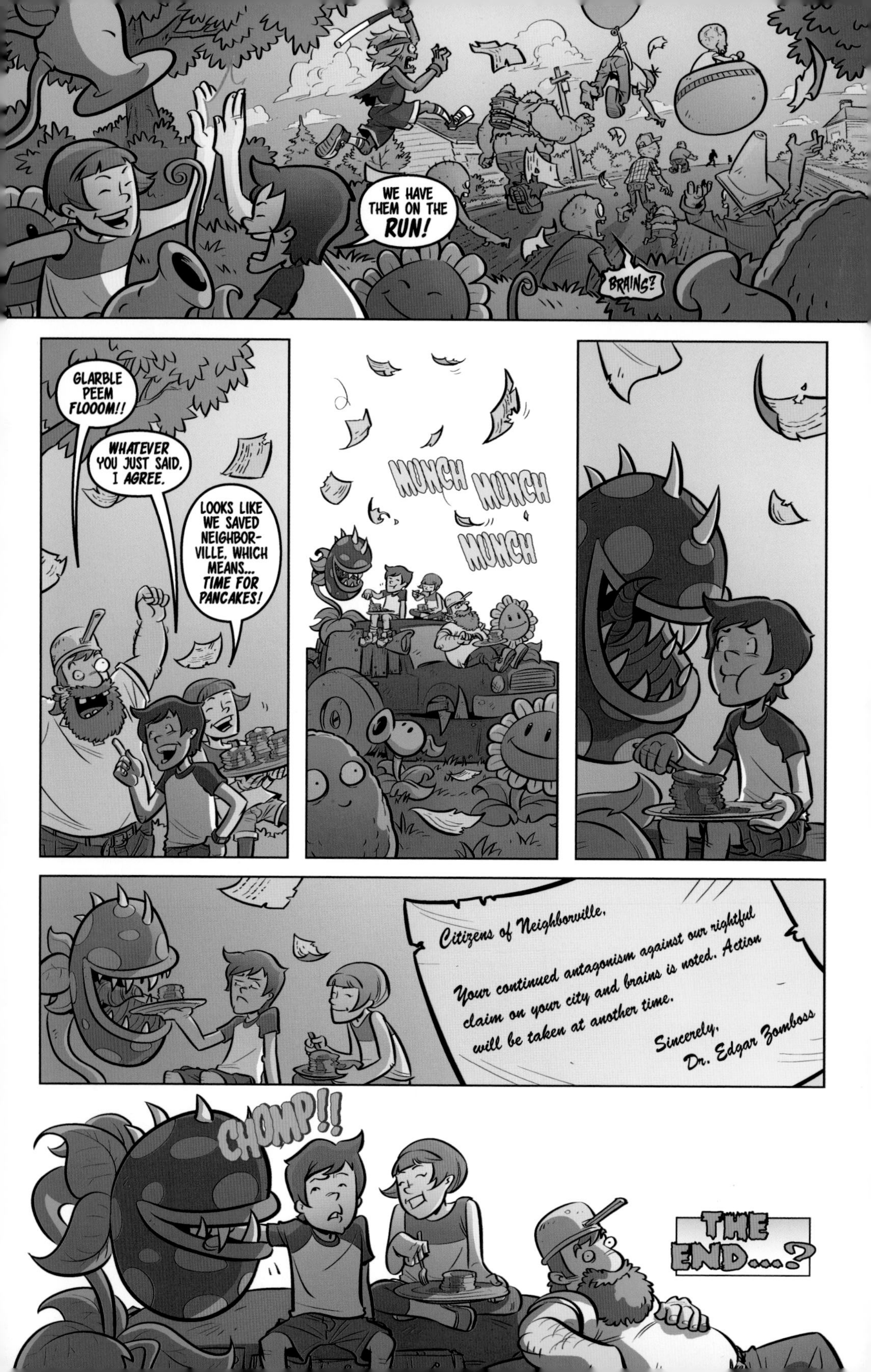

WE HAVE THEM ON THE RUN!
BRAINS?
GLARBLE PEEM FLOOOM!!
WHATEVER YOU JUST SAID, I AGREE.
LOOKS LIKE WE SAVED NEIGHBOR-VILLE, WHICH MEANS... TIME FOR PANCAKES!
MUNCH MUNCH MUNCH
Citizens of Neighborville,
Your continued antagonism against our rightful claim on your city and brains is noted. Action will be taken at another time.
Sincerely,
Dr. Edgar Zomboss
CHOMP!!
THE END...?

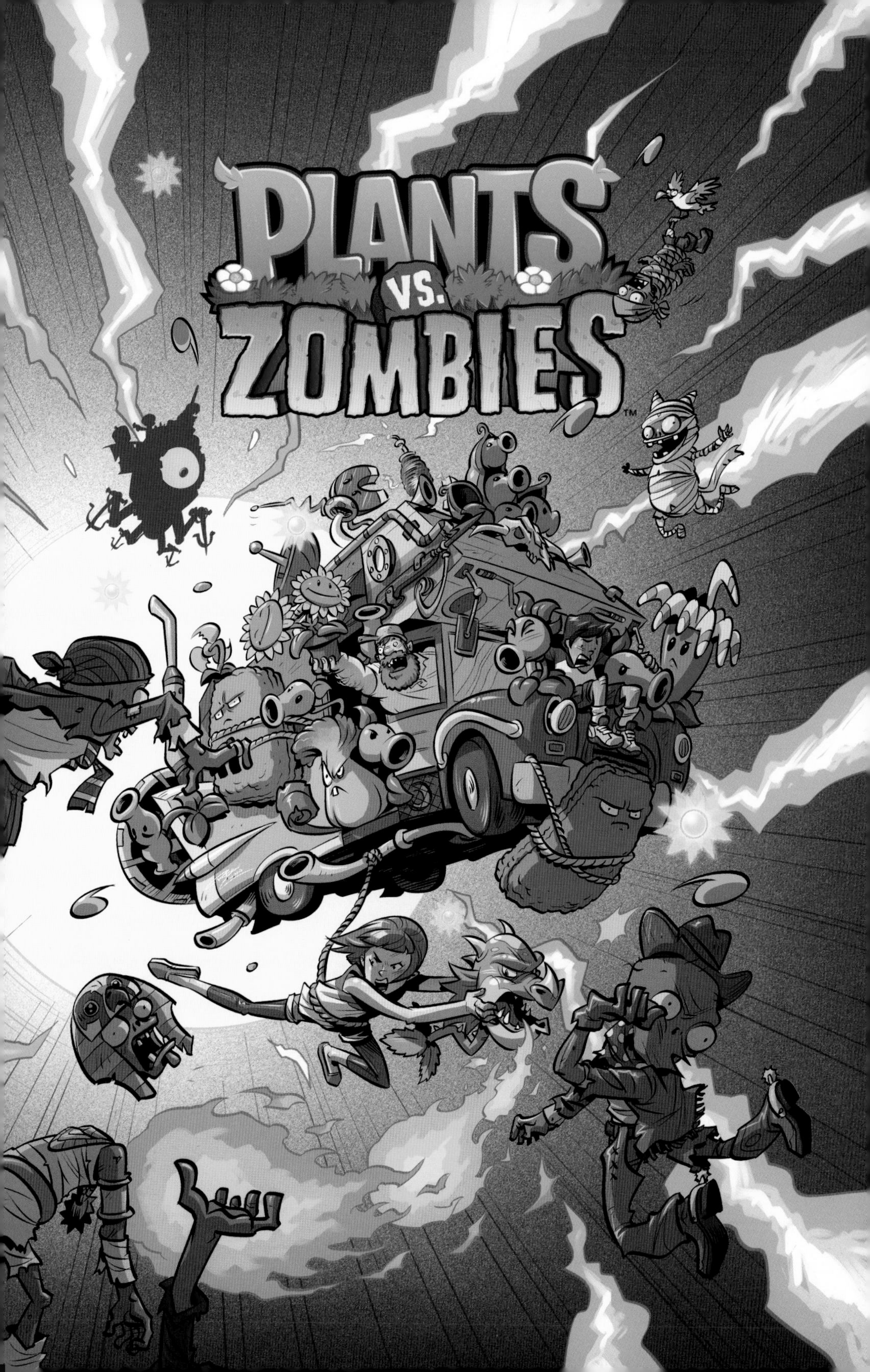
PLANTS
VS.
ZOMBIES
™

TIMEPOCALYPSE

Written by PAUL TOBIN

Art by RON CHAN

Colors by MATT J. RAINWATER

Letters by STEVE DUTRO

Plants vs. Zombies: Timepocalypse #1 cover art
(previous page) by Ron Chan

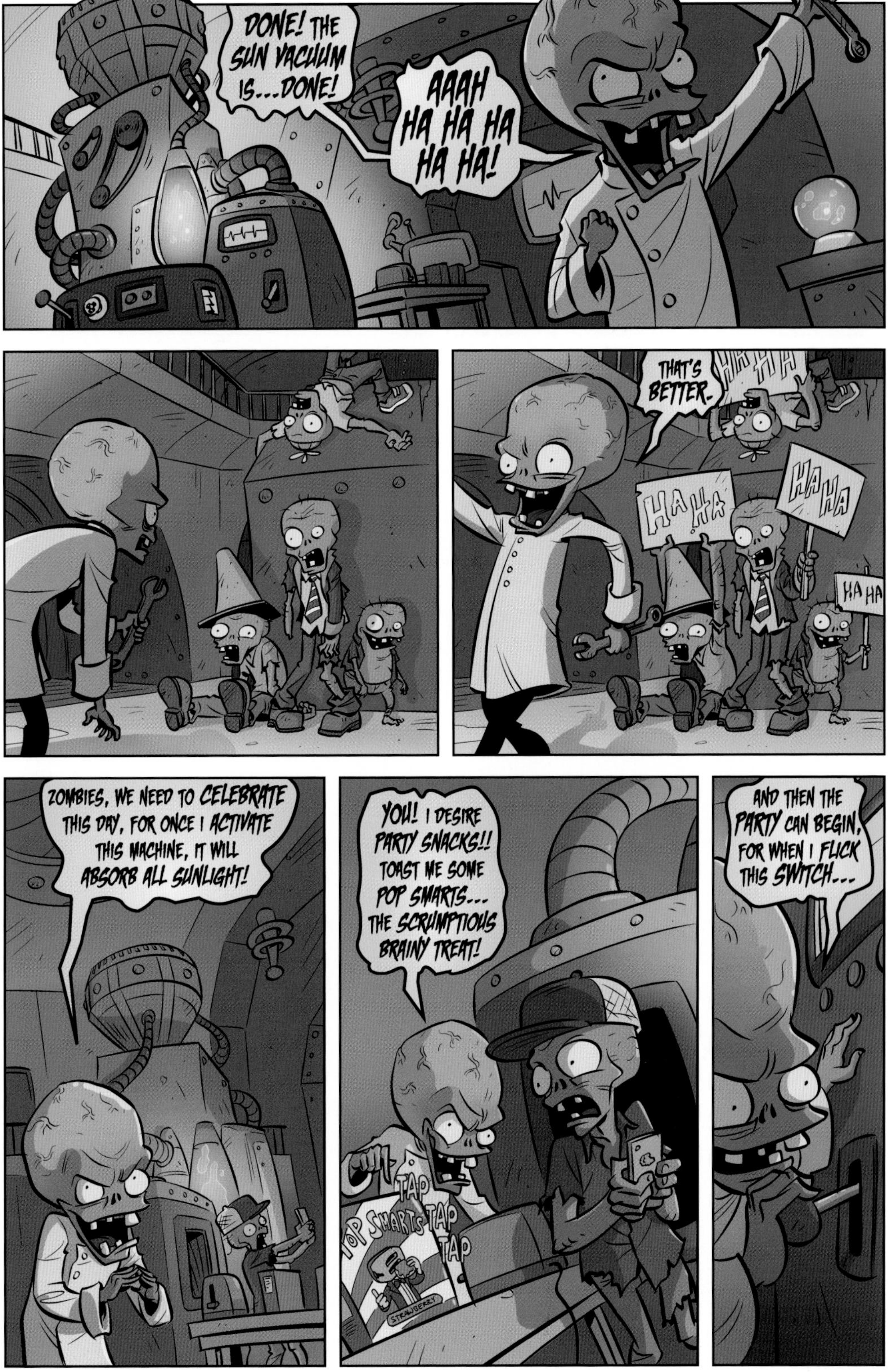
DONE! THE SUN VACUUM IS...DONE!
AAAH HA HA HA HA HA!
THAT'S BETTER.
HA HA
HA HA
HA HA
ZOMBIES, WE NEED TO CELEBRATE THIS DAY, FOR ONCE I ACTIVATE THIS MACHINE, IT WILL ABSORB ALL SUNLIGHT!
YOU! I DESIRE PARTY SNACKS!! TOAST ME SOME POP SMARTS... THE SCRUMPTIOUS BRAINY TREAT!
TAP
POP SMARTS
TAP
TAP
STRAWBERRY
AND THEN THE PARTY CAN BEGIN, FOR WHEN I FLICK THIS SWITCH...

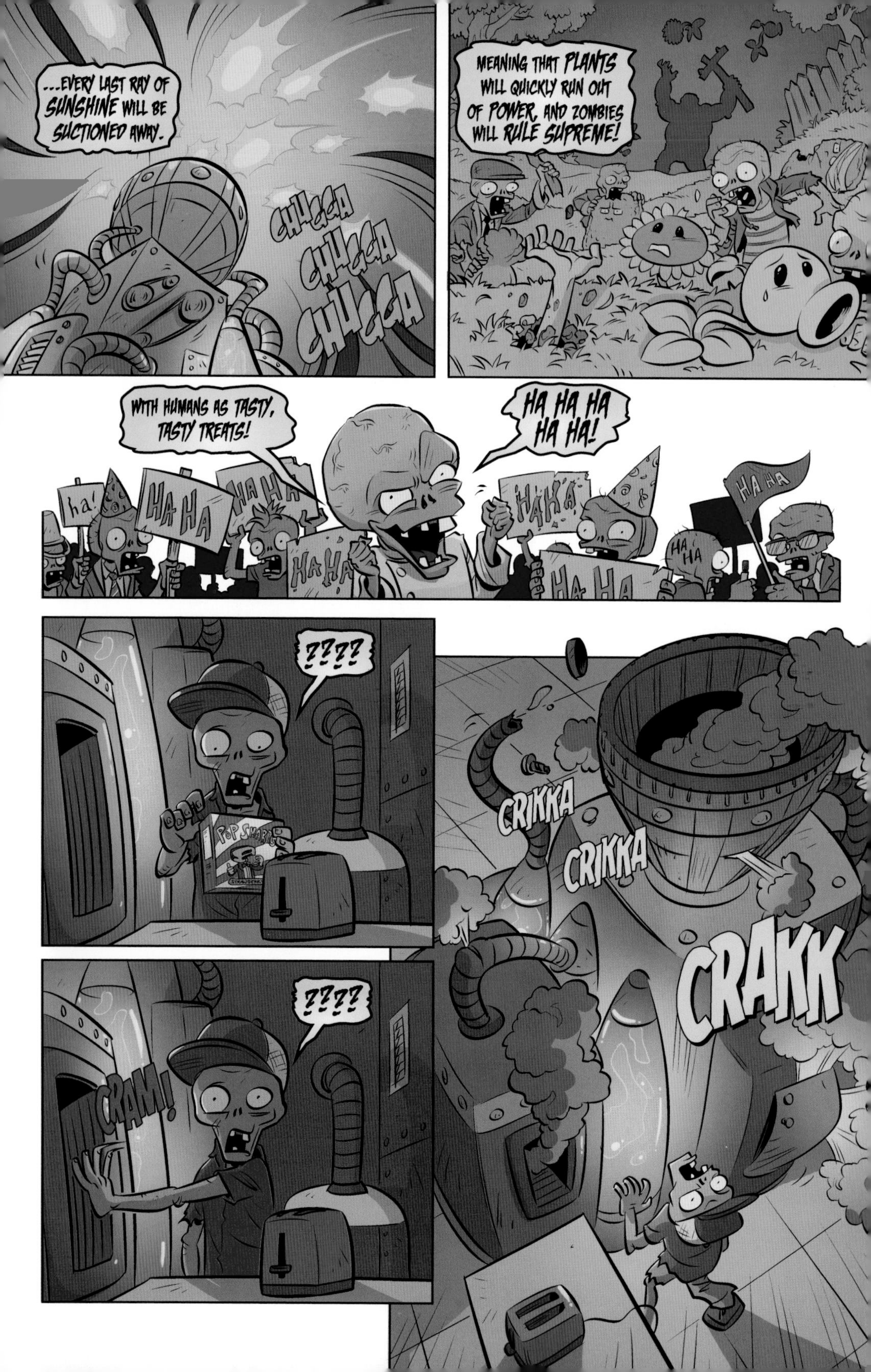

...EVERY LAST RAY OF SUNSHINE WILL BE SUCTIONED AWAY.
CHUGGA CHUGGA CHUGGA
MEANING THAT PLANTS WILL QUICKLY RUN OUT OF POWER, AND ZOMBIES WILL RULE SUPREME!
WITH HUMANS AS TASTY, TASTY TREATS!
HA HA HA HA HA!
ha!
HA HA
HA HA
HA HA
HA HA
HA HA
HA HA
HA HA
HA HA
????
POP SHARKS
????
CRAM!
CRIKKA
CRIKKA
CRAKK

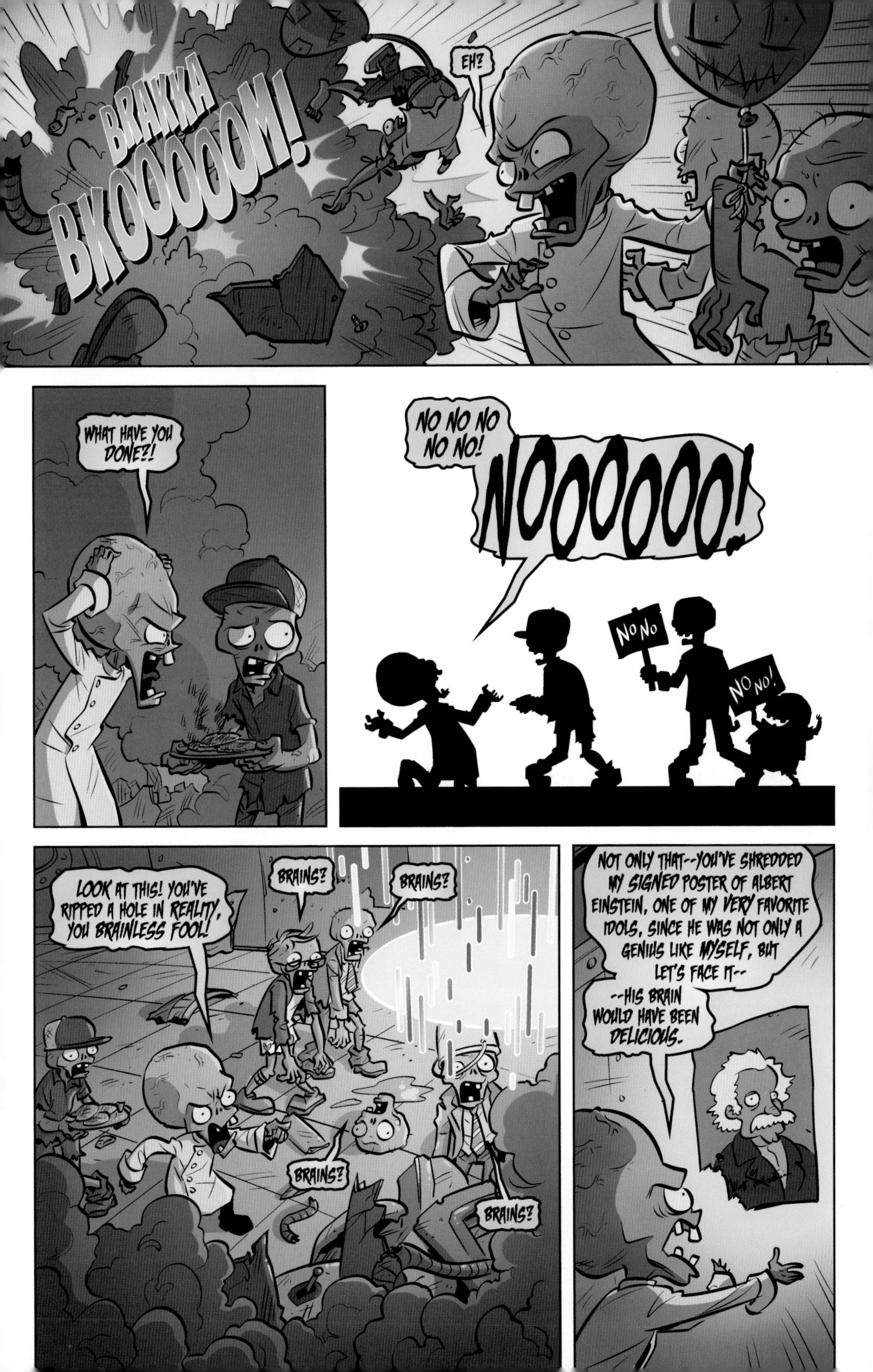
BRAKKA BKOOOOOM!
EH?
WHAT HAVE YOU DONE?!
NO NO NO NO NO! NOOOOOO!
NO NO
NO NO!
LOOK AT THIS! YOU'VE RIPPED A HOLE IN REALITY, YOU BRAINLESS FOOL!
BRAINS?
BRAINS?
BRAINS?
BRAINS?
NOT ONLY THAT--YOU'VE SHREDDED MY SIGNED POSTER OF ALBERT EINSTEIN, ONE OF MY VERY FAVORITE IDOLS, SINCE HE WAS NOT ONLY A GENIUS LIKE MYSELF, BUT LET'S FACE IT--
--HIS BRAIN WOULD HAVE BEEN DELICIOUS.

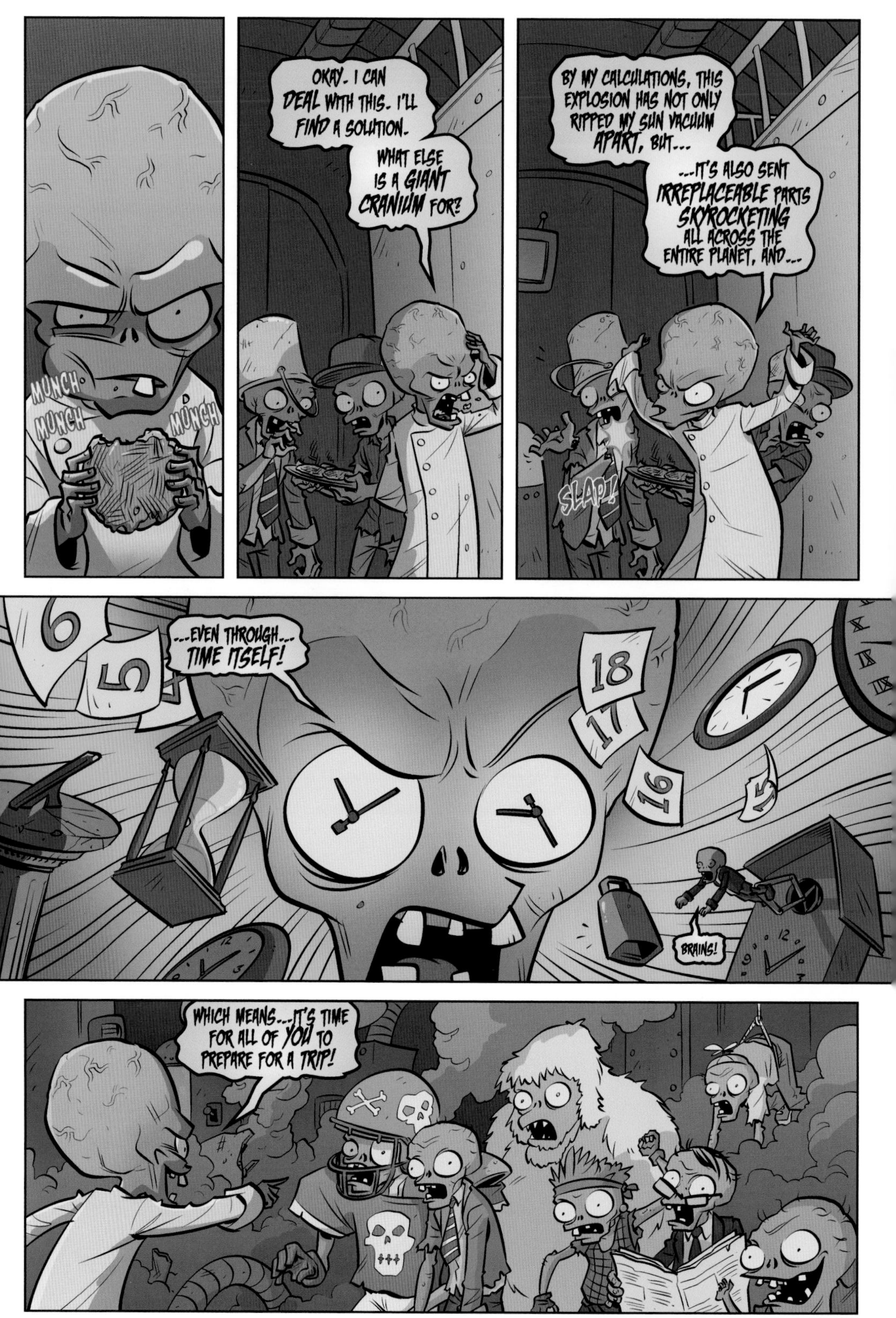
MUNCH
MUNCH
MUNCH
OKAY. I CAN DEAL WITH THIS. I'LL FIND A SOLUTION.
WHAT ELSE IS A GIANT CRANIUM FOR?
BY MY CALCULATIONS, THIS EXPLOSION HAS NOT ONLY RIPPED MY SUN VACUUM APART, BUT...
...IT'S ALSO SENT IRREPLACEABLE PARTS SKYROCKETING ALL ACROSS THE ENTIRE PLANET, AND...
SLAP!
...EVEN THROUGH... TIME ITSELF!
BRAINS!
WHICH MEANS...IT'S TIME FOR ALL OF YOU TO PREPARE FOR A TRIP!

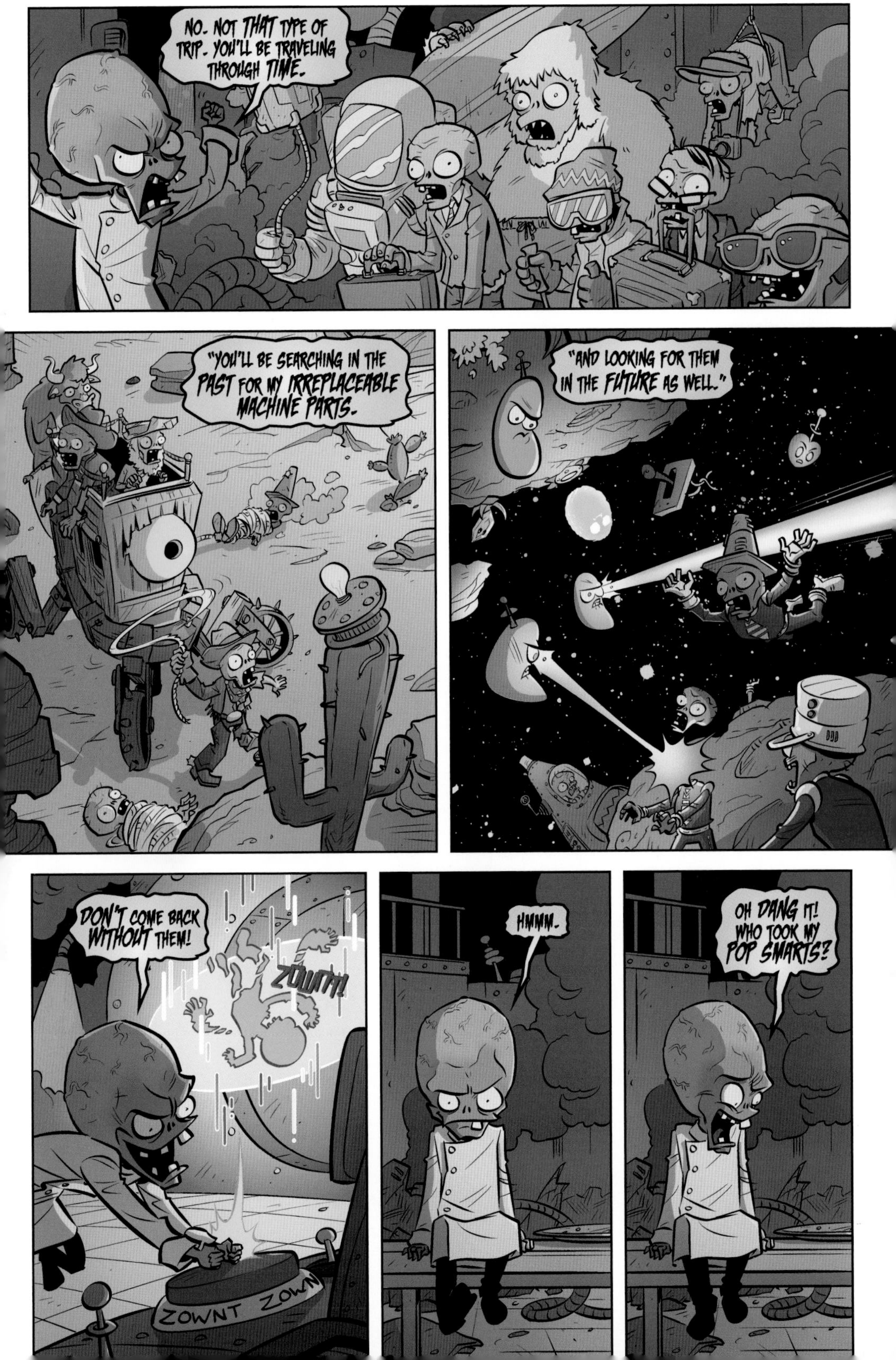
NO. NOT THAT TYPE OF TRIP. YOU'LL BE TRAVELING THROUGH TIME.
"YOU'LL BE SEARCHING IN THE PAST FOR MY IRREPLACEABLE MACHINE PARTS.
"AND LOOKING FOR THEM IN THE FUTURE AS WELL."
DON'T COME BACK WITHOUT THEM!
ZOWNT ZOWN
ZOWNT ZOWN
HMMM.
OH DANG IT! WHO TOOK MY POP SMARTS?

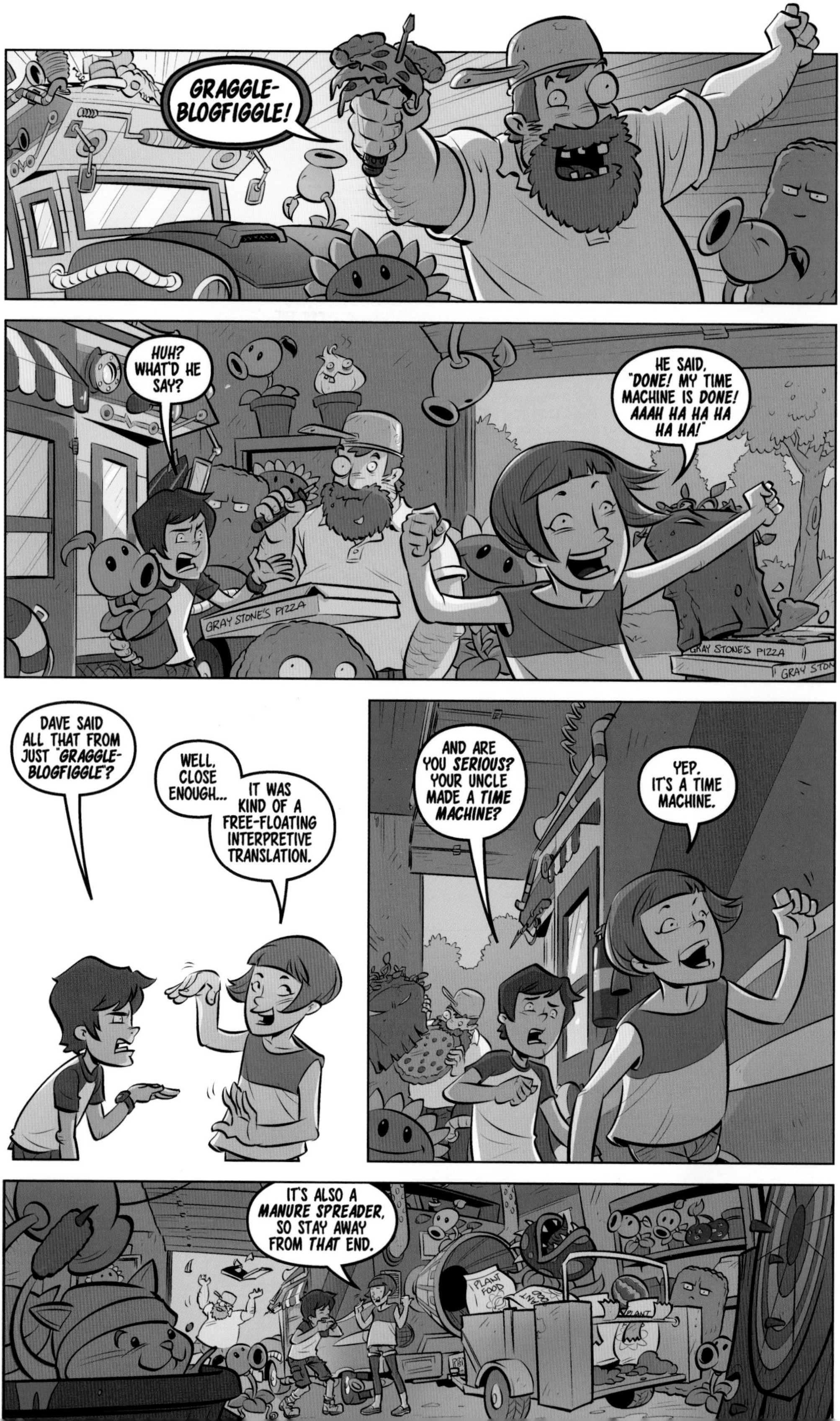
GRAGGLE-BLOGFIGGLE!
HUH? WHAT'D HE SAY?
HE SAID, "DONE! MY TIME MACHINE IS DONE! AAAH HA HA HA HA HA!"
GRAY STONE'S PIZZA
GRAY STONE'S PIZZA
DAVE SAID ALL THAT FROM JUST "GRAGGLE-BLOGFIGGLE"?
WELL, CLOSE ENOUGH...
IT WAS KIND OF A FREE-FLOATING INTERPRETIVE TRANSLATION.
AND ARE YOU SERIOUS? YOUR UNCLE MADE A TIME MACHINE?
YEP. IT'S A TIME MACHINE.
IT'S ALSO A MANURE SPREADER, SO STAY AWAY FROM THAT END.
PLANT FOOD

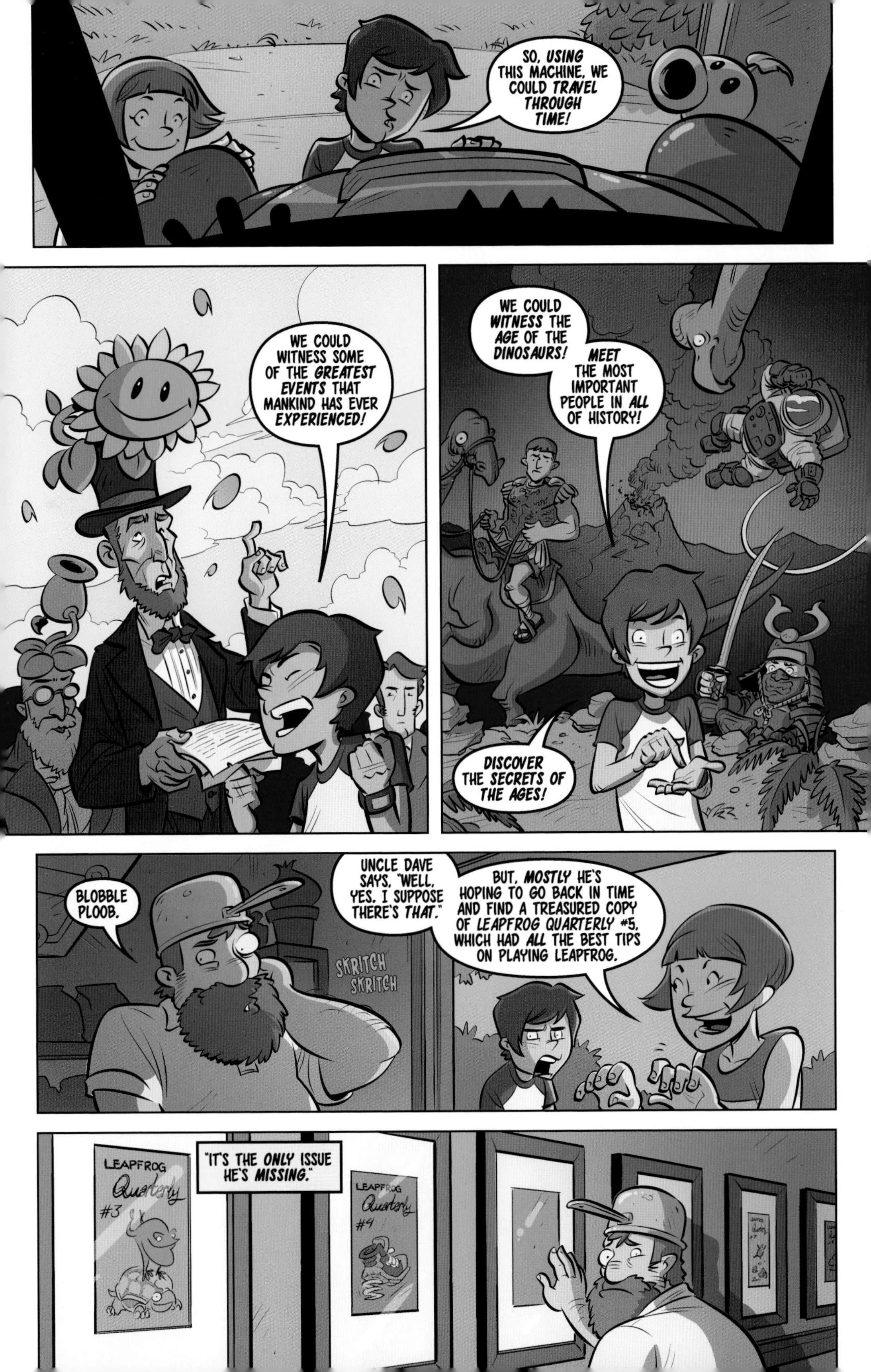
SO, USING THIS MACHINE, WE COULD TRAVEL THROUGH TIME!
WE COULD WITNESS SOME OF THE GREATEST EVENTS THAT MANKIND HAS EVER EXPERIENCED!
WE COULD WITNESS THE AGE OF THE DINOSAURS!
MEET THE MOST IMPORTANT PEOPLE IN ALL OF HISTORY!
DISCOVER THE SECRETS OF THE AGES!
BLOBBLE PLOOB.
SKRITCH SKRITCH
UNCLE DAVE SAYS, "WELL, YES. I SUPPOSE THERE'S THAT."
BUT, MOSTLY HE'S HOPING TO GO BACK IN TIME AND FIND A TREASURED COPY OF LEAPFROG QUARTERLY #5, WHICH HAD ALL THE BEST TIPS ON PLAYING LEAPFROG.
LEAPFROG Quarterly #3
"IT'S THE ONLY ISSUE HE'S MISSING."
LEAPFROG Quarterly #4

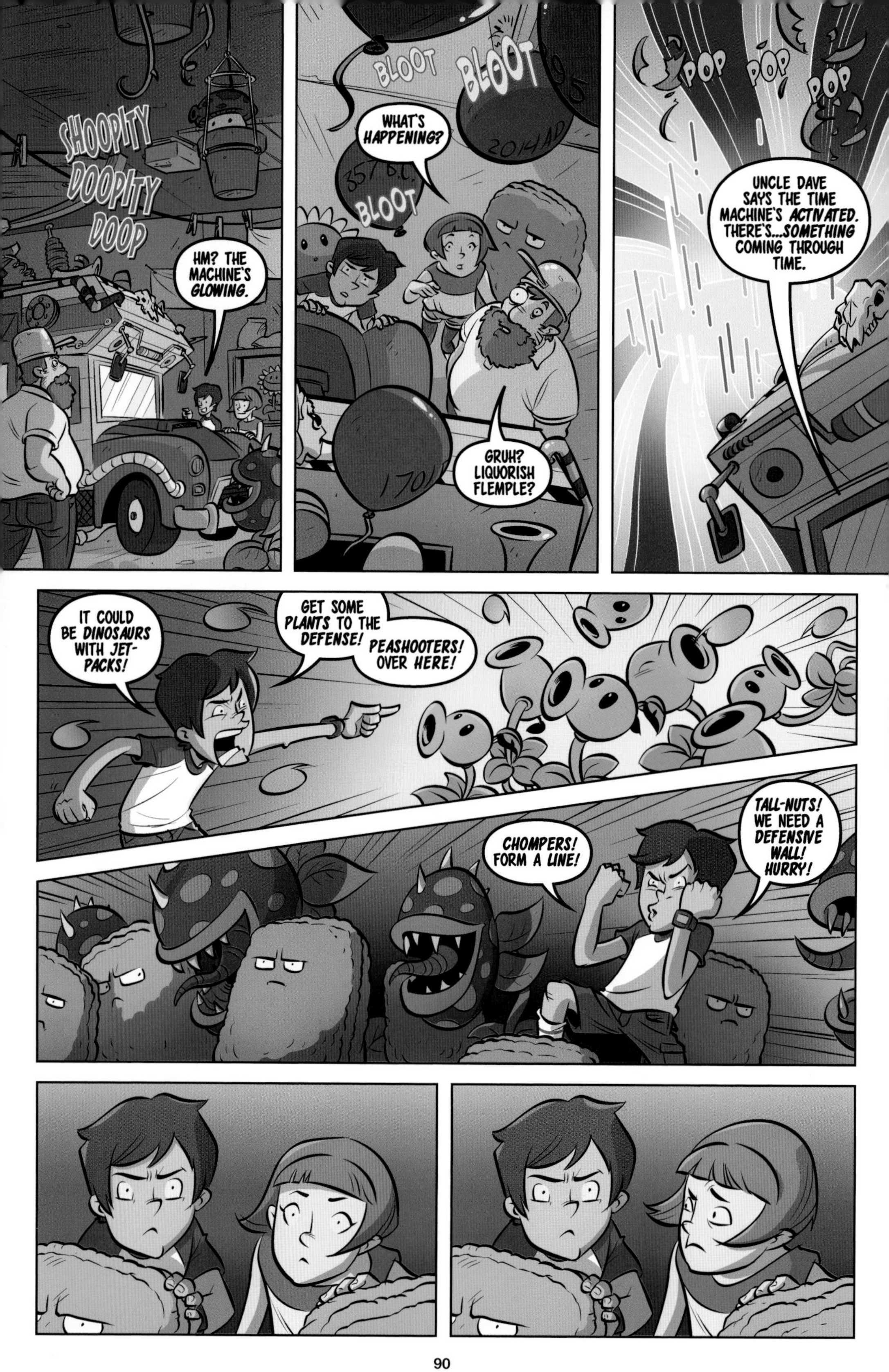
SHOOPITY DOOPITY DOOP
HM? THE MACHINE'S GLOWING.
BLOOT
BLOOT
WHAT'S HAPPENING?
BLOOT
GRUH? LIQUORISH FLEMPLE?
POP POP POP
UNCLE DAVE SAYS THE TIME MACHINE'S ACTIVATED. THERE'S...SOMETHING COMING THROUGH TIME.
IT COULD BE DINOSAURS WITH JET-PACKS!
GET SOME PLANTS TO THE DEFENSE!
PEASHOOTERS! OVER HERE!
CHOMPERS! FORM A LINE!
TALL-NUTS! WE NEED A DEFENSIVE WALL! HURRY!

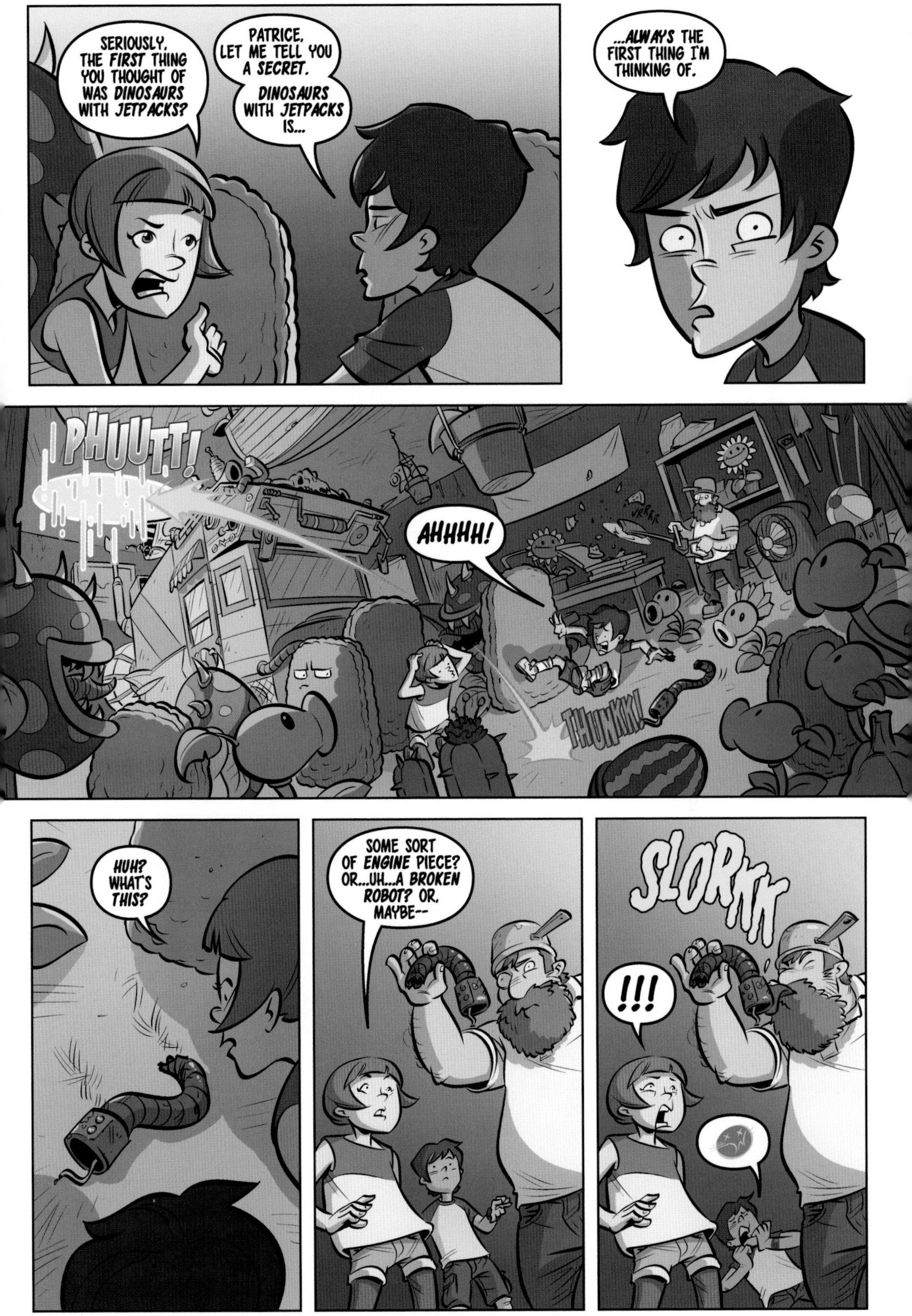
SERIOUSLY, THE FIRST THING YOU THOUGHT OF WAS DINOSAURS WITH JETPACKS?
PATRICE, LET ME TELL YOU A SECRET.
DINOSAURS WITH JETPACKS IS...
...ALWAYS THE FIRST THING I'M THINKING OF.
PHUUTT!
AHHHH!
VRRRR
THUNKKK!
HUH? WHAT'S THIS?
SOME SORT OF ENGINE PIECE? OR...UH...A BROKEN ROBOT? OR, MAYBE--
SLORKK
!!!

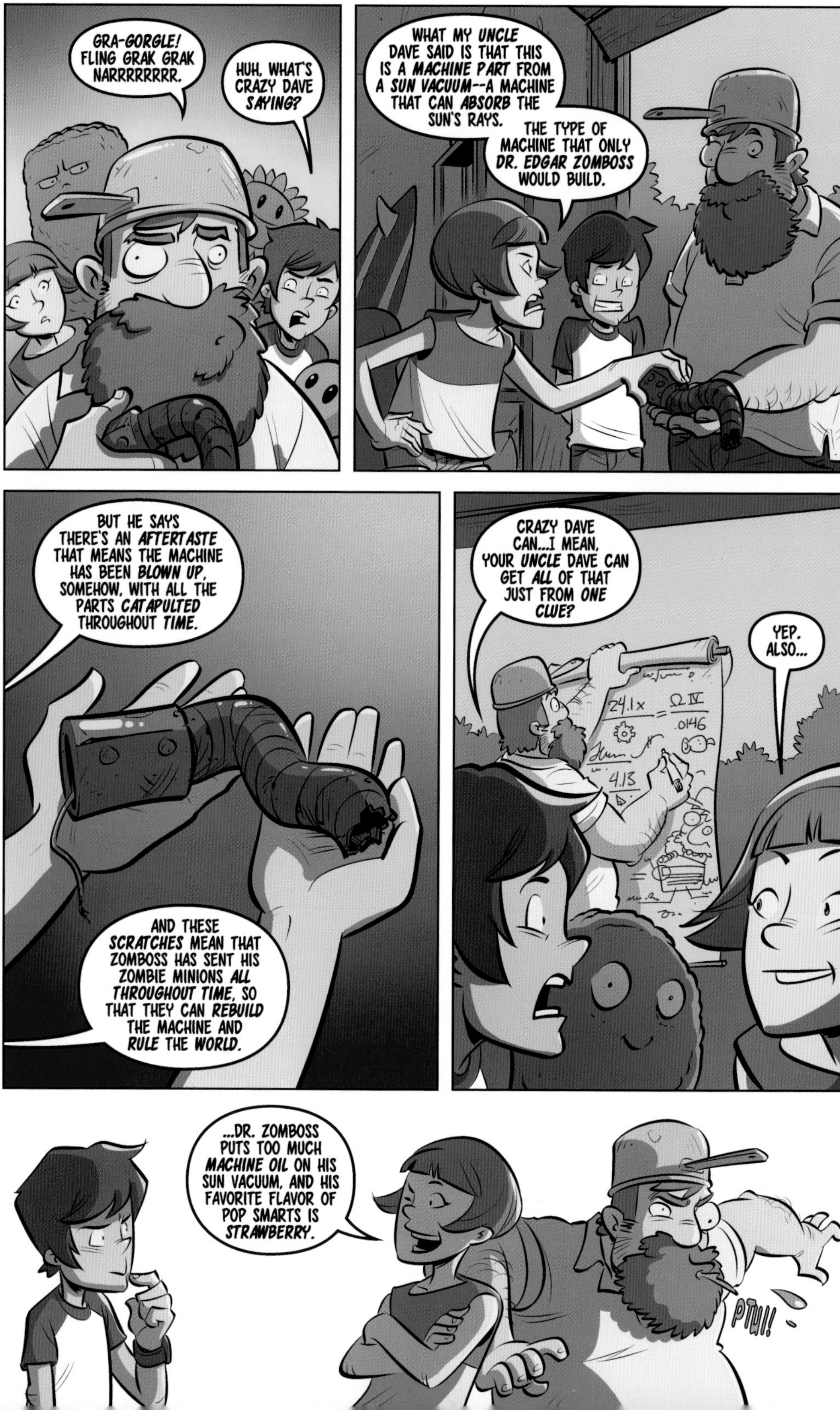
GRA-GORGLE! FLING GRAK GRAK NARRRRRRRR.
HUH, WHAT'S CRAZY DAVE SAYING?
WHAT MY UNCLE DAVE SAID IS THAT THIS IS A MACHINE PART FROM A SUN VACUUM--A MACHINE THAT CAN ABSORB THE SUN'S RAYS.
THE TYPE OF MACHINE THAT ONLY DR. EDGAR ZOMBOSS WOULD BUILD.
BUT HE SAYS THERE'S AN AFTERTASTE THAT MEANS THE MACHINE HAS BEEN BLOWN UP, SOMEHOW, WITH ALL THE PARTS CATAPULTED THROUGHOUT TIME.
AND THESE SCRATCHES MEAN THAT ZOMBOSS HAS SENT HIS ZOMBIE MINIONS ALL THROUGHOUT TIME, SO THAT THEY CAN REBUILD THE MACHINE AND RULE THE WORLD.
CRAZY DAVE CAN...I MEAN, YOUR UNCLE DAVE CAN GET ALL OF THAT JUST FROM ONE CLUE?
YEP. ALSO...
...DR. ZOMBOSS PUTS TOO MUCH MACHINE OIL ON HIS SUN VACUUM, AND HIS FAVORITE FLAVOR OF POP SMARTS IS STRAWBERRY.
PTUI!

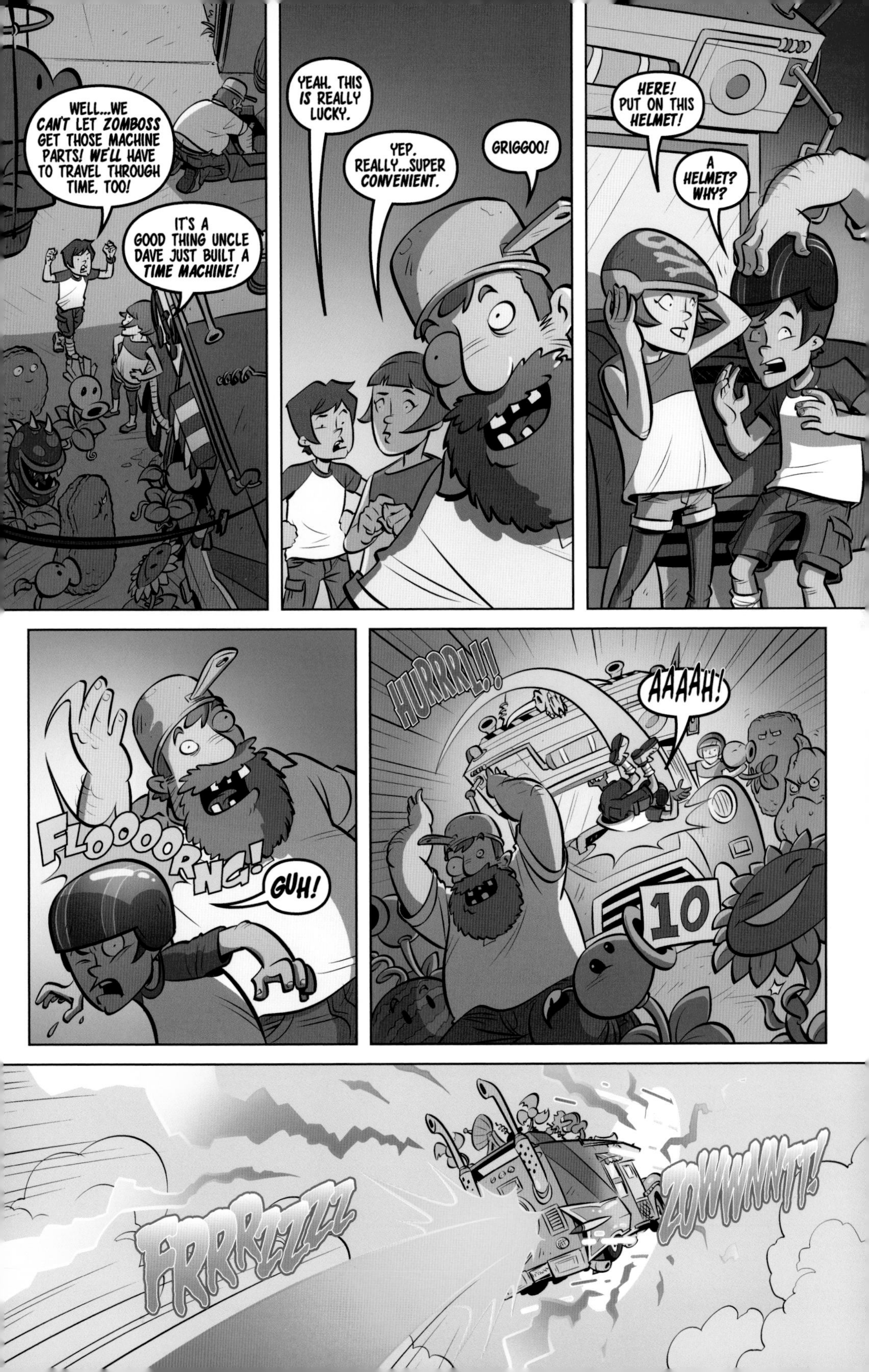

WELL...WE CAN'T LET ZOMBOSS GET THOSE MACHINE PARTS! WE'LL HAVE TO TRAVEL THROUGH TIME, TOO!
IT'S A GOOD THING UNCLE DAVE JUST BUILT A TIME MACHINE!
YEAH. THIS IS REALLY LUCKY.
YEP. REALLY...SUPER CONVENIENT.
GRIGGOO!
HERE! PUT ON THIS HELMET!
A HELMET? WHY?
FLOOOORNG!
GUH!
HURRRL!!
AAAAH!
10
FRRRZZZZ
ZOWWNNT!

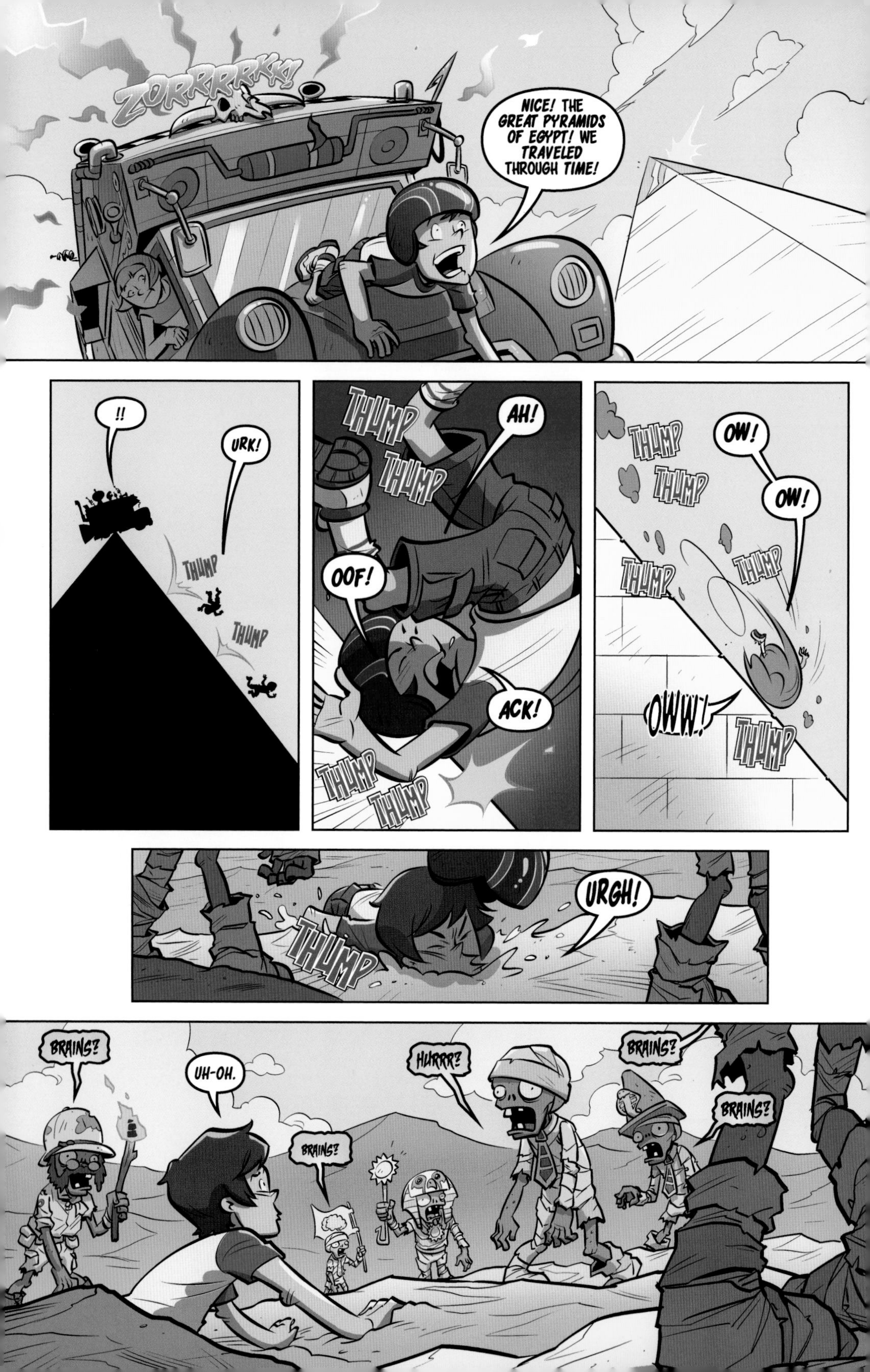
ZORRRRKK!
NICE! THE GREAT PYRAMIDS OF EGYPT! WE TRAVELED THROUGH TIME!
!!
URK!
THUMP
THUMP
THUMP
AH!
THUMP
OOF!
ACK!
THUMP
THUMP
THUMP
OW!
THUMP
OW!
THUMP
THUMP
OWW!
THUMP
THUMP
URGH!
BRAINS?
UH-OH.
BRAINS?
HURRR?
BRAINS?
BRAINS?

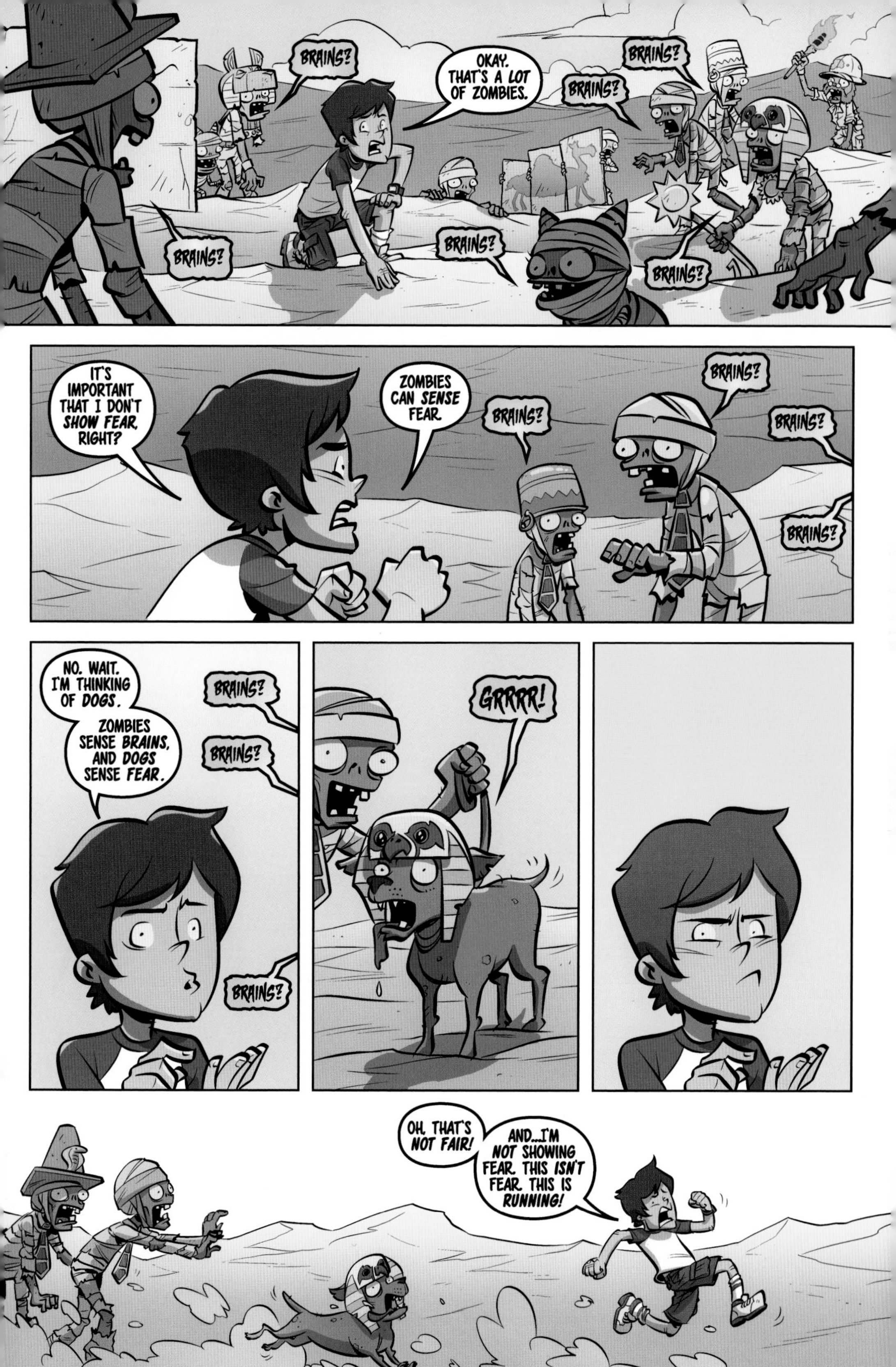
BRAINS?
OKAY. THAT'S A LOT OF ZOMBIES.
BRAINS?
BRAINS?
BRAINS?
BRAINS?
BRAINS?
IT'S IMPORTANT THAT I DON'T SHOW FEAR, RIGHT?
ZOMBIES CAN SENSE FEAR.
BRAINS?
BRAINS?
BRAINS?
BRAINS?
NO. WAIT. I'M THINKING OF DOGS.
ZOMBIES SENSE BRAINS, AND DOGS SENSE FEAR.
BRAINS?
BRAINS?
BRAINS?
GRRRR!
OH, THAT'S NOT FAIR!
AND...I'M NOT SHOWING FEAR. THIS ISN'T FEAR. THIS IS RUNNING!

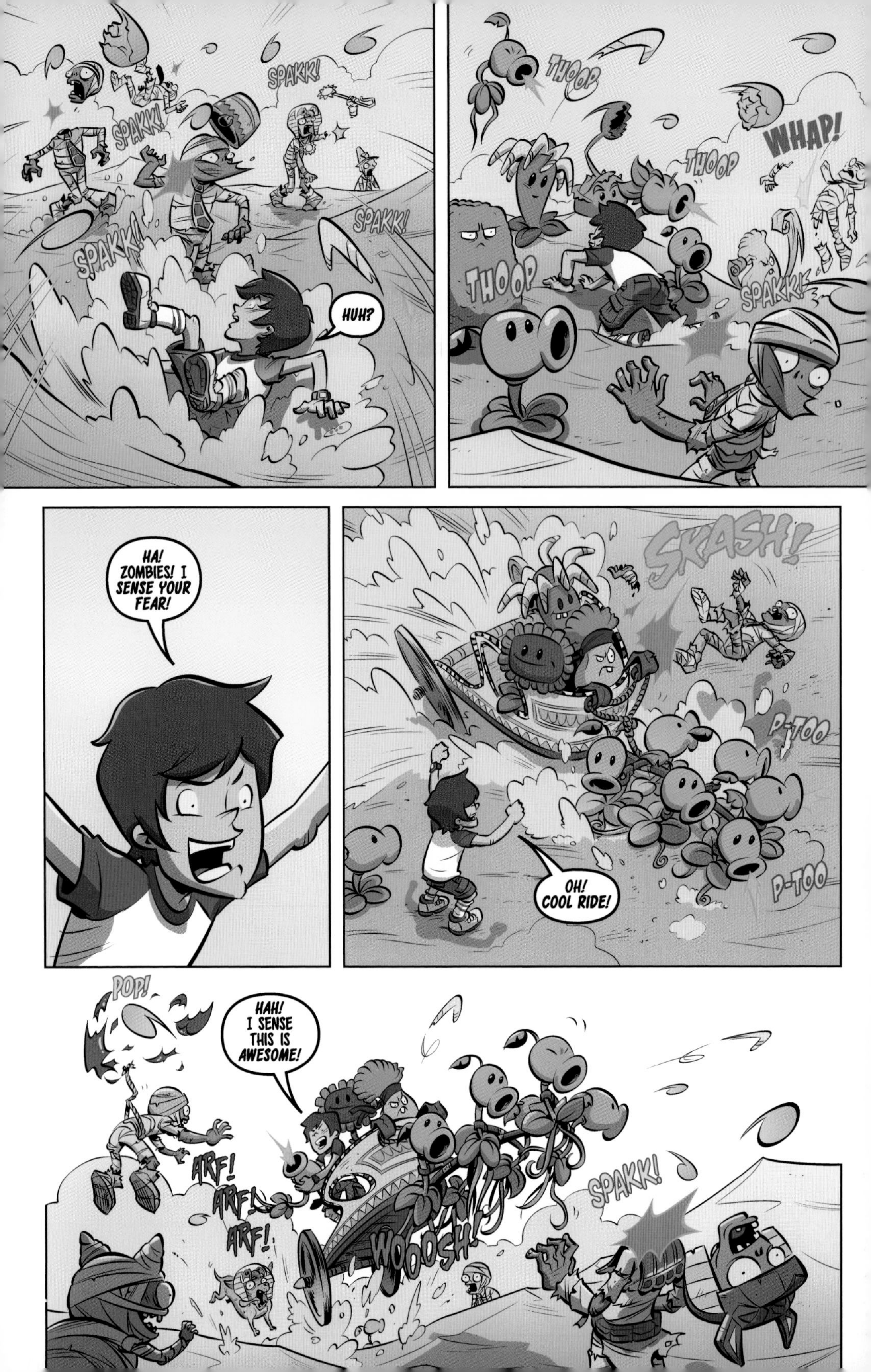
SPAKK!
SPAKK!
SPAKK!
SPAKK!
HUH?
THOOP
THOOP
WHAP!
THOOP
SPAKK!
HA! ZOMBIES! I SENSE YOUR FEAR!
SKASH!
P-TOO
P-TOO
OH! COOL RIDE!
POP!
HAH! I SENSE THIS IS AWESOME!
ARF!
ARF!
ARF!
WOOOSH!
SPAKK!

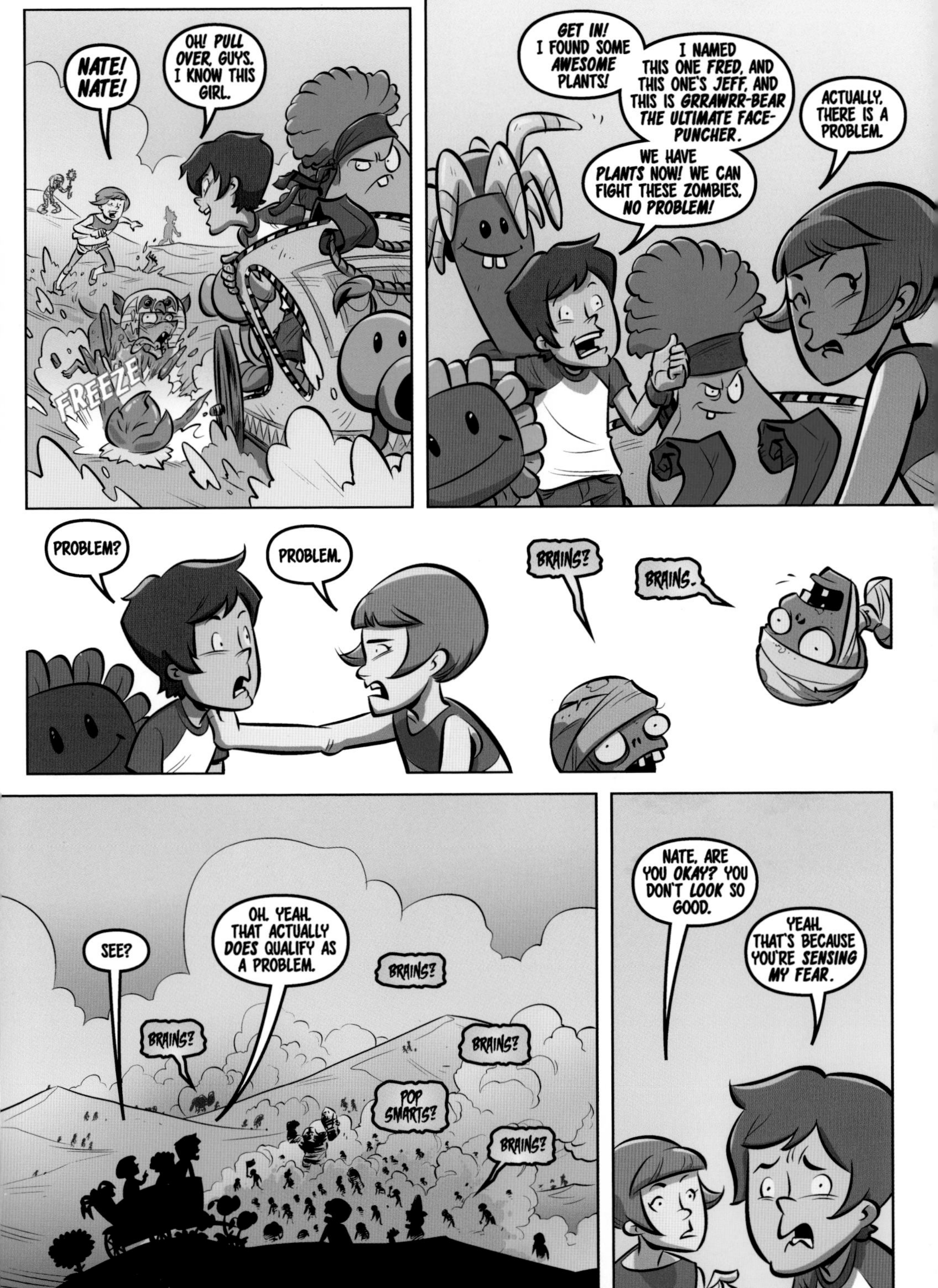
NATE! NATE!
OH! PULL OVER, GUYS. I KNOW THIS GIRL.
FREEZE
GET IN! I FOUND SOME AWESOME PLANTS!
I NAMED THIS ONE FRED, AND THIS ONE'S JEFF, AND THIS IS GRRAWRR-BEAR THE ULTIMATE FACE-PUNCHER.
WE HAVE PLANTS NOW! WE CAN FIGHT THESE ZOMBIES, NO PROBLEM!
ACTUALLY, THERE IS A PROBLEM.
PROBLEM?
PROBLEM.
BRAINS?
BRAINS.
SEE?
OH. YEAH. THAT ACTUALLY DOES QUALIFY AS A PROBLEM.
BRAINS?
BRAINS?
BRAINS?
POP SMARTS?
BRAINS?
NATE, ARE YOU OKAY? YOU DON'T LOOK SO GOOD.
YEAH. THAT'S BECAUSE YOU'RE SENSING MY FEAR.

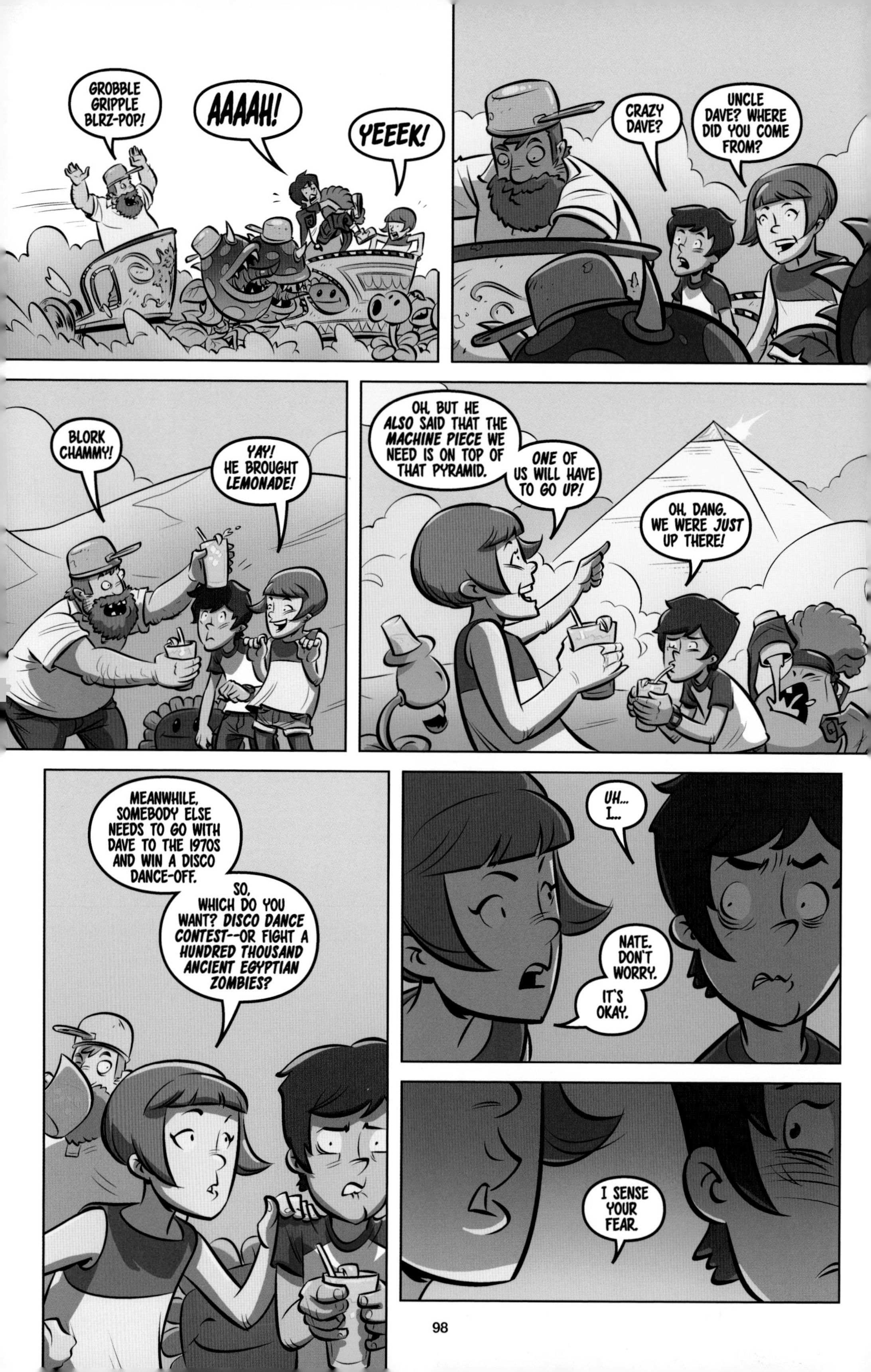
GROBBLE GRIPPLE BLRZ-POP!
AAAAH!
YEEEK!
CRAZY DAVE?
UNCLE DAVE? WHERE DID YOU COME FROM?
BLORK CHAMMY!
YAY! HE BROUGHT LEMONADE!
OH, BUT HE ALSO SAID THAT THE MACHINE PIECE WE NEED IS ON TOP OF THAT PYRAMID.
ONE OF US WILL HAVE TO GO UP!
OH, DANG. WE WERE JUST UP THERE!
MEANWHILE, SOMEBODY ELSE NEEDS TO GO WITH DAVE TO THE 1970S AND WIN A DISCO DANCE-OFF.
SO, WHICH DO YOU WANT? DISCO DANCE CONTEST--OR FIGHT A HUNDRED THOUSAND ANCIENT EGYPTIAN ZOMBIES?
UH... I...
NATE. DON'T WORRY.
IT'S OKAY.
I SENSE YOUR FEAR.

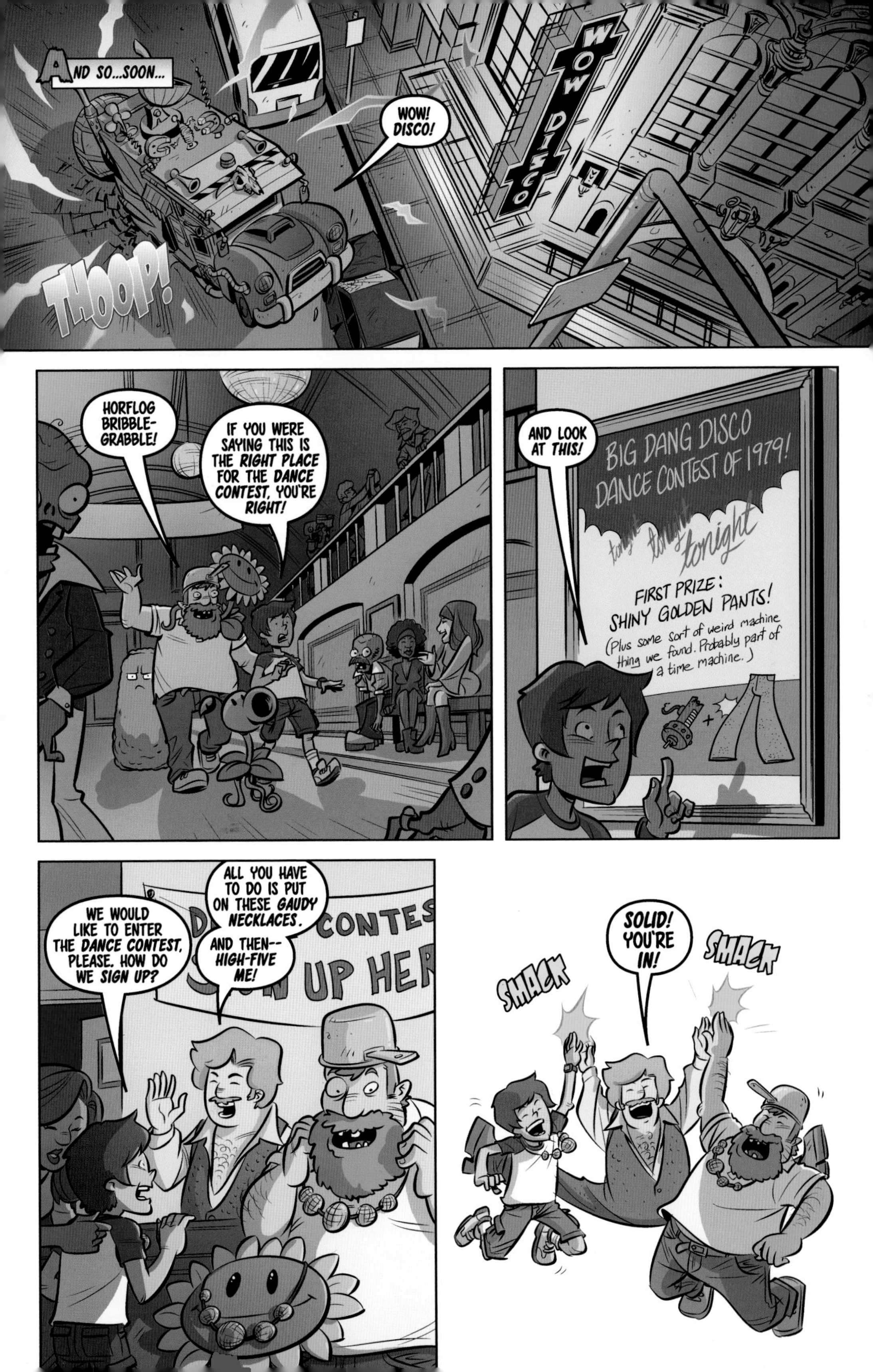
AND SO...SOON...
WOW! DISCO!
THOOIP!
WOW DISCO
HORFLOG BRIBBLE-GRABBLE!
IF YOU WERE SAYING THIS IS THE RIGHT PLACE FOR THE DANCE CONTEST, YOU'RE RIGHT!
AND LOOK AT THIS!
BIG DANG DISCO DANCE CONTEST OF 1979!
tonight tonight tonight
FIRST PRIZE: SHINY GOLDEN PANTS!
(Plus some sort of weird machine thing we found. Probably part of a time machine.)
WE WOULD LIKE TO ENTER THE DANCE CONTEST, PLEASE. HOW DO WE SIGN UP?
ALL YOU HAVE TO DO IS PUT ON THESE GAUDY NECKLACES.
AND THEN-- HIGH-FIVE ME!
SOLID! YOU'RE IN!
SMACK
SMACK

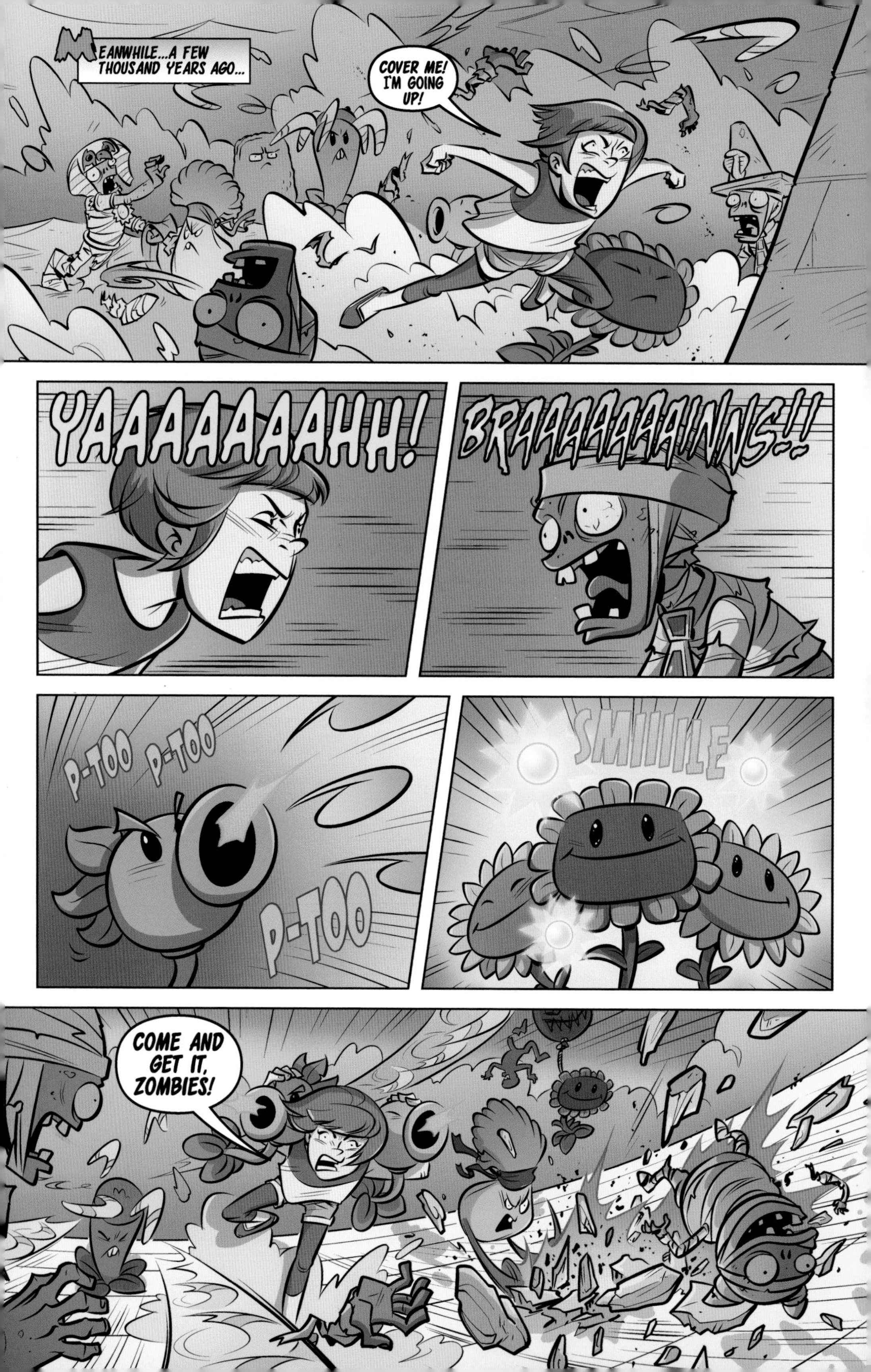
MEANWHILE...A FEW THOUSAND YEARS AGO...
COVER ME! I'M GOING UP!
YAAAAAAAHH!
BRAAAAAAAAINNS!!
P-TOO P-TOO
P-TOO
SMIIIILE
COME AND GET IT, ZOMBIES!

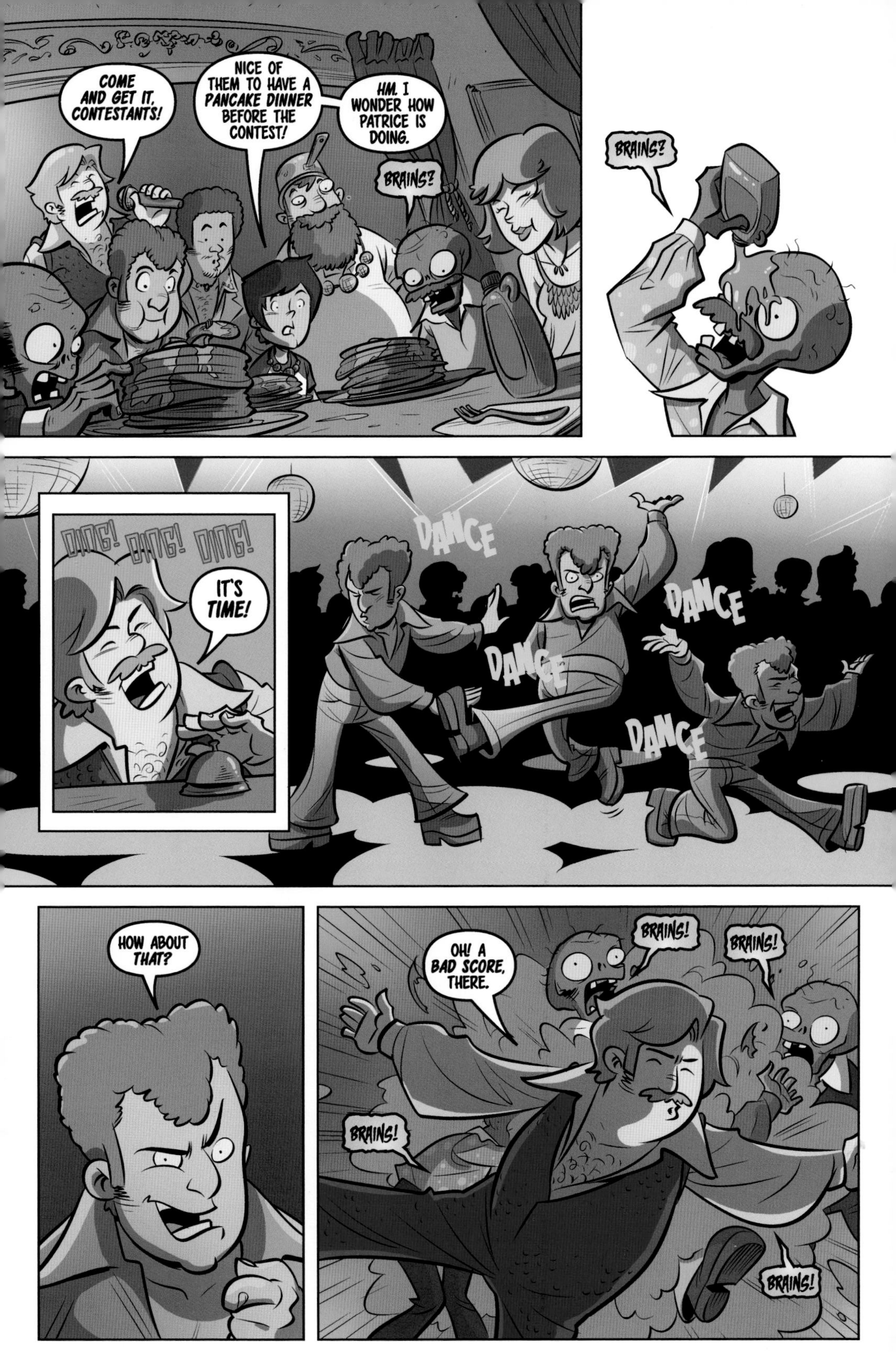
COME AND GET IT, CONTESTANTS!
NICE OF THEM TO HAVE A PANCAKE DINNER BEFORE THE CONTEST!
HM. I WONDER HOW PATRICE IS DOING.
BRAINS?
BRAINS?
DING! DING! DING!
IT'S TIME!
DANCE
DANCE
DANCE
DANCE
HOW ABOUT THAT?
OH! A BAD SCORE, THERE.
BRAINS!
BRAINS!
BRAINS!
BRAINS!

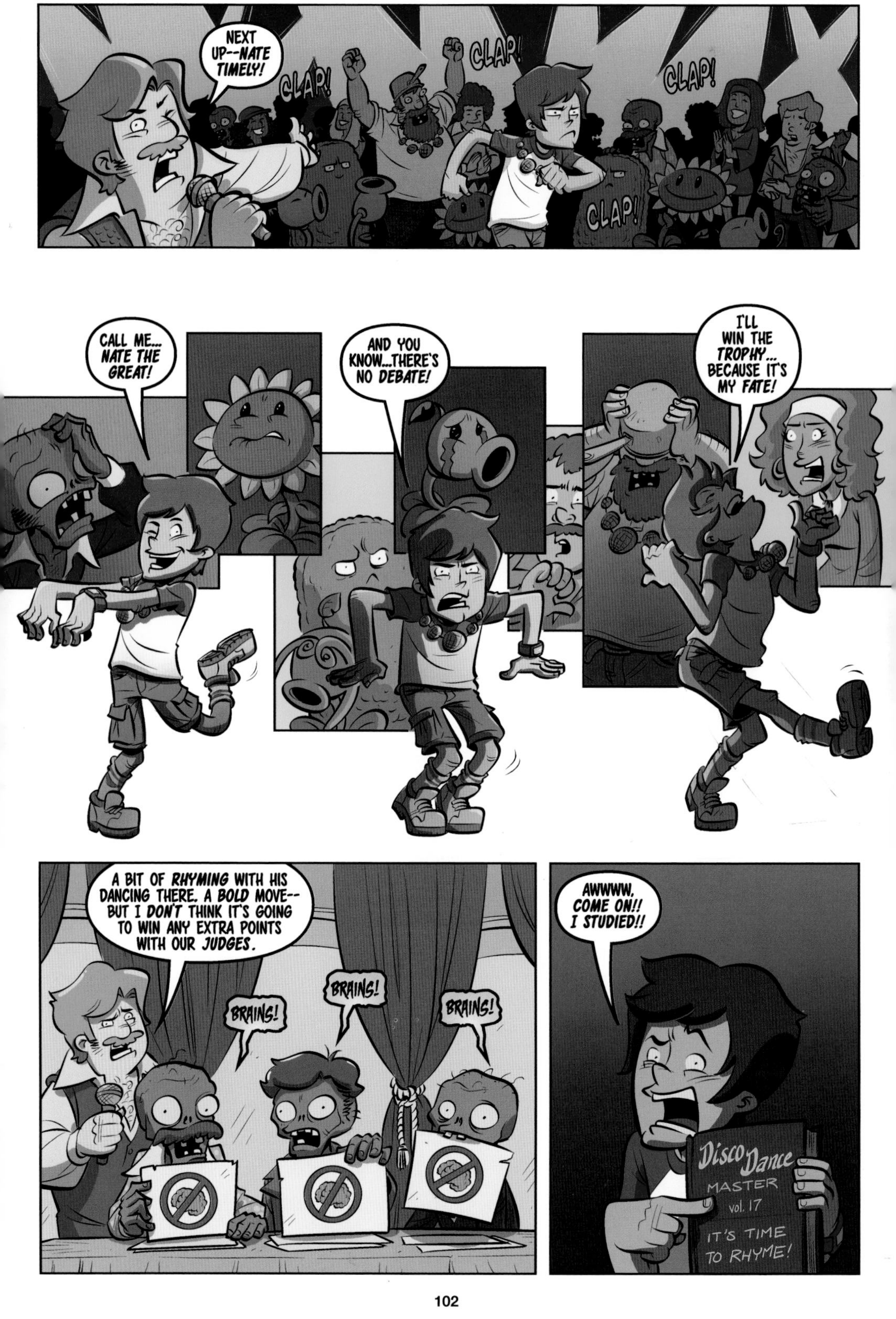
NEXT UP--NATE TIMELY!
CLAP!
CLAP!
CLAP!
CLAP!
CALL ME... NATE THE GREAT!
AND YOU KNOW...THERE'S NO DEBATE!
I'LL WIN THE TROPHY... BECAUSE IT'S MY FATE!
A BIT OF RHYMING WITH HIS DANCING THERE. A BOLD MOVE--BUT I DON'T THINK IT'S GOING TO WIN ANY EXTRA POINTS WITH OUR JUDGES.
BRAINS!
BRAINS!
BRAINS!
AWWWW, COME ON!! I STUDIED!!
Disco Dance MASTER vol. 17
IT'S TIME TO RHYME!

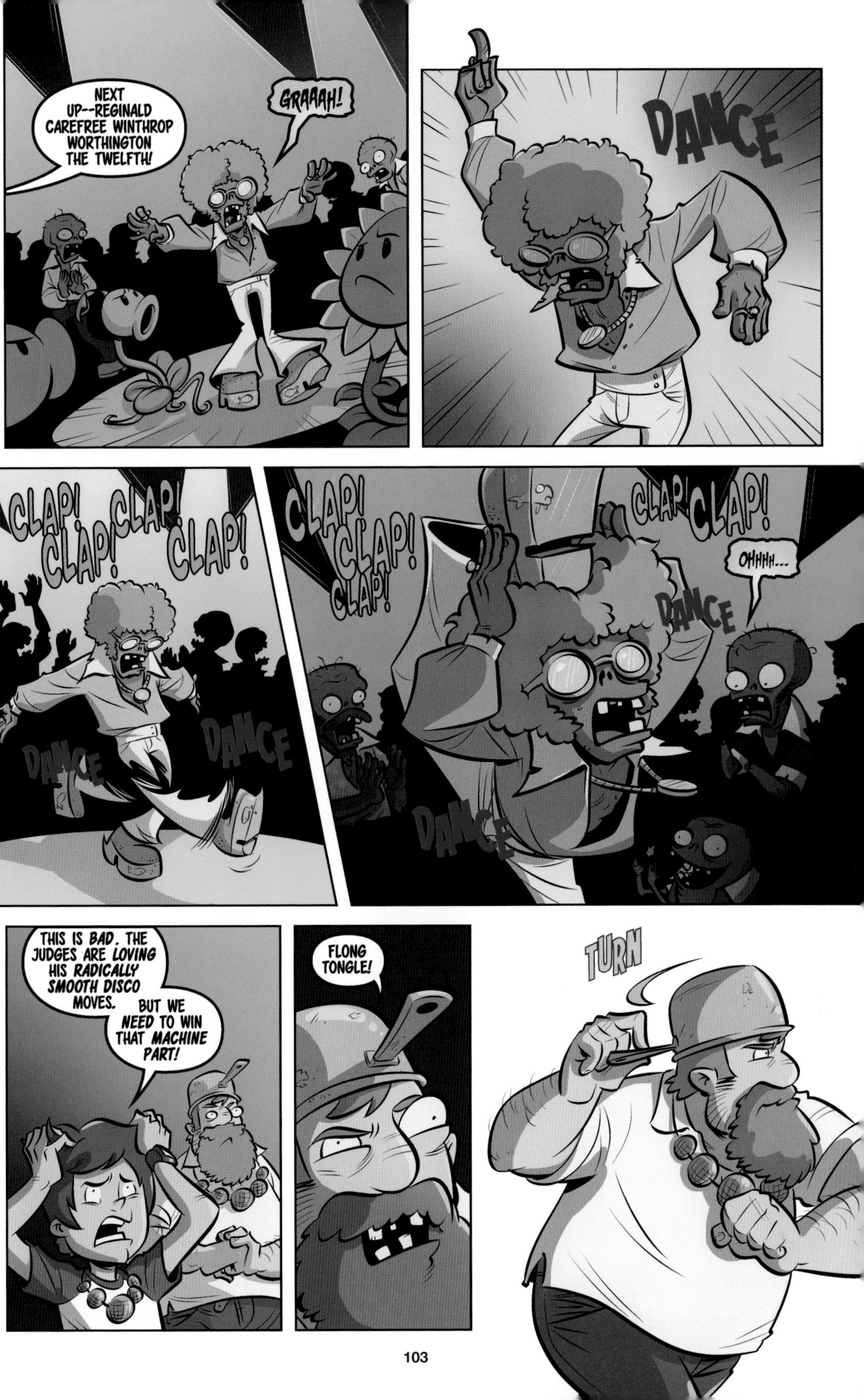
NEXT UP--REGINALD CAREFREE WINTHROP WORTHINGTON THE TWELFTH!
GRAAAAH!
DANCE
CLAP! CLAP! CLAP! CLAP!
DANCE
DANCE
CLAP! CLAP! CLAP!
CLAP CLAP!
OHHHH...
DANCE
DANCE
THIS IS BAD. THE JUDGES ARE LOVING HIS RADICALLY SMOOTH DISCO MOVES.
BUT WE NEED TO WIN THAT MACHINE PART!
FLONG TONGLE!
TURN

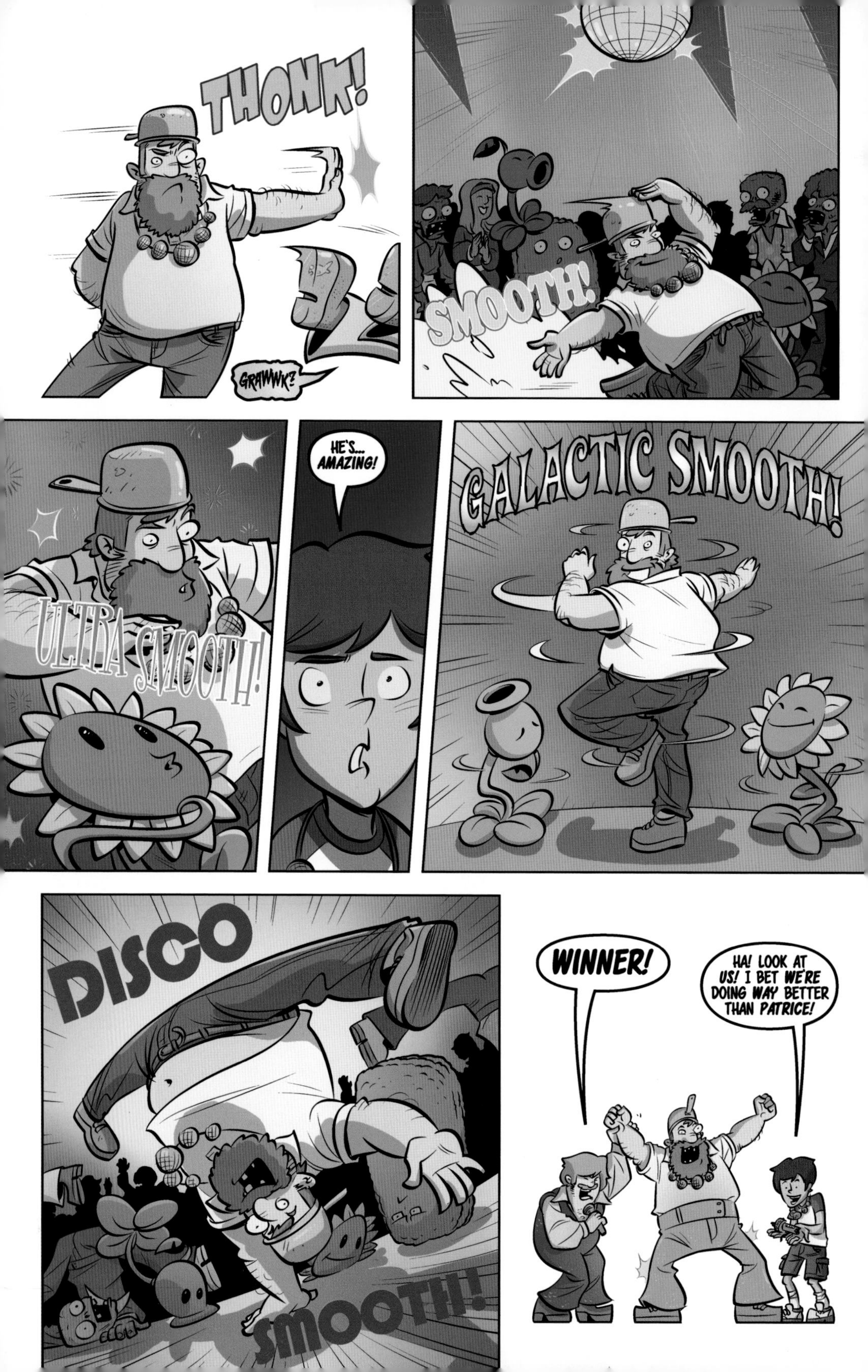
THONK!
GRAWWK?
SMOOTH!
ULTRA SMOOTH!
HE'S... AMAZING!
GALACTIC SMOOTH!
DISCO
SMOOTH!
WINNER!
HA! LOOK AT US! I BET WE'RE DOING WAY BETTER THAN PATRICE!

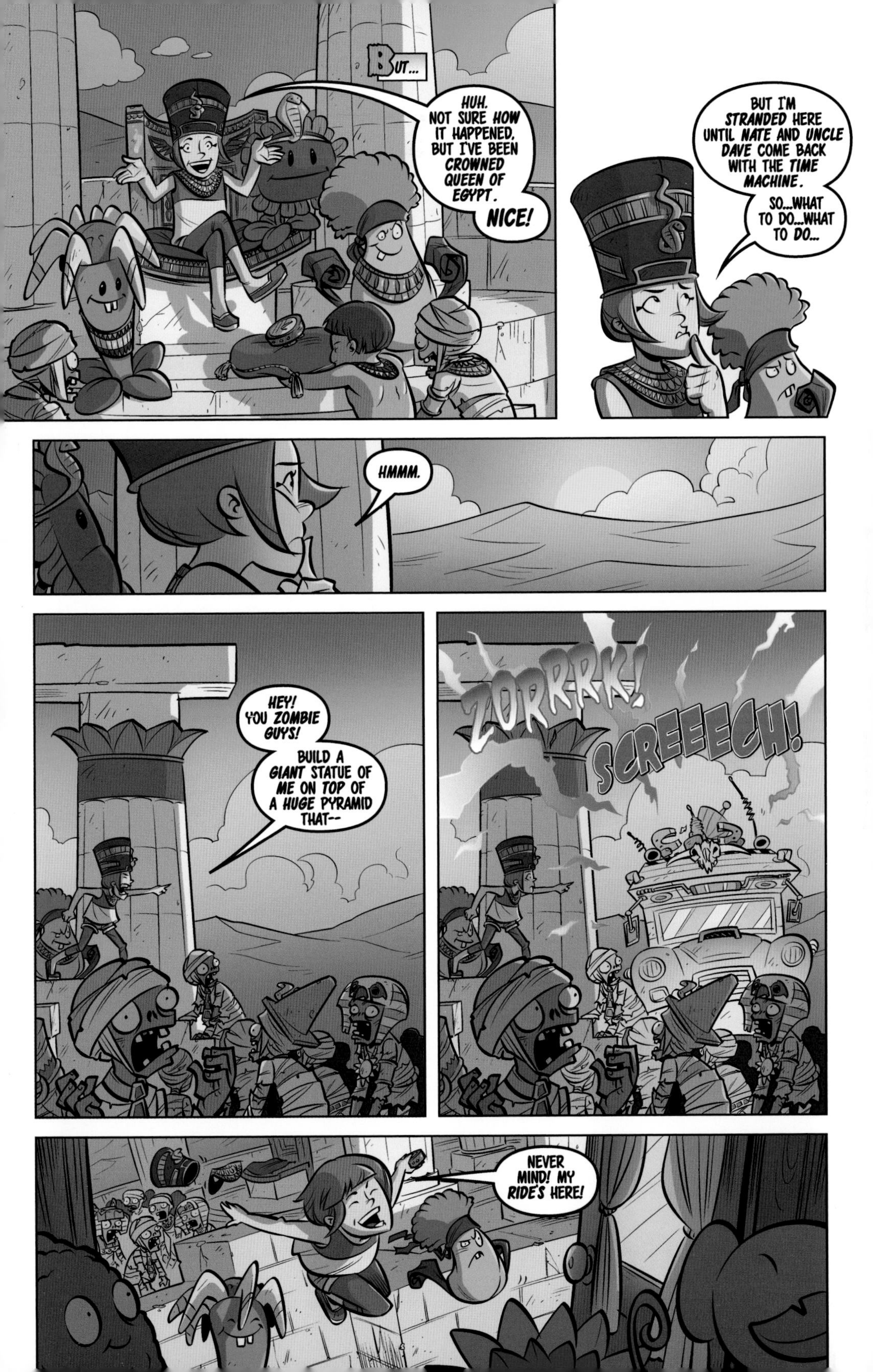
BUT...
HUH. NOT SURE HOW IT HAPPENED, BUT I'VE BEEN CROWNED QUEEN OF EGYPT.
NICE!
BUT I'M STRANDED HERE UNTIL NATE AND UNCLE DAVE COME BACK WITH THE TIME MACHINE.
SO...WHAT TO DO...WHAT TO DO...
HMMM.
HEY! YOU ZOMBIE GUYS!
BUILD A GIANT STATUE OF ME ON TOP OF A HUGE PYRAMID THAT--
ZORRRK!
SCREEEECH!
NEVER MIND! MY RIDE'S HERE!

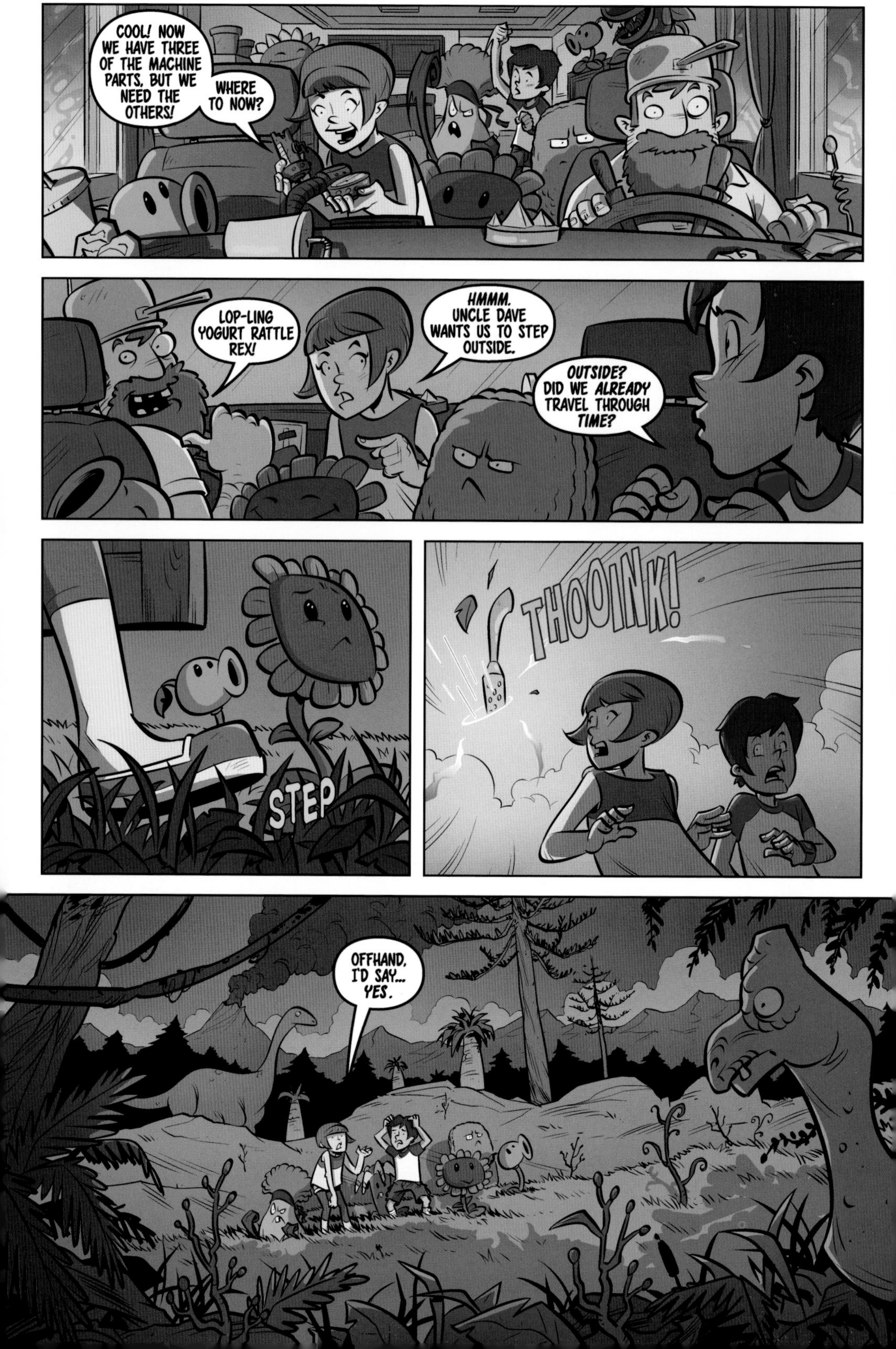
COOL! NOW WE HAVE THREE OF THE MACHINE PARTS, BUT WE NEED THE OTHERS!
WHERE TO NOW?
LOP-LING YOGURT RATTLE REX!
HMMM. UNCLE DAVE WANTS US TO STEP OUTSIDE.
OUTSIDE? DID WE ALREADY TRAVEL THROUGH TIME?
STEP
THOOINK!
OFFHAND, I'D SAY... YES.

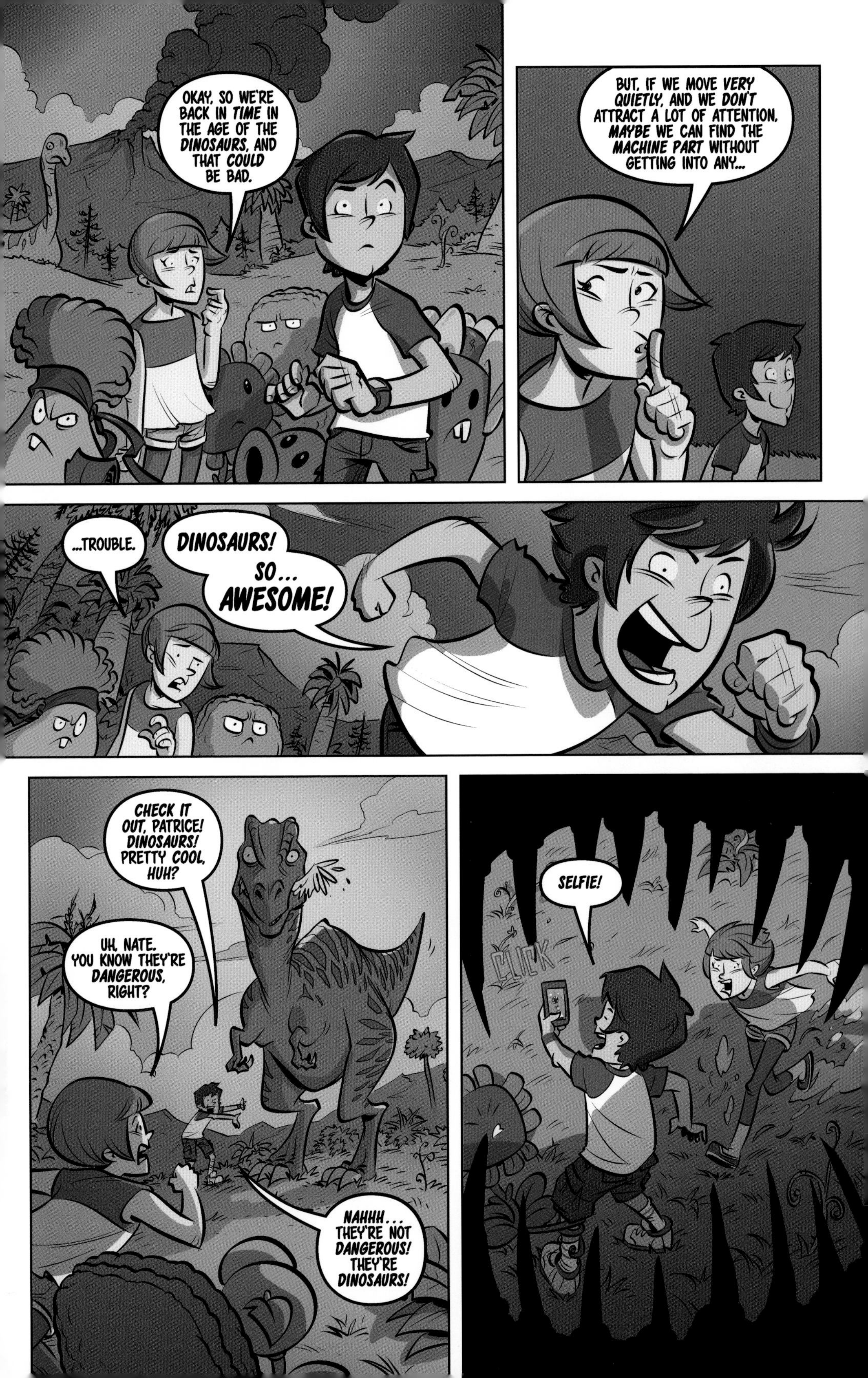
OKAY, SO WE'RE BACK IN TIME IN THE AGE OF THE DINOSAURS, AND THAT COULD BE BAD.
BUT, IF WE MOVE VERY QUIETLY, AND WE DON'T ATTRACT A LOT OF ATTENTION, MAYBE WE CAN FIND THE MACHINE PART WITHOUT GETTING INTO ANY...
...TROUBLE.
DINOSAURS! SO... AWESOME!
CHECK IT OUT, PATRICE! DINOSAURS! PRETTY COOL, HUH?
UH, NATE. YOU KNOW THEY'RE DANGEROUS, RIGHT?
NAHHH... THEY'RE NOT DANGEROUS! THEY'RE DINOSAURS!
SELFIE!
CLICK

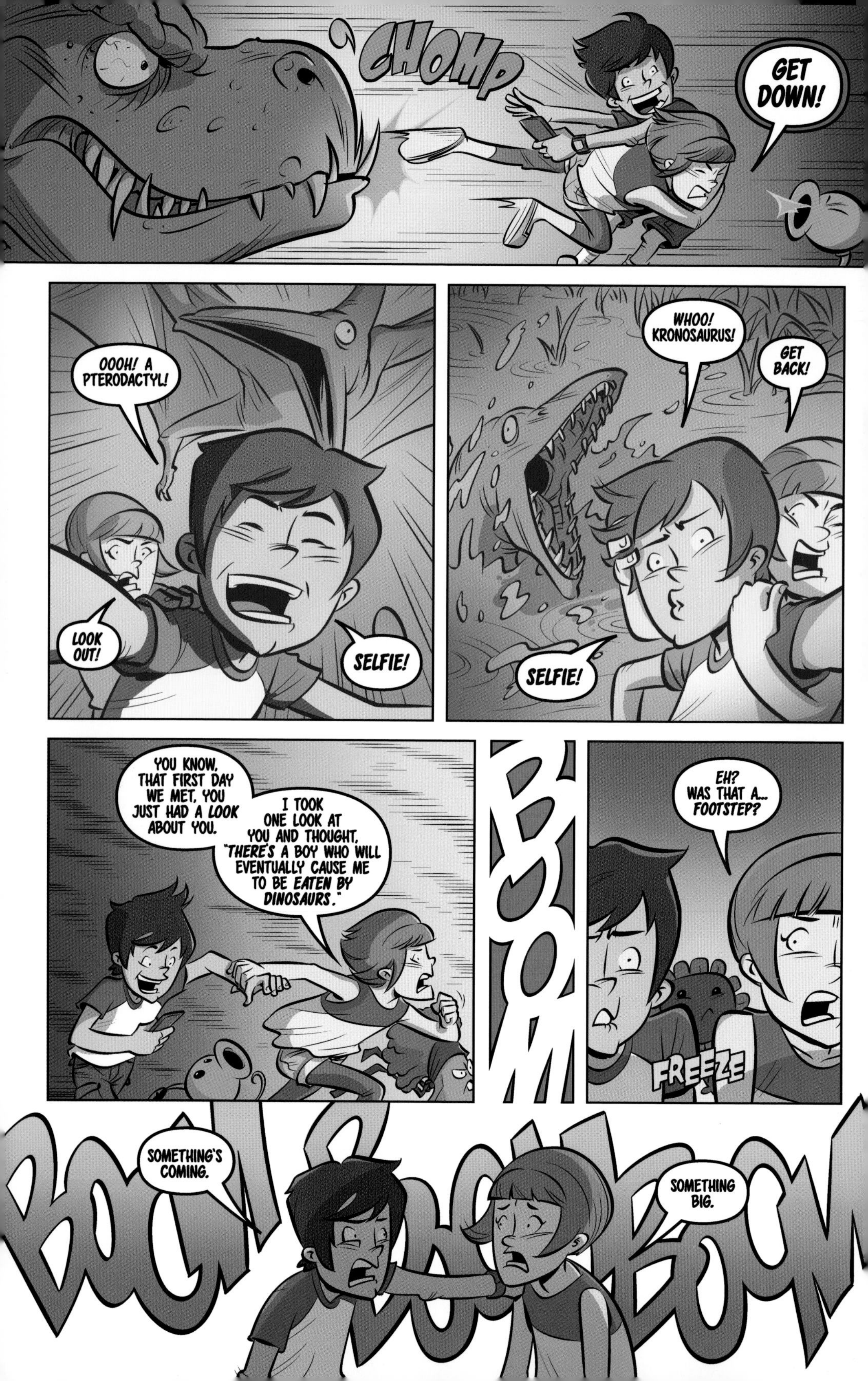
CHOMP
GET DOWN!
OOOH! A PTERODACTYL!
LOOK OUT!
SELFIE!
WHOO! KRONOSAURUS!
GET BACK!
SELFIE!
YOU KNOW, THAT FIRST DAY WE MET, YOU JUST HAD A *LOOK* ABOUT YOU.
I TOOK ONE LOOK AT YOU AND THOUGHT, "*THERE'S* A BOY WHO WILL EVENTUALLY CAUSE ME TO BE *EATEN* BY *DINOSAURS*."
BOOM
EH? WAS THAT A... FOOTSTEP?
FREEZE
BOOM BOOM BOOM
SOMETHING'S COMING.
SOMETHING BIG.

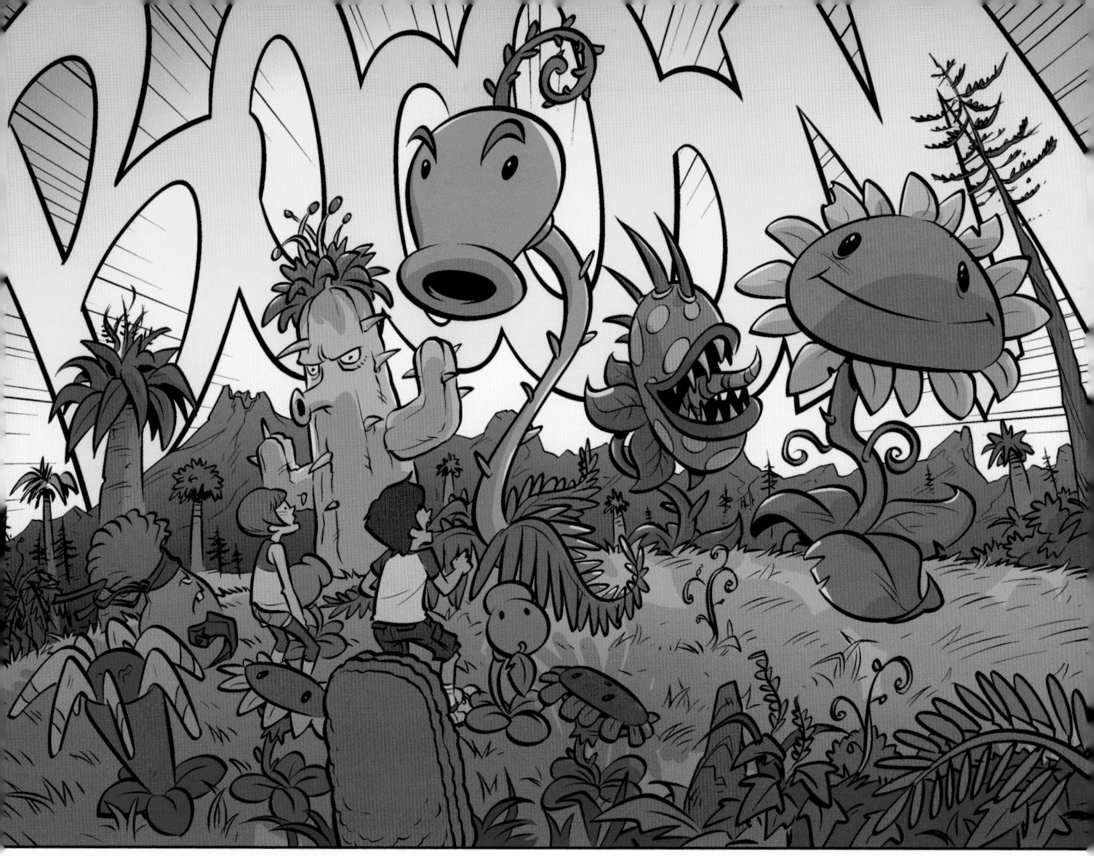

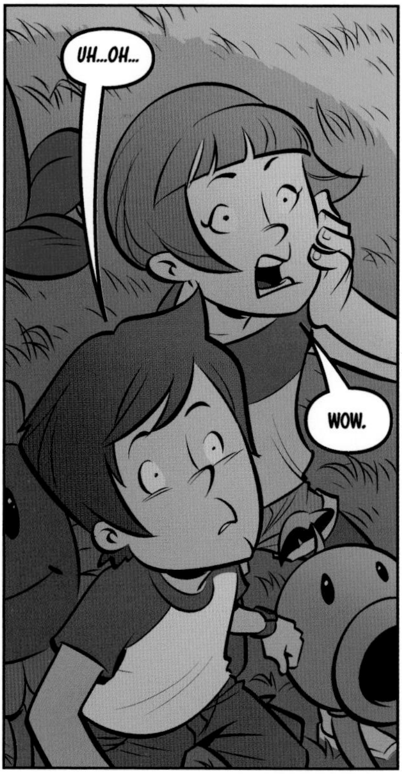
UH...OH...
WOW.

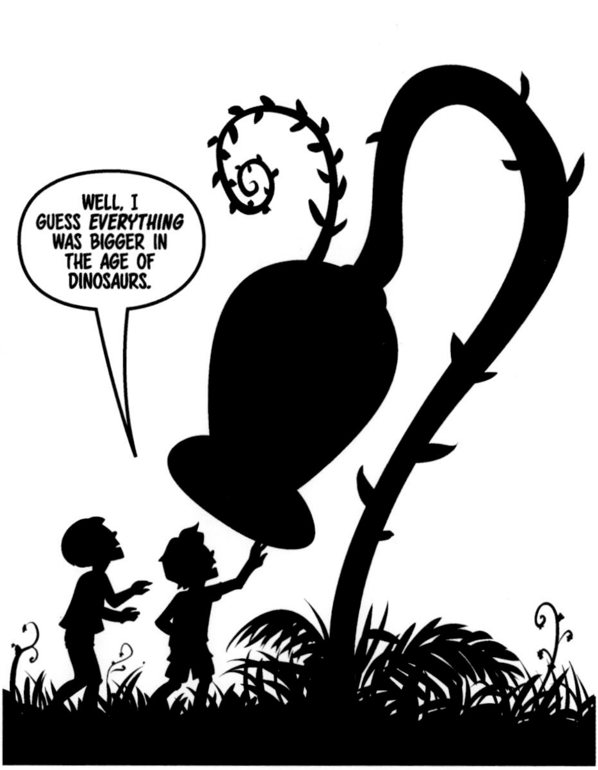
WELL, I GUESS EVERYTHING WAS BIGGER IN THE AGE OF DINOSAURS.

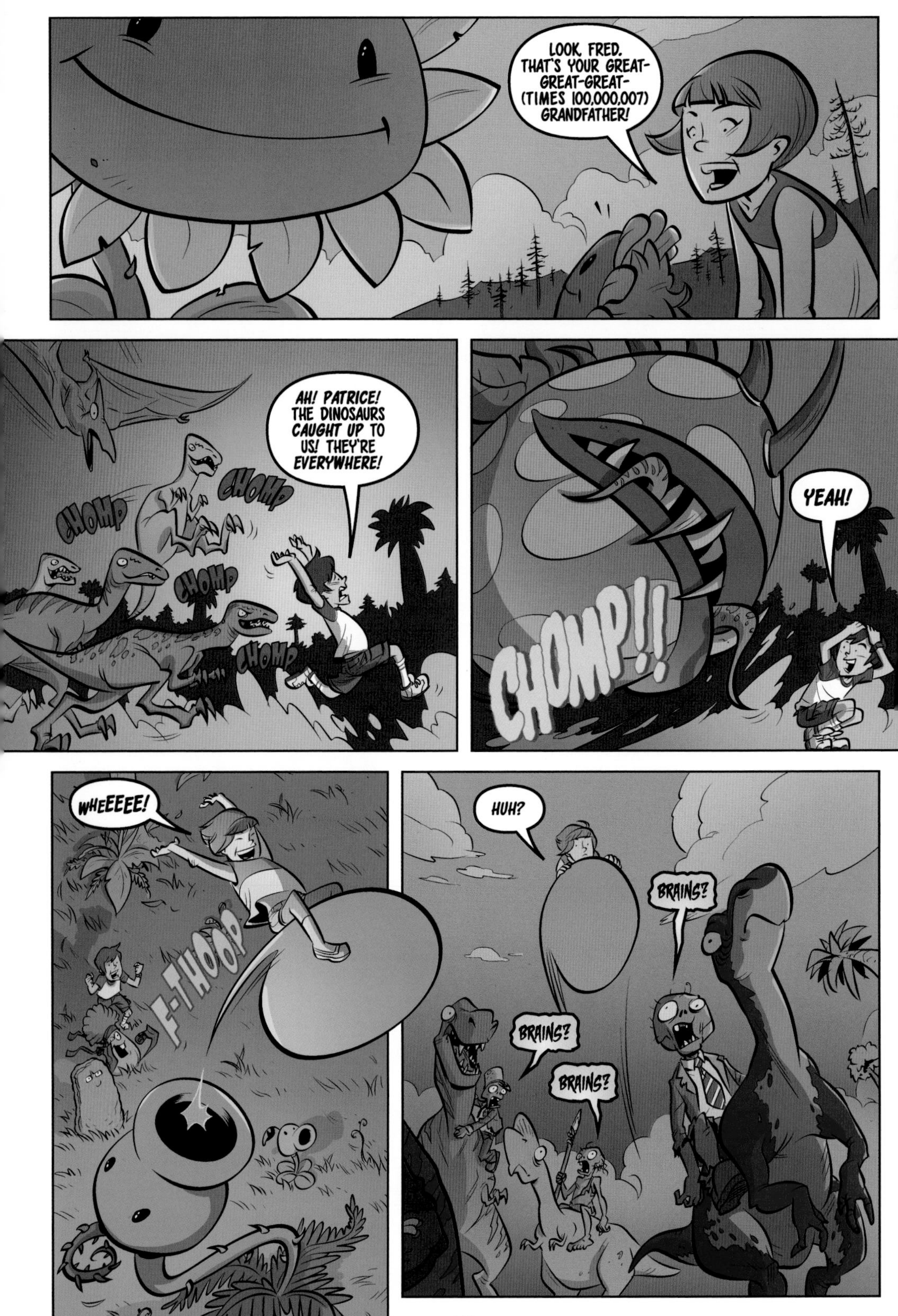
LOOK, FRED. THAT'S YOUR GREAT-GREAT-GREAT-(TIMES 100,000,007) GRANDFATHER!
AH! PATRICE! THE DINOSAURS CAUGHT UP TO US! THEY'RE EVERYWHERE!
CHOMP
CHOMP
CHOMP
CHOMP
CHOMP!!
YEAH!
WHEEEEE!
F-THOOP
HUH?
BRAINS?
BRAINS?
BRAINS?

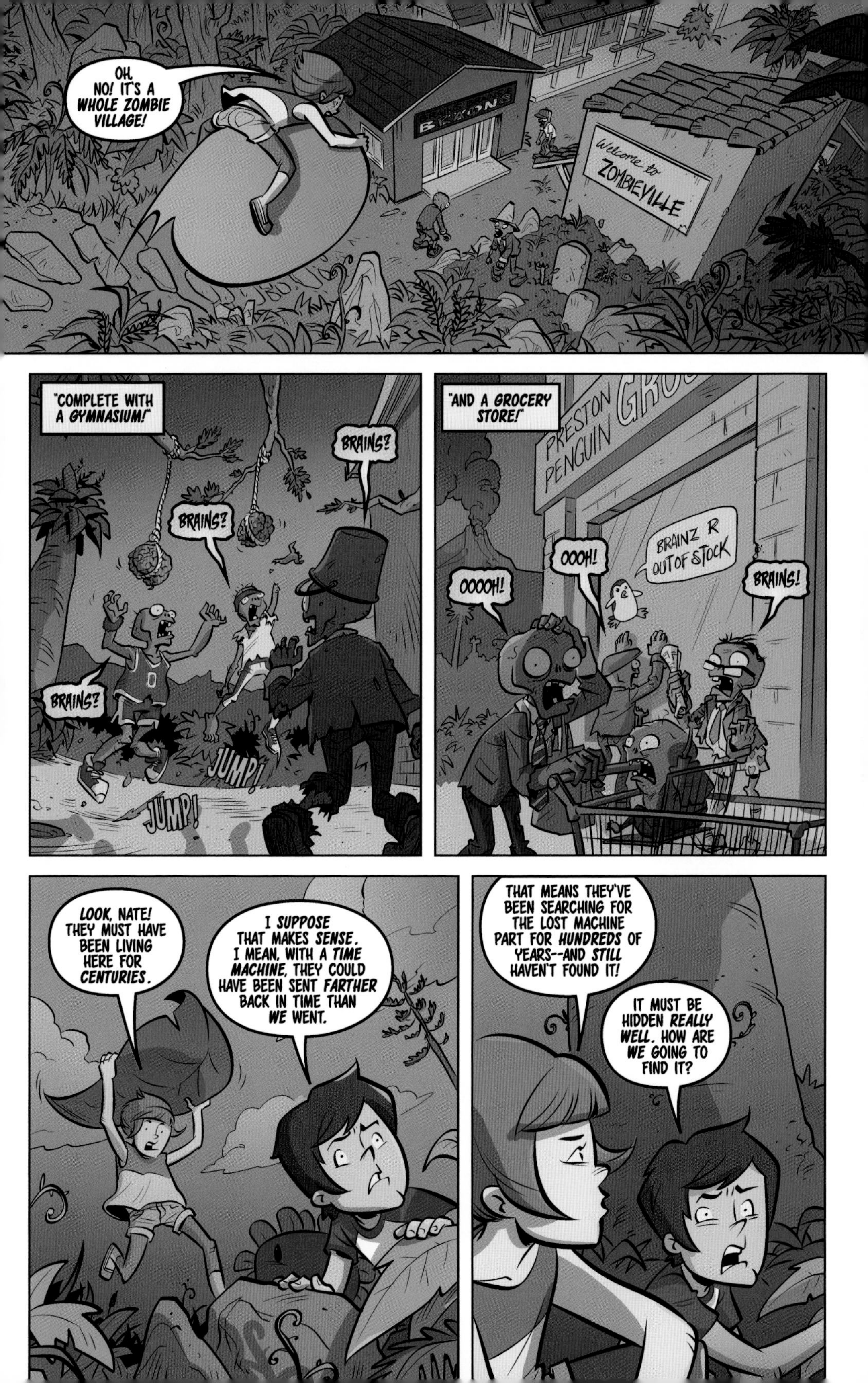
OH, NO! IT'S A WHOLE ZOMBIE VILLAGE!
Welcome to ZOMBIEVILLE
"COMPLETE WITH A GYMNASIUM!"
BRAINS?
BRAINS?
BRAINS?
JUMP!
JUMP!
"AND A GROCERY STORE!"
PRESTON PENGUIN
OOOOH!
OOOH!
BRAINZ R OUT OF STOCK
BRAINS!
LOOK, NATE! THEY MUST HAVE BEEN LIVING HERE FOR CENTURIES.
I SUPPOSE THAT MAKES SENSE. I MEAN, WITH A TIME MACHINE, THEY COULD HAVE BEEN SENT FARTHER BACK IN TIME THAN WE WENT.
THAT MEANS THEY'VE BEEN SEARCHING FOR THE LOST MACHINE PART FOR HUNDREDS OF YEARS--AND STILL HAVEN'T FOUND IT!
IT MUST BE HIDDEN REALLY WELL. HOW ARE WE GOING TO FIND IT?

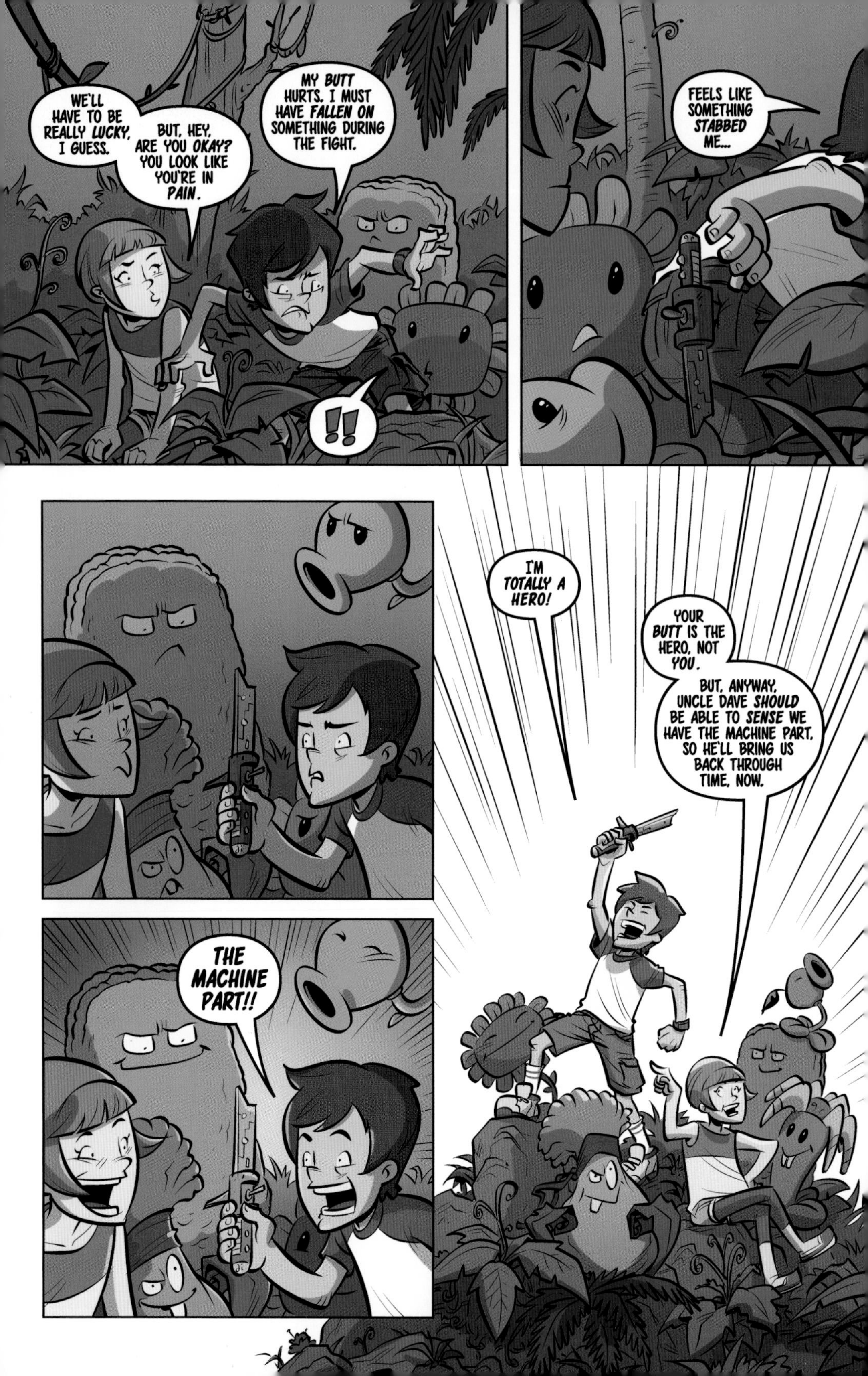
WE'LL HAVE TO BE REALLY LUCKY, I GUESS.
BUT, HEY, ARE YOU OKAY? YOU LOOK LIKE YOU'RE IN PAIN.
MY BUTT HURTS. I MUST HAVE FALLEN ON SOMETHING DURING THE FIGHT.
!!
FEELS LIKE SOMETHING STABBED ME...
THE MACHINE PART!!
I'M TOTALLY A HERO!
YOUR BUTT IS THE HERO, NOT YOU.
BUT, ANYWAY, UNCLE DAVE SHOULD BE ABLE TO SENSE WE HAVE THE MACHINE PART, SO HE'LL BRING US BACK THROUGH TIME, NOW.

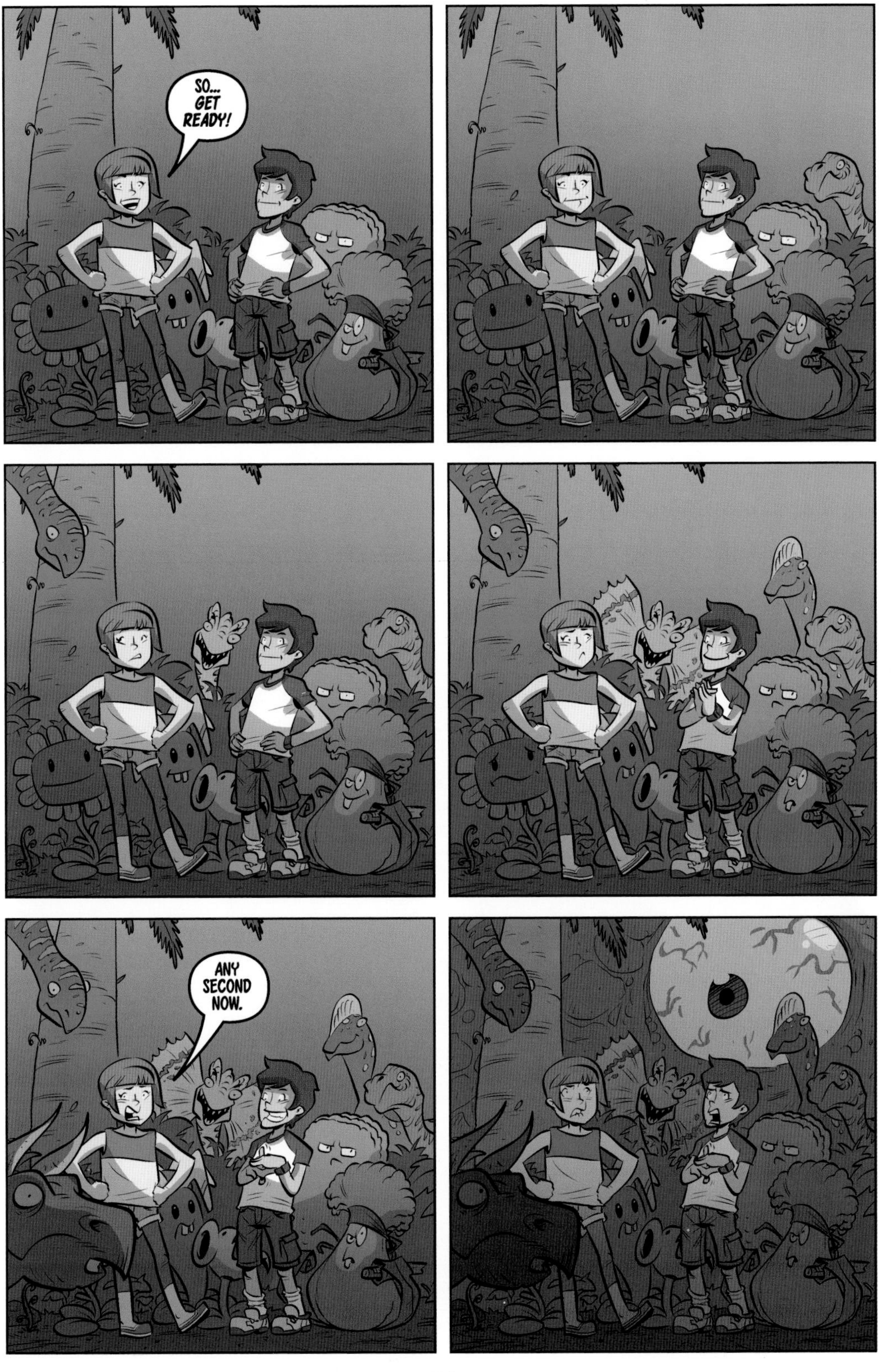
SO... GET READY!
ANY SECOND NOW.

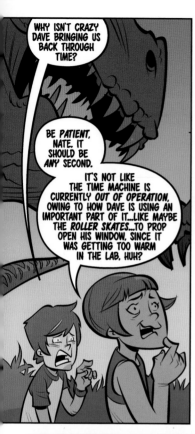

WHY ISN'T CRAZY DAVE BRINGING US BACK THROUGH TIME?

BE PATIENT, NATE. IT SHOULD BE ANY SECOND.

IT'S NOT LIKE THE TIME MACHINE IS CURRENTLY *OUT OF OPERATION*, OWING TO HOW DAVE IS USING AN IMPORTANT PART OF IT...LIKE MAYBE THE *ROLLER SKATES*...TO PROP OPEN HIS WINDOW, SINCE IT WAS GETTING TOO WARM IN THE LAB, HUH?

EANWHILE, MILLIONS OF YEARS IN THE FUTURE...

LA, LA, LA! GARBLE-GRABBLE LA!

OH, THAT'S *TOTALLY* HAPPENING.

OKAY, SO YOU AND I HAVE TO SURVIVE *LONG ENOUGH* FOR DAVE TO REMEMBER THAT HE SENT US BACK TO THE *AGE OF THE DINOSAURS* IN AN ATTEMPT TO *SAVE* THE WORLD.

YOU KNOW, THAT'S SOMETHING THAT *MOST* OF US, QUITE FRANKLY, WOULD *REMEMBER*.

WELL, WE NEED TO REMEMBER TO *FIGHT!*

FIGHT? I THOUGHT WE WERE GOING TO RUN.

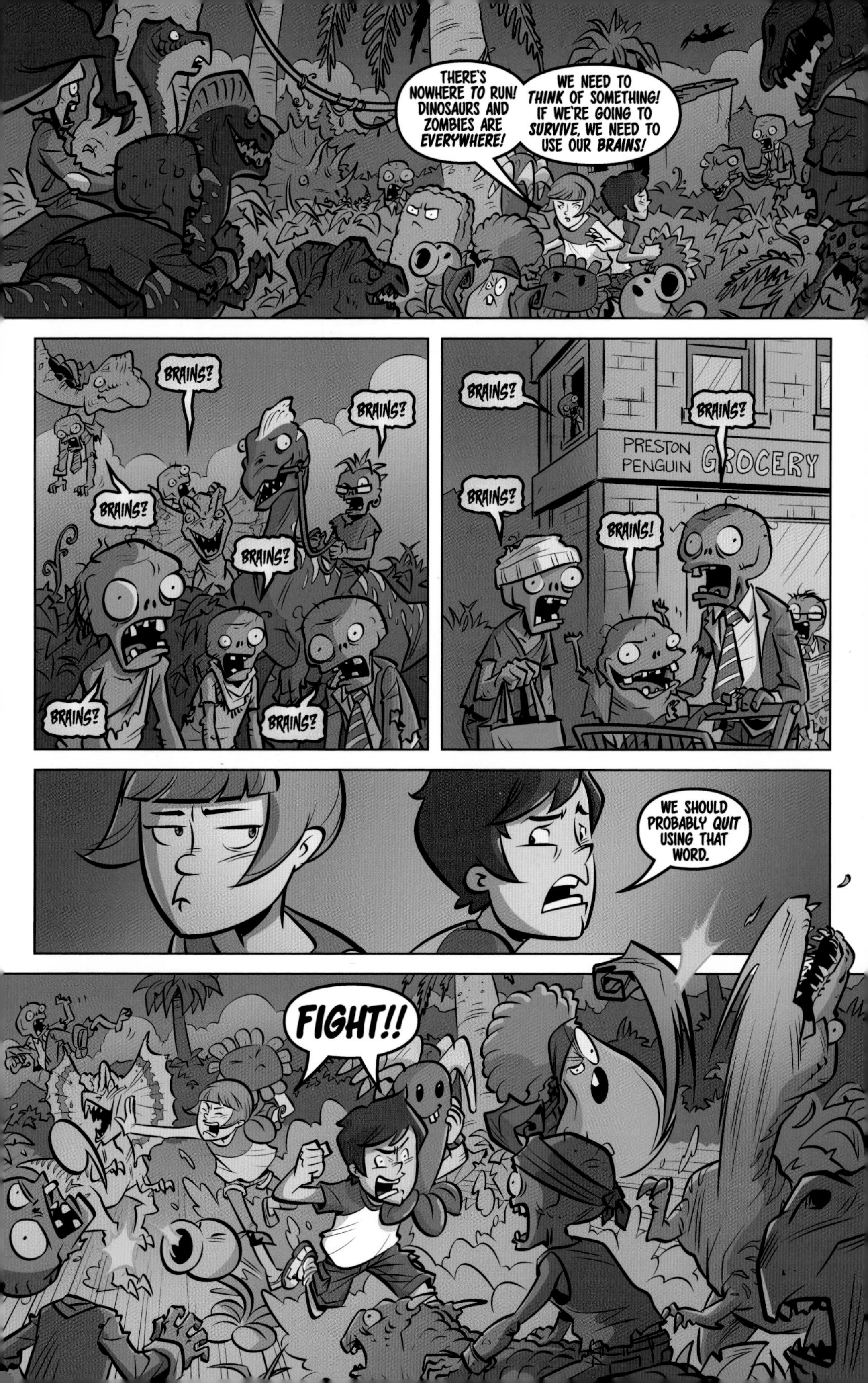

THERE'S NOWHERE TO RUN! DINOSAURS AND ZOMBIES ARE EVERYWHERE!
WE NEED TO THINK OF SOMETHING! IF WE'RE GOING TO SURVIVE, WE NEED TO USE OUR BRAINS!
BRAINS?
BRAINS?
BRAINS?
BRAINS?
BRAINS?
BRAINS?
BRAINS?
BRAINS?
PRESTON PENGUIN GROCERY
BRAINS?
BRAINS!
WE SHOULD PROBABLY QUIT USING THAT WORD.
FIGHT!!

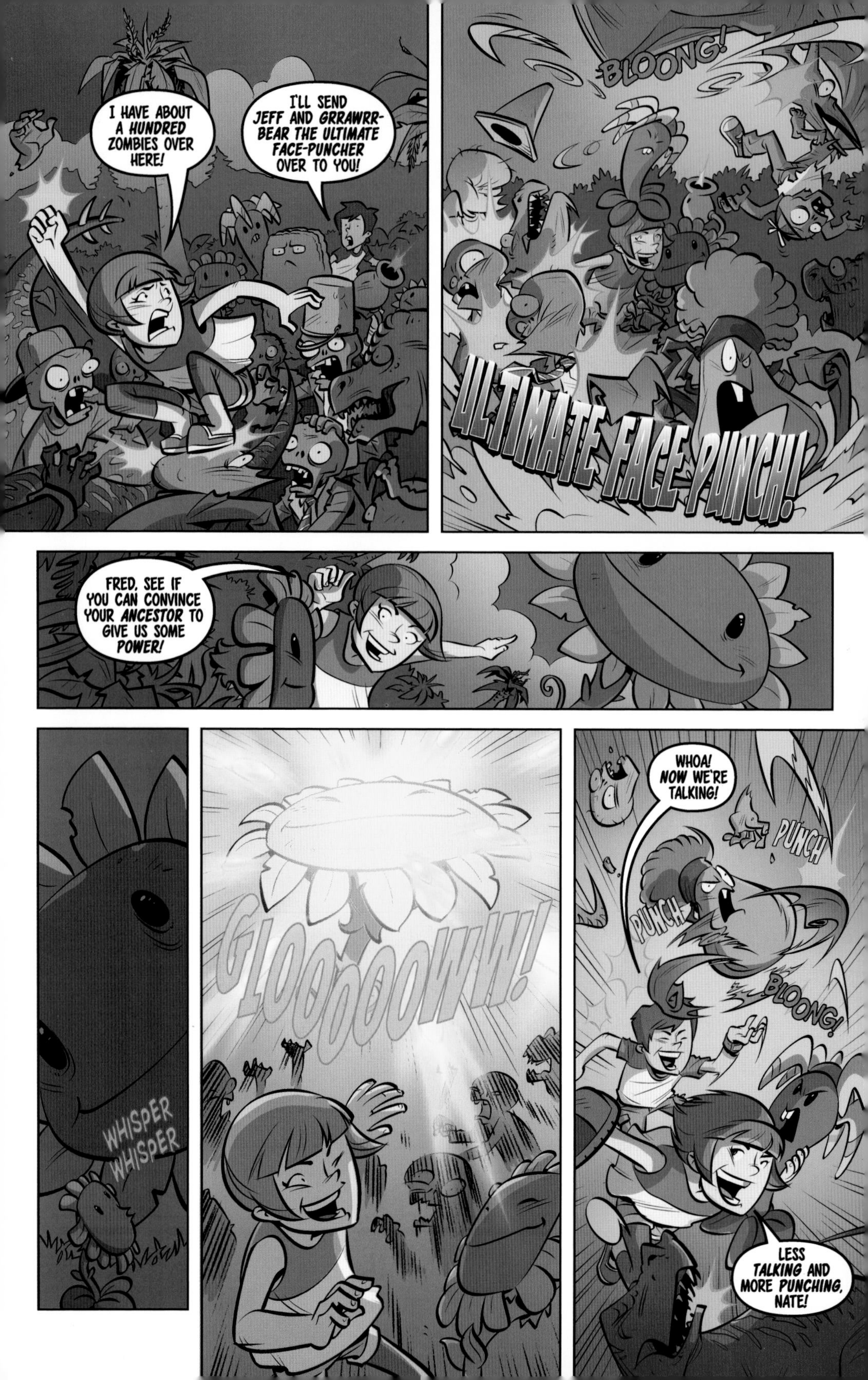
I HAVE ABOUT A HUNDRED ZOMBIES OVER HERE!
I'LL SEND JEFF AND GRRAWRR-BEAR THE ULTIMATE FACE-PUNCHER OVER TO YOU!
BLOONG!
ULTIMATE FACE PUNCH!
FRED, SEE IF YOU CAN CONVINCE YOUR ANCESTOR TO GIVE US SOME POWER!
WHISPER WHISPER
GLOOOOOOWW!
WHOA! NOW WE'RE TALKING!
PUNCH
PUNCH
BLOONG!
LESS TALKING AND MORE PUNCHING, NATE!

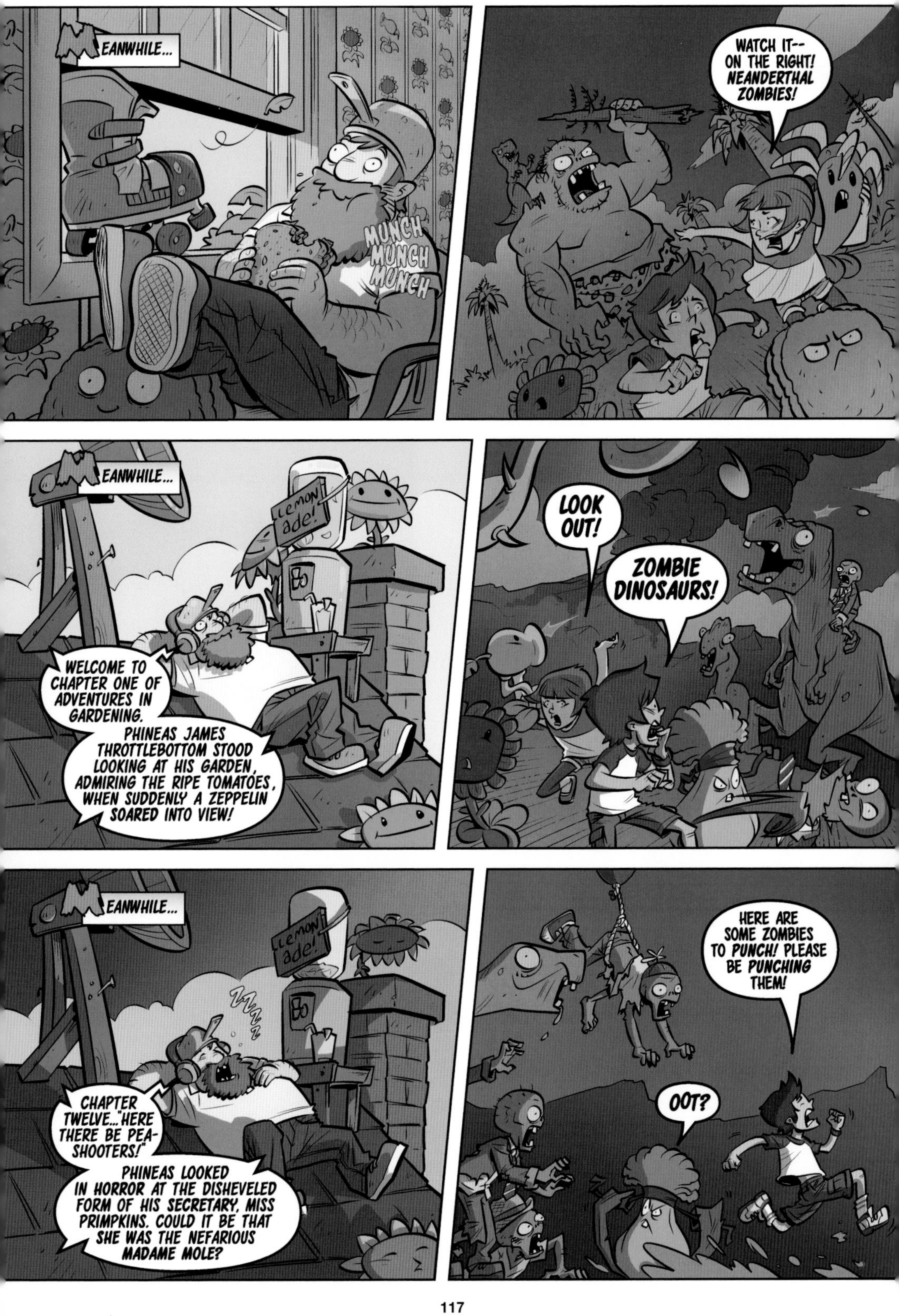
MEANWHILE...
MUNCH MUNCH MUNCH
WATCH IT-- ON THE RIGHT! NEANDERTHAL ZOMBIES!
MEANWHILE...
LEMON ADE!
WELCOME TO CHAPTER ONE OF ADVENTURES IN GARDENING.
PHINEAS JAMES THROTTLEBOTTOM STOOD LOOKING AT HIS GARDEN, ADMIRING THE RIPE TOMATOES, WHEN SUDDENLY A ZEPPELIN SOARED INTO VIEW!
LOOK OUT!
ZOMBIE DINOSAURS!
MEANWHILE...
LEMON ADE!
ZZZZ
CHAPTER TWELVE..."HERE THERE BE PEA-SHOOTERS!"
PHINEAS LOOKED IN HORROR AT THE DISHEVELED FORM OF HIS SECRETARY, MISS PRIMPKINS. COULD IT BE THAT SHE WAS THE NEFARIOUS MADAME MOLE?
HERE ARE SOME ZOMBIES TO PUNCH! PLEASE BE PUNCHING THEM!
OOT?

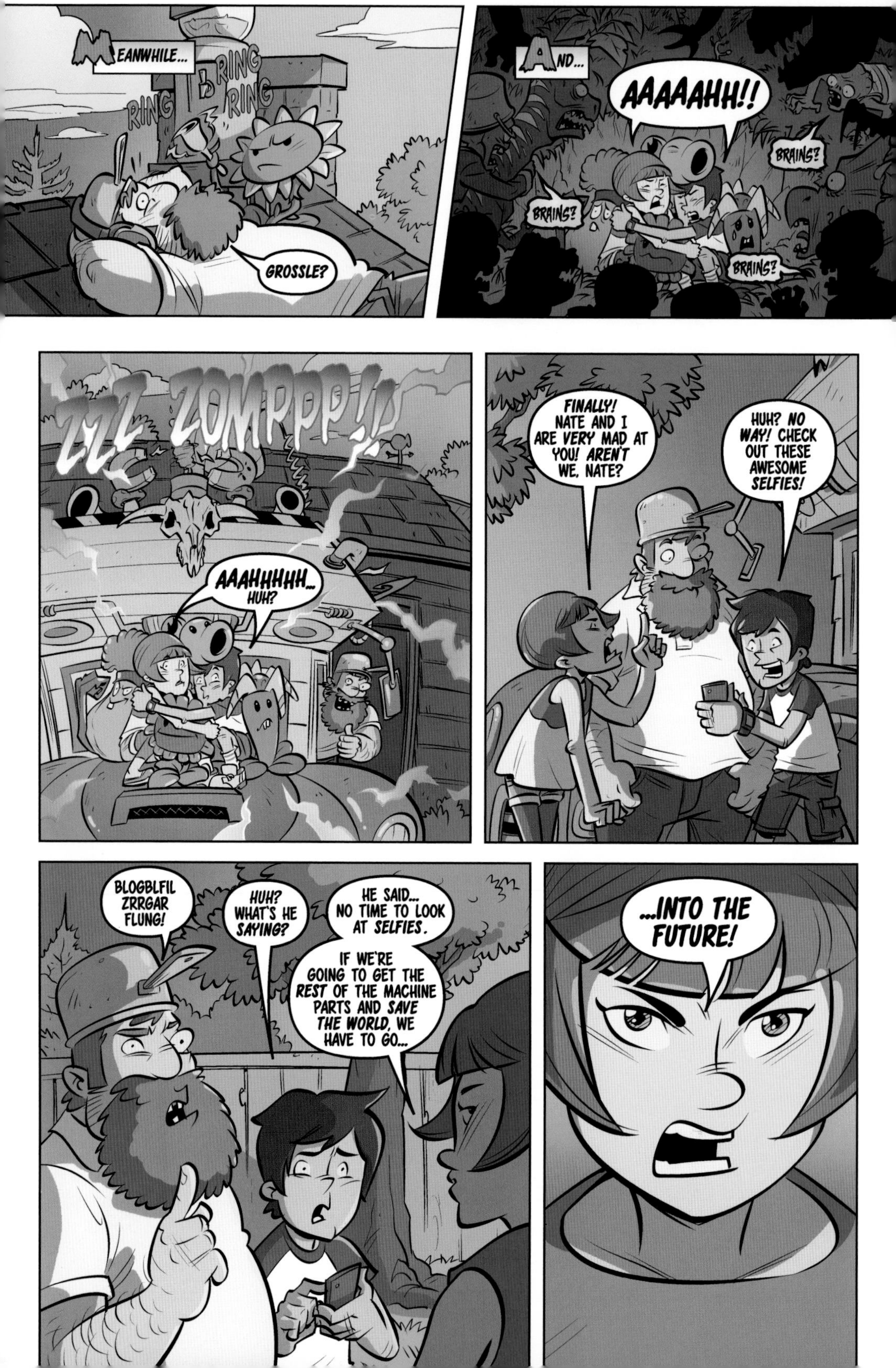
MEANWHILE...
RING
BRING
RING
GROSSLE?
AND...
AAAAAHH!!
BRAINS?
BRAINS?
BRAINS?
ZZZ ZOMPPP!!!
AAAHHHH... HUH?
FINALLY! NATE AND I ARE VERY MAD AT YOU! AREN'T WE, NATE?
HUH? NO WAY! CHECK OUT THESE AWESOME SELFIES!
BLOGBLFIL ZRRGAR FLUNG!
HUH? WHAT'S HE SAYING?
HE SAID... NO TIME TO LOOK AT SELFIES.
IF WE'RE GOING TO GET THE REST OF THE MACHINE PARTS AND SAVE THE WORLD, WE HAVE TO GO...
...INTO THE FUTURE!

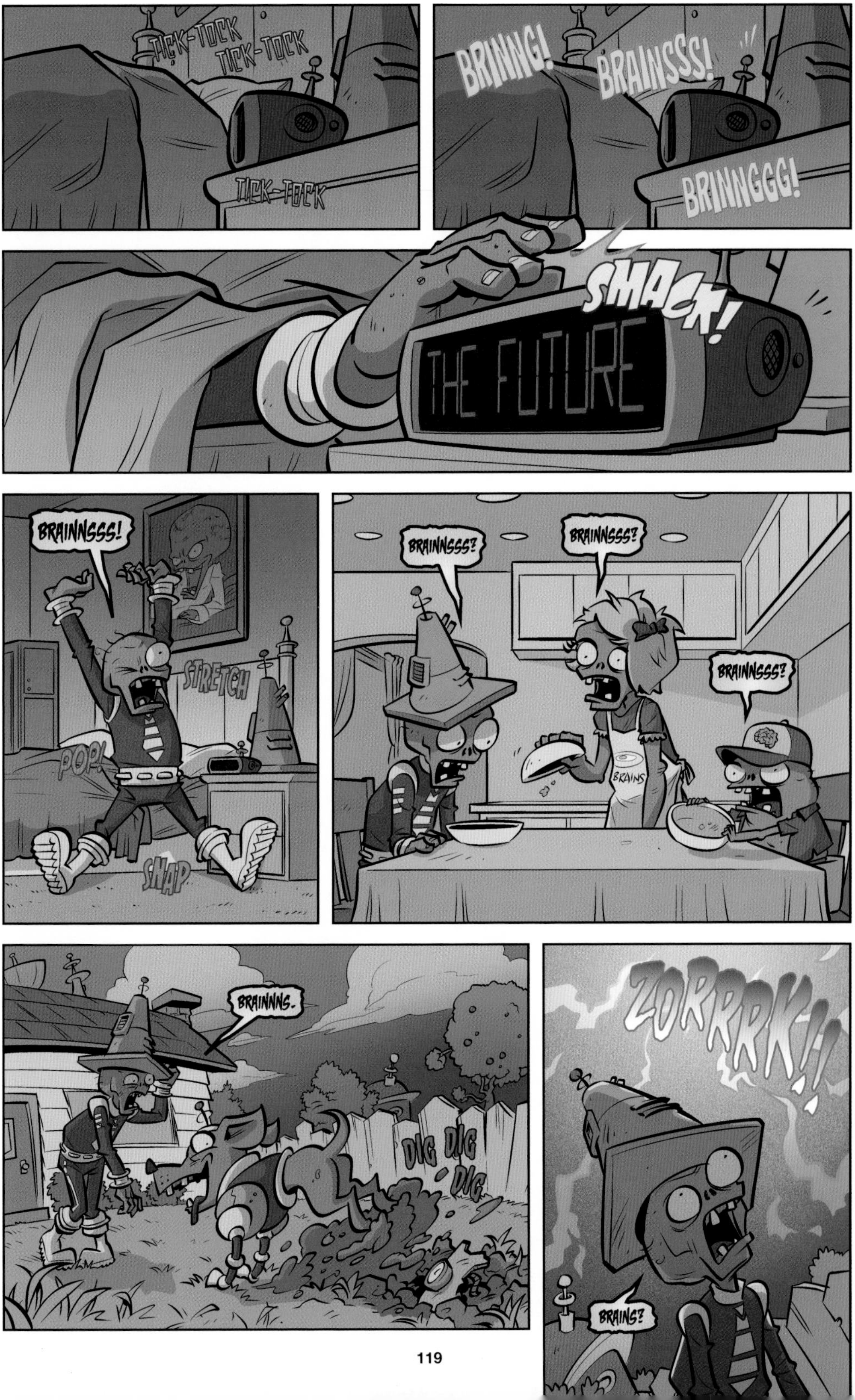
TICK-TOCK
TICK-TOCK
TICK-TOCK
BRINNG!
BRAINSSS!
BRINNGGG!
SMACK!
THE FUTURE
BRAINNSSS!
STRETCH
POP!
SNAP
BRAINNSSS?
BRAINNSSS?
BRAINS
BRAINNSSS?
BRAINNNS.
DIG DIG
DIG
DIG
ZORRRK!!
BRAINS?

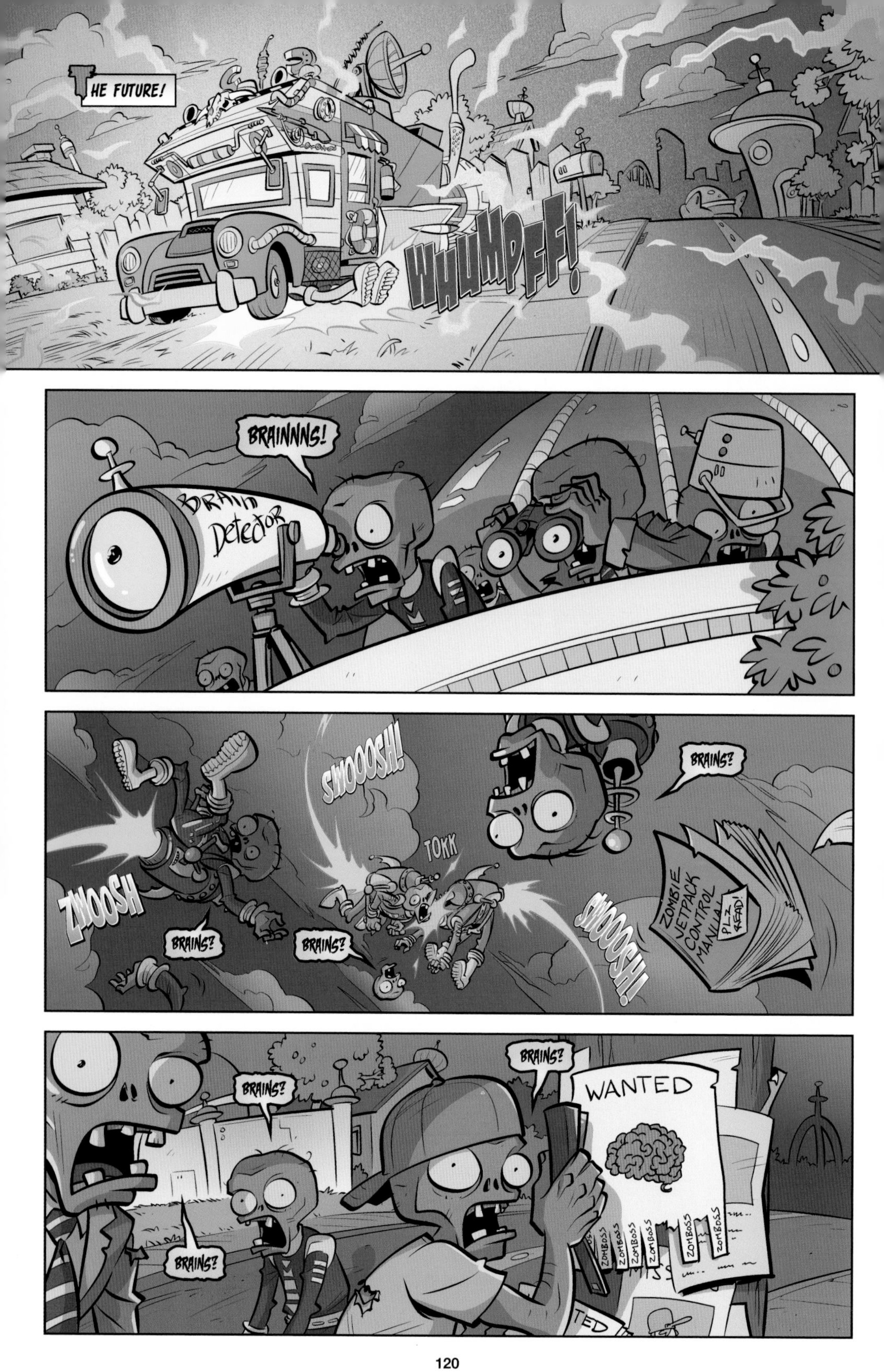
THE FUTURE!
WHUMPFF!
BRAINNNS!
BRAIN DETECTOR
SWOOOSH!
BRAINS?
TOKK
ZWOOSH
SWOOOSH!
BRAINS?
BRAINS?
ZOMBIE JETPACK CONTROL MANUAL
PLZ READ!
BRAINS?
BRAINS?
WANTED
ZOMBOSS
BRAINS?

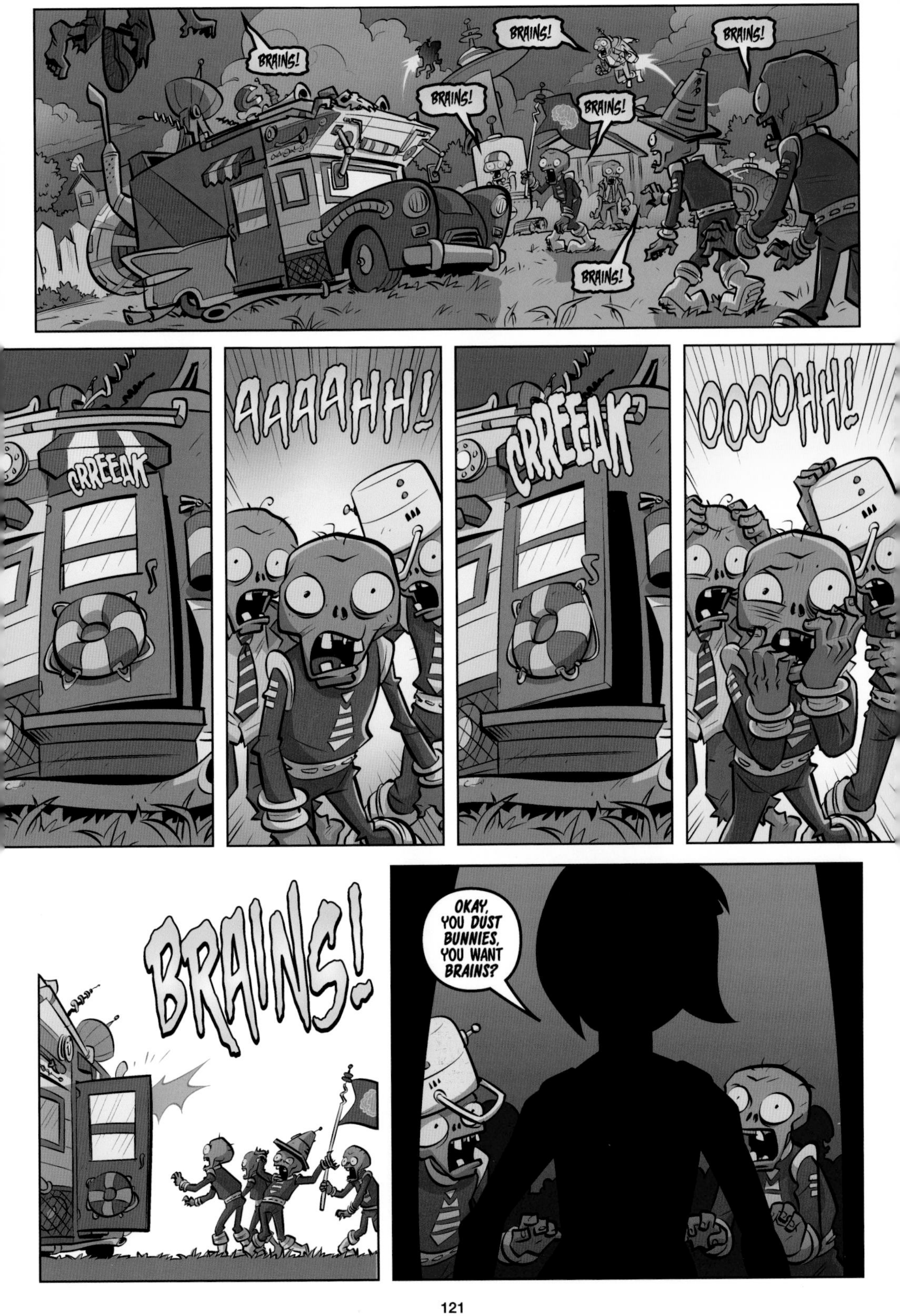

BRAINS!
BRAINS!
BRAINS!
BRAINS!
BRAINS!
BRAINS!
CRREEAK
AAAAHH!
CRREEAK
OOOOHH!
BRAINS!
OKAY, YOU DUST BUNNIES, YOU WANT BRAINS?

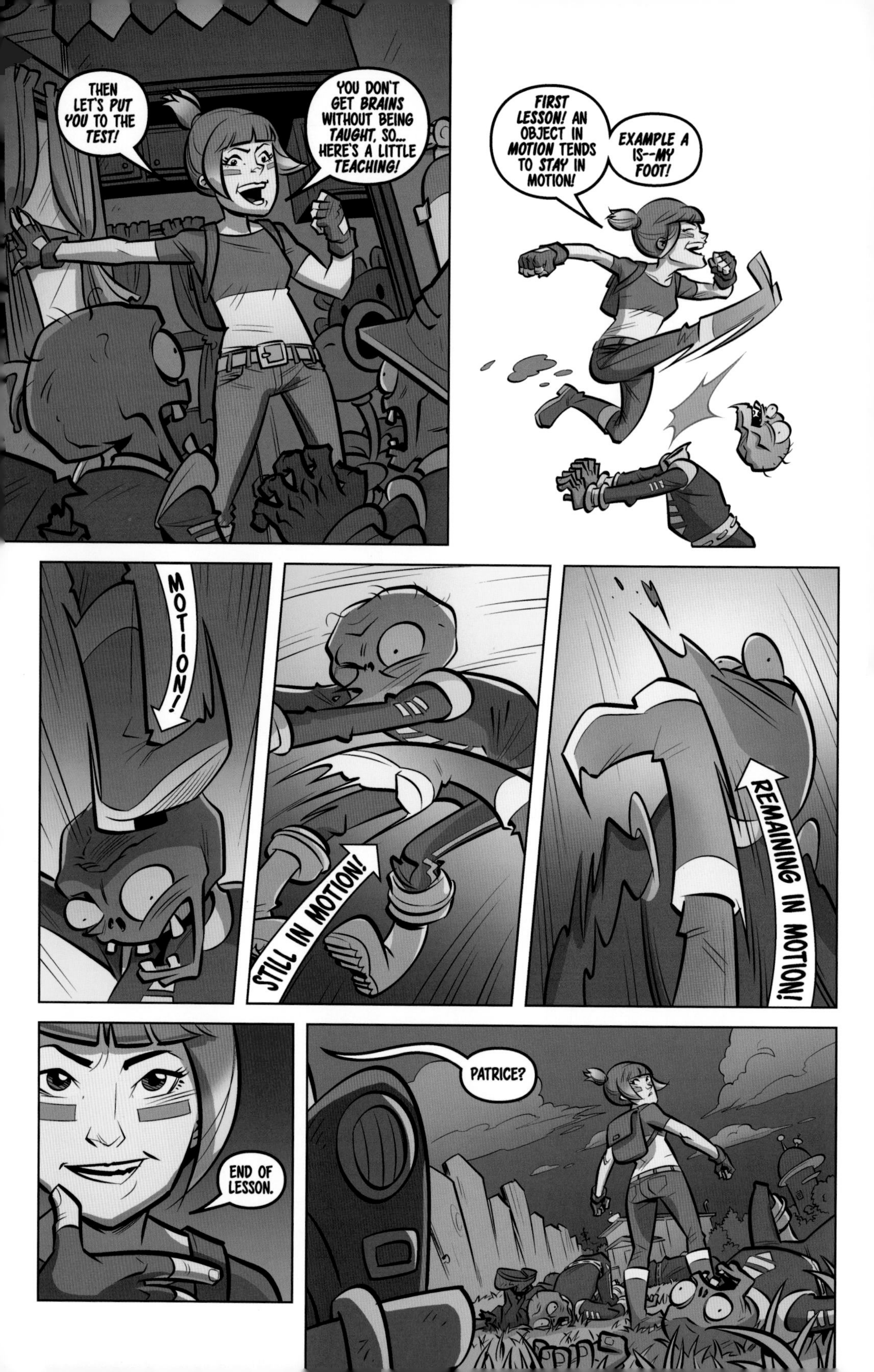
THEN LET'S PUT YOU TO THE TEST!
YOU DON'T GET BRAINS WITHOUT BEING TAUGHT, SO... HERE'S A LITTLE TEACHING!
FIRST LESSON! AN OBJECT IN MOTION TENDS TO STAY IN MOTION!
EXAMPLE A IS--MY FOOT!
MOTION!
STILL IN MOTION!
REMAINING IN MOTION!
END OF LESSON.
PATRICE?

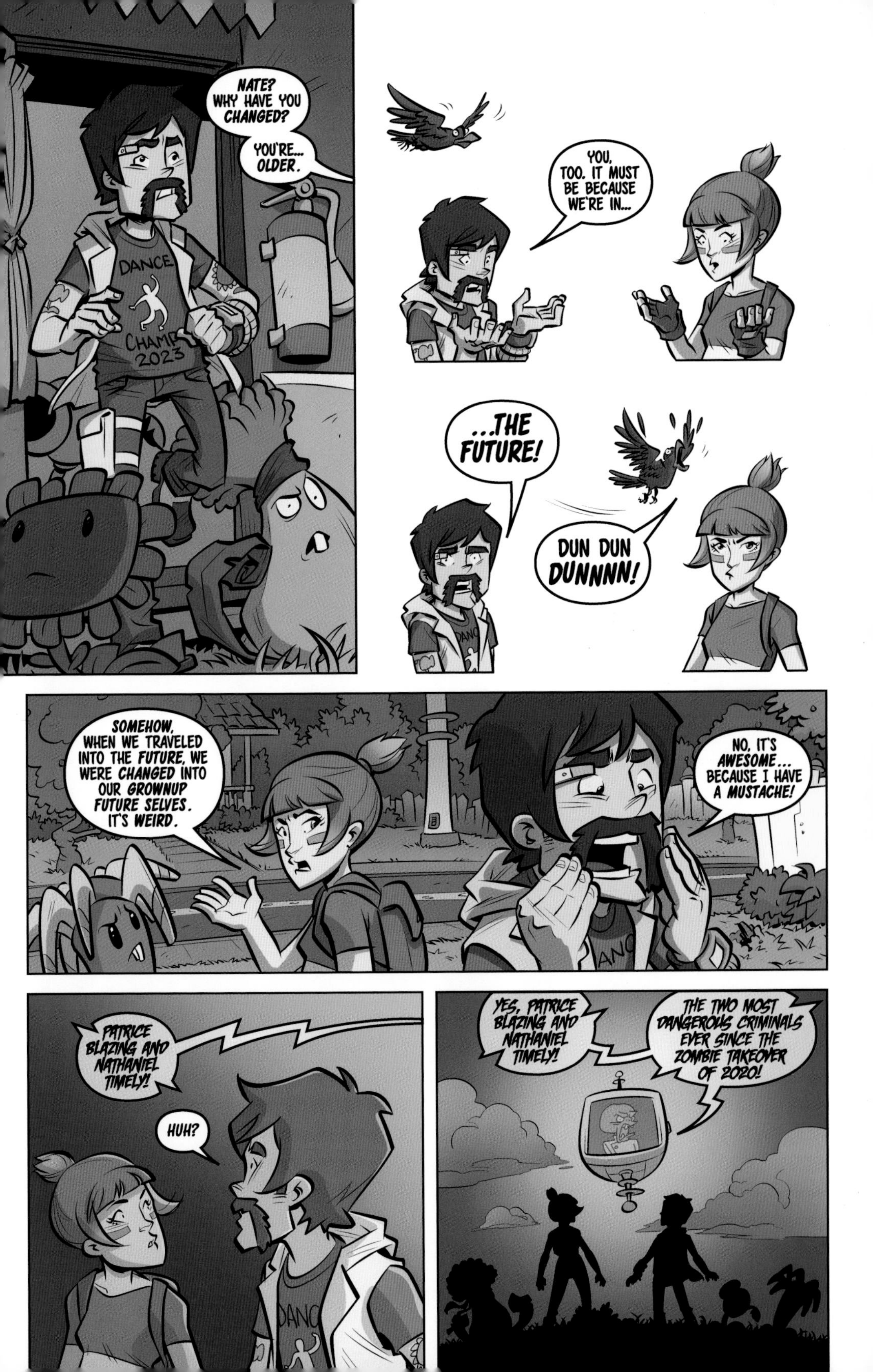
NATE? WHY HAVE YOU CHANGED?
YOU'RE... OLDER.
DANCE CHAMP 2023
YOU, TOO. IT MUST BE BECAUSE WE'RE IN...
...THE FUTURE!
DUN DUN DUNNNN!
SOMEHOW, WHEN WE TRAVELED INTO THE FUTURE, WE WERE CHANGED INTO OUR GROWNUP FUTURE SELVES. IT'S WEIRD.
NO, IT'S AWESOME... BECAUSE I HAVE A MUSTACHE!
PATRICE BLAZING AND NATHANIEL TIMELY!
HUH?
YES, PATRICE BLAZING AND NATHANIEL TIMELY!
THE TWO MOST DANGEROUS CRIMINALS EVER SINCE THE ZOMBIE TAKEOVER OF 2020!

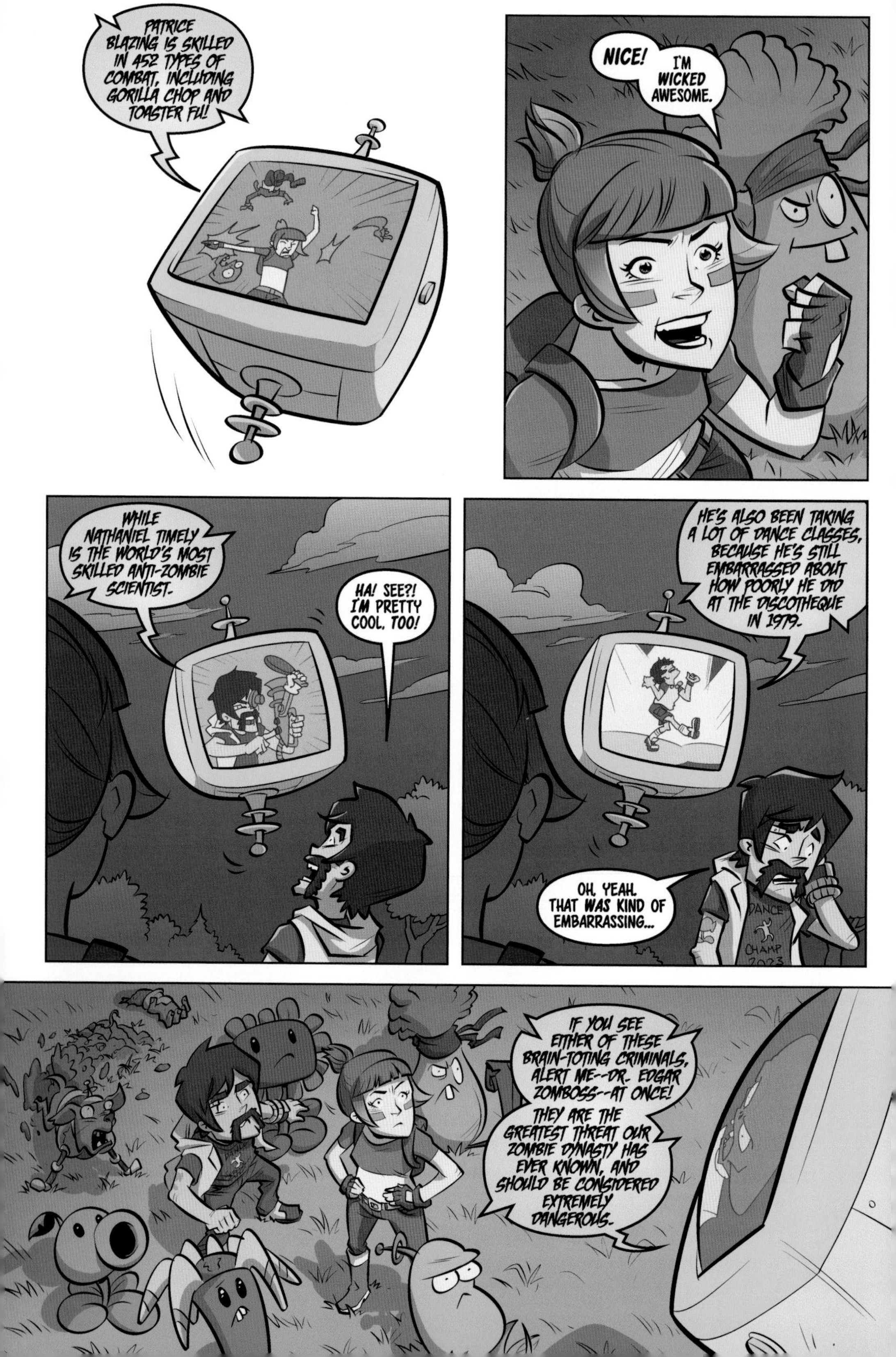
PATRICE BLAZING IS SKILLED IN 452 TYPES OF COMBAT, INCLUDING GORILLA CHOP AND TOASTER FU!
NICE!
I'M WICKED AWESOME.
WHILE NATHANIEL TIMELY IS THE WORLD'S MOST SKILLED ANTI-ZOMBIE SCIENTIST.
HA! SEE?! I'M PRETTY COOL, TOO!
HE'S ALSO BEEN TAKING A LOT OF DANCE CLASSES, BECAUSE HE'S STILL EMBARRASSED ABOUT HOW POORLY HE DID AT THE DISCOTHEQUE IN 1979.
OH, YEAH. THAT WAS KIND OF EMBARRASSING...
DANCE CHAMP 2023
IF YOU SEE EITHER OF THESE BRAIN-TOTING CRIMINALS, ALERT ME--DR. EDGAR ZOMBOSS--AT ONCE!
THEY ARE THE GREATEST THREAT OUR ZOMBIE DYNASTY HAS EVER KNOWN, AND SHOULD BE CONSIDERED EXTREMELY DANGEROUS.

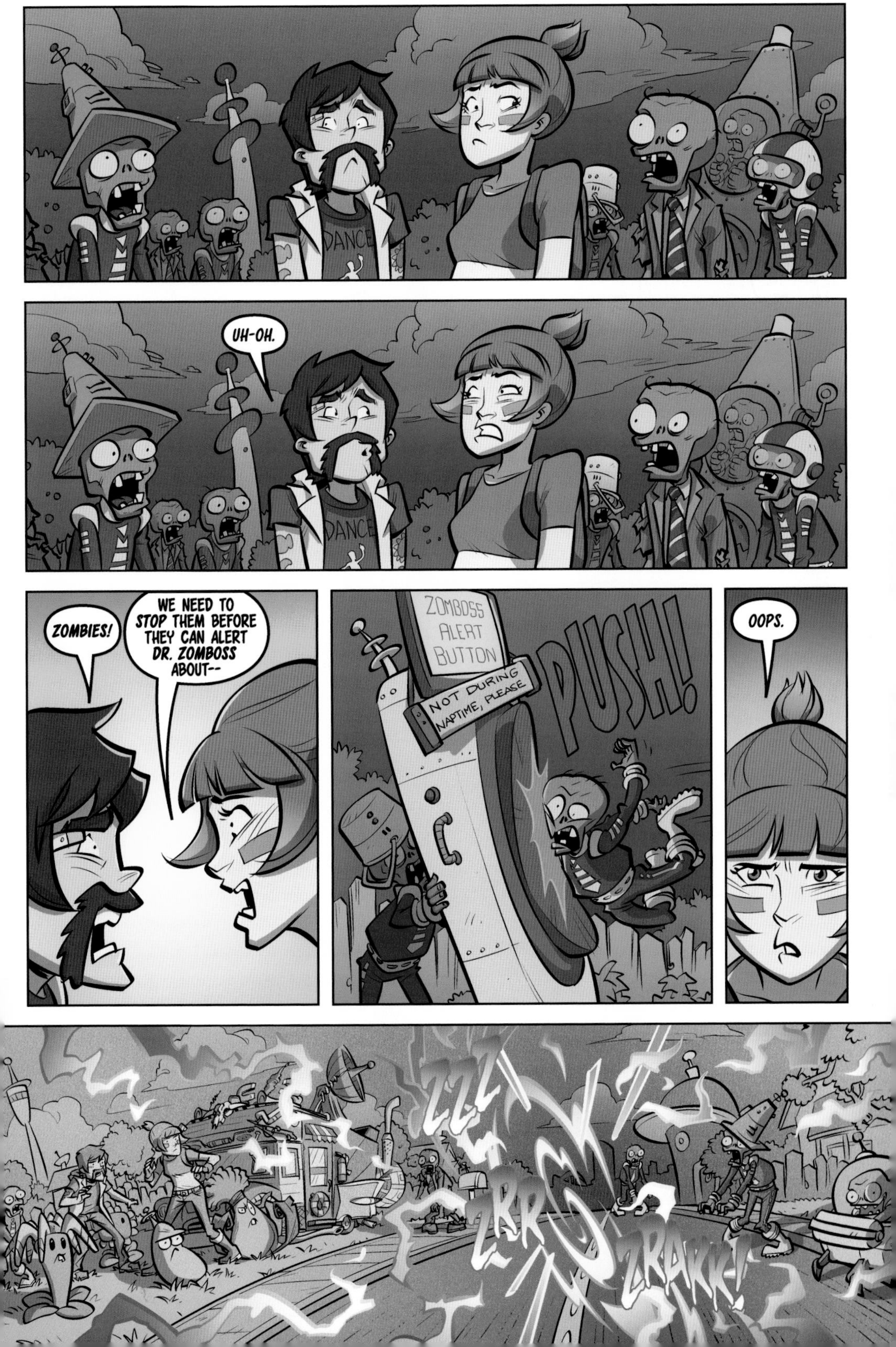
DANCE
UH-OH.
ZOMBIES!
WE NEED TO STOP THEM BEFORE THEY CAN ALERT DR. ZOMBOSS ABOUT--
ZOMBOSS ALERT BUTTON
NOT DURING NAPTIME, PLEASE
PUSH!
OOPS.
ZZZ
ZRR
ZRAKK!

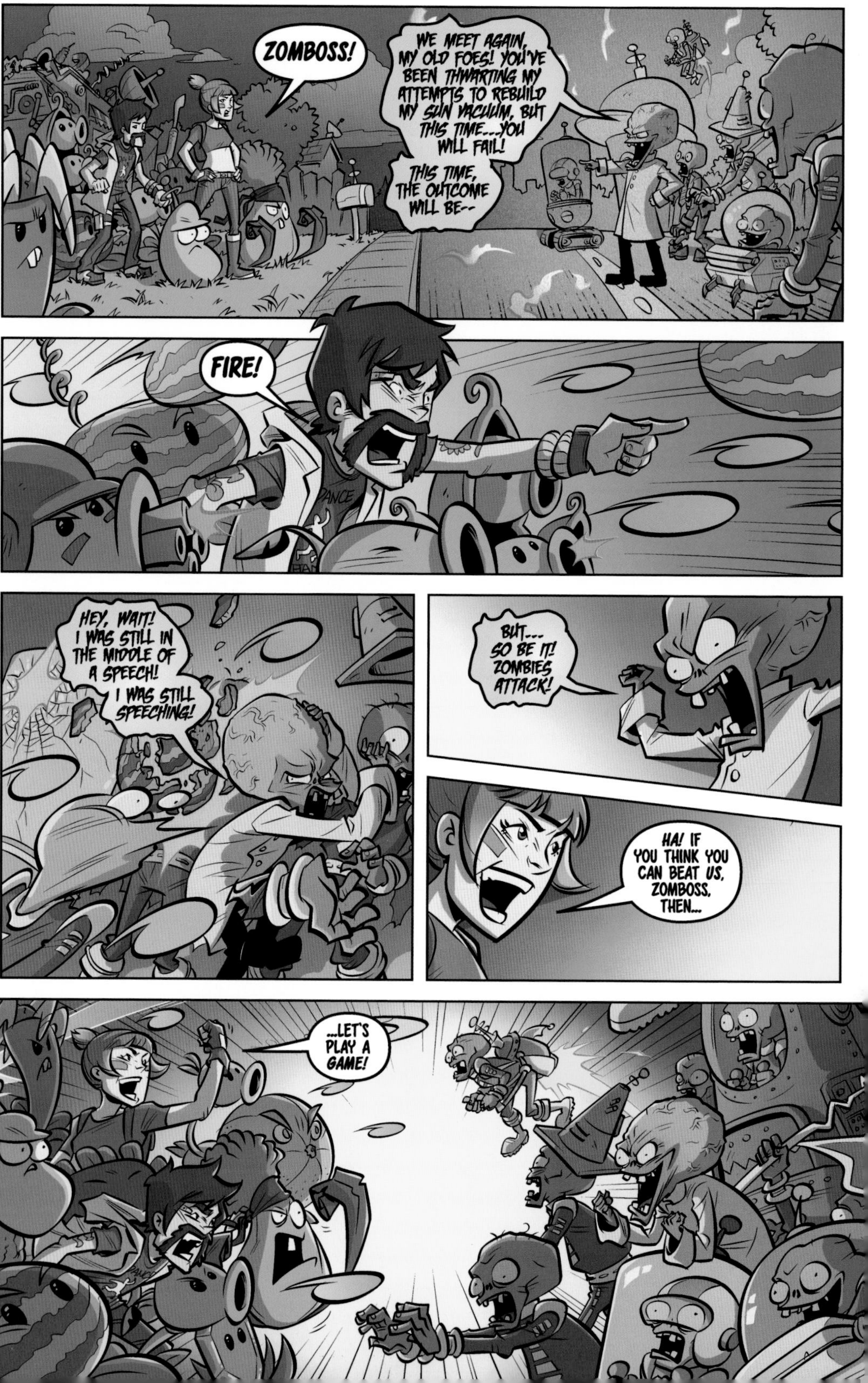
ZOMBOSS!
WE MEET AGAIN, MY OLD FOES! YOU'VE BEEN THWARTING MY ATTEMPTS TO REBUILD MY SUN VACUUM, BUT THIS TIME...YOU WILL FAIL!
THIS TIME, THE OUTCOME WILL BE--
FIRE!
HEY, WAIT! I WAS STILL IN THE MIDDLE OF A SPEECH!
I WAS STILL SPEECHING!
BUT... SO BE IT! ZOMBIES ATTACK!
HA! IF YOU THINK YOU CAN BEAT US, ZOMBOSS, THEN...
...LET'S PLAY A GAME!

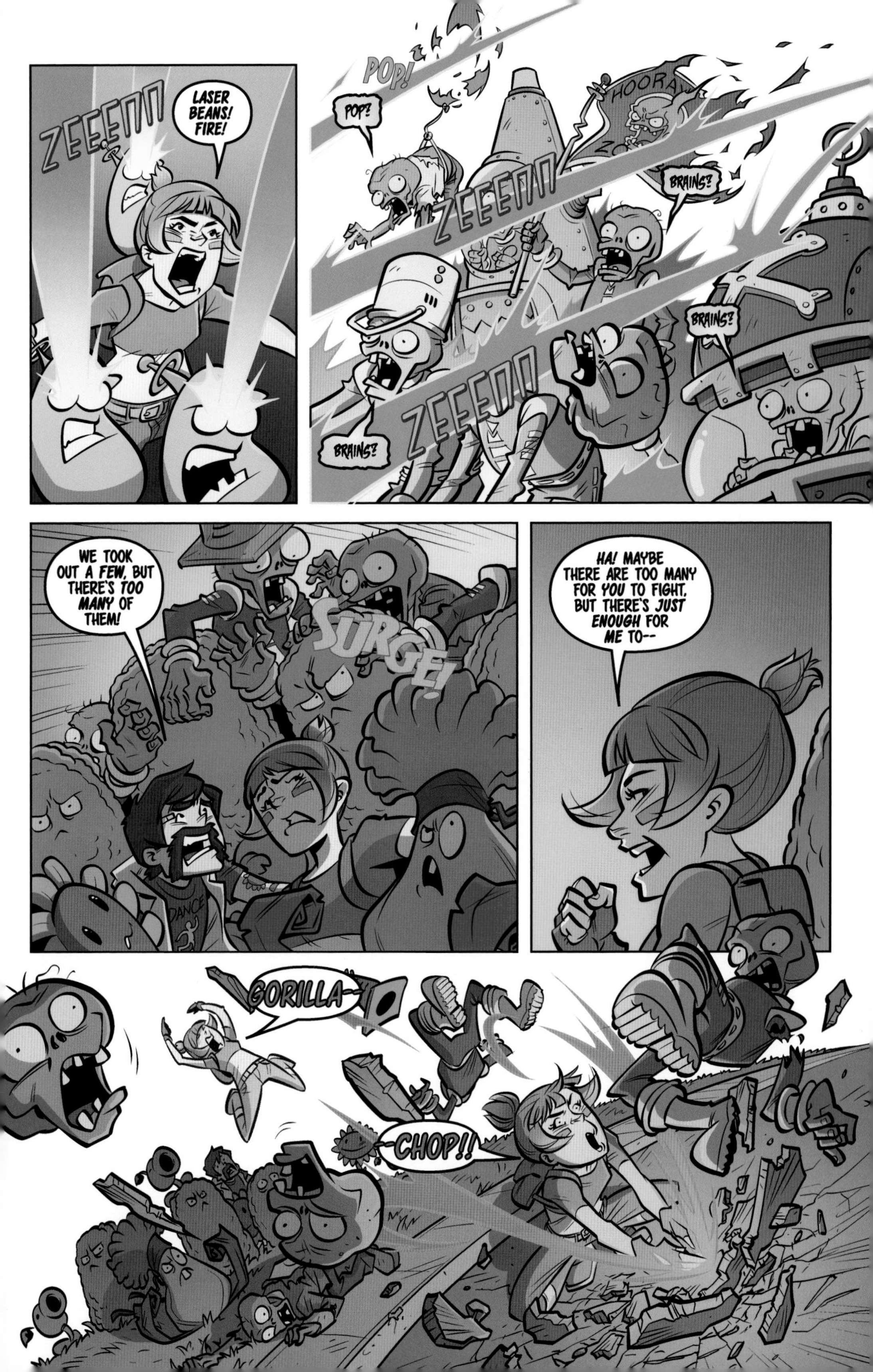
ZEEENN
LASER BEANS! FIRE!
POP!
POP?
HOORA
ZEEENN
BRAINS?
BRAINS?
ZEEENN
BRAINS?
WE TOOK OUT A FEW, BUT THERE'S TOO MANY OF THEM!
SURGE!
HA! MAYBE THERE ARE TOO MANY FOR YOU TO FIGHT, BUT THERE'S JUST ENOUGH FOR ME TO--
DANCE
GORILLA--
--CHOP!!

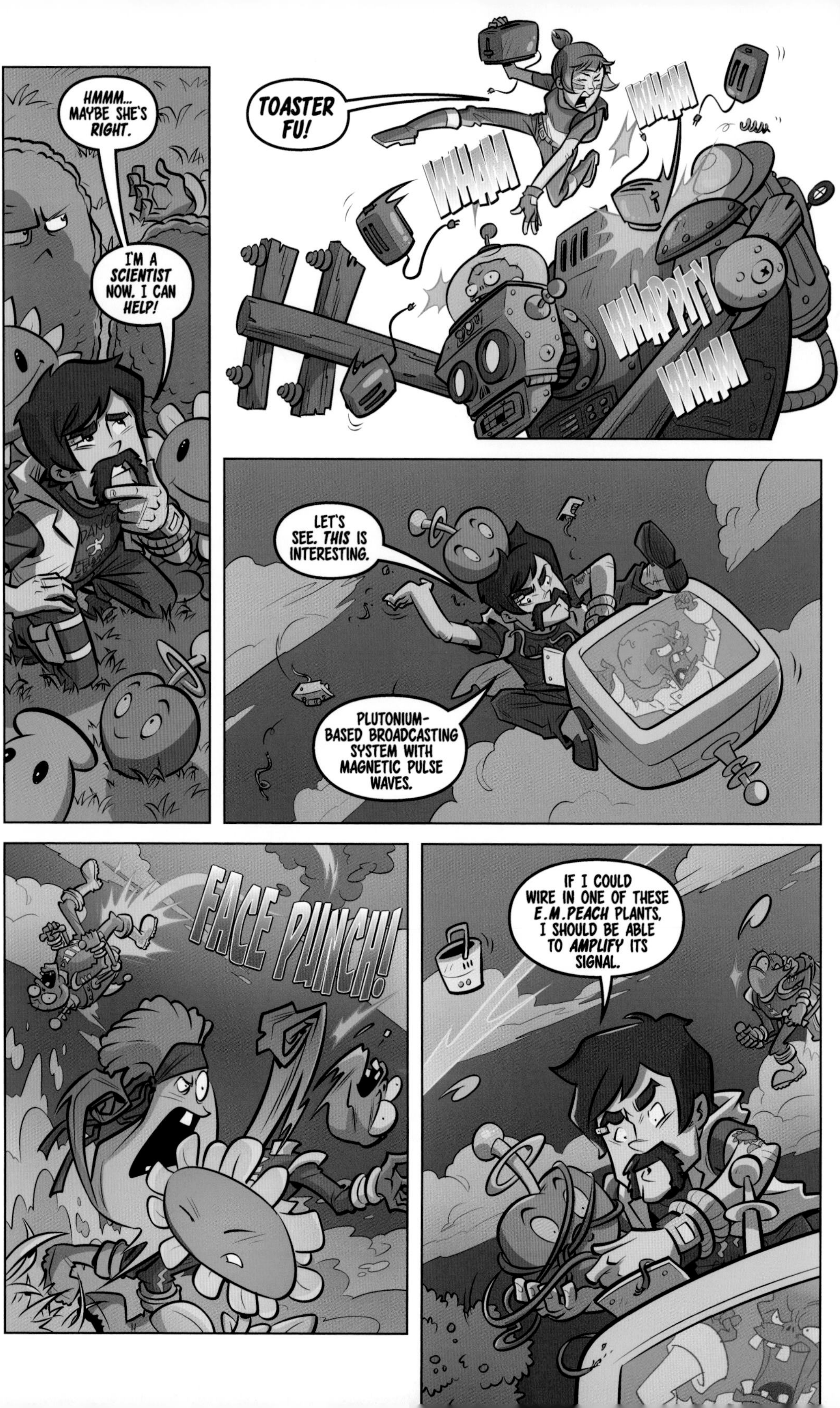
HMMM... MAYBE SHE'S RIGHT.
I'M A SCIENTIST NOW. I CAN HELP!
TOASTER FU!
WHAM
WHAM
WHAPPITY WHAM
LET'S SEE. THIS IS INTERESTING.
PLUTONIUM-BASED BROADCASTING SYSTEM WITH MAGNETIC PULSE WAVES.
FACE PUNCH!
IF I COULD WIRE IN ONE OF THESE E.M.PEACH PLANTS, I SHOULD BE ABLE TO AMPLIFY ITS SIGNAL.

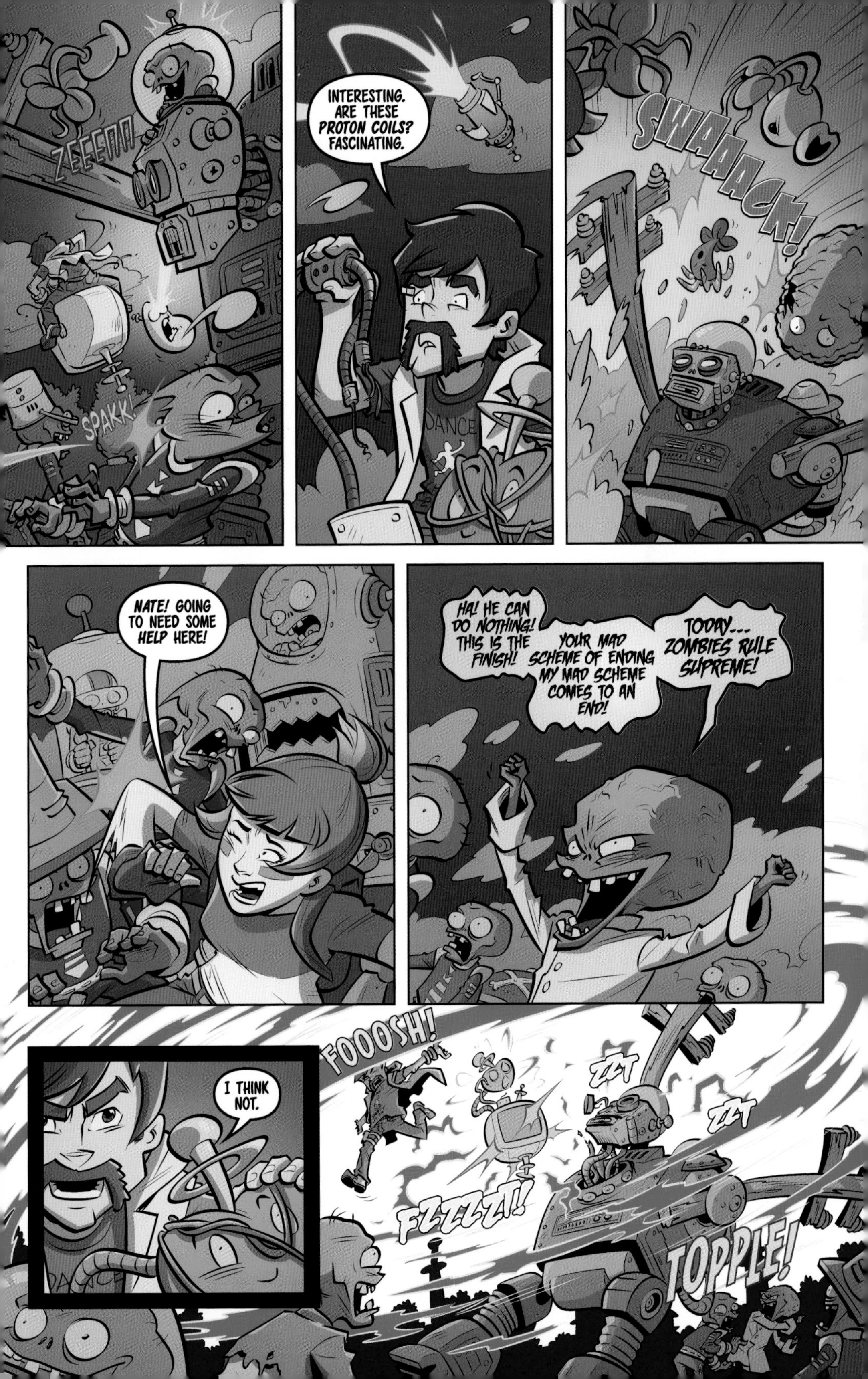
ZEEEMM
SPAKK!
INTERESTING. ARE THESE PROTON COILS? FASCINATING.
SWAAACK!
NATE! GOING TO NEED SOME HELP HERE!
HA! HE CAN DO NOTHING! THIS IS THE FINISH!
YOUR MAD SCHEME OF ENDING MY MAD SCHEME COMES TO AN END!
TODAY... ZOMBIES RULE SUPREME!
I THINK NOT.
FOOOSH!
ZZT
ZZT
FZZZZT!
TOPPLE!

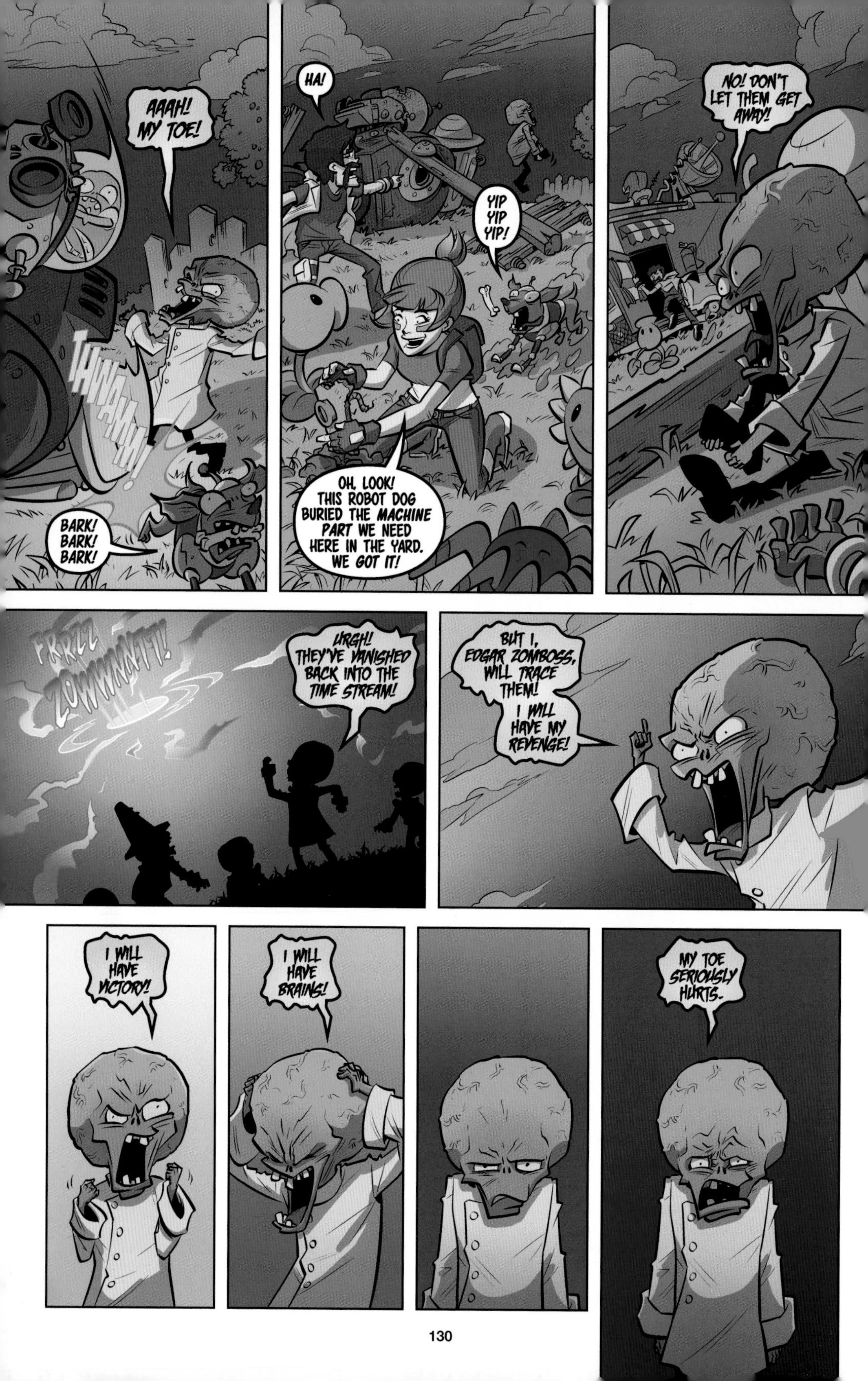
AAAH! MY TOE!
THWAMM!
BARK! BARK! BARK!
HA!
YIP YIP YIP!
OH, LOOK! THIS ROBOT DOG BURIED THE MACHINE PART WE NEED HERE IN THE YARD. WE GOT IT!
NO! DON'T LET THEM GET AWAY!
FRRZZ ZOWWWNTT!
URGH! THEY'VE VANISHED BACK INTO THE TIME STREAM!
BUT I, EDGAR ZOMBOSS, WILL TRACE THEM!
I WILL HAVE MY REVENGE!
I WILL HAVE VICTORY!
I WILL HAVE BRAINS!
MY TOE SERIOUSLY HURTS.

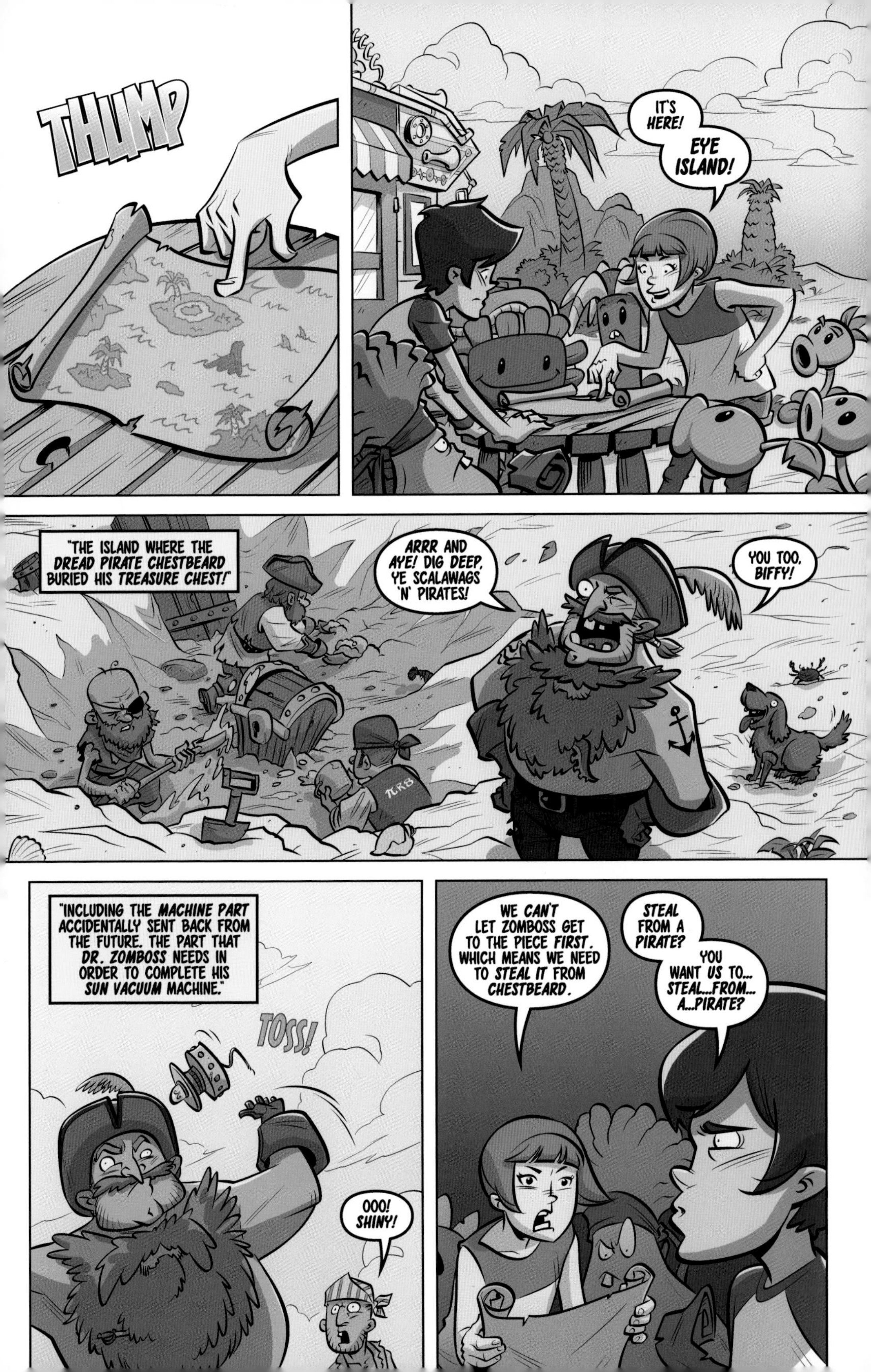
THUMP
IT'S HERE! EYE ISLAND!
"THE ISLAND WHERE THE DREAD PIRATE CHESTBEARD BURIED HIS TREASURE CHEST!"
ARRR AND AYE! DIG DEEP, YE SCALAWAGS 'N' PIRATES!
YOU TOO, BIFFY!
"INCLUDING THE MACHINE PART ACCIDENTALLY SENT BACK FROM THE FUTURE. THE PART THAT DR. ZOMBOSS NEEDS IN ORDER TO COMPLETE HIS SUN VACUUM MACHINE."
TOSS!
OOO! SHINY!
WE CAN'T LET ZOMBOSS GET TO THE PIECE FIRST. WHICH MEANS WE NEED TO STEAL IT FROM CHESTBEARD.
STEAL FROM A PIRATE?
YOU WANT US TO... STEAL...FROM... A...PIRATE?

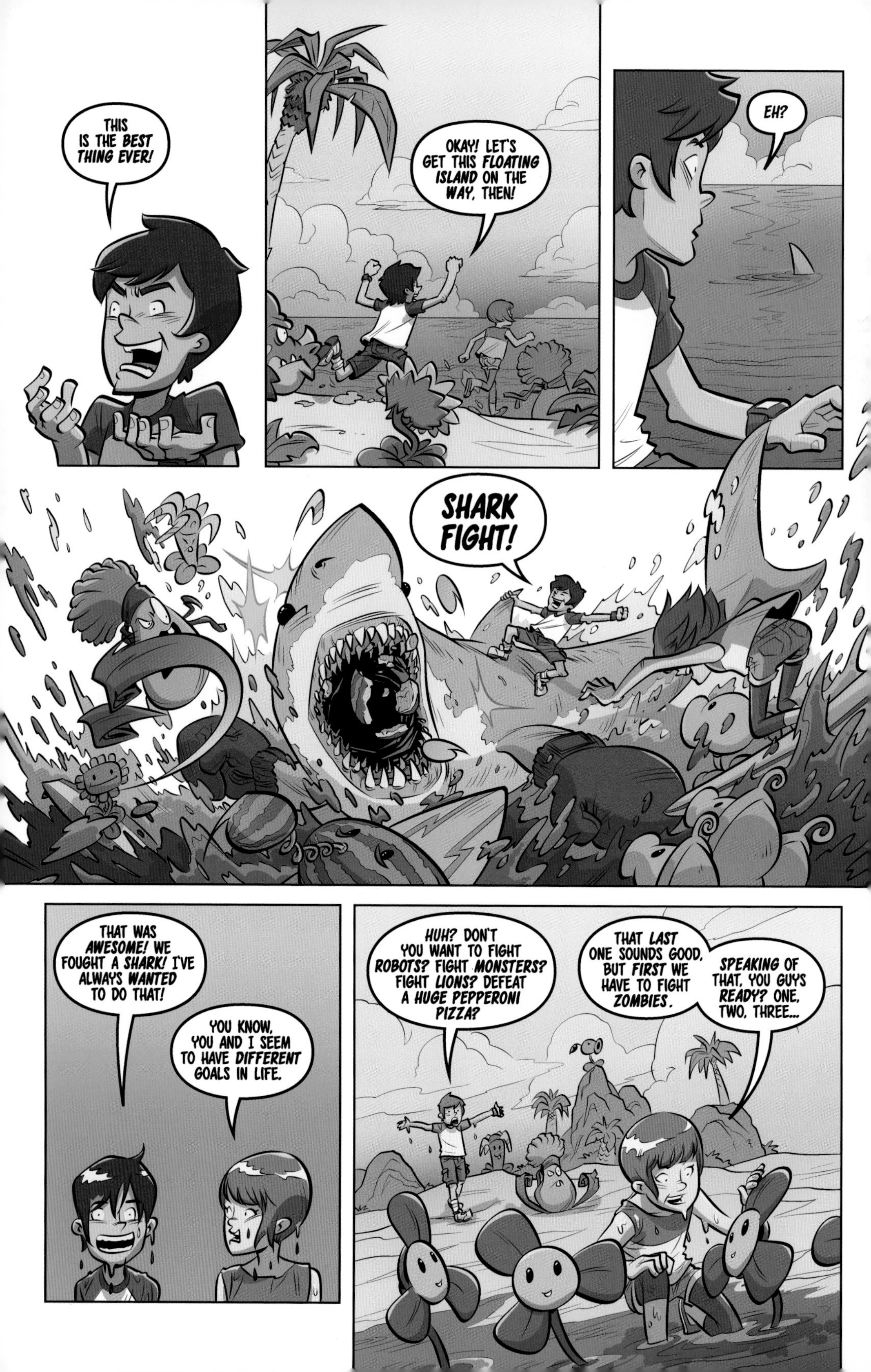
THIS IS THE BEST THING EVER!
OKAY! LET'S GET THIS FLOATING ISLAND ON THE WAY, THEN!
EH?
SHARK FIGHT!
THAT WAS AWESOME! WE FOUGHT A SHARK! I'VE ALWAYS WANTED TO DO THAT!
YOU KNOW, YOU AND I SEEM TO HAVE DIFFERENT GOALS IN LIFE.
HUH? DON'T YOU WANT TO FIGHT ROBOTS? FIGHT MONSTERS? FIGHT LIONS? DEFEAT A HUGE PEPPERONI PIZZA?
THAT LAST ONE SOUNDS GOOD, BUT FIRST WE HAVE TO FIGHT ZOMBIES.
SPEAKING OF THAT, YOU GUYS READY? ONE, TWO, THREE...

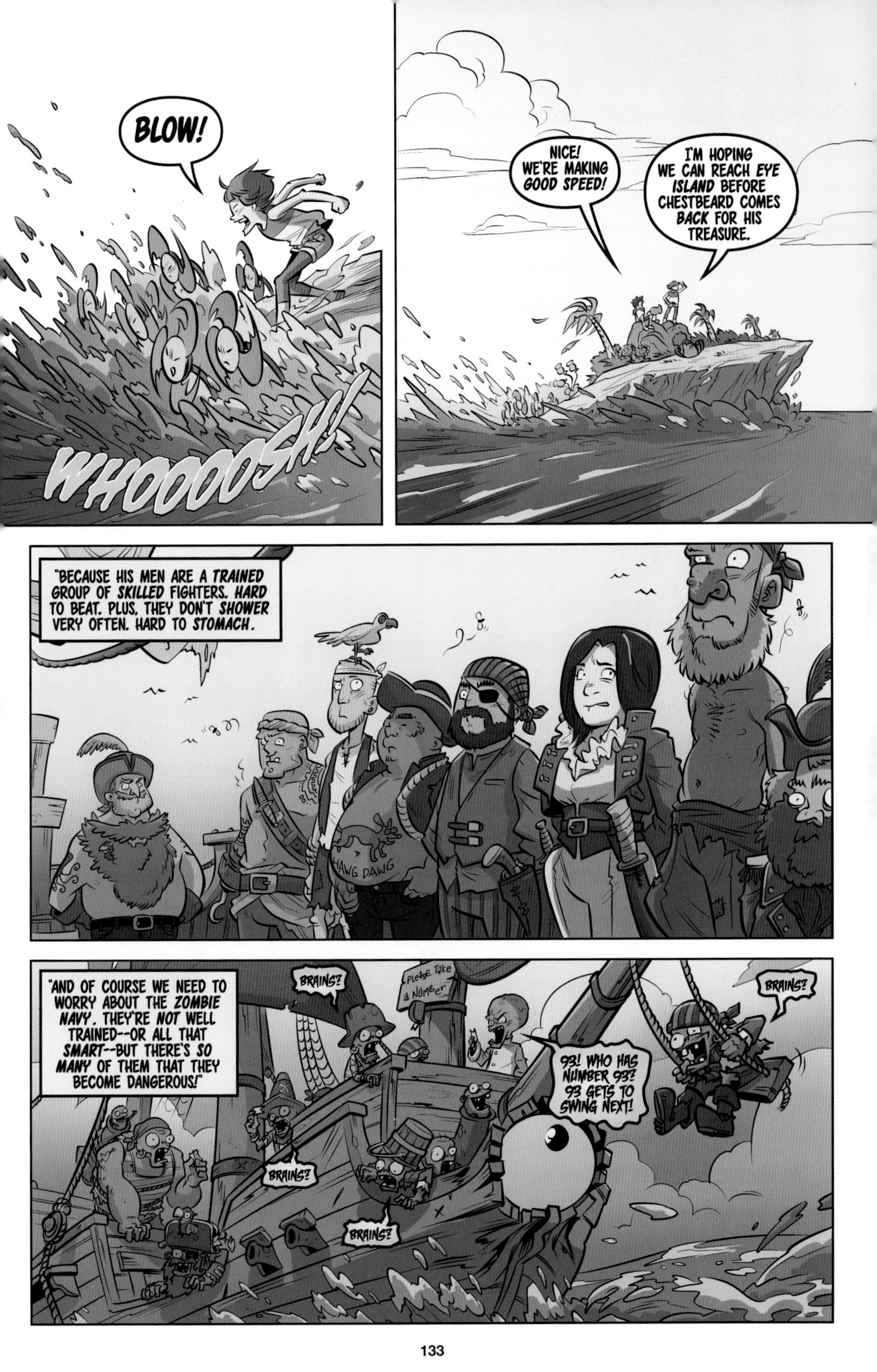
BLOW!
WHOOOOOSH!
NICE! WE'RE MAKING GOOD SPEED!
I'M HOPING WE CAN REACH EYE ISLAND BEFORE CHESTBEARD COMES BACK FOR HIS TREASURE.
"BECAUSE HIS MEN ARE A TRAINED GROUP OF SKILLED FIGHTERS. HARD TO BEAT. PLUS, THEY DON'T SHOWER VERY OFTEN. HARD TO STOMACH.
HAWG DAWG
"AND OF COURSE WE NEED TO WORRY ABOUT THE ZOMBIE NAVY. THEY'RE NOT WELL TRAINED--OR ALL THAT SMART--BUT THERE'S SO MANY OF THEM THAT THEY BECOME DANGEROUS!"
BRAINS?
Please Take a Number
BRAINS?
93! WHO HAS NUMBER 93? 93 GETS TO SWING NEXT!
BRAINS?
BRAINS?

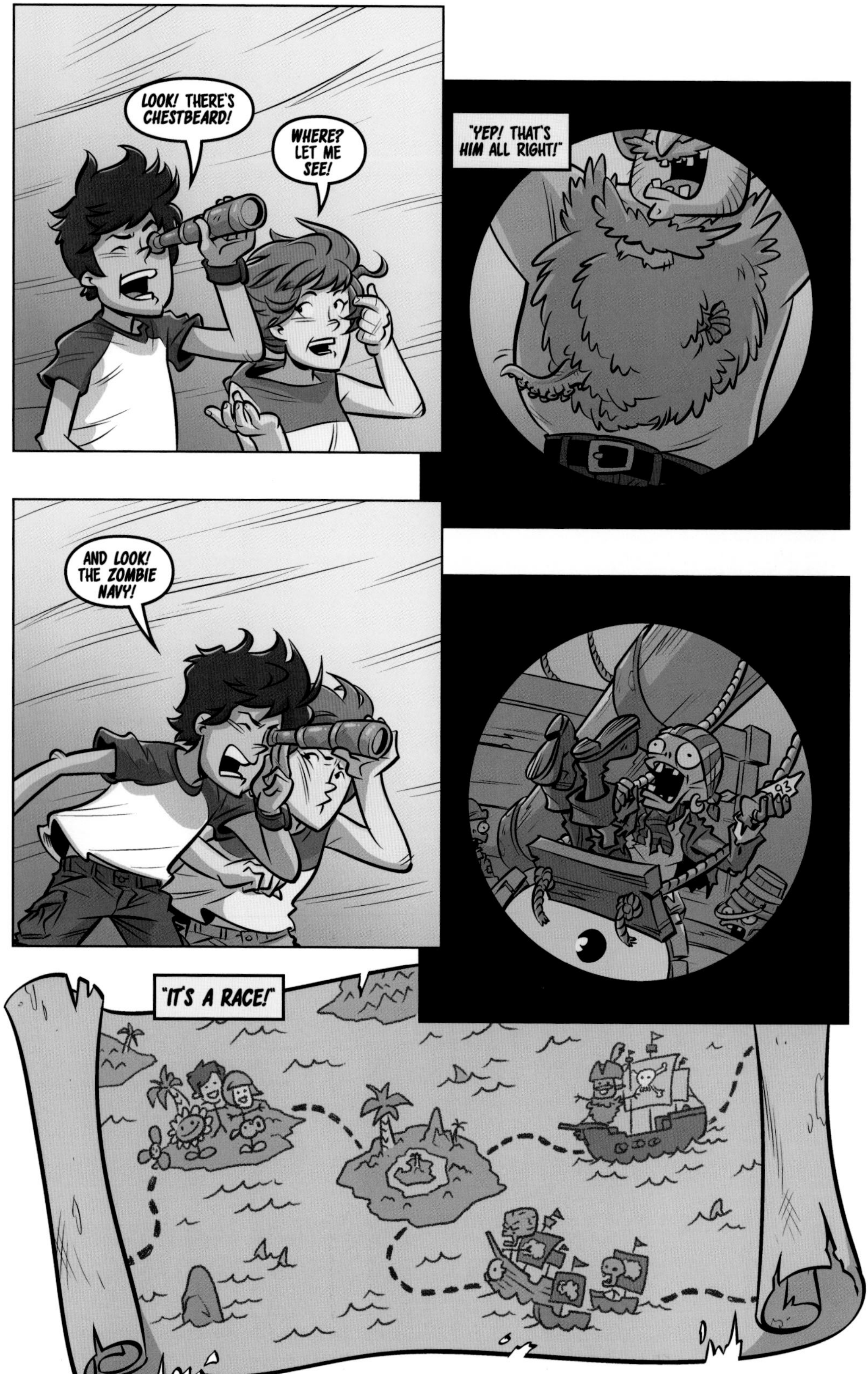
LOOK! THERE'S CHESTBEARD!
WHERE? LET ME SEE!
"YEP! THAT'S HIM ALL RIGHT!"
AND LOOK! THE ZOMBIE NAVY!
"IT'S A RACE!"

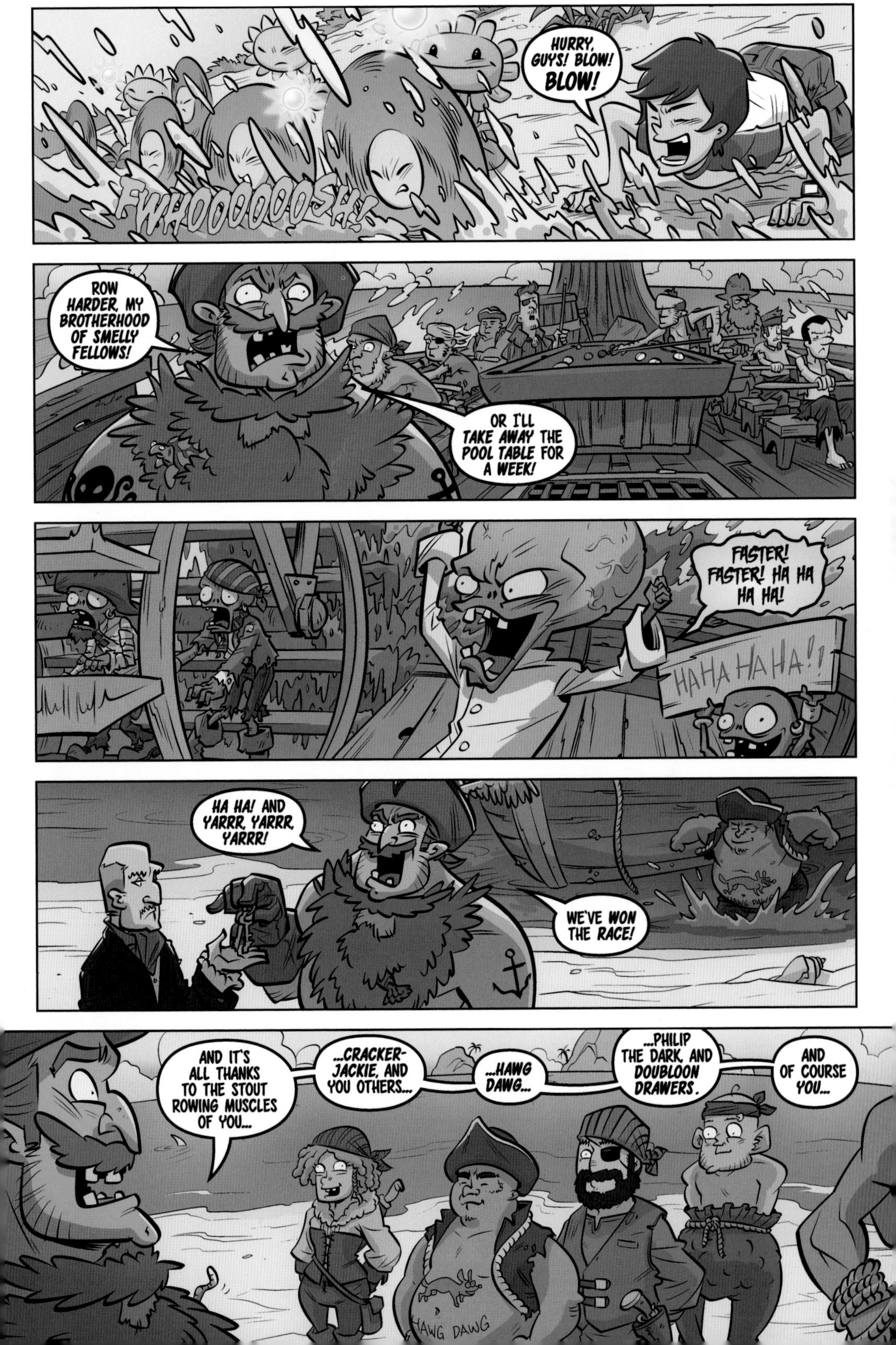
HURRY, GUYS! BLOW! BLOW!
FWHOOOOOOSH!
ROW HARDER, MY BROTHERHOOD OF SMELLY FELLOWS!
OR I'LL TAKE AWAY THE POOL TABLE FOR A WEEK!
FASTER! FASTER! HA HA HA HA!
HAHA HAHA!!
HA HA! AND YARRR, YARRR, YARRR!
WE'VE WON THE RACE!
HAWG DAWG
AND IT'S ALL THANKS TO THE STOUT ROWING MUSCLES OF YOU...
...CRACKER-JACKIE, AND YOU OTHERS...
...HAWG DAWG...
...PHILIP THE DARK, AND DOUBLOON DRAWERS.
AND OF COURSE YOU...
HAWG DAWG

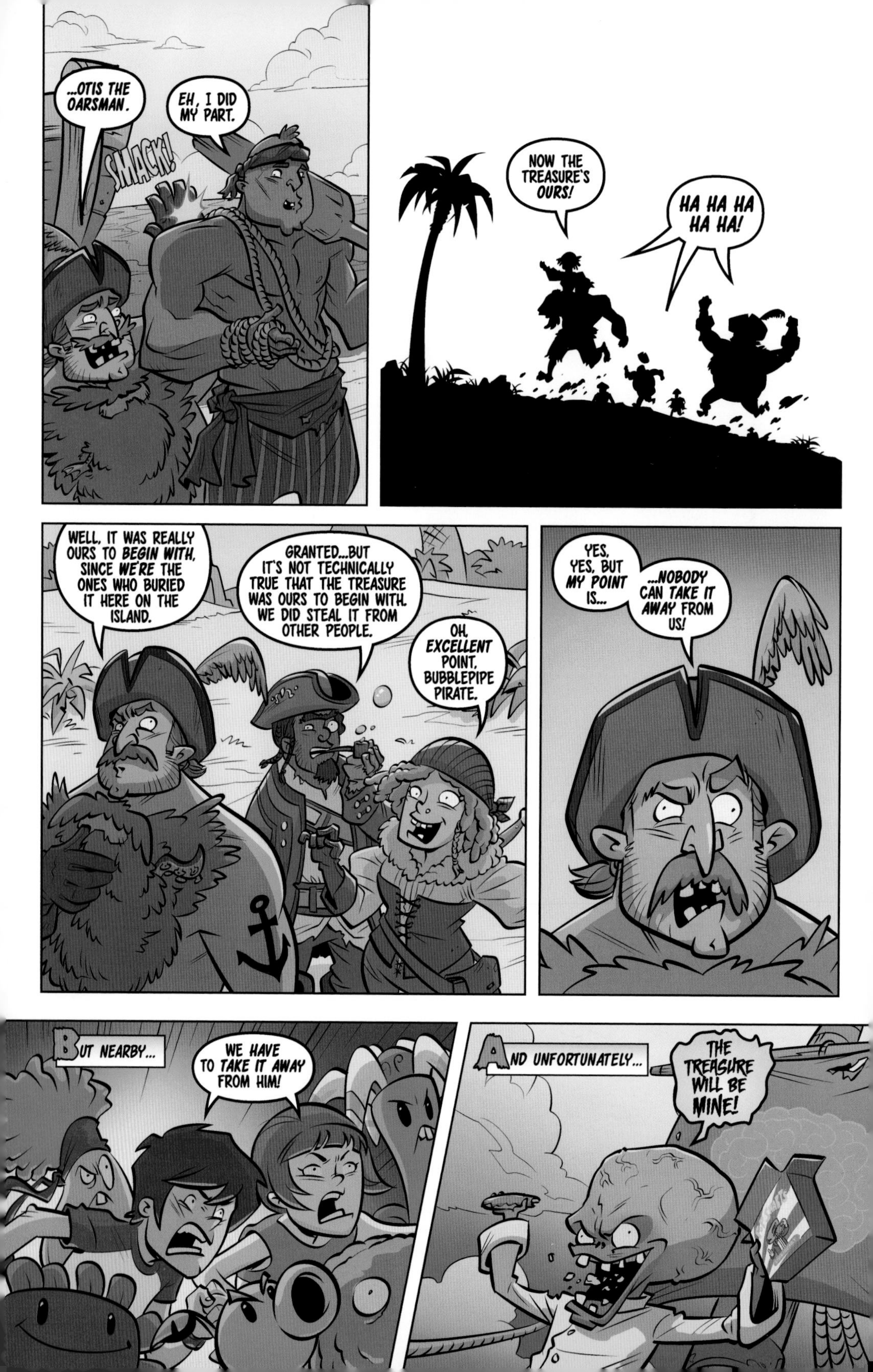
...OTIS THE OARSMAN.
SMACK!
EH, I DID MY PART.
NOW THE TREASURE'S OURS!
HA HA HA HA HA!
WELL, IT WAS REALLY OURS TO BEGIN WITH, SINCE WE'RE THE ONES WHO BURIED IT HERE ON THE ISLAND.
GRANTED...BUT IT'S NOT TECHNICALLY TRUE THAT THE TREASURE WAS OURS TO BEGIN WITH. WE DID STEAL IT FROM OTHER PEOPLE.
OH, EXCELLENT POINT, BUBBLEPIPE PIRATE.
YES, YES, BUT MY POINT IS...
...NOBODY CAN TAKE IT AWAY FROM US!
BUT NEARBY...
WE HAVE TO TAKE IT AWAY FROM HIM!
AND UNFORTUNATELY...
THE TREASURE WILL BE MINE!

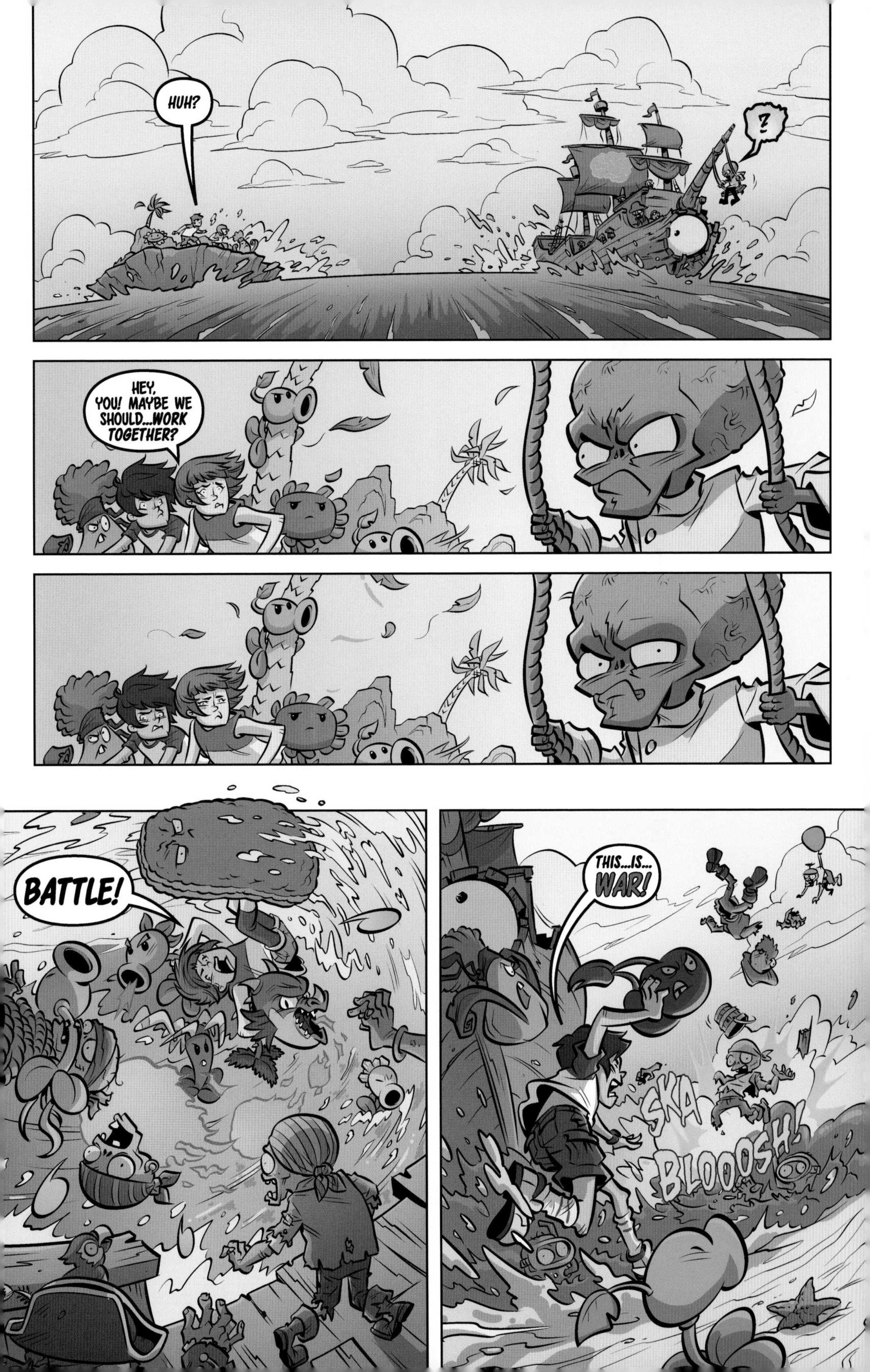
HUH?
?
HEY, YOU! MAYBE WE SHOULD...WORK TOGETHER?
BATTLE!
THIS...IS... WAR!
SKA
BLOOOSH!

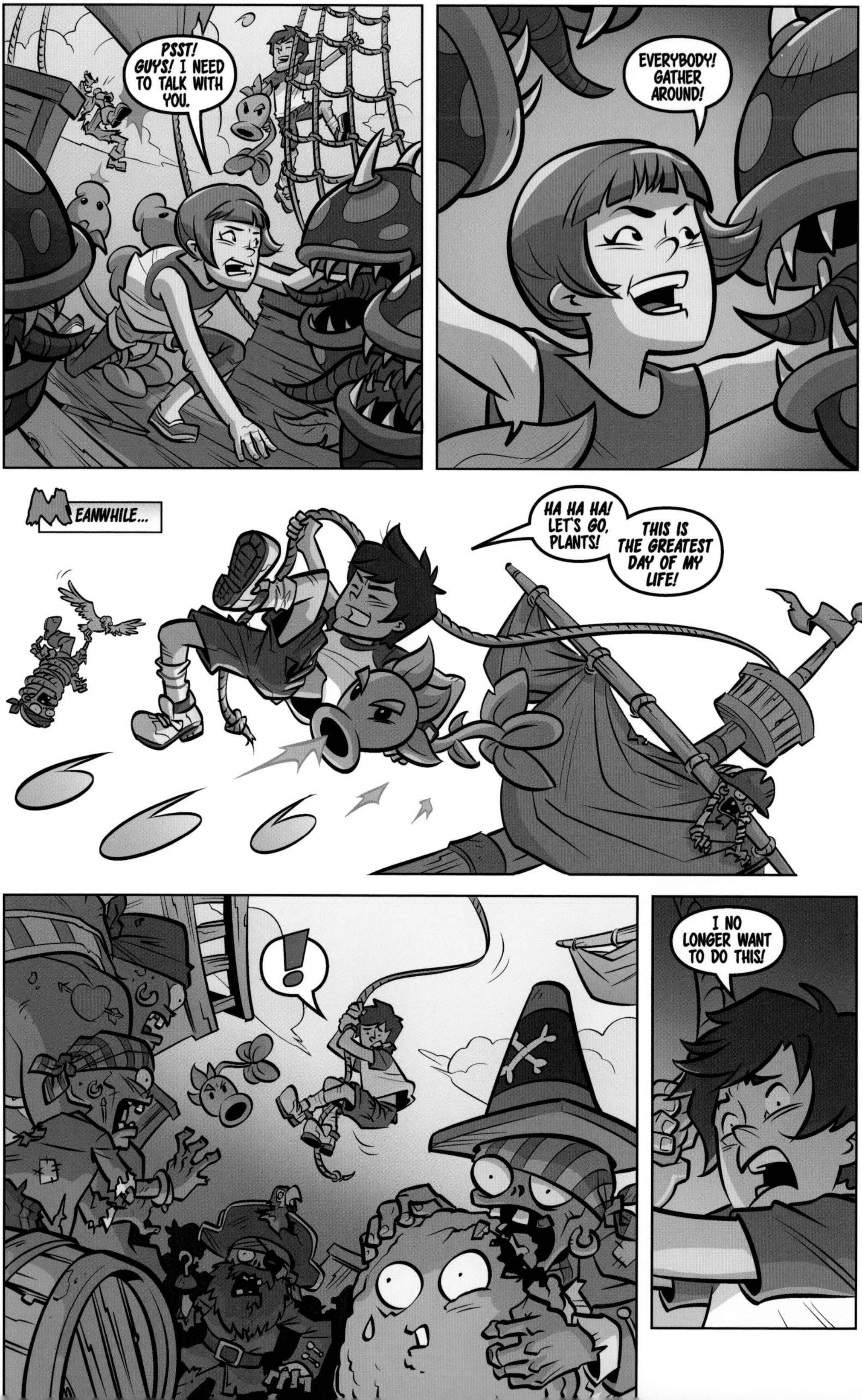
PSST! GUYS! I NEED TO TALK WITH YOU.
EVERYBODY! GATHER AROUND!
MEANWHILE...
HA HA HA! LET'S GO, PLANTS!
THIS IS THE GREATEST DAY OF MY LIFE!
!
I NO LONGER WANT TO DO THIS!

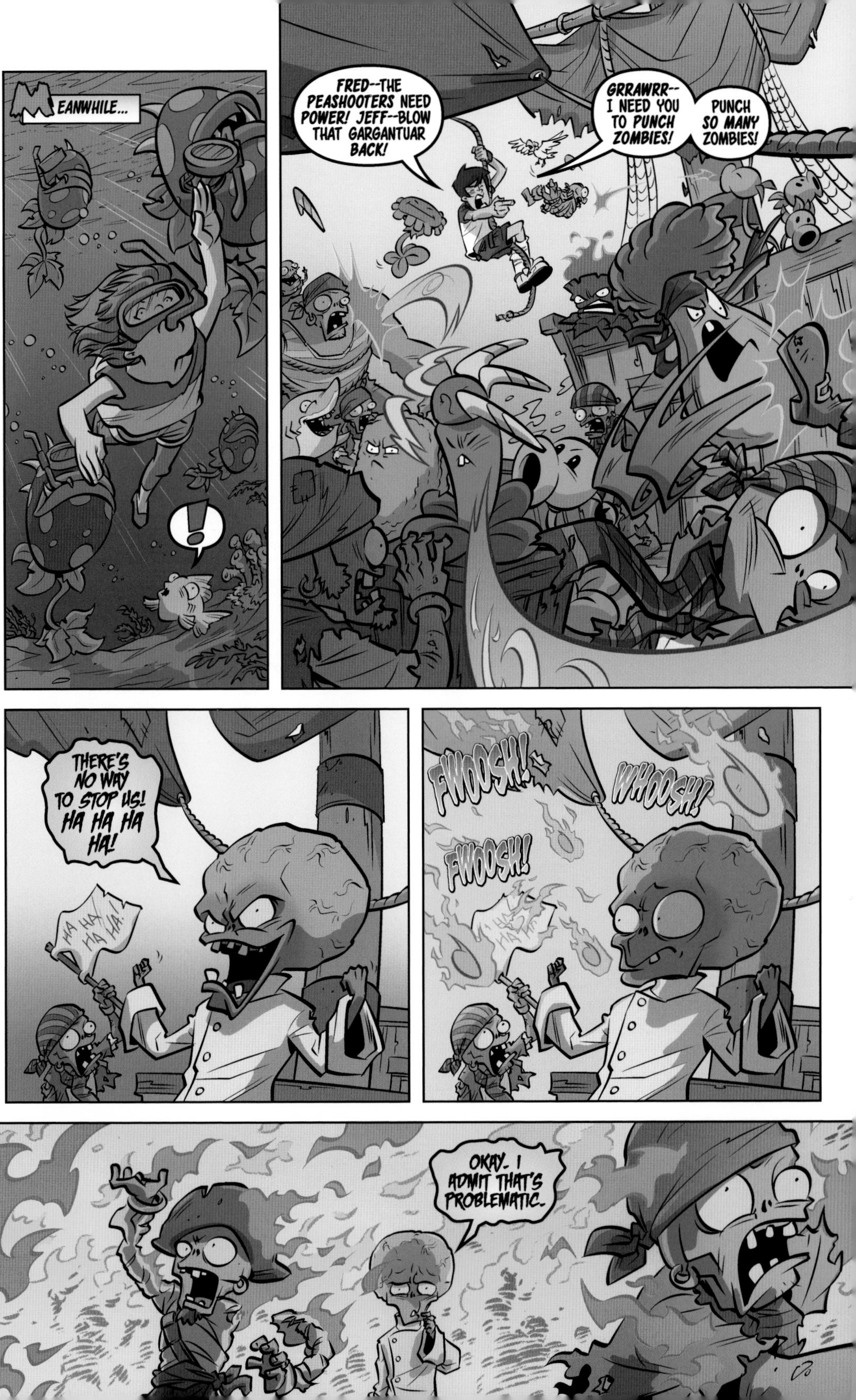
MEANWHILE...
FRED--THE PEASHOOTERS NEED POWER! JEFF--BLOW THAT GARGANTUAR BACK!
GRRAWRR-- I NEED YOU TO PUNCH ZOMBIES!
PUNCH SO MANY ZOMBIES!
!
THERE'S NO WAY TO STOP US! HA HA HA HA!
HA HA HA HA!
FWOOSH!
WHOOSH!
FWOOSH!
OKAY. I ADMIT THAT'S PROBLEMATIC.

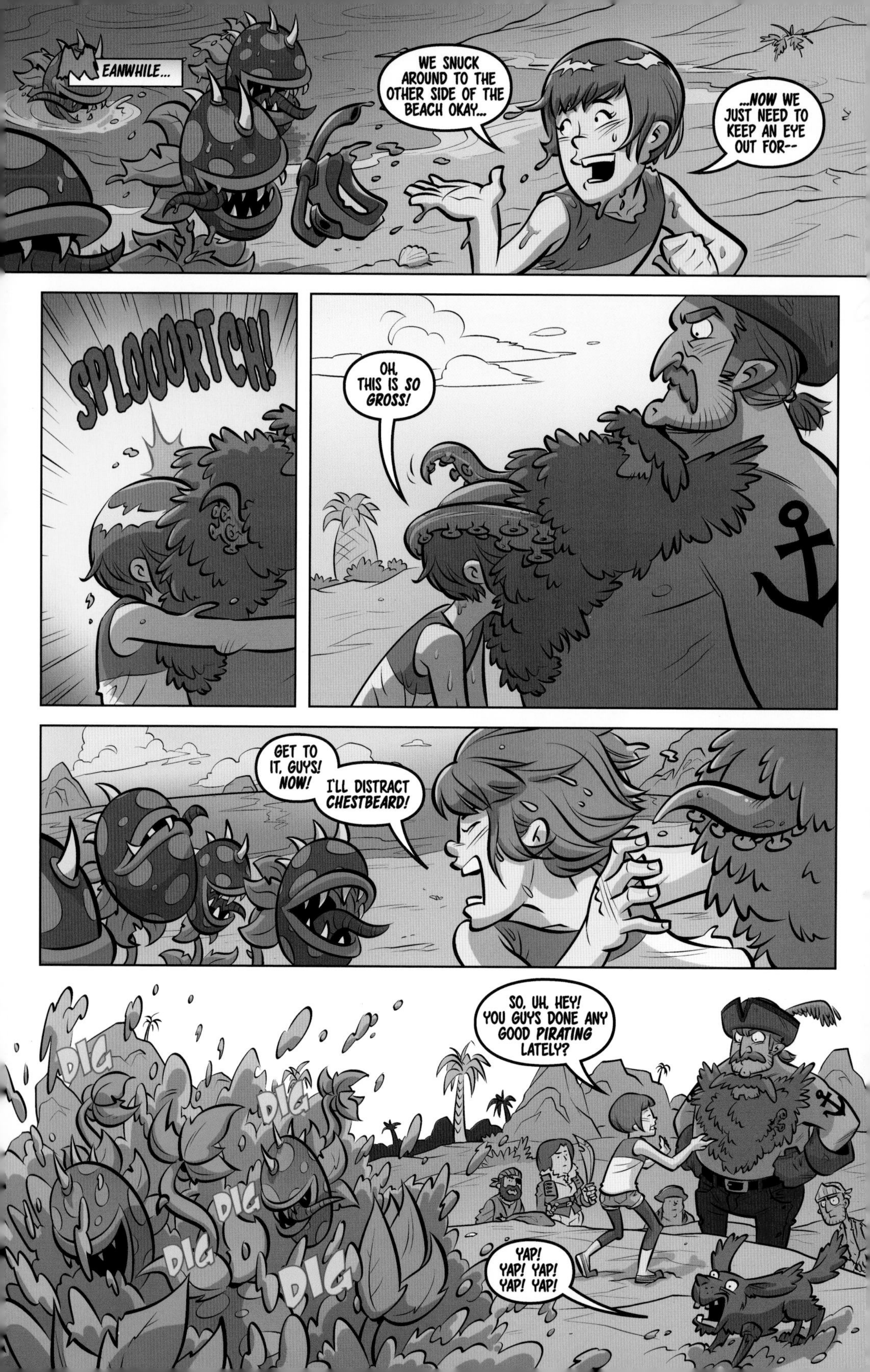
EANWHILE...
WE SNUCK AROUND TO THE OTHER SIDE OF THE BEACH OKAY...
...NOW WE JUST NEED TO KEEP AN EYE OUT FOR--
SPLOOORTCH!
OH, THIS IS SO GROSS!
GET TO IT, GUYS! NOW!
I'LL DISTRACT CHESTBEARD!
DIG
DIG
DIG
DIG
DIG
SO, UH, HEY! YOU GUYS DONE ANY GOOD PIRATING LATELY?
YAP! YAP! YAP! YAP! YAP!

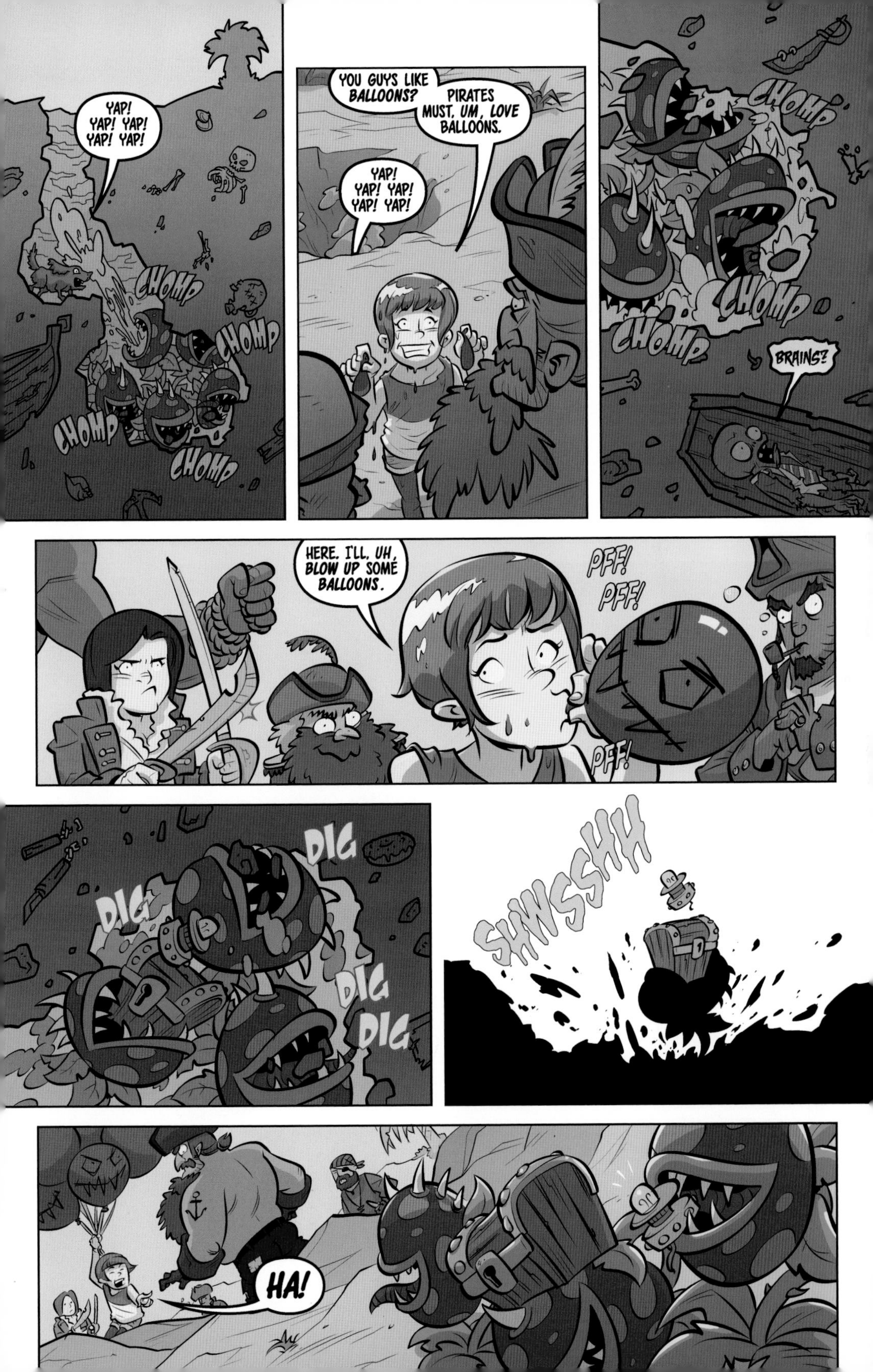
YAP! YAP! YAP! YAP! YAP!
CHOMP
CHOMP
CHOMP
CHOMP
YOU GUYS LIKE BALLOONS?
PIRATES MUST, UM, LOVE BALLOONS.
YAP! YAP! YAP! YAP! YAP!
CHOMP
CHOMP
CHOMP
BRAINS?
HERE. I'LL, UH, BLOW UP SOME BALLOONS.
PFF!
PFF!
PFF!
DIG
DIG
DIG
DIG
SHWSSHH
HA!

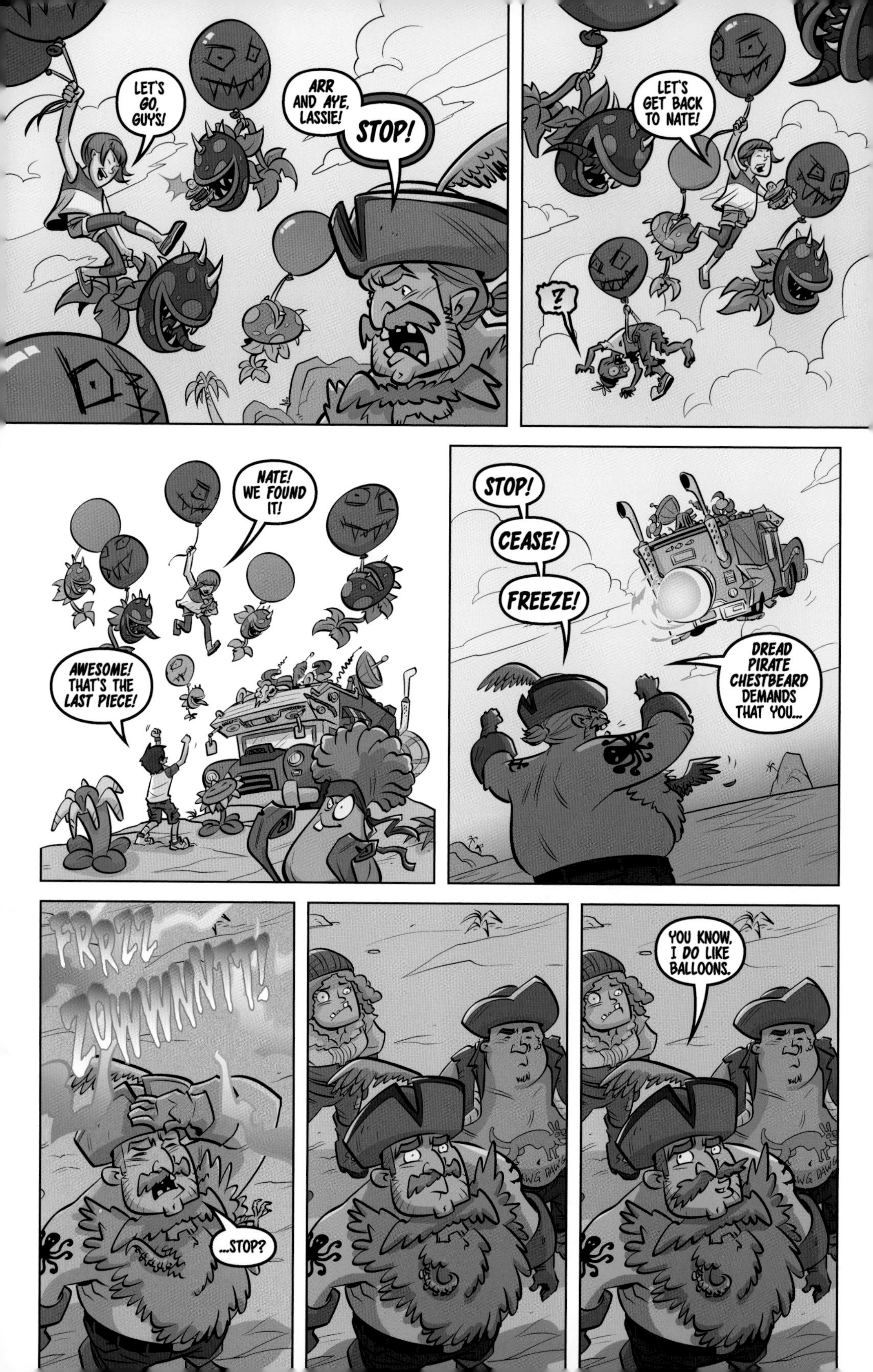
LET'S GO, GUYS!
ARR AND AYE, LASSIE!
STOP!
LET'S GET BACK TO NATE!
?
NATE! WE FOUND IT!
AWESOME! THAT'S THE LAST PIECE!
STOP!
CEASE!
FREEZE!
DREAD PIRATE CHESTBEARD DEMANDS THAT YOU...
FRRZZ ZOWWNNTT!
...STOP?
YOU KNOW, I DO LIKE BALLOONS.

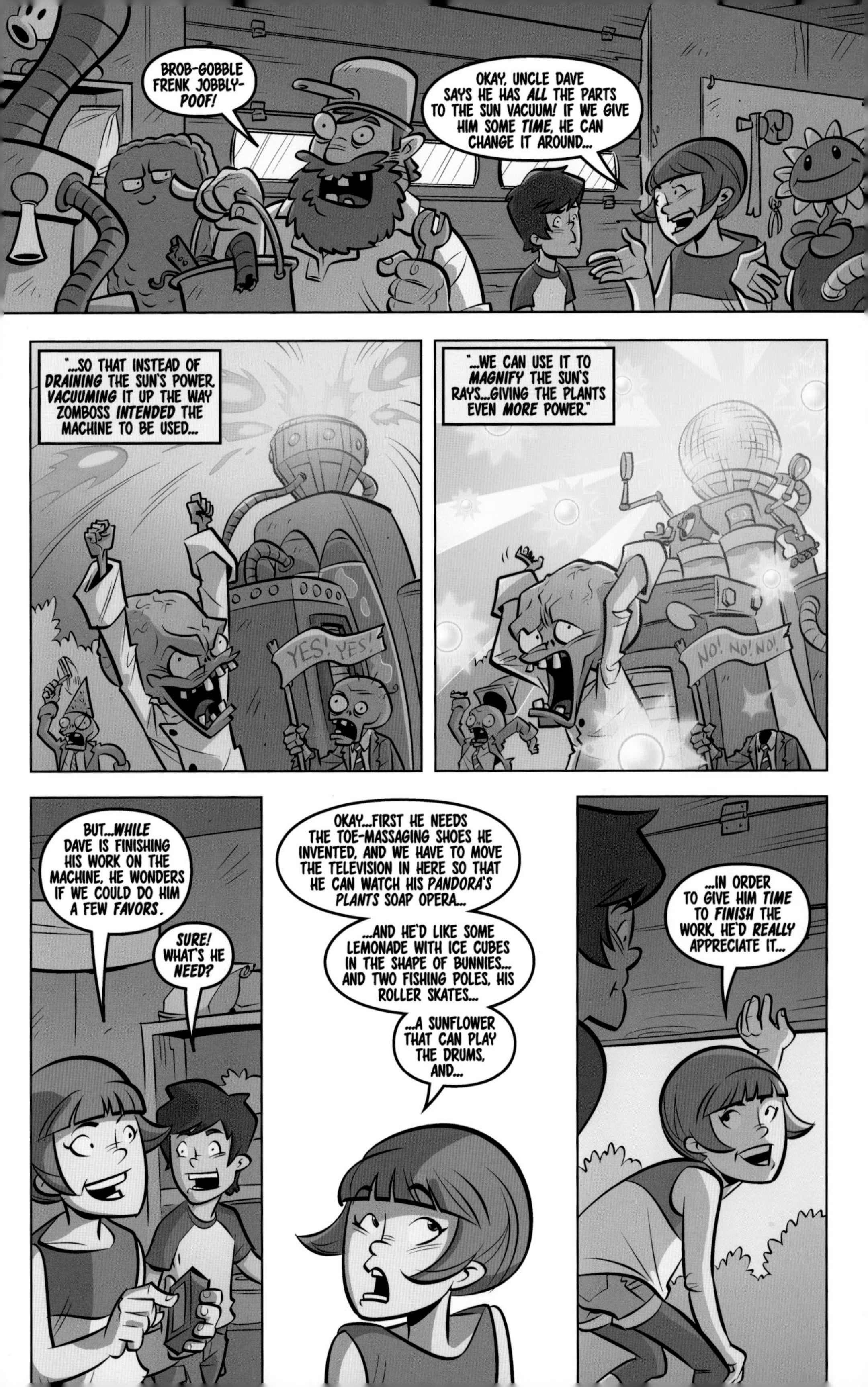
BROB-GOBBLE FRENK JOBBLY-POOF!
OKAY, UNCLE DAVE SAYS HE HAS ALL THE PARTS TO THE SUN VACUUM! IF WE GIVE HIM SOME TIME, HE CAN CHANGE IT AROUND...
"...SO THAT INSTEAD OF DRAINING THE SUN'S POWER, VACUUMING IT UP THE WAY ZOMBOSS INTENDED THE MACHINE TO BE USED...
YES! YES!
"...WE CAN USE IT TO MAGNIFY THE SUN'S RAYS...GIVING THE PLANTS EVEN MORE POWER."
NO! NO! NO!
BUT...WHILE DAVE IS FINISHING HIS WORK ON THE MACHINE, HE WONDERS IF WE COULD DO HIM A FEW FAVORS.
SURE! WHAT'S HE NEED?
OKAY...FIRST HE NEEDS THE TOE-MASSAGING SHOES HE INVENTED, AND WE HAVE TO MOVE THE TELEVISION IN HERE SO THAT HE CAN WATCH HIS PANDORA'S PLANTS SOAP OPERA...
...AND HE'D LIKE SOME LEMONADE WITH ICE CUBES IN THE SHAPE OF BUNNIES... AND TWO FISHING POLES, HIS ROLLER SKATES...
...A SUNFLOWER THAT CAN PLAY THE DRUMS, AND...
...IN ORDER TO GIVE HIM TIME TO FINISH THE WORK, HE'D REALLY APPRECIATE IT...

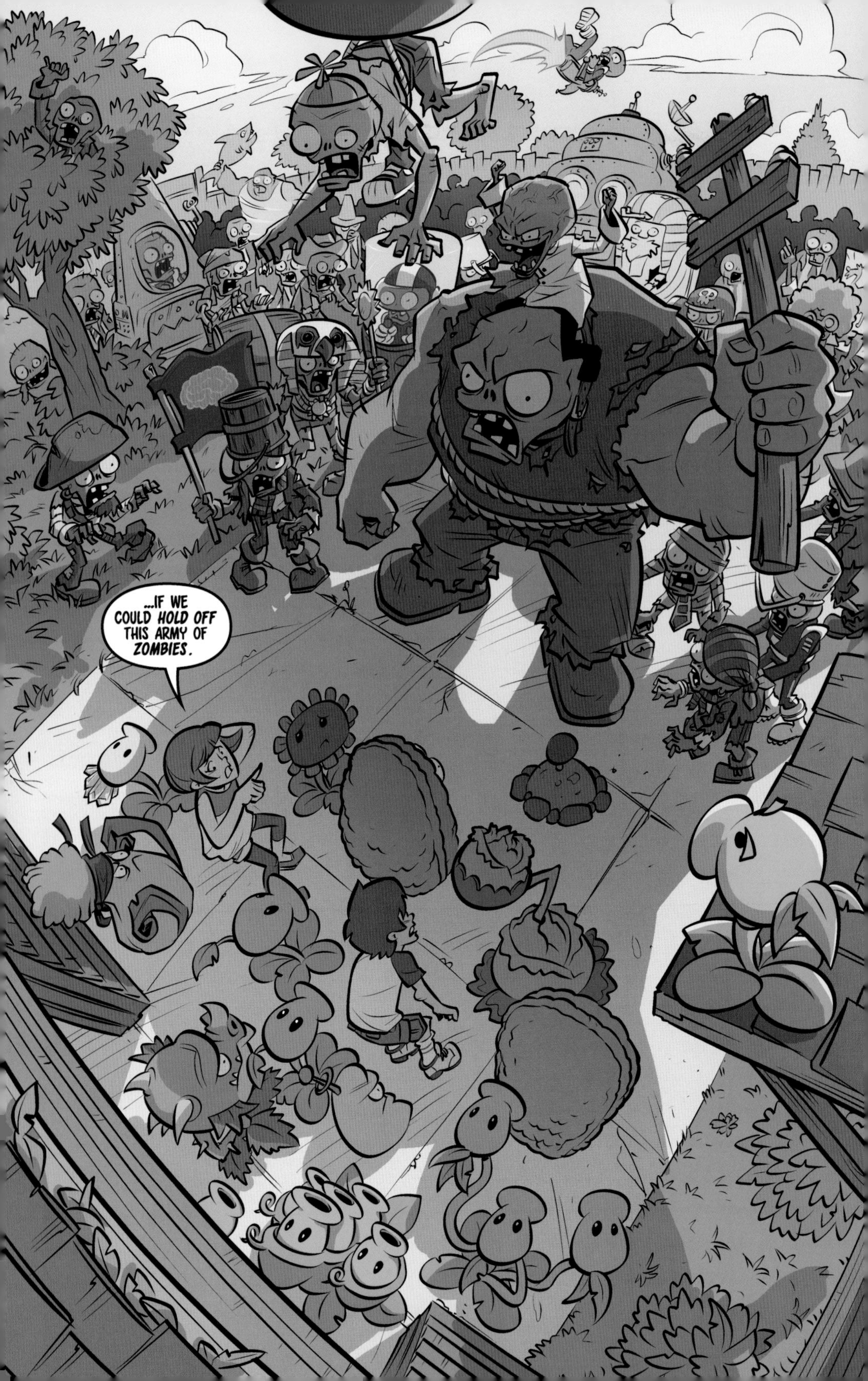
...IF WE COULD HOLD OFF THIS ARMY OF ZOMBIES.

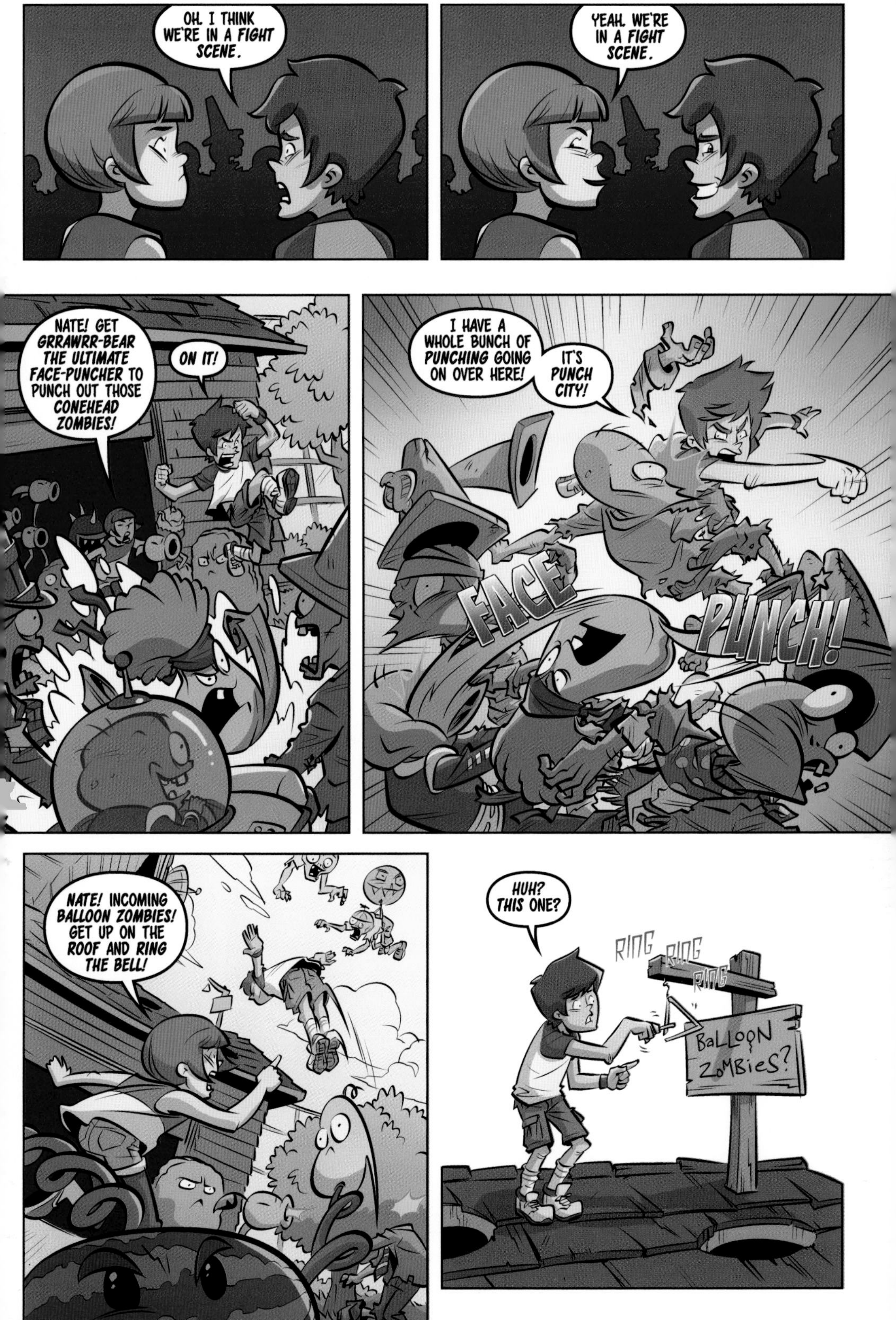
OH. I THINK WE'RE IN A FIGHT SCENE.
YEAH. WE'RE IN A FIGHT SCENE.
NATE! GET GRRAWRR-BEAR THE ULTIMATE FACE-PUNCHER TO PUNCH OUT THOSE CONEHEAD ZOMBIES!
ON IT!
I HAVE A WHOLE BUNCH OF PUNCHING GOING ON OVER HERE!
IT'S PUNCH CITY!
FACE
PUNCH!
NATE! INCOMING BALLOON ZOMBIES! GET UP ON THE ROOF AND RING THE BELL!
HUH? THIS ONE?
RING RING RING
BALLOON ZOMBIES?

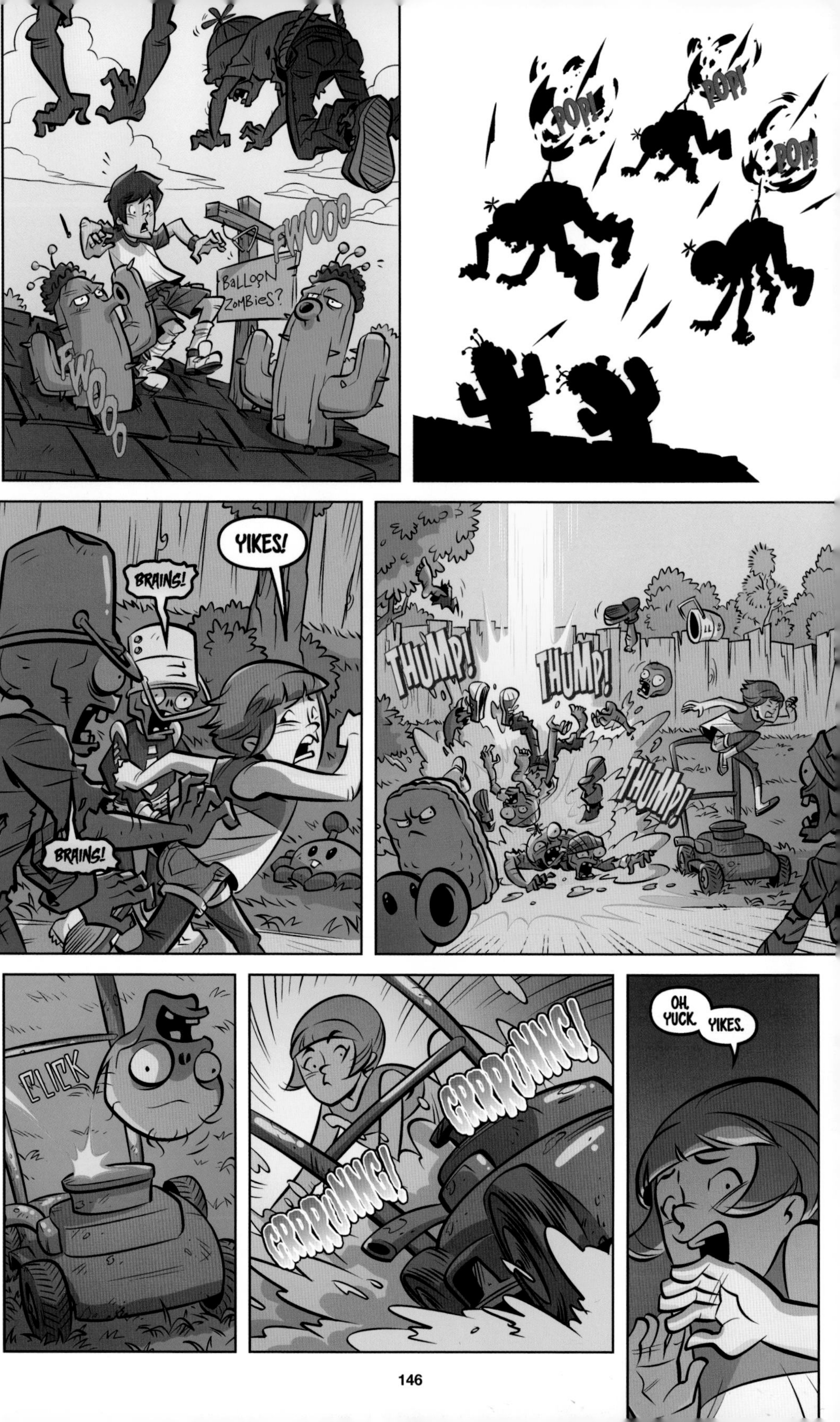
FWOOO
BALLOON ZOMBIES?
FWOOO
POP!
POP!
POP!
BRAINS!
YIKES!
BRAINS!
THUMP!
THUMP!
THUMP!
CLICK
CRRRUNNG!
CRRRUNNG!
OH, YUCK.
YIKES.

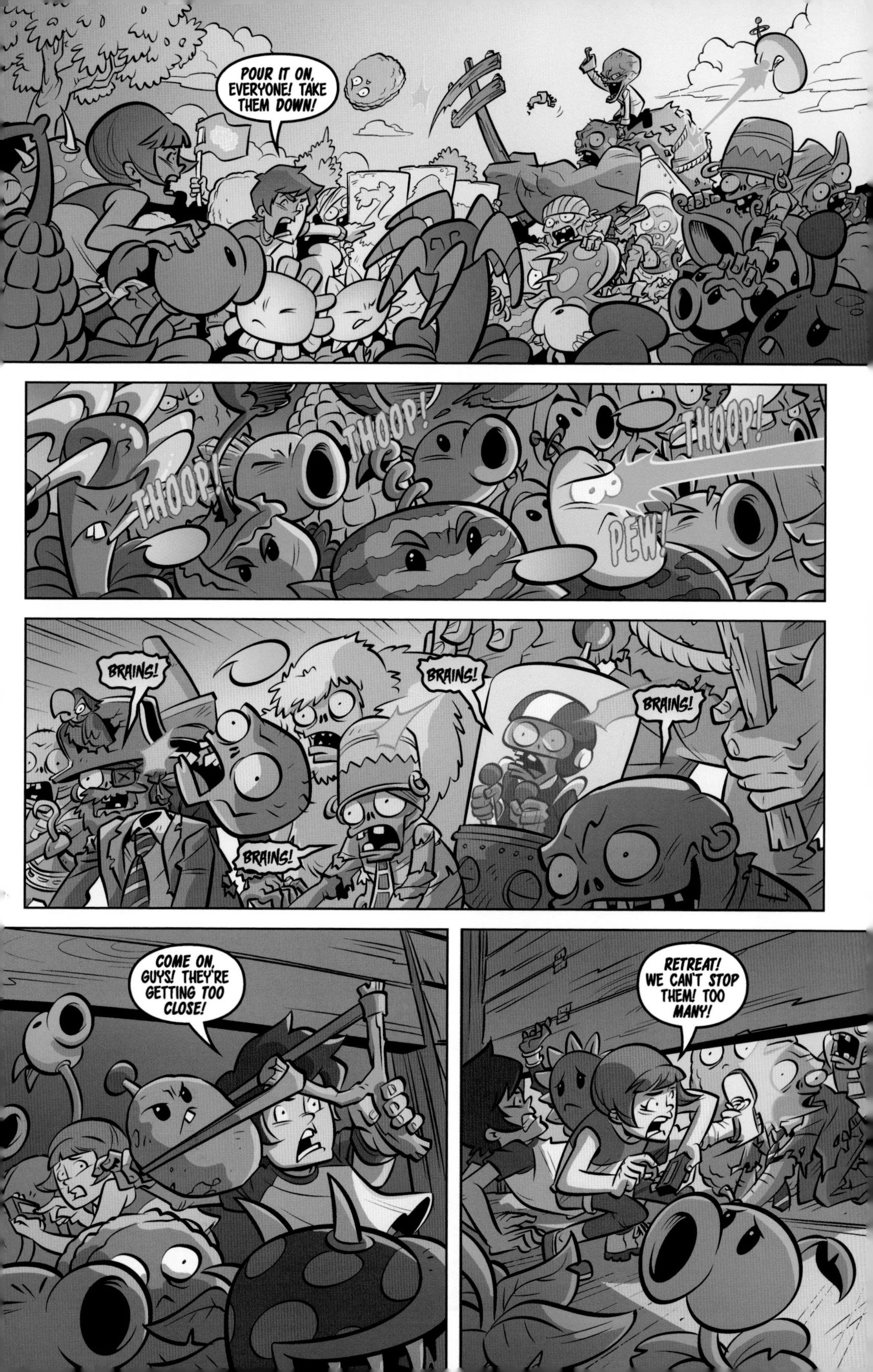
POUR IT ON, EVERYONE! TAKE THEM DOWN!
THOOP!
THOOP!
THOOP!
PEW!
BRAINS!
BRAINS!
BRAINS!
BRAINS!
COME ON, GUYS! THEY'RE GETTING TOO CLOSE!
RETREAT! WE CAN'T STOP THEM! TOO MANY!

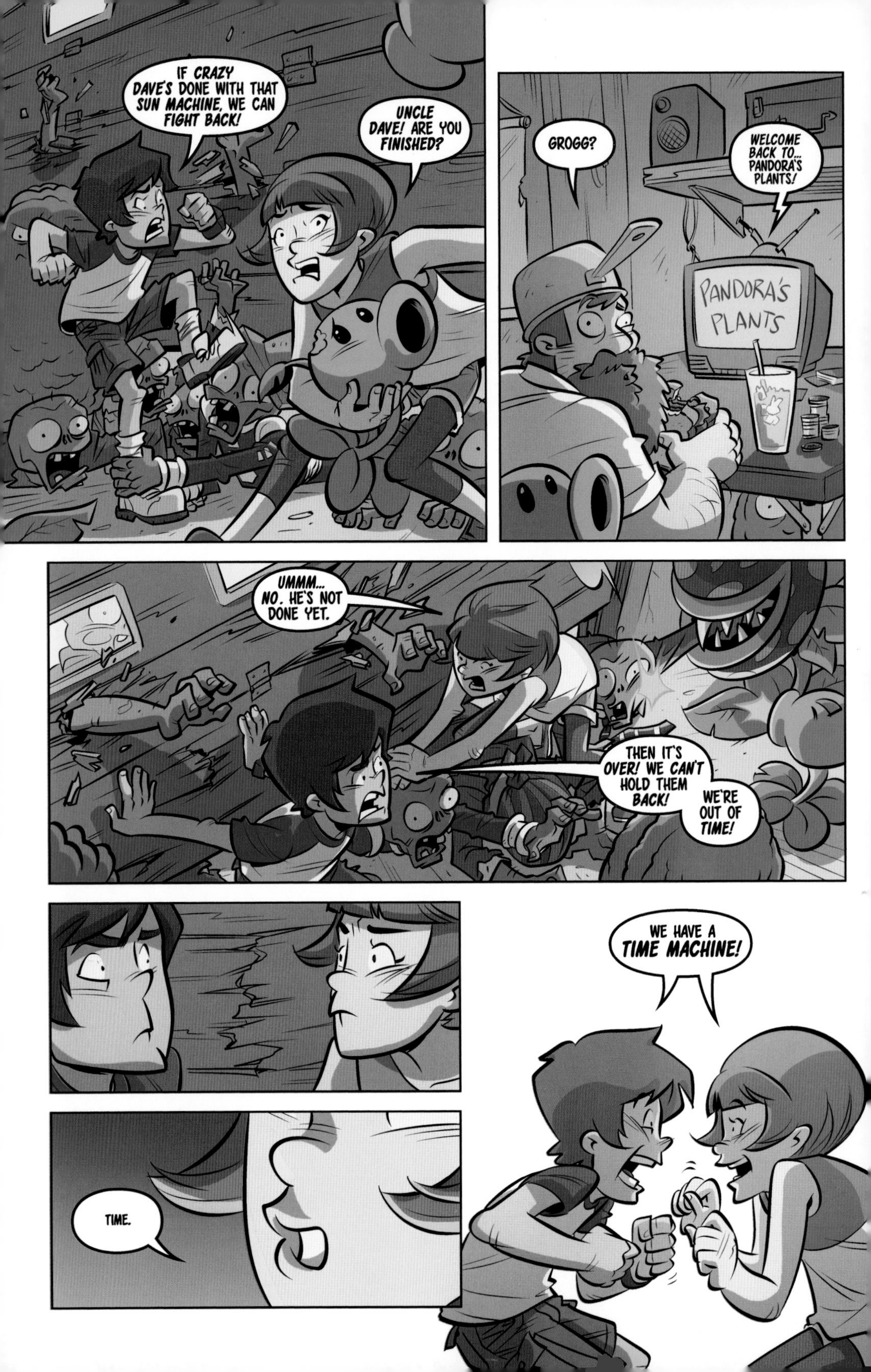
IF CRAZY DAVE'S DONE WITH THAT SUN MACHINE, WE CAN FIGHT BACK!
UNCLE DAVE! ARE YOU FINISHED?
GROGG?
WELCOME BACK TO... PANDORA'S PLANTS!
PANDORA'S PLANTS
UMMM... NO. HE'S NOT DONE YET.
THEN IT'S OVER! WE CAN'T HOLD THEM BACK!
WE'RE OUT OF TIME!
TIME.
WE HAVE A TIME MACHINE!

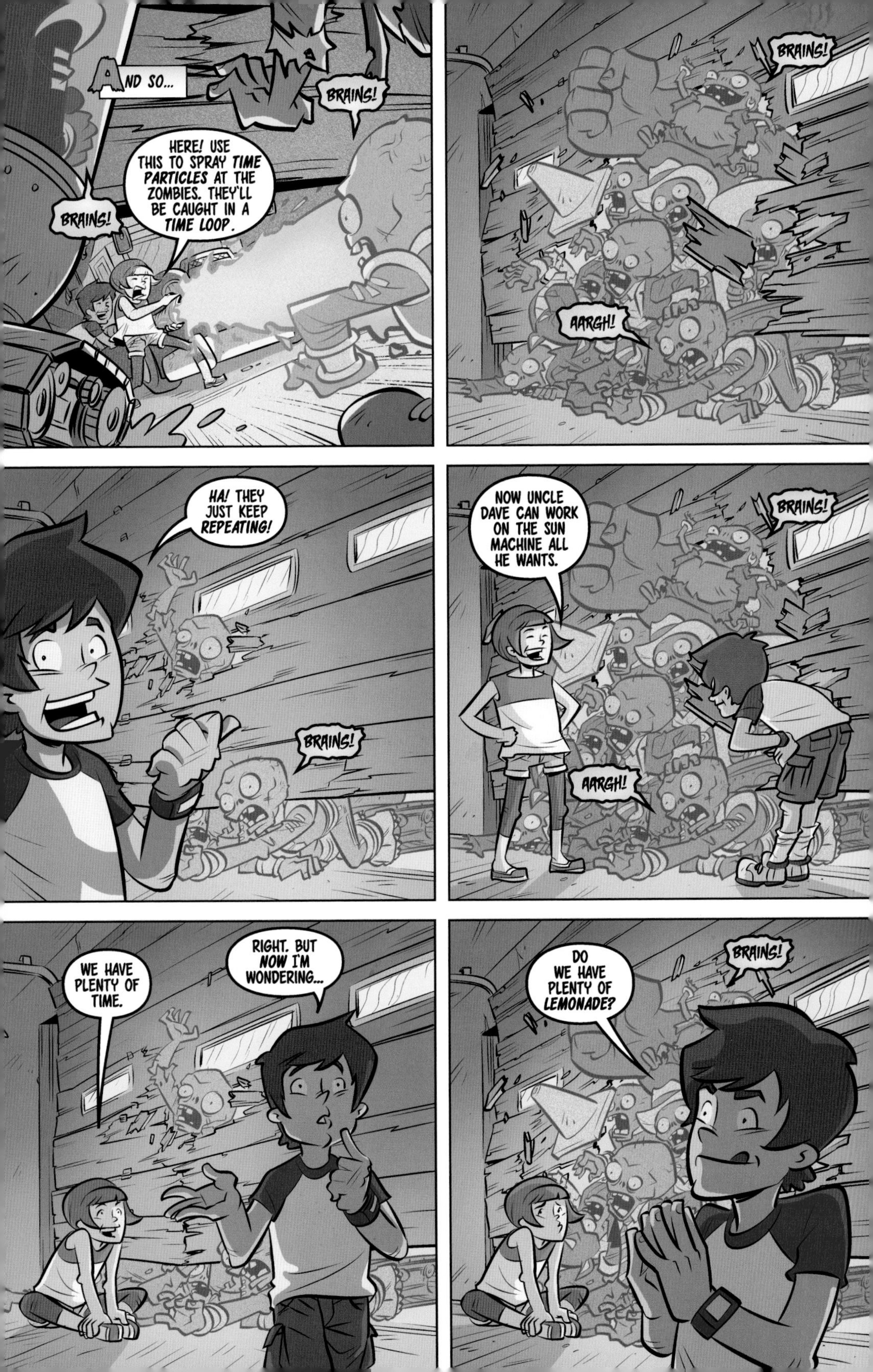
AND SO...
BRAINS!
HERE! USE THIS TO SPRAY TIME PARTICLES AT THE ZOMBIES. THEY'LL BE CAUGHT IN A TIME LOOP.
BRAINS!
BRAINS!
AARGH!
HA! THEY JUST KEEP REPEATING!
BRAINS!
NOW UNCLE DAVE CAN WORK ON THE SUN MACHINE ALL HE WANTS.
BRAINS!
AARGH!
WE HAVE PLENTY OF TIME.
RIGHT. BUT NOW I'M WONDERING...
DO WE HAVE PLENTY OF LEMONADE?
BRAINS!

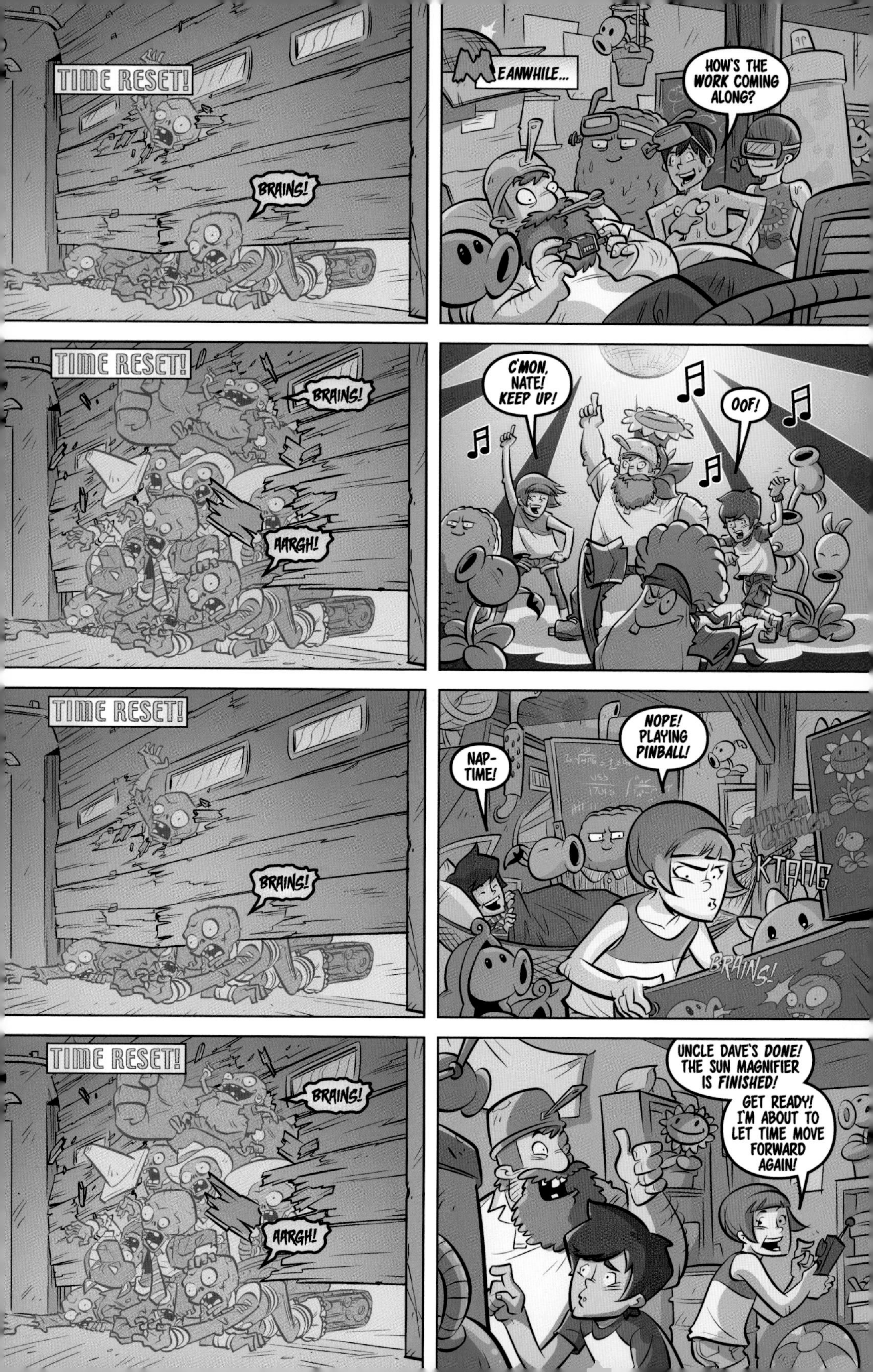
TIME RESET!
BRAINS!
MEANWHILE...
HOW'S THE WORK COMING ALONG?
TIME RESET!
BRAINS!
AARGH!
C'MON, NATE! KEEP UP!
OOF!
TIME RESET!
BRAINS!
NAP-TIME!
NOPE! PLAYING PINBALL!
KTANG
BRAINS!
TIME RESET!
BRAINS!
AARGH!
UNCLE DAVE'S DONE! THE SUN MAGNIFIER IS FINISHED!
GET READY! I'M ABOUT TO LET TIME MOVE FORWARD AGAIN!

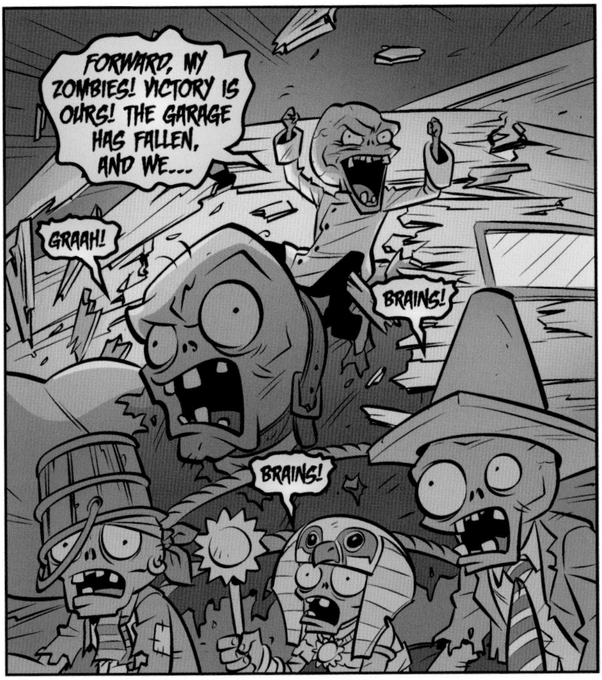
FORWARD, MY ZOMBIES! VICTORY IS OURS! THE GARAGE HAS FALLEN, AND WE...
GRAAH!
BRAINS!
BRAINS!

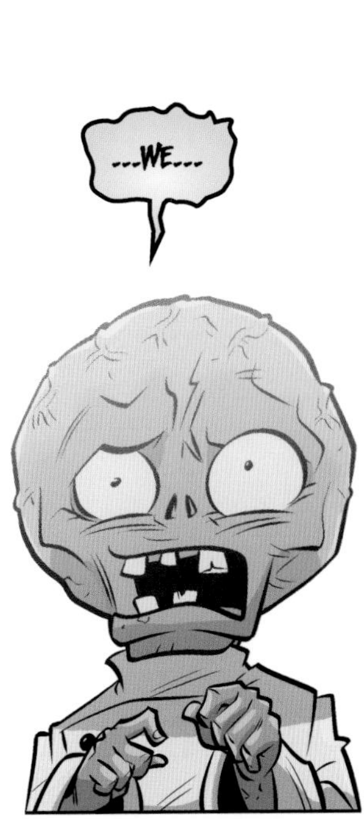
...WE...

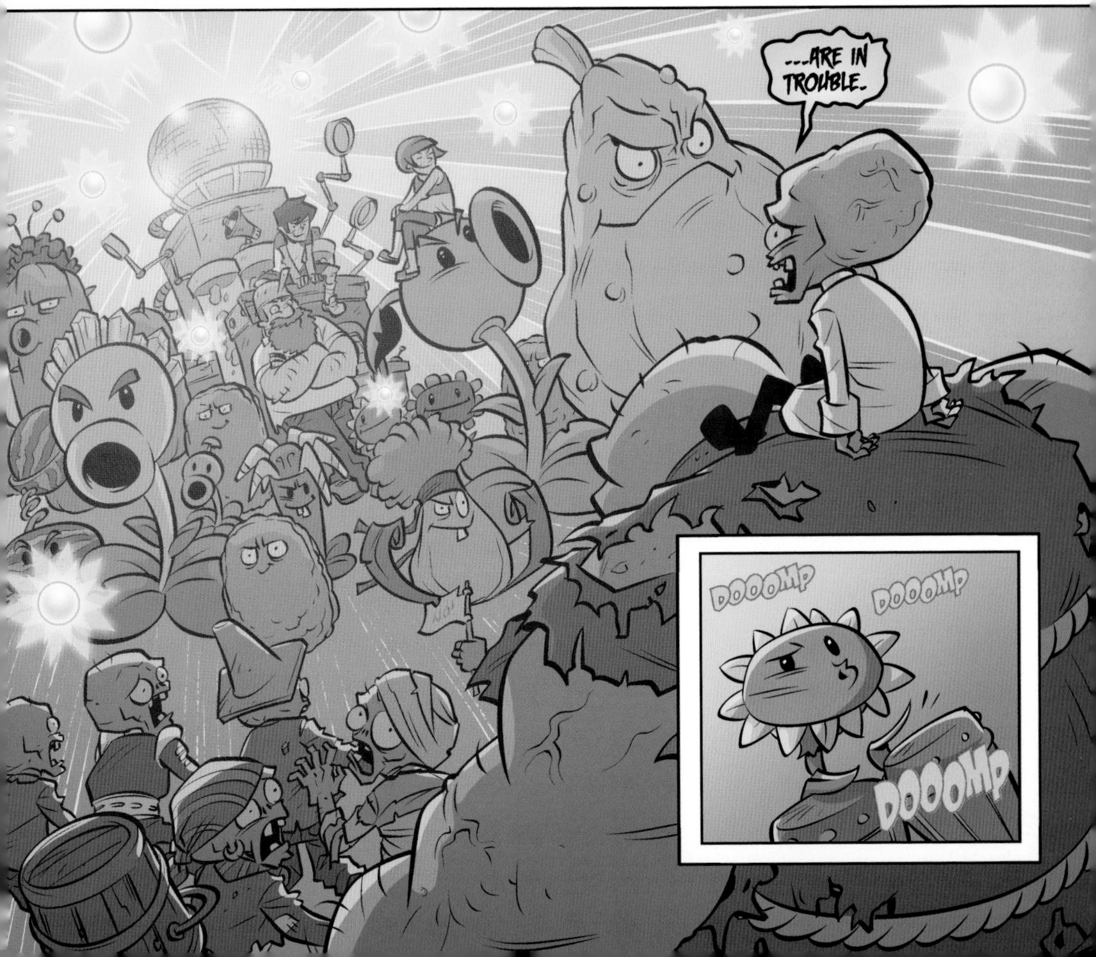
...ARE IN TROUBLE.
DOOOMP
DOOOMP
DOOOMP

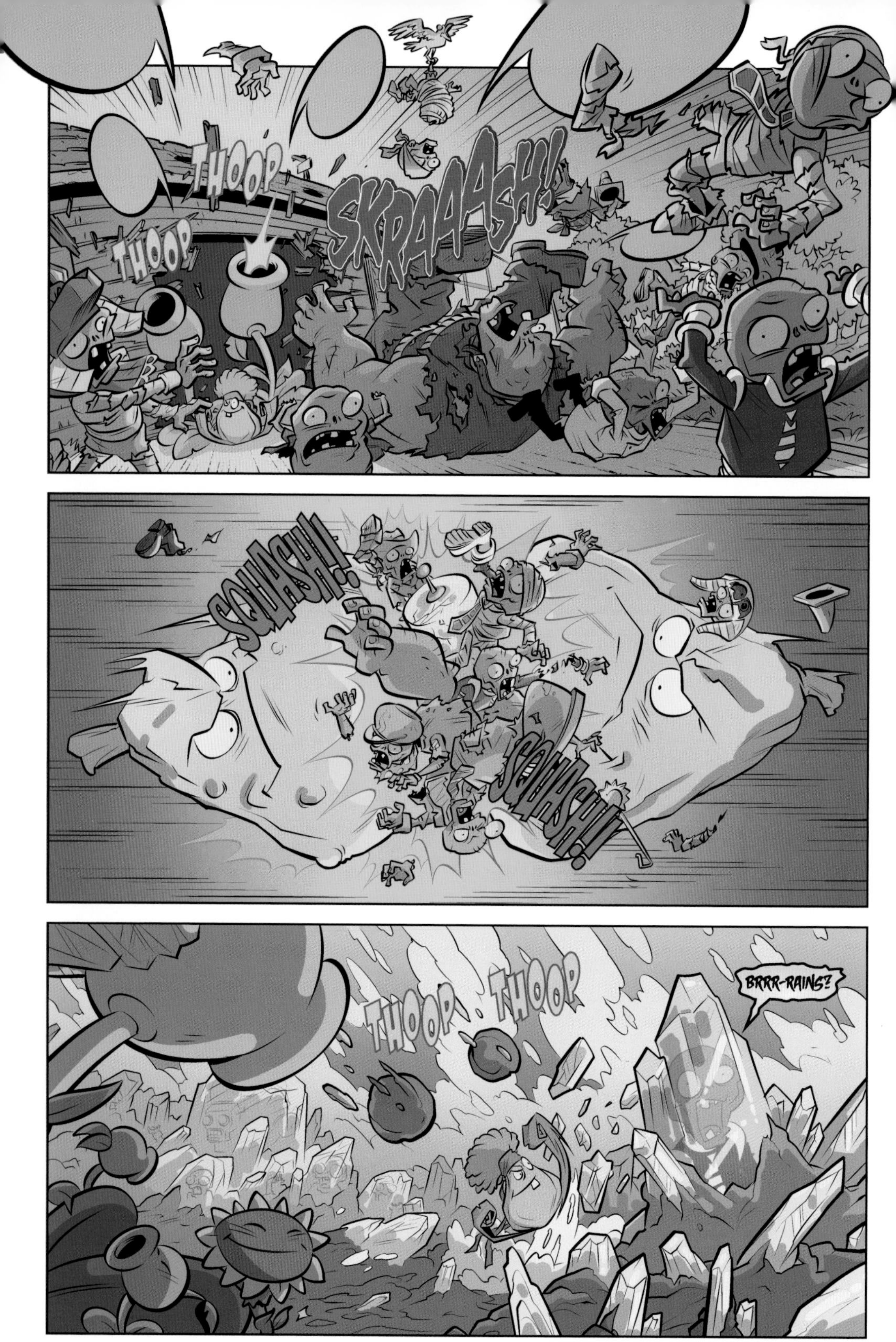
THOOP
THOOP
SKRAAAASH!!
SQUASH!!
SQUASH!!
THOOP
THOOP
BRRR-RAINS?

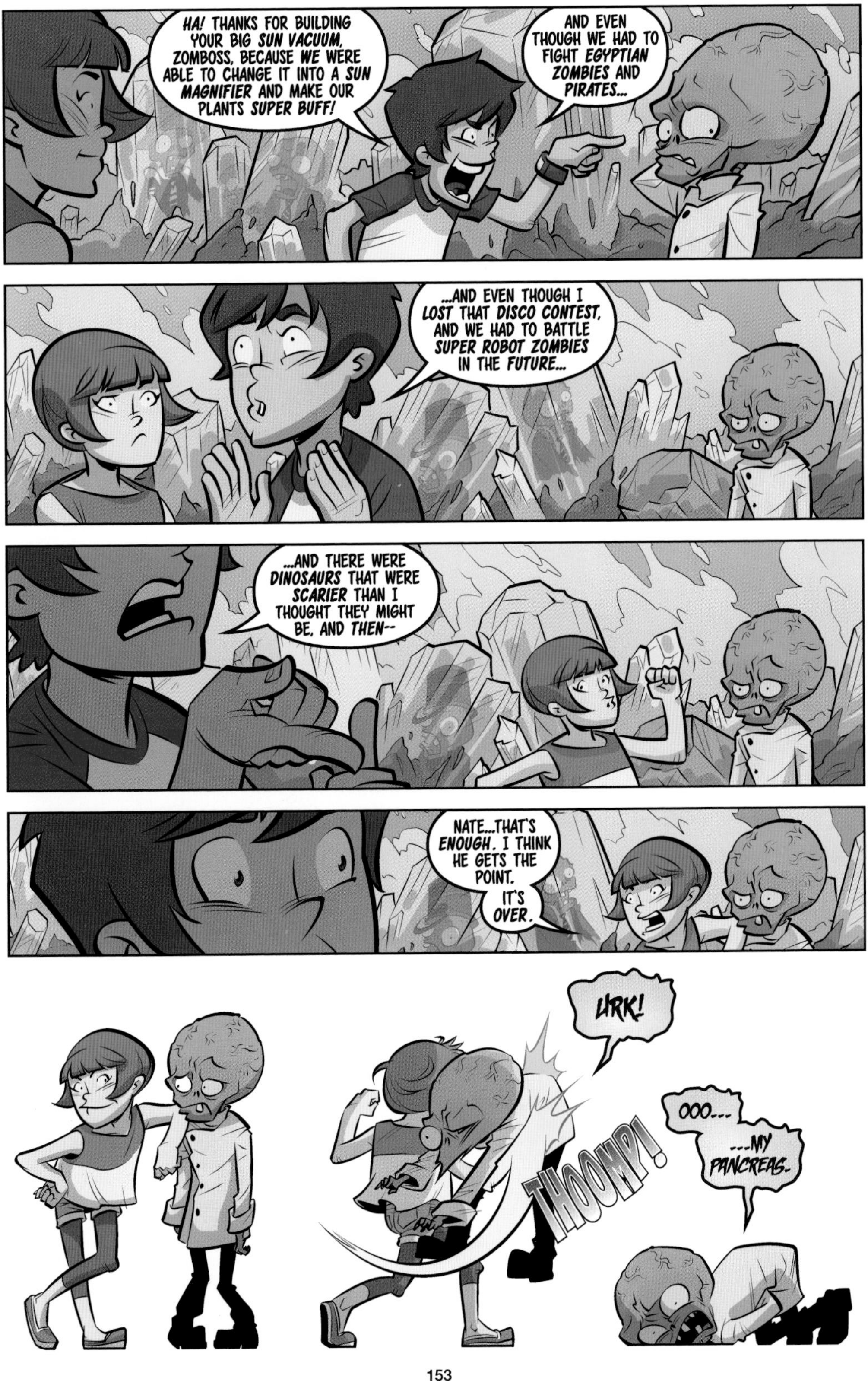
HA! THANKS FOR BUILDING YOUR BIG SUN VACUUM, ZOMBOSS, BECAUSE WE WERE ABLE TO CHANGE IT INTO A SUN MAGNIFIER AND MAKE OUR PLANTS SUPER BUFF!
AND EVEN THOUGH WE HAD TO FIGHT EGYPTIAN ZOMBIES AND PIRATES...
...AND EVEN THOUGH I LOST THAT DISCO CONTEST, AND WE HAD TO BATTLE SUPER ROBOT ZOMBIES IN THE FUTURE...
...AND THERE WERE DINOSAURS THAT WERE SCARIER THAN I THOUGHT THEY MIGHT BE, AND THEN--
NATE...THAT'S ENOUGH. I THINK HE GETS THE POINT.
IT'S OVER.
URK!
THOOMP!
OOO...
...MY PANCREAS.

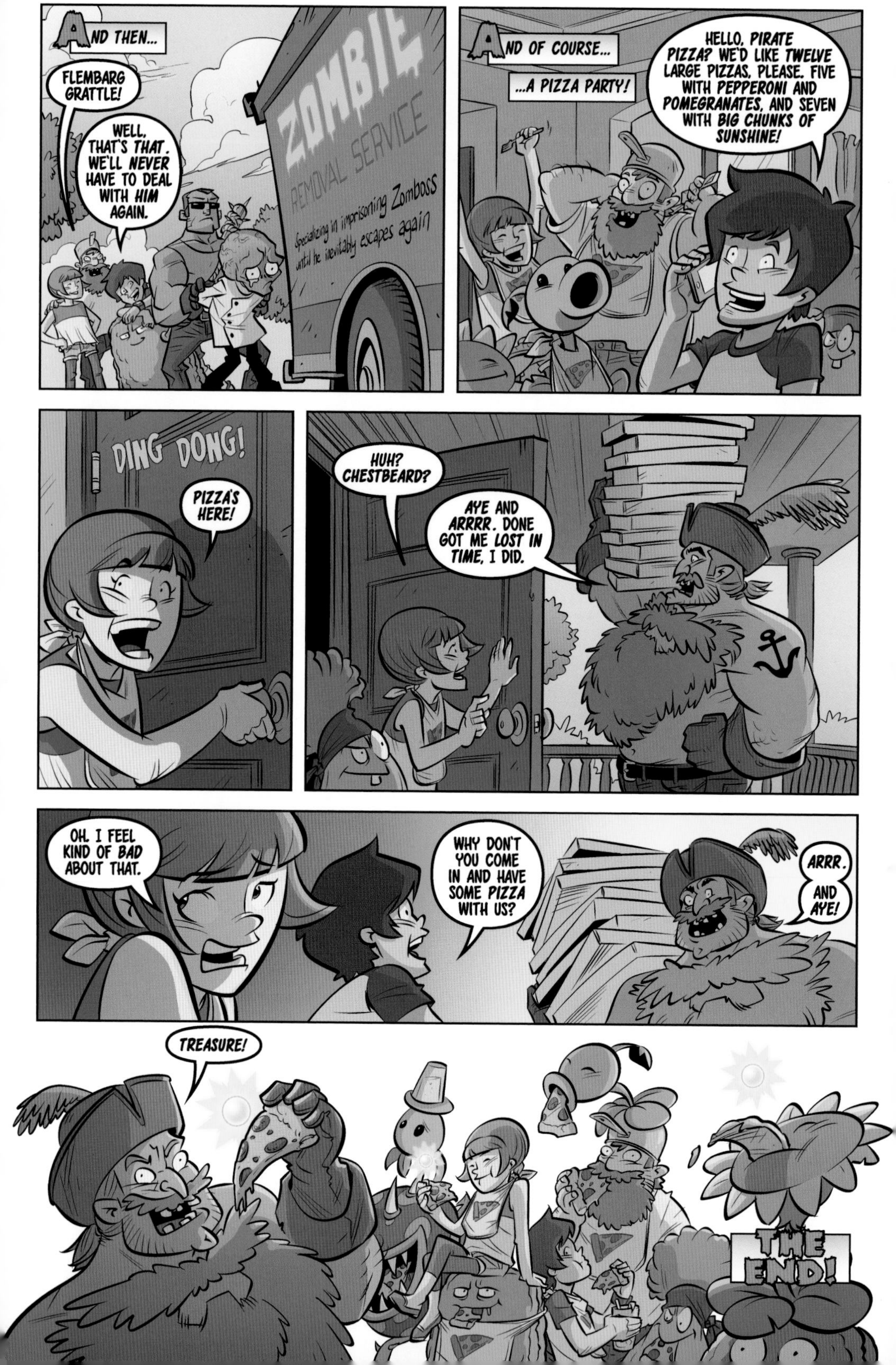
AND THEN...
FLEMBARG GRATTLE!
WELL, THAT'S THAT. WE'LL NEVER HAVE TO DEAL WITH HIM AGAIN.
ZOMBIE REMOVAL SERVICE
Specializing in imprisoning Zomboss until he inevitably escapes again
AND OF COURSE...
...A PIZZA PARTY!
HELLO, PIRATE PIZZA? WE'D LIKE TWELVE LARGE PIZZAS, PLEASE. FIVE WITH PEPPERONI AND POMEGRANATES, AND SEVEN WITH BIG CHUNKS OF SUNSHINE!
DING DONG!
PIZZA'S HERE!
HUH? CHESTBEARD?
AYE AND ARRRR. DONE GOT ME LOST IN TIME, I DID.
OH. I FEEL KIND OF BAD ABOUT THAT.
WHY DON'T YOU COME IN AND HAVE SOME PIZZA WITH US?
ARRR.
AND AYE!
TREASURE!
THE END!

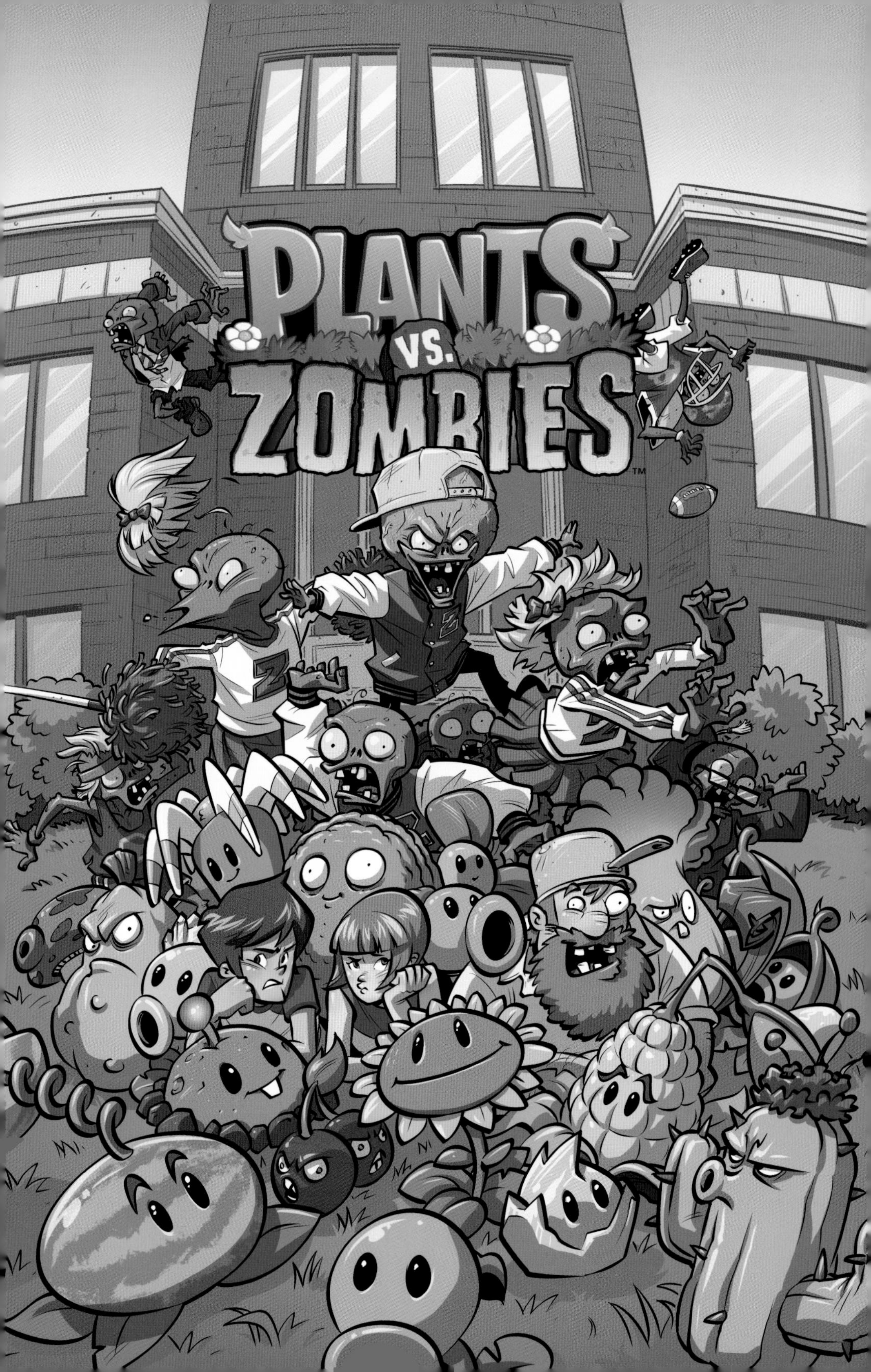
PLANTS VS. ZOMBIES™

BULLY FOR YOU

Written by **PAUL TOBIN**

Art by **RON CHAN**

Colors by **MATT J. RAINWATER**

Letters by **STEVE DUTRO**

Plants vs. Zombies: Bully For You #1 cover art
(previous page) by Ron Chan

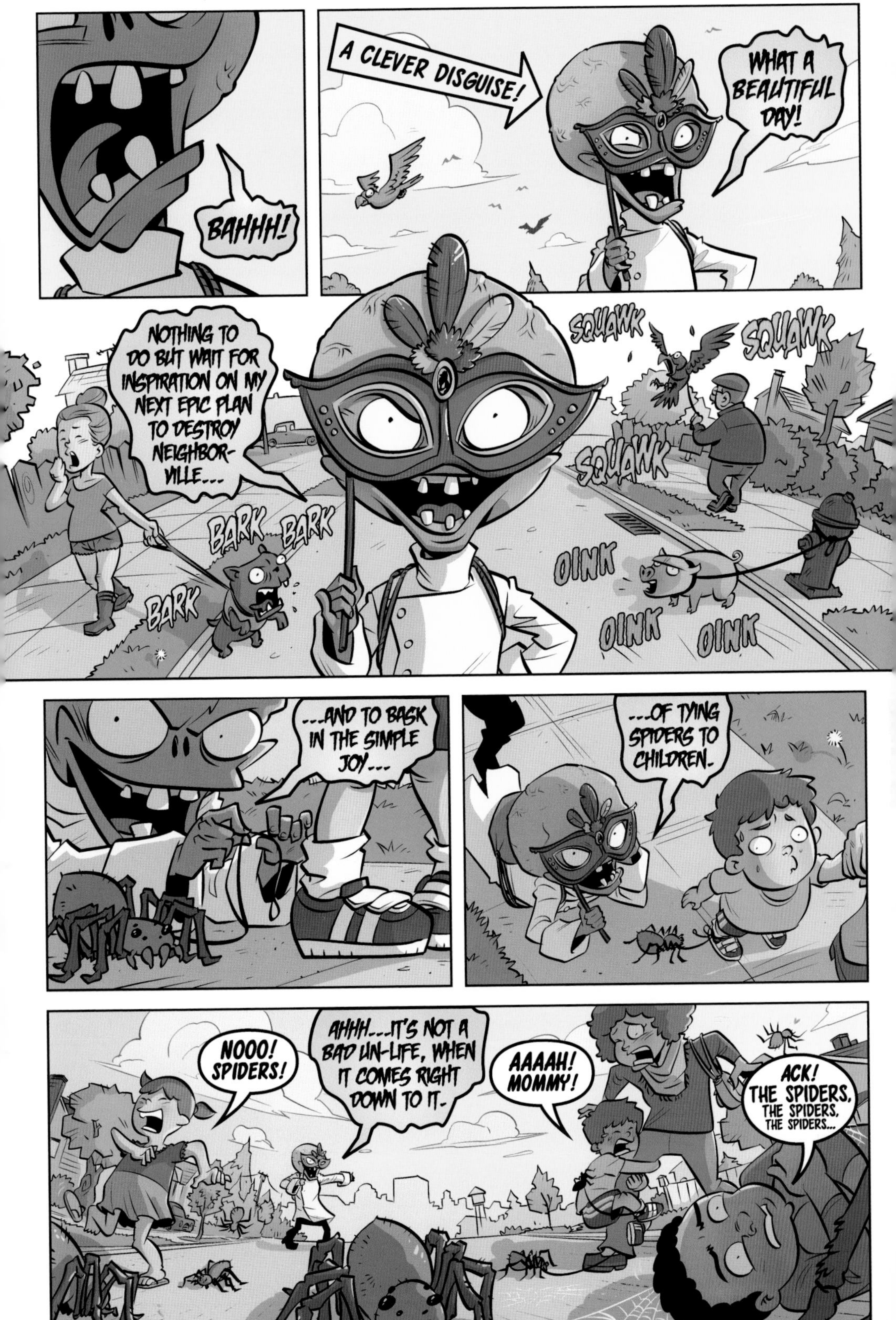
BAHHH!
A CLEVER DISGUISE!
WHAT A BEAUTIFUL DAY!
NOTHING TO DO BUT WAIT FOR INSPIRATION ON MY NEXT EPIC PLAN TO DESTROY NEIGHBOR-VILLE...
SQUAWK
SQUAWK
SQUAWK
BARK
BARK
BARK
OINK
OINK
OINK
...AND TO BASK IN THE SIMPLE JOY...
...OF TYING SPIDERS TO CHILDREN.
NOOO! SPIDERS!
AHHH... IT'S NOT A BAD UN-LIFE, WHEN IT COMES RIGHT DOWN TO IT.
AAAAH! MOMMY!
ACK! THE SPIDERS, THE SPIDERS, THE SPIDERS...

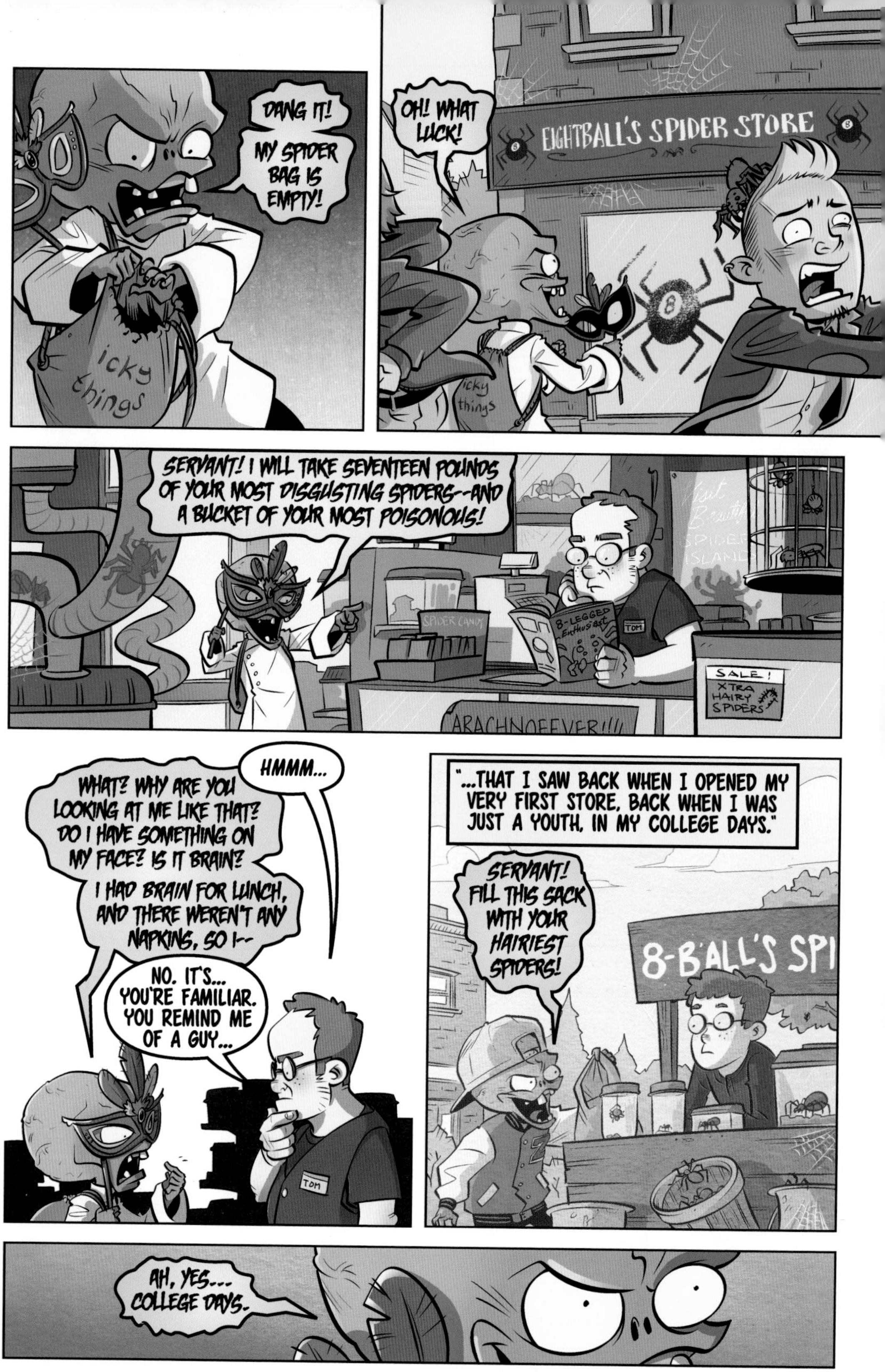
DANG IT!
MY SPIDER BAG IS EMPTY!
icky things
OH! WHAT LUCK!
EIGHTBALL'S SPIDER STORE
icky things
SERVANT! I WILL TAKE SEVENTEEN POUNDS OF YOUR MOST DISGUSTING SPIDERS--AND A BUCKET OF YOUR MOST POISONOUS!
SPIDER CANDY
8-LEGGED Enthusiast
TOM
SALE! XTRA HAIRY SPIDERS
ARACHNOFEVER!!!
HMMM...
WHAT? WHY ARE YOU LOOKING AT ME LIKE THAT? DO I HAVE SOMETHING ON MY FACE? IS IT BRAIN?
I HAD BRAIN FOR LUNCH, AND THERE WEREN'T ANY NAPKINS, SO I--
NO. IT'S... YOU'RE FAMILIAR. YOU REMIND ME OF A GUY...
TOM
"...THAT I SAW BACK WHEN I OPENED MY VERY FIRST STORE, BACK WHEN I WAS JUST A YOUTH, IN MY COLLEGE DAYS."
SERVANT! FILL THIS SACK WITH YOUR HAIRIEST SPIDERS!
8-B'ALL'S SPI
AH, YES... COLLEGE DAYS.

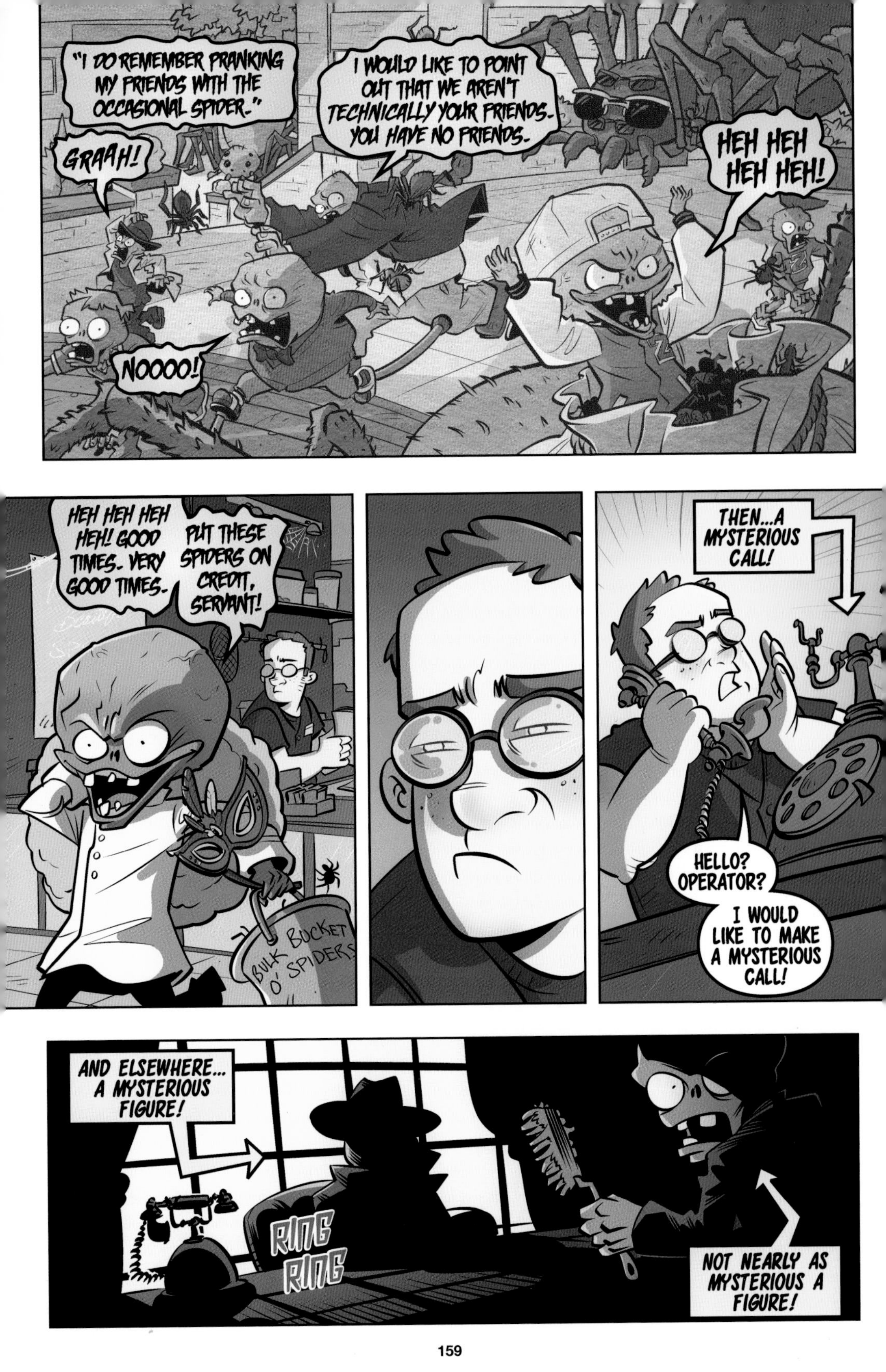
"I DO REMEMBER PRANKING MY FRIENDS WITH THE OCCASIONAL SPIDER."
I WOULD LIKE TO POINT OUT THAT WE AREN'T TECHNICALLY YOUR FRIENDS. YOU HAVE NO FRIENDS.
GRAAH!
HEH HEH HEH HEH!
NOOOO!
HEH HEH HEH HEH! GOOD TIMES. VERY GOOD TIMES.
PUT THESE SPIDERS ON CREDIT, SERVANT!
BULK BUCKET O' SPIDERS
THEN...A MYSTERIOUS CALL!
HELLO? OPERATOR?
I WOULD LIKE TO MAKE A MYSTERIOUS CALL!
AND ELSEWHERE... A MYSTERIOUS FIGURE!
RING RING
NOT NEARLY AS MYSTERIOUS A FIGURE!

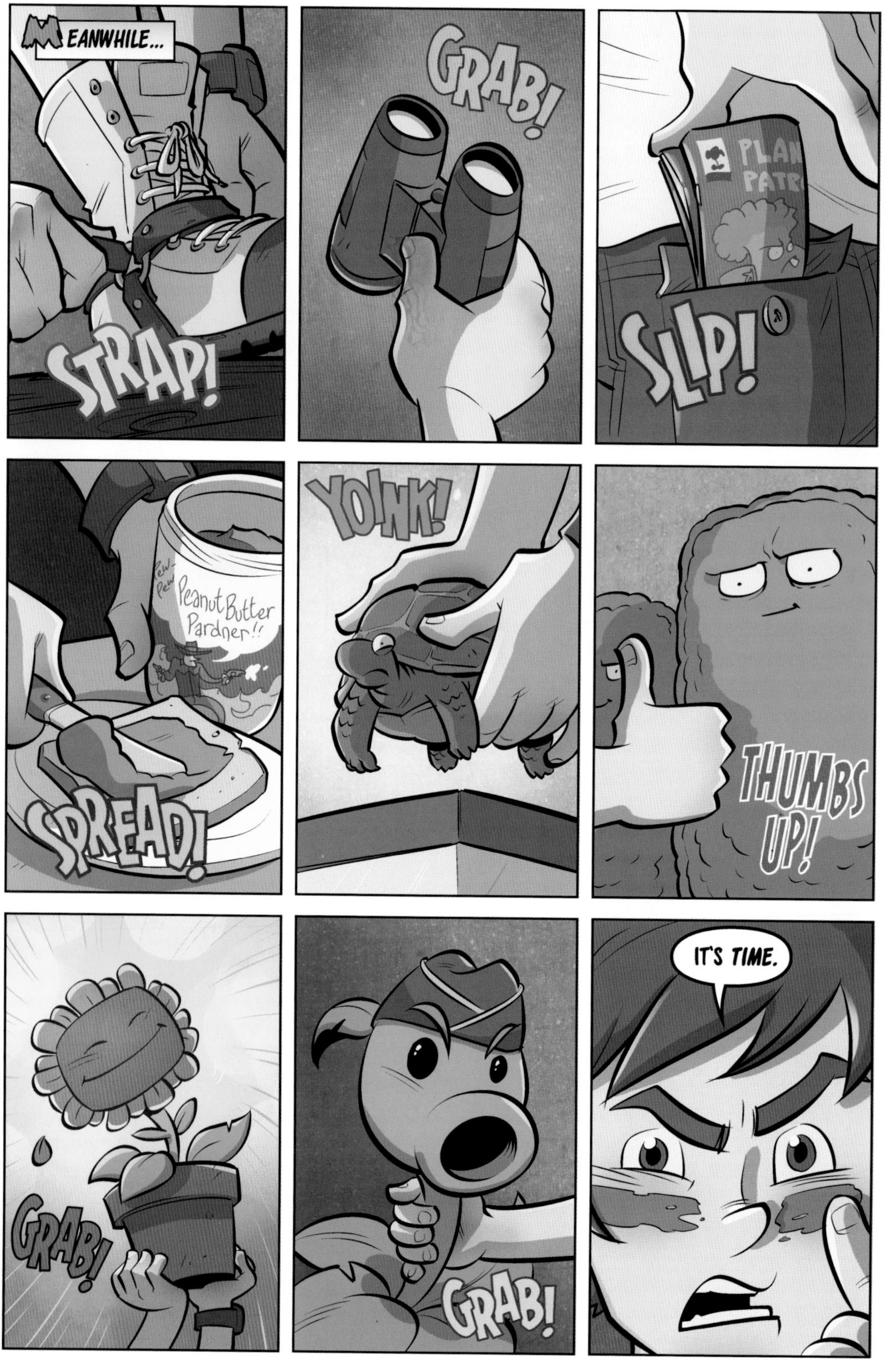
MEANWHILE...
STRAP!
GRAB!
PLAN
PATR
SLIP!
Pew-Pew-
Peanut Butter Pardner!!
SPREAD!
YOINK!
THUMBS UP!
GRAB!
GRAB!
IT'S TIME.

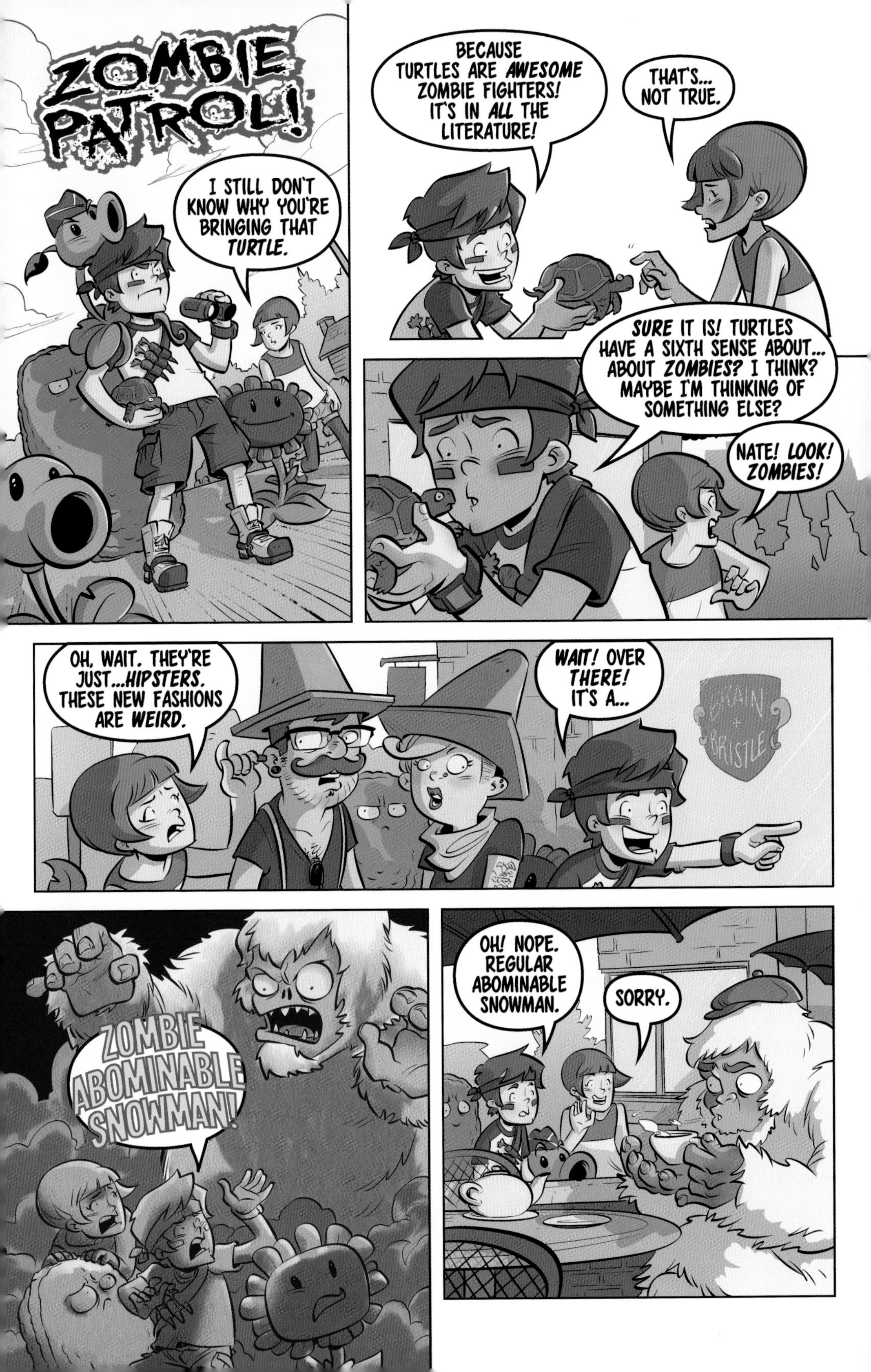
ZOMBIE PATROL!
I STILL DON'T KNOW WHY YOU'RE BRINGING THAT TURTLE.
BECAUSE TURTLES ARE AWESOME ZOMBIE FIGHTERS! IT'S IN ALL THE LITERATURE!
THAT'S... NOT TRUE.
SURE IT IS! TURTLES HAVE A SIXTH SENSE ABOUT... ABOUT ZOMBIES? I THINK? MAYBE I'M THINKING OF SOMETHING ELSE?
NATE! LOOK! ZOMBIES!
OH, WAIT. THEY'RE JUST...HIPSTERS. THESE NEW FASHIONS ARE WEIRD.
WAIT! OVER THERE! IT'S A...
BRAIN + BRISTLE
ZOMBIE ABOMINABLE SNOWMAN!
OH! NOPE. REGULAR ABOMINABLE SNOWMAN.
SORRY.

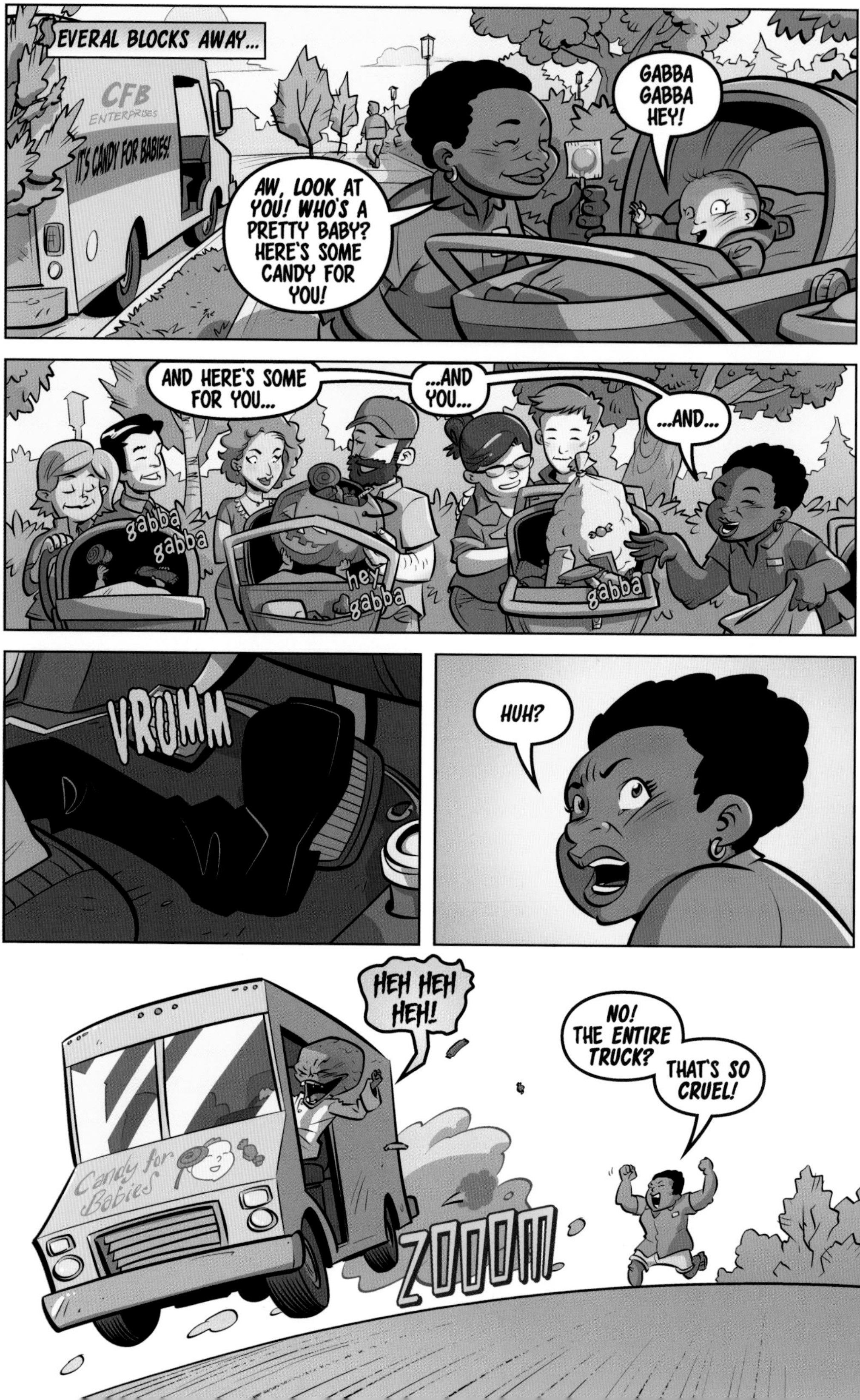
SEVERAL BLOCKS AWAY...
CFB ENTERPRISES
IT'S CANDY FOR BABIES!
GABBA GABBA HEY!
AW, LOOK AT YOU! WHO'S A PRETTY BABY? HERE'S SOME CANDY FOR YOU!
AND HERE'S SOME FOR YOU...
...AND YOU...
...AND...
gabba gabba
hey gabba
gabba
VRUMM
HUH?
HEH HEH HEH!
NO! THE ENTIRE TRUCK?
THAT'S SO CRUEL!
Candy for Babies
ZOOOM

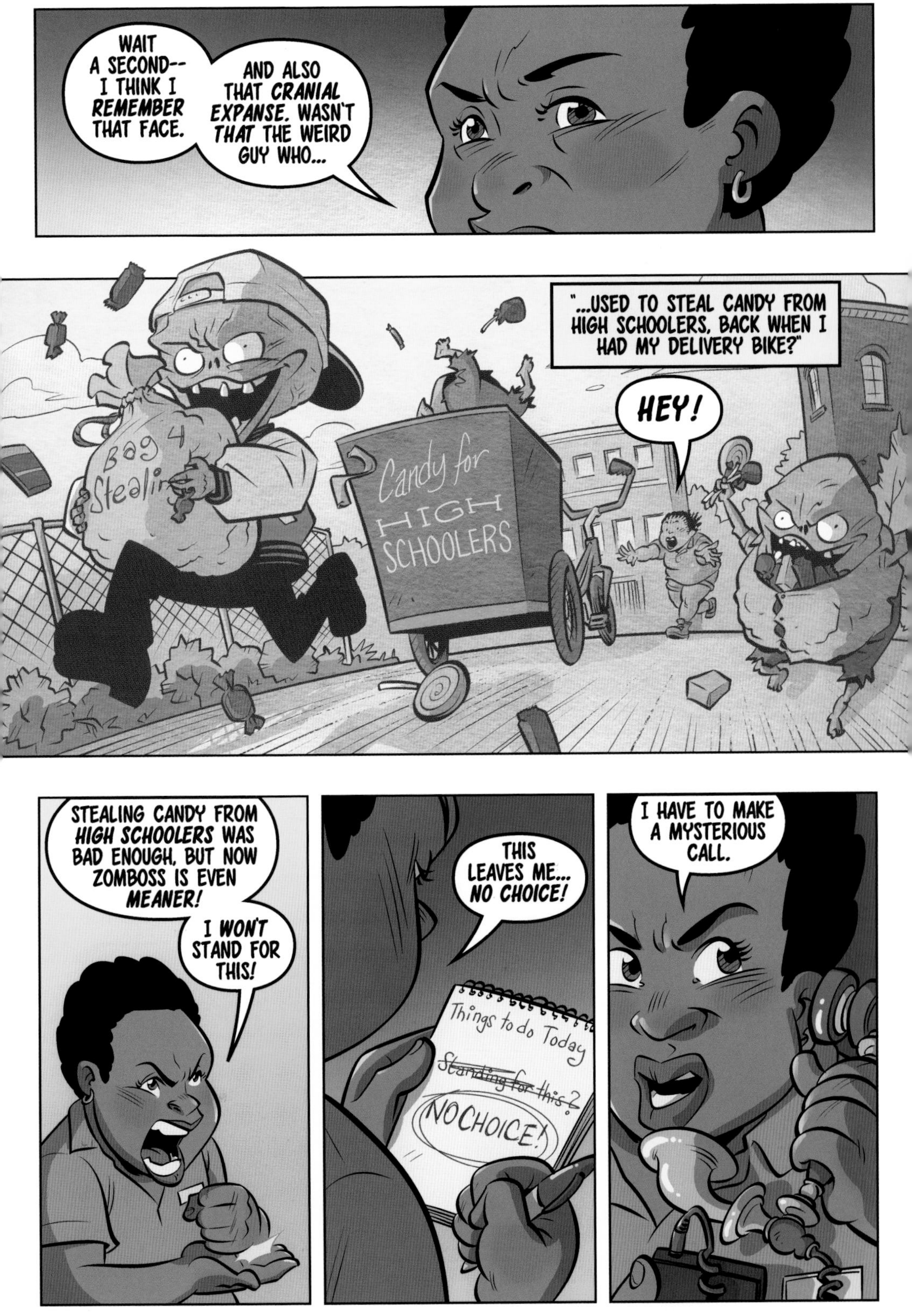

WAIT A SECOND-- I THINK I REMEMBER THAT FACE.
AND ALSO THAT CRANIAL EXPANSE. WASN'T THAT THE WEIRD GUY WHO...
"...USED TO STEAL CANDY FROM HIGH SCHOOLERS, BACK WHEN I HAD MY DELIVERY BIKE?"
Bag 4 Stealin
Candy for HIGH SCHOOLERS
HEY!
STEALING CANDY FROM HIGH SCHOOLERS WAS BAD ENOUGH, BUT NOW ZOMBOSS IS EVEN MEANER!
I WON'T STAND FOR THIS!
THIS LEAVES ME... NO CHOICE!
Things to do Today
Standing for this?
NO CHOICE!
I HAVE TO MAKE A MYSTERIOUS CALL.

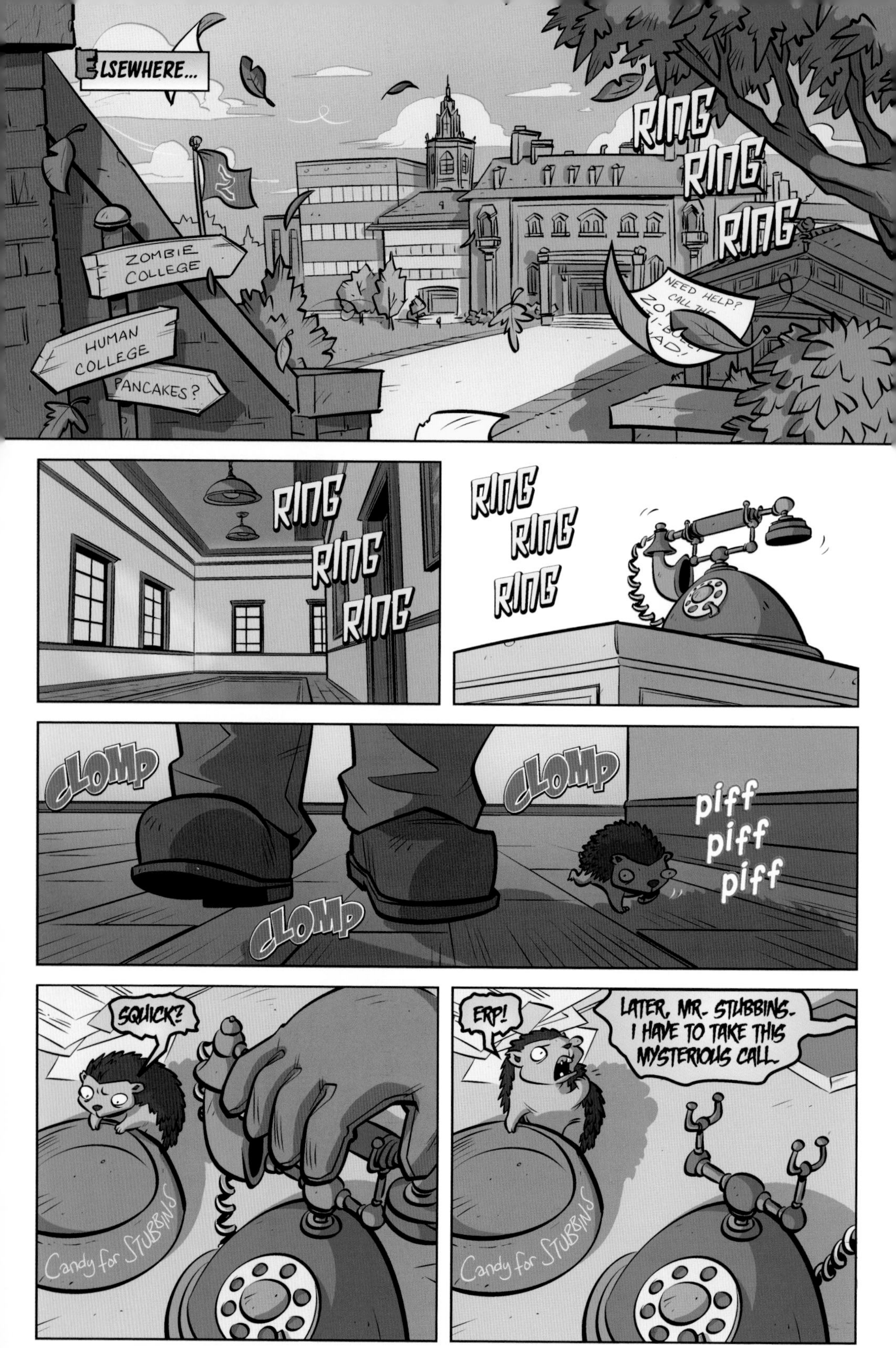
ELSEWHERE...
ZOMBIE COLLEGE
HUMAN COLLEGE
PANCAKES?
RING RING RING
NEED HELP? CALL THE
RING RING RING
RING RING RING
CLOMP
CLOMP
CLOMP
piff piff piff
SQUICK?
Candy for STUBBINS
ERP!
LATER, MR. STUBBINS. I HAVE TO TAKE THIS MYSTERIOUS CALL.
Candy for STUBBINS

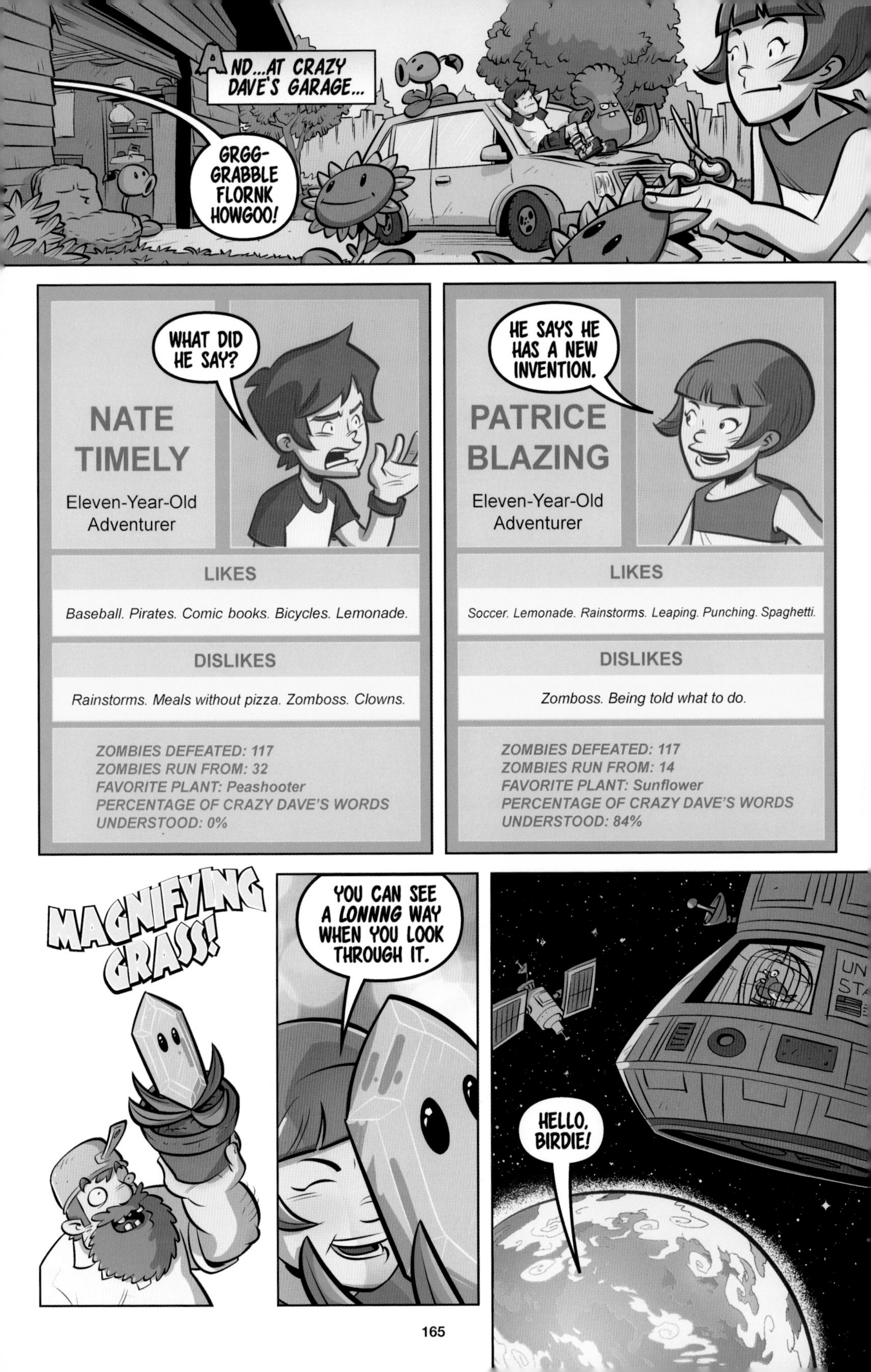
AND...AT CRAZY DAVE'S GARAGE...
GRGG-GRABBLE FLORNK HOWGOO!
WHAT DID HE SAY?
NATE TIMELY
Eleven-Year-Old Adventurer
LIKES
Baseball. Pirates. Comic books. Bicycles. Lemonade.
DISLIKES
Rainstorms. Meals without pizza. Zomboss. Clowns.
ZOMBIES DEFEATED: 117
ZOMBIES RUN FROM: 32
FAVORITE PLANT: Peashooter
PERCENTAGE OF CRAZY DAVE'S WORDS UNDERSTOOD: 0%
HE SAYS HE HAS A NEW INVENTION.
PATRICE BLAZING
Eleven-Year-Old Adventurer
LIKES
Soccer. Lemonade. Rainstorms. Leaping. Punching. Spaghetti.
DISLIKES
Zomboss. Being told what to do.
ZOMBIES DEFEATED: 117
ZOMBIES RUN FROM: 14
FAVORITE PLANT: Sunflower
PERCENTAGE OF CRAZY DAVE'S WORDS UNDERSTOOD: 84%
MAGNIFYING GRASS!
YOU CAN SEE A LONNNG WAY WHEN YOU LOOK THROUGH IT.
HELLO, BIRDIE!

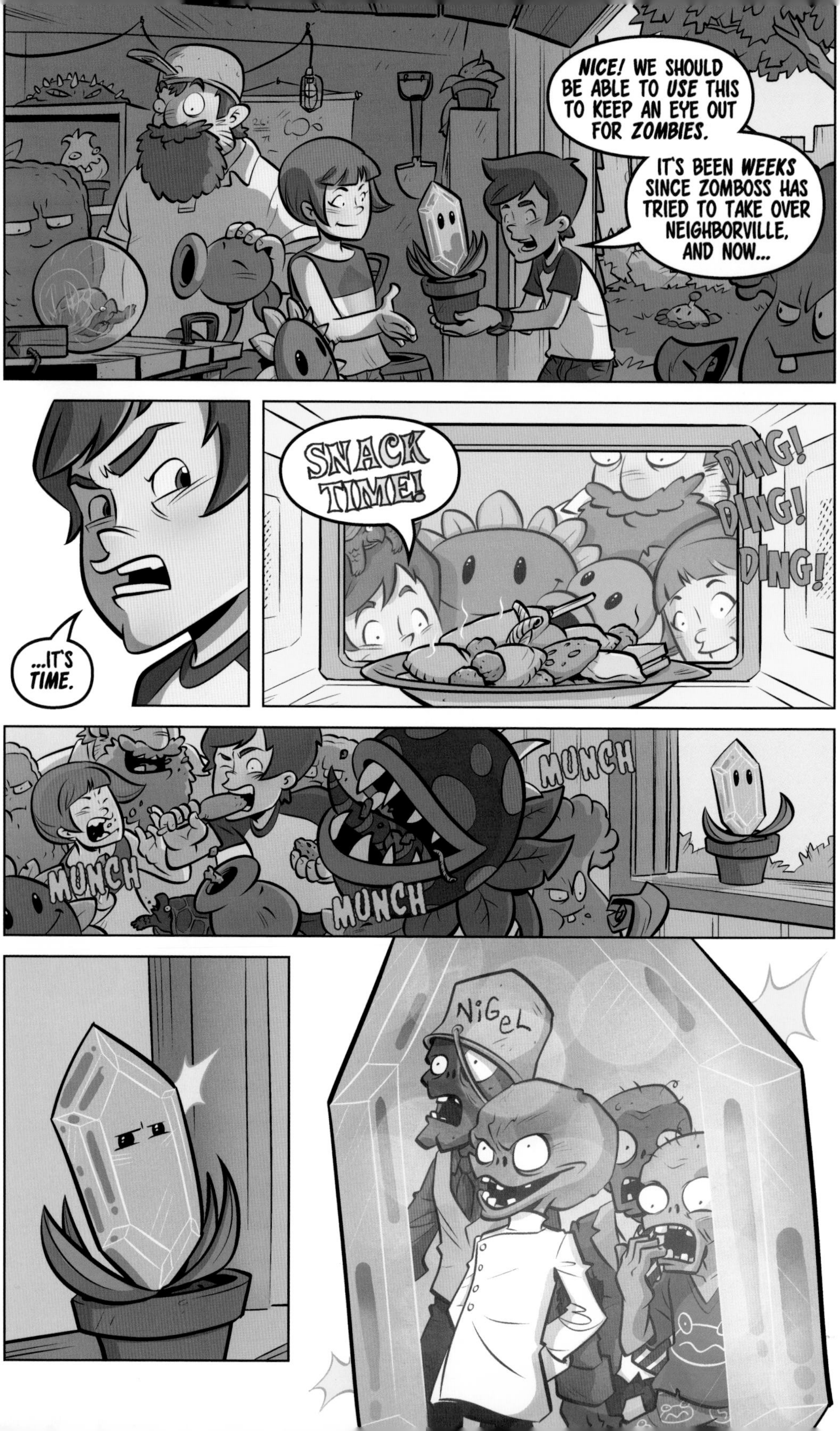
NICE! WE SHOULD BE ABLE TO USE THIS TO KEEP AN EYE OUT FOR ZOMBIES.
IT'S BEEN WEEKS SINCE ZOMBOSS HAS TRIED TO TAKE OVER NEIGHBORVILLE, AND NOW...
...IT'S TIME.
SNACK TIME!
DING! DING! DING!
MUNCH
MUNCH
MUNCH
NiGeL

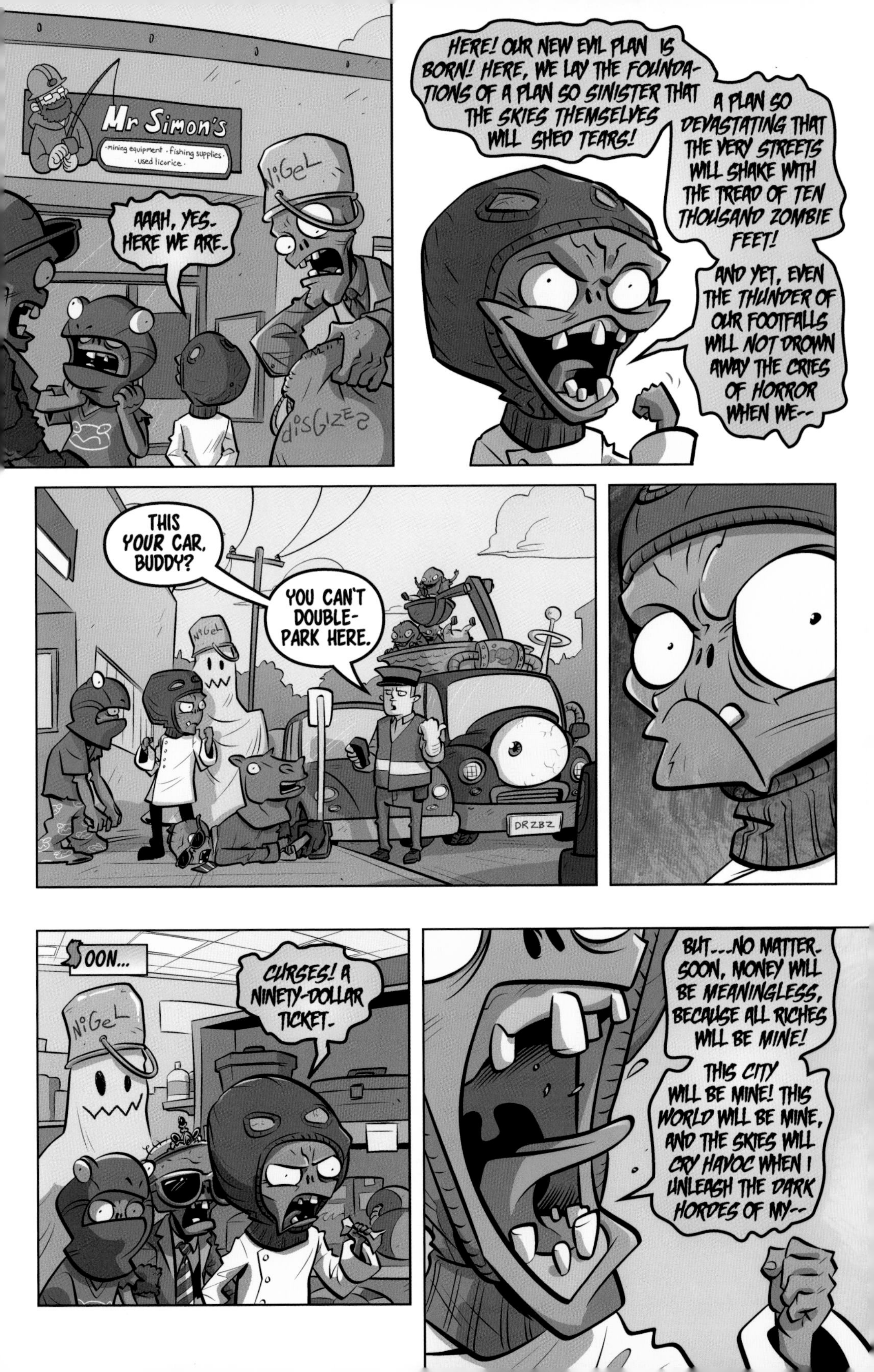
Mr Simon's
·mining equipment · fishing supplies · used licorice·
NiGeL
AAAH, YES. HERE WE ARE.
disGIZEs
HERE! OUR NEW EVIL PLAN IS BORN! HERE, WE LAY THE FOUNDATIONS OF A PLAN SO SINISTER THAT THE SKIES THEMSELVES WILL SHED TEARS!
A PLAN SO DEVASTATING THAT THE VERY STREETS WILL SHAKE WITH THE TREAD OF TEN THOUSAND ZOMBIE FEET!
AND YET, EVEN THE THUNDER OF OUR FOOTFALLS WILL NOT DROWN AWAY THE CRIES OF HORROR WHEN WE--
THIS YOUR CAR, BUDDY?
YOU CAN'T DOUBLE-PARK HERE.
NiGeL
DRZBZ
SOON...
CURSES! A NINETY-DOLLAR TICKET.
NiGeL
BUT...NO MATTER. SOON, MONEY WILL BE MEANINGLESS, BECAUSE ALL RICHES WILL BE MINE!
THIS CITY WILL BE MINE! THIS WORLD WILL BE MINE, AND THE SKIES WILL CRY HAVOC WHEN I UNLEASH THE DARK HORDES OF MY--

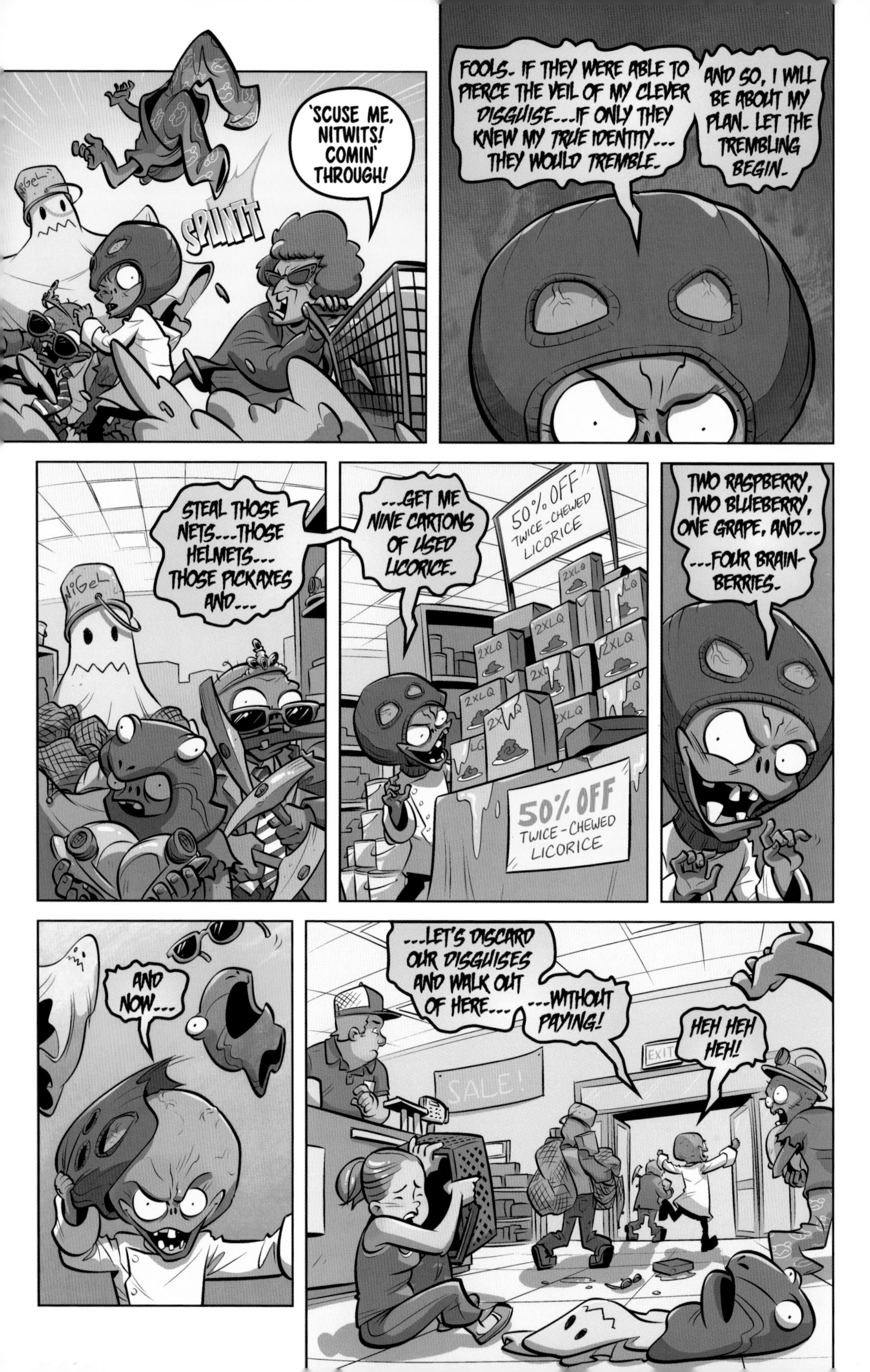
'SCUSE ME, NITWITS! COMIN' THROUGH!
SPLNTT
FOOLS. IF THEY WERE ABLE TO PIERCE THE VEIL OF MY CLEVER DISGUISE...IF ONLY THEY KNEW MY TRUE IDENTITY... THEY WOULD TREMBLE.
AND SO, I WILL BE ABOUT MY PLAN. LET THE TREMBLING BEGIN.
NiGeL
STEAL THOSE NETS...THOSE HELMETS... THOSE PICKAXES AND...
...GET ME NINE CARTONS OF USED LICORICE.
50% OFF TWICE-CHEWED LICORICE
2XLQ
50% OFF TWICE-CHEWED LICORICE
TWO RASPBERRY, TWO BLUEBERRY, ONE GRAPE, AND...
...FOUR BRAIN-BERRIES.
AND NOW...
...LET'S DISCARD OUR DISGUISES AND WALK OUT OF HERE...
...WITHOUT PAYING!
HEH HEH HEH!
EXIT
SALE!

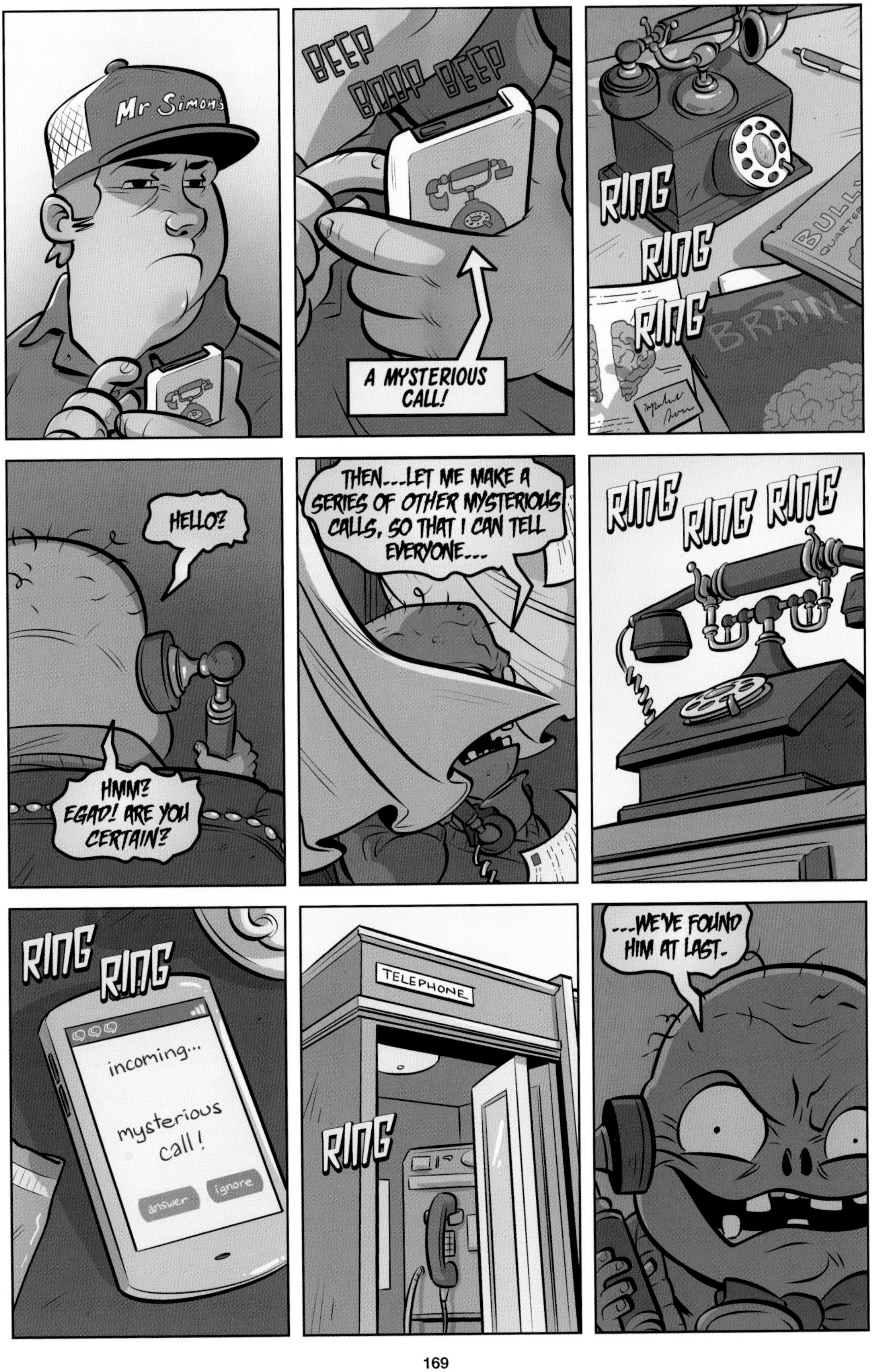
Mr Simon's
BEEP
BOOP BEEP
A MYSTERIOUS CALL!
RING
RING
RING
HELLO?
HMM? EGAD! ARE YOU CERTAIN?
THEN...LET ME MAKE A SERIES OF OTHER MYSTERIOUS CALLS, SO THAT I CAN TELL EVERYONE...
RING
RING RING
RING
RING
incoming...
mysterious call!
answer
ignore
TELEPHONE
RING
...WE'VE FOUND HIM AT LAST.

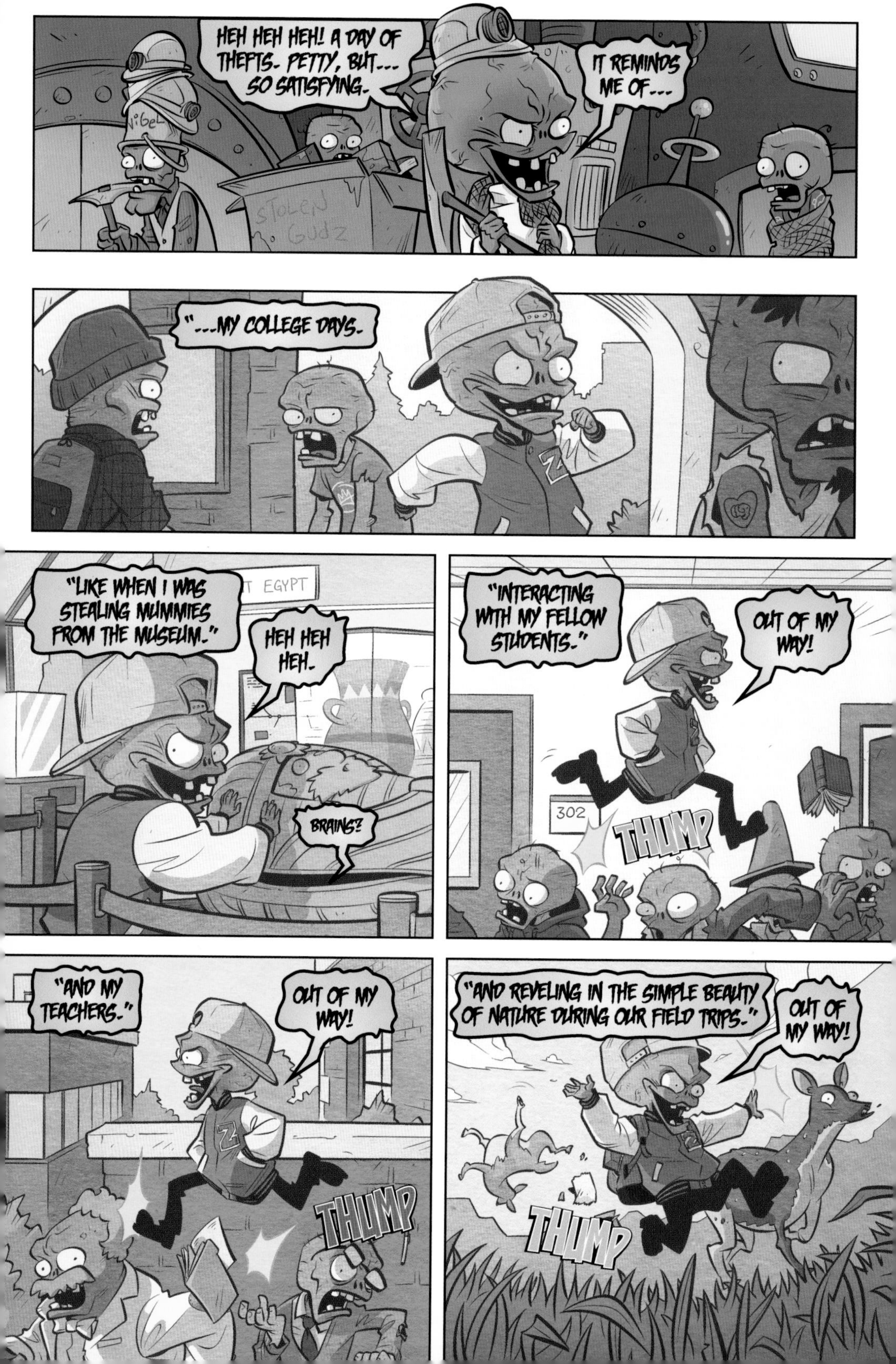

HEH HEH HEH! A DAY OF THEFTS. PETTY, BUT... SO SATISFYING.
IT REMINDS ME OF...
STOLEN GUDZ
"...MY COLLEGE DAYS.
"LIKE WHEN I WAS STEALING MUMMIES FROM THE MUSEUM."
T EGYPT
HEH HEH HEH.
BRAINS?
"INTERACTING WITH MY FELLOW STUDENTS."
OUT OF MY WAY!
302
THUMP
"AND MY TEACHERS."
OUT OF MY WAY!
THUMP
"AND REVELING IN THE SIMPLE BEAUTY OF NATURE DURING OUR FIELD TRIPS."
OUT OF MY WAY!
THUMP

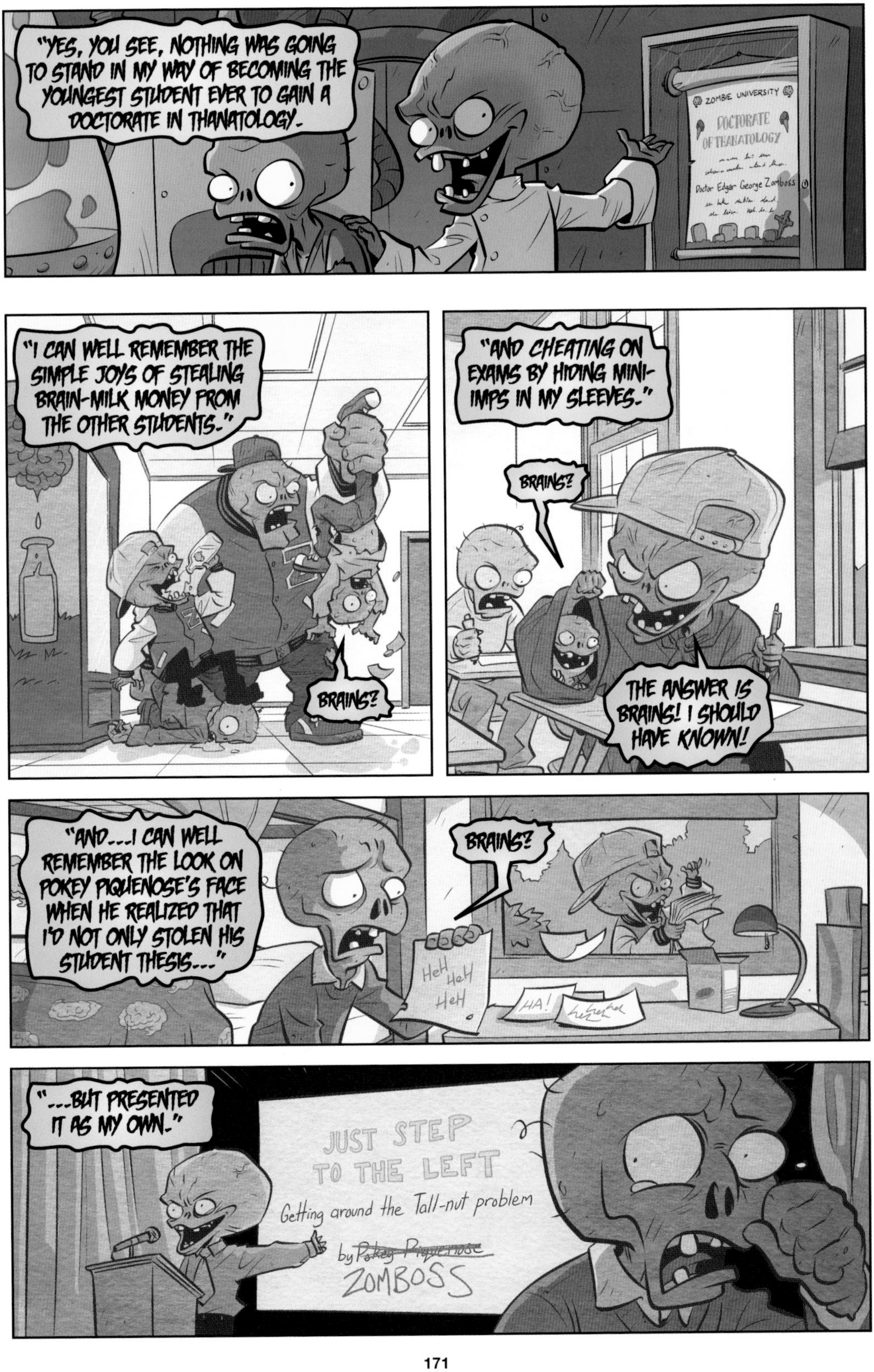
"YES, YOU SEE, NOTHING WAS GOING TO STAND IN MY WAY OF BECOMING THE YOUNGEST STUDENT EVER TO GAIN A DOCTORATE IN THANATOLOGY.
ZOMBIE UNIVERSITY
DOCTORATE OF THANATOLOGY
Doctor Edgar George Zomboss
"I CAN WELL REMEMBER THE SIMPLE JOYS OF STEALING BRAIN-MILK MONEY FROM THE OTHER STUDENTS."
BRAINS?
"AND CHEATING ON EXAMS BY HIDING MINI-IMPS IN MY SLEEVES."
BRAINS?
THE ANSWER IS BRAINS! I SHOULD HAVE KNOWN!
"AND...I CAN WELL REMEMBER THE LOOK ON POKEY PIQUENOSE'S FACE WHEN HE REALIZED THAT I'D NOT ONLY STOLEN HIS STUDENT THESIS..."
BRAINS?
HeH HeH HeH
HA!
"...BUT PRESENTED IT AS MY OWN."
JUST STEP TO THE LEFT
Getting around the Tall-nut problem
by ~~Pokey Piquenose~~
ZOMBOSS

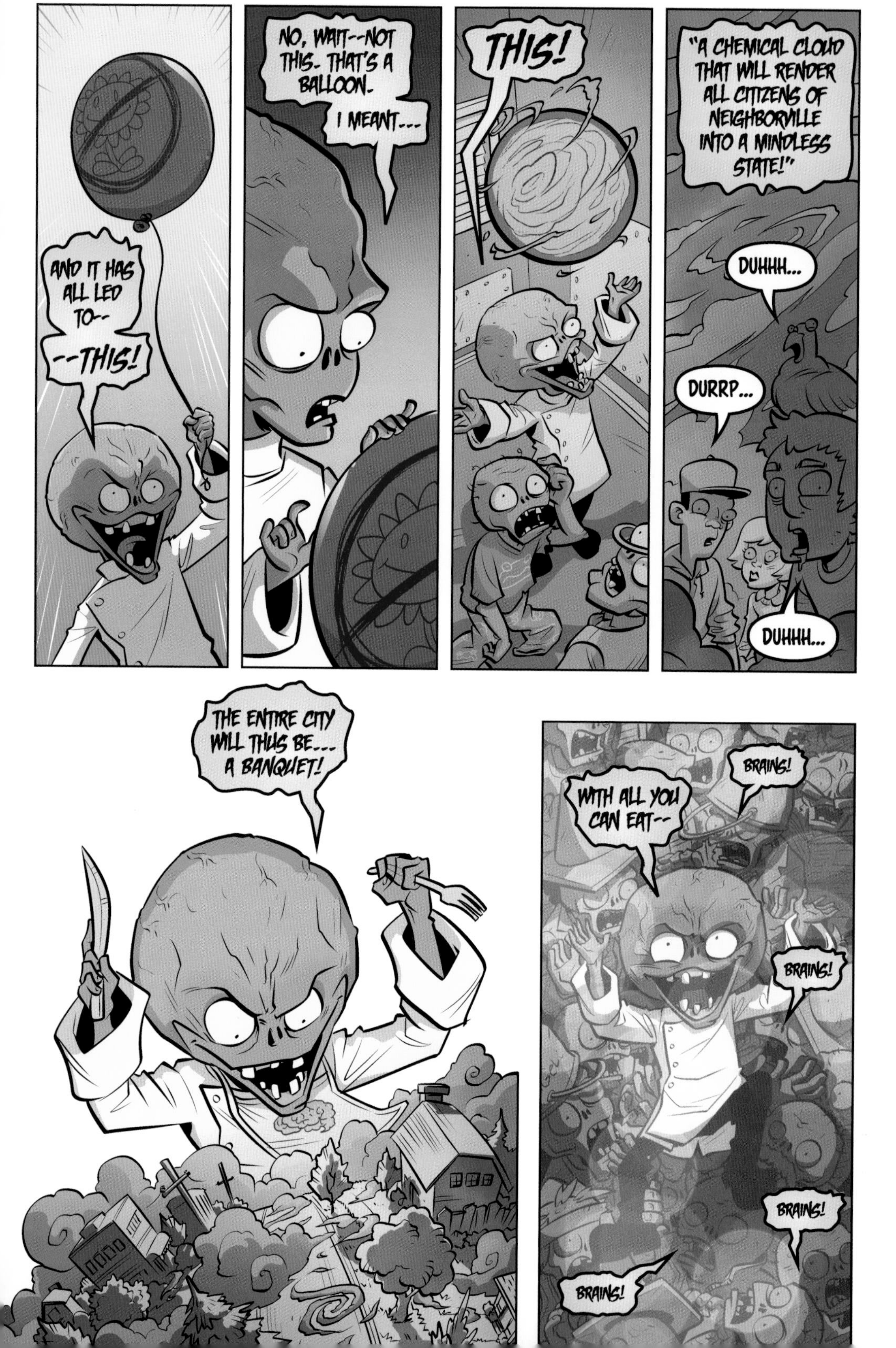
AND IT HAS ALL LED TO--
--THIS!
NO, WAIT--NOT THIS. THAT'S A BALLOON.
I MEANT...
THIS!
"A CHEMICAL CLOUD THAT WILL RENDER ALL CITIZENS OF NEIGHBORVILLE INTO A MINDLESS STATE!"
DUHHH...
DURRP...
DUHHH...
THE ENTIRE CITY WILL THUS BE... A BANQUET!
WITH ALL YOU CAN EAT--
BRAINS!
BRAINS!
BRAINS!
BRAINS!

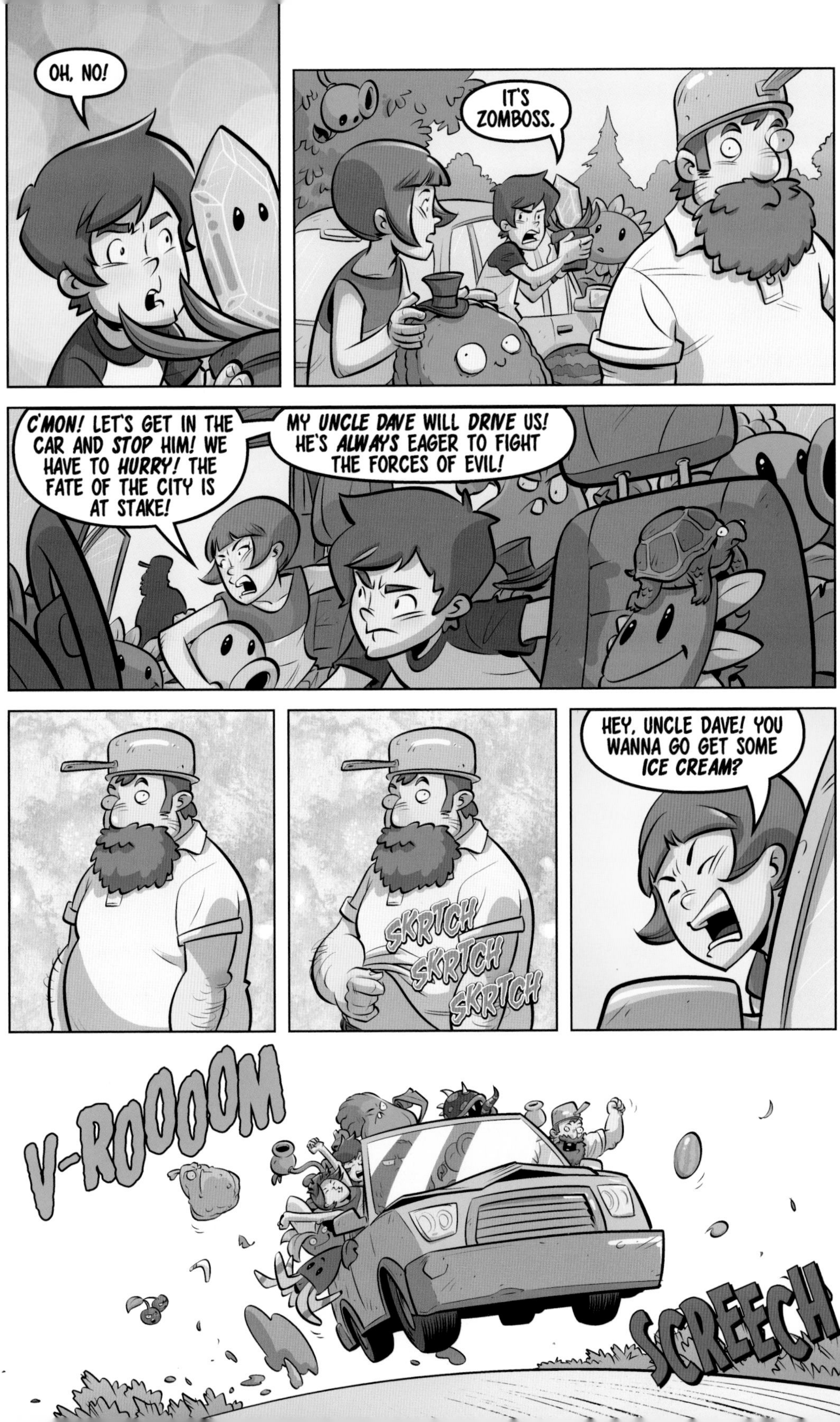
OH, NO!
IT'S ZOMBOSS.
C'MON! LET'S GET IN THE CAR AND STOP HIM! WE HAVE TO HURRY! THE FATE OF THE CITY IS AT STAKE!
MY UNCLE DAVE WILL DRIVE US! HE'S ALWAYS EAGER TO FIGHT THE FORCES OF EVIL!
SKRTCH
SKRTCH
SKRTCH
HEY, UNCLE DAVE! YOU WANNA GO GET SOME ICE CREAM?
V-ROOOOM
SCREECH

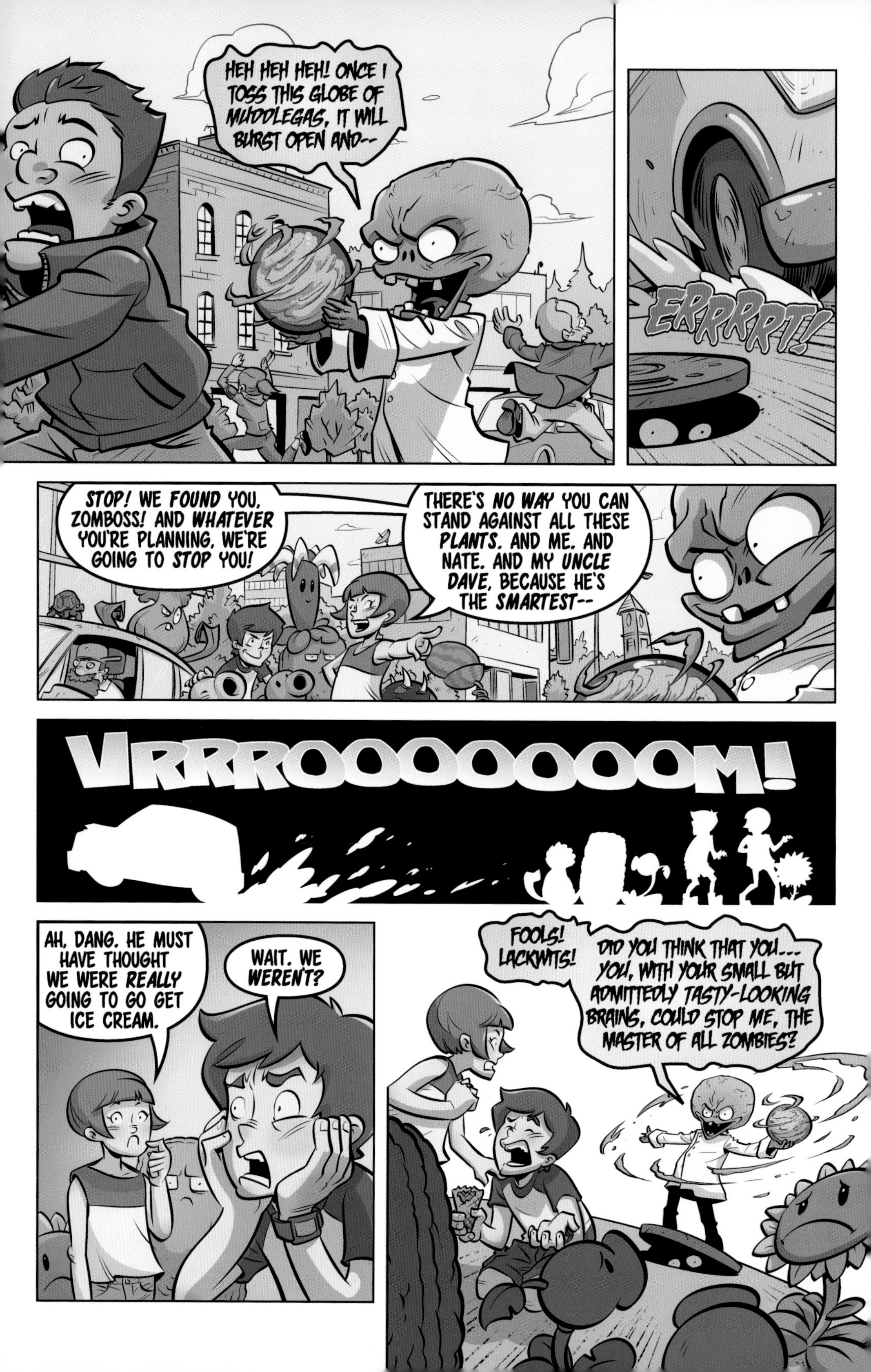
HEH HEH HEH! ONCE I TOSS THIS GLOBE OF MUDDLEGAS, IT WILL BURST OPEN AND--
ERRRRT!
STOP! WE FOUND YOU, ZOMBOSS! AND WHATEVER YOU'RE PLANNING, WE'RE GOING TO STOP YOU!
THERE'S NO WAY YOU CAN STAND AGAINST ALL THESE PLANTS. AND ME. AND NATE. AND MY UNCLE DAVE, BECAUSE HE'S THE SMARTEST--
VRRROOOOOOOOM!
AH, DANG. HE MUST HAVE THOUGHT WE WERE REALLY GOING TO GO GET ICE CREAM.
WAIT. WE WERENT?
FOOLS! LACKWITS!
DID YOU THINK THAT YOU... YOU, WITH YOUR SMALL BUT ADMITTEDLY TASTY-LOOKING BRAINS, COULD STOP ME, THE MASTER OF ALL ZOMBIES?

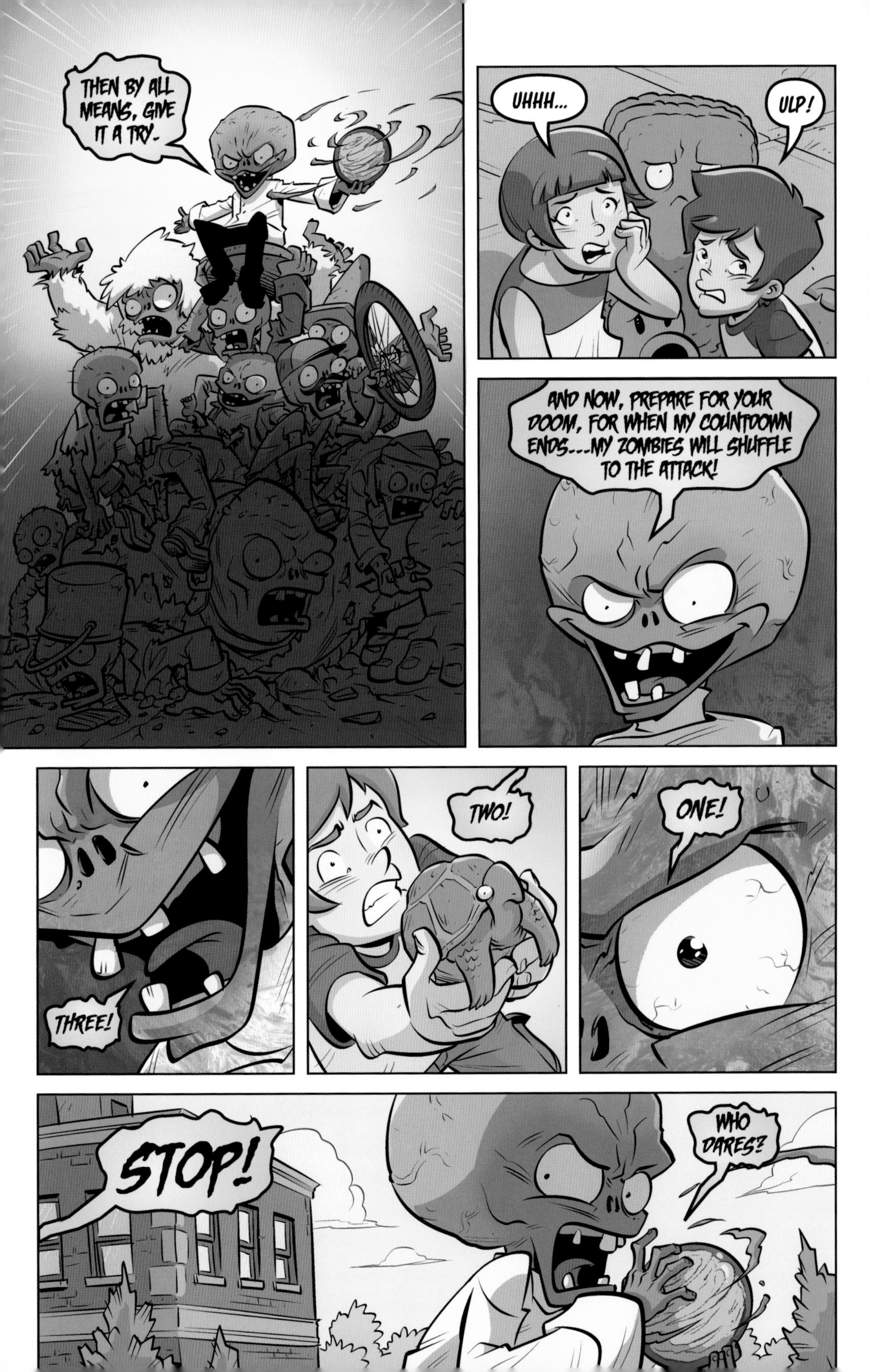
THEN BY ALL MEANS, GIVE IT A TRY.
UHHH...
ULP!
AND NOW, PREPARE FOR YOUR DOOM, FOR WHEN MY COUNTDOWN ENDS...MY ZOMBIES WILL SHUFFLE TO THE ATTACK!
THREE!
TWO!
ONE!
STOP!
WHO DARES?

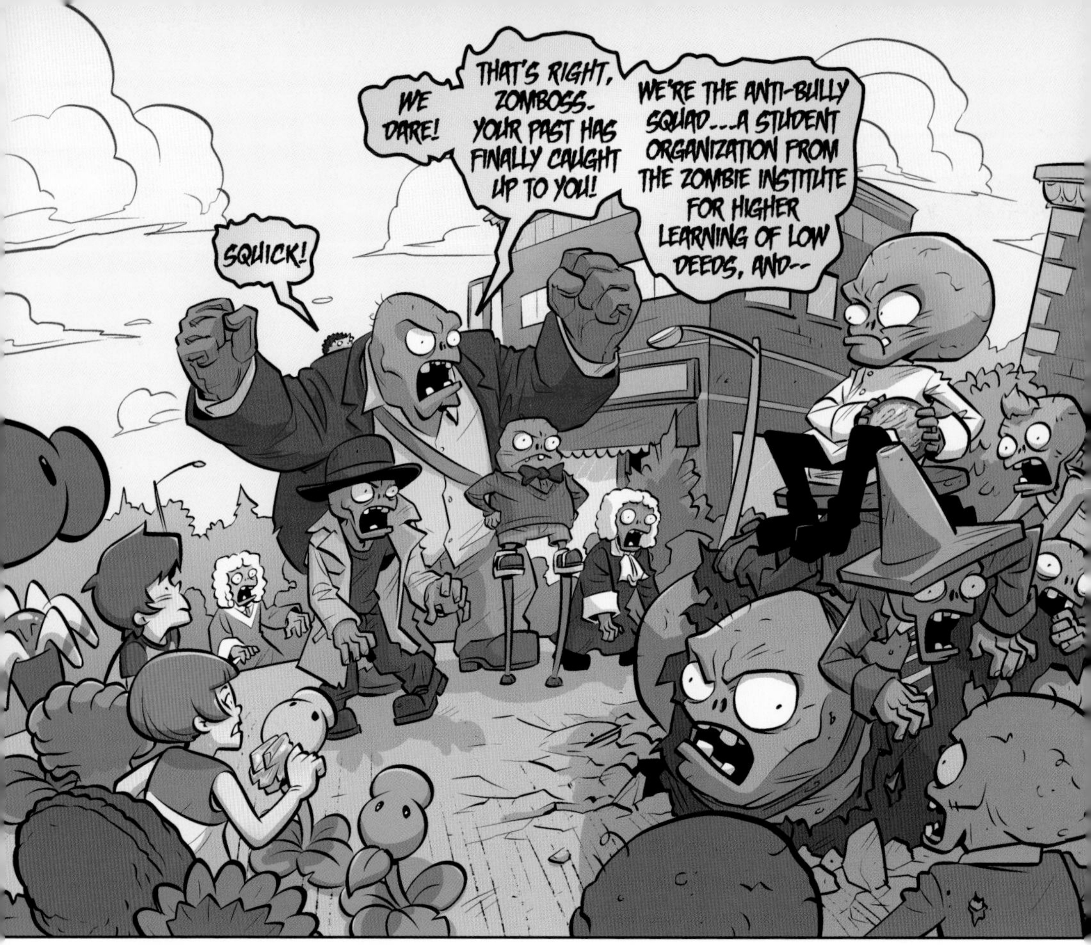

SQUICK!
WE DARE!
THAT'S RIGHT, ZOMBOSS. YOUR PAST HAS FINALLY CAUGHT UP TO YOU!
WE'RE THE ANTI-BULLY SQUAD...A STUDENT ORGANIZATION FROM THE ZOMBIE INSTITUTE FOR HIGHER LEARNING OF LOW DEEDS, AND--

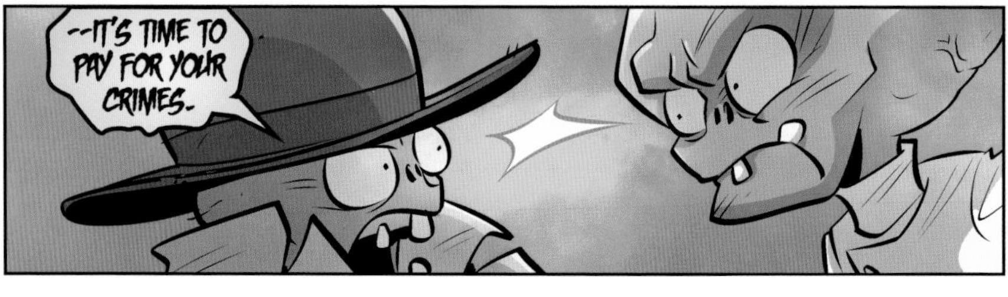

--IT'S TIME TO PAY FOR YOUR CRIMES.

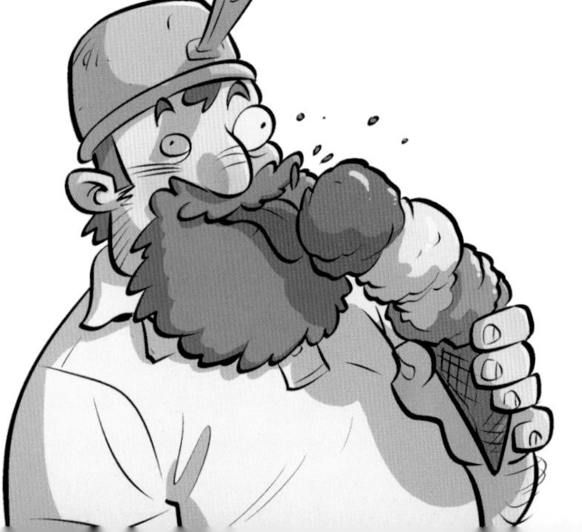

CRAZY DAVE'S ICE-CREAM FACTS

DID YOU KNOW THAT ICE CREAM WAS INVENTED BY PENGUINS? IT'S TRUE! MAYBE. I DON'T KNOW. MAYBE ICE CREAM INVENTED PENGUINS? I LIKE THEM BOTH! HAVE YOU EVER SEEN AN ICE-CREAM-CONE-HEAD ZOMBIE? I HAVEN'T EITHER. STRAWBERRY ICE CREAM IS THE BEST FOR FUELING YOUR TIME MACHINE. *THESE ARE FACTS!*

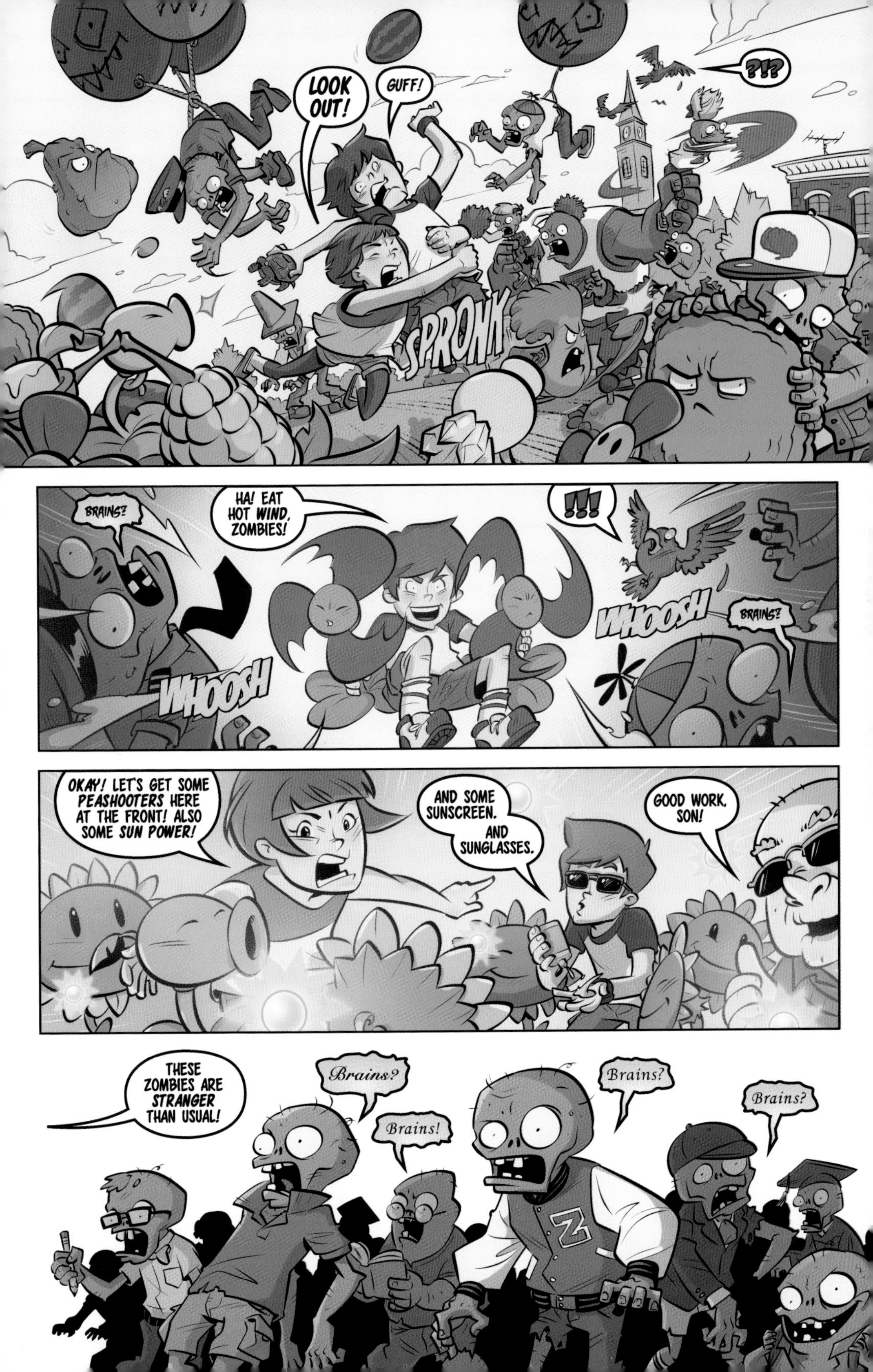
LOOK OUT!
GUFF!
?!?
SPRONK
BRAINS?
HA! EAT HOT WIND, ZOMBIES!
!!!
WHOOSH
WHOOSH
BRAINS?
OKAY! LET'S GET SOME PEASHOOTERS HERE AT THE FRONT! ALSO SOME SUN POWER!
AND SOME SUNSCREEN.
AND SUNGLASSES.
GOOD WORK, SON!
THESE ZOMBIES ARE STRANGER THAN USUAL!
Brains?
Brains!
Brains?
Brains?

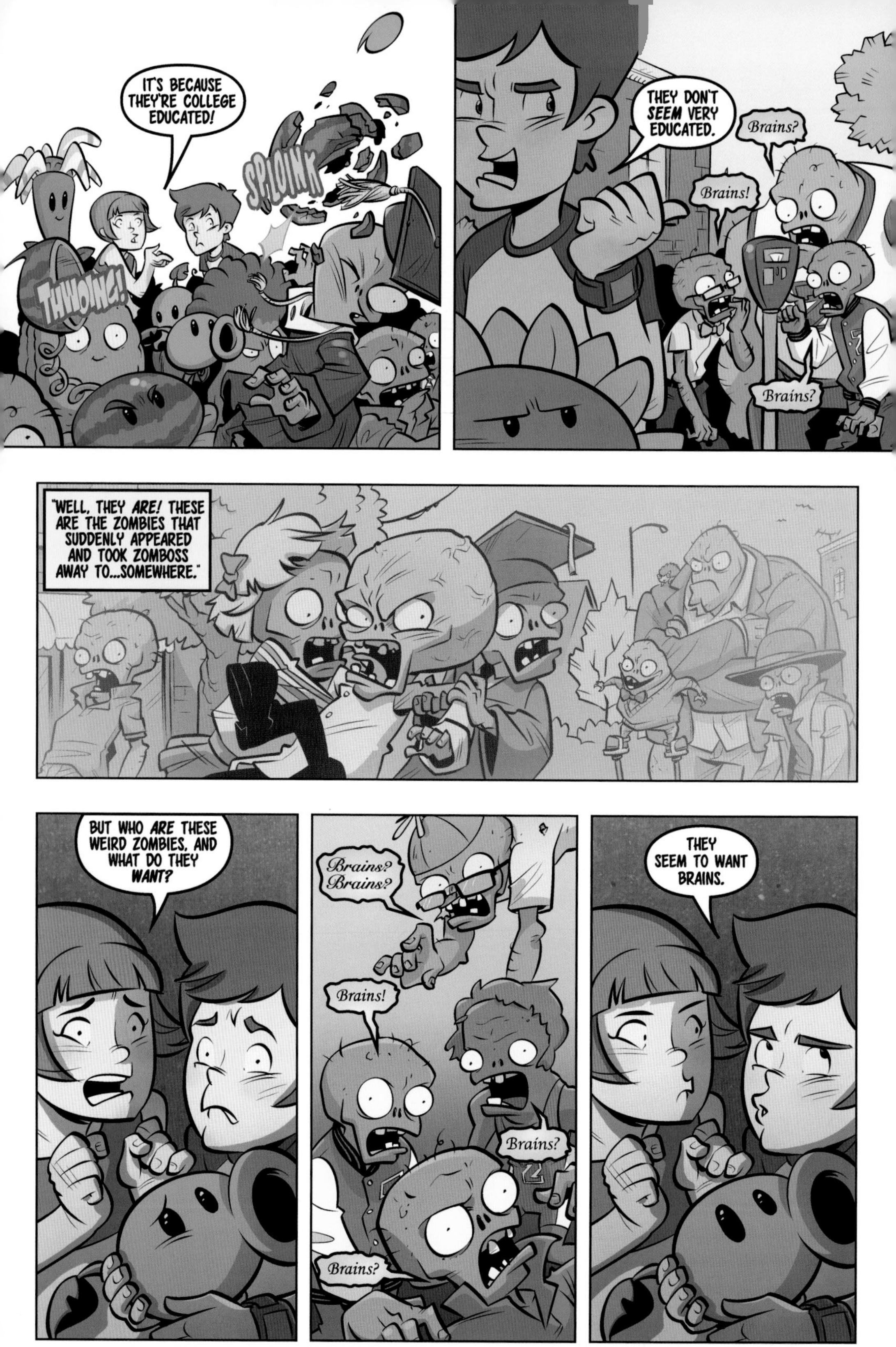
IT'S BECAUSE THEY'RE COLLEGE EDUCATED!
SPLOINK
THWOING!
THEY DON'T SEEM VERY EDUCATED.
Brains?
Brains!
Brains?
"WELL, THEY ARE! THESE ARE THE ZOMBIES THAT SUDDENLY APPEARED AND TOOK ZOMBOSS AWAY TO...SOMEWHERE."
BUT WHO ARE THESE WEIRD ZOMBIES, AND WHAT DO THEY WANT?
Brains? Brains?
Brains!
Brains?
Brains?
THEY SEEM TO WANT BRAINS.

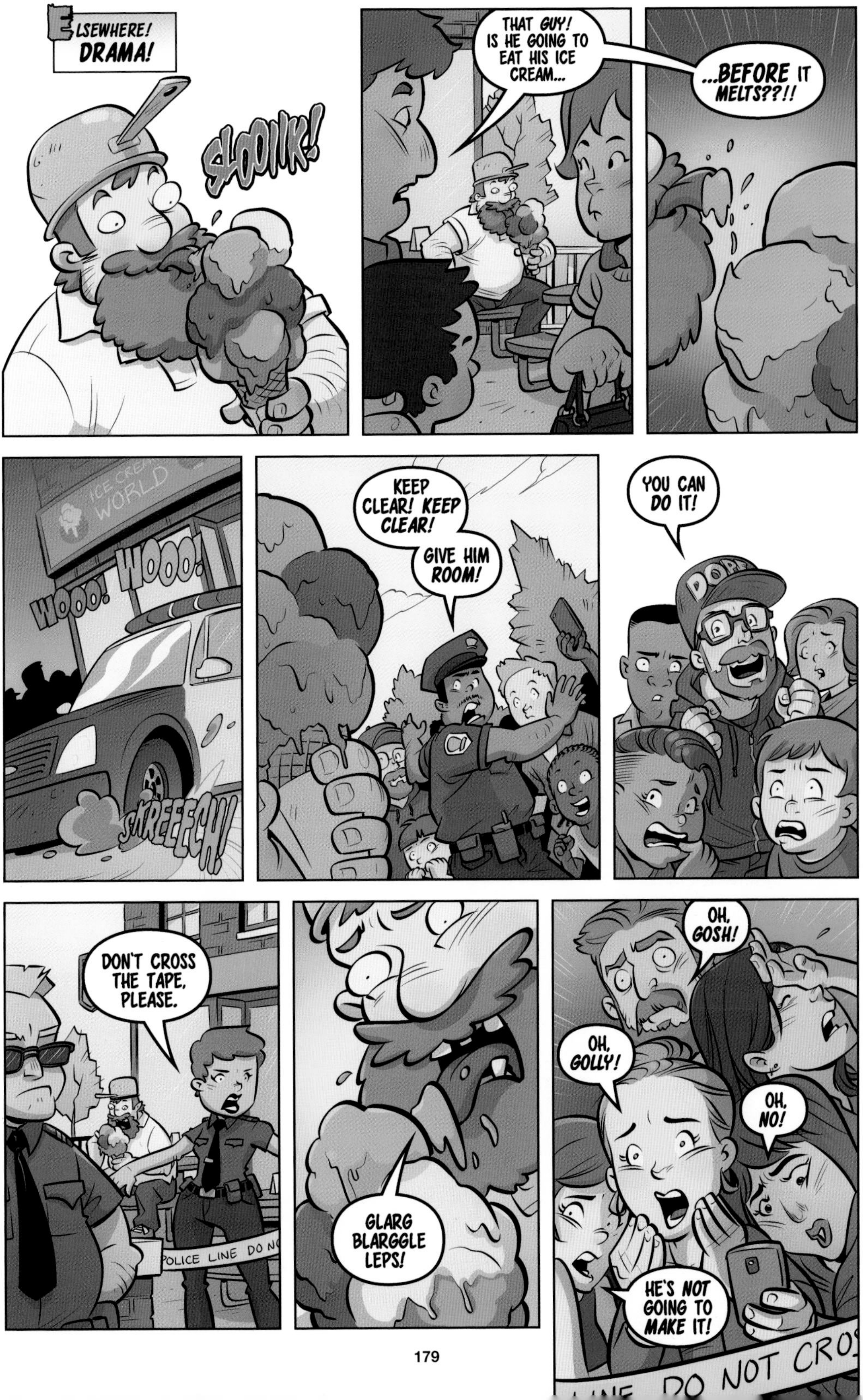
ELSEWHERE! DRAMA!
SLOOIIK!
THAT GUY! IS HE GOING TO EAT HIS ICE CREAM...
...BEFORE IT MELTS??!!
ICE CREAM WORLD
WOOO! WOOO!
SKREEECH!
KEEP CLEAR! KEEP CLEAR!
GIVE HIM ROOM!
YOU CAN DO IT!
DOPE
DON'T CROSS THE TAPE, PLEASE.
POLICE LINE DO NO
GLARG BLARGGLE LEPS!
OH, GOSH!
OH, GOLLY!
OH, NO!
HE'S NOT GOING TO MAKE IT!
LINE DO NOT CROS

MEANWHILE...

YOU CAN'T LEAVE ME ROTTING IN JAIL!

LET ME OUT!

OR AT LEAST GET ME SOME DIFFERENT READING MATERIAL!

JAIL QUARTERLY
The Magazine All About Rotting in Jail!

101 NEW WAYS TO ROT!

How to embrace boredom

Find Joy with pebble collecting

ALSO MEANWHILE...

HERE THEY COME!

BIRD SEED

"GET READY WITH THE BIRDSEED!"

JAIL QUARTERLY
The Magazine All About Rotting in Jail!

THROWWW!

HURL!

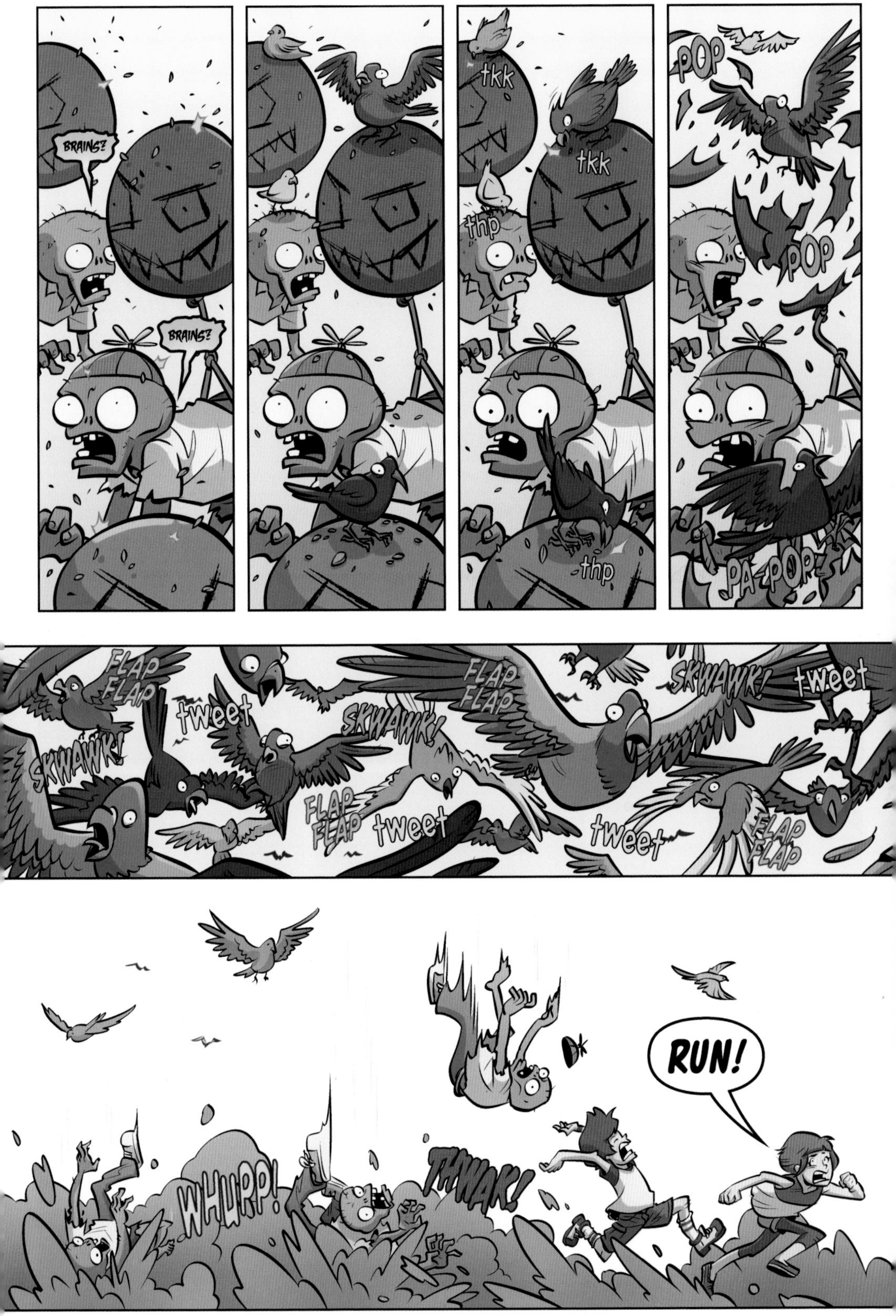
BRAINS?
BRAINS?
tkk
tkk
thp
thp
POP
POP
PA-POP!
FLAP FLAP
tweet
SKWAWK!
SKWAWK!
FLAP FLAP
SKWAWK!
tweet
FLAP FLAP
tweet
tweet
FLAP FLAP
RUN!
WHUPP!
THWAK!

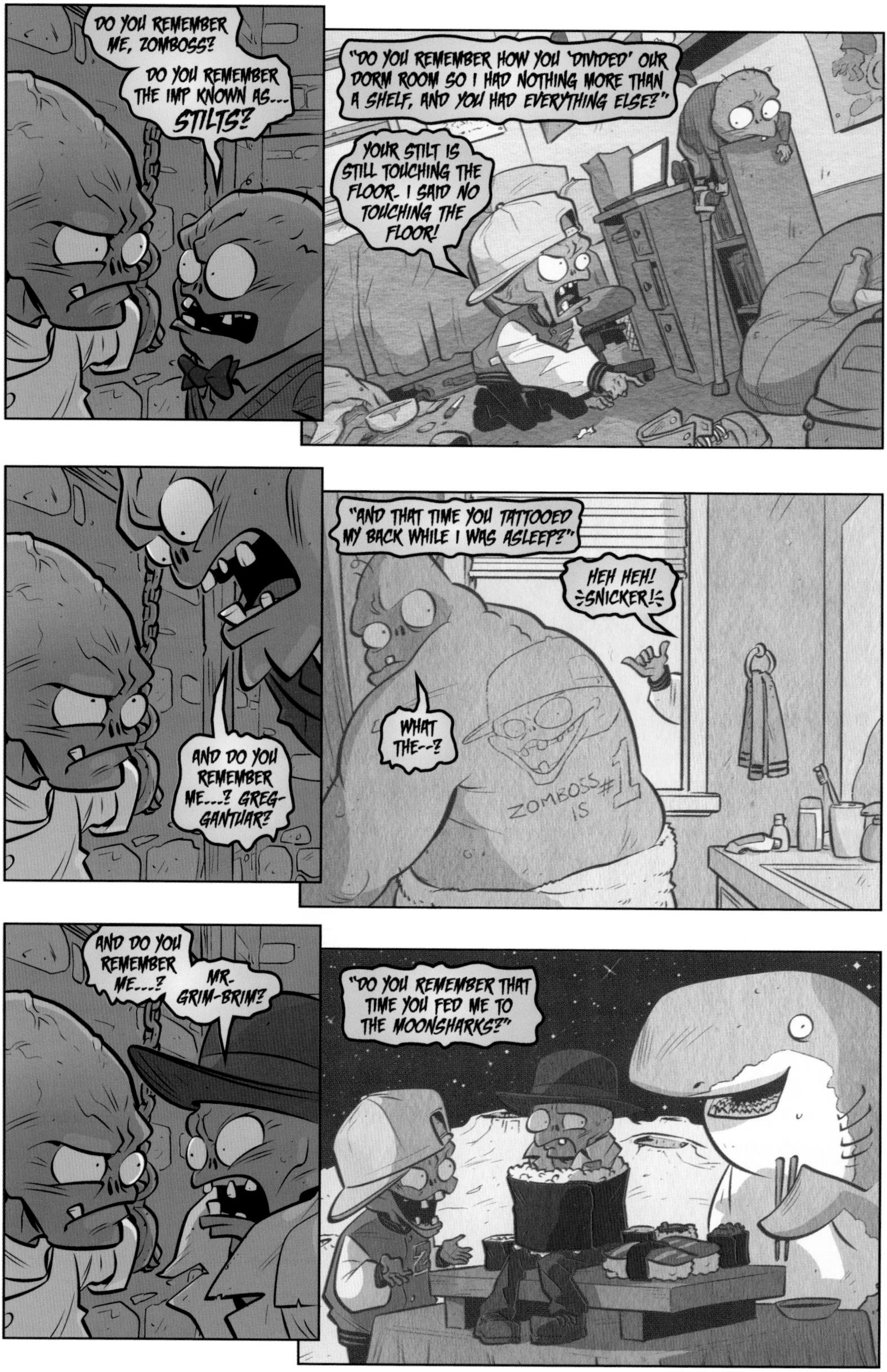
DO YOU REMEMBER ME, ZOMBOSS?
DO YOU REMEMBER THE IMP KNOWN AS... STILTS?
"DO YOU REMEMBER HOW YOU 'DIVIDED' OUR DORM ROOM SO I HAD NOTHING MORE THAN A SHELF, AND YOU HAD EVERYTHING ELSE?"
YOUR STILT IS STILL TOUCHING THE FLOOR. I SAID NO TOUCHING THE FLOOR!
AND DO YOU REMEMBER ME...? GREG-GANTUAR?
"AND THAT TIME YOU TATTOOED MY BACK WHILE I WAS ASLEEP?"
HEH HEH! SNICKER!
WHAT THE--?
ZOMBOSS IS #1
AND DO YOU REMEMBER ME...?
MR. GRIM-BRIM?
"DO YOU REMEMBER THAT TIME YOU FED ME TO THE MOONSHARKS?"

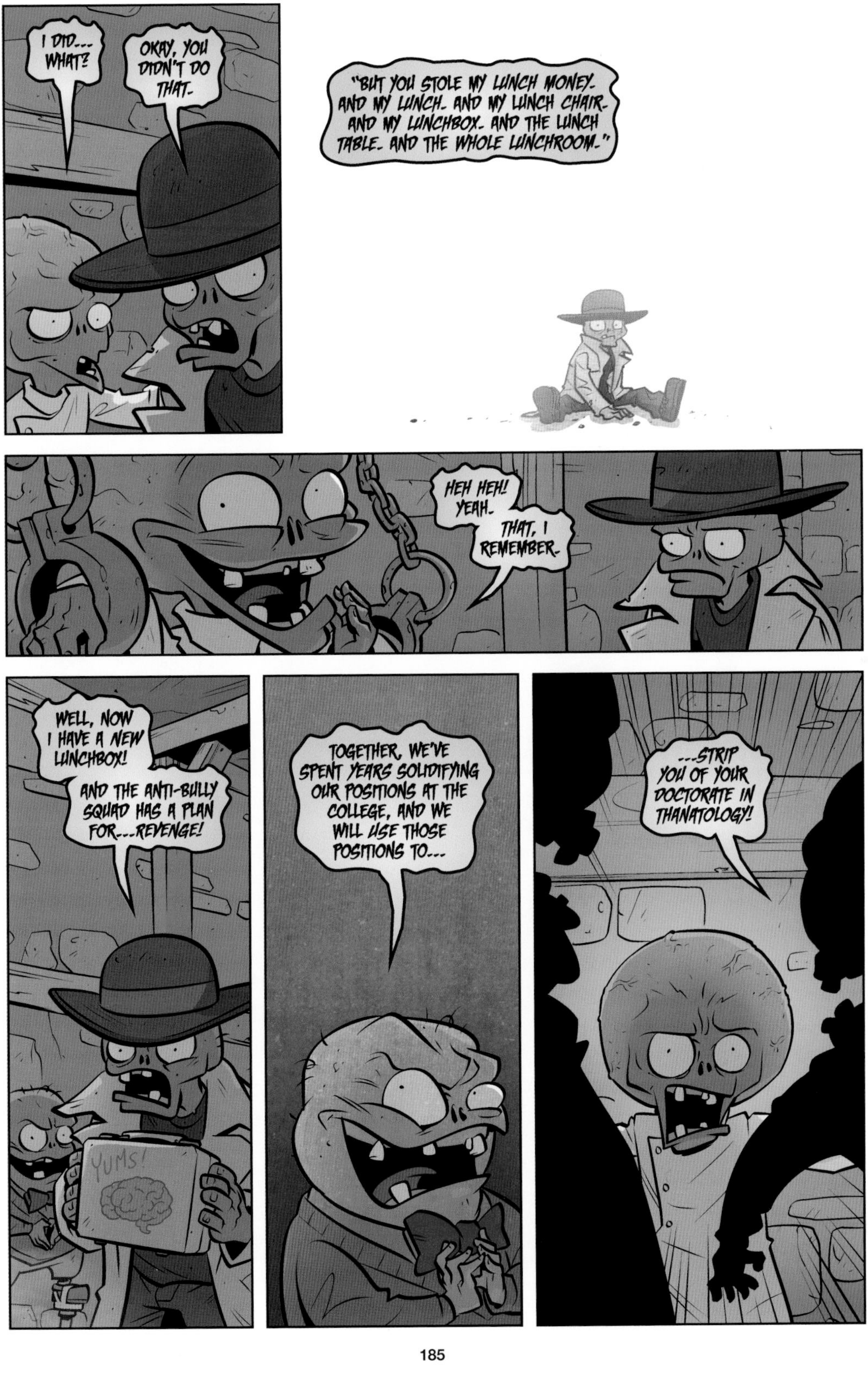
I DID... WHAT?
OKAY, YOU DIDN'T DO THAT.
"BUT YOU STOLE MY LUNCH MONEY. AND MY LUNCH. AND MY LUNCH CHAIR. AND MY LUNCHBOX. AND THE LUNCH TABLE. AND THE WHOLE LUNCHROOM."
HEH HEH! YEAH.
THAT, I REMEMBER.
WELL, NOW I HAVE A NEW LUNCHBOX!
AND THE ANTI-BULLY SQUAD HAS A PLAN FOR...REVENGE!
YUMS!
TOGETHER, WE'VE SPENT YEARS SOLIDIFYING OUR POSITIONS AT THE COLLEGE, AND WE WILL USE THOSE POSITIONS TO...
...STRIP YOU OF YOUR DOCTORATE IN THANATOLOGY!

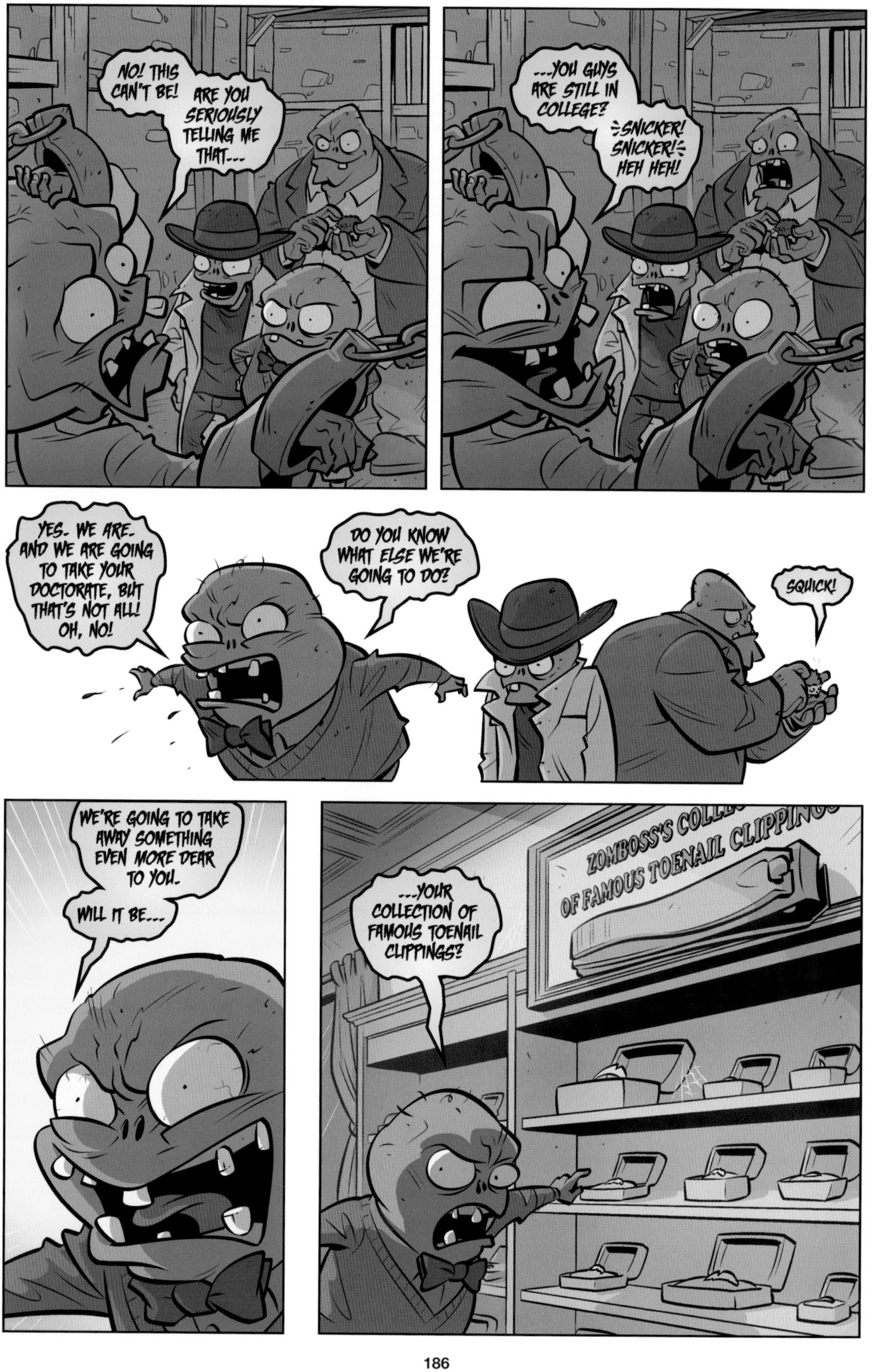
NO! THIS CAN'T BE!
ARE YOU SERIOUSLY TELLING ME THAT...
...YOU GUYS ARE STILL IN COLLEGE?
SNICKER! SNICKER! HEH HEH!
YES. WE ARE. AND WE ARE GOING TO TAKE YOUR DOCTORATE, BUT THAT'S NOT ALL! OH, NO!
DO YOU KNOW WHAT ELSE WE'RE GOING TO DO?
SQUICK!
WE'RE GOING TO TAKE AWAY SOMETHING EVEN MORE DEAR TO YOU.
WILL IT BE...
...YOUR COLLECTION OF FAMOUS TOENAIL CLIPPINGS?
ZOMBOSS'S COLLE
OF FAMOUS TOENAIL CLIPPINGS

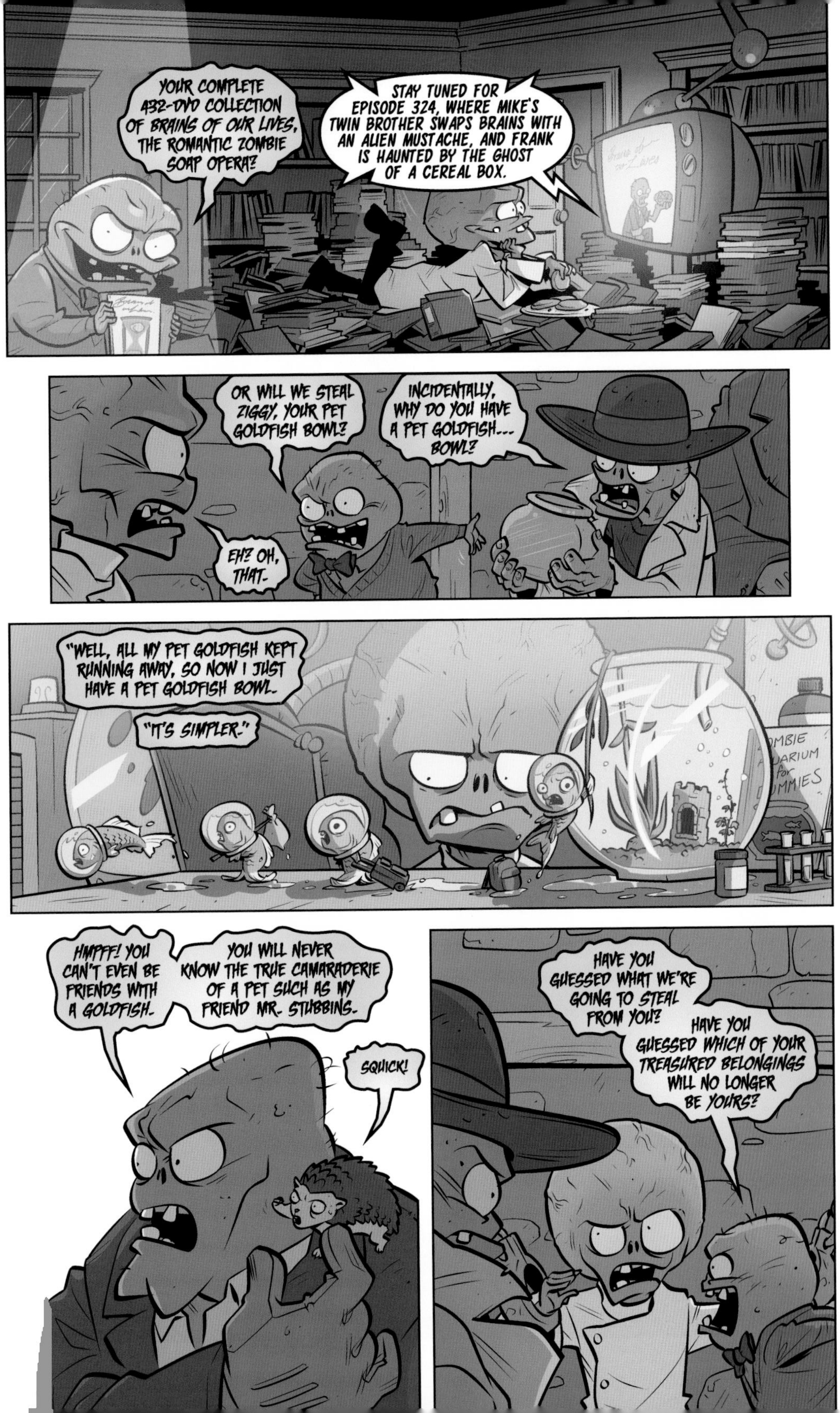
YOUR COMPLETE 432-DVD COLLECTION OF BRAINS OF OUR LIVES, THE ROMANTIC ZOMBIE SOAP OPERA?
STAY TUNED FOR EPISODE 324, WHERE MIKE'S TWIN BROTHER SWAPS BRAINS WITH AN ALIEN MUSTACHE, AND FRANK IS HAUNTED BY THE GHOST OF A CEREAL BOX.
OR WILL WE STEAL ZIGGY, YOUR PET GOLDFISH BOWL?
INCIDENTALLY, WHY DO YOU HAVE A PET GOLDFISH... BOWL?
EH? OH, THAT.
"WELL, ALL MY PET GOLDFISH KEPT RUNNING AWAY, SO NOW I JUST HAVE A PET GOLDFISH BOWL.
"IT'S SIMPLER."
HMPFF! YOU CAN'T EVEN BE FRIENDS WITH A GOLDFISH.
YOU WILL NEVER KNOW THE TRUE CAMARADERIE OF A PET SUCH AS MY FRIEND MR. STUBBINS.
SQUICK!
HAVE YOU GUESSED WHAT WE'RE GOING TO STEAL FROM YOU?
HAVE YOU GUESSED WHICH OF YOUR TREASURED BELONGINGS WILL NO LONGER BE YOURS?

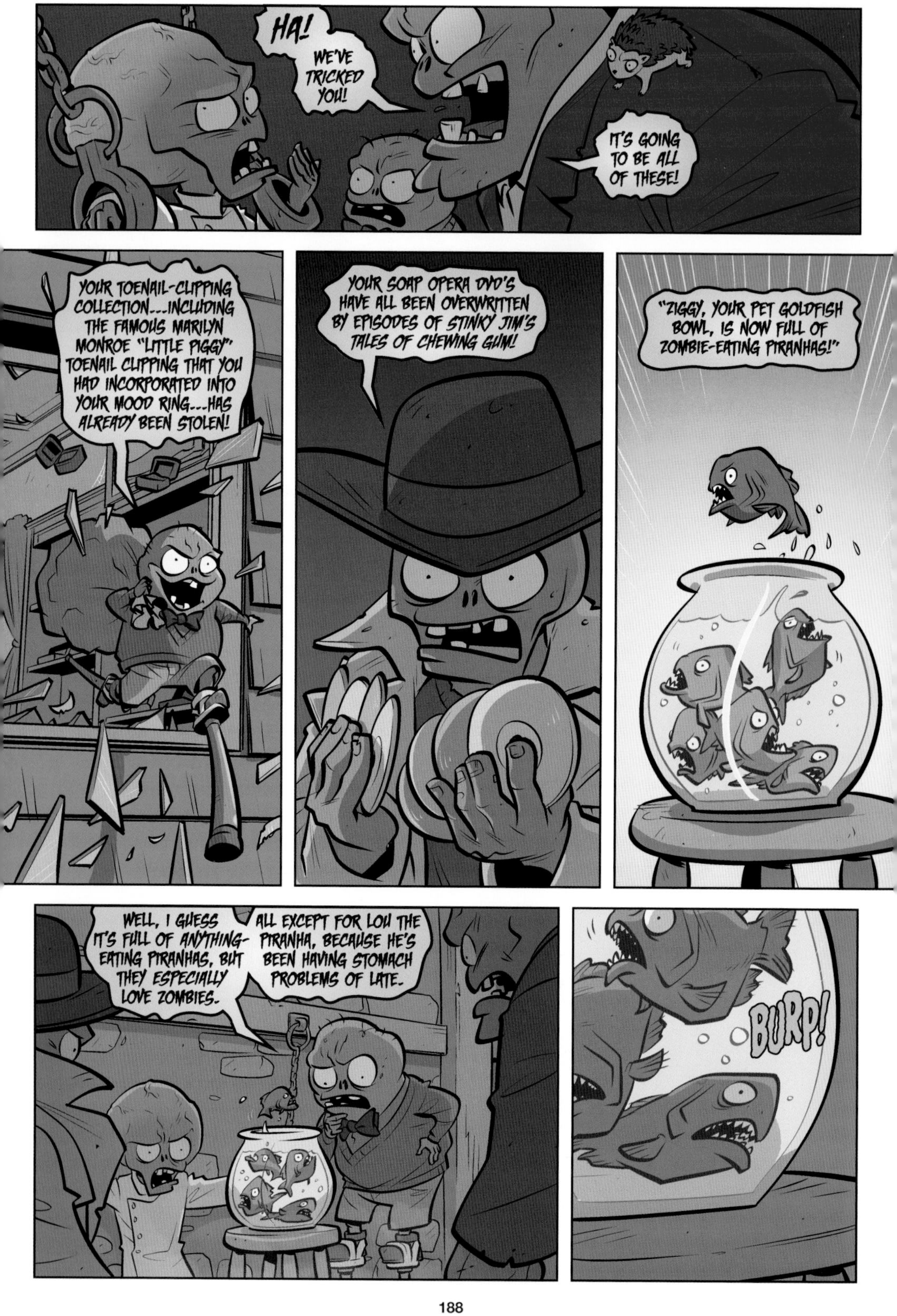
HA!
WE'VE TRICKED YOU!
IT'S GOING TO BE ALL OF THESE!
YOUR TOENAIL-CLIPPING COLLECTION...INCLUDING THE FAMOUS MARILYN MONROE "LITTLE PIGGY" TOENAIL CLIPPING THAT YOU HAD INCORPORATED INTO YOUR MOOD RING...HAS ALREADY BEEN STOLEN!
YOUR SOAP OPERA DVD'S HAVE ALL BEEN OVERWRITTEN BY EPISODES OF STINKY JIM'S TALES OF CHEWING GUM!
"ZIGGY, YOUR PET GOLDFISH BOWL, IS NOW FULL OF ZOMBIE-EATING PIRANHAS!"
WELL, I GUESS IT'S FULL OF ANYTHING-EATING PIRANHAS, BUT THEY ESPECIALLY LOVE ZOMBIES.
ALL EXCEPT FOR LOU THE PIRANHA, BECAUSE HE'S BEEN HAVING STOMACH PROBLEMS OF LATE.
BURP!

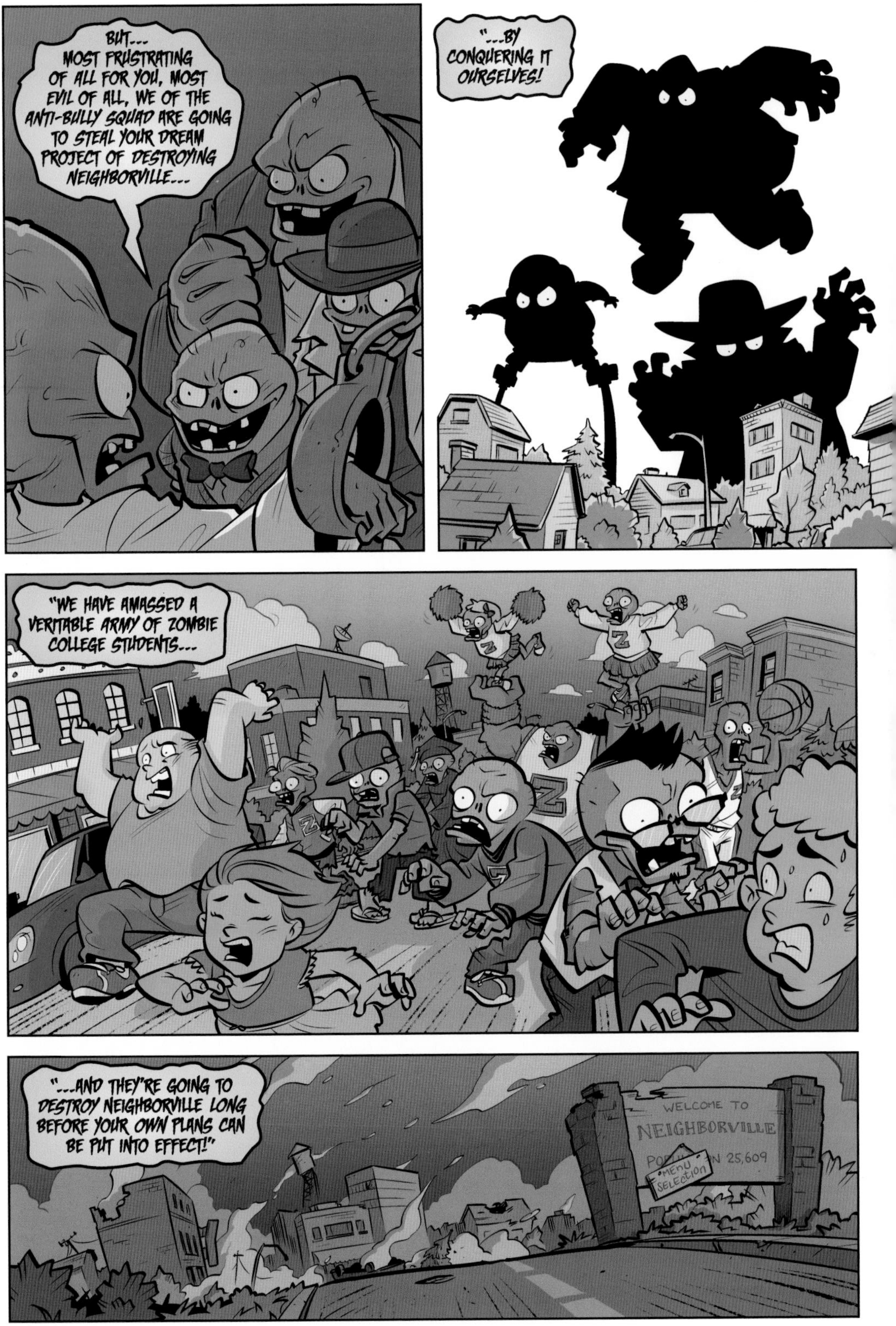
BUT... MOST FRUSTRATING OF ALL FOR YOU, MOST EVIL OF ALL, WE OF THE ANTI-BULLY SQUAD ARE GOING TO STEAL YOUR DREAM PROJECT OF DESTROYING NEIGHBORVILLE...
"...BY CONQUERING IT OURSELVES!
"WE HAVE AMASSED A VERITABLE ARMY OF ZOMBIE COLLEGE STUDENTS...
"...AND THEY'RE GOING TO DESTROY NEIGHBORVILLE LONG BEFORE YOUR OWN PLANS CAN BE PUT INTO EFFECT!"
WELCOME TO
NEIGHBORVILLE
"MENU" SELECTION

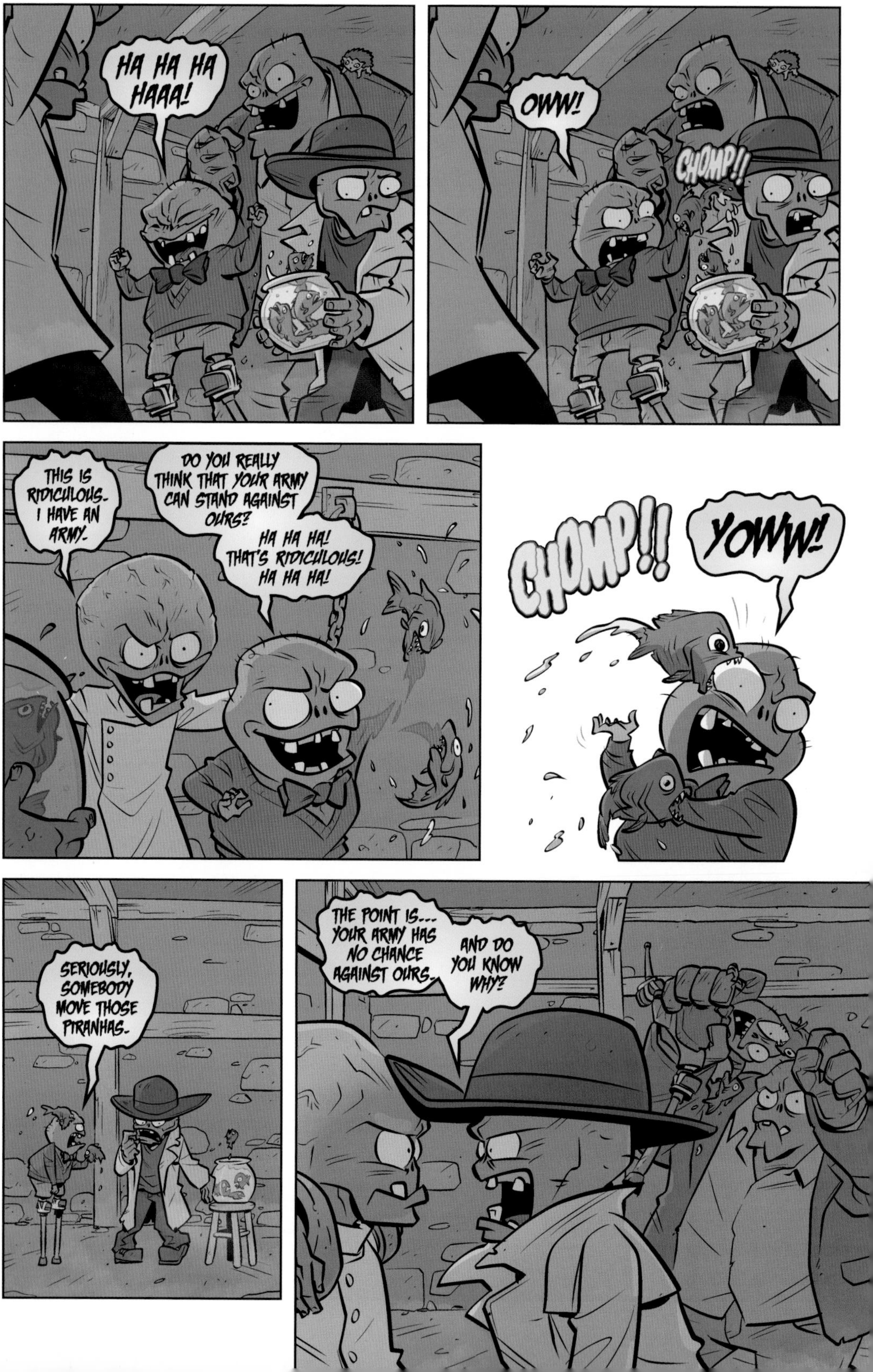
HA HA HA HAAA!
OWW!
CHOMP!!
THIS IS RIDICULOUS. I HAVE AN ARMY.
DO YOU REALLY THINK THAT YOUR ARMY CAN STAND AGAINST OURS?
HA HA HA! THAT'S RIDICULOUS! HA HA HA!
CHOMP!!
YOWW!
SERIOUSLY, SOMEBODY MOVE THOSE PIRANHAS.
THE POINT IS... YOUR ARMY HAS NO CHANCE AGAINST OURS.
AND DO YOU KNOW WHY?

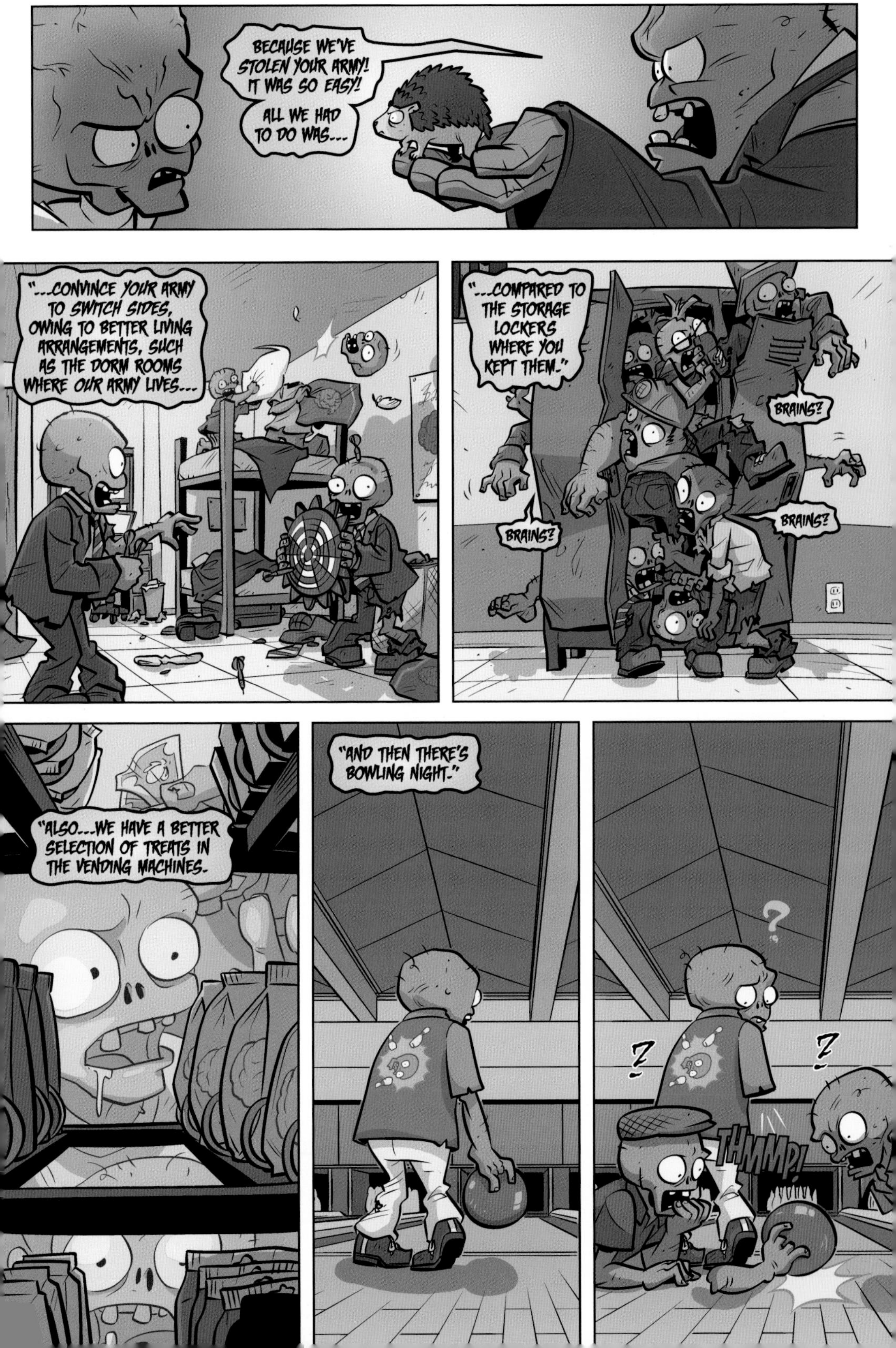
BECAUSE WE'VE STOLEN YOUR ARMY! IT WAS SO EASY!
ALL WE HAD TO DO WAS...
"...CONVINCE YOUR ARMY TO SWITCH SIDES, OWING TO BETTER LIVING ARRANGEMENTS, SUCH AS THE DORM ROOMS WHERE OUR ARMY LIVES...
"...COMPARED TO THE STORAGE LOCKERS WHERE YOU KEPT THEM."
BRAINS?
BRAINS?
BRAINS?
"ALSO...WE HAVE A BETTER SELECTION OF TREATS IN THE VENDING MACHINES.
"AND THEN THERE'S BOWLING NIGHT."
?
Z
Z
THMMP!

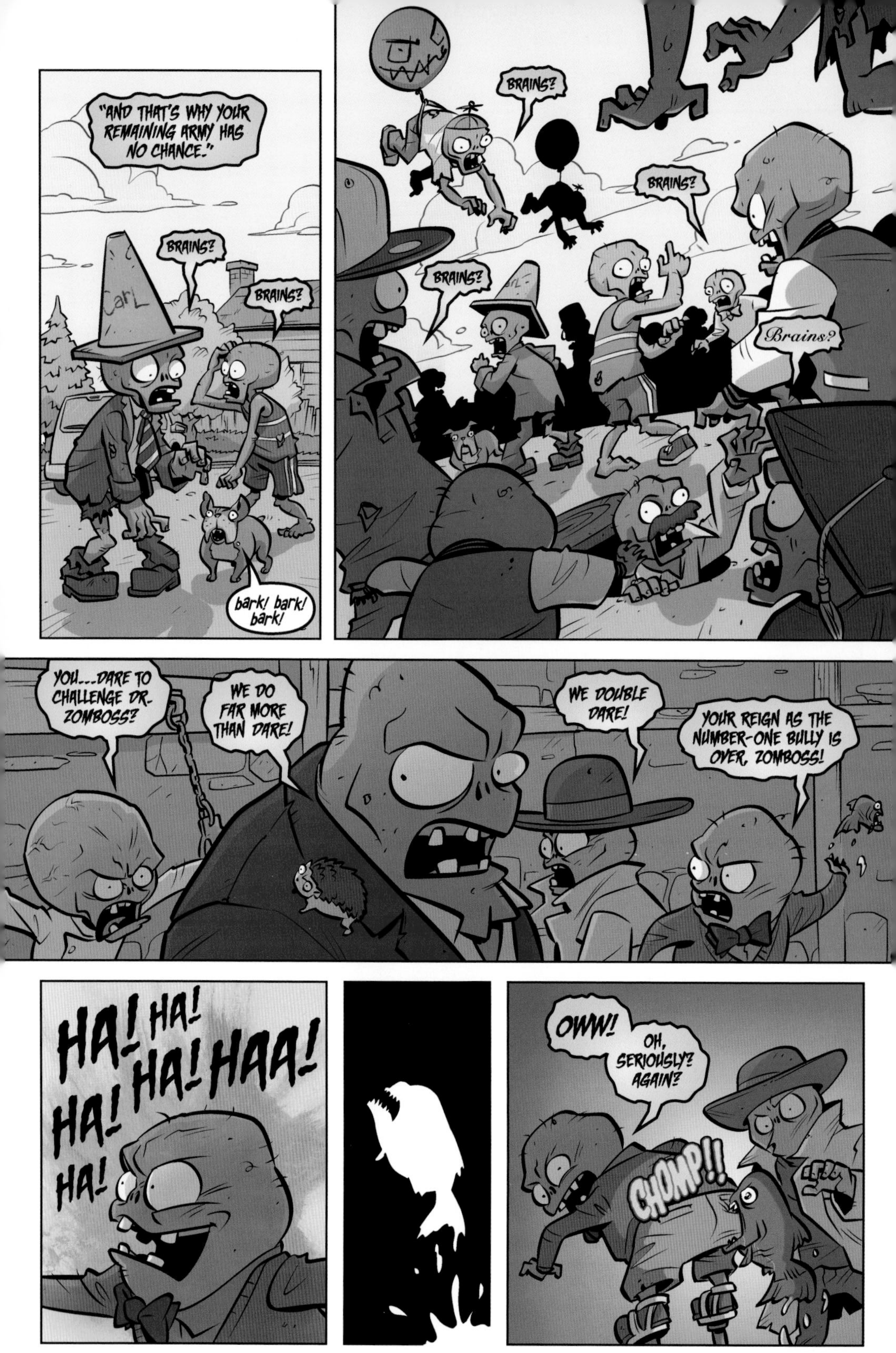
"AND THAT'S WHY YOUR REMAINING ARMY HAS NO CHANCE."
BRAINS?
BRAINS?
bark! bark! bark!
BRAINS?
BRAINS?
BRAINS?
Brains?
YOU...DARE TO CHALLENGE DR. ZOMBOSS?
WE DO FAR MORE THAN DARE!
WE DOUBLE DARE!
YOUR REIGN AS THE NUMBER-ONE BULLY IS OVER, ZOMBOSS!
HA! HA! HA! HA! HAA! HA!
OWW!
OH, SERIOUSLY? AGAIN?
CHOMP!!

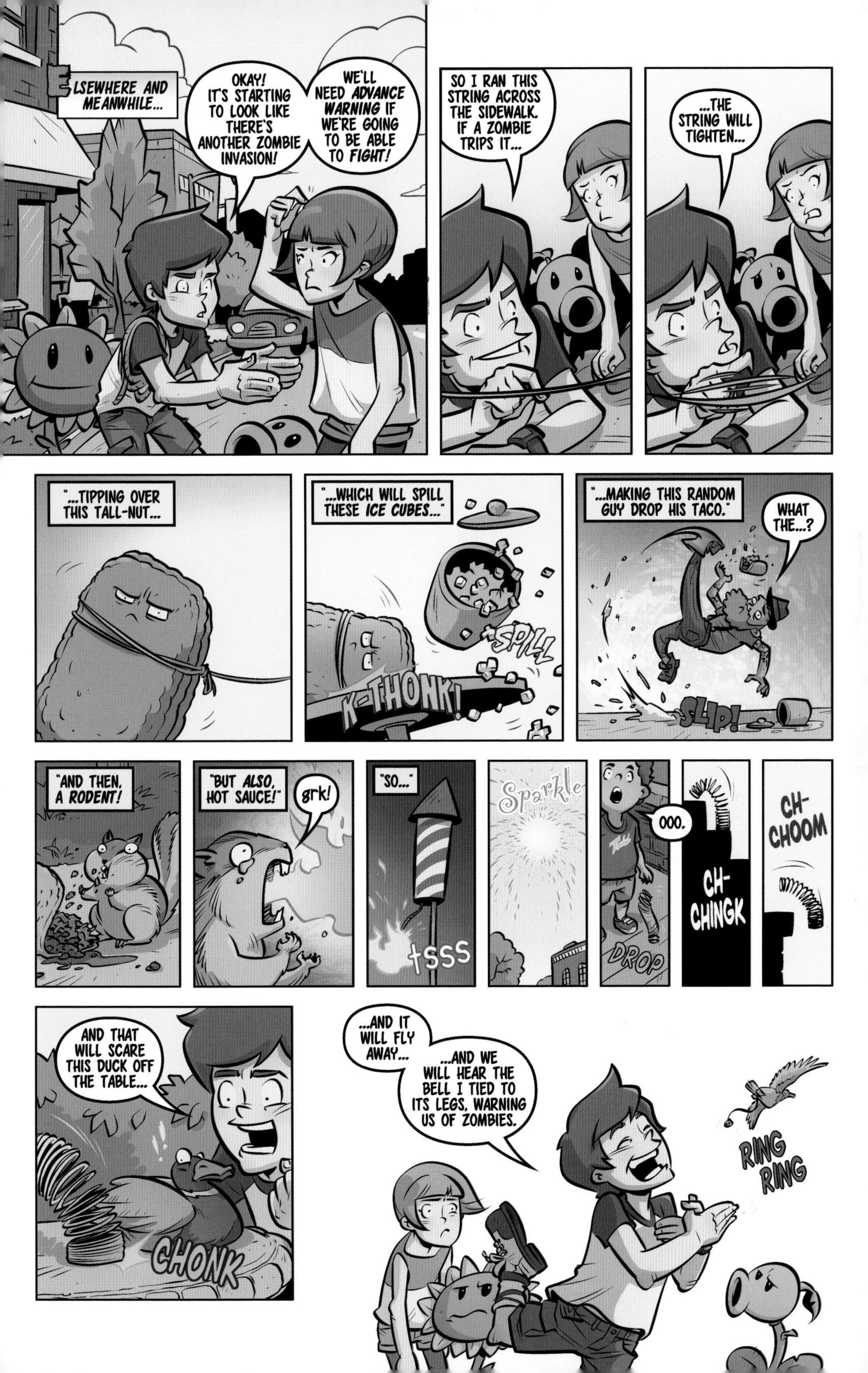
ELSEWHERE AND MEANWHILE...
OKAY! IT'S STARTING TO LOOK LIKE THERE'S ANOTHER ZOMBIE INVASION!
WE'LL NEED ADVANCE WARNING IF WE'RE GOING TO BE ABLE TO FIGHT!
SO I RAN THIS STRING ACROSS THE SIDEWALK. IF A ZOMBIE TRIPS IT...
...THE STRING WILL TIGHTEN...
"...TIPPING OVER THIS TALL-NUT...
"...WHICH WILL SPILL THESE ICE CUBES..."
SPILL
K-THONK!
"...MAKING THIS RANDOM GUY DROP HIS TACO."
WHAT THE...?
SLIP!
"AND THEN, A RODENT!
"BUT ALSO, HOT SAUCE!"
grk!
"SO..."
tsss
Sparkle
OOO.
DROP
CH-CHINGK
CH-CHOOM
AND THAT WILL SCARE THIS DUCK OFF THE TABLE...
!!
CHONK
...AND IT WILL FLY AWAY...
...AND WE WILL HEAR THE BELL I TIED TO ITS LEGS, WARNING US OF ZOMBIES.
RING RING

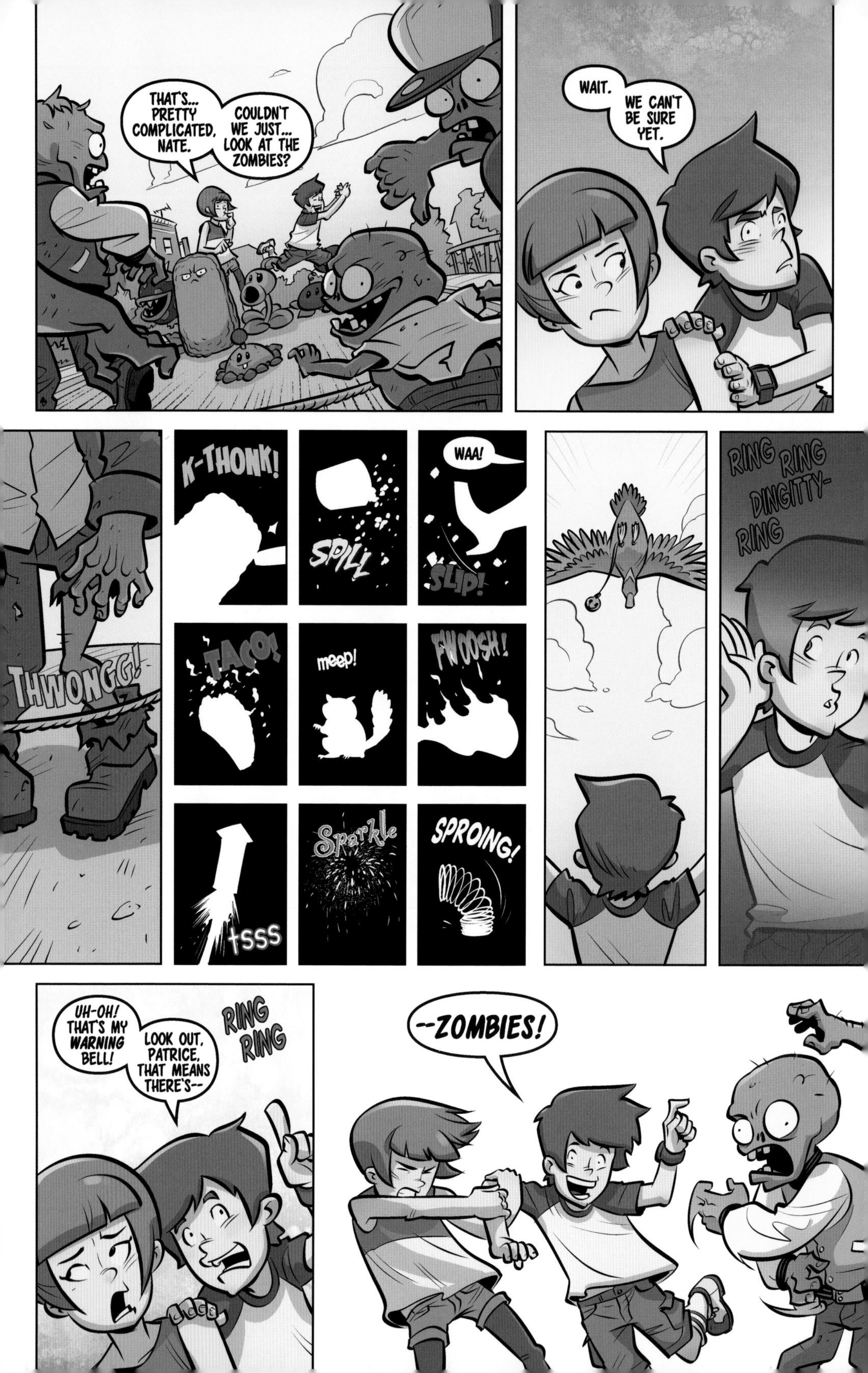
THAT'S... PRETTY COMPLICATED, NATE.
COULDN'T WE JUST... LOOK AT THE ZOMBIES?
WAIT.
WE CAN'T BE SURE YET.
THWONGG!
K-THONK!
SPILL
WAA!
SLIP!
TACO!
meep!
FWOOSH!
tsss
Sparkle
SPROING!
RING RING DINGITTY-RING
UH-OH! THAT'S MY WARNING BELL!
LOOK OUT, PATRICE, THAT MEANS THERE'S--
RING RING
--ZOMBIES!

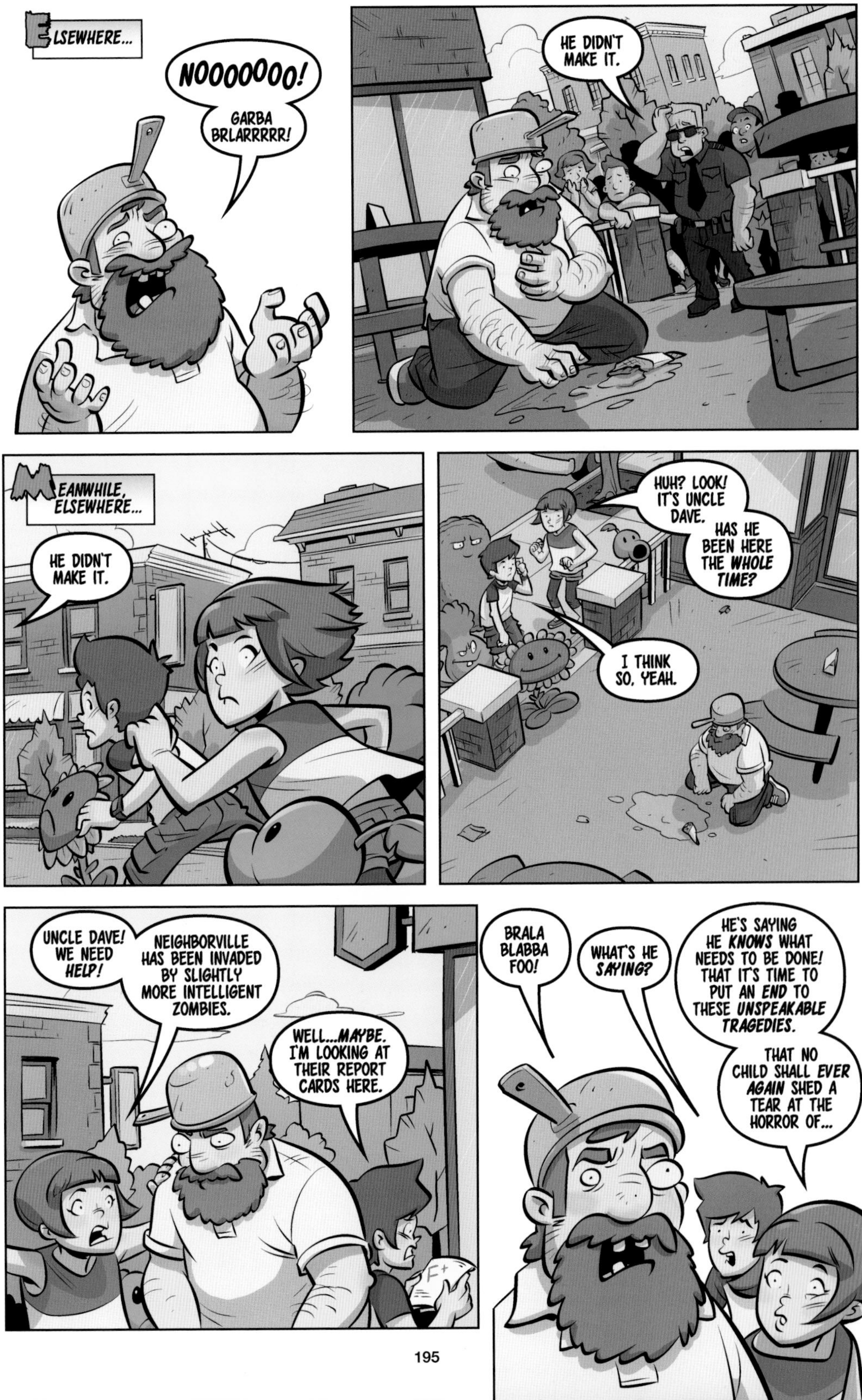
ELSEWHERE...
NOOOOOOO!
GARBA BRLARRRRR!
HE DIDN'T MAKE IT.
MEANWHILE, ELSEWHERE...
HE DIDN'T MAKE IT.
HUH? LOOK! IT'S UNCLE DAVE.
HAS HE BEEN HERE THE WHOLE TIME?
I THINK SO, YEAH.
UNCLE DAVE! WE NEED HELP!
NEIGHBORVILLE HAS BEEN INVADED BY SLIGHTLY MORE INTELLIGENT ZOMBIES.
WELL...MAYBE. I'M LOOKING AT THEIR REPORT CARDS HERE.
F+
BRALA BLABBA FOO!
WHAT'S HE SAYING?
HE'S SAYING HE KNOWS WHAT NEEDS TO BE DONE! THAT IT'S TIME TO PUT AN END TO THESE UNSPEAKABLE TRAGEDIES.
THAT NO CHILD SHALL EVER AGAIN SHED A TEAR AT THE HORROR OF...

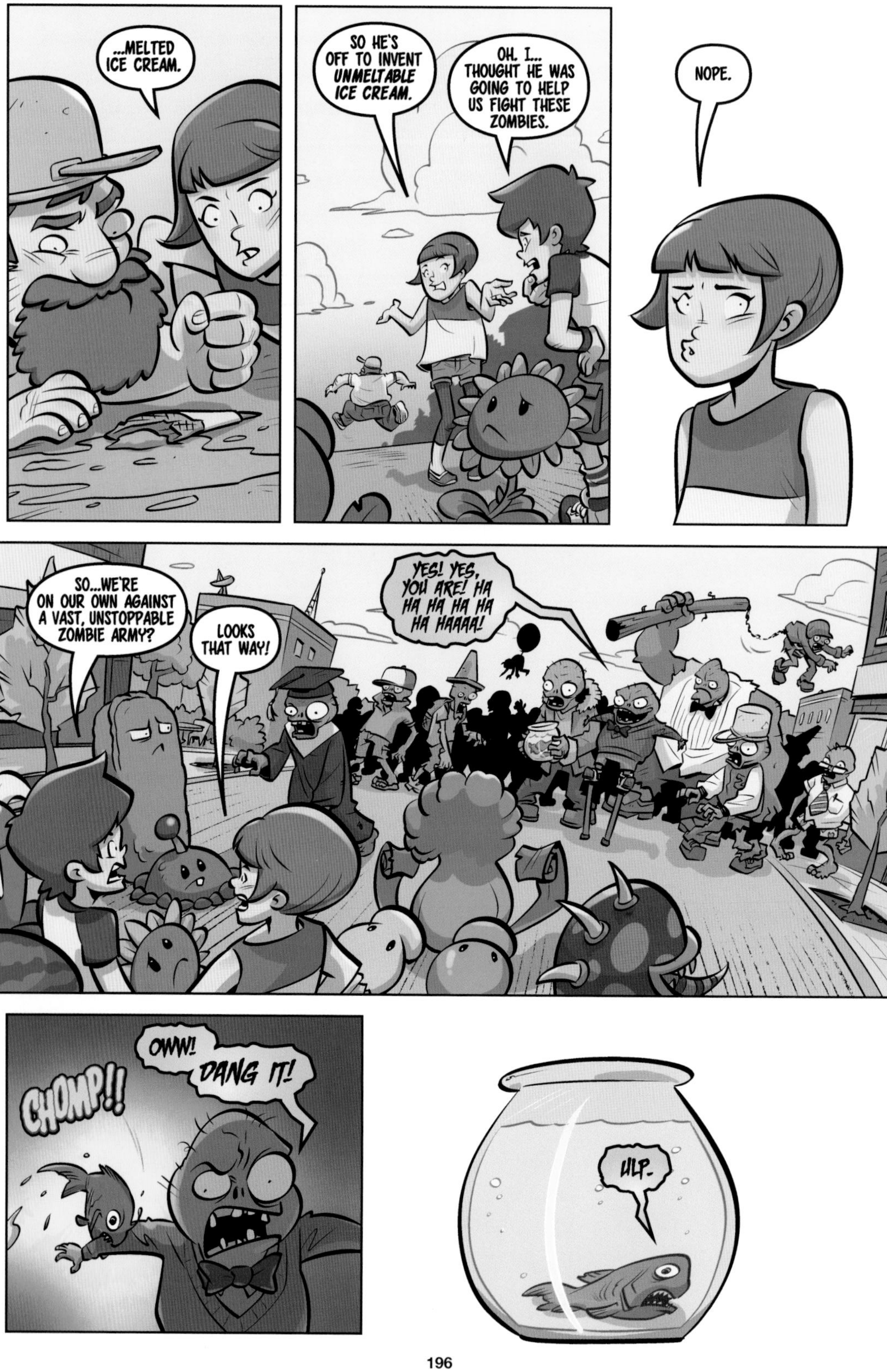
...MELTED ICE CREAM.
SO HE'S OFF TO INVENT *UNMELTABLE* ICE CREAM.
OH. I... THOUGHT HE WAS GOING TO HELP US FIGHT THESE ZOMBIES.
NOPE.
SO...WE'RE ON OUR OWN AGAINST A VAST, UNSTOPPABLE ZOMBIE ARMY?
LOOKS THAT WAY!
YES! YES, YOU ARE! HA HA HA HA HA HA HAAAA!
CHOMP!!
OWW!
DANG IT!
ULP.

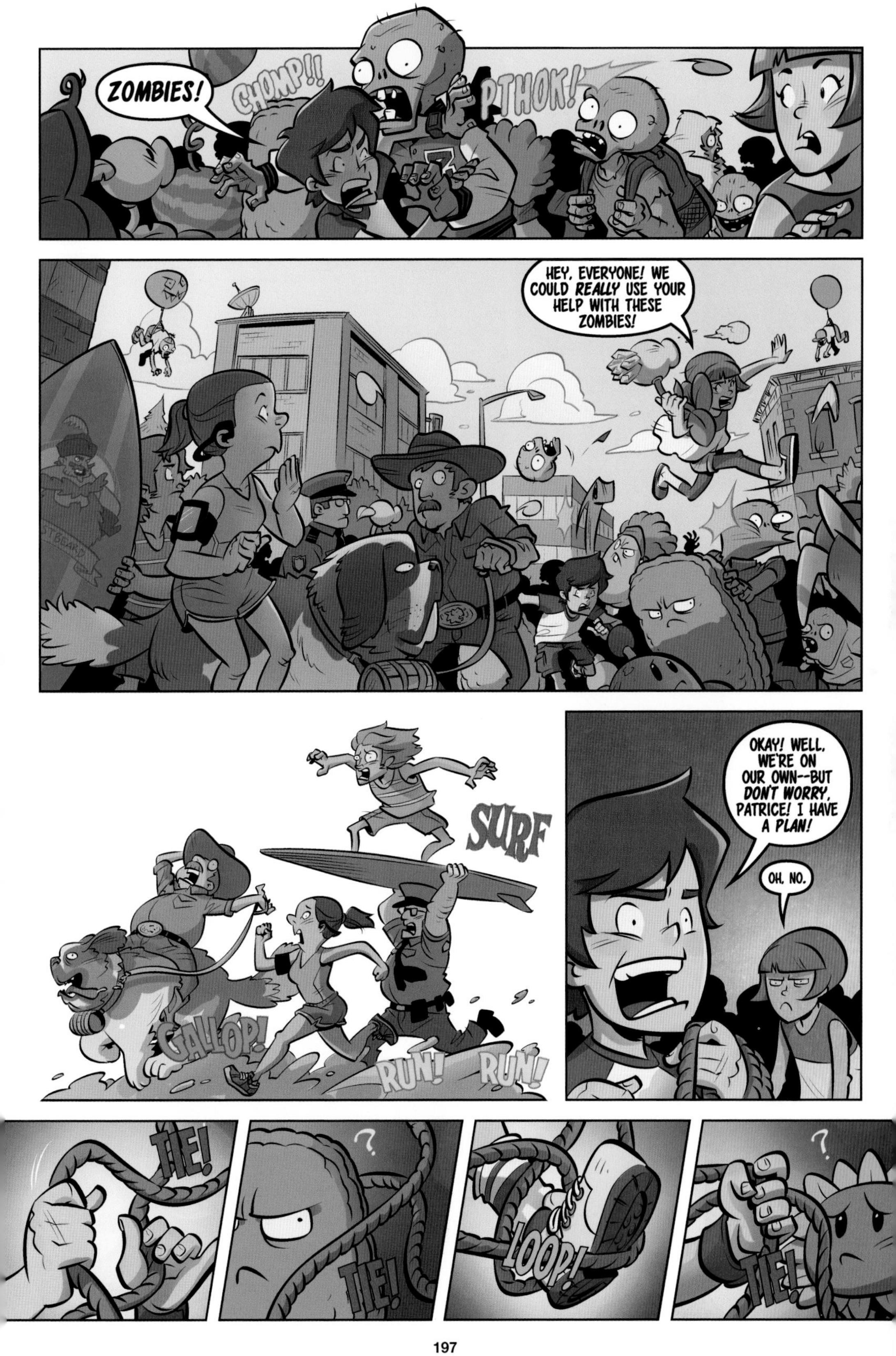
ZOMBIES!
CHOMP!!
PTHOK!
HEY, EVERYONE! WE COULD REALLY USE YOUR HELP WITH THESE ZOMBIES!
SURF
GALLOP!
RUN!
RUN!
OKAY! WELL, WE'RE ON OUR OWN--BUT DON'T WORRY, PATRICE! I HAVE A PLAN!
OH, NO.
TIE!
?
TIE!
LOOP!
?
TIE!

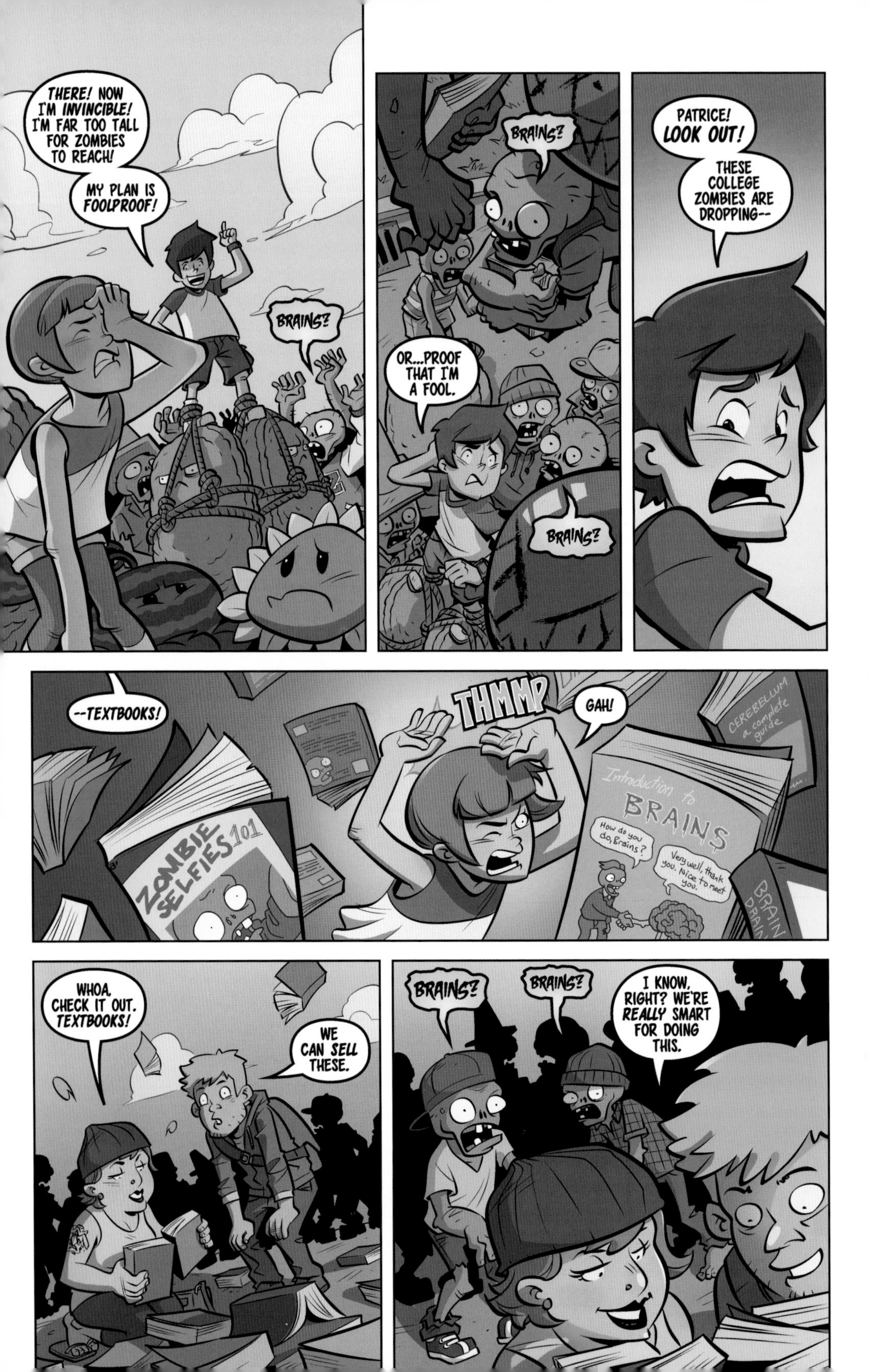
THERE! NOW I'M INVINCIBLE! I'M FAR TOO TALL FOR ZOMBIES TO REACH!
MY PLAN IS FOOLPROOF!
BRAINS?
BRAINS?
OR...PROOF THAT I'M A FOOL.
BRAINS?
PATRICE! LOOK OUT!
THESE COLLEGE ZOMBIES ARE DROPPING--
--TEXTBOOKS!
THMMP
GAH!
ZOMBIE SELFIES 101
Introduction to BRAINS
How do you do, Brains?
Very well, thank you. Nice to meet you.
CEREBELLUM a complete guide
BRAIN DRAIN
WHOA, CHECK IT OUT. TEXTBOOKS!
WE CAN SELL THESE.
BRAINS?
BRAINS?
I KNOW, RIGHT? WE'RE REALLY SMART FOR DOING THIS.

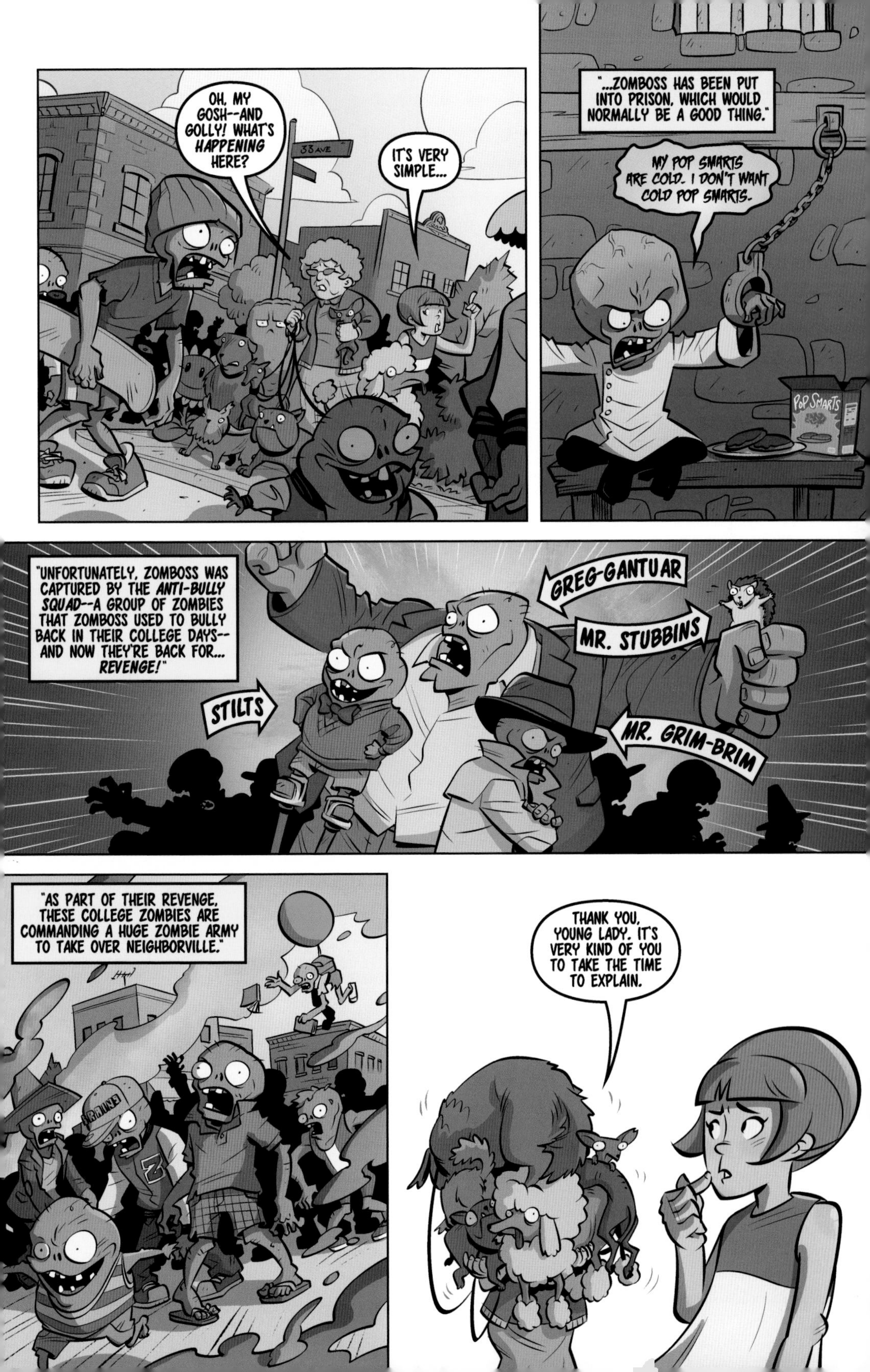
OH, MY GOSH--AND GOLLY! WHAT'S HAPPENING HERE?
33 AVE
IT'S VERY SIMPLE...
"...ZOMBOSS HAS BEEN PUT INTO PRISON, WHICH WOULD NORMALLY BE A GOOD THING."
MY POP SMARTS ARE COLD. I DON'T WANT COLD POP SMARTS.
POP SMARTS
"UNFORTUNATELY, ZOMBOSS WAS CAPTURED BY THE ANTI-BULLY SQUAD--A GROUP OF ZOMBIES THAT ZOMBOSS USED TO BULLY BACK IN THEIR COLLEGE DAYS--AND NOW THEY'RE BACK FOR... REVENGE!"
GREG-GANTUAR
MR. STUBBINS
STILTS
MR. GRIM-BRIM
"AS PART OF THEIR REVENGE, THESE COLLEGE ZOMBIES ARE COMMANDING A HUGE ZOMBIE ARMY TO TAKE OVER NEIGHBORVILLE."
THANK YOU, YOUNG LADY. IT'S VERY KIND OF YOU TO TAKE THE TIME TO EXPLAIN.

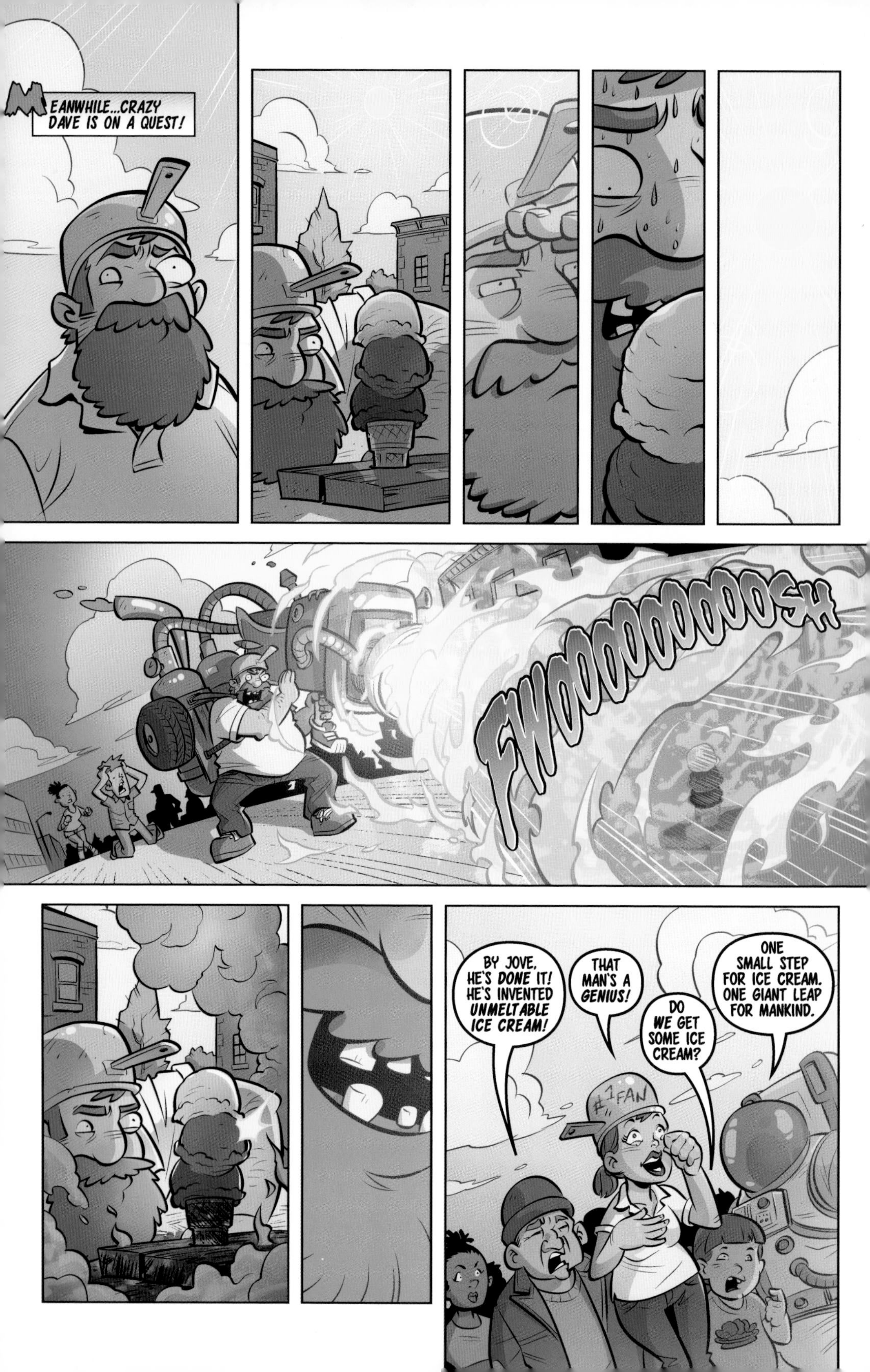
MEANWHILE...CRAZY DAVE IS ON A QUEST!
FWOOOOOOOOOOSH
BY JOVE, HE'S DONE IT! HE'S INVENTED UNMELTABLE ICE CREAM!
THAT MAN'S A GENIUS!
DO WE GET SOME ICE CREAM?
ONE SMALL STEP FOR ICE CREAM. ONE GIANT LEAP FOR MANKIND.
#1 FAN

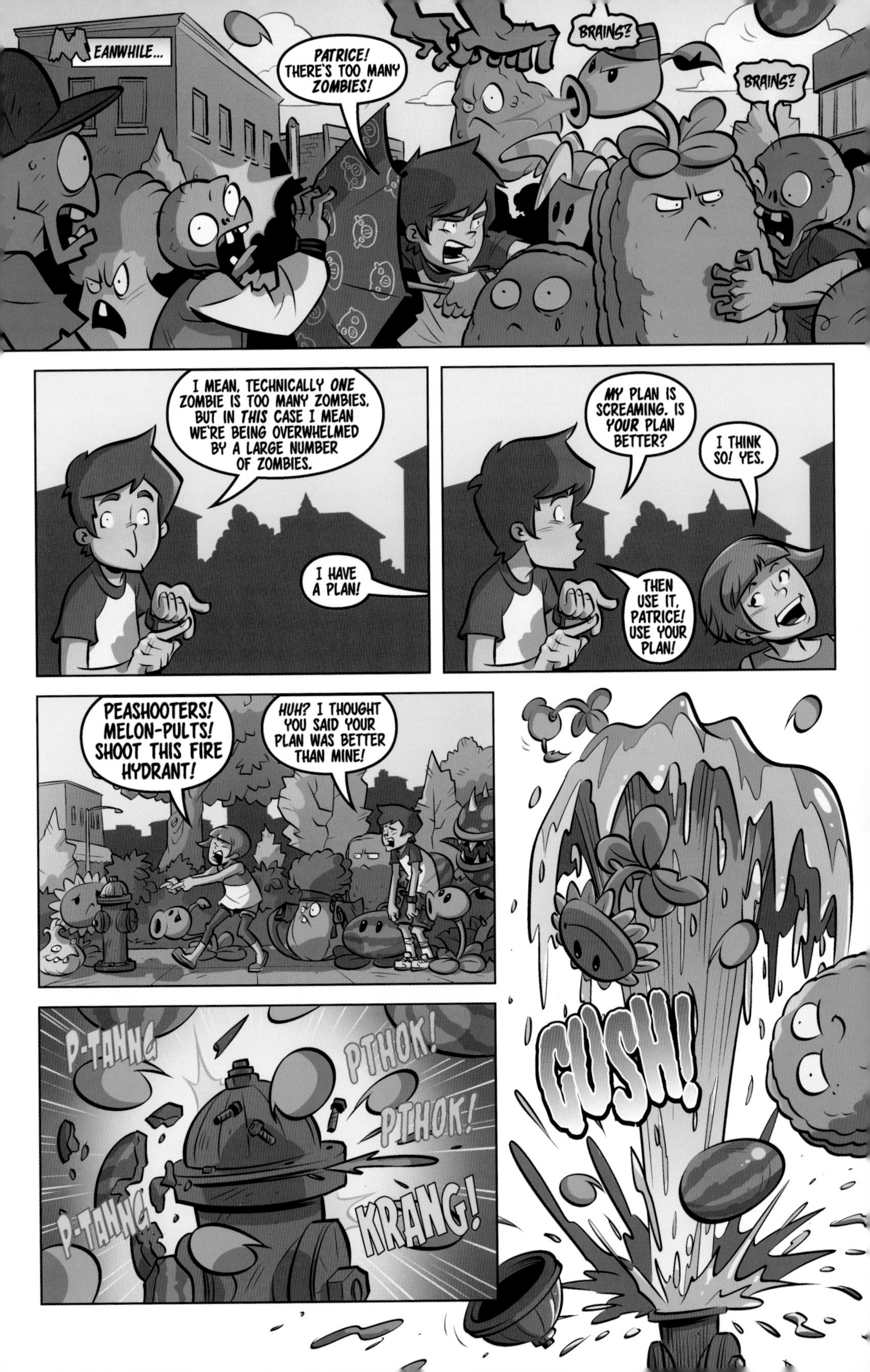
MEANWHILE...
PATRICE! THERE'S TOO MANY ZOMBIES!
BRAINS?
BRAINS?
I MEAN, TECHNICALLY ONE ZOMBIE IS TOO MANY ZOMBIES, BUT IN THIS CASE I MEAN WE'RE BEING OVERWHELMED BY A LARGE NUMBER OF ZOMBIES.
I HAVE A PLAN!
MY PLAN IS SCREAMING. IS YOUR PLAN BETTER?
I THINK SO! YES.
THEN USE IT, PATRICE! USE YOUR PLAN!
PEASHOOTERS! MELON-PULTS! SHOOT THIS FIRE HYDRANT!
HUH? I THOUGHT YOU SAID YOUR PLAN WAS BETTER THAN MINE!
P-TAHNG
PTHOK!
PTHOK!
P-TAHNG
KRANG!
GUSH!

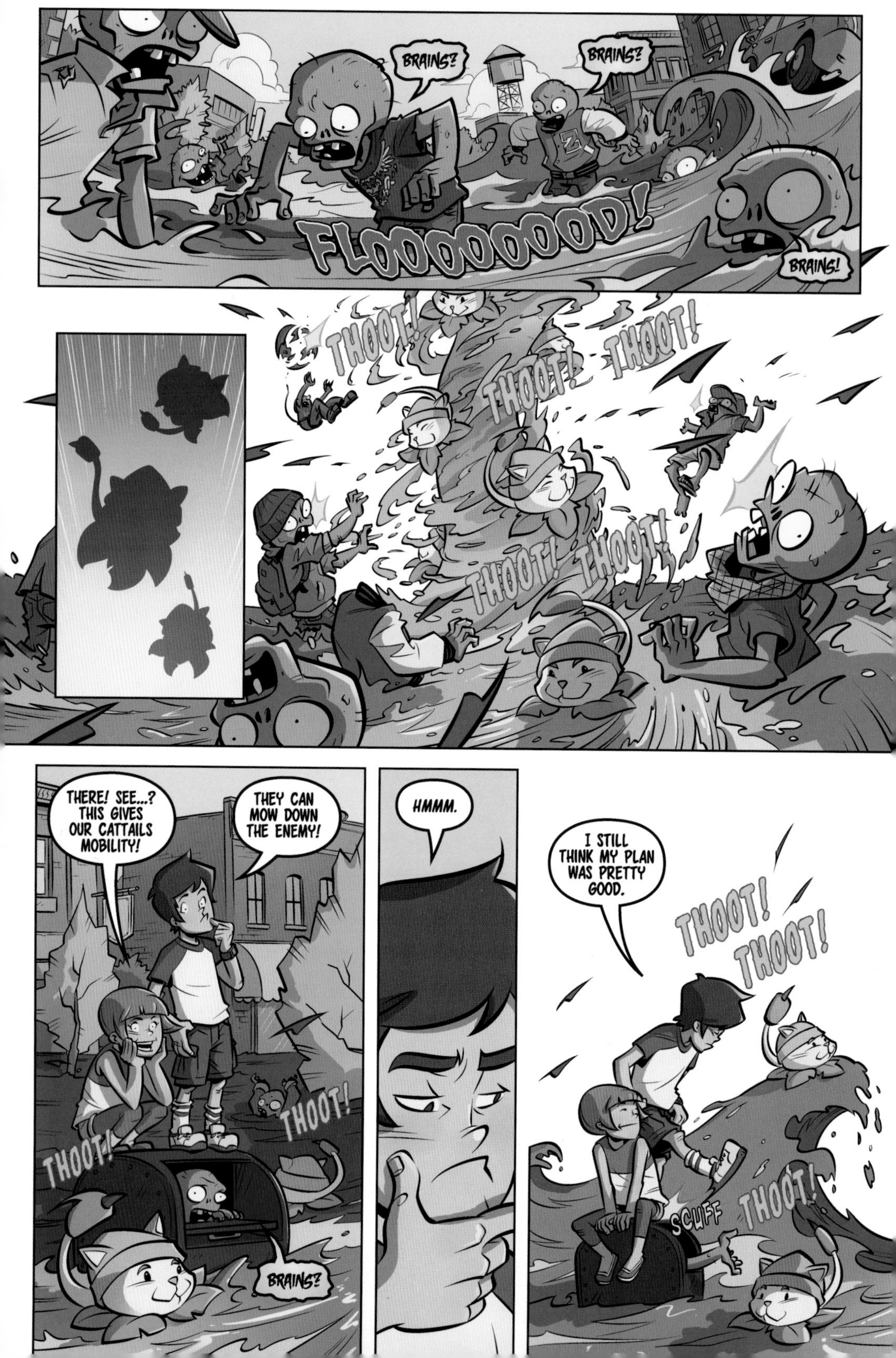
BRAINS?
BRAINS?
FLOOOOOOOD!
BRAINS!
THOOT!
THOOT!
THOOT!
THOOT!
THOOT!
THERE! SEE...? THIS GIVES OUR CATTAILS MOBILITY!
THEY CAN MOW DOWN THE ENEMY!
THOOT!
THOOT!
BRAINS?
HMMM.
I STILL THINK MY PLAN WAS PRETTY GOOD.
THOOT!
THOOT!
SCUFF
THOOT!

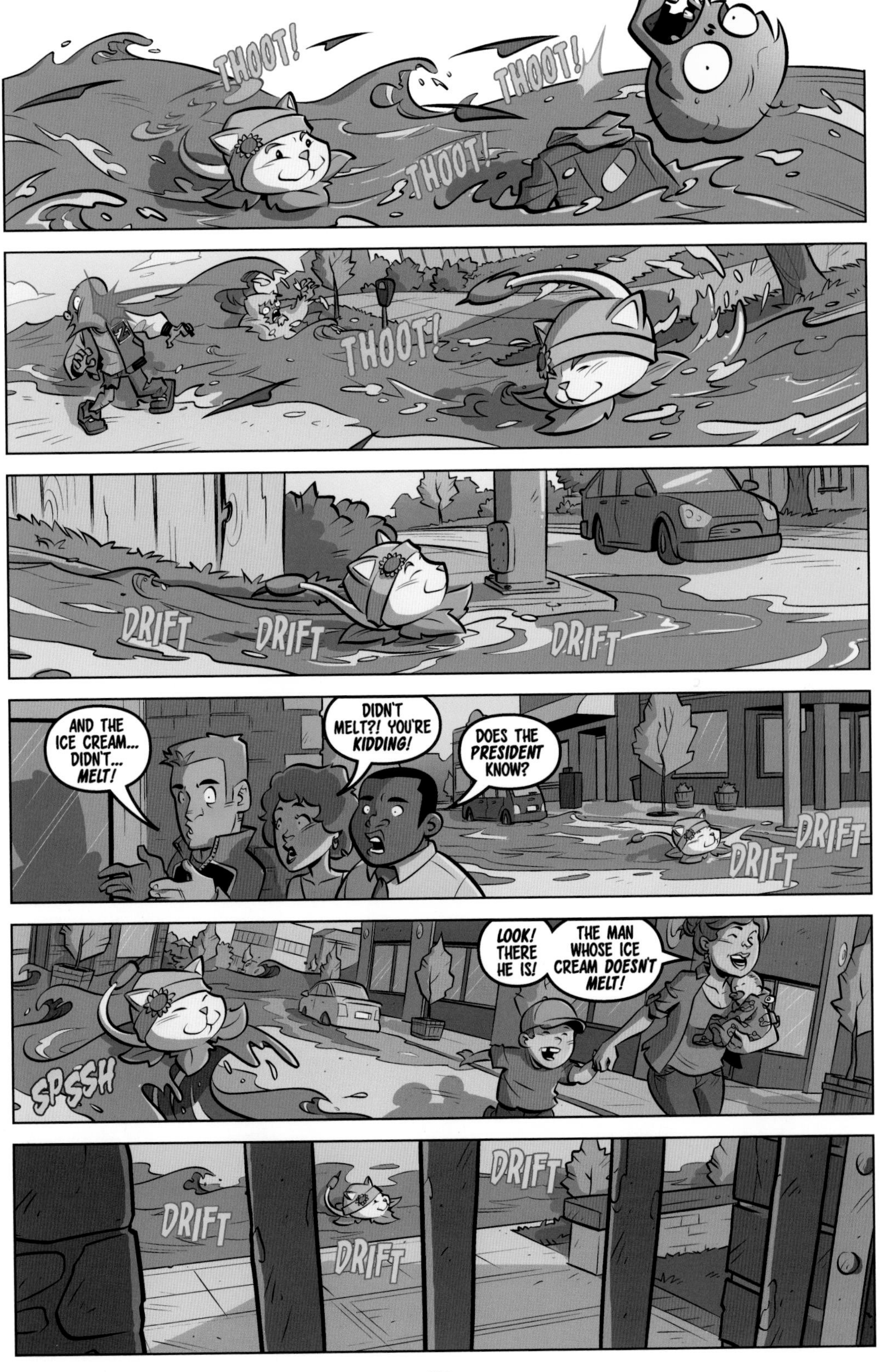
THOOT!
THOOT!
THOOT!
THOOT!
DRIFT
DRIFT
DRIFT
AND THE ICE CREAM... DIDN'T... MELT!
DIDN'T MELT?! YOU'RE KIDDING!
DOES THE PRESIDENT KNOW?
DRIFT
DRIFT
SPSSH
LOOK! THERE HE IS!
THE MAN WHOSE ICE CREAM DOESN'T MELT!
DRIFT
DRIFT
DRIFT

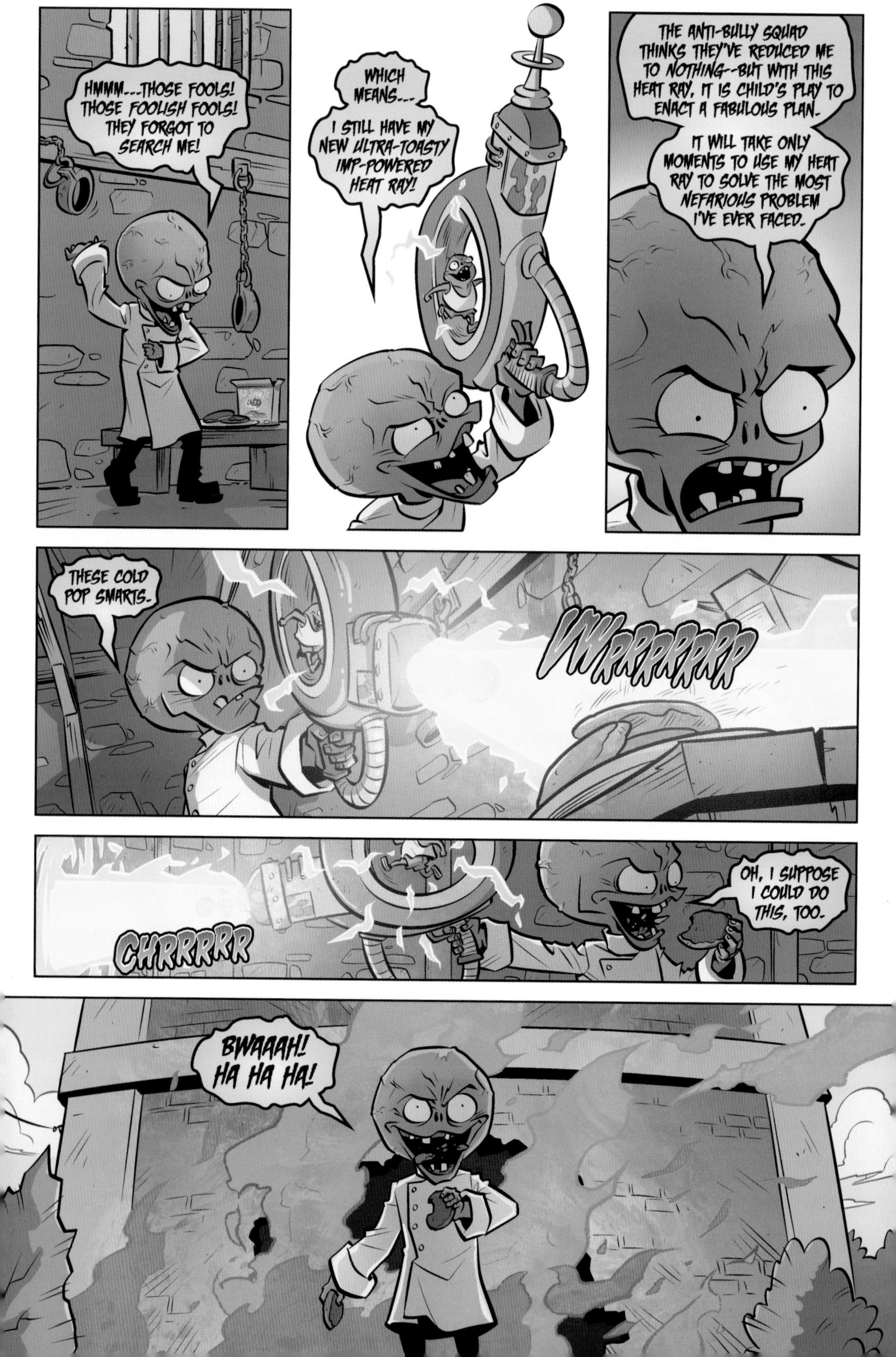

HMMM...THOSE FOOLS! THOSE FOOLISH FOOLS! THEY FORGOT TO SEARCH ME!
WHICH MEANS...
I STILL HAVE MY NEW ULTRA-TOASTY IMP-POWERED HEAT RAY!
THE ANTI-BULLY SQUAD THINKS THEY'VE REDUCED ME TO NOTHING--BUT WITH THIS HEAT RAY, IT IS CHILD'S PLAY TO ENACT A FABULOUS PLAN.
IT WILL TAKE ONLY MOMENTS TO USE MY HEAT RAY TO SOLVE THE MOST NEFARIOUS PROBLEM I'VE EVER FACED.
THESE COLD POP SMARTS.
VWRRRRRRR
CHRRRRR
OH, I SUPPOSE I COULD DO THIS, TOO.
BWAAAH! HA HA HA!

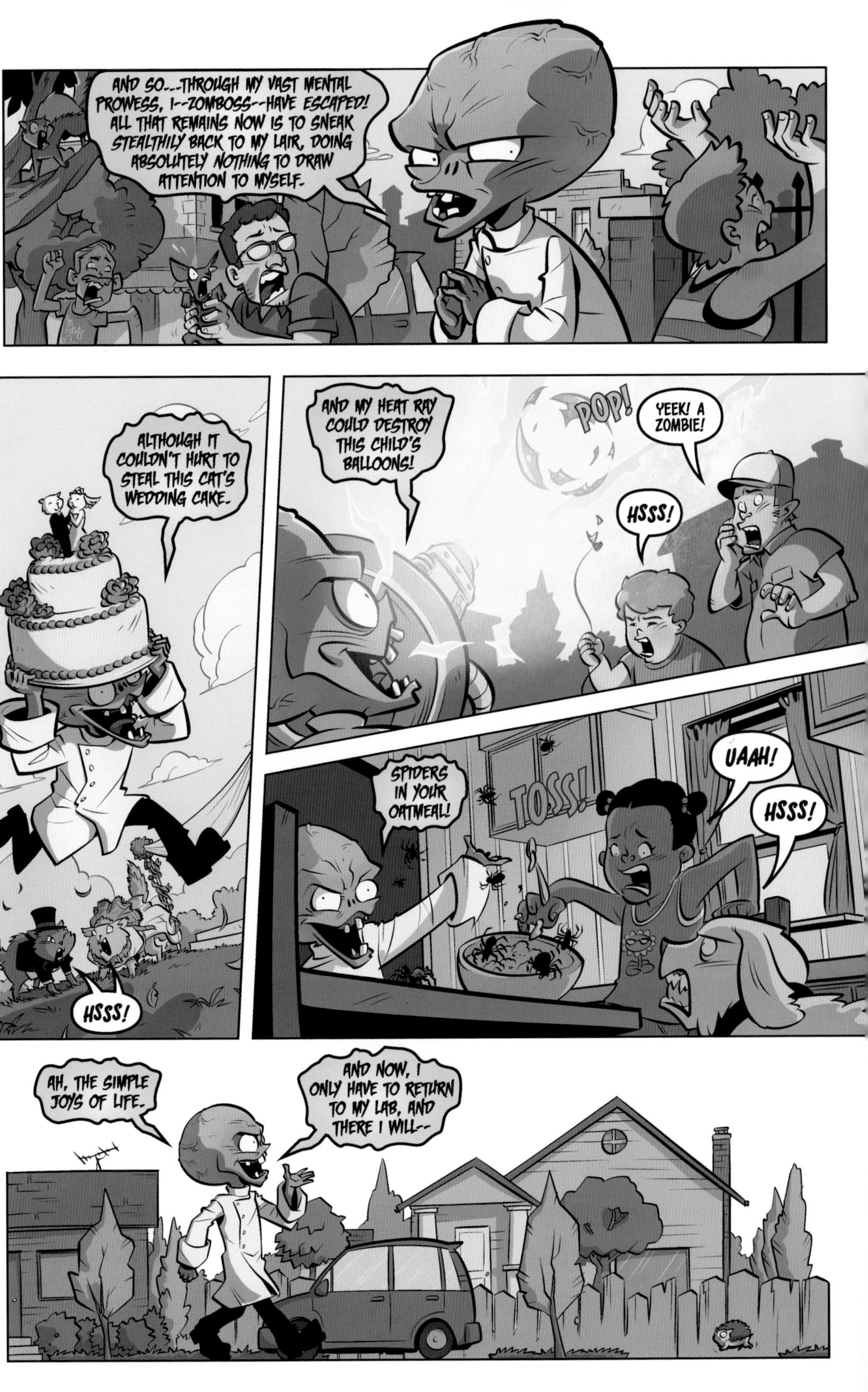
AND SO...THROUGH MY VAST MENTAL PROWESS, I--ZOMBOSS--HAVE ESCAPED! ALL THAT REMAINS NOW IS TO SNEAK STEALTHILY BACK TO MY LAIR, DOING ABSOLUTELY NOTHING TO DRAW ATTENTION TO MYSELF.
ALTHOUGH IT COULDN'T HURT TO STEAL THIS CAT'S WEDDING CAKE.
HSSS!
AND MY HEAT RAY COULD DESTROY THIS CHILD'S BALLOONS!
POP!
YEEK! A ZOMBIE!
HSSS!
SPIDERS IN YOUR OATMEAL!
TOSS!
UAAH!
HSSS!
AH, THE SIMPLE JOYS OF LIFE.
AND NOW, I ONLY HAVE TO RETURN TO MY LAB, AND THERE I WILL--

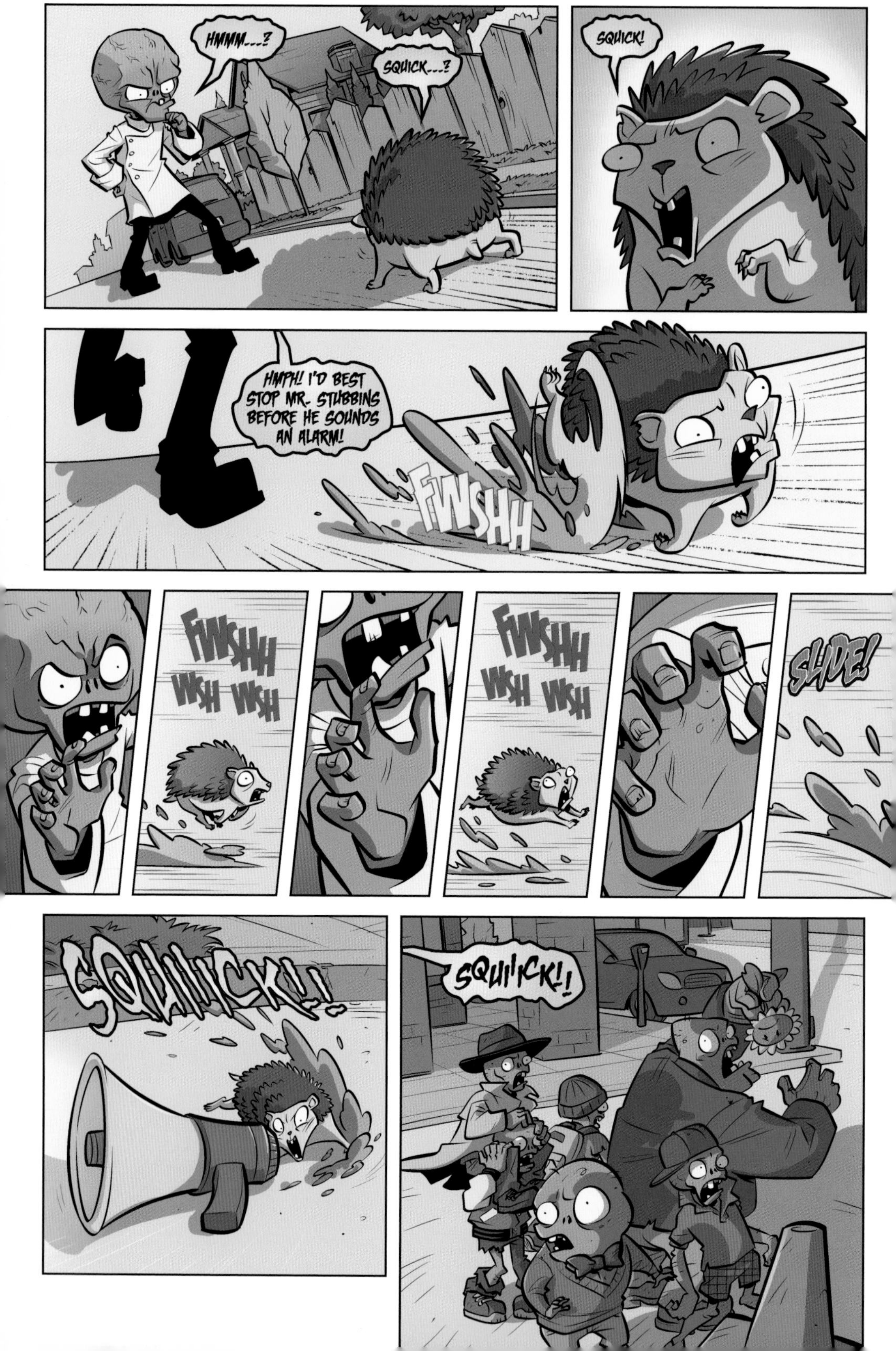

HMMM...?
SQUICK...?
SQUICK!
HMPH! I'D BEST STOP MR. STUBBINS BEFORE HE SOUNDS AN ALARM!
FWSHH
FWSHH
WSH WSH
FWSHH
WSH WSH
SLIDE!
SQUIICK!!
SQUIICK!!

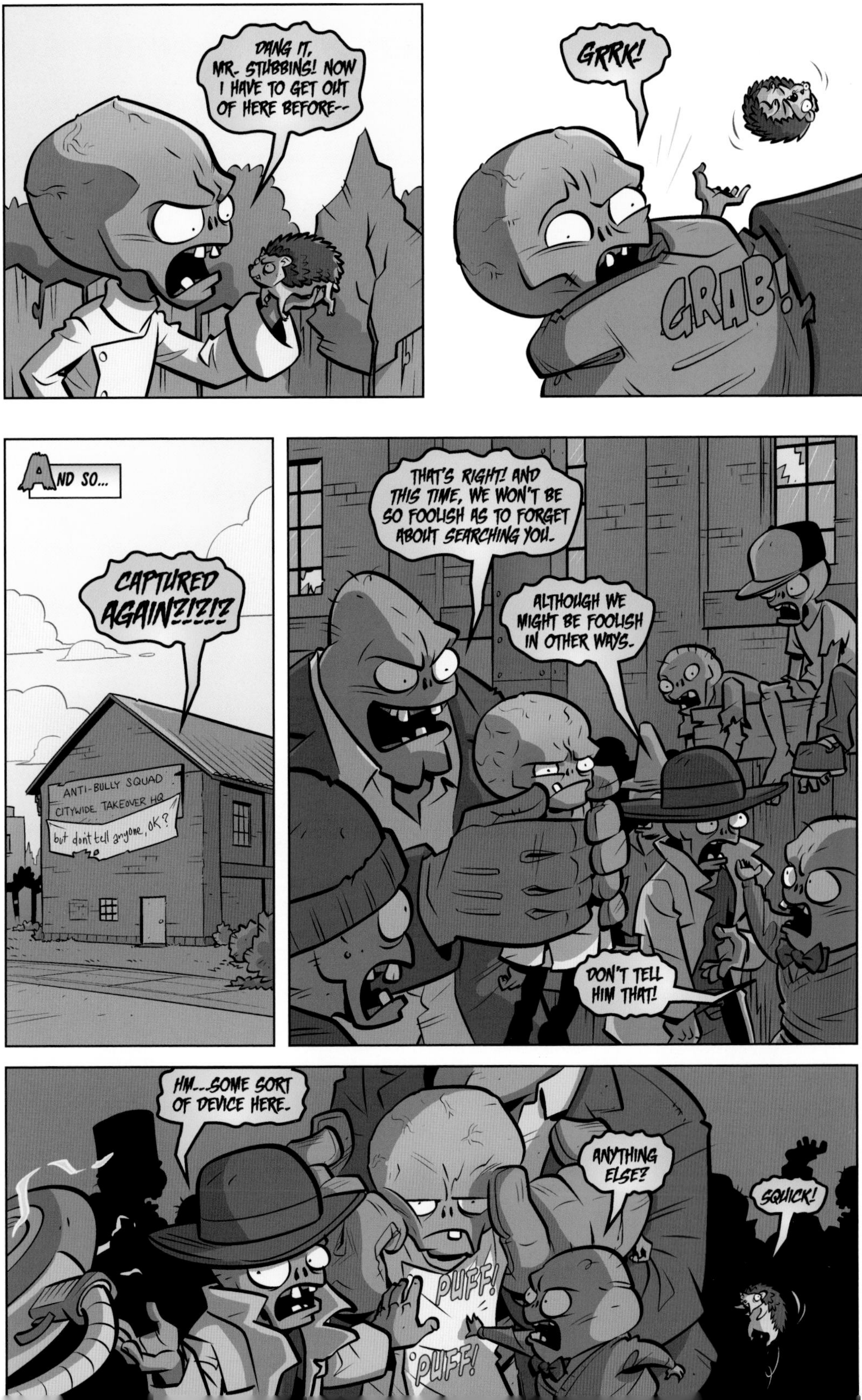
DANG IT, MR. STUBBINS! NOW I HAVE TO GET OUT OF HERE BEFORE--
GRRK!
GRAB!
AND SO...
CAPTURED AGAIN?!?!?!?
ANTI-BULLY SQUAD
CITYWIDE TAKEOVER HQ
but don't tell anyone, OK?
THAT'S RIGHT! AND THIS TIME, WE WON'T BE SO FOOLISH AS TO FORGET ABOUT SEARCHING YOU.
ALTHOUGH WE MIGHT BE FOOLISH IN OTHER WAYS.
DON'T TELL HIM THAT!
HM...SOME SORT OF DEVICE HERE.
ANYTHING ELSE?
SQUICK!
PUFF!
PUFF!

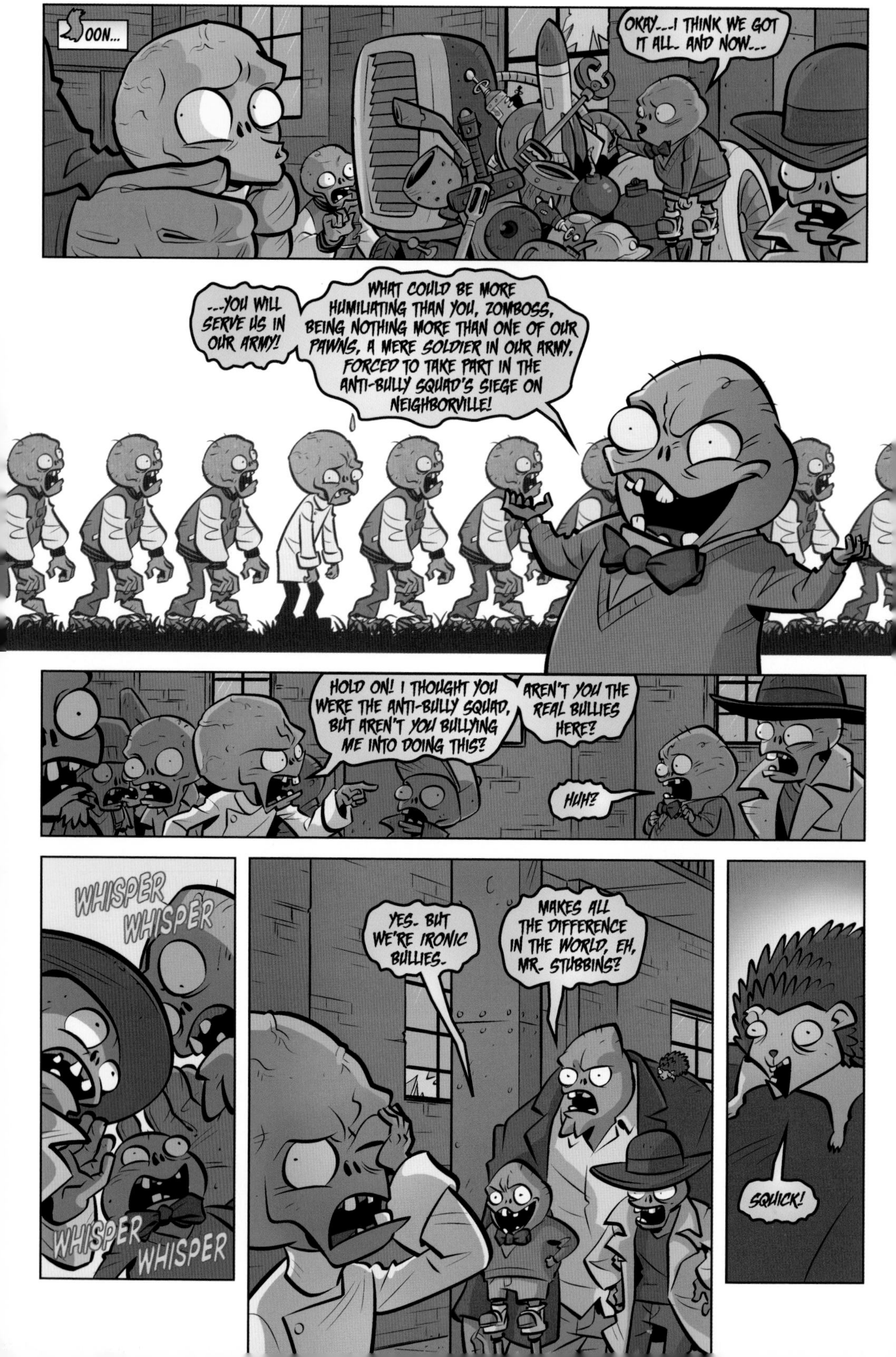
SOON...
OKAY...I THINK WE GOT IT ALL. AND NOW...
...YOU WILL SERVE US IN OUR ARMY!
WHAT COULD BE MORE HUMILIATING THAN YOU, ZOMBOSS, BEING NOTHING MORE THAN ONE OF OUR PAWNS, A MERE SOLDIER IN OUR ARMY, FORCED TO TAKE PART IN THE ANTI-BULLY SQUAD'S SIEGE ON NEIGHBORVILLE!
HOLD ON! I THOUGHT YOU WERE THE ANTI-BULLY SQUAD, BUT AREN'T YOU BULLYING ME INTO DOING THIS?
AREN'T YOU THE REAL BULLIES HERE?
HUH?
WHISPER WHISPER
WHISPER WHISPER
YES. BUT WE'RE IRONIC BULLIES.
MAKES ALL THE DIFFERENCE IN THE WORLD, EH, MR. STUBBINS?
SQUICK!

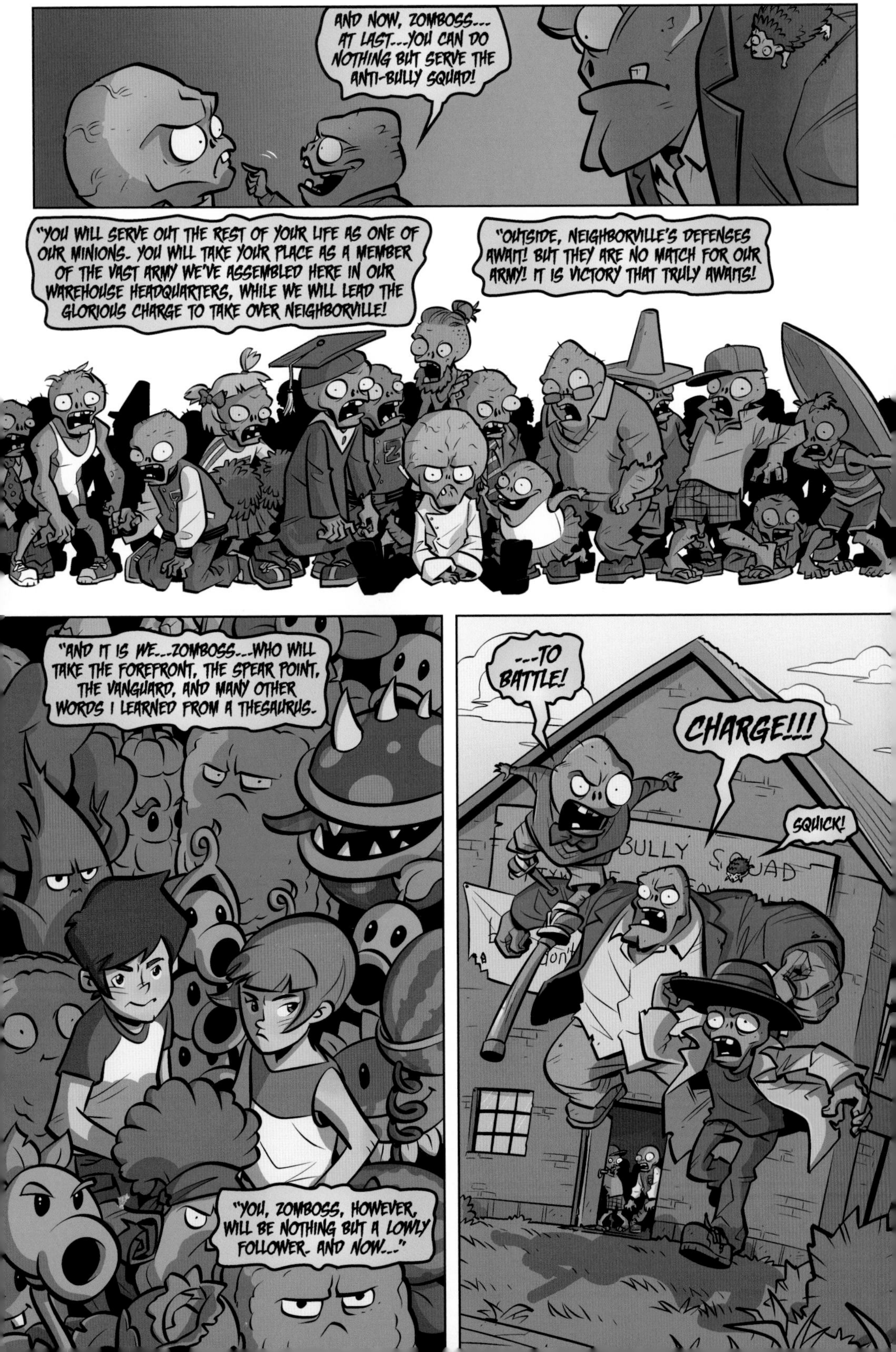
AND NOW, ZOMBOSS... AT LAST...YOU CAN DO NOTHING BUT SERVE THE ANTI-BULLY SQUAD!
"YOU WILL SERVE OUT THE REST OF YOUR LIFE AS ONE OF OUR MINIONS. YOU WILL TAKE YOUR PLACE AS A MEMBER OF THE VAST ARMY WE'VE ASSEMBLED HERE IN OUR WAREHOUSE HEADQUARTERS, WHILE WE WILL LEAD THE GLORIOUS CHARGE TO TAKE OVER NEIGHBORVILLE!
"OUTSIDE, NEIGHBORVILLE'S DEFENSES AWAIT! BUT THEY ARE NO MATCH FOR OUR ARMY! IT IS VICTORY THAT TRULY AWAITS!
"AND IT IS WE...ZOMBOSS...WHO WILL TAKE THE FOREFRONT, THE SPEAR POINT, THE VANGUARD, AND MANY OTHER WORDS I LEARNED FROM A THESAURUS.
"YOU, ZOMBOSS, HOWEVER, WILL BE NOTHING BUT A LOWLY FOLLOWER. AND NOW..."
...TO BATTLE!
CHARGE!!!
SQUICK!
BULLY SQUAD

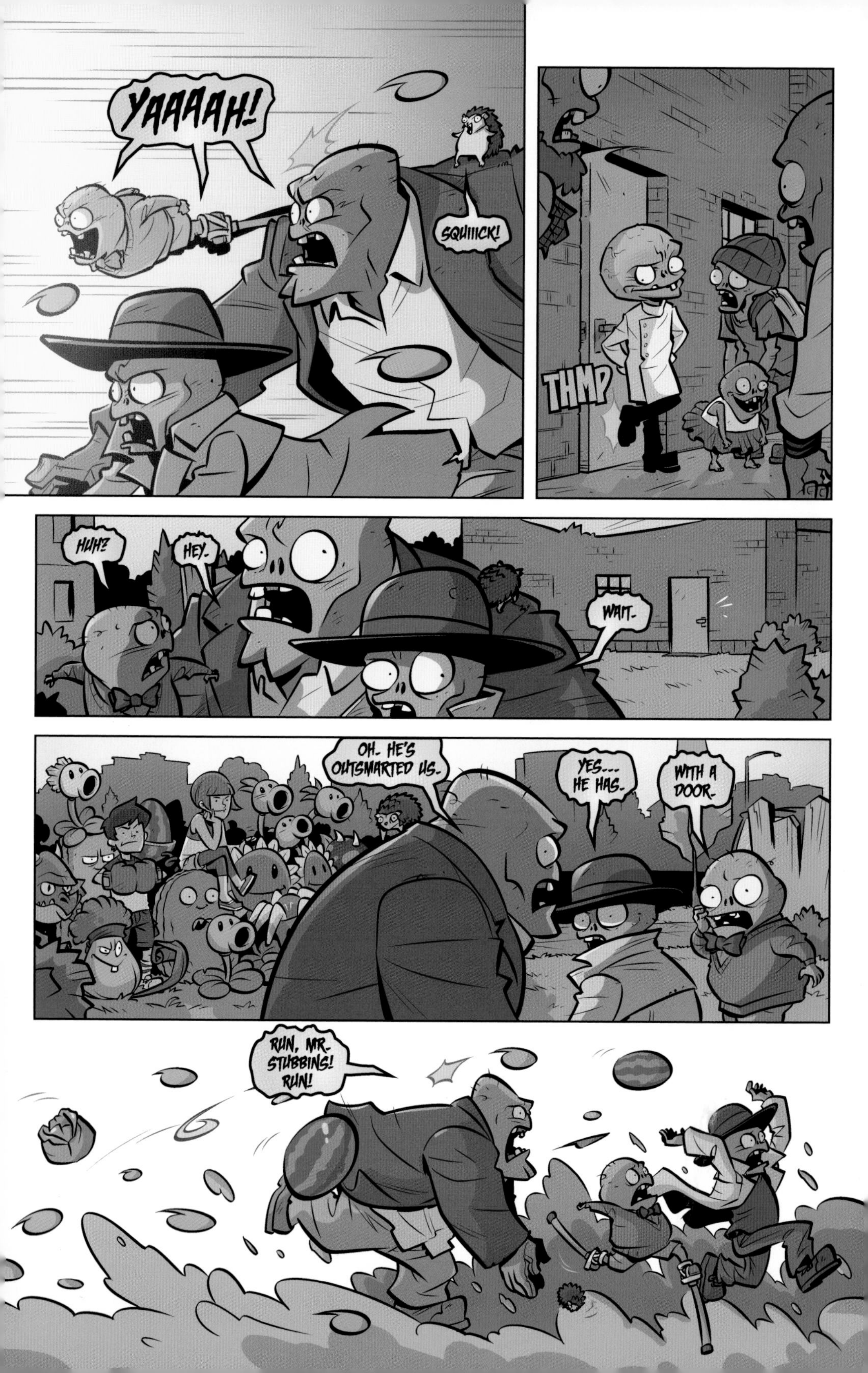
YAAAAH!
SQUIIICK!
THMP
HUH?
HEY.
WAIT.
OH. HE'S OUTSMARTED US.
YES... HE HAS.
WITH A DOOR.
RUN, MR. STUBBINS! RUN!

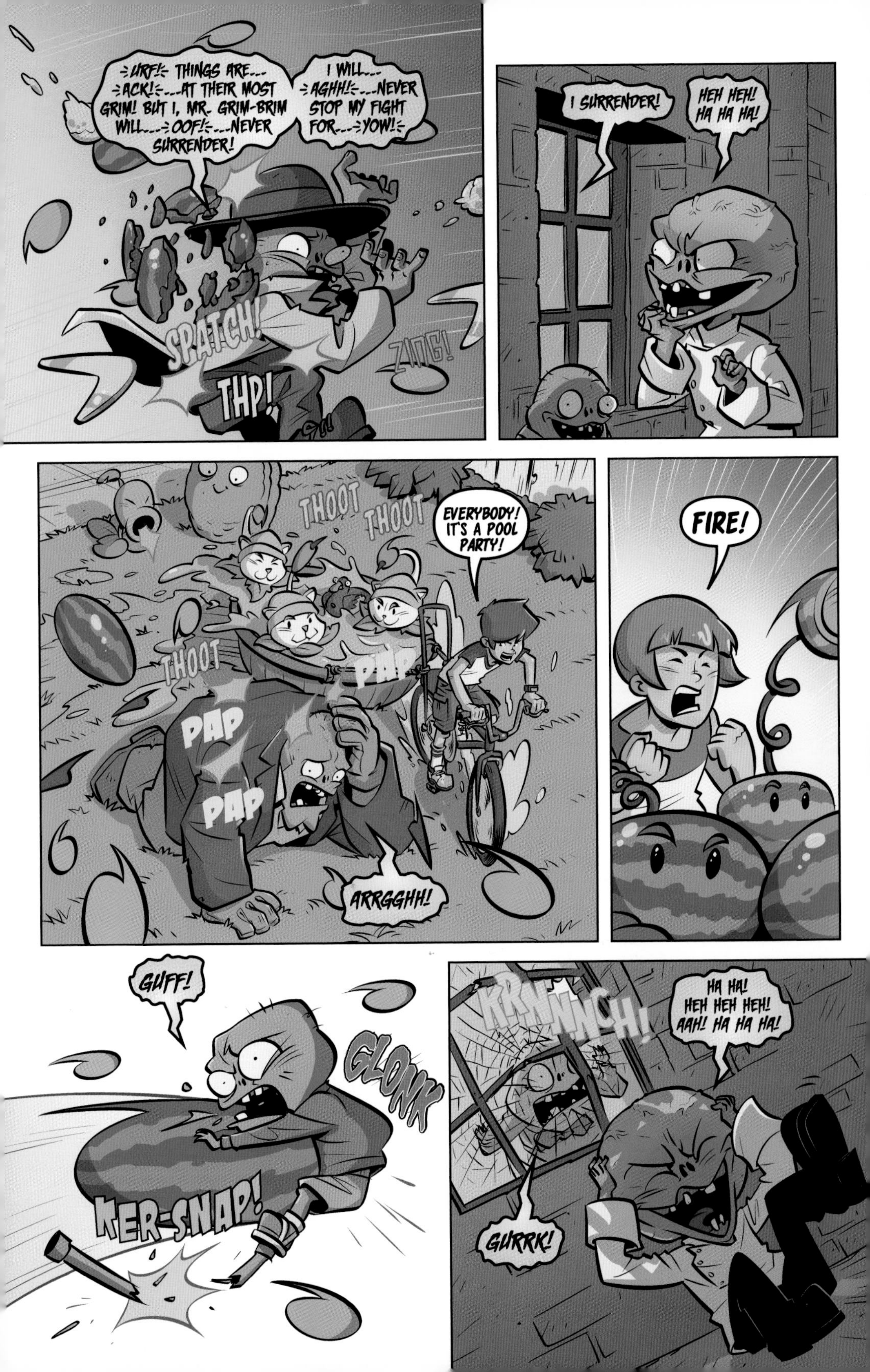

-URF!- THINGS ARE... -ACK!- ...AT THEIR MOST GRIM! BUT I, MR. GRIM-BRIM WILL... -OOF!- ...NEVER SURRENDER!
I WILL... -AGHH!- ...NEVER STOP MY FIGHT FOR... -YOW!-
SPATCH!
ZING!
THP!
I SURRENDER!
HEH HEH! HA HA HA!
THOOT THOOT
EVERYBODY! IT'S A POOL PARTY!
THOOT
PAP
PAP
PAP
ARRGGHH!
FIRE!
GUFF!
GLONK
KER-SNAP!
KRNNNCH!
HA HA! HEH HEH HEH! AAH! HA HA HA!
GURRK!

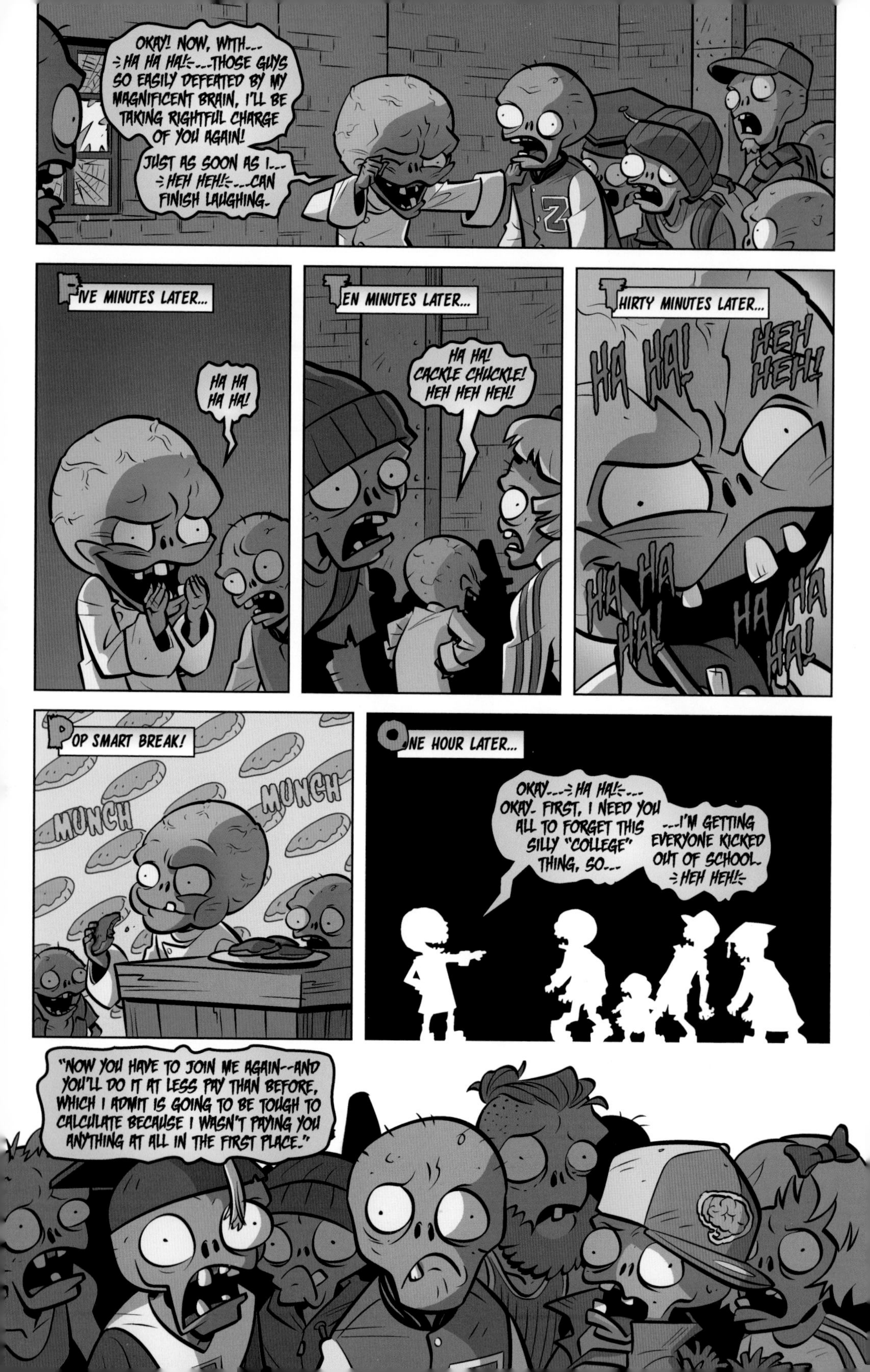
OKAY! NOW, WITH... ≈HA HA HA!≈ ...THOSE GUYS SO EASILY DEFEATED BY MY MAGNIFICENT BRAIN, I'LL BE TAKING RIGHTFUL CHARGE OF YOU AGAIN!
JUST AS SOON AS I... ≈HEH HEH!≈ ...CAN FINISH LAUGHING.
FIVE MINUTES LATER...
HA HA HA HA!
TEN MINUTES LATER...
HA HA! CACKLE CHUCKLE! HEH HEH HEH!
THIRTY MINUTES LATER...
HA HA!
HEH HEH!
HA HA HA!
HA HA HA!
POP SMART BREAK!
MUNCH
MUNCH
ONE HOUR LATER...
OKAY... ≈HA HA!≈ ... OKAY. FIRST, I NEED YOU ALL TO FORGET THIS SILLY "COLLEGE" THING, SO...
...I'M GETTING EVERYONE KICKED OUT OF SCHOOL. ≈HEH HEH!≈
"NOW YOU HAVE TO JOIN ME AGAIN--AND YOU'LL DO IT AT LESS PAY THAN BEFORE, WHICH I ADMIT IS GOING TO BE TOUGH TO CALCULATE BECAUSE I WASN'T PAYING YOU ANYTHING AT ALL IN THE FIRST PLACE."

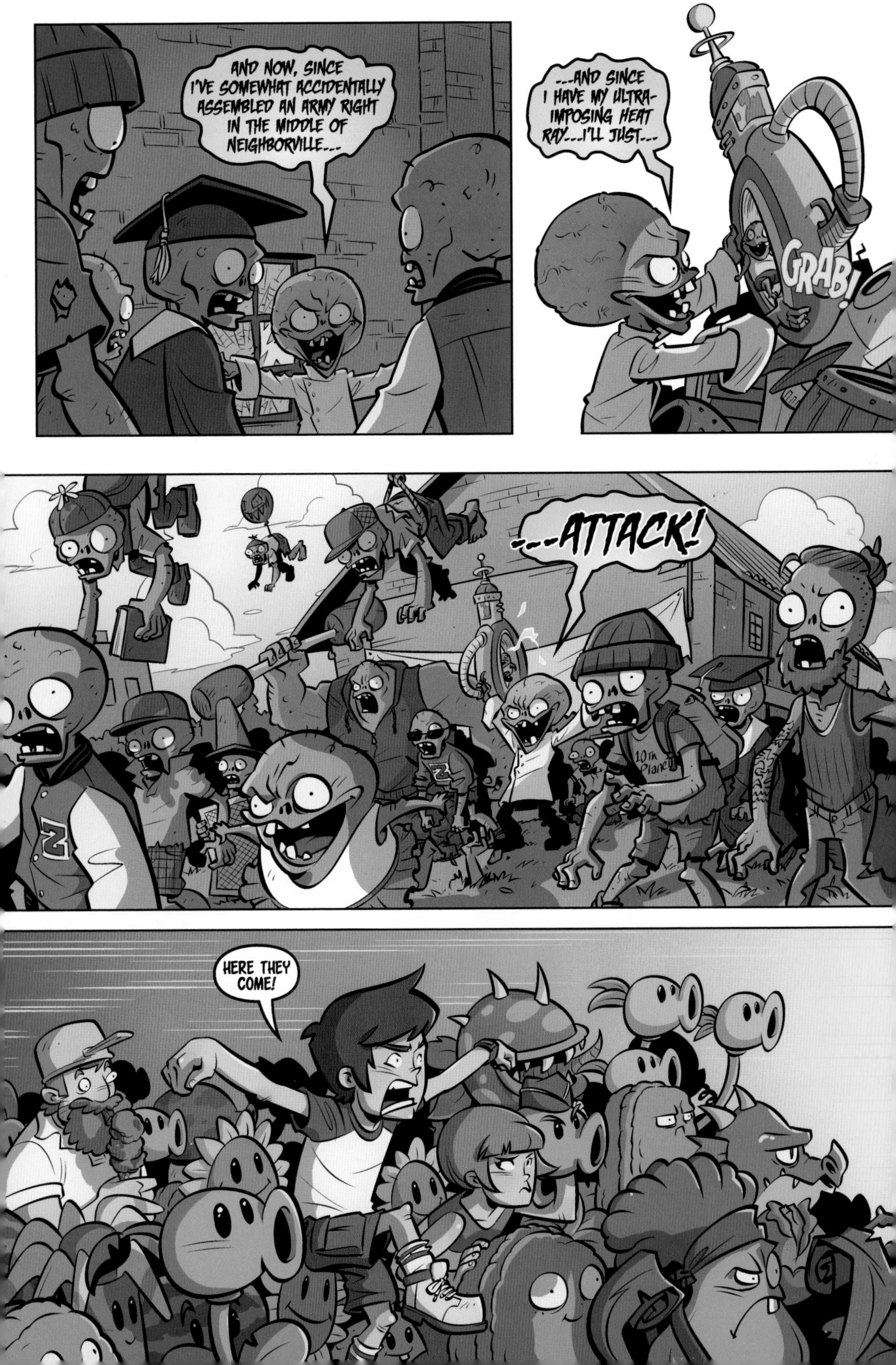
AND NOW, SINCE I'VE SOMEWHAT ACCIDENTALLY ASSEMBLED AN ARMY RIGHT IN THE MIDDLE OF NEIGHBORVILLE...
...AND SINCE I HAVE MY ULTRA-IMPOSING HEAT RAY...I'LL JUST...
GRAB!
...ATTACK!
10th Planet
HERE THEY COME!

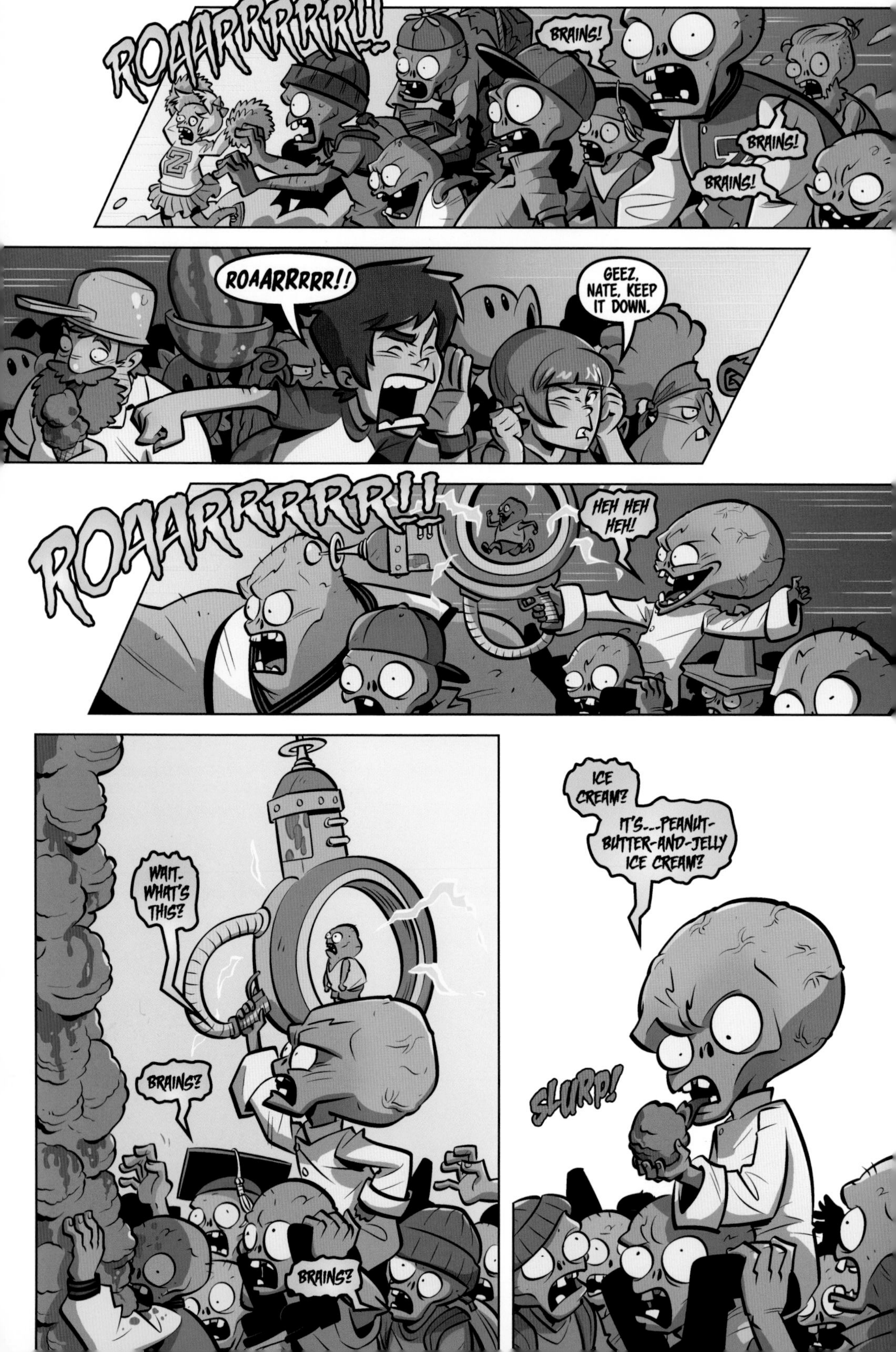
ROAARRRRRR!!
BRAINS!
BRAINS!
BRAINS!
ROAARRRRR!!
GEEZ, NATE, KEEP IT DOWN.
ROAARRRRRR!!
HEH HEH HEH!
WAIT. WHAT'S THIS?
BRAINS?
BRAINS?
ICE CREAM?
IT'S...PEANUT-BUTTER-AND-JELLY ICE CREAM?
SLURP!

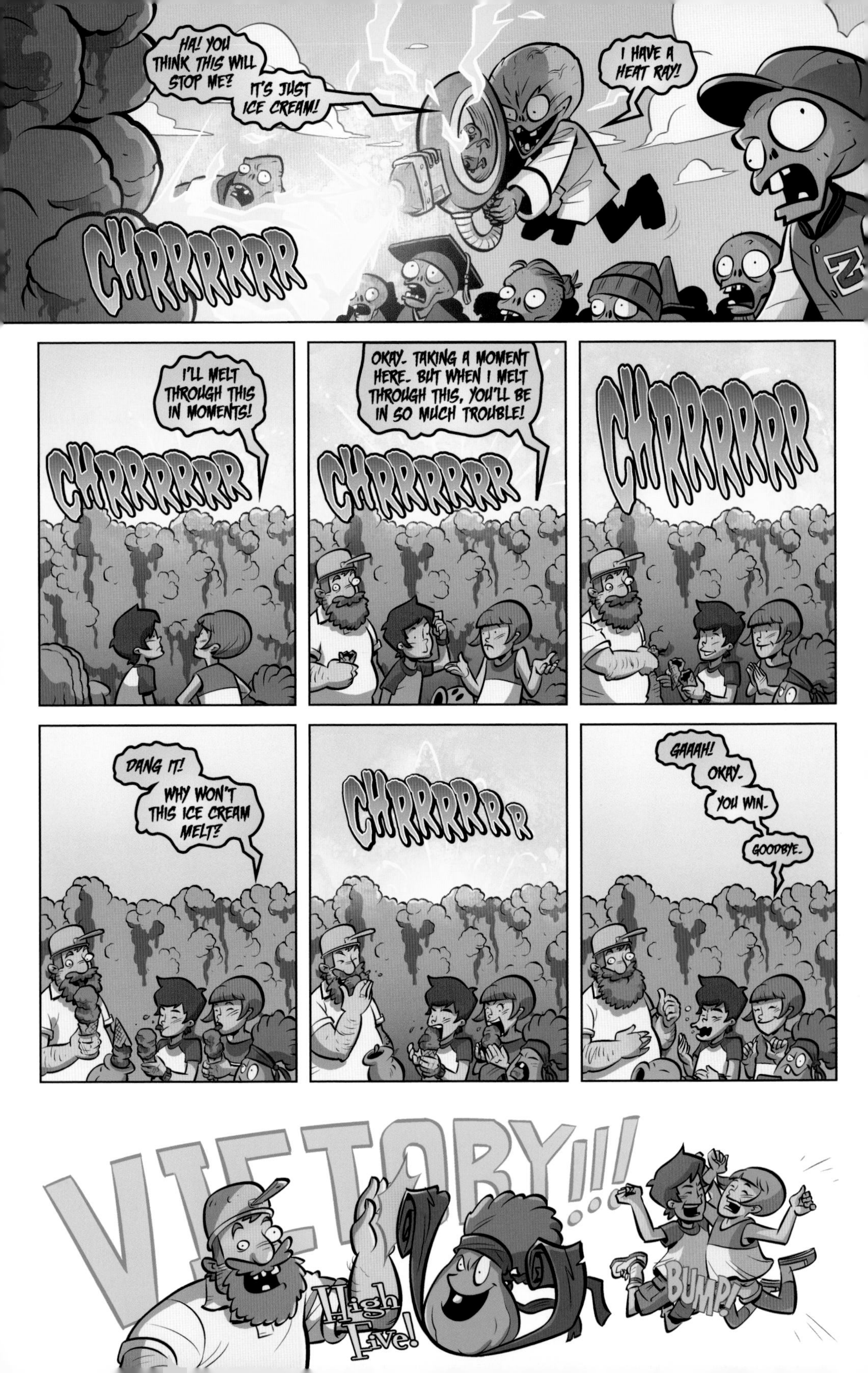
HA! YOU THINK THIS WILL STOP ME?
IT'S JUST ICE CREAM!
I HAVE A HEAT RAY!
CHRRRRRR
I'LL MELT THROUGH THIS IN MOMENTS!
CHRRRRRR
OKAY. TAKING A MOMENT HERE. BUT WHEN I MELT THROUGH THIS, YOU'LL BE IN SO MUCH TROUBLE!
CHRRRRRR
CHRRRRRR
DANG IT!
WHY WON'T THIS ICE CREAM MELT?
CHRRRRRRR
GAAAH!
OKAY.
YOU WIN.
GOODBYE.
VICTORY!!!
High Five!
BUMP!

ONE WEEK LATER...

SO... WE WERE EXPELLED?

AND NOW WE HAVE TO TAKE COLLEGE ALL OVER AGAIN?

THAT'S WHAT THE LETTERS SAID. WE HAVE TO RETAKE ALL OF OUR CLASSES, INCLUDING...

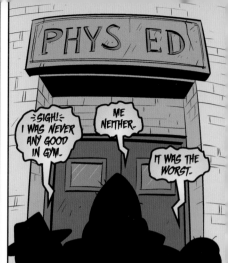

PHYS ED

=SIGH!= I WAS NEVER ANY GOOD IN GYM.

ME NEITHER.

IT WAS THE WORST.

I HEAR THERE'S A NEW SUBSTITUTE COACH. MAYBE HE'LL BE NICE?

I HOPE SO. MAYBE WE CAN JUST--

HA HA HA!

THAT... LAUGHTER? NO! IT CAN'T BE!

HA HA! HA HA!

HA!

HA HA HA!

ZOMBOSS!

HELLO, ANTI-BULLY SQUAD. WELCOME TO GYM CLASS, WHERE WE'RE GOING TO PLAY...

SQUICK!

...DODGEBALL.

THE END!

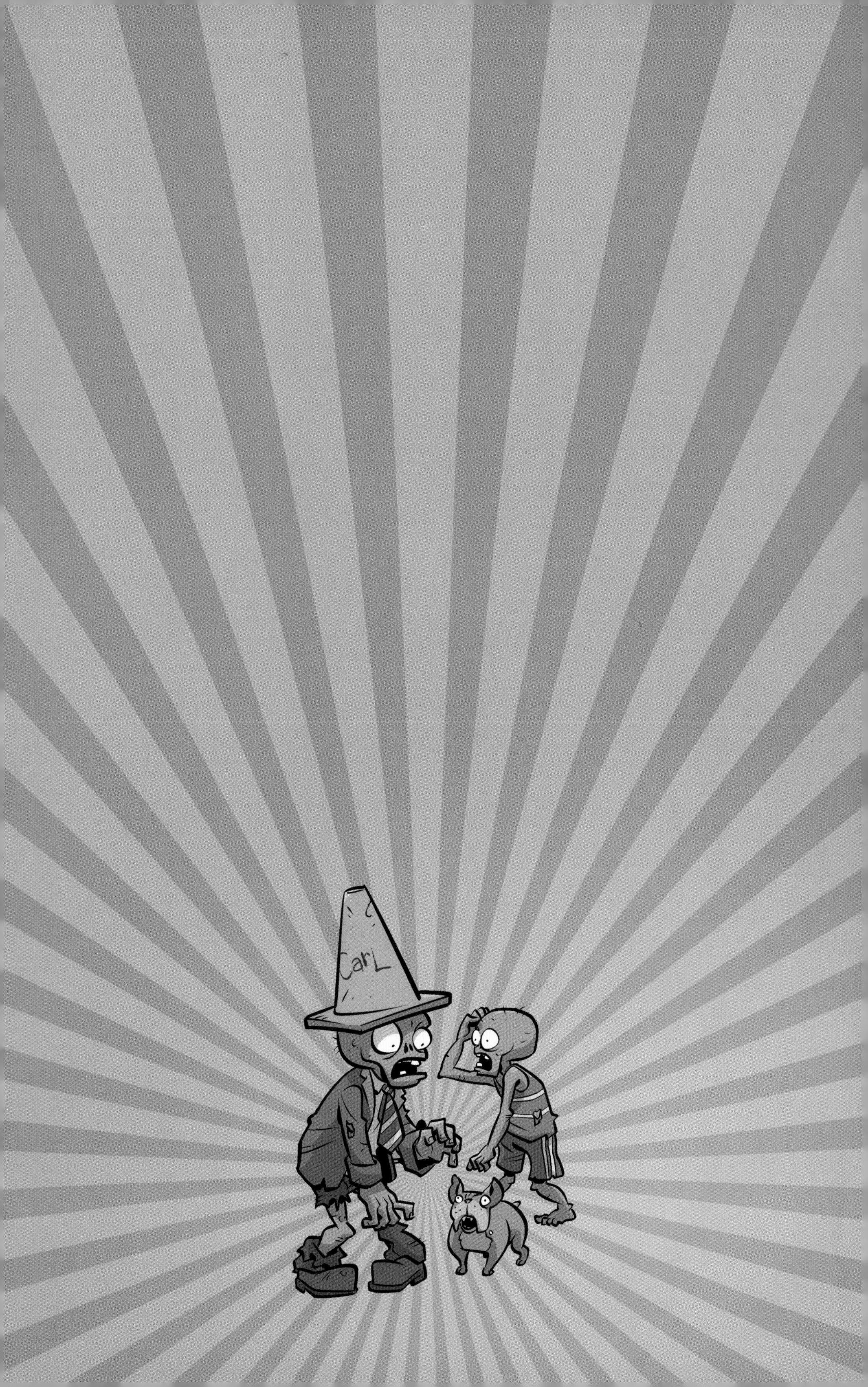
CarL

PLANTS vs. ZOMBIES™

THE CURSE OF THE FLOWER-BOT

Written by **PAUL TOBIN**
Art by **RON CHAN**
Colors by **MATT J. RAINWATER**
Letters by **STEVE DUTRO**

FREE COMIC BOOK DAY

The Free Comic Book Day story that introduced Tugboat, Frogpants, and Nigel Blimpbottom!

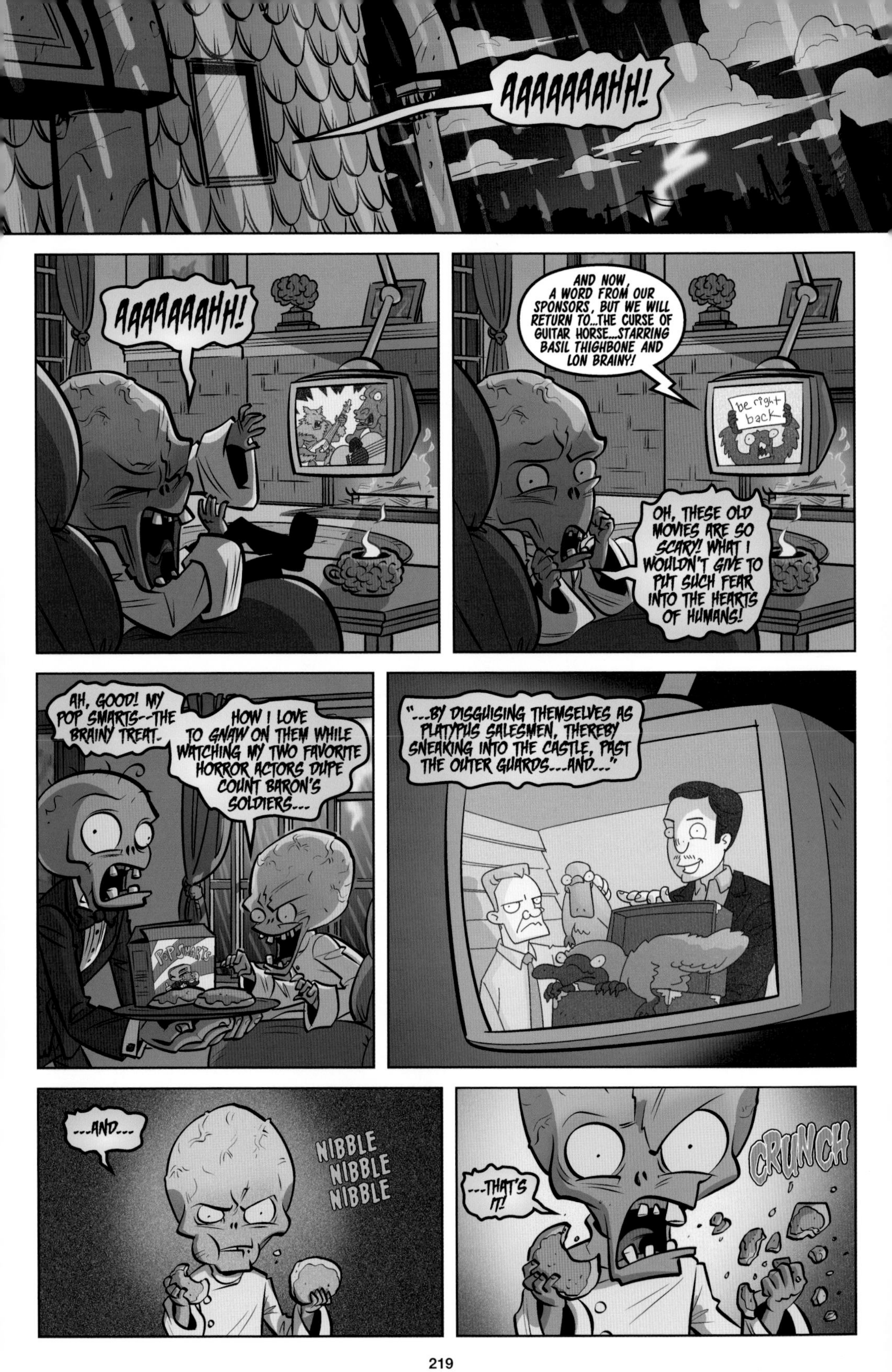
AAAAAAAHH!
AAAAAAAHH!
AND NOW, A WORD FROM OUR SPONSORS, BUT WE WILL RETURN TO...THE CURSE OF GUITAR HORSE...STARRING BASIL THIGHBONE AND LON BRAINY!
be right back
OH, THESE OLD MOVIES ARE SO SCARY! WHAT I WOULDN'T GIVE TO PUT SUCH FEAR INTO THE HEARTS OF HUMANS!
AH, GOOD! MY POP SMARTS--THE BRAINY TREAT.
HOW I LOVE TO GNAW ON THEM WHILE WATCHING MY TWO FAVORITE HORROR ACTORS DUPE COUNT BARON'S SOLDIERS...
POP SMARTS
"...BY DISGUISING THEMSELVES AS PLATYPUS SALESMEN, THEREBY SNEAKING INTO THE CASTLE, PAST THE OUTER GUARDS...AND..."
...AND...
NIBBLE NIBBLE NIBBLE
...THAT'S IT!
CRUNCH

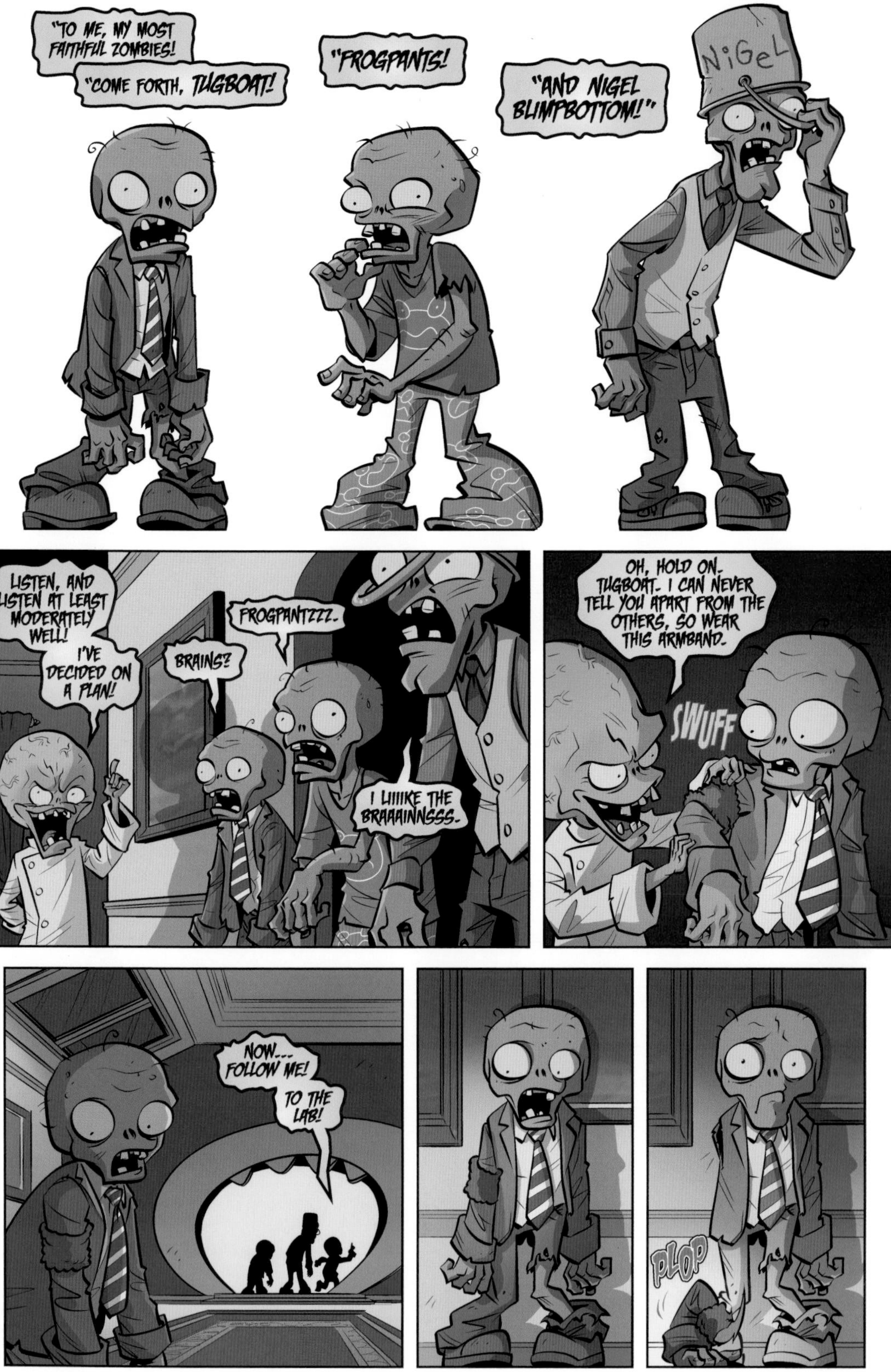
"TO ME, MY MOST FAITHFUL ZOMBIES!
"COME FORTH, TUGBOAT!
"FROGPANTS!
"AND NIGEL BLIMPBOTTOM!"
NiGeL
LISTEN, AND LISTEN AT LEAST MODERATELY WELL!
I'VE DECIDED ON A PLAN!
BRAINS?
FROGPANTZZZ.
I LIIIIKE THE BRAAAINNSSS.
OH, HOLD ON. TUGBOAT. I CAN NEVER TELL YOU APART FROM THE OTHERS, SO WEAR THIS ARMBAND.
SWUFF
NOW... FOLLOW ME!
TO THE LAB!
PLOP

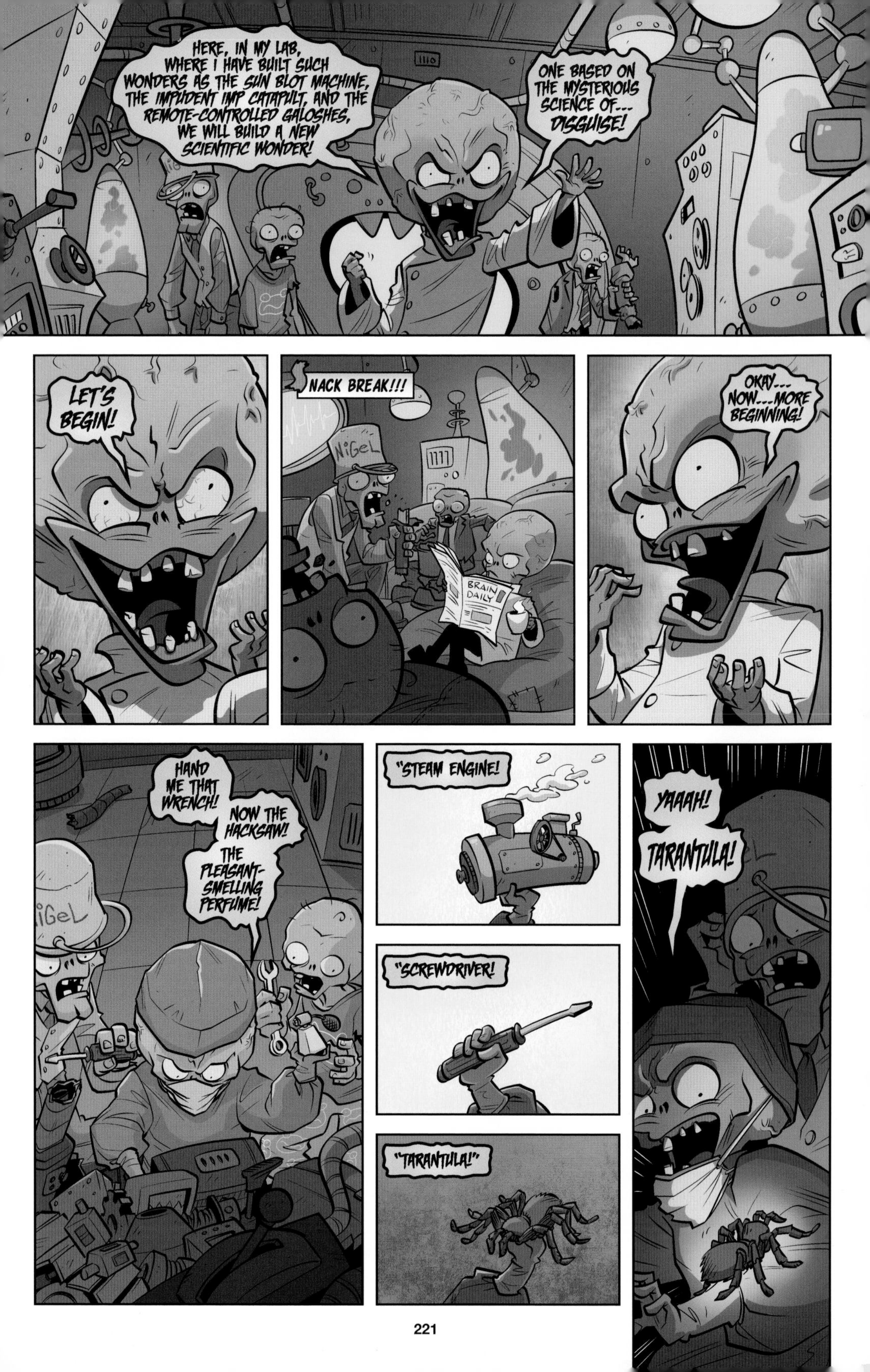
HERE, IN MY LAB, WHERE I HAVE BUILT SUCH WONDERS AS THE SUN BLOT MACHINE, THE IMPUDENT IMP CATAPULT, AND THE REMOTE-CONTROLLED GALOSHES, WE WILL BUILD A NEW SCIENTIFIC WONDER!
ONE BASED ON THE MYSTERIOUS SCIENCE OF... DISGUISE!
LET'S BEGIN!
NACK BREAK!!!
BRAIN DAILY
OKAY... NOW... MORE BEGINNING!
HAND ME THAT WRENCH!
NOW THE HACKSAW!
THE PLEASANT-SMELLING PERFUME!
"STEAM ENGINE!
"SCREWDRIVER!
"TARANTULA!"
YAAAH!
TARANTULA!

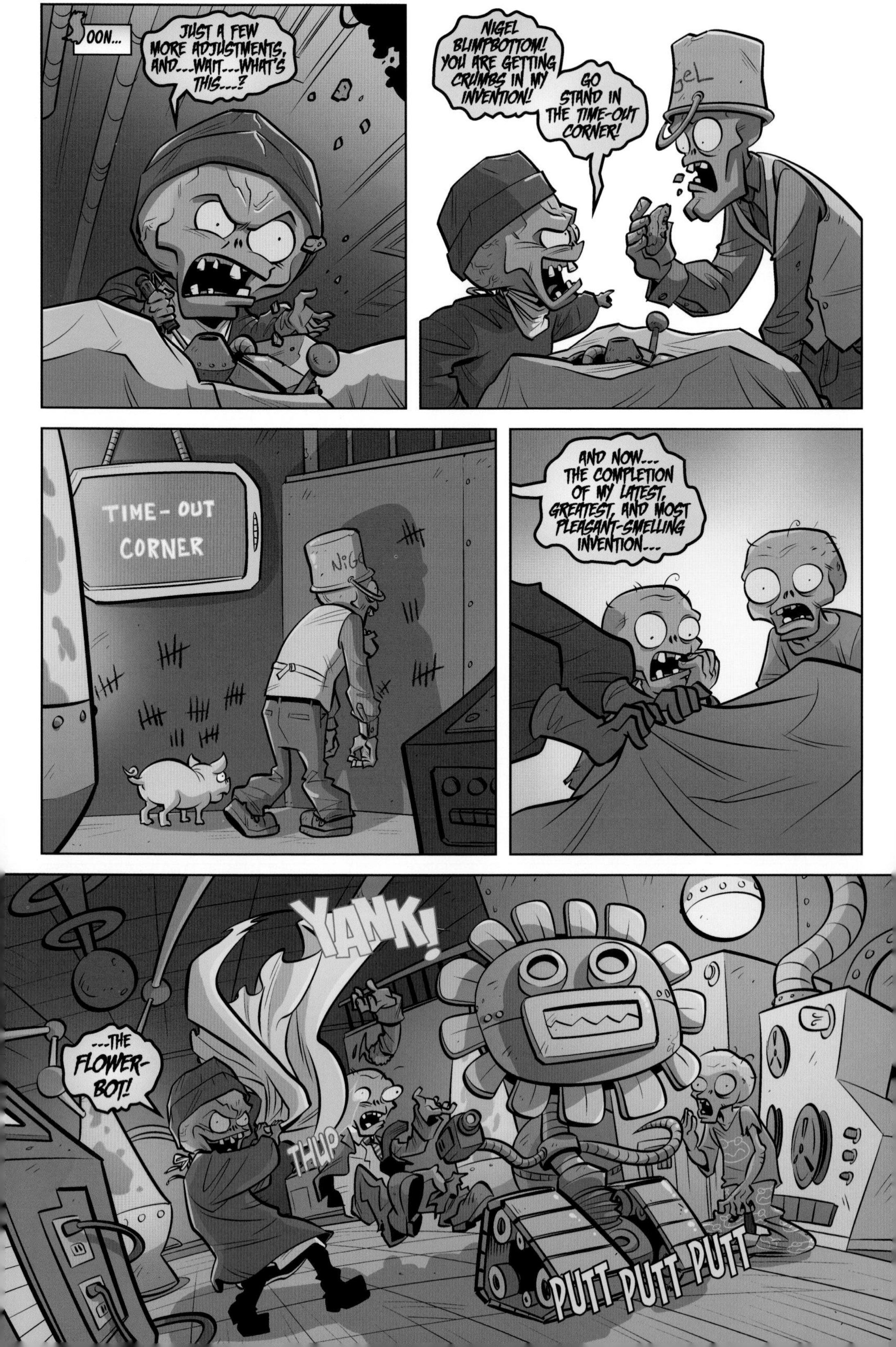
SOON...
JUST A FEW MORE ADJUSTMENTS, AND...WAIT...WHAT'S THIS...?
NIGEL BLIMPBOTTOM! YOU ARE GETTING CRUMBS IN MY INVENTION!
GO STAND IN THE TIME-OUT CORNER!
TIME-OUT CORNER
AND NOW... THE COMPLETION OF MY LATEST, GREATEST, AND MOST PLEASANT-SMELLING INVENTION...
YANK!
...THE FLOWER-BOT!
THUP
PUTT PUTT PUTT

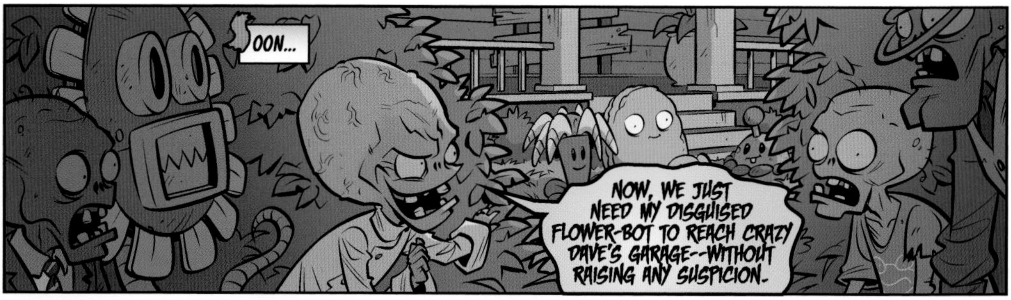
OON...
NOW, WE JUST NEED MY DISGUISED FLOWER-BOT TO REACH CRAZY DAVE'S GARAGE--WITHOUT RAISING ANY SUSPICION.

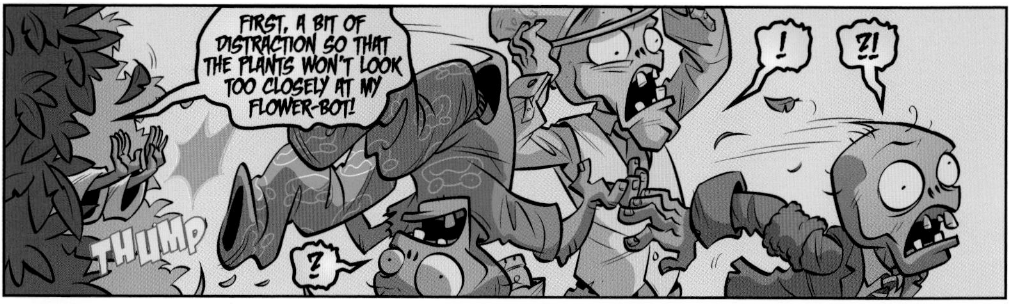
FIRST, A BIT OF DISTRACTION SO THAT THE PLANTS WON'T LOOK TOO CLOSELY AT MY FLOWER-BOT!
!
?!
THUMP
?

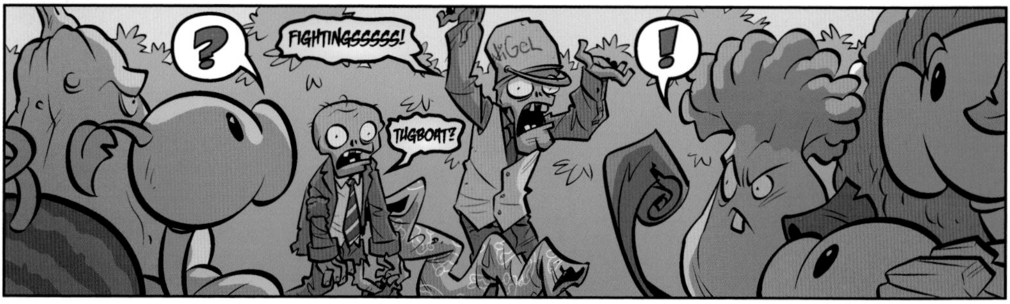
?
FIGHTINGSSSSS!
!
TUGBOAT?

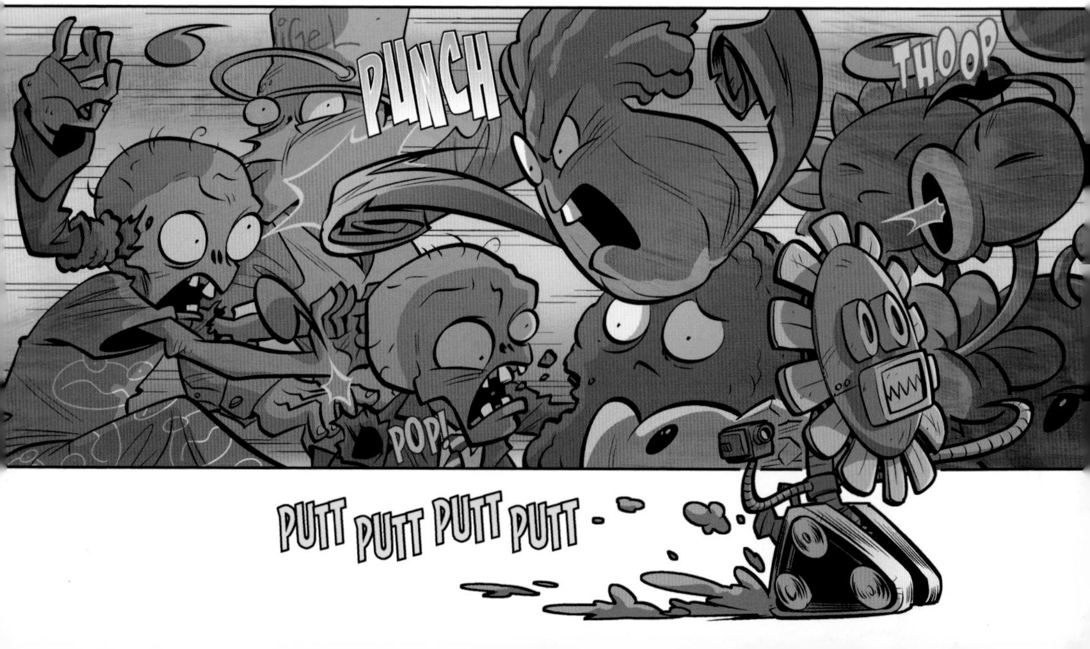
PUNCH
THOOP
POP!
PUTT PUTT PUTT PUTT

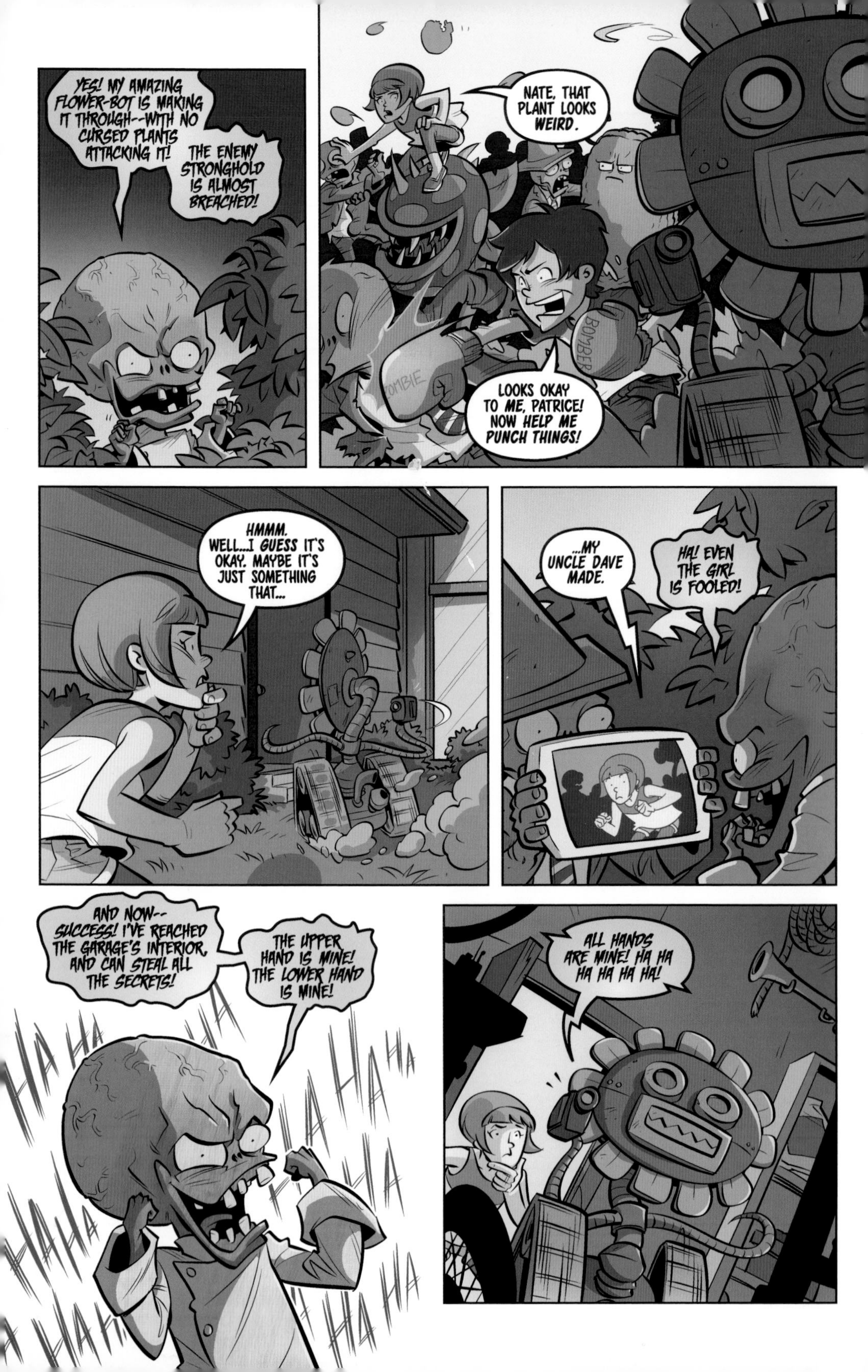
YES! MY AMAZING FLOWER-BOT IS MAKING IT THROUGH--WITH NO CURSED PLANTS ATTACKING IT!
THE ENEMY STRONGHOLD IS ALMOST BREACHED!
NATE, THAT PLANT LOOKS WEIRD.
BOMBER
ZOMBIE
LOOKS OKAY TO ME, PATRICE! NOW HELP ME PUNCH THINGS!
HMMM. WELL...I GUESS IT'S OKAY. MAYBE IT'S JUST SOMETHING THAT...
...MY UNCLE DAVE MADE.
HA! EVEN THE GIRL IS FOOLED!
AND NOW--SUCCESS! I'VE REACHED THE GARAGE'S INTERIOR, AND CAN STEAL ALL THE SECRETS!
THE UPPER HAND IS MINE! THE LOWER HAND IS MINE!
HA HA HA HA HA HA HA HA HA HA HA HA
ALL HANDS ARE MINE! HA HA HA HA HA HA!

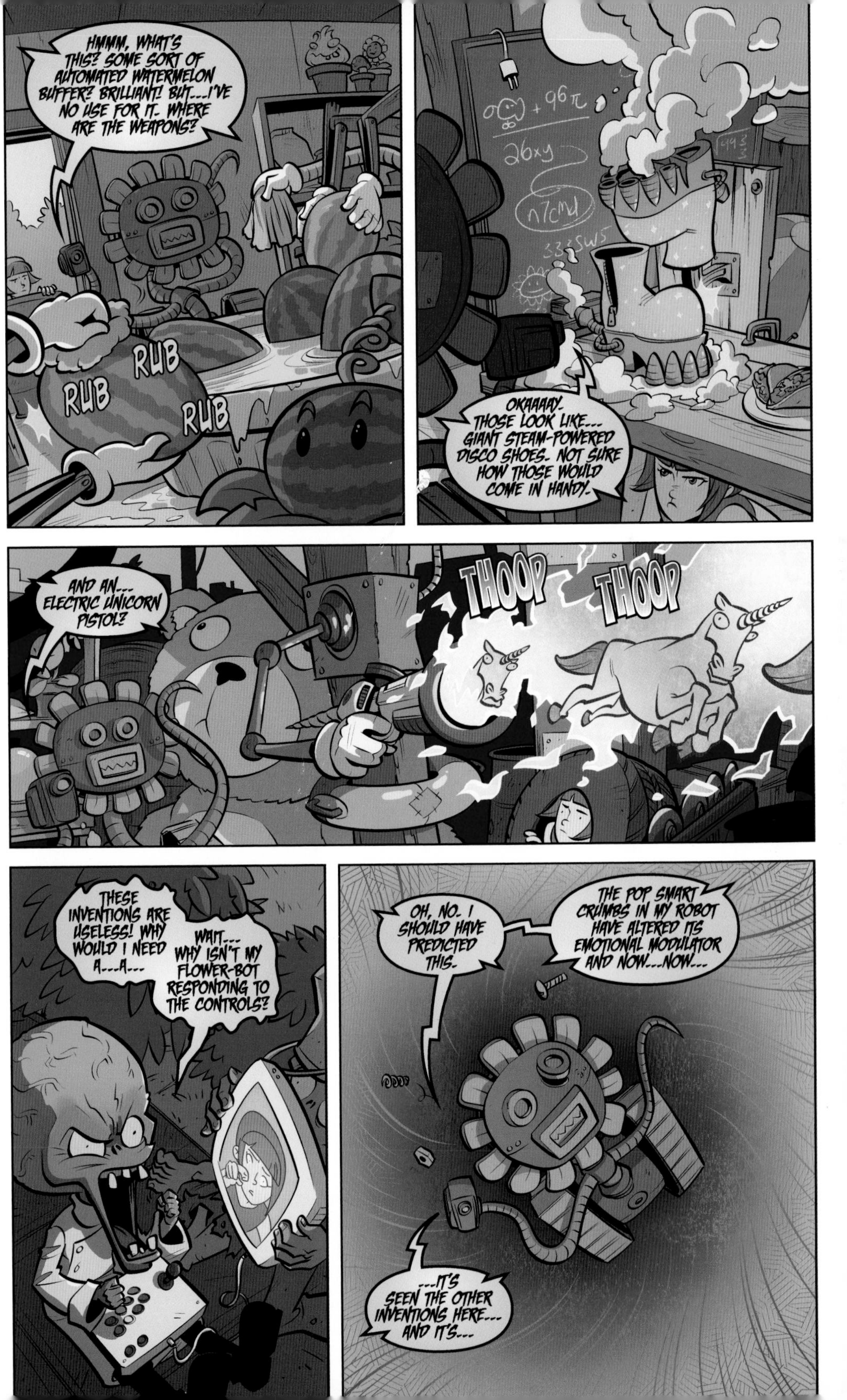
HMMM, WHAT'S THIS? SOME SORT OF AUTOMATED WATERMELON BUFFER? BRILLIANT! BUT...I'VE NO USE FOR IT. WHERE ARE THE WEAPONS?
RUB
RUB
RUB
OKAAAAY. THOSE LOOK LIKE... GIANT STEAM-POWERED DISCO SHOES. NOT SURE HOW THOSE WOULD COME IN HANDY.
AND AN... ELECTRIC UNICORN PISTOL?
THOOP
THOOP
THESE INVENTIONS ARE USELESS! WHY WOULD I NEED A...A...
WAIT... WHY ISN'T MY FLOWER-BOT RESPONDING TO THE CONTROLS?
OH, NO. I SHOULD HAVE PREDICTED THIS.
THE POP SMART CRUMBS IN MY ROBOT HAVE ALTERED ITS EMOTIONAL MODULATOR AND NOW...NOW...
...IT'S SEEN THE OTHER INVENTIONS HERE... AND IT'S...

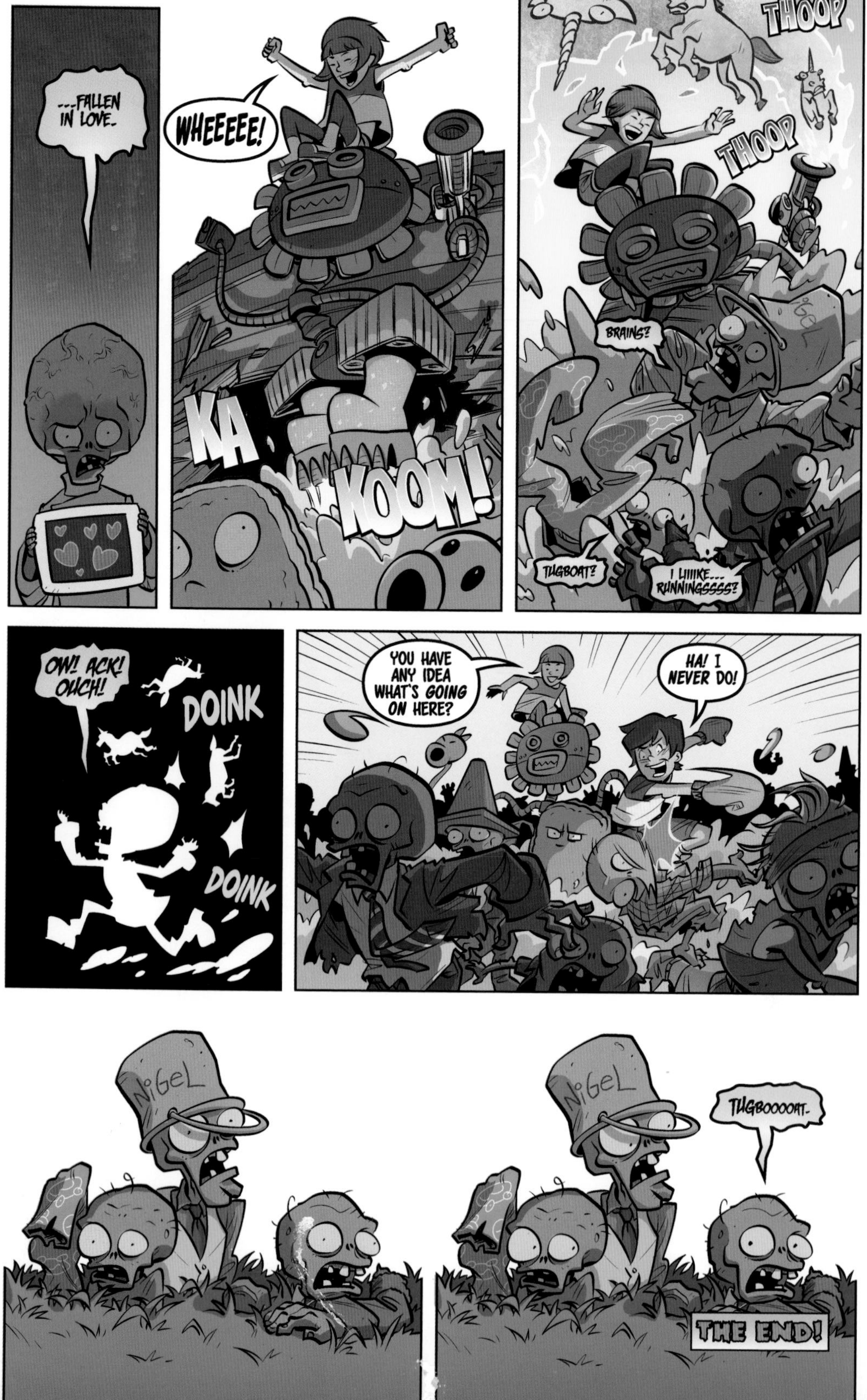

...FALLEN IN LOVE.
WHEEEEE!
KA
KOOM!
THOOP
THOOP
BRAINS?
TUGBOAT?
I LIIIIKE... RUNNINGSSSS?
OW! ACK! OUCH!
DOINK
DOINK
YOU HAVE ANY IDEA WHAT'S GOING ON HERE?
HA! I NEVER DO!
NIGEL
NIGEL
TUGBOOOOAT.
THE END!

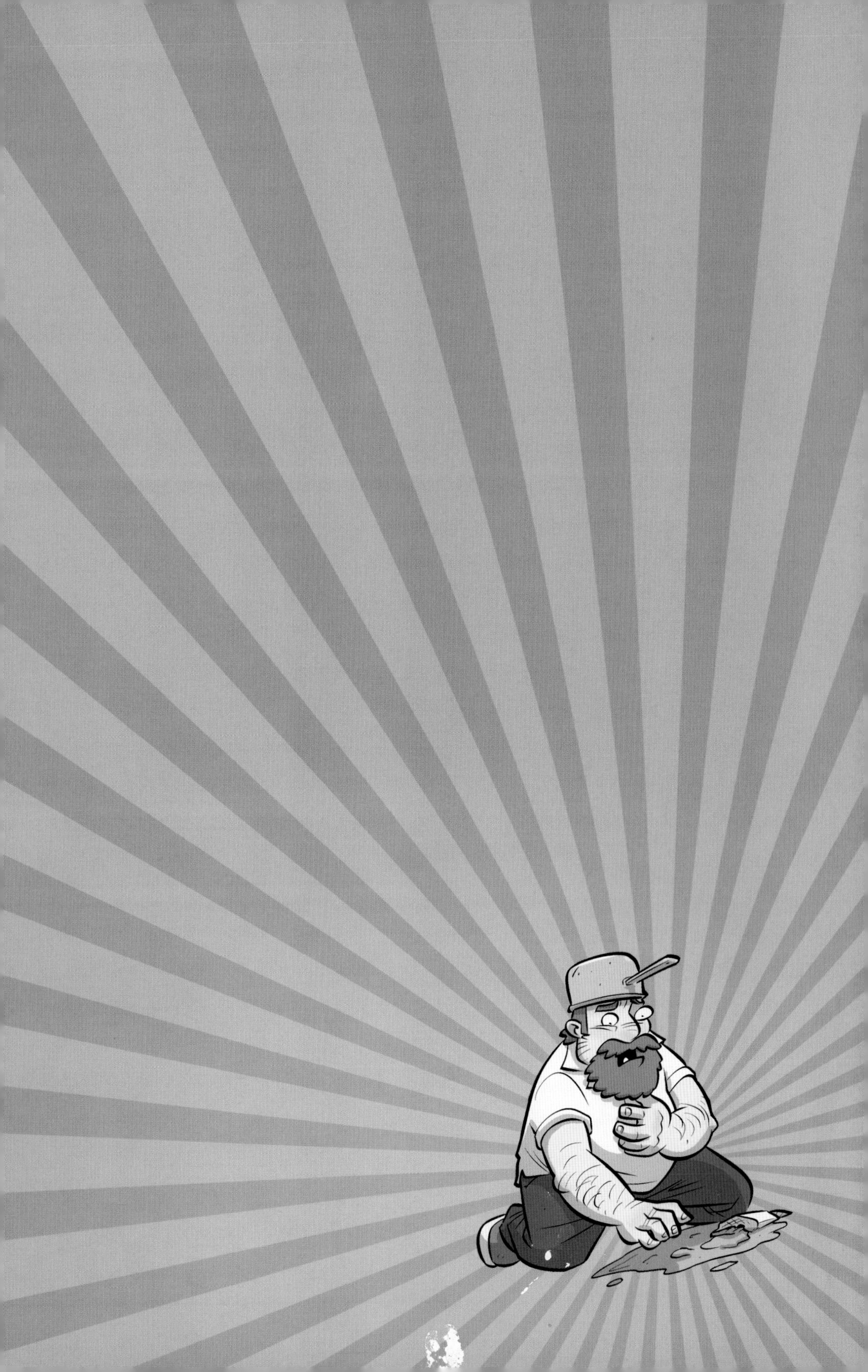

BONUS STORIES

POKEY PIQUENOSE

Written by PAUL TOBIN
Art by DUSTIN NGUYEN
Letters by STEVE DUTRO

BONK CHOY BRO-DOWN!

Written by PAUL TOBIN
Art by DUSTIN NGUYEN
Letters by STEVE DUTRO

BLOWN AWAY

Written by PAUL TOBIN
Art by JENNIFER L. MEYER
Letters by STEVE DUTRO

THE SUNFROWNER

Written by PAUL TOBIN
Art by JENNIFER L. MEYER
Letters by STEVE DUTRO

THE EMPTINESS

Written by PAUL TOBIN
Art and letters by PETER BAGGE

MR. STUBBINS'S ADVENTURES

Written by PAUL TOBIN
Art and letters by PETER BAGGE

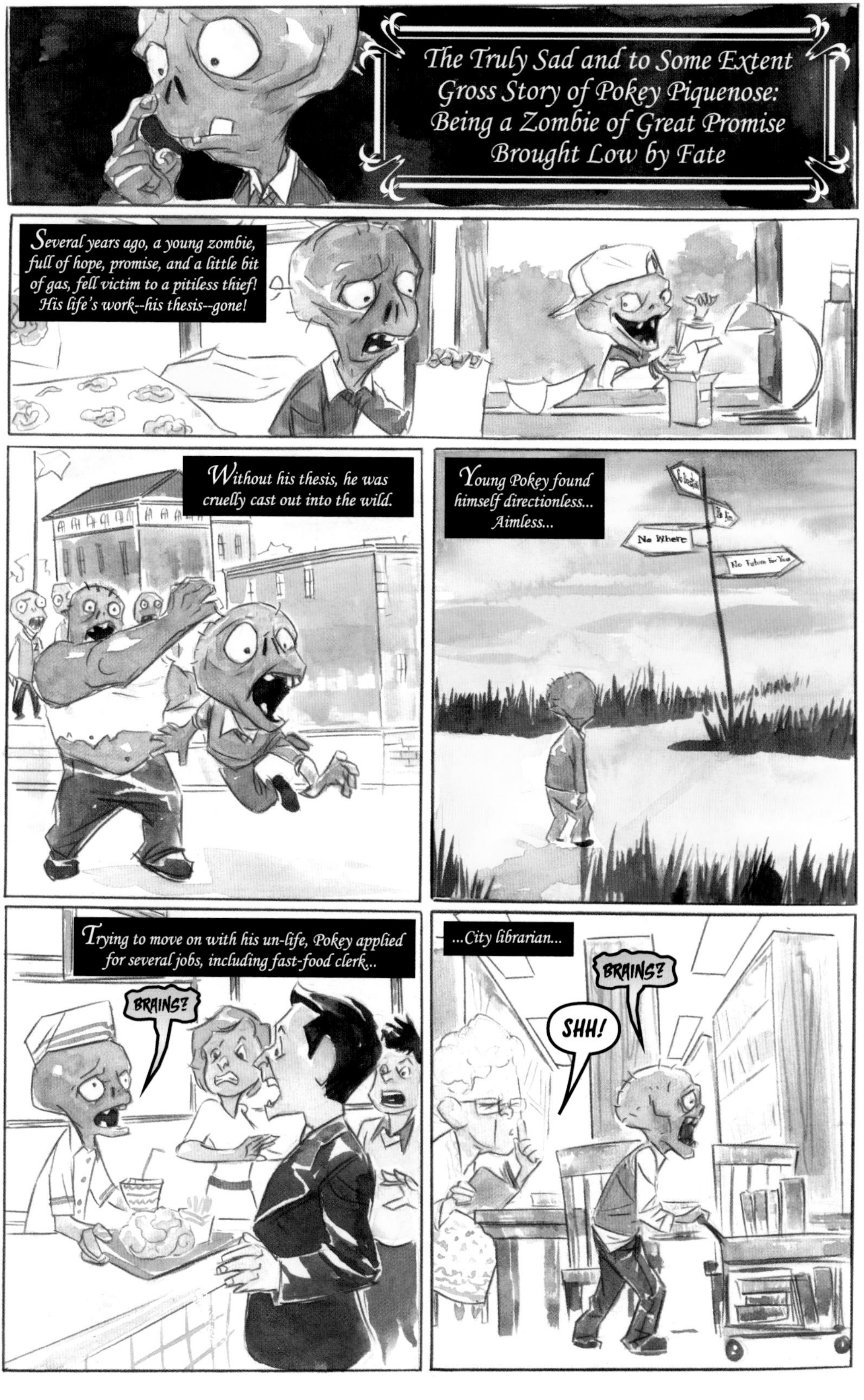

The Truly Sad and to Some Extent Gross Story of Pokey Piquenose: Being a Zombie of Great Promise Brought Low by Fate
Several years ago, a young zombie, full of hope, promise, and a little bit of gas, fell victim to a pitiless thief! His life's work--his thesis--gone!
Without his thesis, he was cruelly cast out into the wild.
Young Pokey found himself directionless... Aimless...
No Where
No Future For You
Trying to move on with his un-life, Pokey applied for several jobs, including fast-food clerk...
BRAINS?
...City librarian...
BRAINS?
SHH!

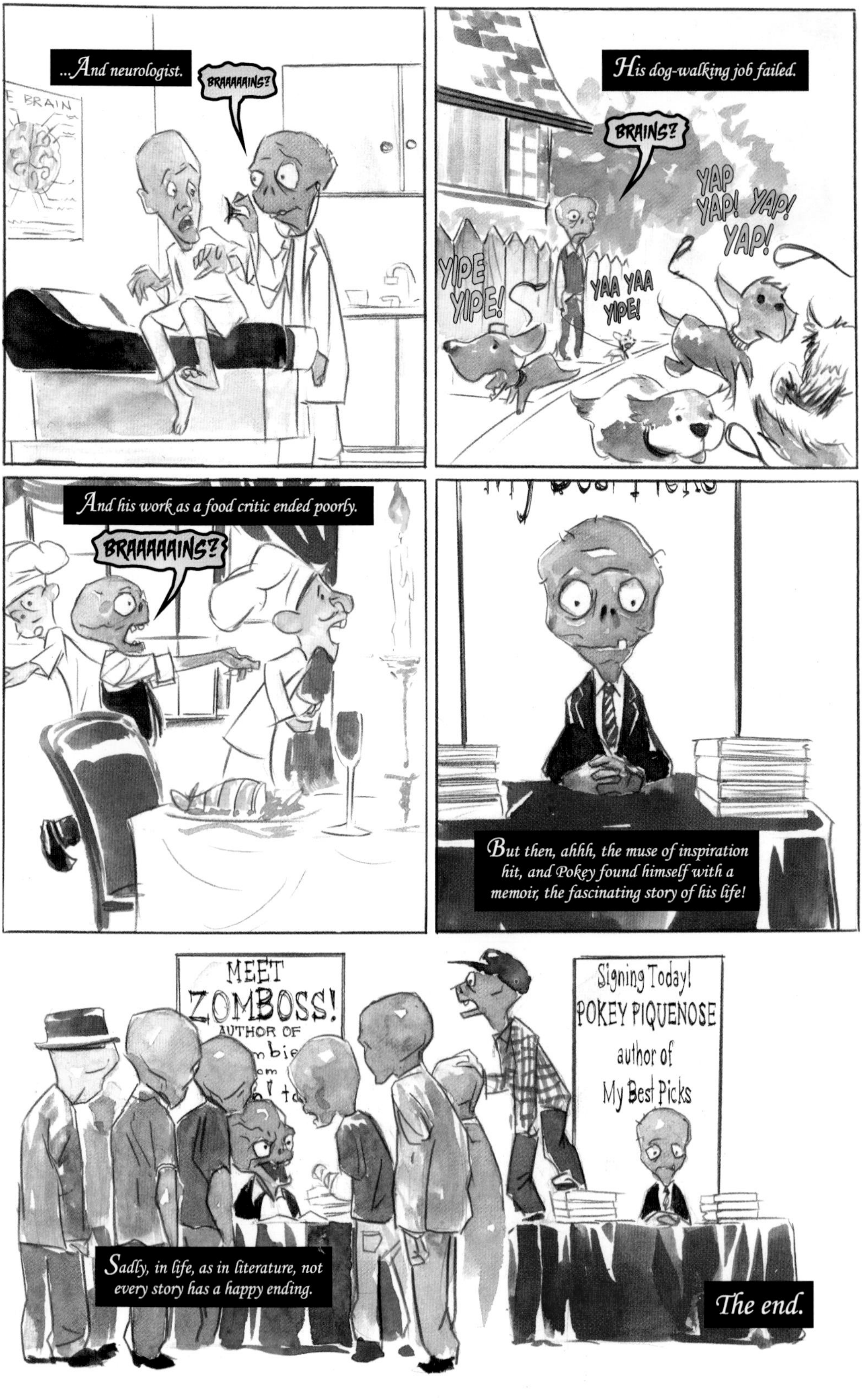
...And neurologist.
BRAAAAAINS?
E BRAIN
His dog-walking job failed.
BRAINS?
YAP YAP! YAP! YAP!
YIPE YIPE!
YAA YAA YIPE!
And his work as a food critic ended poorly.
BRAAAAAINS?
But then, ahhh, the muse of inspiration hit, and Pokey found himself with a memoir, the fascinating story of his life!
MEET
ZOMBOSS!
AUTHOR OF
Signing Today!
POKEY PIQUENOSE
author of
My Best Picks
Sadly, in life, as in literature, not every story has a happy ending.
The end.

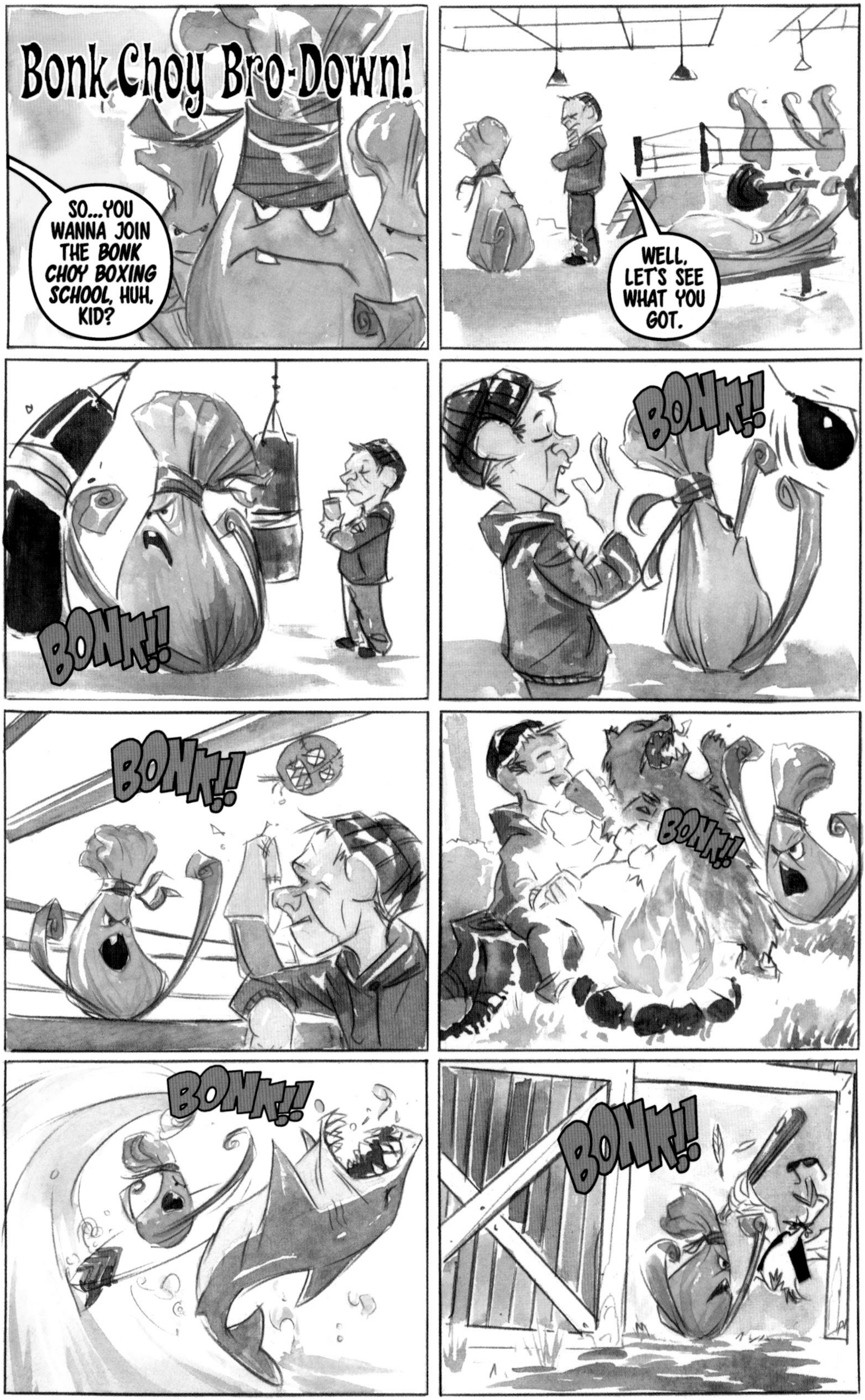
Bonk Choy Bro-Down!
SO...YOU WANNA JOIN THE BONK CHOY BOXING SCHOOL, HUH, KID?
WELL, LET'S SEE WHAT YOU GOT.
BONK!!
BONK!!
BONK!!
BONK!!
BONK!!
BONK!!

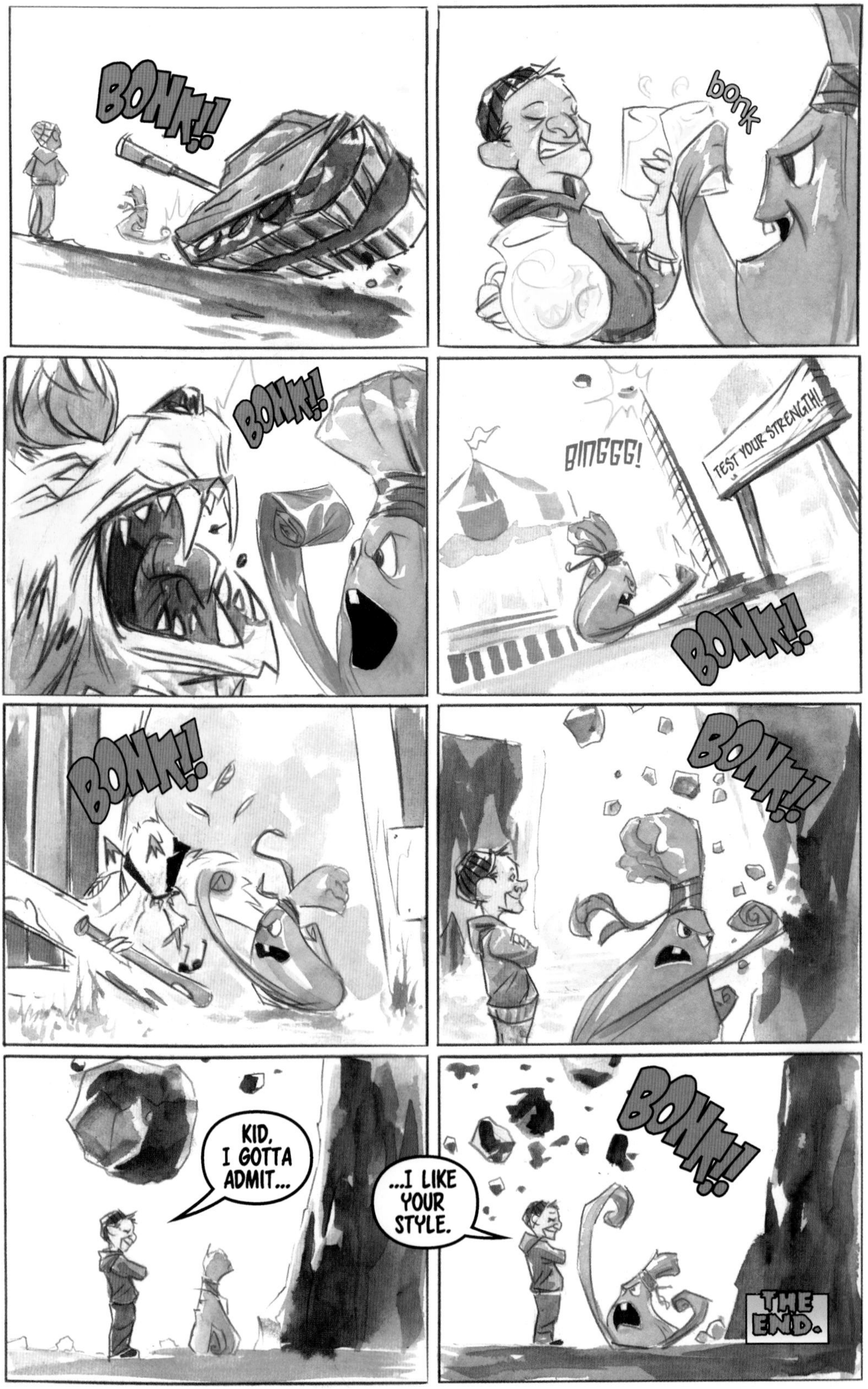
BONK!!
bonk
BONK!!
BINGGG!
TEST YOUR STRENGTH!
BONK!!
BONK!!
BONK!!
KID, I GOTTA ADMIT...
...I LIKE YOUR STYLE.
BONK!!
THE END.

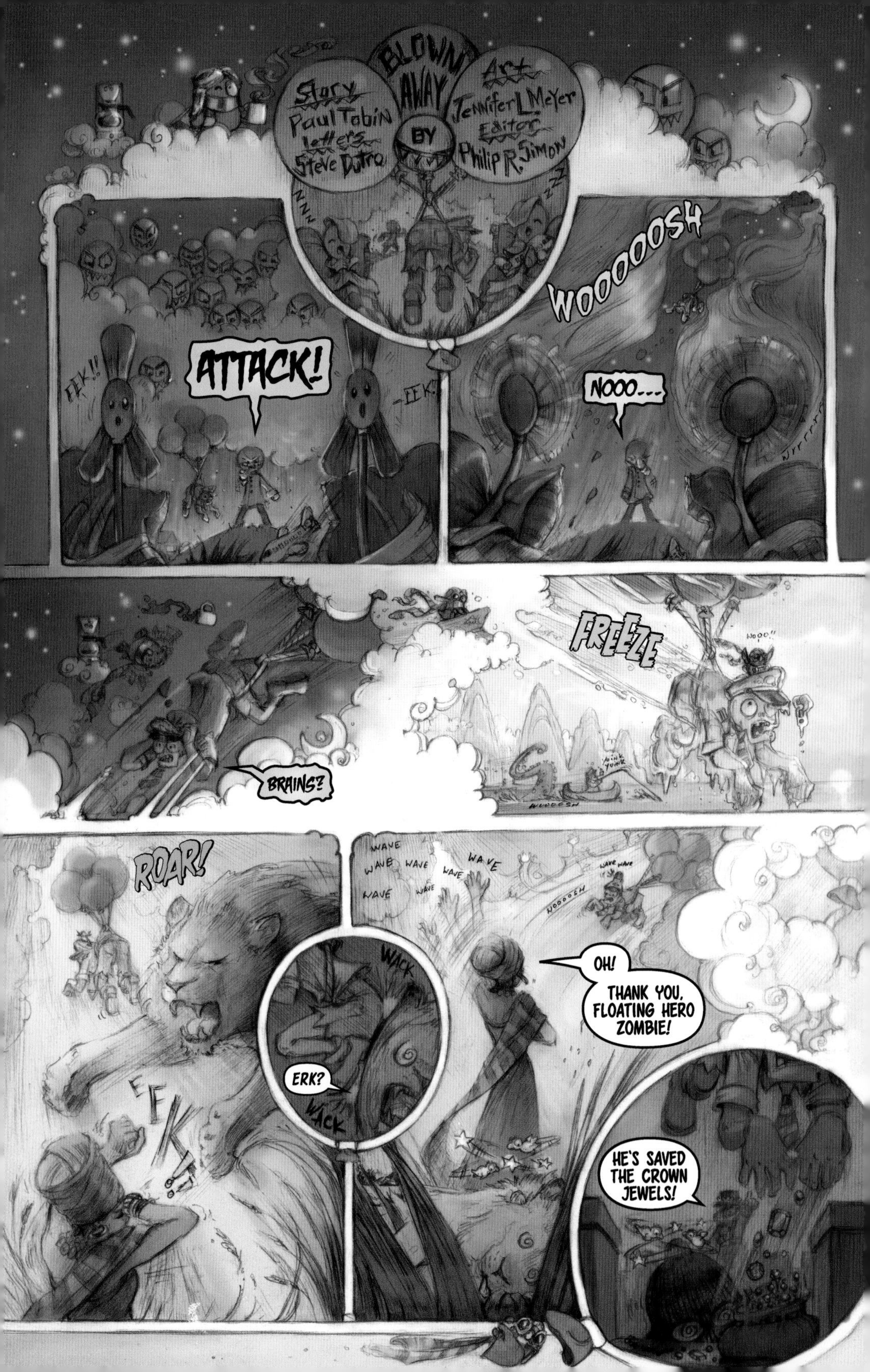
BLOWN AWAY
Story Paul Tobin
Letters Steve Dutro
BY
Art Jennifer L. Meyer
Editor Philip R. Simon
ATTACK!
EEK!!
EEK!!
WOOOOOOSH
NOOO...
BRAINS?
FREEZE
NOOO!!
ROAR!
WAVE WAVE WAVE WAVE WAVE WAVE WAVE
WACK
ERK?
WACK
EEK
OH!
THANK YOU, FLOATING HERO ZOMBIE!
HE'S SAVED THE CROWN JEWELS!

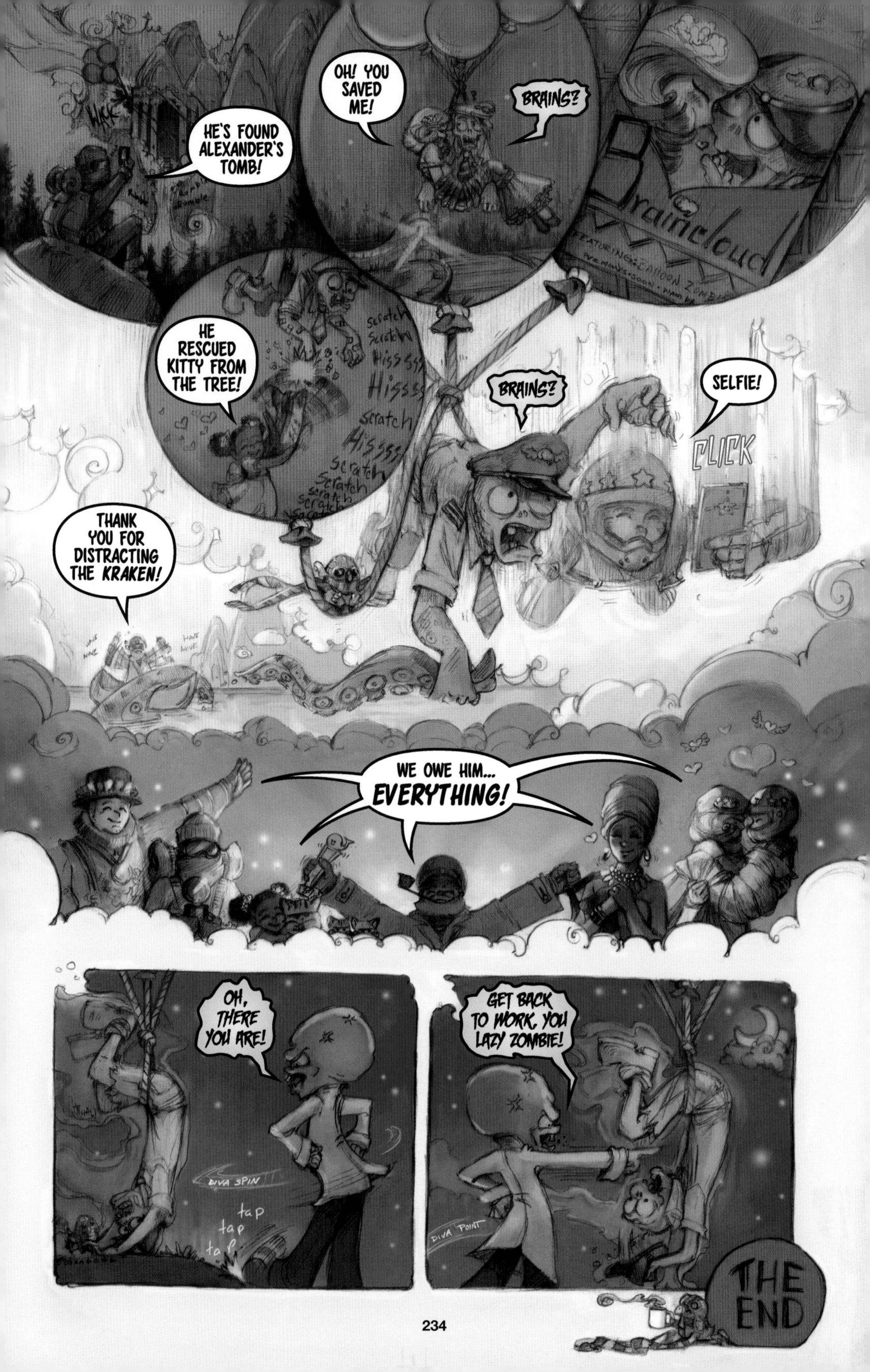
HE'S FOUND ALEXANDER'S TOMB!
OH! YOU SAVED ME!
BRAINS?
HE RESCUED KITTY FROM THE TREE!
scratch scratch Hissss Hissss scratch Hissss scratch scratch scratch scratch
BRAINS?
SELFIE!
CLICK
THANK YOU FOR DISTRACTING THE KRAKEN!
WE OWE HIM... EVERYTHING!
OH, THERE YOU ARE!
DIVA SPIN
tap tap tap
GET BACK TO WORK, YOU LAZY ZOMBIE!
DIVA POINT
THE END

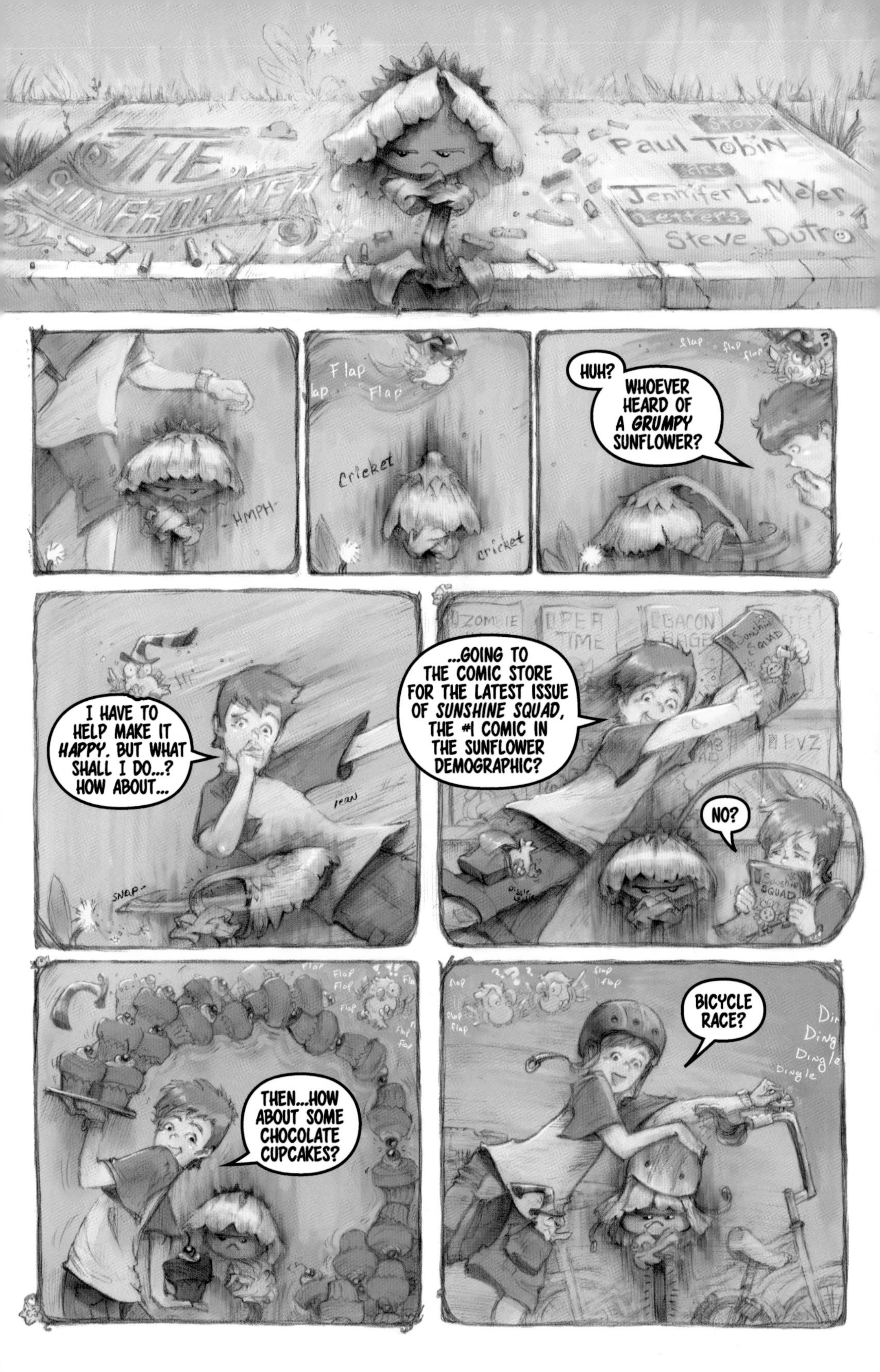
THE SUNFROWNER
STORY
Paul Tobin
ART
Jennifer L. Meyer
LETTERS
Steve Dutro
HMPH
Flap
Flap
Flap
Cricket
cricket
flap
flap
flap
HUH?
WHOEVER HEARD OF A GRUMPY SUNFLOWER?
I HAVE TO HELP MAKE IT HAPPY. BUT WHAT SHALL I DO...? HOW ABOUT...
SNAP
...GOING TO THE COMIC STORE FOR THE LATEST ISSUE OF SUNSHINE SQUAD, THE #1 COMIC IN THE SUNFLOWER DEMOGRAPHIC?
ZOMBIE
TIME
BACON
Sunshine Squad
PVZ
NO?
Sunshine SQUAD
THEN...HOW ABOUT SOME CHOCOLATE CUPCAKES?
BICYCLE RACE?
Ding
Dingle
Dingle

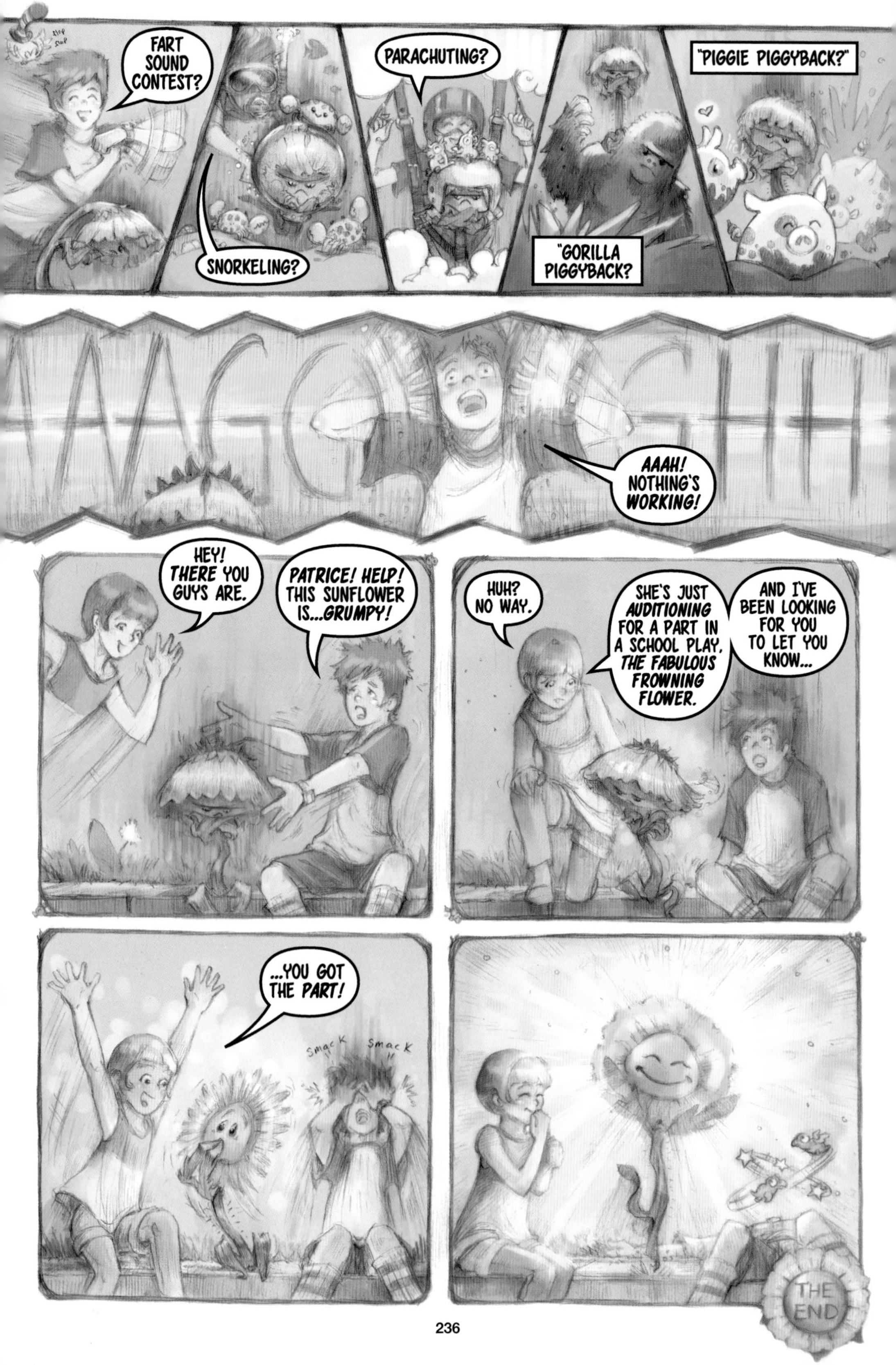

FART SOUND CONTEST?
SNORKELING?
PARACHUTING?
"GORILLA PIGGYBACK?
"PIGGIE PIGGYBACK?"
AAAH! NOTHING'S WORKING!
HEY! THERE YOU GUYS ARE.
PATRICE! HELP! THIS SUNFLOWER IS...GRUMPY!
HUH? NO WAY.
SHE'S JUST AUDITIONING FOR A PART IN A SCHOOL PLAY, THE FABULOUS FROWNING FLOWER.
AND I'VE BEEN LOOKING FOR YOU TO LET YOU KNOW...
...YOU GOT THE PART!
Smack Smack
THE END

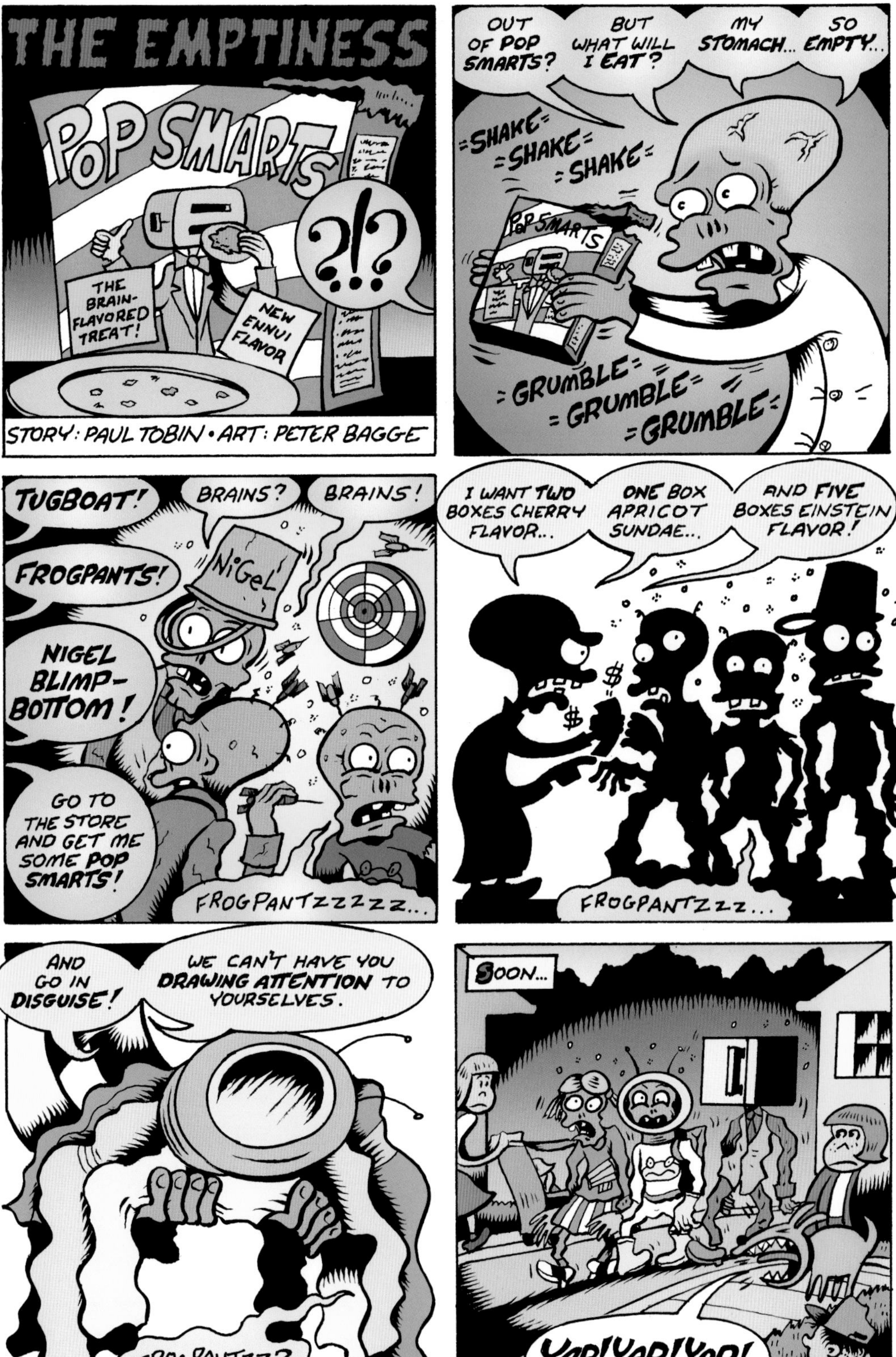
THE EMPTINESS
POP SMARTS
THE BRAIN-FLAVORED TREAT!
NEW ENNUI FLAVOR
?!?
STORY: PAUL TOBIN • ART: PETER BAGGE
OUT OF POP SMARTS?
BUT WHAT WILL I EAT?
MY STOMACH... SO EMPTY...
SHAKE SHAKE SHAKE
POP SMARTS
GRUMBLE GRUMBLE GRUMBLE
TUGBOAT!
BRAINS?
BRAINS!
NiGeL
FROGPANTS!
NIGEL BLIMP-BOTTOM!
GO TO THE STORE AND GET ME SOME POP SMARTS!
FROGPANTZZZZZ...
I WANT TWO BOXES CHERRY FLAVOR...
ONE BOX APRICOT SUNDAE...
AND FIVE BOXES EINSTEIN FLAVOR!
FROGPANTZZZ...
AND GO IN DISGUISE!
WE CAN'T HAVE YOU DRAWING ATTENTION TO YOURSELVES.
FROGPANTZZ?
SOON...
YAP! YAP! YAP!

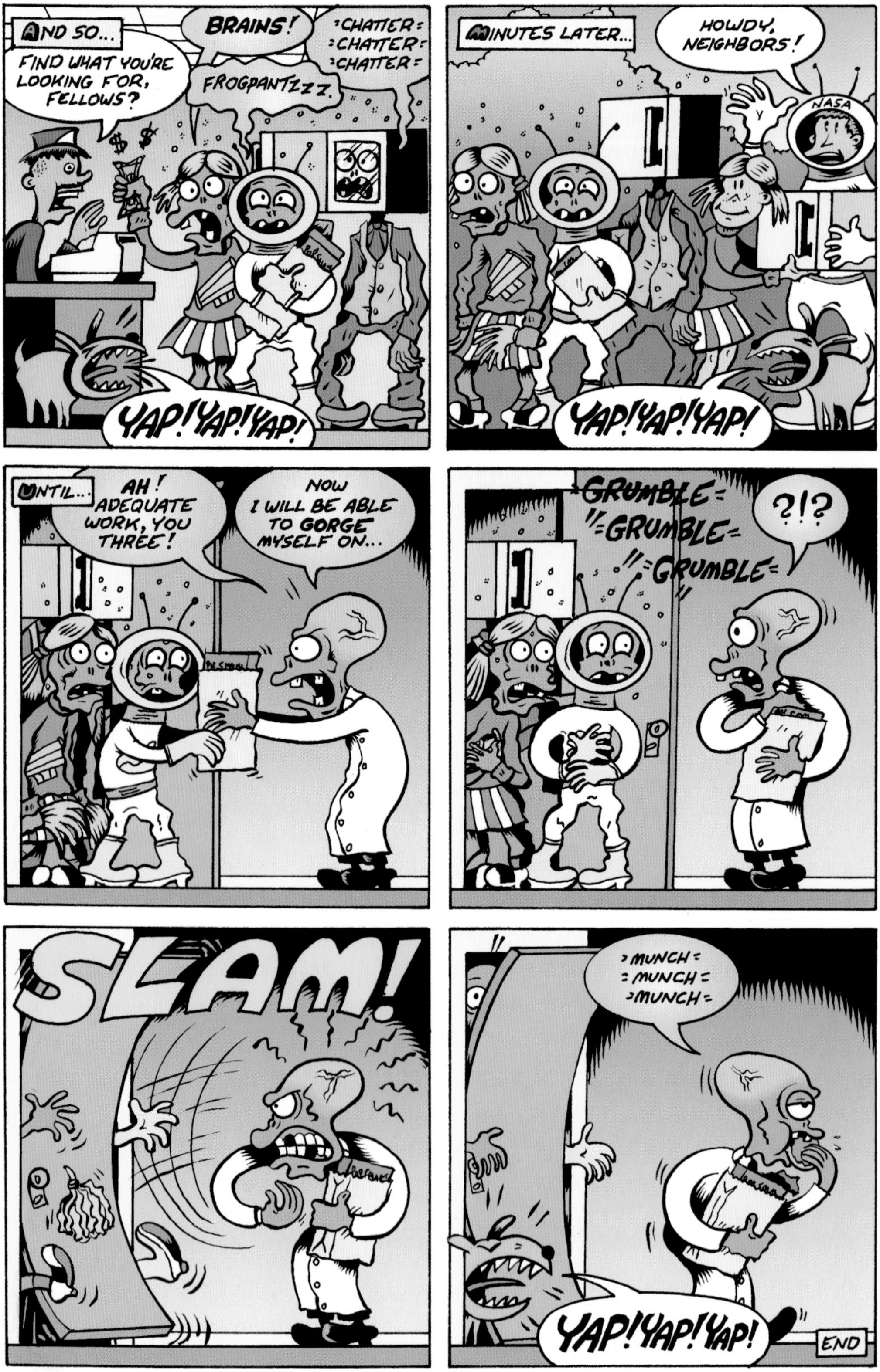
AND SO...
FIND WHAT YOU'RE LOOKING FOR, FELLOWS?
BRAINS!
FROGPANTZzz.
CHATTER CHATTER CHATTER
YAP! YAP! YAP!
MINUTES LATER...
HOWDY, NEIGHBORS!
NASA
YAP! YAP! YAP!
UNTIL...
AH! ADEQUATE WORK, YOU THREE!
NOW I WILL BE ABLE TO GORGE MYSELF ON...
GRUMBLE
GRUMBLE
GRUMBLE
?!?
SLAM!
MUNCH MUNCH MUNCH
YAP! YAP! YAP!
END

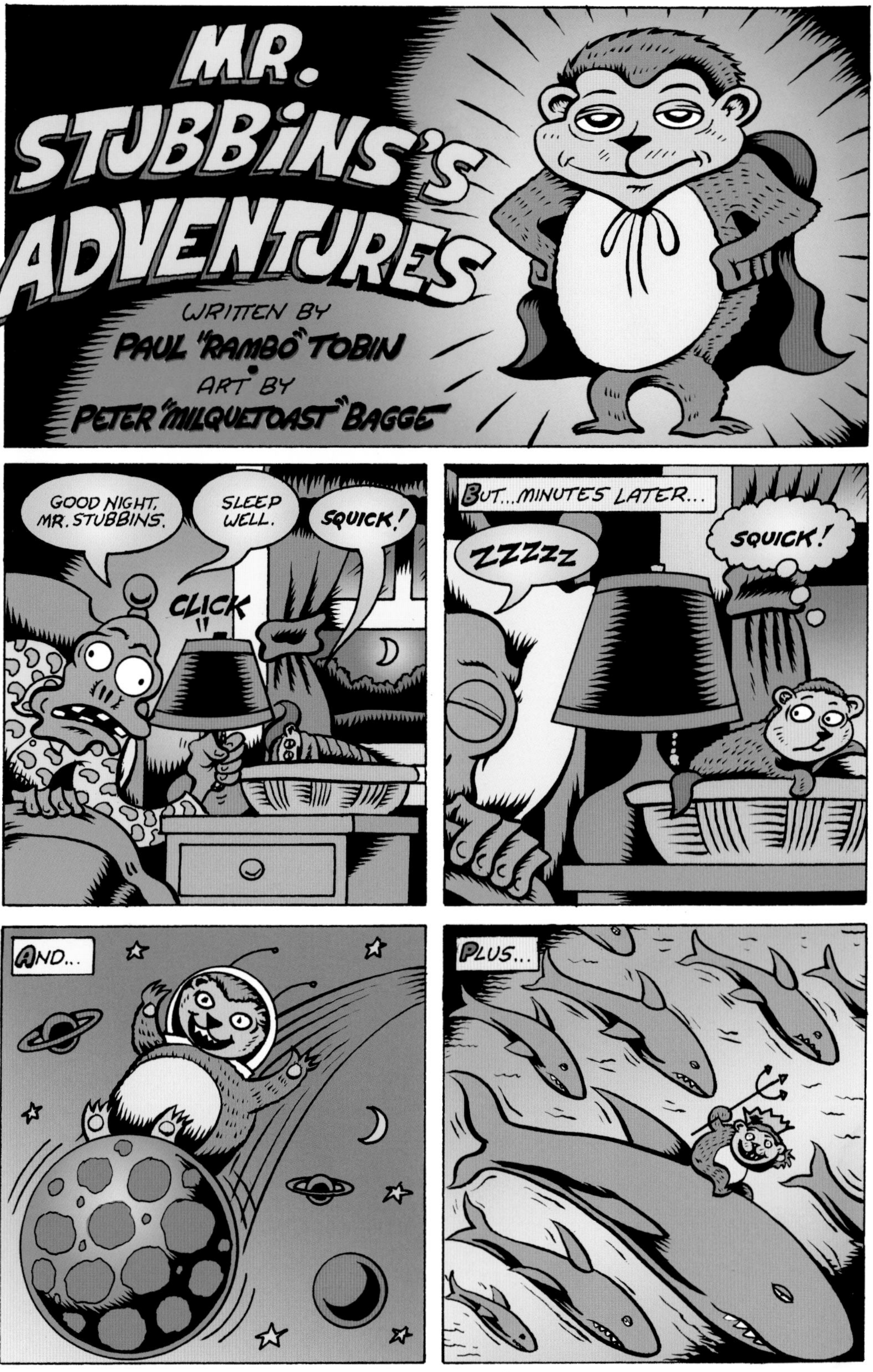
MR. STUBBINS'S ADVENTURES
WRITTEN BY
PAUL "RAMBO" TOBIN
ART BY
PETER "MILQUETOAST" BAGGE
GOOD NIGHT, MR. STUBBINS.
SLEEP WELL.
SQUICK!
CLICK
BUT...MINUTES LATER...
ZZZZZ
SQUICK!
AND...
PLUS...

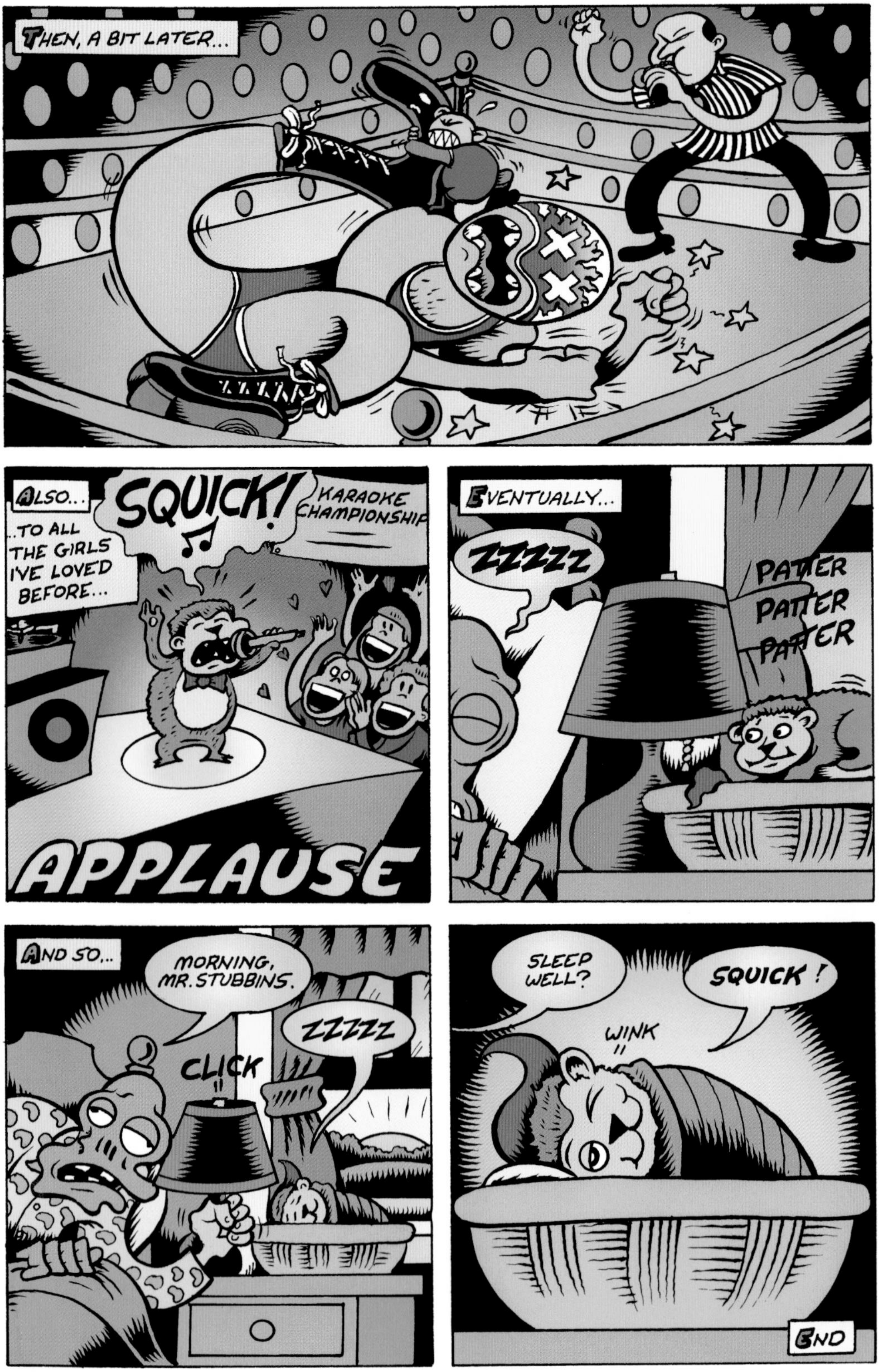
THEN, A BIT LATER...
ALSO...
SQUICK!
KARAOKE CHAMPIONSHIP
..TO ALL THE GIRLS I'VE LOVED BEFORE...
APPLAUSE
EVENTUALLY...
ZZZZZ
PATTER PATTER PATTER
AND SO...
MORNING, MR. STUBBINS.
CLICK
ZZZZZ
SLEEP WELL?
SQUICK!
WINK
END

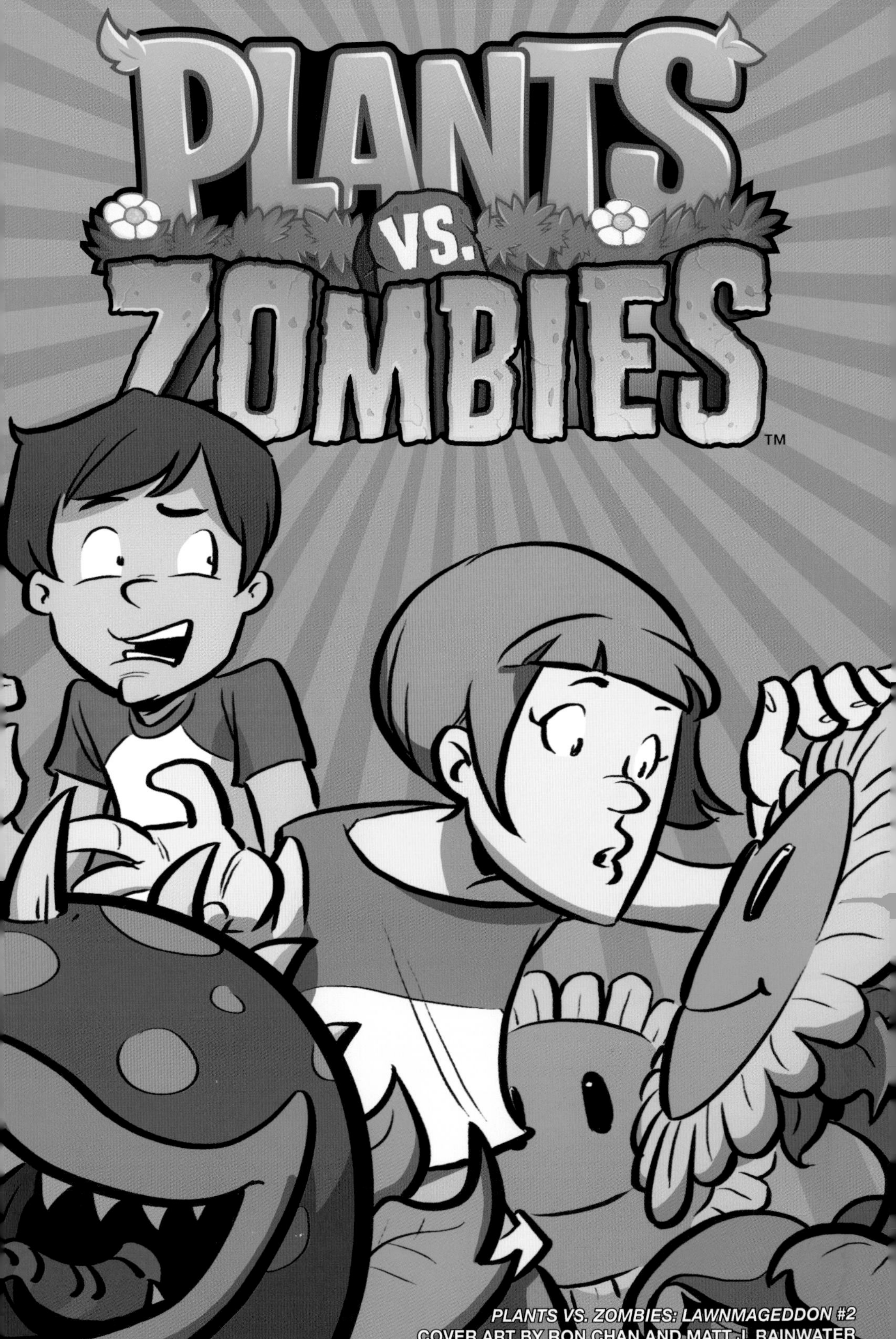
PLANTS
VS.
ZOMBIES

PLANTS VS. ZOMBIES: LAWNMAGEDDON #2
COVER ART BY RON CHAN AND MATT J. RAINWATER

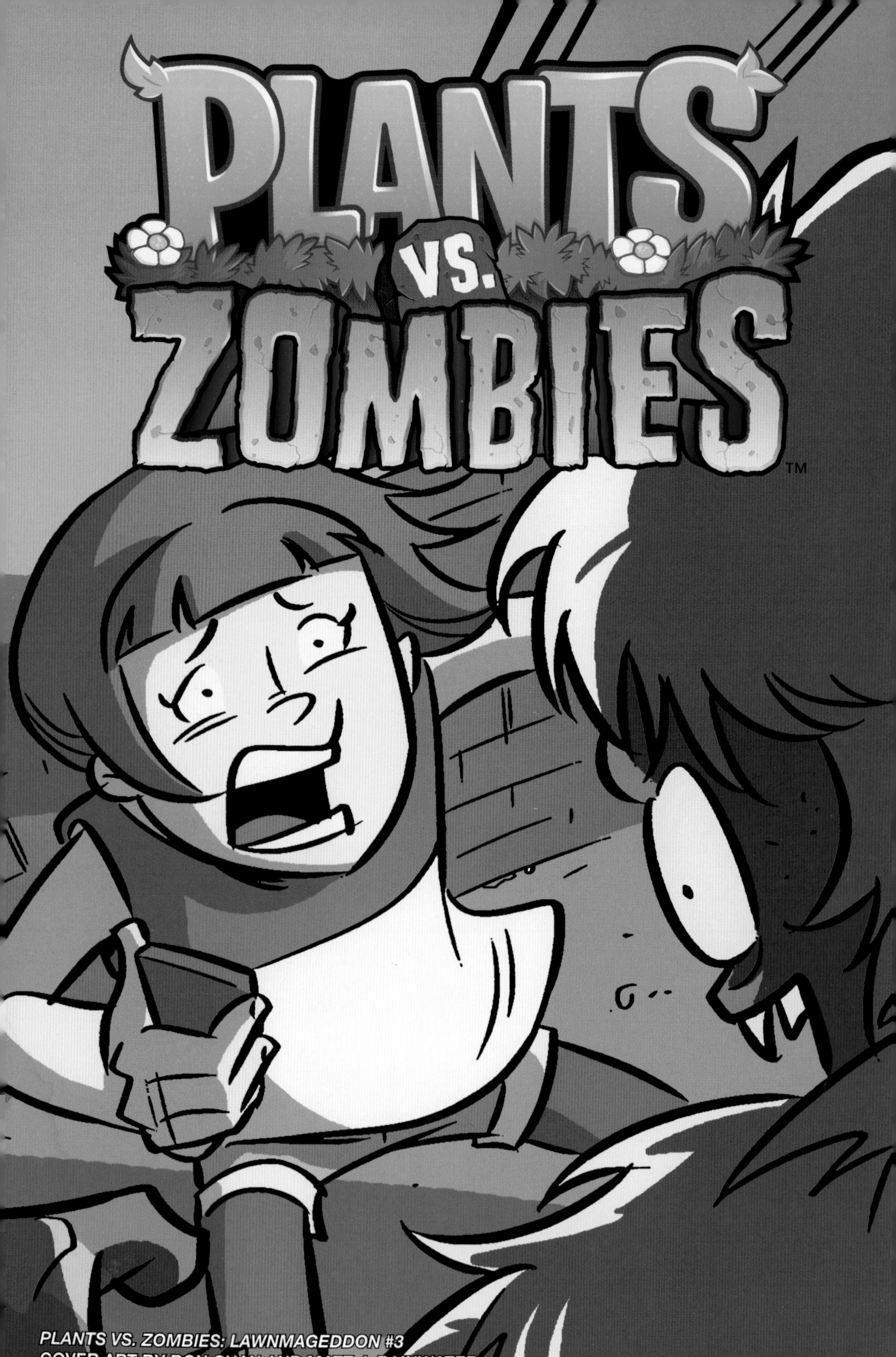
PLANTS VS. ZOMBIES™

PLANTS VS. ZOMBIES: LAWNMAGEDDON #3
COVER ART BY RON CHAN AND MATT J. RAINWATER

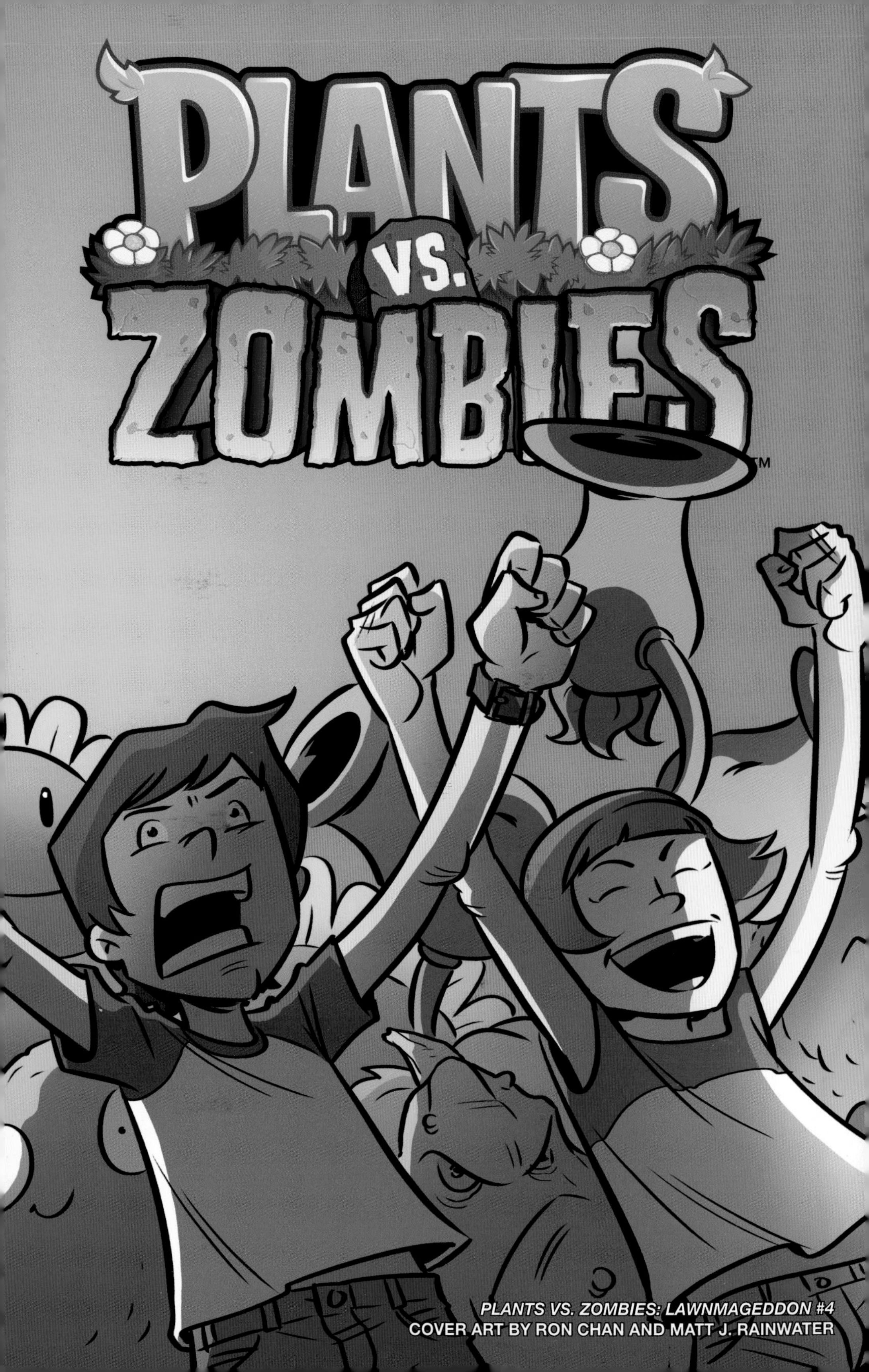
PLANTS VS. ZOMBIES™

PLANTS VS. ZOMBIES: LAWNMAGEDDON #4
COVER ART BY RON CHAN AND MATT J. RAINWATER

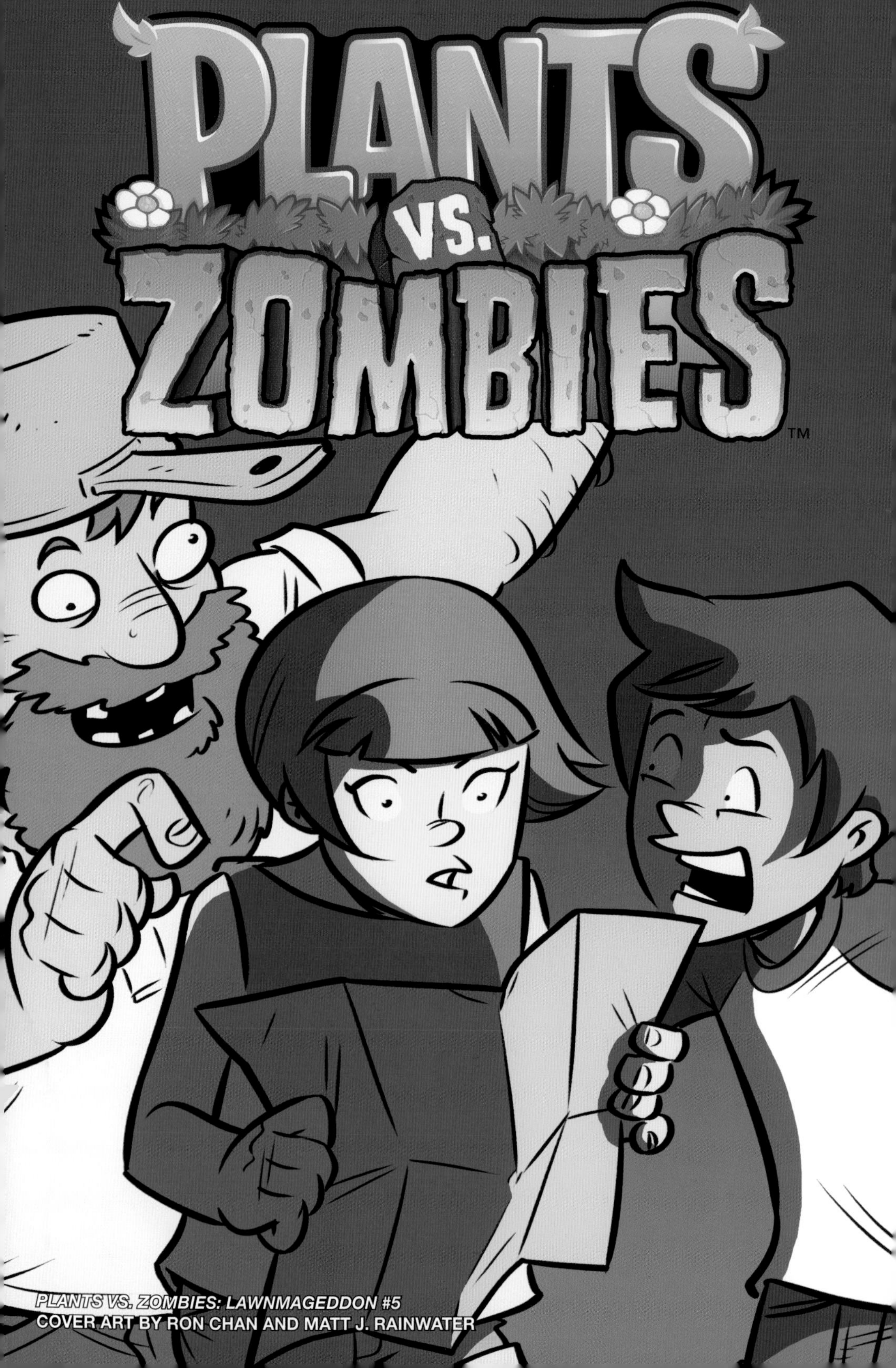
PLANTS VS. ZOMBIES
TM

PLANTS VS. ZOMBIES: LAWNMAGEDDON #5
COVER ART BY RON CHAN AND MATT J. RAINWATER

PLANTS VS. ZOMBIES: LAWNMAGEDDON #6
COVER ART BY RON CHAN AND MATT J. RAINWATER

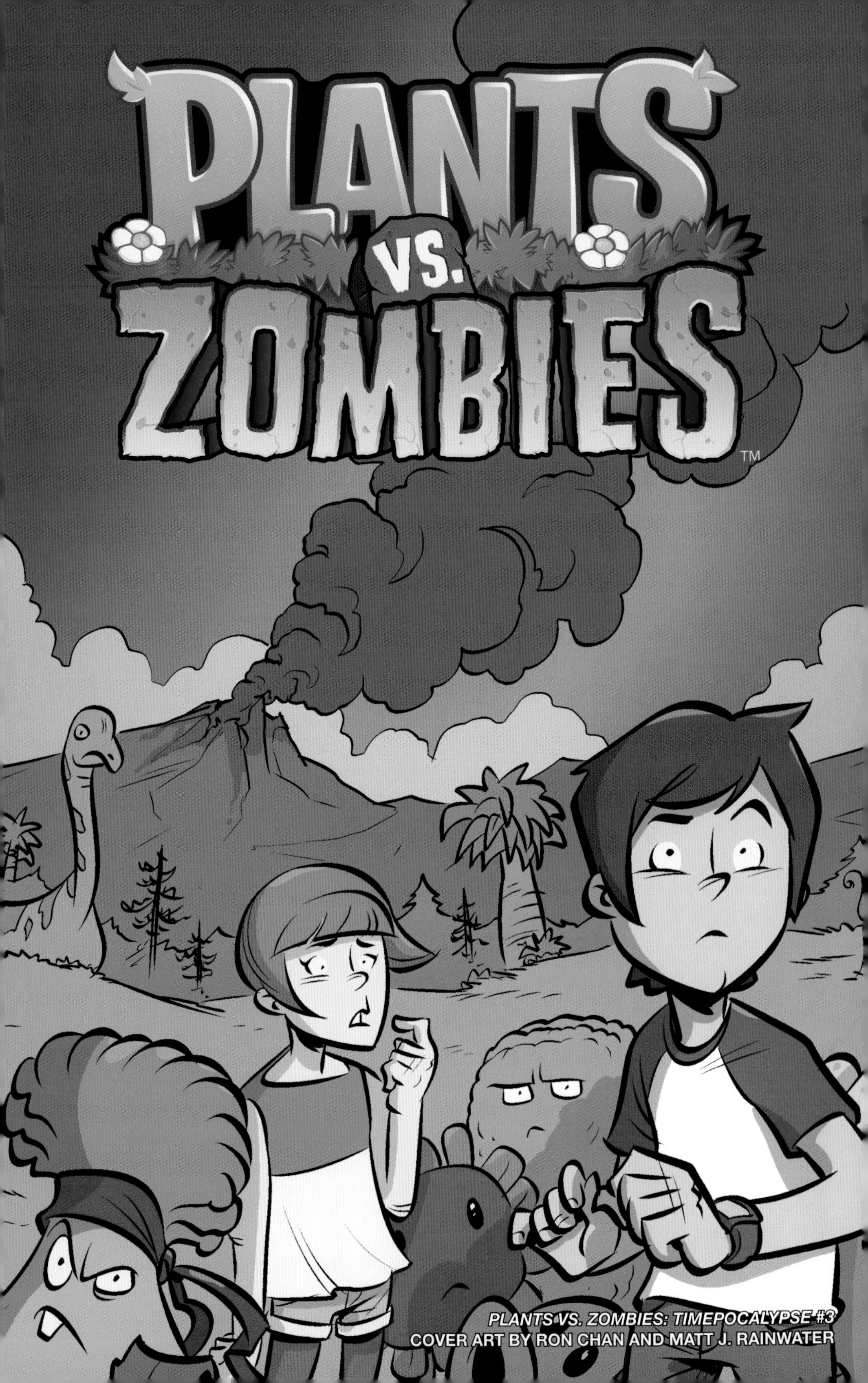
PLANTS VS. ZOMBIES™

PLANTS VS. ZOMBIES: TIMEPOCALYPSE #3
COVER ART BY RON CHAN AND MATT J. RAINWATER

PLANTS VS. ZOMBIES: TIMEPOCALYPSE #4
COVER ART BY RON CHAN AND MATT J. RAINWATER

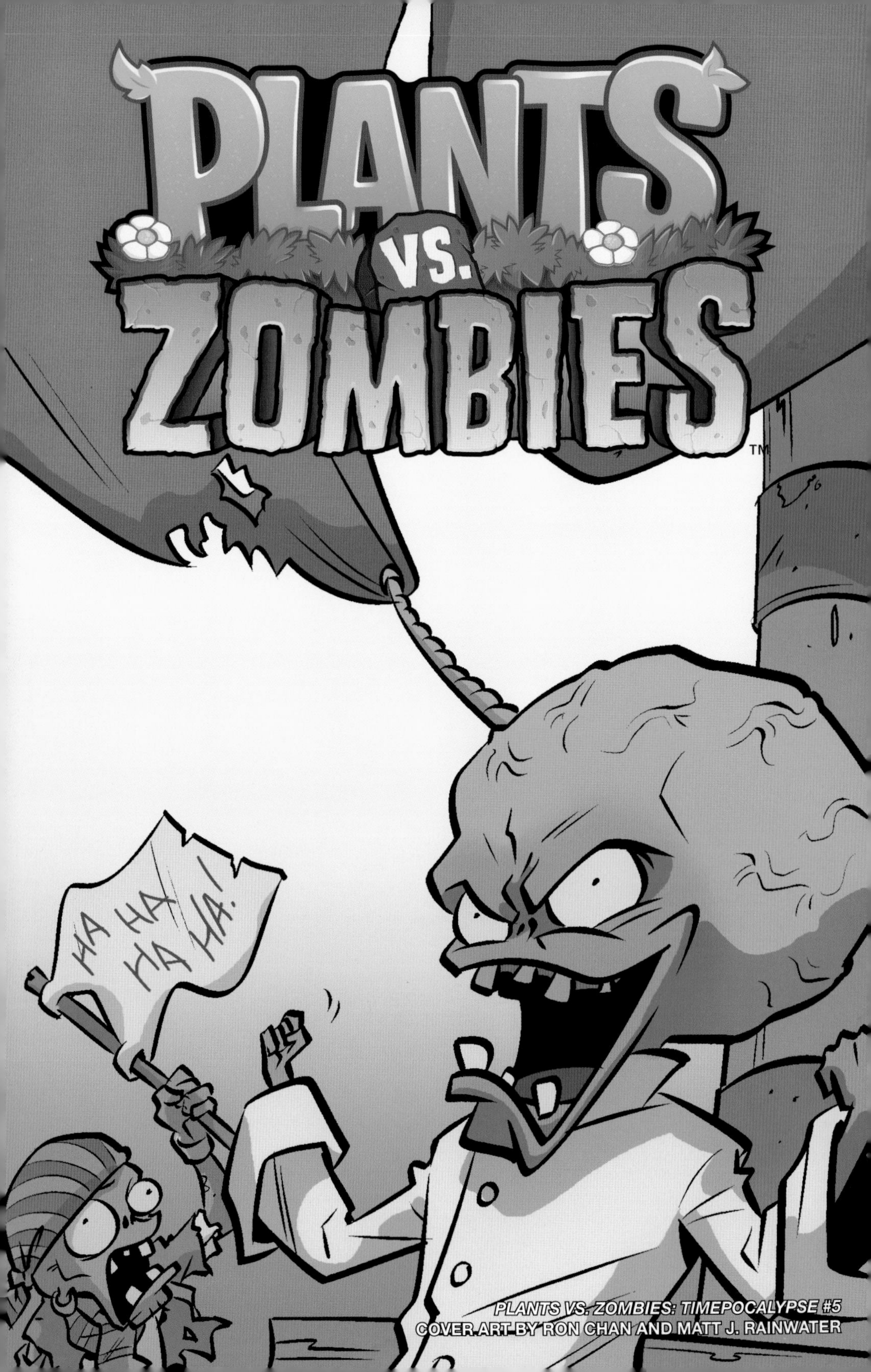
PLANTS VS. ZOMBIES™
HA HA HA HA!

PLANTS VS. ZOMBIES: TIMEPOCALYPSE #5
COVER ART BY RON CHAN AND MATT J. RAINWATER

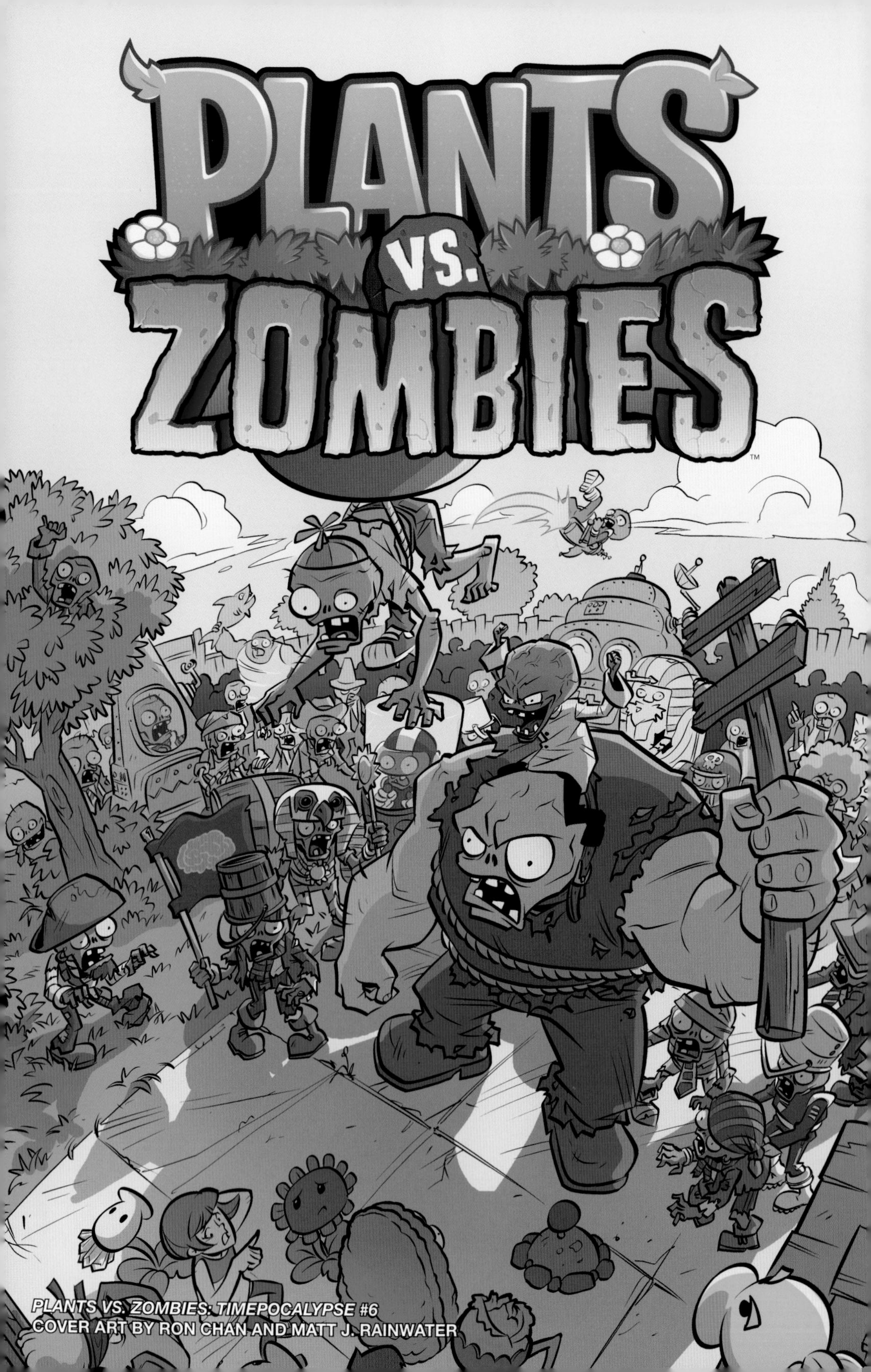
PLANTS VS. ZOMBIES

PLANTS VS. ZOMBIES: TIMEPOCALYPSE #6
COVER ART BY RON CHAN AND MATT J. RAINWATER

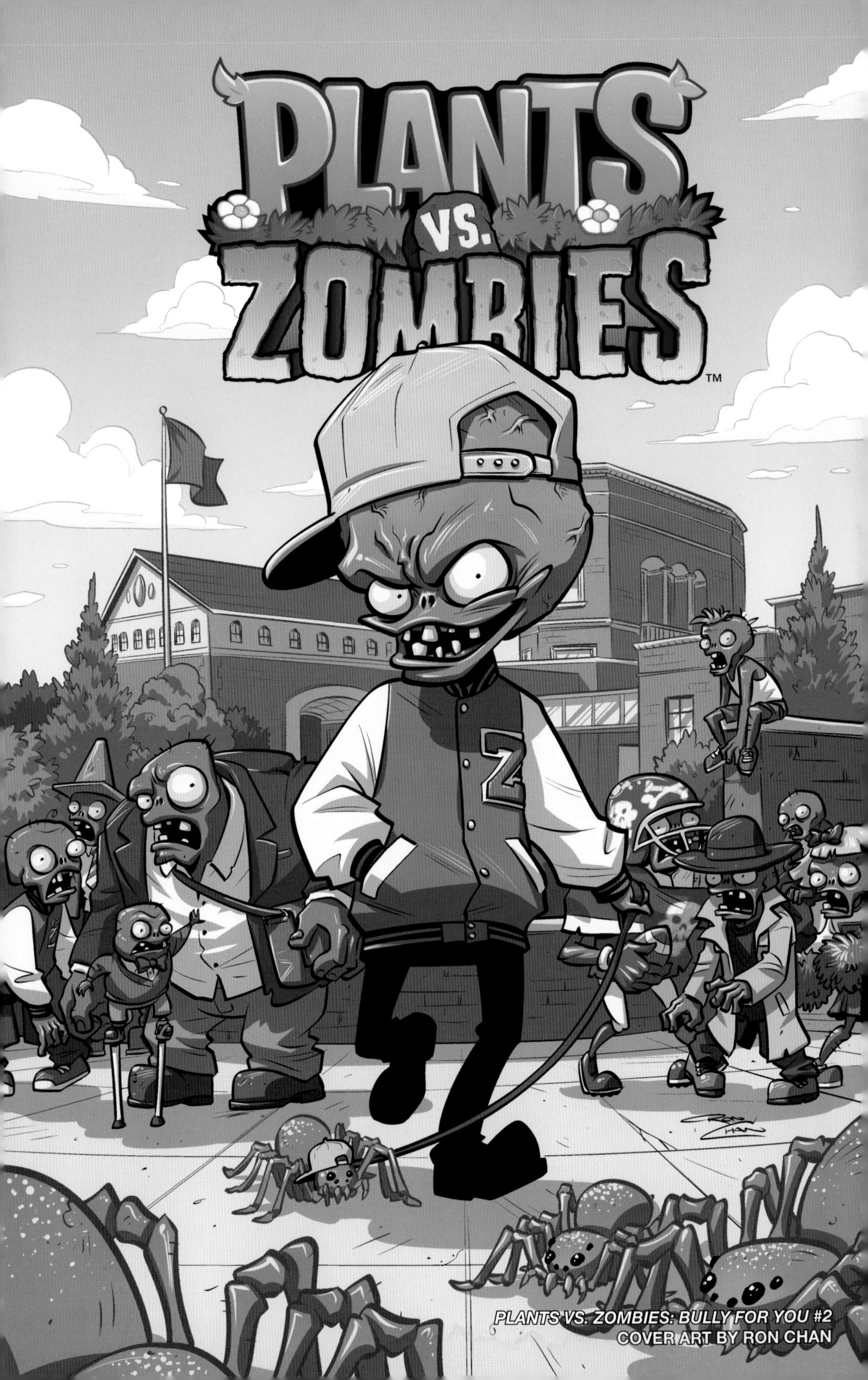
PLANTS VS. ZOMBIES™

PLANTS VS. ZOMBIES: BULLY FOR YOU #2
COVER ART BY RON CHAN

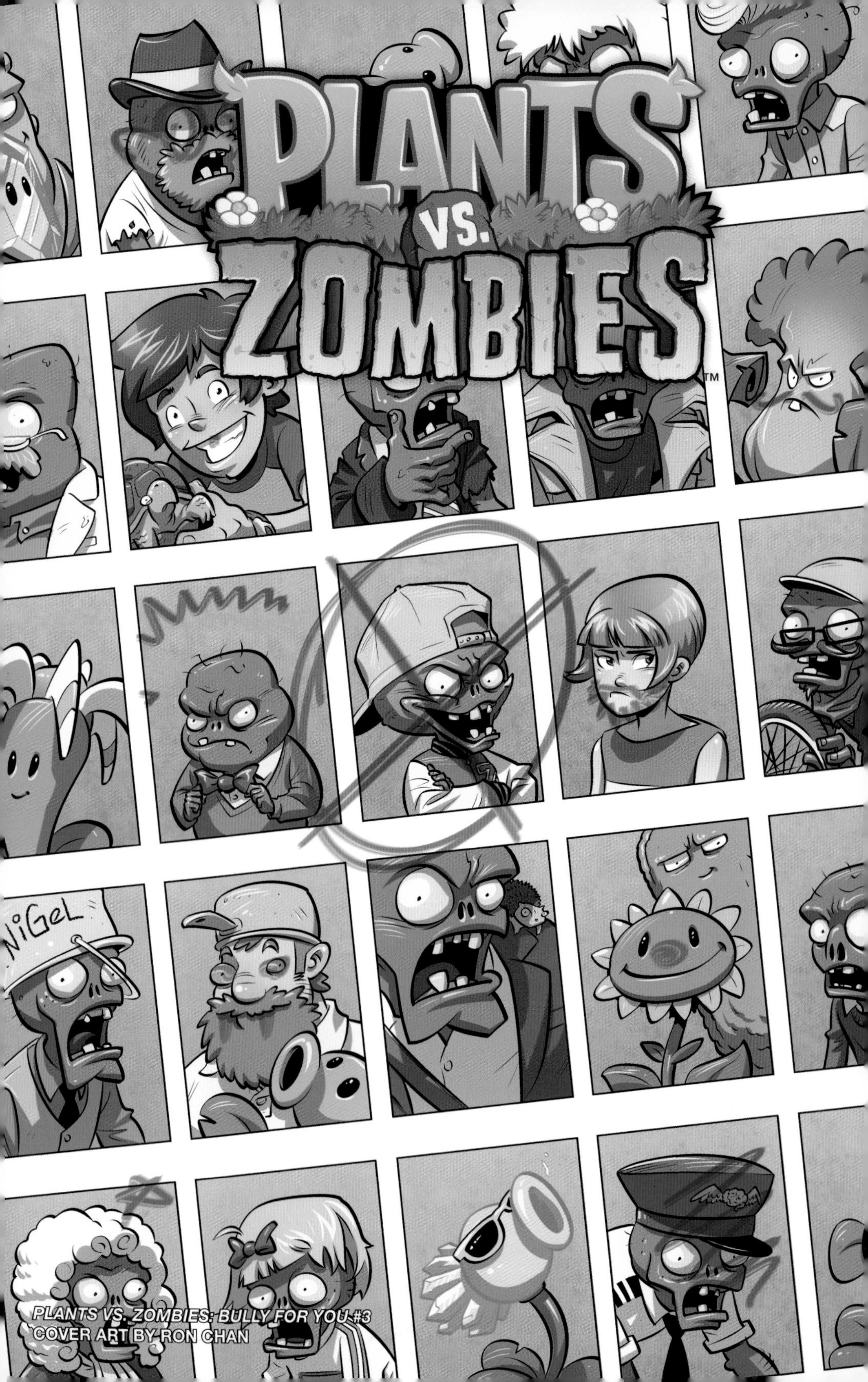
PLANTS VS. ZOMBIES™
NiGeL

PLANTS VS. ZOMBIES: BULLY FOR YOU #3
COVER ART BY RON CHAN

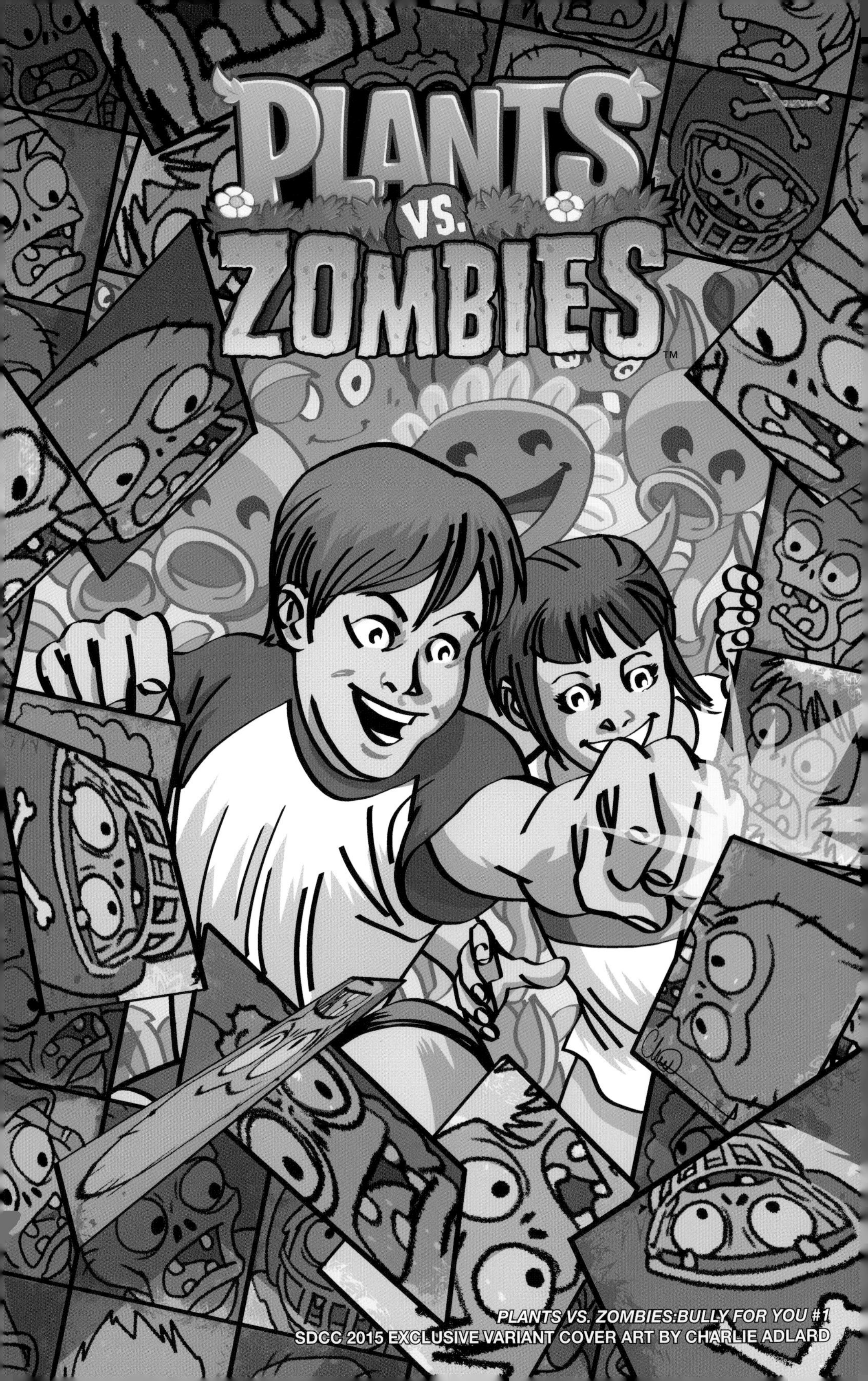
PLANTS
VS.
ZOMBIES™

PLANTS VS. ZOMBIES:BULLY FOR YOU #1
SDCC 2015 EXCLUSIVE VARIANT COVER ART BY CHARLIE ADLARD

CREATOR BIOS

Paul Tobin

PAUL TOBIN is a 12th level writer and a 15th level cookie eater. He begins each morning in the manner we all do, by battling those zombies that have strayed too close to his pillow fort. Between writing all the *Plants vs. Zombies* comics and taking four naps a day, he's also found time to write the *Genius Factor* series of novels, the ape-filled *Banana Sunday* graphic novel, the award-winning *Bandette* series, the *Wrassle Castle* and *Earth Boy* graphic novels, and many other works. He has ridden a giant turtle and an elephant on purpose, and a tornado by accident.

Ron Chan

RON CHAN is a comic book and storyboard artist, video game fan, and occasional jujitsu practitioner. He was born and raised in Portland, Oregon, where he still lives and works as a member of the local artist collective Helioscope Studio. His comics work has been published by Dark Horse, Marvel, and Image Comics, and storyboarding work includes boards for 3-D animation, gaming, user-experience design, and advertising for clients such as Microsoft, Amazon Kindle, Nike, and Sega. He really likes drawing Bonk Choys. (He also enjoys eating actual bok choy in real life.)

Matt J. Rainwater

MATT J. RAINWATER is a freelance illustrator whose work has been featured in advertising, web design, and independent video games. On top of this, he also self-publishes several comic books, including *Trailer Park Warlock*, *Garage Raja*, and *The Feeling Is Multiplied*—all of which can be found at MattJRainwater.com. His favorite zombie-bashing strategy utilizes a line of Bonk Choys with a Wall-nut front guard and Threepeater covering fire.

Steve Dutro

STEVE DUTRO is a pinball fan and an Eisner Award-nominated comic book letterer from Redding, California, who can also drive a tractor. He graduated from the Kubert School and has been lettering comics since the days when foil-embossed covers were cool, working for Dark Horse (*The Fifth Beatle*, *I Am a Hero*, *StarCraft*, *Star Wars*, *Witcher*), Viz, Marvel, and DC Comics. He has submitted a request to the Department of Homeland Security that in the event of a zombie apocalypse he be put in charge of all digital freeway signs so citizens can be alerted to avoid nearby brain-eatings and the like. He finds the *Plants vs. Zombies* game to be a real stress-fest, but highly recommends the *Plants vs. Zombies* table on *Pinball FX2* for game-room hipsters.

ALSO AVAILABLE FROM DARK HORSE!
THE HIT VIDEO GAME CONTINUES ITS COMIC BOOK INVASION!

THE ART OF PLANTS VS. ZOMBIES
Part zombie memoir, part celebration of zombie triumphs, and part anti-plant screed, *The Art of Plants vs. Zombies* is a treasure trove of never-before-seen concept art, character sketches, and surprises from PopCap's popular *Plants vs. Zombies* games!
ISBN 978-1-61655-331-9 | $10.99

PLANTS VS. ZOMBIES: LAWNMAGEDDON
Crazy Dave—the babbling-yet-brilliant inventor and top-notch neighborhood defender—helps young adventurer Nate fend off a zombie invasion that threatens to overrun the peaceful town of Neighborville in *Plants vs. Zombies: Lawnmageddon!* Their only hope is a brave army of chomping, squashing, and pea-shooting plants! A wacky adventure for zombie zappers young and old!
ISBN 978-1-61655-192-6 | $10.99

PLANTS VS. ZOMBIES: TIMEPOCALYPSE
Crazy Dave helps Patrice and Nate Timely fend off Zomboss' latest attack in *Plants vs. Zombies: Timepocalypse!* This new standalone tale will tickle your funny bones and thrill your brains through any timeline!
ISBN 978-1-61655-621-1 | $10.99

PLANTS VS. ZOMBIES: BULLY FOR YOU
Patrice and Nate are ready to investigate a strange college campus to keep the streets safe from zombies!
ISBN 978-1-61655-889-5 | $10.99

PLANTS VS. ZOMBIES: GARDEN WARFARE VOLUME 1
Based on the hit video game, this comic tells the story leading up to the events in *Plants vs. Zombies: Garden Warfare 2!*
ISBN 978-1-61655-946-5 | $10.99

VOLUME 2 ISBN 978-1-50670-548-4 | $10.99

VOLUME 3 ISBN 978-1-50670-837-9 | $10.99

PLANTS VS. ZOMBIES: GROWN SWEET HOME
With newfound knowledge of humanity, Dr. Zomboss strikes at the heart of Neighborville . . . sparking a series of plant-versus-zombie brawls!
ISBN 978-1-61655-971-7 | $10.99

PLANTS VS. ZOMBIES: PETAL TO THE METAL
Crazy Dave takes on the tough *Don't Blink* video game—and challenges Dr. Zomboss to a race to determine the future of Neighborville!
ISBN 978-1-61655-999-1 | $10.99

PLANTS VS. ZOMBIES: BOOM BOOM MUSHROOM
The gang discover Zomboss' secret plan for swallowing the city of Neighborville whole! A rare mushroom must be found in order to save the humans aboveground!
ISBN 978-1-50670-037-3 | $10.99

PLANTS VS. ZOMBIES: BATTLE EXTRAVAGONZO
Zomboss is back, hoping to buy the same factory that Crazy Dave is eyeing! Will Crazy Dave and his intelligent plants beat Zomboss and his zombie army to the punch?
ISBN 978-1-50670-189-9 | $10.99

PLANTS VS. ZOMBIES: LAWN OF DOOM
With Zomboss filling everyone's yards with traps and special soldiers, will he and his zombie army turn Halloween into their zanier Lawn of Doom celebration?!
ISBN 978-1-50670-204-9 | $10.99

PLANTS VS. ZOMBIES: THE GREATEST SHOW UNEARTHED
Dr. Zomboss believes that all humans hold a secret desire to run away and join the circus, so he aims to use his "Big Z's Adequately Amazing Flytrap Circus" to lure Neighborville's citizens to their doom!
ISBN 978-1-50670-298-8 | $10.99

PLANTS VS. ZOMBIES: RUMBLE AT LAKE GUMBO
The battle for clean water begins! Nate, Patrice, and Crazy Dave spot trouble and grab all the Tangle Kelp and Party Crabs they can to quell another zombie attack!
ISBN 978-1-50670-497-5 | $10.99

PLANTS VS. ZOMBIES: WAR AND PEAS
When Dr. Zomboss and Crazy Dave find themselves members of the same book club, a literary war is inevitable! The position of leader of the book club opens up and Zomboss and Crazy Dave compete for the top spot in a scholarly scuffle for the ages!
ISBN 978-1-50670-677-1 | $10.99

PLANTS VS. ZOMBIES: DINO-MIGHT
Dr. Zomboss sets his sights on destroying the yards in town and rendering the plants homeless—and his plans include dogs, cats, rabbits, hammock sloths, and, somehow, dinosaurs . . . !
ISBN 978-1-50670-838-6 | $10.99

PLANTS VS. ZOMBIES: SNOW THANKS
Dr. Zomboss invents a Cold Crystal capable of freezing Neighborville, burying the town in snow and ice! It's up to the humans and the fieriest plants to save Neighborville—with the help of pirates!
ISBN 978-1-50670-839-3 | $10.99

PLANTS VS. ZOMBIES: A LITTLE PROBLEM
Will an invasion of teeny-tiny miniature zombies mean the party for Crazy Dave's two-hundred-year-old pants gets canceled?
ISBN 978-1-50670-840-9 | $10.99

PLANTS VS. ZOMBIES: BETTER HOMES AND GUARDENS
Nate and Patrice try thwarting zombie attacks by putting defending "Guardens" plants *inside* homes as well as in yards! But as soon as Dr. Zomboss finds out, he's determined to circumvent this plan with an epically evil one of his own . . .
ISBN 978-1-50671-305-2 | $10.99

PLANTS VS. ZOMBIES: MULTI-BALL-ISTIC
Dr. Zomboss turns the entirety of Neighborville into a giant, fully functional pinball machine! Nate, Patrice, and their plant posse must find a way to halt this uniquely horrifying zombie invasion. Will the battle go full-tilt zombies?!
ISBN 978-1-50671-307-6 | $10.99

PLANTS VS. ZOMBIES: CONSTRUCTIONARY TALES
A behind-the-scenes look at the secret schemes and craziest contraptions concocted by Zomboss, as he proudly leads around a film crew from the Zombie Broadcasting Network!
ISBN 978-1-50672-091-3 | $10.99

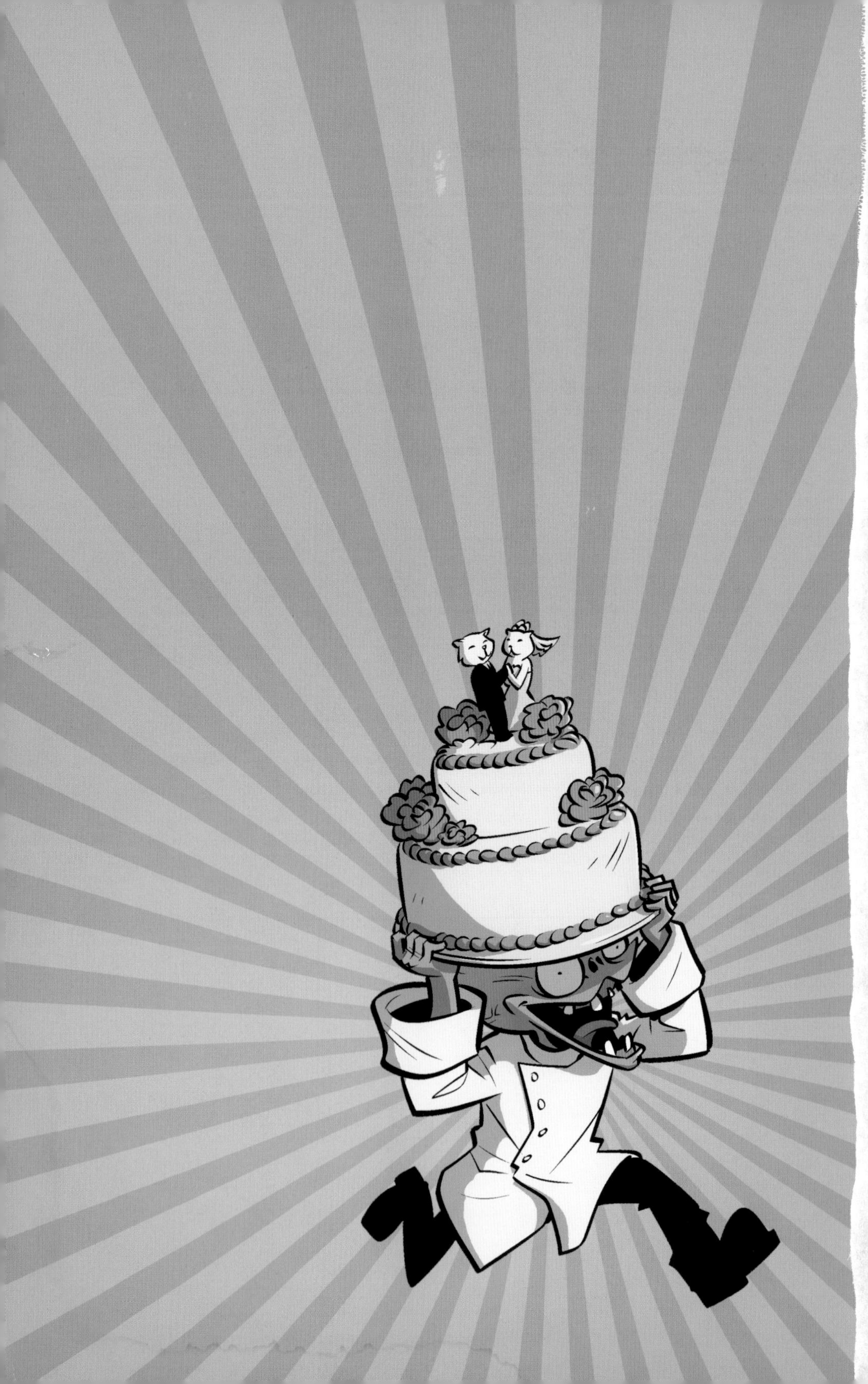

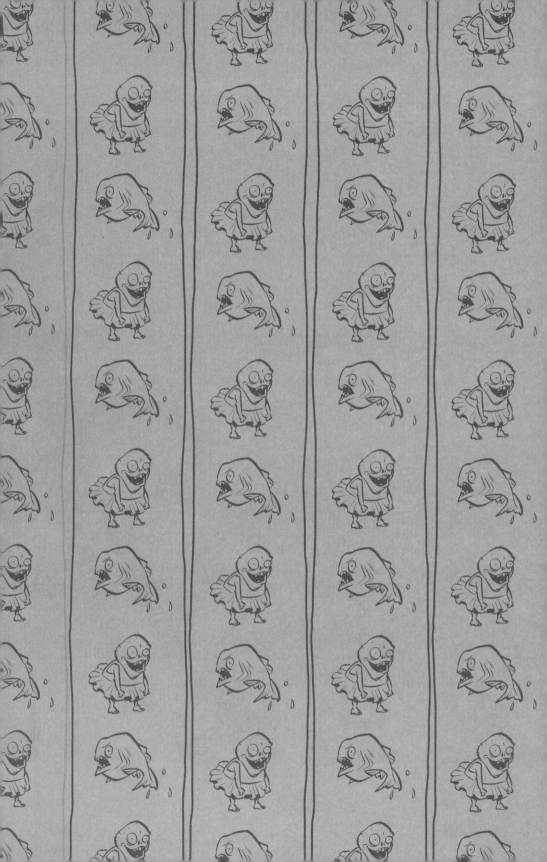